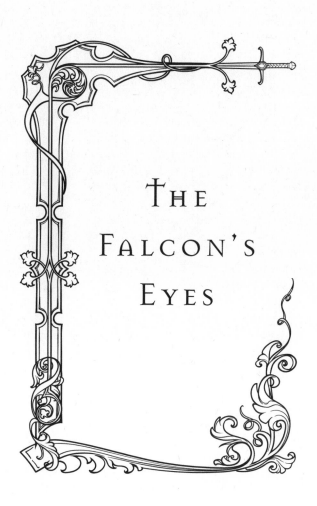

# THE FALCON'S EYES

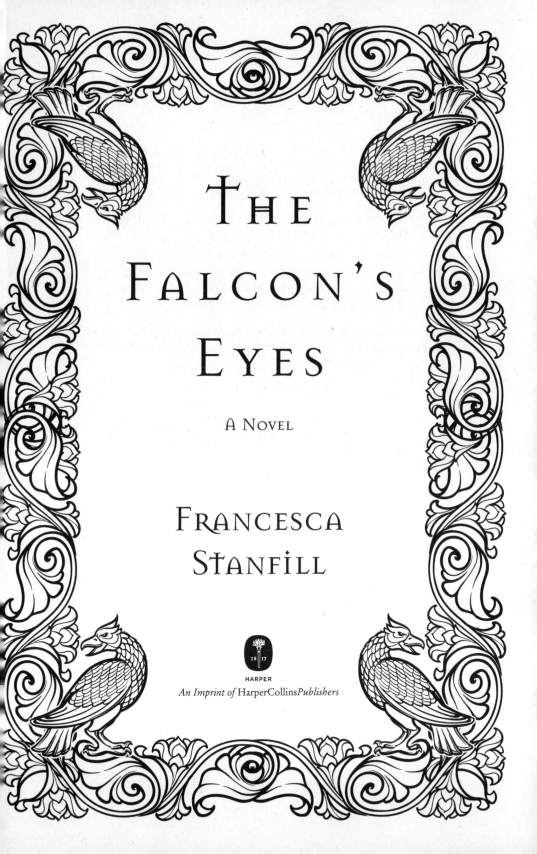

# THE FALCON'S EYES

A Novel

FRANCESCA STANFILL

HARPER

*An Imprint of* HarperCollins*Publishers*

THE FALCON'S EYES. Copyright © 2022 by Francesca Stanfill. All rights reserved. Printed in the United States of America. No part of this book may be used or reproduced in any manner whatsoever without written permission except in the case of brief quotations embodied in critical articles and reviews. For information, address HarperCollins Publishers, 195 Broadway, New York, NY 10007.

HarperCollins books may be purchased for educational, business, or sales promotional use. For information, please email the Special Markets Department at SPsales@harpercollins.com.

FIRST EDITION

*Designed by Nancy Singer*

*Interior art @aen_seidhe/stock.adobe.com*

Library of Congress Cataloging-in-Publication Data has been applied for.

ISBN 978-0-06-307422-4

22 23 24 25 26 LSC 10 9 8 7 6 5 4 3 2 1

# To RBN
*magna gratia et caritate*

As for birds, they were a medieval obsession. They are the subject of one of the earliest medieval sketchbooks, and they fill the borders of manuscripts. . . . they had become symbols of freedom. Under feudalism men and animals were tied to the land: very few people could move about—only artists and birds.

—Kenneth Clark, *Civilisation*

Queen Eleanor, a matchless woman, beautiful and chaste, powerful and modest, meek and eloquent, who was advanced in years enough to have had two husbands and two sons crowned kings, still indefatigable for every undertaking, whose power was the admiration of her age. . . . Let none speak more thereof; I also know well. Be silent.

—Richard of Devizes, *Chronicle,*
*Concerning the Deeds of Richard the First,*
*King of England,* ca. 1192

Brutal, hard

blood shed.

No warning.

Eyes see.

Talons take.

—"On a Hawk" by Ibn al-Mu'tazz,
Arabic poet, ninth century. Trans. by
Professor James E. Montgomery, 2020,
University of Cambridge

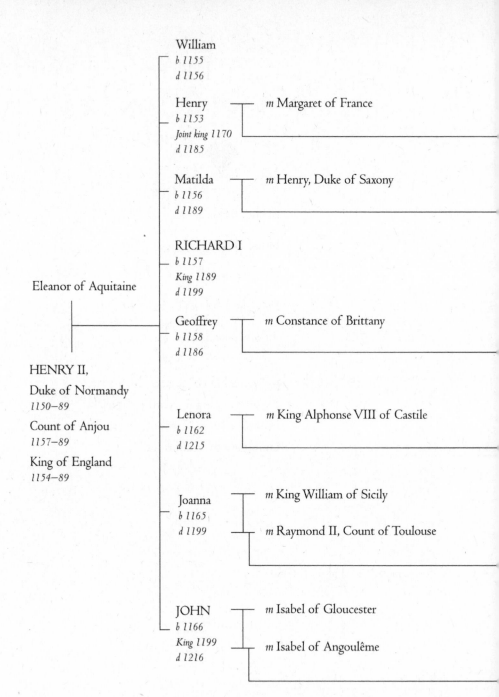

Eleanor of Aquitaine

HENRY II,
Duke of Normandy
*1150–89*

Count of Anjou
*1157–89*

King of England
*1154–89*

William
*b 1155*
*d 1156*

Henry
*b 1153*
*Joint king 1170*
*d 1185*
— m Margaret of France

Matilda
*b 1156*
*d 1189*
— m Henry, Duke of Saxony

RICHARD I
*b 1157*
*King 1189*
*d 1199*

Geoffrey
*b 1158*
*d 1186*
— m Constance of Brittany

Lenora
*b 1162*
*d 1215*
— m King Alphonse VIII of Castile

Joanna
*b 1165*
*d 1199*
— m King William of Sicily
— m Raymond II, Count of Toulouse

JOHN
*b 1166*
*King 1199*
*d 1216*
— m Isabel of Gloucester
— m Isabel of Angoulême

# THE
# PLANTAGENETS
### NORMAN AND ANGEVIN
### KINGS OF ENGLAND

William,
*died at birth*

Henry,
Count Palatinate of the Rhine

Otto of Brunswick,
King of Germany and Emperor

Eleanor

Arthur of Brittany
*1187–1202*

Berenger

Blanca — *m* King Louis VIII of France

Urraque

Eleanor

Henry

Raymond VII, Count of Toulouse

KING HENRY III
*King 1216–1272*

Richard

Joan

Isabel

Eleanor

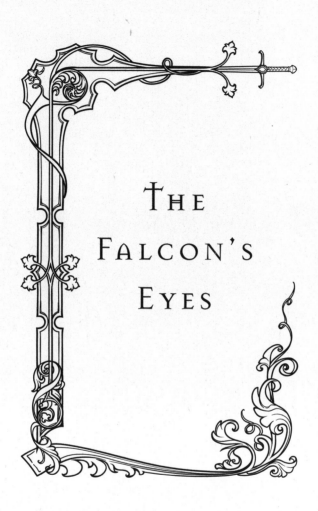

# The
# Falcon's
# Eyes

# PROLOGUE

FONTEVRAUD ABBEY
LOIRE VALLEY, FRANCE
*Thursday, the first of April*
*Anno Domini 1204*

The queen, my queen, died shortly before dusk.

Darkness has descended with her death, and with it all the warmth of her beloved Aquitaine. Her hand rests in mine, her fingers colder than the cloister's stone. Gently I draw the sable about her neck and shoulders; it has been a frigid month, and it comforts me to know the cloak will enshroud her still. She goes to a realm of radiance, they say, yet a desolate part of me fears it will be icy, lightless. Even for her, Eleanor, queen of England and France, the fabled Duchess of Aquitaine.

Her smile is serene, her brow tranquil, the expression of her eyes poignantly questioning. How wondrous that her face hardly betrays the tumult of these years! That she should go to the afterlife with some vestige of her beauty would have gladdened her, no doubt—*vanitas vanitatum*, she would have quipped. It is only her hands that suggest the weighty procession of eight decades. Her fingers are gnarled and heavy; I touch the bloodred signet ring, then the others, glimmering with the seals of Athena and Aphrodite.

Earlier I had summoned Father Luke to issue the last rites. Flickering images return to me: a flock of black-robed figures in the mauve light, the host placed upon her tongue, the gold crucifix studded with amethysts pressed into her hands, now as pale and translucent as the wafer itself. We, her companions of many years, had knelt by her side in desolation, murmuring the words of the viaticum we know all too well. Instants later, she drew her last breath. Silence fell, followed by stifled sobs and the bittersweet strains of our voices as we intoned a *planctus*.

For one phantasmal moment it had seemed she merely slept. I had drawn closer, touched her arm, and murmured, "My lady," as if to waken her. Suddenly I had felt a hand upon my shoulder: the Abbess Mathilda. "Remember the queen and her example," the abbess said, with a firmness that was not without compassion. I turned away from the body in order to regain my composure. It would be my duty, as the one closest to the queen, to lead us in the rituals that would follow.

Even so, I begged the abbess for a few final moments alone with the queen: a time to reflect, I explained, to bid *adieu* and to assemble the mantle, crown, and the keepsakes that would accompany her on this, the final voyage of a queen who had known so many. The abbess and the others—even Sister Alix, the queen's granddaughter—had no idea of my other mission.

Others had already done the work of anointing her body with holy unguents and precious scents. I had watched from a distance as they performed the morbid tasks, all the while recalling other perfumes, those she had used in her lifetime with abandon. How unlike those, today, with their dark, funereal purpose!

Turning to me as she prepared to leave, the abbess gently said, "We will leave you, Isabelle, to close the queen's eyes. It is only right and fitting that you do so."

I glanced at Sister Alix, who stood close to the abbess. "But surely, it should be *you*, her granddaughter," I entreated.

"No," Alix replied. "We know the queen would have wanted you to do it."

I gave a mournful nod of acquiescence before curtseying and making the sign of the cross. Then the sisters filed out—a noiseless phalanx, phantomlike, followed by the abrupt sound of the door closing.

Now, when the moment comes for me to close those vivid eyes, I find even my own strength faltering. Several times I steel myself, only to turn away, unable to touch her lids. Still hesitating, I make my way from the coffin to the prie-dieu before the altar. Banks of tapers burn before me. I gaze at them hungrily, as a starving person might a feast; perhaps part of me hopes their fire will burn away my sadness. I draw my hand close, searing one finger in a flame before dipping another into hot molten wax. The pain seems to jolt me past inaction.

I return to her, implore God for strength, and force myself to seal her eyes shut.

Those eyes! I dare not think what they had witnessed during her long life—even I, who know so much. The anointing of two husbands as kings, of two sons as kings, the crowning of two daughters, the murders of bishops, the betrayals of children, the passionate love affairs, the perilous journeys across storm-wracked seas and menacing mountains. All the bitter cares and struggles, which she had, throughout the years, confided to me. All now subsided into chilling silence.

Would she were still here to guide me! Would it were day, for I long for the orderly light of morning and the call of matins.

I turn once more to gaze upon her face: it seems scarcely less imperious with its shuttered orbs. Eleanor, the great queen whom Egyptian slave traders in Messina had likened to the goddess Isis and called the "shameless, magnificent one." "The comparison does not seem to displease you," I had teased, when she had related this story. "Many would say far more *shameless* than magnificent!" she had replied with a rueful laugh. "About that I have no illusion. But if I were to be compared to a goddess, let it at least be Helen!" Now, at this dark hour, it comforts me to remember those moments of mirth, those larksome references to the Trojan princess who had enthralled her since childhood.

In her final weeks, I begged the queen not to leave me, all the while knowing my entreaties were futile. She knew her time had come, and greeted death as she did all journeys, with courage and resolute, albeit somber, preparation. All the while she tried to cheer me, offering me the jewels and finery she knew my station would not permit. She had the grace never to acknowledge what she had from the first intuited: my fascination with such things. "Keep them as *relics* then," she said with a conspiratorial smile, pressing some lustrous pearls into my palm. "If you do not see them as frivolous and vain, then I doubt God will either." It was her wont, her way of summoning the transformative power of the mind. Willful to the end, she seldom doubted that the Lord would accede to her wishes.

She had honed this turn of mind in England during the long years of captivity. I remember that bleak November afternoon when we walked together within the grounds of Winchester and she told me, "Before this time, it was always my bodily strength that sustained me through the pregnancies year after year, and the pain of childbirth. Yet both were welcome to me, for each creature wrenched from my womb meant another successor to the throne. But in these past years, it is my *mind* which has anchored me. I have learned to have faith and be patient. So perhaps I should thank Henry for this ordeal, after all?"

The years I spent with her, during her imprisonment in England, passed slowly, dimly, in turreted monotony. We spent the time telling tales; it was then she began to relate the story of her life. At the beginning, this was simply a way to flee the moated towers, to escape the knights engaged by King Henry, and to distract us from the sentinels who were always at the ready, suspicious of us women, suspicious of our motives and movements. The stories were a way to bend our minds to freedom—the freedom she prized above all else—and to wrest ourselves from the savage cold of Britain to distant sunny climes. To a Sicily of lemon trees and doves; to Aquitaine with its fields of lavender and skies scattered with purple starlings; to sea-sparkling Cyprus, and to Antioch, with its sensual pleasures and scintillating mosaics.

She told me of the lost weeks in Ephesus during the Second Holy War, with King Louis. It was Christmastime; she and her husband, the king, had set up camp below the ramparts. Few among the soldiers had chosen to venture to the ancient Roman city, as she had, if only to escape the smell of roasting flesh—the detritus from the disaster of the preceding weeks. There, in the Holy Land, she first saw the ancient tombs, which so impressed her, and which would become the inspiration for her own. They reminded her of other tombs, vacant and crumbling, that she had seen as a girl in the Aquitaine, her homeland. The Aquitaine, with its tantalizing echoes of the pagan world, which had fascinated us both.

Hence the singular plan for her tomb, which she has left with me, and that the artisans at the abbey, who both feared and worshipped her, will implement. It seems logical that she, who adored the ballads of the troubadours and who had herself sparked so many stanzas, should be portrayed holding an open book. "Let them think it is a prayer book," she told me with a mischievous glance. "But you and I know better."

She entrusted me with its completion. "Leave the rest to me," I told her, my brisk tone masking sadness; never had my own words resounded with such dreadful finality. She knew I would have the tomb executed to her liking, and that I would also gather the requisite talismans to accompany her to the afterlife. Her simplest crown, "to keep me company" she had instructed; her favorite rings, a lock of her daughter Joanna's hair, the signet of Richard's reign, a carnelian scarab given to her by her father, who had been given it by his. The pilgrim shell from Santiago de Compostela and the Becket casket she had already bequeathed to me.

She was, by then, that darkest January, nearly sightless. "Give me music," she commanded one especially dismal afternoon. Thus, as I had done before, I summoned Alardus the minstrel to play her favorite songs—the music she had heard as a girl in the courts of her father and grandfather, the dukes of Aquitaine. There was no need to ask Mother Mathilda to grant permission for this irregular act: this was a request from the dying queen, after all. "As queen, I overrule the abbess," she once told me, adding with characteristic realism, "and in any case, even *here* the highborn have privileges—surely you, as a countess, must at least tacitly acknowledge that." And if I were, one day, to take the veil? I asked somewhat slyly. To this she merely responded with a sphinxlike smile.

During that week we burned many of the queen's private letters and documents. "You have burned them *all*," she said to me several times; this was framed as royal dictum, rather than question. Over the years she had entrusted me with preserving, and sometimes copying, her most important letters—as keepsakes, as evidence, as means of vengeance. The letters to and from Hildegard of Bingen, for instance; others from Richard when he was held for ransom by the Holy Roman Emperor, still others from the queen's daughter Joanna when she was married to William of Sicily. Letters the queen had either written or dictated herself, or received from friends, lovers, and conspirators.

Her sight had nearly failed by that time—that gray afternoon in early March—when, one by one, I pitched rolls of parchment into the fire as she sipped mulled wine. As the flames crackled, she asked again with unnerving insistence whether "*all* the letters and documents" were burning. Yes, I confirmed, keeping my voice steady as I lied, for I was no stranger to dissembling.

"Can you not smell the parchment burning?" I asked coolly enough. Satisfied, she nodded—unaware, of course, that I had tossed blank parchment into the fire. To reassure her, I took her frail hand, filling its palm with still warm ashes, as further "proof."

I hold my head in my hands now, trembling, every time I think of that moment when I had lied to her, when I had pretended to obey. *I saved the letters and papers she had ordered me to destroy.* I have committed many other sins, but few as haunting. The betrayal pierced me with guilt I could not eradicate even by fasting: in the weeks that followed I began to starve myself, as if in self-deprivation I would find some peace, some penance.

Clementia and Marie had noticed how thin I had become and mentioned it to the queen, who could not, of course, discern the changes in me herself. "I hear you are not eating," she told me with concern, groping for my gaunt hand. I told her it was nothing—I often lost my appetite in winter. All the while, I kept my voice steady, composed, opaque.

I tell myself ad infinitum that my intentions were honorable, that it was better she go to her grave unaware of the only sin for which she would never have forgiven me. The sin that I cannot confess, for it would be too dangerous, especially here, at Fontevraud, where King John's men encircle us and where his other henchmen wait nearby in expectation. At other moments, still searching for absolution, I comfort myself with the notion that my seeming to obey her last commands gave her the forbearance to survive another month. In my heart I realize this is only a delusion. Personal slights, even calumnies, she could bear: any violation of her legacy as queen, or that of the Plantagenets, was unforgivable.

But now I hear the strains of the funeral chant, Dies Irae, come closer: *Lacrimosa dies illa / qua resurgent ex favilla.* I must work quickly to carry out the queen's commands.

All she had requested must be tucked deep within the silken folds of her coffin. And then the forbidden book itself—the copy I created, my final gift to her, for it seemed unthinkable that she should go to the afterlife without it by her side. As for the other, the original—that is hidden here with me, with the letters and papers I have secretly preserved. I must safeguard all when we leave for Castile, to her daughter's court. Word of the queen's death will soon reach King John, and spies tell me his henchmen, awaiting the signal in Chinon, will then advance to the abbey. Among them may be—no, I dare not think of it now.

Kneeling by her, I utter one final prayer. May God protect her and forgive her all her sins. May He grant peace eternal to her, Eleanora Regina, queen of England and France, and Duchess of Aquitaine. May He also forgive me my trespasses, and for the sinful acts that I kept even from her.

The footsteps of the monks draw close. Then—at the door—the three knocks I have both anticipated and dreaded.

They have come to take the body. *Sauve qui peut.*

# PART I

# Chapter I

It is past midnight; the funeral vigil for the queen is underway. I am alone in my chamber, thinking of the perilous journey ahead. I must try to sleep.

The bronze falcon sits beside me, on the table by my bed. Aiglette placed it there yesterday, thinking it would comfort me. I was ambivalent about the falcon when he gave it to me: it was a gift I had never wanted, and was, at first, almost wary of. Yet the passing years and the perception of others have changed my way of perceiving this fanciful creature, with its gilded wings and enigmatic gaze. But then, time has altered so much.

Would it were morning, would that sunlight might banish my disquiet! Even my prayers have been fruitless: God and the Virgin seem to have forsaken me. I must seek another way to find peace.

Throughout my life, I have always found solace in stories. Storytelling was how my brother and I would pass time together in childhood; and how, later, at Château Ravinour, during my marriage, Aiglantine and I would escape from apprehension and tedium. Here at the abbey, when Marie was a little girl, she not only reveled in my tales, but also came to love creating her own. When, one day, she found herself unable to begin, I proposed "the game of the first line": she was to start with one sentence, I would supply the next, and so forth; then, almost magically it seemed, she would be able to spin the story by herself. From that moment on, whenever she was frustrated, I would remind her: "It is always the first line, the first stroke, that is the hardest."

Tonight, more than ever, I long to soothe myself by storytelling. Yet, for once, I have no ability to invent; fear and sadness have rendered me barren of imagination. There is only one story I burn to tell: a *real* story, my own.

And if I were to tell that story—the story of my life—how would I begin? "Take a deep breath and steel your mind," the queen would have exhorted me. But surely it is my own advice to Marie that I ought to take heed of now: "It is that first sentence which matters most. The rest will follow."

IT WAS MARRIAGE TO A stranger, a lord whose land lay to the north, that brought me to this place and, ultimately, to the queen, to Eleanor. . . .

My family was of noble name, but it lacked real riches. We came from the countryside in the region of Nîmes, not far from Uzès. I was the youngest of four children. My two brothers had come first, then my sister, Amélie, who thought me an odd creature. "Your head is too much in books and stories, Isabelle," she would scold, "and your strange ideas are worse than useless!" I was her bête noire, and the quarrels that erupted between us were fierce and frequent. "Everyone cried the day you were born," she would taunt me, spitefully aware that my parents had been praying for a son.

My early childhood was encircled by a nimbus of disappointment. My mother had little use for daughters who required dowries we could scarcely afford, and even less patience with me, the youngest, whose constant questions irritated her beyond all measure. Most maddening to her was my curiosity about things which, to her, were of no consequence: the lore of our region among them—that of the cities of Nîmes and Arles, where the ancient people, the Greeks and Romans, had left their mark.

When I was conceived, she once admitted, God cursed her by depriving her of another son. The infant boy who had preceded my birth had died, as had another, born when I was five years old. For years I would remember the terrifying screams of my mother through the long hours of that searing night, and how, in early morning, the wizened midwives finally emerged, brandishing rags soaked with blood as they conveyed word that the baby boy was stillborn.

My mother recovered from that ordeal, but her attitude toward me ever after changed and hardened. I never knew the warmth that she bestowed upon my siblings, especially my brothers. I learned to evoke feeling from her by other means. I would disobey her, or mock her behind her back, or stick my tongue out when she spouted a favorite precept warning us about Héloïse and the perils of the flesh, or when she extolled Saint Ursula, the virgin martyr, as an exemplar for us, her daughters. Then I would give full rein to mischief and impertinence, for it was not lost on me that my fearlessness frightened her. "The little vixen," she would call me, her violet eyes alight with fury. This gave me a fleeting sense of victory, for at such moments she did show me something, even if it was rage.

IT WAS MY BROTHERS I admired, and who took me hawking and riding; yet even from them I hid much of my secret life. The eldest, Guy, a pragmatist, would have scoffed at my incessant wonderings. But Arnaut seemed to understand my fascination with adventure and tales of the pagan people. He had been told about that lost world by my grandfather, who had been told those stories by his. These tales became the first of many codes between Arnaut and me, a vernacular of our own.

It was with my brothers that I first went to the city of Nîmes by horseback one crystalline day in May decades ago. I was twelve at the time of this, my first great adventure. I had heard about Nîmes and its Roman monuments; even so, I was unprepared for the moment when we first glimpsed the stupendous arches of the Pont du Gard reflected in the glassy river. I remember how small I felt, how paltry and overpowered, as we gazed above in wonder at the gigantic arches against the clear blue sky.

We stopped at noontime by the edge of the river, the aqueduct looming above us. We were thirsty and hot from hours of riding; even now I remember how delicious the food tasted, how icy and fresh the spring water tasted as I gulped it from cupped hands. I gazed at the looming arches as I bit into the bread and pungent cheese, savoring the breezes, which wafted the fragrance of mimosa toward us from the riverbank.

We finished eating and resumed our journey to Nîmes along the old Roman road, the Via Domitia. Pilgrims passed us: old men in ragged clothes, picking out their steps along the path with crooked staffs, beggars with missing limbs. Then came merchants with bolts of cloth, peddlers hawking relics of saints, mercenaries with unsightly scars, and, one moment, a haughty legate from Rome—or so my brothers told me—who rode on horseback with vivid pennants of white and scarlet.

AT LAST WE CAME TO the city itself: bustling, clamorous, dusty, and teeming with crowds. We went first, of course, to the cathedral, where we asked the Lord's blessings for our family. I did not like the cathedral, which seemed a chilly, fear-inducing place, vaguely resonant of my mother. It brought to mind her sharp looks when I asked about things she deemed improper, and the fearsome blows she dealt me when I had disobeyed.

Arnaut had told me stories of *other* places: we would go to these on our own without Guy, he had confided in the low, thrilling voice of a conspirator. Take me, I had begged him: show me all that is forbidden, show me all you know of that other world. And so we left Guy, with the excuse that we would go to another church for confession, and would meet him later.

He led me to an ancient shrine which had long figured in his stories—"the temple of Diana," he called it. As I gazed, awestruck, at the entrance, and then began to ascend the expanse of marble steps, I wondered with a shiver how many sacrificial virgins had proceeded up them in centuries past. Yet once I entered the serene white sanctuary, how enveloped I felt, how safe! Then, as now, this was the effect of ancient beauty upon me.

Through twisting streets next, through sun and lacy shade, we approached the Roman amphitheater: an imperious skeleton of stone. During many cold winter nights as children in Provence, while the wind blew and the fire crackled with olive wood, Arnaut had told me stories of the savage games that had once taken place in this arena—of the carnage, and the lusty people who clapped while men were torn to pieces by roaring lions and exotic beasts from Africa. How those in the audience would cheer, carousing with food and drink while the combatants, their blood trailing in the ravaged sand, met their fate below.

We arrived at the massive arch framing the entrance: how incongruous it seemed to find wildflowers blossoming in the crevices between the layers of cold stone. I plucked a few flowers, crushing them in my hand so that my palms were sticky and moist as I stepped inside. The sun was still hot and strong when we entered the antechambers, the two of us alone in the silent, dusky labyrinth. We walked slowly through, still leading our horses through long, dank tunnels matted with oozing kernels and errant vines. A few times I stopped to touch the icy wall, closing my eyes as I tried to imagine the echo of ancient voices and the footsteps of victors, victims, untamed animals, and emperors ravenous for the bloody confirmation of their power. Even now I can remember the smell of that place, for it was the smell of death itself—icy, alien, fetid.

A sharp wheeling sound above, in the sky, frightened me, wrenching me from reverie: the circling of swallows with whirling, bladelike wings. I took a deep breath, steadying myself, though I was reluctant to lean against the beady wall, as if mere contact with it might suck me into an inferno. Yet the sound of the swallows had also reassured me—soaring high above that ominous place, they were a sign of life after all, and of freedom.

At last we came to a long passageway where, to each side, crude pits were hacked from stone. A sudden gust of wind seemed to propel us forward into that dark universe, with its intimations of cruelty. I looked to each side at the cavelike cells, which had once held men, and then at Arnaut. We stood close together in a place where the light was so dim that even his bright red hair looked murky.

"This is where the gladiators were kept," he whispered, "where they would wait until they were summoned."

"By whom?" I asked, even though I already knew the answer: I merely wanted him to repeat it.

"By the emperor," he replied, "or by his surrogate." He repeated the story recited to him by our grandfather: these men, these gladiators gathered from every corner of the empire would stare into the scorching sun, bend their glistening shaven heads, and utter the chilling words: "We who are about to die salute you."

WHEN WE RETURNED HOME, I tried as best I could to stifle my questions and resume my chores. I thought incessantly of Nîmes—the amphitheater and the temple of Diana—and pretended that I was once more walking through the dim tunnels that led to the arena, or I would venture far away, to the edge of our property, to climb my favorite tree, a lovely sturdy oak that had been my refuge from my prying sister and hectoring mother for years. There, hidden and safe among its branches, I would look down over the land and pretend I glimpsed a phalanx of advancing Roman soldiers, or that I was a scribe to Julius Caesar.

This is another memory of a childhood spent yearning for the *elsewhere.*

AFTER NÎMES, THERE FOLLOWED A deepening closeness with Arnaut, the closeness that comes when one has shared a momentous experience. I wonder if the rest of our family suspected what the journey to Nîmes had meant to us. I doubt it: we took care to conceal it, for the two of us stirred to the clandestine as much as we did to adventure.

Since early childhood Arnaut and I had been fascinated by spies and codes. Indeed, we had already evolved secret ways of communicating, often involving messages by code. It was a way of engaging our imaginations, I suppose, of passing the interminable winter nights, of evading our parents' control. Our schemes had begun with letters written in a primitive code, sometimes in the form of an anagram.

One day, when Arnaut returned from a visit to my grandfather's library, he told me that he had come upon a detail in a volume of a Roman writer, Pliny: the milk of the tithymalus plant could be used as invisible ink. He explained that the fluid would be invisible after drying, but afterward, if held over gentle heat, it would turn brown and become legible. The name of the plant seemed so exotic that I never thought we would find it, but Arnaut proved me wrong. He learned that the euphorbia bush, abundant in our region, was a member of the same genus.

After this discovery, we raced outside to pick some flowering branches of euphorbia, crushed the blossoms, and concocted our own "ink." For weeks we delighted in sending each other scraps of parchment which appeared to be blank, but on which, after being held over a low flame, words magically sprang to life.

Little by little the messages evolved. At first, they were merely childish and silly; as we grew older, they became a way of communicating much that we could not outwardly express. Mine were often reflections of a rebellious girl: "I am going to get my revenge on Amélie tomorrow"; "Let us meet later in the stables and hide there until supper so no one can find us"; "I never want to be like our mother when I grow up"; or "I wish I were like young Queen Eleanor and could set off to the Holy Land."

My brother's messages were of another order. Some were passages from stories he had read or heard: "He who caused the wound must heal it" or "They can because they think they can." It was others of his own, at once edifying and imaginative, which resonated with me long afterward: "Guilt is sloth by another name," "Life must be an adventure, above all," and lastly, and perhaps most indelibly: "Whenever you are in despair, invent."

Most of all I wanted to read books that contained the secrets of the ancient world. For I, too, could read: my father and my grandfather had insisted that the girls of our family should learn, though my mother hardly saw the need of it.

During the weeks following the visit to Nîmes, I decided to ask my grandfather whether I might be permitted to use his library. I was full of trepidation, for I knew that it was a sacred place, the domain of men, of learning. I rehearsed posing the question to him many times, pacing the grounds near our orchard as I did so. Yet I was also bolstered by my confidence in my grandfather's love, for I knew I was his favorite. It was he who had taught me not only to read but also to write. He, like Arnaut, never disparaged my curiosity.

One day that summer I rode to his manor and crept into the library so quietly that I caught Grandfather unawares. Embracing him, I caught the familiar scent of lavender from his tunic; great, purply bushes of lavender grew in abundance in his garden, a paradise of vivid, orderly profusion. His simple, rough-hewn clothes were at variance with his elegant chiseled features, his accent that of an older epoch before the penetration of the Angevins. He had created a wondrous universe in his library. The light that filtered through the room was perpetually golden even in the dead of winter, as if imbued by the radiance of knowledge, of learning.

He told me my father had mentioned our journey to Nîmes, and asked, "Did Amélie accompany you and your brothers?"

"No. Amélie stayed home to do her chores and to help Mother. 'Goody goody Saint Amélie' I call her behind her back. I make up little rhymes about her, too, she annoys me so."

"What kind of rhymes?" he asked with a patient smile.

"One like this: 'Amélie is so perfect and so sweet / Even boar would kiss her feet!'" Then, with childish savagery: "I *hate* her!"

Even to my forgiving grandfather, however, I did not dare disclose what I had recently done to my sister when she humiliated me in front of my parents. I had plotted my revenge: I would tuck a few dead mice under the coverlet of her bed that night. Oh, her fury when she discovered them! As she screamed, I had stuck out my tongue and chanted: "Amélie, Amélie, what a coward in our house / Frightened by a little mouse!"

"And what do you think she makes of you?" my grandfather asked, interrupting my vengeful reverie.

"I'm the little devil. The vixen. That is what Mother calls me." I paused, adding, "Mother wanted another son, and instead she got me. Sometimes when she presses those awful poultices upon my face to rid me of my freckles, she says, 'Oh, what a nuisance you can be, Isabelle!' Everything I am, she dislikes."

"I doubt that is so—" he remonstrated.

"Oh yes, it is," I replied. "I know it. Arnaut knows it, too, although he does not admit it. But he understands. He understands *everything.*"

Grandfather seemed to reflect on this. "How much do you know about your mother, and her life, and what made her what she is?"

I shrugged. "Nothing."

"Ah, then that is something you might consider. You see, your mother never knew her own mother. Her own mother left her family and ran away to a nunnery. No one ever spoke of her again, nor did her children ever see her again."

"Do you mean," I said, slowly absorbing this revelation, "that since my mother never knew her own mother, that perhaps she does not know how to be a good mother to me?"

He kissed my forehead. "You are a wise little thing, beyond your years."

This startled me: I had never been called wise. Many other things—reckless, disobedient, brave (this, from Arnaut)—but wise, *never.*

"But she never talks about these things, about her childhood," I mused, returning to the subject of my mother. "Father sometimes does. She never does."

"And you never thought to ask her?"

"No," I replied, for this seemed a preposterous notion. I spoke with my mother of chores, or of my wretched sewing, or of ways to tame my wayward hair, but never of her life. My conversations with her were always tense and infected by her disappointment in me.

"One day you might ask about her own life," my grandfather gently suggested.

"Why? It would do no good, Grandfather. So I won't."

"You are a stubborn little thing," he replied, with an indulgent smile. "It can be useful, that stubbornness. And so can your willfulness. But there will be times in life when you must try your best to pull back, and think: Is this the best way to act? Is this the best *strategy?*"

He said no more. He had set forth this empowering idea gently, merely suggesting that the control of my thoughts and actions lay with me, not with others. Hence his words carried a weight no one else's did. And, of course, the word *strategy* was a brilliant way to frame a new approach to thinking and acting, for *strategy* was a magic word to me, a worldly word, a word I associated with kings and queens, with people of power and learning.

On that still, hot summer afternoon, Grandfather sat by the end of the long table where he habitually studied and wrote. A stylus was poised in his frail, freckled hand, and on one finger, an ancient ring set with a translucent green intaglio. He had bought it as a young man, from a trader south of Rome. It had long fascinated me. Sometimes he would take it off and permit me to hold it so that I might examine the carving more closely. It depicted the Emperor Hadrian, or so my grandfather said, offering a laurel wreath to the goddess Athena, who stood by an olive tree. It was the only possession to which my grandfather had any attachment, other than his books. "My talisman," he called it.

I took a deep breath, my fingers nervously tracing a circle on the table, and asked, "One day, Grandfather, might I be permitted to use your library?"

"I was only wondering *when* you would ask, not *if,* my dear girl!" he exclaimed, with a smile. "Of course, of course you can! If you had not asked me, I would have suggested it soon enough."

In the next few weeks and months, as if he were unveiling rubies from Constantinople or pearls from the eastern seas, he shared his greatest treasures. He introduced me to texts by Cicero, Pliny, and Tacitus, and when I was a bit older, to the splendid poems of Ovid (though only those that he deemed fit for a girl). I was also obliged to study the work of Boethius—my grandfather insisted upon it—but I admit that the *Consolation of Philosophy* interested me little. It was the heroic tales of ancient adventures that enthralled me, and which I read again and again: the stories of the Trojan War—of Helen and Paris and the warrior Agamemnon—and my very favorite, that of Aeneas and his journeys.

In other ways he forever influenced me, opening my eyes to beauty and the wider world beyond. He told me tales of churches being built in other parts of France in a new style, with marble columns carved to resemble figures of men and saints. "Some are not so different," he said, "from the statues made by the ancient peoples." He was much traveled, my grandfather: he had glimpsed the culture and richness of the Burgundian court, to the north, and even the royal court, in Paris. He had been to the Abbey of Saint-Denis, and described its sparkling, colored windows to me—how light filtered through glass panes where stories were depicted in hues as rich as gemstones. This splendid church, he said, had been built according to the plan of the Abbot Suger. It was Suger's idea that beauty and the sacred *could* coexist, that in fact they may be one and the same.

He had seen the sea. Tell me more, I would entreat him, and he told me how he had traveled to Britain and thought the people rich and clever, but savage. There was a wall on the border near Scotland, he said, which had been built by the Emperor Hadrian to sever the Roman world from the wild tribes to the north. He recalled a place called Northumberland as a beautiful, wild land; to me its rich, rolling name alone seemed redolent of mystery. It was rumored Roman treasure was buried there, he said, and hoards of silver left by fleeing peoples in the chaos of later centuries. He told me about the fleets of vessels at Barfleur, as well, and how these daunting ships, which often carried King Henry's men, would cross that unruly stretch of water until they reached the shore of England.

To his stories, I bent my ear; they changed me.

I LOVED THAT LAND, THE land that I would cross by horseback on my visits to my grandfather. I knew its trees, hillocks, valleys, and streams well, so well that I never feared being lost, despite the land's vastness. Even now, when I have traveled far and seen so much, I have moments when I suddenly recall, with an inner passionate welling up, the rough beauty of that terrain crisscrossed by well-worn paths and stone walls, a land of orchards and olive trees, this most ancient part of our country, the land that had been Roman Gaul. Sometimes here at the abbey in the winter when the wind howls, when it is so cold my breath appears as white clouds before me, I think back on the realm of my childhood, and of fields tremulous with bloodred poppies warmed by the southern sun.

So little was I attended to during my girlhood that I could disappear for hours, indeed almost an entire day. Often no one knew, save Arnaut, what I had been doing when I later returned home, scraped and dirty from my adventures.

Not far from my grandfather's manor I had come across the ruins of a pagan sanctuary: here I created my own secret paradise. I had discovered that there were treasures to be found deep within the soil—bits of stone, bronze, and marble, vestiges of the ancient people. I began to collect these remnants, hoarding them in a cave near a copse of bay trees. A fragment of a small stone head, a bit of black and red pottery painted with warriors whom I fantasized to be Trojan, a small vessel of frosty bluish glass. These became my cherished possessions, my private cache. I guarded them fiercely, for they were my greatest treasures, survivors of a vanished world. Often reckless and impatient, I became quiet and focused during these forays, my mind stilled to such a degree that hours would pass without my realizing.

One afternoon on a scalding day in late August, just past the feast of Saint Radegonde, my favorite saint, on the thirteenth, I brought a small shovel from the stable so that I might dig deeper and see what else the earth might yield up. (I had told my parents I needed the shovel for some planting, only one of the many instances when I had lied to them.) Hours later, just at the point of giving up, I struck something hard. I shall never forget that sharp, exultant sound! Slowly, ever so slowly, I pulled the thing forth—a fragile, very beautiful bronze hand, which seemed to beckon upward toward eternity, its slender fingers and wrist encircled by delicate gold bands. No midwife seeing the limbs of an infant emerge from its mother's womb could have been more thrilled!

I cradled the discovery in my hands, wondering how it had survived. As I cleaned the encrustations of centuries off each finger, I marveled who had crafted the hand, and why, and how it had come to rest in this place. This was a young woman's hand, surely. Perhaps she had been only slightly older than myself; perhaps she, too, had longed to escape, but had found her escape only in death.

Hours later, when the sun began to descend, I placed the hand with the rest of my treasures deep within the cave, hiding the entrance with a camouflage I had spent hours creating from pieces of stone and torn branches. When, later that evening, I returned home—much later than was customary—my mother, her face distorted with fury, demanded an explanation. For once, I had failed to dupe her.

"Beat her," my mother insisted.

"Is such a punishment *necessary*?" resisted my father, with a deep sigh.

"Yes. Is it the only way she will learn."

He walked slowly to the wall where the black strap reserved for such punishments was suspended and took it in hand. My skirt was pulled down. I was placed over his knees and given five strokes, which left fearsome red marks across my buttocks for days. Staggering up the steps on the way to my chamber, I tried to *think* my way out of humiliation. I imagined I was a female saint who had been unjustly treated, and for whom God would wreak revenge on my captors. I thought of Héloïse and all she had suffered in her love for Abelard. These were absurd comparisons—I think I realized it even then—but they assuaged the inner pain.

That night I wept myself to sleep: my tears were hot, and my fury great, but never did I reveal my hurt and rage, not even to Arnaut. Indeed, part of me felt weirdly triumphant: my secret cave and my treasures, after all, remained hidden and safe.

FROM MY MOTHER I HEARD tales of Queen Eleanor: her scandals and sins. My mother would recall how Eleanor, as the young queen, had left for the Holy War with her women—all of them richly caparisoned and hungry for adventure. "The queen and her ladies—and the *whores*," my mother would say to me and Amélie. She would repeat rumors of the queen's dalliances with her uncle Raymond in Antioch while in the Holy Land, and in Paris, with Geoffrey of Anjou, the father of her now estranged husband, King Henry. I drank in these stories as greedily as I had the water from the spring near Nîmes.

My mother despised the queen, whom she considered "sinful" and "unwomanly." That Eleanor divorced King Louis and then plotted her marriage to Henry Plantagenet was "unseemly," a scandal for which God would punish her.

"Eleanor was born of a line of devils, and will go to the devil," my mother would say. "Her grandfather Duke William was an adulterer, after all, and her father was cursed by Bernard of Clairvaux." At the mention of Bernard, whom she revered, she would make the sign of the cross.

"No wonder," she would continue contemptuously, "that Eleanor has never been able to bear a son for Louis! This was a sign from God, punishing her for her wickedness. It is no wonder the Holy War they led had been such a disaster, and that it brought shame upon the Franks!"

IT WAS FROM MY MOTHER, as well, that I first heard about the Abbey of Fontevraud, which lay on the border of Poitou, not far from Saumur. This is where queen Eleanor would occasionally reside, my mother said, the holy place that she and the Plantagenets had endowed, and where the queen, and other noblewomen of high rank, would find refuge. Women who had been discarded or abused by their husbands, highborn women who had the means to choose another path, or wealthy widows who had retreated from the world. At Fontevraud, Mother said, with a cluck of disapproval, there was an unusual arrangement: it was the abbess who ruled over both the monks and sisters.

The abbey had been endowed by the queen's grandfather, I was to learn—the wicked Duke William IX, he of the ribald verses and shameless womanizing. Its founder, Robert d'Arbrissel, had been a wandering hermit whose first followers had been fallen women—women who worshipped at the shrine of Mary Magdalene.

WHEN I WAS THIRTEEN, I came of age. The flood of blood between my thighs frightened me, filled me with shame, and rendered several nights sleepless. Surely, I imagined, the bleeding was due to sin—for my reading, my secrets, my wayward thoughts. I prayed to my favorite saints to cure me of the bloody wound: to Saint Radegonde, to Saint Michael the archangel, he who had done battle with the devil; and then, for good measure, to the Virgin.

Too frightened to remain silent, I finally sought out my mother early one morning. She sat by the hearth, sewing, hoop in hand. I told her about the dreadful bleeding and confessed that all my underclothes were soiled.

She looked up, needle poised in hand. "Surely you must know what this means," she said with some impatience.

I shook my head.

"This is your monthly bleeding," she said, resuming her sewing. "It is a sign from God that you are now a woman. Did not Amélie tell you about this?" She seemed irritated.

"No," I replied, both confused and ashamed of my ignorance.

"She ought to have." Then she called for Hortense, the maid.

"Give Isabelle some fresh under linens and show her how to use them," she directed, in the same voice she would use to order a chicken plucked, or have a floor swept of dirty rush.

"I will, my lady," said Hortense.

"And if the bleeding should become copious, boil a toad, dry it, and place its powder in a pouch that Isabelle will carry at her waist." She stood up, tossed her hoop on the chair, and left us, the red tassels of her pointed sleeves trailing behind her.

# CHAPTER 2

A few years later, Amélie married a pompous knight, Balduin, from the region of Albi. She now enjoyed the fripperies of a household on the edge of court life, a position that imbued her with a maddening air of superiority. It irked me that Guy, who had always been close to Amélie, seemed inordinately impressed by her new position—"You would do well to think of your sister as an example, Isabelle," he would say, to my annoyance. When she returned once to visit, I thought her newly acquired clothes, her prattle about domestic matters, and her painted face, all quite insufferable.

With her absence, the chores normally heaped upon me—gathering kindling, doing the simplest mending—had doubled, leaving me little time for walks or visits to my grandfather. One cold afternoon in autumn, I returned to our manor bearing branches and twigs for kindling. Gusts of wind had propelled me home, and a gray sky bore down on the ragged outlines of our manor.

I entered the house, turning into the hall, which led to a room deep within, which was separated by a rough wool curtain the color of crushed berries. I overheard my parents speaking: "Isabelle"—"Dowry"—"Would she were." I crept closer to listen.

"She is headstrong and disobedient," I heard my mother say.

"But she is clever," said my father.

"And what will *cleverness* achieve for her?" retorted my mother. "And *us*?"

There was a long pause before my father replied, "Intelligence is not a small thing, even for a woman."

My mother then began to recite a litany of my deficiencies: I was secretive, I was rebellious—

"Some would say spirited," interrupted my father. "And many call Isabelle lovely in face and form."

"She is not without admirers and can be winsome when she chooses," conceded my mother. "But it is her *manner* which is so maddening. Her tendency to willfulness and disobedience." She paused, uttering the little clucking noise that often accompanied her dicta. "She has none of the decorous qualities of Amélie. The sooner we can make provisions for Isabelle, the better. After all, she has no dowry to speak of. And we have not the means to send her to the abbey." Then, in the accusatory tone she often used: "You know that as well as I do." Our lack of riches was at once a wound she never failed to remind him of and a weapon she wielded when it served her purpose.

There fell a long silence before my father said, "Given our circumstances, what makes you think he would agree to wed her—"

"He is rich, but his family was only recently granted a title. It would be important to him that Isabelle has noble lineage, that she is a countess," she added proudly.

A slight pause. "What is known of his character?" my father asked, in a rather timorous voice.

"That he is well respected, and not unkindly," she replied. Then, shrilly: "Well, what say you, husband?"

My father sighed. "So be it." There was the thud of wood being tossed into the fire; then he said, "Tell me what I should do."

"Nothing at the moment," replied my mother, before adding, peremptorily, "leave it all to me."

I crept upstairs to the chamber I had once shared with my sister. Outside, wind howled, and menacing clouds gathered in the evening sky. I crawled into my bed, drawing my cat, Cachette, close under the quilt as I wiped my tears and listlessly stroked her fur. Hurt swept through every pore of my body.

Of course I had always known that marriage loomed. *It was beyond my control*—five words that engulfed me with terror. Had I a choice? No, I had no choice except—except—and here my thoughts swerved—except *in my way of facing it*. I began to pace the room, treading quietly so as not to wake the household, Cachette still cradled in my arms. I thought of Saint Radegonde, married at thirteen to Clotaire, the Merovingian king; I thought of Queen Eleanor, married at about my age to Louis of France. I thought of Helen, shipped off to Troy to marry Menelaus. They were queens, of course, and I was not—but still they were young women, perhaps not so different from myself.

What would *they* have done? I asked myself. Surely they would not have cowered. They would have seized this impending marriage and cloaked it in a different guise: not as an imprisonment, but as an act that could conceivably set them free. An escape.

WHEN, THE FOLLOWING MONTH, I was promised in marriage to Gerard, Lord de Meurtaigne, I still struggled to submit. It was my fate, I continued to tell myself (the idea of *fate* seemed to have a certain grandeur). One afternoon in mid-December, my father quietly took me aside to tell me of the man to whom I was betrothed, a newly rich knight who lived near the port of La Rochelle, and who had use for my title, as countess, and noble name. I would learn more about Gerard de Meurtaigne, my future husband, from Guy, who had met him in Troyes. Guy seemed to greatly admire him. "Château Ravinour is renowned for its luxury, and its falcon hunts," he told me reverently. Lord de Meurtaigne, he went on to say, was the younger son of a father who had been raised from a minor baron to a knight. He had made his early fortune by the importation of textiles and spices from the East, from the Holy Land, before expanding into the wine trade and the cultivation of woad, the plant stuff used to make dyes for the newly fashionable color blue—the celestial blue of the Virgin, the brilliant heavenly blue of the stained-glass windows of Abbot Suger's Saint-Denis.

It was my grandfather who had first told me about men who were becoming rich from trade in the color blue. "Rich from the blue of the Virgin?" I had asked him, for the notion of earthly riches tied to the holy realm seemed quite implausible. "Yes, even so," he had replied. "Celestial blue, and the Blessed Virgin's it may be. But the trade in it has also created some worldly fortunes, ones quite apart from the spirit of the Holy Church."

IN THE MONTH THAT PRECEDED the marriage, a midwife came to examine me. "Be not afraid," she said, unaware that it was humiliation, not fear, that I struggled with. After ordering me to undress, she proceeded to inspect my breasts, my stomach, and my hips; then, forcing me to open my legs, she drew them apart to see "the fork," she called it, in such a way that shame overcame me and I prayed to God that this should end.

She pronounced me healthy and told my parents, who had waited outside the door, that I was ready for the "act of Venus" and well able to produce a child.

Then it was my mother's turn to prepare me for my new life. She took me into her bedchamber after the midwife departed.

"Sit down," she said, her mouth set rather tensely, "and let us talk."

I did so, nervously. She took a seat opposite, her hands tightly folded in her lap.

"It is time for you to know what is required in marriage," she began. "You must learn to curb your tongue, be obedient, and assume a gentler mien. That will not be easy for you, admittedly. But you must remember how fortunate you are that we have been able to arrange this marriage for you. You have no dower lands to offer, after all—only your noble name and bloodline. Your first duty is to produce a child. The man you are to marry requires an heir. He lost his first wife in childbirth. Do you understand, Isabelle?"

I nodded.

From the pocket of her tunic she took an ex-voto of beaten silver stamped with the impression of a baby boy. "You must place this in your husband's chapel the morning after the wedding night," she said, handing it to me.

Of the details of the wedding night she said nothing else, nor were they ever discussed. Indeed, when I later asked Hortense, the usually talkative servant girl, what would happen, she only stammered a response, her face flushing as she made a veiled reference to animals in our barn-yard.

IT WAS ARNAUT, MY CHERISHED brother, who seemed most reticent on the subject of my marriage. One day, after he returned from a ride to the village on a cold day with a churlish sky, I noticed that he was uncommonly quiet. As we walked toward the stable, I looked at him closely, trying to memorize the color of his burnished red hair, the in-vincible way he walked, and the strength of his slender fingers as he held the reins of his mount.

He loved music, Arnaut did, and sometimes, when he returned from the village, he would tell me of new songs or verses he had heard. But on that day he was alarmingly quiet.

I asked what was troubling him.

"Your leaving," he said, looking away.

"But we knew the time would come," I murmured, in a low, choked voice.

"Yes, of course, but the man you are marrying—he is greatly older than you. And you know very little of the world."

He dismounted; then, after helping me, we continued on foot, in silence, until we caught sight of our house in the distance. He stopped suddenly, turning to me, his blue-gray eyes intent. "We must think of a way we can exchange letters," he said. "There may be times when we use our code, or invisible ink, perhaps."

I did not voice what I was thinking: this seemed, even to me, rather improbable. "But who will carry our letters?" I asked. "Messengers are very costly." For I recalled occasions when my parents had sent a letter to Amélie—how painstakingly they had parceled out the payment to the messenger, and how my mother had complained about the expense.

When I reminded him of this, he seemed surprised by my concern. "That will not be the issue for you—the expense." He paused again. "It will be the *contriving* to do so I expect."

"Well, then!" I replied, relieved.

He seemed not to hear me, so absorbed was he in thinking. Then, suddenly, turning to me, he announced: "Yes, we must find a way to write each other privately, if need be. Let me think upon it."

AND SO I PREPARED TO leave my home, my family, and the beloved countryside where I had known some freedom, for the journey to my new home to the north—to Château Ravinour, in the region of La Rochelle. I gathered my few clothes, my cherished book on the history of Troy from my grandfather, and the tiny statuette of Saint Radegonde, which I kept by my bed. But it was the idea of preserving my treasures in the cave that obsessed me. There are times when obsession can be useful, diverting one's mind from pain.

I asked Arnaut to help me collect my treasures. With great care he helped me gather the objects, swaddling them in old bits of cloth and wool, which we packed in saddlebags for the ride home. I asked him to keep one of them as a keepsake: he chose a small black pottery vase with grimacing warriors painted in red. One side depicted a journey, the other a galley manned by oarsmen. "A harbinger of future journeys," he observed with a smile, marveling at it. Only now do I realize he was speaking of his own life.

During the following weeks, he crafted a small casket to protect my keepsakes for my journey north. It was hewn in walnut and painted with our family shield—a motif of laurel leaves encircling the motto VIRTUTE OMNIBUS SUPEREMINET, which he had carved on its lid. A gift of precious jewels or gold-threaded silk could not have touched me as much! Even now when I glimpse the box—for it has survived all these years—I remember the joy, yet also the unutterable sadness, I felt in receiving it.

Within it lay a roll of parchment that appeared to have nothing written on it but my name. I, of course, knew better. When, later, I held the sheet to a low steady flame, I watched as a message flickered across the page: "Never forget the motto upon this box: 'Courage above all else.'"

ON THE EVE OF MY departure, our family gathered for supper; it was our custom to exchange keepsakes before momentous journeys. From my father, a medal of the Virgin; from Guy, a well-worn Psalter; and from Arnaut, a Roman coin engraved with a crocodile and serpent, the ancient insignia of Nîmes, which he had threaded through a silk ribbon. "May it always remind you of our visit there," he said, placing it around my neck. "I shall give you my gift tomorrow," my mother told me.

The following morning, just past dawn, my family and our servants gathered together in the courtyard. I remember how bitterly I cried when Hortense wrested Cachette from my arms; how I knelt to pat Petru, my father's devoted dog, one last time. I remember the solemn faces of the grooms and stableboys as they bid me adieu, for they had known me since birth. The sky threatened snow, and the pavement of the court-yard was ice crackled and treacherous. I slipped as I approached my horse, trembling as I looked at Arnaut, who lent me his hand. He stood by me, one hand on my horse's flank; then he stole a glance at Guy, who signaled it was time. It was Guy, as the eldest brother, who would accompany me to my new home.

I turned first to Arnaut. "And so—" he said, holding me tight, his voice choking as I wept.

"To the next adventure," I replied, trying desperately to be brave as I wiped my tears. He kissed both my cheeks and murmured, "Never forget the words on the casket I gave you—"

"'Courage above all else,'" I choked out, embracing him. Then Guy quickly drew me away.

My father held me and kissed me, and then Grandfather, whose embrace almost crushed me with its power, for he knew the terrible unspoken truth—that it was unlikely I should ever see him again. "Al-ways remember our times reading together, and your favorite stories of adventure," he entreated me. "Think of heroes setting off on journeys, think of your beloved Aeneas—" Then, in a low rich voice, he began to recite a familiar passage from *The Aeneid*: "'Let us go, goddess-born, where the Fates, in their ebb and flow, draw us—'" At this he paused, grasping my hands in his so tightly I felt his signet ring cut into my fingers. "Continue, darling girl," he murmured, my hands still in his.

Struggling to speak, I haltingly resumed the verse: "'Come what may, endurance must master every fortune—'" At that, I gave in to sobs, hugging him with all my might. I felt his whiskers upon my cheeks as he returned my embrace, I remember catching a whiff of lavender, the scent that I would forever associate with him.

"It is time," Guy said, taking me by the shoulders. I wiped my face of tears and drew on my gloves. He cupped his hands for me to use as a stirrup; I mounted.

At last I turned to face my mother, a tall figure draped in crimson. Her face, with its wide dark brow, was calm and composed. I had thought that she might embrace me, but she did not. She took my gloved hand for a moment, pressing upon its palm a seal with the image of Saint Ursula, the martyred saint. "This is my gift to you," she said.

The next moment she gave a quick, sharp nod in Guy's direction: "Now it is time for you to leave," a measure of relief and triumph in her eyes. She flung her red shawl across her shoulder and commanded, "Set off."

This was January in the year of our grace, 1178. I was seventeen.

CHAPTER 3

It was approaching nightfall when we first caught sight of Château Ravinour in the distance. A light, scrim-like snow partly obscured its outlines, and I remember drawing back my woolen hood so that I might see ahead more clearly. We had ridden long and hard, my body and hands ached with cold, yet at that moment all normal sensation seemed to have left me, so intent was I on the ghostly structure in the distance. I stopped, overcome with nervous excitement, glancing to the side, to my brother, for reassurance. I had learned that Guy knew my future husband from tournaments, for it appeared that Lord de Meurtaigne belonged to the circle of noblemen who surrounded the Young King, Queen Eleanor's eldest son, Henry—part of the gilded youth of Angevin France to which Guy greatly aspired. Some, like himself, were of ancient name; others were newly rich and able to fund the Young King's appetite for luxury.

"Not long now," Guy said, stopping beside me. "Are you ready?"

I nodded, uttering "yes" in as hearty a voice as I could summon, for I did not want Guy to know how terrified I was, and how I dreaded the thought of his leaving me in this foreign place.

Soon phalanxes of torches moved closer, as if borne by phantoms; only as they came closer could I see the faces of the men who bore them slowly coming into focus. Next, the sonorous horns signaling the lowering of the drawbridge; the furious sound of our horses' hooves upon the wood as we crossed the frozen moat, then a great clamor of shouted instructions that accompanied our arrival into the courtyard, as stable hands and servants greeted us and helped us to dismount.

We were led down a long passageway, into a great hall lit by clusters of tapers and warmed by a roaring fire, the walls hung with damasks, the stone pavement scattered with fragrant fresh rush. But it was the profusion of color, of walls covered with fabrics glittering with golden threads intertwined with blue, that lent the great room a luxurious, phantasmagoric quality.

Water from a golden ewer was brought so that we might wash our hands, the vessel itself fashioned in the shape of a strange creature with a long, lascivious tongue as a spout. Servants offered savory hot wine in silver cups, warm and comforting in my grasp. The next moment the steward, a slight dark-haired man, led us to a table piled with enormous platters of food, pitchers of drink, and an array of expensive spices— ground pepper, and cumin, and cinnamon, spices I had only known from feast days, and even then, never in abundance. I remember how liberally and with what abandon I sprinkled them on the capon cakes and the roasted breasts of duck. How I gorged myself that night!

As dazzled as I, but straining to appear nonchalant, Guy inquired when we would see Gerard de Meurtaigne himself. The steward told us Lord de Meurtaigne had traveled to Aigues-Mortes for a meeting with merchants from Genoa. Assuming all went well, he would return the following day.

After an hour or so, and sated by supper, we were escorted to our bedchambers, down a passageway painted with frescoes that seemed to come to life by the light of tapers—patterns of vivid blues, and green twisting vines, and arabesques in red and violet. My steps were unsteady from fatigue and wine as I was led up a series of twisting steps to an upper chamber where a young woman, a servant, awaited me.

"My lady," she said, with a deep bow.

I smiled in return, cheered by her sweet face, which was nevertheless not without a trace of sadness. She was very fair, with hair the color of palest wheat; but it was her eyes that arrested me, for each was a different hue: one golden brown, the other blue. Below the outer corner of the brown eye was a small, deep purple, birthmark.

I asked her name, guessing she was only slightly older than I. "Aiglantine," she said, her eyes cast down.

She helped me with my cape, brushing off the last vestiges of snow

before she led me to the roaring fire opposite, all the while asking me
what she could fetch for me, or prepare for me, always prefacing her entreaties with "Perhaps the countess—" Finally I turned to her, and with
a smile of reassurance, I said I required little other than to warm my
frozen body. As I held my hands before the fire, I asked where she was
from, and how long she had served this household.

"Since the Lord de Meurtaigne took a wife," she replied.

"And when was that?" I asked.

"Five years ago. It was about the time—" But here, overcome by
shyness, she stopped, only to say, "I will help you undress."

MORNING CAME—FRIGID AND BRIGHT, THE sky scattered with
clouds like great swollen blossoms. I walked to the window, gathering a
wool shawl around me as I looked outside at fields thick with snow, the
trees to one side by the orchard clipped and stunted. From this vantage
point I could see that the property was vast and perhaps beautiful in
springtime, but on that morning, it simply looked forbidding.

I glanced around the room where I found myself and where, the
previous night, I had fallen asleep almost in a delirium. I looked above,
at the painted arched ceiling, fingered the silken surface of the bedcover,
and felt the soft carpet beneath my feet. But most of all it was the
profusion of enameled objects that fascinated me: an elaborate jewel
casket upon a table, a cup embellished with a design of tendrils, and a
glimmering oval tray with a falcon etched at its center. Even the lock on
the chamber door was a precious thing, for it was fashioned in gold to
resemble a griffin, with wings enameled in brilliant hues of red, blue,
and green. Rest and warmth had restored me; fear had given way to a
surge of curiosity.

LATER THAT DAY, SHORTLY BEFORE the winter sun began to set, I
heard a great commotion—dogs barking, the clamor of horns, the fierce
pounding of hoofbeats—the sounds of horses and of men approaching. Aiglantine, her face flushed with excitement, came to tell me that
I was wanted in the hall, that my brother had ordered me to descend. I

pinched my cheeks to give them some color and asked her to arrange the ribbons plaited in my hair, for my own hands were far too skittish to do so. Then I followed her down the steps, my heart beating fast.

Gerard de Meurtaigne stood to the left side of the hall, pulling off one glove, then another as he addressed his groom and the household marshal in a voice that was low, rich, and incisive rather than elegant, with a thunderclap intensity. He issued one dictum, then another, with such authority that I continued to stand apart, hesitant to approach. It did not seem that he was waiting for me at all.

Finally he turned, approaching me as my brother led me forward to curtsey before him. I was a frightened girl standing between two men—both tall, assured, and seasoned in the ways of the world. I was but seventeen; Gerard de Meurtaigne was twenty-nine. How worldly and self-possessed he seemed to me!

His few glances in my direction seemed desultory and aloof; his attention continued to be directed to Guy, who seemed rather slavishly attentive to him. He asked about our journey north, whether we had been comfortable the previous night, whether Guy would participate in a tournament the following month not far from Poitiers. There was, as I recall, much talk of hawking, and of intricate bargaining for some rare gyrfalcons that Gerard de Meurtaigne had acquired. I remember how this piqued Guy's interest and, I daresay, even envy: these were costly hawks, the sort my family never could have afforded.

The next moment Lord de Meurtaigne asked—commanded, rather—that we go into supper.

Pages in red embroidered surcoats stood at the entrance of the hall, silver jugs of water in one hand, linen towels in the other. The steward—the slight, dark-haired man with a pointed face—directed the many servants who attended to the guests—folk of high rank from the region, I assumed, who glanced at me and my provincial clothes with curiosity. All the while I looked at Guy rather uncertainly, following his lead as I offered my hands to be cleansed, the first of many unfamil-iar rituals. Then through a passageway into the hall itself—a splendid sight! The long tables, covered with heavy white cloths, glimmered with silver plate and golden water vessels shaped like dragons and falcons; a tasseled silken canopy, emblazoned with his family's insignia—the falcon and the phoenix—hovered over our places in the center. We took our seats, and I remember Lord de Meurtaigne's concern that I be comfortably settled on the soft crimson cushion.

He was seated beside me. To my other side sat the bishop, a short rotund man who reeked of costly sandalwood and who proceeded to give a blessing, the length of which was only matched by its pomposity. At one point I glanced up and caught the eyes of Aiglantine, who stood to one corner, and who returned my glance with a slight, shy smile.

Lord de Meurtaigne signaled that the feast begin. Minstrels roaming the outer edges of the hall began to play; wine to flow; and the great hall burst into sudden, giddy animation.

I had little appetite that night, but the savory wine had relaxed me. I looked about the vast hall flickering with torchlight, and at the silken figures of attendants who moved among us, proffering more wine. For the first time since my arrival, I felt a modicum of ease: it was then I looked more closely at the man who would, the following day, become my husband.

His hair was thick and dark, his eyes a deep blue, the blue of Norman blood, the blue that had first come from the Norsemen. But what struck me most was his intense, assessing gaze, noticeable even in profile, perhaps most of all in profile, for at certain angles his fine, high-bridged nose gave him an aristocratic mien which seemed at odds with the rest—from the compressed energy of his gait to his voice, with its hint of alien inflection. One would never have met him and said, as one would have said of my brothers, "Ah, this is a knight of ancient stock." I sensed at once that Gerard de Meurtaigne was of another breed entirely.

There was no detail of the meal he did not notice. All the while he spoke to us, he would reprove a servant for spilling a bit of sauce, or call to another for more wine, the excellent and very costly wine of Saint-Pourçain from the Auvergne, which I had never tasted before; or suggest we try a lumpy white substance called "sugar," a delicacy from the Levant; or extol a dish that his cooks had labored over (at one point, memorably, a dazzling stuffed peacock with purply, outspread plumage). Even then I sensed that largesse was, to him, a far more complicated matter than to most—that it was as much a question of *amour propre* as it was of generosity.

Nothing prepared me for the confection, which culminated the procession of so many: a huge pastry in the shape of a crown, which was borne by a quartet of servants and presented directly to the host. A triumphant blaring of horns preceded it; then our host stood up, brandishing a dagger as he slit open the center of the pie, releasing in that instant the flock of tiny birds that had been held within. The next moment his falconers, who had stood motionless to one side, sprang into action. The falcons at their wrists were let loose to hunt their prey; the tiny fluttering birds were duly caught and killed, before they were roasted, heaped on immense gilded trays, and then served to us.

Sweetmeats eventually followed—sugared pears and the drink known then as "yellow water" and which we now call brandy. Jongleurs had arrived and serenaded us with melodious songs, some of which I knew; some of which, being bawdier, made me blush.

Some guests began to dance; I tapped my foot as I watched them. I longed to join in and hoped that my future husband would ask me, for my sister, who knew such things, had taught me a few of the new dances that had come into vogue. But I waited in vain; it was Guy who finally asked me—a way no doubt, for my brother, overweeningly anxious to please our host, to demonstrate my proficiency in dancing. After we finished our turn and sat down, I took a napkin to my perspiring brow.

"I gather you like to dance," Lord de Meurtaigne said.

I looked down and bit my lip, wondering if I should have asked his permission. "I do, my lord." Then, shyly, I ventured: "And you?"

He shook his head. "No," he replied, his eyes continuing to scan the scene. "It gives me more pleasure to watch."

WE WERE MARRIED THE FOLLOWING day in the chapel of the castle. Of the marriage ceremony itself I remember little, save for the acrid scent of incense and herbs, the blur of flickering tapers, the tightness of the white bodice of my pearl-encrusted robe, and how, after it had been fastened upon me, I felt the coin that Arnaut had given me—the coin with the crocodile and the serpent—pressed deep against my flesh.

The day was shrouded in the fear of what was to come later—the wedding night itself, which remains lodged in memory as a chaotic succession of images. My fumbling fingers unbuckling the jeweled bridal girdle, Aiglantine of the melancholy eyes coming to help me undress, the pulsing reflection of torchlight against the walls; then the waiting, the terror of waiting, my heart beating in fear as my husband approached, as I tried in vain to hide the flush of shame upon my face. Next, the extinguishing of light, followed by the awkward, hectic fumbling in the dark; the groping of thighs; and then, finally, a burst of pain.

I was alone when I awakened the following morning; my brother had departed after the marriage ceremony, and my husband was nowhere to be seen. I sat up in bed, reflecting on the wedding night with bewilderment, disappointment, and shame. Was this what awaited me in the years ahead? I wondered with despair. I pulled the coverlet away and stood up rather unsteadily: there were spots of red upon the sheet.

Soon afterward, Aiglantine appeared with a basin of water and a cup of milk. She was silent, her eyes cast down—whether out of shyness or embarrassment, I was not certain.

I opened the small casket with my keepsakes and took out the ex-voto, which my mother had given me. I held it in my palm for a moment, my finger tracing the image of a baby boy that was raised in relief on the beaten silver.

Turning to Aiglantine, I asked, "Would you come with me to the chapel this morning? I was told I must place this on the altar today."

"Of course, my lady." She smiled shyly. "But now I must help you dress. Your hair, first."

She led me to a small table near the window; a long, oval mirror edged in blue and gold, and a hairbrush with a carved ivory handle, lay upon it. "How lovely these are!" I murmured. They were among the chamber's many luxuries to which I was unaccustomed—the sumptuous coverlet, the intricately woven carpets, the splendid wall hangings. I picked up the brush and began to pull it through my hair.

"No, that is for me to do, my lady," she said gently, taking the brush from me. I smiled awkwardly, then picked up the mirror—this, another unfamiliar luxury. I looked into the glass with wonder, even trepidation, as if unsure that a familiar face would greet me, so changed did I feel by the marriage ceremony and the dark tumbling strangeness of the wedding night.

Finally, my toilette finished, I rose to my feet. "Will you help me choose a dress?" I asked.

She selected one of deep green—my finest dress—and helped me don it. "Yes, that will do very well, my lady," she said, standing a few steps back.

"Are you sure this is suitable for day?"

She nodded. "Lord de Meurtaigne sets great store by dress."

"When will I next see my husband?" I had paused almost imperceptibly before uttering those last, still alien, two words.

"I do not know," she replied. "Raoul told me that Lord de Meurtaigne has gone out riding. He did not say when he would return."

I considered this—at once relieved and disappointed—before asking, "And Raoul is—"

"The steward, my lady."

"The slight man with the face like an ermine's?"

I saw her suppress a smile. "Yes, that would be Raoul."

"Has he served here a long time?"

"Yes. Though not as long as others. Millicent has been here the longest. She was here when Lord de Meurtaigne was a child."

"I do not think I have yet met her."

"You may not have remembered, since there were so many of us. She is an older woman—tiny, with white hair. She will attend you, as well. Especially when the time comes, God willing."

"What do you mean?"

"When you are with child, my lady. She has much experience in such things. And she is the only one among us who is allowed to assist the midwives in the birthing chamber."

I walked to the window; it was snowing gently. "Perhaps we should go to the chapel now. To place the votive."

"I will gather your cloak. First you must eat something—you must be very hungry. I have brought you some bread and cheese."

DURING MUCH OF THE MORNING I was occupied, with Aiglantine, as she helped me unpack my clothing and arrange my things. I longed to explore on my own but soon realized this was not possible; given the weather—it was bitter cold and had begun to snow—I had no choice but to remain inside. When, at noon, we descended the long, twisting stairwell to the hall for the midday meal, I felt the eyes of the servants, ever curious, watching me. Raoul hovered about, as did the decidedly talkative Millicent, who seemed quite intent on asking me about my family, my patron saint, whether this was my first journey to this region. . . . At first I welcomed her questions, but as the conversation wore on, I found myself drawing back.

The rest of the time passed in nervous tedium as I awaited the arrival of my husband; trying to sew, I sat alone in my chamber, all the while fighting loneliness and isolation. At one point, searching for the familiar, I opened the casket from my brother and ran my fingers across the words carved upon it—"Courage above all else"—but the dictum only fleetingly comforted me.

I had been alone several hours when, in the middle of the afternoon, came a knocking at the door: Aiglantine, announcing that Lord de Meurtaigne had returned. Moments later, we heard the strident sounds of footsteps approaching. The door opened; it was my husband—his cheeks were ruddy, his dark hair dusted with snow; one hand clenched gloves.

I set the hoop aside and curtseyed before resuming my seat. I felt bashful, uncertain how to behave, and pretended to busy myself with stitching; but I suspect that he discerned my nervousness.

"All is well?" he asked, in a kindly manner.

"Yes, my lord."

"And you have been comfortable, and have been provided with everything you need?"

"Yes—I have never seen such a lovely bedchamber."

He smiled, as if this gratified him, then glanced at Aiglantine. "Leave us now," he told her peremptorily, tossing his gloves on the table.

I felt his eyes upon me as we waited for the door to close behind her. "Are you fond of stitching?" he asked, glancing at the hoop in my lap.

"I cannot say it is my very favorite pastime," I admitted, all too aware that my reply would have appalled my mother.

"An honest answer." He seemed amused. "What *are* your favorites, then?"

"I like stories. And I like to ride."

"So your brother told me. He said you were an able rider, for a woman. Come"—he offered his hand, beckoning me to rise—"and we will go to the stables. I have chosen a mount for you, and I want you to see her."

Now we stood face-to-face, my hand in his, but only momentarily. "It is very cold," he said. "You shall need your cloak. Where is it?"

"Over there, on the bench."

He placed it around my shoulders and then carefully fastened the ties. "It is a rather meager cloak for such weather," he remarked. "You have no other?"

I shook my head.

"I shall get you one far warmer. Lined with marten, or sable. Something more suitable, and in heavier wool."

"But I have always found this quite warm enough," I assured him almost pleadingly. I dared not say that I cherished the cloak because of its associations: my grandfather had given it to me, and I had worn it on adventures with Arnaut, and on the last, momentous journey from my home.

"We shall see," he said. "But now—to the stables."

He walked ahead quickly, with the strong, decisive step I would come to recognize so well. We descended the stairwell, and then made our way from the great hall to the outside, across the snow-dusted ground to the stables.

Once inside, he led me to a stall with a splendid pale gray steed. "She is beautiful, is she not?" His eyes shone with a different expression, that of a child seeking approval.

"I have never seen such a beauty!" I exclaimed, stroking her mane.

"I leave it to you to name her. What shall it be?"

I felt his eyes fixed upon me. Having already sensed he was by nature impatient, I did not want to displease him by seeming indecisive. But names were magical things to me, and not to be given casually. I forced myself to think hard, and quickly. "Juno. Yes—Juno!"

"Why 'Juno'?"

"The queen of the gods. In the story by the Roman poet that I used to read with my brother," I stammered. "Not Guy—my *other* brother, Arnaut." All the while, as he watched, Juno nuzzled my hand. "I cannot really believe she will be mine," I murmured, turning to him with a smile.

"I am glad she pleases you."

"How amazed my brothers and sister would be, to see me on such a mount!" I exclaimed. "Have you any brothers, or sisters, my lord?"

"Only one brother. He was killed in the lists years ago. He fell, and his horse trampled him and broke his neck." He had said this with scarcely any emotion, yet I sensed it was a deep and secret wound.

"How terrible," I murmured. "Were you there, at the tournament, when he was killed?"

"No. I was far away. In the East. Trying to make my fortune in Outremer."

I was fascinated by the way he pronounced "Outremer"—by the lulling emphasis he had given it. "Will you tell me, one day, what it was like there—"

"In Outremer? Does it interest you?" He seemed almost surprised.

"Very much!"

"Then one day soon I shall. But now you must say goodbye to Juno.

It has grown too cold to stay here." Darkness was falling. The grooms, who had been standing at attention in the back, had begun to light some lanterns,

"We will go inside and sit awhile by the fire," he said. "I shall ask Raoul to bring us wine." He took my hand, and it remained in his until we were inside the great hall.

LITTLE BY LITTLE, DAY BY day, conversation by conversation, I came to know the man who was my husband—Gerard, I now called him, at his insistence. Fearful at first that he would rebuff my questions, I came to realize that he welcomed them; indeed my curiosity, my love of stories—most of all his own story—seemed to amuse, even intrigue, him.

I soon learned more about his family: his adored mother had died when he was a little boy; he had hated his father; and he had always admired his brother, Roger. Roger—handsome, affable, ambitious and daring—had been the eldest, the favorite.

In our family, I told him, it was always Amélie who had been favored. "But unlike you, with Roger," I added, "I never admired her. I only resented her." Then—for he had become less intimidating to me by that time—I added, "But you never talk about Roger with resentment. Ever."

"The thought never occurred to me," he said so conclusively that I was almost embarrassed for having made the observation.

ONE EVENING, ABOUT TWO WEEKS after my arrival, we sat in the great hall after supper. Wine had made me pleasantly drowsy. The fire blazed, and a minstrel strummed in a distant corner.

"You said you would tell me about Outremer one day." I leaned forward and stroked his hand; I now not only enjoyed his touch but had even come to seek it out. "Why not now? Tell me," I said, leaning forward, "where did you go first?"

"Sicily. A land I came to love, and where I first encountered the Arabs. I spent some time there, and then took ship to Cyprus. . . ." As he described his travels—the people he had met, and his experiences—I began to discern that the East was the other great influence in his life, the first being his position as the second son. The East, and the ways of Outremer and the Holy Land, and the encounters with the Arab world had had a profound effect upon him, something akin to a cataclysm. It was Eastern learning and scholarship he admired, Eastern luxury he aspired to, and it was also unspoken, but evident to me, that it was a certain sensuousness that drew him to that other world in a way that our own mores did not. If anything, I sensed his contempt for what he considered our "backwater" customs and the "coarseness" of our daily life. His attitude fascinated me; my own impression of the Infidel's land— those exotic kingdoms beyond the Middle Sea—was of a dangerous and sordid realm. But that was not at all the way my husband conjured up the Muslim world.

He described its gardens, its rooms with walls trembling with mosaics, and its inner courtyards lulled by the voluptuous sound of fountains; he told me of banquets served on silken divans and punctuated by goblets of fruit ices transported from distant snowcapped mountains. He had traveled to glorious cities in the desert and to an ancient Roman trading city in Syria where the stone, at sunset, turned to a burnished rose color, and the wind whistled through arcades of marble columns and splendid arches. "You must understand," he explained in a thrilling, confiding voice, "the desert is their sea."

"Tell me more," I implored.

"The women," he said, "wore tunics of silk so fine, so transparent, that one could almost see the flesh beneath." I blushed.

"You see, they are not prudish like Frankish women," he told me. Indeed, he went on to say, many titled Frankish ladies from families who had settled in the Holy Land—those who had been there for generations—had come to adopt these ways, living the life of the quasi-harem with all its refinements, secrecies, and obliqueness. They, too, would rim their eyes in kohl and keep their faces half-covered so that their painted mouths were never revealed to those beyond the inner sanctum.

Then he went on to recount how he had once met an Egyptian

sage in the market of Damascus—a withered old man who sat on the ground, his pet cobra coiled beside him. "He fed him milk from a copper jug. I remember that well," he added. The man told him his fortune: wealth and power would be his, he augured. Heartened by the prophecy, he gave the old man some coins in payment, only to pause the next instant to watch a covey of hooded Muslim women filing past. "You are wondering why the Infidels cover their women," observed the sage, who had been following the direction of Gerard's gaze. "It is the eye which leads to Eros."

"More about Eros," I rejoined at once with a mischievous smile. It was not the response my husband had anticipated, clearly, for his expression showed that I had taken him by surprise.

BUT I SOON LEARNED THAT the Outremer of his experience was not only the land of fountains, and falconry, and vast, wind-whipped deserts he had conjured up so vividly, but also a place of teeming cities, of fabled markets, of commerce—the place, most importantly, where he had made his early fortune from the trade of silk. "It was in Palermo," he told me, "where I was first exposed to the possibilities of commerce on a significant level—in silk, and luxury goods." He described the gossamer fabrics woven by the Jews of Thebes, and how these artisans had been brought by the rulers of Sicily to establish royal workshops in Palermo. "Having seen what they produced—silks finer than anything woven in the West—made me desirous to learn more. And so I journeyed to the East. To Syria first." To this he added, with a touchingly proud smile, "It did not take me long to be successful."

From there, intent on expanding his commerce to other luxury goods—gemstones and spices—he had ventured to Antioch. What I knew about Antioch came from stories my parents had told me about the travels of Saint Paul, and the hallowed sites he had visited. Had he been to those holy places? I asked. At this my husband only scoffed. Saint Paul hardly interested him; indeed, for the Church he had nothing but scorn—"A corrupt institution, like any other," he called it.

My husband's attitude both shocked and fascinated me, as did much else about him: never had I met anyone with such contempt for what I had been taught to hold dear. But Gerard cared little, in this way at least, for what others thought. I eventually came to tease him, wondering why he bothered to attend Mass in his chapel—not without his prized falcon splendidly appareled on his wrist—or to make the sign of the cross, when he was so skeptical about the ways of our Lord. To this, he merely laughed. Only much later would I realize that, while he did not believe in our Lord and his teachings, he was too superstitious to tempt the fates by refusing to perform the rituals under which his own earthly fortune had flourished.

It was the world of hard bargains, and of commodities that could be shipped from place to place, which consumed him, and which had brought him freedom and riches. With those riches had come power, and access to those at the highest level of the court. Henry, the Young King, Gerard explained, had a "prodigious appetite for costly things"— for tournaments, for treasure. "And he is not averse," he added, "to consorting with those, like myself, who can help provide them."

My own appetite for tales of Gerard's adventures seemed at first to surprise, then delight, him. We had been married a month when, one evening, after he recounted more of what I came to dub his "silk stories," he suddenly said, "Enough *talk* about these places and their fabled silk. It is time I gave you some." The next day, as Aiglantine raptly watched, he presented me with a ravishing piece of damask, its pattern of leopards and palm trees woven in a wondrous way, so that the gold gleamed and the leopards appeared to prance; a few days later, a length of the finest linen with a border the Arab artisans called a *tiraz*. For days afterward, that redolent word, *tiraz*, would reverberate in my mind. I would drape myself with those fabrics, as if they would impart to me the same allure of the women he had so vividly described.

He derived pleasure in decking me in the finery and jewels which, he said, became my new station. Only once, in the early months of our marriage, when we held a sumptuous dinner in honor of merchants from Marseilles, did I unwittingly displease him in this way: I had chosen an unadorned robe of patternless blue silk, which was among my own favorites; and with it, a sole ornament—the necklace with the ancient coin that Arnaut had given me.

Gerard waited for me below: a look of anger crossed his face the moment he glimpsed me. "You must change your robe at once," he reprimanded. "You do not look nearly elegant enough—you are far too simply dressed."

I repaired at once to my chamber, trembling, perplexed, and inwardly angry. Aiglantine was summoned and helped me undress. She then fetched a robe made of Byzantine purple edged with ermine from Russian traders and, as a final touch, wound my neck with long strands of pearls intertwined with rubies.

When I reappeared, Gerard scrutinized me and pronounced me "perfect." As we stepped into the hall itself, he turned to me with this final admonition: "You must never forget who I am, and what you represent."

Yet I do not want to give the impression that it was only Gerard who introduced me to new worlds, that it was only he who taught me. There were ways he learned from me as well. I think of this with some pride, for I realize now, far more than I did then, that I brought much to the marriage, however intangible.

He drew pleasure from my family's noble lineage, from the fact that I was not only a countess, but well-read and could converse with ease among his peers and those with whom he did commerce: traders from Egypt and Tyre, men who ran the fairs at Troyes, merchants from La Rochelle. The court of Henry II and his counselors had made literacy not only fashionable, but also *necessary* for worldly success.

My husband knew how to read, but not to write; he had scribes to whom he dictated the messages or letters that were delivered by courier. But one day, as he entered my chamber and I, with quill in hand, was penning a letter to my family, he sat down and watched silently, and with such intense focus, that I turned to him and said: "Surely for a man of your position, you should not be ignorant of knowing how to write." He denied needing to, yet I could tell it irked him that I had this skill, and he did not. He was by nature fiercely competitive.

"Come on then," I cajoled, tugging playfully at his sleeve. "Try a little with me tomorrow. A little every day, this winter, and by springtime you will be quite proficient."

And so in this way our "lessons" began. At first—and not with great success—I selected a psalm for him to copy, but since the verses bored him and only provoked jokes about my strict provincial upbringing, I searched for another text that would pique his interest and spur him on to copy the letters.

I knew that one of his heroes was Duke William IX of Aquitaine, the grandfather of our Queen Eleanor—the irreverent duke, warrior and poet. And so quietly, and without my husband knowing, I asked one of the household minstrels to find me one of Duke William's songs: he did so, and as he sang, I copied its verses and kept one as a writing exercise for my husband.

*And so it went:*
*From her, where grace and beauty spring*
*No word's come and no signet ring*
*My heart won't rest and can't exult*
*I don't dare move or take a stand*
*Until I know our strife's result*
*And if she'll yield to my demands. . . .*

That I had done this delighted my husband. He willingly copied the verses, sitting with me at the writing table throughout many afternoons that March and April. He was quick to master the quill and soon developed a script which, though not as fluid and graceful as mine, was compelling and distinctive.

GRADUALLY, OVER THOSE FIRST FEW months, my feelings for him developed into something I had never known before—something preoccupying and powerful. I struggle now to understand precisely what it was. A fascination for his mind, perhaps, his temperament, and unquestionably a powerful attraction—here I must force myself to continue—

to his body. For he was strong, lean, purposeful, and all the evidence of his struggles and tests in realms so apart from anything I could fathom drew me to him: the deep scar that ran across his back, and another, rough and meandering, on his right forearm where he had been struck during a tournament. His sheer physicality, his courage—one might even say recklessness—in the face of danger, his lust for foreign places—these I found thrilling. The steeliness, which other women might have found daunting, I found wondrous: I sensed it was the key to his survival in the wider world.

He offered to me a glimpse of that world. His mind, restless and probing, challenged my own; and if, as part of this bargain, he exerted a strict control over me, in the early days I did not mind it. There was even a modicum of comfort in it. "Comfort," I say; but is that not really dissembling, transmuting what I experienced into something more palatable? In his control over me, his demands on all levels, I had discovered in those early days a new and intoxicating form of pleasure, pure and—simple, I was on the verging of saying. But no, it was not simple at all; it would take me a long time to decipher it, if ever I would.

I sometimes wonder, thinking back, what he really thought of me. Certainly, in the earliest days, he viewed me with a certain aloofness, save for our private moments, in bed. And yet, I daresay that as the months progressed that first year, I felt something from him akin to love. Never before, he once confided to me in an unguarded moment, had he so enjoyed talking to a woman, and teaching her about his world—about hunting, falconry, the ways of trade. Yet, the instant he revealed this to me, his expression changed, and he removed his hand from mine.

I could not help but wonder if he had always been thus: whether his late wife, the woman whose place I had taken, had also found him hard to fathom. Her name was never mentioned. There seemed no trace of her in the castle itself, though of course I could not help but wonder about her. What she had looked like, where she had come from, what had made her laugh and cry . . .

I knew from Guy that she had been about twenty-four years of age, and that her death had been a cruel blow. Guy had seen her once, at a tournament, and told me that she was very fair "like an angel"—this, uttered in a tone that roundly implied that I was not. And then, a few days before I had left my family's home, my mother had taken me aside to reiterate that the subject was still so painful to my future husband that I must never, ever bring it up—precisely the sort of admonishment which, particularly coming from my mother, had only piqued my curiosity.

LATE ONE AFTERNOON THAT FIRST February, I stood by the window in the bedchamber, looking out at fields suffocated by snow, while Aiglantine swept the hearth. It was so quiet, so still, that the sound of the straw bristles brushing stone remains vivid to me even now. The wind had come up, and the bitter cold made me draw away from my perch and move toward the fire while Aiglantine continued her work, only stopping on occasion to blow on her frozen fingers.

Aiglantine was only slightly older than I, yet I sensed she had seen far more of life. This was merely intuition on my part, for she had never revealed much, if anything, about her background or family. She came from a village near Saumur, in the Loire Valley, the eldest of seven children, and her father was a blacksmith. She was someone, I sensed, who had long ago succeeded in quelling her own curiosity and native intelligence. I had come little by little to trust her, even to confide in her. Lately, to my delight, she had even begun to share some of the household gossip with me, just as Hortense had, at my family's home. (My predilection for such gossip was another fault for which my mother had often castigated me.)

I turned from the window to warm myself before the fire, drew up my courage, and asked:

"Why is it that no one ever mentions Lord de Meurtaigne's late wife?"

"It was all very sad, my lady. She—" But here she stopped.

"What was her name? Surely you can tell me that—"

"Gisela."

"Where was she from? Her family?"

"From the north. I do not know exactly where. What region. Only that she came from the north—"

"I have been told she died in childbirth—"

"Yes."

"And the child itself?"

"A boy, who died the following day. She had not carried him the full nine months."

"And Lord de Meurtaigne?"

"He was distraught. His grief was terrible. Most of all he blamed—" She bit her lip, as if realizing she had gone too far.

"Tell me, please"—my voice had risen in insistence—"whom he did blame?"

"The midwives and the doctor who attended her. But most of all, the doctor. The doctor came from another part. He had settled here from Montpelier. Very learned, they said."

"But surely it cannot really have been his fault!"

"There was no telling that to Lord de Meurtaigne. He did not eat for days. He would not see anyone for weeks." She turned to me with a plaintive glance. "I beg you, my lady, never tell anyone what I have said."

"It will remain between us. I promise"—here I touched the small ivory figure of the Madonna that rested on a table—"I swear upon the Virgin."

## Chapter 4

Among the happiest times with my husband were those we spent riding together. His property was vast and exceptionally beautiful: within its bounds were meadows and hills fragrant with wildflowers, poppies, and wild lilies; forests with huge primeval trees; coursing streams; and glades with tall upright stones, arranged in half circles, where ancient fairies were once said to have dwelled. And in winter, there was a luminous beauty about the land and its expansiveness; one could ride for days across that frozen, muted landscape without ever seeing another human being, without ever crossing its boundaries.

Those forays were made all the more joyful by Juno, for I had never ridden a horse so thrillingly attuned to my commands. I doted on her as one would a child: I would keep my pockets full of treats for her—slices of apple, a bit of grain—and only the fiercest weather would keep me from mounting her.

One morning shortly after our marriage, Gerard and I took a long fast ride together, the opaque winter sky pressing down upon us as we galloped, the fields glinting with hoarfrost. It seemed that all of nature—its wily creatures and stalwart flowers, its grains and grasses—all had been put to sleep under icy, sparkling white blankets.

It was so cold that I remember I had to set out wearing two pairs of gloves, a thick woolen set beneath my leather gauntlets. But the ride had been so exhilarating that I had quickly warmed up, and had paused late morning to take off my outer vest.

By noon time we stopped to eat by the edge of a stream beneath the filtered light of towering pines. I remember the intoxicating fresh scent, and how our footsteps made a dry intrusive sound as we walked through the leaves to a protected place. I remember the hooting of owls, the

sharp frantic beating sound of rooks high above us, the scent of burning charcoal from the abandoned fire of a hermit. The sun still shone,
though clouds had begun to appear.

Gerard spread a blanket on the ground, while I began to take out our
food: chunks of savory cheese, ham and bread, extricated with frozen
fingers from my saddlebag. I told him I was famished, and bit into a
piece of bread.

"You must be thirsty, too," he said, offering me some barley water. I
took great gulps as he watched me, smiling and almost amused.

We began to talk, to reminisce. I told him about my visit to Nîmes
with my brothers years before—what an adventure it had been, how
much I had loved the journey. He, too, had passed through Nîmes once,
but had not seen, as I had, the temple of Diana or the Roman amphithe-
atre. He listened to my impressions, though I sensed all the while that it
was not the ancient city that really interested him: indeed, he went on to
tell me that what he most remembered about his time in Nîmes were the
merchants he had met there, and the transactions he had made.

He was in the midst of telling me about one such dealing, with a
devious wool merchant from England, when he suddenly stopped mid-
sentence, his attention arrested by something in the sky. "Look," he
said, with intense excitement: "A peregrine—in flight." Above us, soaring, coiling with regal purpose, was indeed a falcon. "It is hunting," he
told me as he continued to follow the path.

"How do you know?"

"The swoop, the shape of its flight pattern, the way the wings are
positioned. It is alert to kill."

Guy had told me, with more than a grain of envy, that my future
husband had the means to afford the most expensive birds as well as
skilled falconers and an elaborate mews.

"One day I should like to see the mews," I told Gerard, though
I was not sure he had really heard me. His face was still turned to the
sky until, at last, the falcon disappeared from sight. It was only then
that we resumed talking about Nîmes and then about his own journeys
through Provence. There, he told me, he had encountered Muslim salt

merchants who had told him about parched distant lands, about Egypt and the desert. And he had encountered other traders, too, who had come from the high snowcapped mountains of the distant East bearing strange gilded idols with myriad writhing arms. . . . How I loved those stories! I drank them up greedily, as greedily as I had the barley water.

We finished eating: not a crumb remained, so ravenous had we been. We prepared to set off again, first leading the horses to drink from a stream before we continued our ride, stopping only occasionally when he was roused by a particular view, or a covey of birds, or the tracks of a wild boar in the forest. All the while I watched and listened, transfixed by his observations, by his ability to discern things in the sky and forest I could not.

At last, as light began to fade, we quickened our pace and began to ride home.

We returned by midafternoon, taking great care as we crossed the ice-slicked drawbridge over the moat. The slow, suspended clip-clop of hooves, the sound of our low reassuring voices as we urged our horses on, the gentle guidance of our reins; then the raising of the portcullis, and the sound of the stable boys running to fetch our thirsty horses.

One of the boys, a sturdy sort with red hair, approached to help me dismount. He took my hand, and as I thanked him—we were then standing face-to-face—I was struck by something about him that reminded me of my brother, of Arnaut: his vivid blue eyes had a similar faraway look. I asked his name. "Gallien, my lady," he said, bowing.

I was about to inquire where he was from—for his accent was unfamiliar—but the steward, Raoul, summoned him at that moment. The boy left abruptly, excusing himself with a hurried, "I must be gone now, to help the others, in the hall."

Raoul approached, carrying a cape: "You will need this now, my lady." Gerard took it from him and placed it over my shoulders.

It had begun to snow—luxurious flakes whirling around us and covering the unyielding ground with a thickening, frosty spider's web of white.

"Come, I want to show you something," Gerard said, taking my hand. "The mews." He brushed some snowflakes from my hair. "I want you to see my falcons."

WE WALKED A SHORT WAY, past the stables, and came to a long building with slatted outer walls: its door was painted an inky blue, and within its central panel was the escutcheon with the gilded falcon and the phoenix, now familiar to me.

He unlatched the door; we stepped inside. Before us stretched a central aisle with stone pavement, and to each side, the weathering chambers of the hawks.

I shall never forget my first glimpse of that inner sanctum, most of all the fierce, glittering golden eyes, which met my own. I gazed at a tribe of falcons tethered to blocks and an eagle so fearsome, so majestic, that I stood completely still, quite unable to speak. The birds seemed to have known at once that a stranger had invaded their domain, for they roused, and their necks wrenched about in quick jerking movements as their hostile eyes followed me, followed us. The raw piercing sounds of their mewing rent the air.

Gerard was watching me closely, assessing my reaction—his clear blue eyes amid the gallery of primordial pupils flecked with orange and yellow. He had taken a falconer's glove from a table and put it on his left hand. The wide cuff of the gauntlet covered a great part of his forearm, and the leather itself was splotched with red, and marked with deep chaotic scratches—the insignia of talons and beaks, no doubt, which had ravaged that gloved fist for food. For bits of rabbit, morsels of squirrels, the wing of a pigeon.

"Guy told me about your falcons. But I had no idea there would be so many. Such beautiful ones. And the eagle, as well!"

"So you see," he said proudly, almost boyishly, "this is what I wanted to show you."

"I have never seen such a place," I murmured, continuing to look around: all was perfectly ordered, meticulous. The ground beneath the birds smelled of fresh rush, and the perches were covered with taut leather; in each of the chambers stood a long, low basin with fresh water now turned partly to ice.

"So many splendid falcons," I said almost to myself, still marveling; and then, to him: "A palace of falcons! And I have never seen such an eagle. Not up close. Ever." We stood across from the huge eagle now, its talons digging into the block like two huge, wrinkled yellow hands, and its eyes, its feral eyes, always upon us.

"He knows you," I said, turning to Gerard. "His master."

"He should! I have trained him."

"What is his name?" I asked, sure this fearsome creature, with its proud feathered chest, its formidable beak, and its imperious gaze must have a name.

"Féroce."

I smiled. "It suits him well."

He walked to the eagle while I stood back, waiting and watching. "Good boy, good boy," he murmured, stroking the feathers of Féroce, and then his crest. "We have come to see you." Then, to me: "You would like to see him up close?"

I nodded.

"He must be hooded first. To calm him, since he does not know you. Come." He took my hand.

We walked to the back of the mews, to a workplace with a table carefully arrayed with tools, knives, and big scraps of thin hides ("for the jesses"). Above were shelves arrayed with a collection of hoods in varying sizes and styles. Smaller ones in deep polished brown with tassels ("for the goshawks"); tiny ones for kestrels; an exquisite hood in blue tooled with gold and inset with pearls ("for the peregrine"); and for Féroce, the largest hood of all—a globe of gleaming red leather edged with braided blue, and on top, tall plumes of white feathers. "This," he said, taking it with him, "is the one we need."

He entered the eagle's chamber and stood by him now, speaking to him softly, coaxingly, "Good boy, let's see you now, be good for our visitor" while I waited at a distance. The next instant Féroce had leaped to his gloved wrist, and for several thrilling moments as Gerard manned him, I saw the full extent of his wingspan and imagined the power of those wings high in the sky, soaring and predatory—a menace to any hapless creature spotted below, on earth.

Gerard had fastened the jess to his cuff and had deftly slipped on the hood before approaching me. Suddenly the eagle seemed to have been transformed into a bizarre masqueraded creature with a preposterous beak. His wings were taut, and he was quiet.

Gerard stroked his feathers and continued to speak to him lullingly, as one would to a child. "We will feed you soon, Féroce—just enough, but not too much, so you will be ready to hunt."

"How do you know when he is ready?"

"We can tell, partly by his weight, when he is in *yarak*."

"In—"

"In *yarak*. An Arab word. We owe much to the Arabs in matters of falconry. It means when he is ready to hunt. Rapacious and ready." Another stroke. "Too much food and he will be sated. Indifferent."

"And you do not like indifference," I said, somewhat teasingly.

He laughed, arching one brow. "Not in hunting, *ever*." Then, pensively: "It is hard for me to think of a time when I would willingly choose indifference."

"Over what?"

"Over passionate commitment," he replied, adding, "to a purpose. A desire. For better or worse." He stroked the bird's chest, and without looking at me directly: "And you?"

"I have always thought of indifference as"—I struggled to alight on the right word—"the enemy."

"That does not surprise me," he said, with a glance that was not without tenderness.

There was a sudden sound of the door opening, and a gust of icy air. A tall, burly man with the white-blond hair of a Northman had entered and strode toward us.

"My lord," he said, in a deep, slightly guttural accent. He had a wide, flaccid face and wary light eyes under brows so pale they were almost invisible. I had seen men like him at home, in the south: mercenaries from the Brabant, mostly, or adventurers from Norway. He wore a tunic of ancient, scratched leather and on his left hand, a massive falconer's glove.

"This is Ragnar," said Gerard, "the master falconer."

Ragnar bowed slightly, but I sensed at once it was not his habit to be deferential, least of all to a woman. He was so imposing that I found myself resisting the impulse to curtsey.

"Where is Arnulf?" Gerard asked in an even voice. "Why is he not here?"

"He is growing old. He has a weakness of the muscles, feels pain in his hands. He cannot work as he used to. He will have to be replaced."

"Have you found someone?"

"Not yet. I will."

"But I assume that all else—"

"Yes. Everything is in order."

"Of that I have no doubt," replied Gerard almost deferentially.

"The birds were taken out earlier. And they have been fed."

"Good." Gerard had taken my hand. "I wanted Lady Isabelle to see them. Or perhaps I should say that I wanted to introduce her to them."

I smiled, perhaps a bit too eagerly. Ragnar remained impassive.

"I will leave you while I work, my lord," was all he said. He took some thin, supple pieces of leather from his pocket. "I found some good skins for more jesses. And some rope, too. Good rope, strong and flexible, for new creances." He bowed slightly. "And I will light the lamps for you. It is growing dark." He left us.

One by one, the oil lamps were lit, and a hazy greenish light illuminated things I had not been able to see earlier.

I noticed that each railing was subtly inset with a small panel indicating each hawk's name: Guiscard ("for the Norman adventurer" Gerard told me); Palmyra ("after the city in the desert"), Bror, Lady Danger . . .

We came to a chamber fluttering with velvety white doves, comforting in their gentleness. I stood before them for many moments, watching them flit about. How different they were from the falcons, how companionable, how benign! "And these," I said, turning to him. "Not for hunting surely!"

"For beauty. And I find them calming."

"I would fear for them here. With the others."

"No need. We keep them safe and protected. Woe to anyone or anything who harms them. Or my hawks. That I promise you."

I continued to walk among the chambers, looking at one bird, then another. Snow fell thickly outside the slatted windows, the wind wuthered, and it was growing very cold.

Questions continued to whirl in my mind. I wondered when he had begun to hunt, when this fascination had been sparked, and by whom, or what, and where. I wondered about Ragnar, for I knew from my brothers that master falconers were a breed apart and highly prized by those who could afford them. And then I began to imagine the hawks released, swooping in the sky, spiraling with deadly speed to the ground, and the men running to the warm, squirming prizes exploding with fur, blood, and feathers: a riot of dismemberment . . .

I turned to my husband. "The doves are beautiful, but it is the falcons and the eagle you love the most. Why?"

"They are wild and free."

"Still they come to you. You and Ragnar have trained them. They do your bidding here, and in the fields, when you hunt."

"Yes, but in the end they could leave at any moment. And some have. One never knows—"

"That would make me uneasy. To love something and to think there was always a chance of losing it."

"True. It is a game of chance. A gamble, but a precise one, with its own rituals and rules. But chance nevertheless."

"So you play at this, the way others play at dice!" And then, half teasingly: "You are a gambler, then. A gambler with falcons."

He smiled. "I have never thought of it that way."

We had come to the first chamber, the one closest to the entrance. Within it was a splendid white female peregrine whom I had not noticed until that moment, so intent had I been, at first, on the eagle. The peregrine peered at us calmly, almost aloofly, yet with an unnerving intensity. There was no indication of a name. I wondered if the exquisite blue hood studded with pearls belonged to her.

"This is the most beautiful falcon of all," I told him.

"And the rarest. She came from the best breeder in Valkenswaard. She is immensely valuable, and when she is hungry, there is no more ferocious hunter. I trained her myself."

"What is her name?"

"Gisela."

Inwardly I started: *Gisela*, the name of his late wife. But I said nothing: I could not betray Aiglantine, for it was she who had disclosed the wife's name to me. And so I merely said: "A lovely name. It suits her as perfectly as Féroce suits the eagle."

"I am glad you think so," he said almost wistfully; then, in his customary, peremptory voice: "It is too cold here for you now." He gathered my cape over my shoulders, fastened the tie, and gently drew the hood over my head.

"I feel as if I were one of the hawks," I said, with a small laugh.

"You are far more valuable," he said, kissing the top of my head. "And even with your hood, you can see." He took my hands, drawing away for a moment, his eyes scanning my shadowed face: "No, you are not a hawk. You are a dove," he mused. "Yes, truly a dove. *My* dove."

WINTER PASSED. LONG, COLD DAYS of precious sun and darkened shadows across desiccated lands; windblown, torchlit corridors. Early spring arrived with a poignant vividness. I remember how images of Persephone emerging from the underworld came to me as I gazed out the window from my chamber. I thought of my grandfather and the stories he had told me about those pagan gods; I thought of my brothers, my home, my beloved little cat, everything I had left behind.

Below, in the garden, green shoots pierced the loosening earth and taunted the elusive sun.

One day in early spring we rode to a site where my husband intended to build new kennels. There he would keep his best hounds, those with "the purest bloodlines," he explained as we dismounted. It was the first time he had shown me the site.

I was touched by his excitement as he began to describe the design: where it would be situated, what kind of stone and timber he would use. To my delight I found that the area was partly encircled by an ancient wall, near which there were the vestiges of a small temple: a few jagged crumbling steps, the sculpted capital of a marble column, and a tilting moss-covered stone tablet, half-covered by weeds, that bore a detailed inscription and a depiction of the goddess Athena. The carving was remarkably crisp, and I could make out her helmet and shield, and the fierceness of her face.

I walked to the column and knelt, carefully brushing away the weeds from the capital, so that, little by little, the intricate leaves of the acanthus emerged. I was so absorbed that I had not noticed Gerard's impatience. But then I heard his voice: a stern voice telling me it was time to leave.

"Might we stay a little while longer?" I asked.

"Why?"

"Because I find these fascinating"—an imploring look in his direction—"and *beautiful*, too, for what they have survived."

"This rubble? These bits of stone?"

"But imagine what they have *survived!*"

"Imagine all you like," he scoffed. "They will be gone soon enough, when my masons come to clear the land." He looked away impatiently, tugging at his reins.

I asked at the very least that the fragments be saved or incorporated, perhaps, into the new design for the kennel. He scoffed again at the idea, but once more, and then again, I implored him. Finally, seeing how obdurate he was, and how unyielding, I proposed instead that I simply keep the remnants for myself, to place in a corner of my own garden.

"A foolish idea," he said. "Foolish and impractical. Better to be rid of them. Or to sell them to traders in these parts who deal in such things. Stone that can be used again, for other buildings. For churches, walls."

I asked who they were, these traders.

"People from the south—Italians, often. What does it matter?"

He pulled his reins tautly: his horse whinnied and the waning sun-light caught its tossing lustrous mane. "It will grow dark soon," he said, digging his heels into the flanks. "We must be off."

But still, stubbornly, I resisted leaving, and it was only when he called me again, this time rather angrily, that I reluctantly mounted my horse for the return home.

A gravid silence fell between us as we rode. His displeasure was palpable, while my own submerged anger had transmuted itself into a hollow, parched feeling: scattered thoughts, tense stomach. Only now do I realize how much the conversation had troubled me: I had smarted at his indifference and had felt belittled by his contempt for what fas-cinated me.

But I made no mention of this then. Instead, I assumed a smile and grasped Gerard's hand as we entered the hall. I told him I would ready myself for the feast that we would hold that night for merchants from Poitiers.

Perhaps it was by way of recompense that I took great pains when I dressed that evening. I asked Aiglantine to weave pearls into my braided hair, scented my wrists with a fragrance of crushed roses, and chose a robe of saffron-colored silk that was among my husband's very favorites.

When he later greeted me with a warm, proud smile—"There, that is better, you look perfect"—I felt a relief so overwhelming, it was as if I could breathe again, live again.

NOT LONG AFTERWARD, MY MONTHLY courses ceased, and I real-ized with a tumult of feelings—excitement, fear, nervousness—that I might be with child.

It was late morning on a day in May; the sky was strewn with form-less clouds. I called Aiglantine at once and told her what I suspected.

"If it is true, then God has blessed you indeed," she said shyly, crossing herself. She asked when I had last had my "monthly flowers," as she put it. I smiled at the expression, for it reminded me of Hortense.

"The last time I remember was during the feast of Saint Joseph," I told Aiglantine, though I did not mention what I recalled so vividly: I had begun to bleed while I was out riding that day and had returned to the castle in embarrassment to find fresh cloths and change my soiled undergarments.

Shyly Aiglantine asked if there were other signs, any change in my body, and in the way I felt.

I told her my breasts seemed tender and slightly swollen, and that I also felt rather unnaturally tired. "Could those be signs?" I asked.

She nodded.

I began to joke a little, for the idea of being with child was at once welcome—the fulfillment of an obligation—and frightening. "Adieu to being a girl," I said as lightheartedly as I could, "adieu to freedom!"

She smiled but did not reply; indeed I remember quite distinctly that she looked away silently, and that her silence left me uneasy. I had expected her to say something comforting; but she did not.

A few moments passed. I went to the window and stood, looking outside, past the gates, my hand running over my stomach, as if it were suddenly a separate entity: an alien vessel where this new being would grow.

"I must tell my lord, my husband, at once," I said, turning to Aiglantine, only to realize that I had been so preoccupied I had not noticed she had left.

Gerard had ridden to the village, for he was to meet that day with his master mason to review the plan for the kennels. All afternoon I waited and waited for him to return, walking in the garden and trying to occupy myself with some stitching. Finally I ventured into the mews, only to find Ragnar feeding the hawks. His face looked bloated, and especially florid, as if he had been drinking. So chilly and unwelcoming was he that I left, hardly even glancing at Féroce, whose stare seemed vaguely hostile.

Restless and quite unable to take up any task, I returned to my chamber. It was still light: the luxuriously painted walls seemed especially vivid, almost animated by the fluctuating rays of sunlight that illuminated the saturated hues of green, red, and blue. I gazed at one high wall painted with a wonderfully lifelike design of swags of silk held by two playful lions; at the swirling tendrils of leaves delineating the outline of one window; and finally at the central mural, a scene of the Annunciation. I looked at it long and hard, as if seeing it for the first time. How cryptic the smile of the Angel Gabriel, how frozen and maddeningly unperturbed the face of the Virgin!

I walked to the table where my hand mirror lay. I picked it up, gazing at my own reflection, as if searching for signs that my face, like my body, had already imperceptibly changed. But it had not: the same rosy cheeks, the same constellation of freckles, the same arch of my brow.

At last, just when the sun began to set, I heard the sound of Gerard and his men returning. The dull grinding noise of the portcullis raising, then the stampede of horses, the shouts of the men and the stable boys. I ran down to the courtyard to meet him.

"Come," I said, tugging at his sleeve, "I have some news to tell you." His cheeks were ruddy, his tunic splattered by mud, and he smelled of fresh grass and the forest.

He stopped at once, facing me, and placed a finger on one of my cheeks, then the other.

"I believe I am with child," I told him in a tremulous voice. He took both my hands, kissing them over and over with such fervor that I almost looked away.

"God willing," I said, "you will have an heir next year, in January."

He called a doctor, rather than a midwife, to examine me a few days later. "Millicent will stay with you, of course, while he examines you," Gerard told me. I had never met a doctor before; in my family, we knew only midwives and healers, rough country people with their own methods and elixirs. The doctor, from the region of Bordeaux, had studied medicine in Salerno, I was told. He had ascetic white skin, fine freckled hands, and a reverent, kindly expression, which put me at ease.

He asked me to take off my outer tunic, and I stood before him in a simple shift, closing my eyes as he touched my stomach, and felt each breast. My initial reticence gave way to curiosity as he asked me questions and looked for the signs of pregnancy. Gerard waited outside the chamber; I could hear the methodical sound of his pacing.

"You are indeed with child," the doctor told me at last.

"Is there"—I hesitated—"is there a way to know if it is a son I carry?"

He smiled gently. "As time passes, look to your right"—he paused, as if hesitant to pronounce the next word—"breast, and if it is larger than the left, then it is likely, very likely, that you carry a son."

"And is this willed by now, the sex of the baby?"

"Not yet, my lady. For the soul has not yet entered the womb. That will come, in time. When you first feel the quickening. You must be patient and trust in faith."

I asked whether it was he who would be with me, when I gave birth.

"No," he replied, "that is women's work. Millicent and the midwives will be with you then." He began to gather his cloak and his implements. "May God grant you an easy confinement, my lady," he said, bowing slightly as he left.

I remember being startled by the word *confinement*, as if it could not really apply to me, to my life. And yet of course it did, and would.

THAT EVENING, AFTER MY HUSBAND and I retired to our chamber, I discovered a silken green parcel, tied with slender ropes of gold, which lay upon the bed like an exotic blossom.

"What is this?" I asked, turning to Gerard.

"For you. A present to celebrate our news today. Open it."

Within the silken folds lay a pair of bracelets of such seraphic splendor that I was, for a moment, too astonished to speak. The bracelets had a supernal beauty, as if they had been crafted in heaven by angels who had deigned to let them spiral to earth.

I held one bracelet, then the other, examining each slowly, as if I were imbibing the luster of pearls, the glimmer of gold, the opalescent hues of enamel. A large, budlike rosette studded with a nacreous pearl and bordered by green enamel anointed the top of each cuff; this in turn was surrounded by smaller rosettes in blue enamel and pearl.

The inner part of each bracelet—the hidden part that would touch my skin—was fashioned as exquisitely as the outer, with an ethereal design of the sun and moon.

"Are these really for me?" I asked.

"I assure you they are," he said, smiling. He told me they had come from old Constantinople and bore the imprint of a fabled imperial workshop.

"Imagine who might have worn them," I mused as he fastened one, then the other, on my wrists. "They are exquisite—the kind of jewel Queen Eleanor herself might even wear!" I held my hands away to gaze at the bracelets, savoring the glint of gold, gems, and pearls against my skin and hands. I had thought the bracelets would feel heavy, for there was a subtle authoritative aura about them, as if they had been worn by a woman accustomed to giving orders. But they were not heavy, indeed they felt strangely light.

"Perhaps," I continued to muse, "they might even have been created for the Empress Theodora." Tales of the wicked Byzantine queen had long fascinated me: my grandfather had told me about her, choosing his words carefully as he described her background and her infamous adventures as a harlot and bear-baiter.

"Theodora?" Gerard replied, bemused. "Doubtful I would give you jewels made for a harlot, my dove!"

"But who knows—if they came from that workshop? Who knows who they were made for, and why?"

"All that matters is that I have been saving them for *you*," he told me, "for such a moment. Let us hope they bring us good fortune." And then, holding me tight as he brushed my face with kisses, "And let us hope most of all that they help bring us a son."

# CHAPTER 5

I was no longer permitted to go riding. The doctor had discerned a certain "fragility of the womb" and advised my husband that horseback riding would present too great a danger. And so my life in those months from late spring through midsummer assumed a different cast. There was the disorienting nausea of the early months; the transformation of my body into that of an alien swollen creature; then the first stirring of movement and life within me. I should have borne these changes proudly, and to some extent I did, though not without a needling ambivalence. There were days when I would almost ostentatiously drape myself in heavy folds of silk that emphasized my growing belly, and other days when, overcome with something approaching revulsion, I only wanted to conceal it.

The memories of my mother giving birth haunted me; the terror of that night, her screams piercing our house, the rags soaked with her blood, and the heap of spoiled linens spilling out of the midwives' hands wrapped with the detritus of the dead infant—these were specters that inundated me in the midst of the most prosaic tasks: when I pierced my finger with my sewing needle and saw drops of blood upon my embroidery, or when one warm, humid afternoon, I caught sight of a coil of rope in the stable only to have it remind me, with a shudder, of a discarded umbilical cord.

What I did not feel—I admit this now—was *joy*. There was the relief, yes, at having fulfilled my duty to my husband and the obligation of marriage, but only here, privately, can I confess how uneasy I felt, how frightened, how many times I longed to flee, to return to childhood, to the gallops across my family's land to see my grandfather and visit my cave.

Most of all I feared what would happen to me if the child were not a son.

SPRINGTIME HAD ARRIVED, PARTICULARLY RAVISHING that year, the earth vivid with green, the fields brilliant with yellow mustard seed. The household stirred to life after a long winter of frozen ponds and frost-glazed fields. News of the world beyond Ravinour slowly began to reach us: messengers could travel with more ease, and ships could navigate the fickle waters of the Channel with less peril.

My husband and his men were to leave for the annual fair at the city of Troyes, to the northeast. I longed to accompany them, if only to hear news of the world beyond, but of course I could not. As "recompense," Gerard promised to bring me a surprise. I entreated him for some books and a chess set, for chess had become fashionable for highborn women.

At dawn on an early May morning cleansed by rain, I saw the men off. The sudden clarity of the weather was at once piercing and ephemeral: clouds were strewn like membranes in the sky, alternately dispersing and gathering. I turned and walked slowly back to my chamber.

As the sun came up, a dismal silence penetrated the castle. Even Aiglantine had left. Days before, she had learned that her father was dying; she had begged us to be allowed to visit him one last time. Gerard had said no at first, but I had insisted that she be allowed to go. "Best she see him," I said, touching Gerard's cheek as I implored him the previous evening, after supper; only reluctantly had he consented.

The day after the men's departure, a letter arrived from Arnaut, the first I had received from him since my departure in January. I remember the precise moment his letter was handed to me: how, as I touched the parchment, I was afire with excitement. I untied the crimson cord: Arnaut's distinctive hand, with its generous loops and expansive capitals, unfurled before me:

*To the Countess Isabelle, Lady de Meurtaigne, health and good tidings*, it began. I remember how this greeting—the intimacy-strangling language of politesse—startled me. But, of course, I was a married woman now, I had assumed another persona, perhaps even to him.

He told me of his adventures. He had been to Britain and had traveled widely there. He had ventured to the north as far as the wall that the Roman emperor Hadrian had built—"The wall Grandfather described to us—a snake of stone beneath a forbidding sky"—which divided his empire from the blue-painted, wild-eyed tribes of the barbarians. He had kept a few small stones from the wall for me, he said, and would give them to me when he next visited, perhaps in summertime. The land was green as emeralds, he continued, with skies of a piercing blue; at dawn, the mist about the River Tyne was thick and ghostly. From Britain he had ventured even farther north, to the Northern Sea, with its cliffs and treacherous water—"The sea that had brought forth hordes of brigands in high-throated boats." It was a churning, icy sea, he wrote—a forbidding sea, unlike our own, the Middle Sea.

He spoke of Britain's richness, its "moody red-haired inhabitants," its raucous cosmopolitan capital, and of the journey he made to Canterbury. There he had encountered pilgrims—some in rags, others richly appareled—kissing the pavement in the cathedral where the martyr, Thomas, had been murdered. He thought the town itself "a wondrous place" and had bought us pilgrim badges emblazoned with shells, for he hoped one day we might make the journey to Santiago de Compostela, as our grandfather had years before.

Amid the jostling crowd near the cathedral, Arnaut had heard men speaking of King Henry, and of his wife, Queen Eleanor, who remained in captivity—whether in the towers of Winchester or Salisbury, they were not certain.

He went on:

When I asked more of this—about the queen—another man, a tanner (or so it seemed, by his raiment) swaggered up to me and asked what had provoked my interest in her. "After all, she is a queen no more," he sneered, "but a common prisoner now, as she deserves to be, harlot that she is!" At this, a fight ensued between him and another, a young man with a lute strapped across his back. Incensed by the words against the queen, he made threatening gestures, but was far too spindly to subdue the tanner. Knowing of your admiration for Queen Eleanor, I leapt to the young man's defense, the result of which is that his honor—and the queen's—were preserved, and I am now the proud possessor of a broken arm and a gash upon my face. But do not let this disquiet you, sister dear, for the wounds are mending well. . . .

Hearing of this incident alarmed me; I feared for my brother and his recklessness, his impulse toward physicality and heroism. I set down the letter, suddenly feeling unsettled and slightly guilty: it was my enduring fascination with the queen, after all, which had prompted his involvement in the sorry incident and placed him in danger.

A moment later, I resumed reading. He had decided to seek his fortune in the East, he continued, lured as so many were, and still are, by the promises of riches in the Holy Land. En route he would venture to Cyprus, perhaps first to Sicily. He had met some wealthy Normans in his travels who had told him stories of the splendid court in Palermo and of the opportunities for ambitious young men in that island ripe with wheat and trade. If he did not succeed in Sicily, there was also land to be had in the province slightly to the north, Apulia: rich Normans there held vast estates. Travelers had also told him that King William of Sicily kept a garrison of Saracens in a place called Lucera, not far from the Adriatic Sea: this too intrigued him. He might set off from there through Brindisi, and then for the Holy Land.

His letter ended:

My dear sister, I think of you often and of your new life, and whether you remain as you were. I wonder whether you have become such a fine married lady that you have forgotten all we used to do together. Your last letter was penned in a voice I hardly recognized, as if it were not your voice at all, but that of an older woman, so different from the voice I remember.

I was beset by a wave of homesickness. Arnaut's observation about my strange new voice had unsettled me. There was no question that my girlhood did seem something from the distant past, like an old fraying robe tossed into a locked cupboard. But the change in my tone—was it solely the effect of marriage and new responsibilities? Or were there other reasons that I could hardly acknowledge, even to myself?

It was at that moment I scanned the surface of the letter, realizing only then that it had come without our family seal; only when I drew it closer did I discern the faintest vestige of red wax. There *had* been a seal, no doubt, but it had been broken and its traces expunged. The cord itself had likely been refastened by someone other than my brother. The discovery confirmed that letters to me were being opened and read before they were given to me, and my own letters were, most likely, subjected to the same scrutiny.

Disquieted, I began to walk nervously about. I then tried to sew a little, but to no avail. I tossed aside my embroidery, bored with its design— an angel with outstretched wings whose petulant face suddenly revolted me. Pacing back and forth, I glanced around the room: a place of luxury, with its brilliant silk hangings and walls painted with a border of twisting laurel leaves. . . .

Nausea came over me. I needed to step outside to collect my thoughts. Gathering my shawl, I walked to the door, my hand resting on its enameled blue and red latch; I remember that the morning light caught it in such a way that its design of intertwined serpents' heads seemed to grimace.

IN THE COURTYARD ALL WAS still, save for the sound of a carpenter repairing a broken gate: the methodical thud of his hammer rent the air, a discordant note on a crisp, sunny morning. I walked about, taking deep breaths, relieved that the nausea seemed to have abated. A savory smell of roasting fowl emanated from the kitchen, and I felt relieved that the smells, which only the week before had turned my stomach, were now welcome, even appetite-inducing.

I stepped into the kitchen, heartened by the gleam of copper pots and the comforting sight of great wooden bowls arrayed on the work-table. Honey cakes were being prepared for the men's return, and partridge was being roasted; the homely sweet scent of baking apples and cinnamon wafted in the air. A young, plump woman with florid skin and curly auburn hair looked up, flustered, when she saw me enter. She had been peeling apples: the bowl beside her was piled high with their lustrous, curling skins. Putting aside her knife, and wiping her hands hurriedly, she curtseyed to me. "My lady," she said. She had a cocked smile, which was not without a certain charm: her small perfect white teeth rescued her from abject homeliness.

"Give me some work," I said quietly, but with an edge of urgency that surprised her. My loneliness was such that it seemed preferable to work in the kitchen, with its warm companionable scents, than to be upstairs in my silent chamber, piercing a needle through a taut circle of linen.

She handed me an apron, watching with some curiosity as I tied it. "A stool for you, my lady?" she asked, clearly still perplexed. I nodded, sat down, and began to peel an apple, watching as the knife cut beneath the surface and the peel spiraled in circles on my lap.

Awkward silent moments passed; I knew she would not speak to me until I addressed her first. Having finished a second apple, I turned to her and asked her name—Agnes—and how old she was—eighteen—and where her family was from—not far from Rochefort.

"Have you and Aiglantine been here about the same time?"

"I came a bit later, my lady."

I continued to peel one apple, then another. I did not work nearly as neatly as Agnes, and the skins had fallen on my lap in a whorling, glistening reddish mass. My thoughts began to wander. I thought of Aiglantine and her melancholia—the despairing looks that would occa-

sionally cross her face, her small fine-boned hands with their nails bitten
to the quick.

"I wonder about Aiglantine," I finally remarked to Agnes. "There is
a certain sadness about her."

Agnes replied in a low confiding voice: "She had a child—"

"Ah, I did not know that." Then: "I did not know Aiglantine was
married."

"She is *not* married, my lady—"

"I see," I replied, embarrassed at my naivete. I looked down at my
lap. "And the father?"

"A local man, a laborer. The son of a serf from our region. So they
say."

"And what happened to the child?"

"She was forced to abandon it. The father would not let her keep it,
he would not admit that it was his own seed. They say she left the child
in a basket in the forest. But no one really knows."

"So this is merely hearsay?"

She nodded. "She asked Lord de Meurtaigne"—but once again, she
seemed to catch herself. "I must fetch some water," she said briskly. A
few moments later she returned with a copper pot filled with water;
into this, she dropped one peeled apple, then another.

"You were saying—" I continued. "About the child. That she had
asked Lord de Meurtaigne . . ."

"I cannot say, my lady." She gave a shrug. "It is only hearsay."

"Then I shall consider it as such." Then, with an imperiousness that
seemed to take her aback: "But tell me even so."

"Aiglantine asked the Lord de Meurtaigne for some fine silk, so that
she might wrap the child with it before she set it in the forest."

I dwelled on this a moment: woeful stories of this kind were not
uncommon. "So that someone who came upon it would think the baby
of noble blood?"

"Yes." She paused, wiping her hands again as she took up another
apple. "The child would have a better chance of survival that way,

swaddled in silk. No one wants a child of unknown blood. It could be the child of the village idiot. Or even of a Jew." She paused, continuing to work, stopping once to wipe her forehead of sweat. "But then, with Jews, they know their own, they say."

Her tone here, its edge of savagery, took me aback, but I managed to hold my voice in check: she was a peasant, after all, with a peasant's prejudices. "And what of the silk?"

"He would not provide it."

"But surely——" I stammered, trying hard to conceal my dismay. I thought of all the bolts of brocade in my own wardrobe, and the lengths of costly damask that were discarded in the making of my gowns. And then, with a pang, I thought of how Aiglantine was sometimes strangely quiet, even melancholy, as she folded the silks, and arranged them in the armoire. "Did my lord give a reason why the fabric should not have been provided?" I asked.

"He said that a child of one station could not presume to be that of another." She gave me a tight, confiding smile; there was something unpleasant and smug in her expression. "This was Aiglantine's child, after all," she continued, "and she herself is lowly born. To pretend anything else would be dishonest, and against the very laws of nature!" She spouted these last words as one would any common dictum as she continued to toss peeled apples into the pot.

I took another apple, holding it tight in one palm, knife poised in hand. "Against the very laws of nature" she had said. I thought of my husband and his obsession with his falcons and hounds: their breeding, their bloodlines. "No creatures of inferior quality," he had told me only days before he had left on his journey. We had been walking in the mews that day, and once more he had proudly shown me those glittering-eyed creatures, tethered to blocks.

So preoccupied was I that I cut my finger, staining my apron. "Enough now, my lady," she said, pressing a cloth to it to staunch the bleeding. "No good for you to hurt yourself. Not in your condition!"

I rinsed my hand in a basin of water she fetched for me. Then I left, giving her the excuse that I needed to take some air.

Walking away from the kitchen, I picked my way through the glistening puddles, some beginning to constrict from the sun. The gossip imparted by Agnes had at once intrigued and disconcerted me. Still lonely and yearning for some company, I decided to go to the stables and visit Juno; perhaps Gallien, the stable boy, would be there. In the earliest days of my marriage, I would often venture to the stables on my own, sometimes in preparation for an outing with my husband, and sometimes, on a bitter cold day, merely to see the mounts when weather forbade riding. And I was always happy to see Gallien, partly because he reminded me of Arnaut in his expression, at times wistful, at other times so penetrating and fierce one felt he were possessed of secret power. It heartened me that my husband seemed fond of him.

Gallien was an orphan, Gerard had told me. He had begun in the household with the lowliest chores, but was so bright and capable that he was quickly elevated to work caring for the prized steeds. "He has a way of communicating with animals—horses, hounds, falcons," my husband told me. "Never have I known anyone as gifted in this way."

Gallien was cleaning out the stall of a sleek dark steed called Raven as I entered, though he was so intent on his work that he was quite unaware of my presence at first. I smiled and bade him good morrow. "No need to stop your work," I told him as he bowed to me. Then I walked along the stalls, savoring the familiar scent of hay and feed, until I came to Juno.

I beckoned Gallien to fetch some oats. "When will my lord return, do they say?" I asked, stroking Juno's head as she ate the oats from my hand.

"In a few days, my lady. Within the week, at the most."

I must have looked pale and drawn, for he asked if I would like to sit down; in truth the conversation with Agnes had unsettled me. "Better for me to stand and walk about," I replied. "I have taken so little exercise these last months." I continued to stroke Juno, who whinnied in delight.

"Lord de Meurtaigne took great care to find you the very best mount," Gallien said, shuffling from one foot to another as he shyly observed me.

"Did he?" I replied absentmindedly, Juno nuzzling my hand.

"My lord is not one to talk of such things." There was a hint of pride in his voice, the pride of a servant for his master.

"How long have you served Lord de Meurtaigne?"

"Four years now."

"Time enough, then."

"Not so long in these parts."

"But you are quite young—you are—"

"Nineteen."

"And from this region?"

"No, not at all. From Britain."

"Ah—from a Norman family then?"

"No. A Saxon family."

This startled me: to be of Saxon origin in a land dominated by Normans was not an easy matter. The Saxons were treated harshly, contemptuously, by those who had conquered their island. I had once seen young Saxon slaves being auctioned in our village—a pitiful sight that had haunted me for days. "But your name is not in the least Saxon."

"Gallien is not my birth name," he said, so softly that I had to strain to hear him. "Lord de Meurtaigne had me take another name. I was born Garulf. My lord did not think it would be seemly for a man of his station to be known to have a Saxon in his household. Not as a groom. Not to tend his horses." He announced this simply, as one would any logical fact.

"So your name was changed to something more 'suitable'?" This was a word I often heard my husband use.

He nodded.

"And how did you come here, to this household?"

"I had been sold to an owner of a ship that crossed the Channel. I worked as a galley hand, my lady. I met Lord de Meurtaigne during one of his voyages. His mount had a bleeding ulcer on a hind leg. When I saw the wound, I offered to make a poultice."

"And you did, and that healed the horse," I rejoined, for I could easily imagine the scene. "And for that my lord was very grateful."

"Yes." His eyes glowed with pride. "He has been good to me. He gave me a chance to do what I love most. Other men of high rank would not have given me such work. Certainly not to tend their mounts." He shrugged. "I might have worked in the fields, but nothing better."

"You are lucky then." I smiled. "Lucky to have found work you love."

"Lucky to have such a master," came his emphatic reply, before he added, "and my lord has promised me something else."

"What is that?"

"That one day I should help him with his falcons. That is what I dream of. Training birds for the hunt and helping in the mews."

"Then I have no doubt you shall."

"God willing, my lady," he replied in a heartfelt voice, casting his eyes down.

"Yes, of course." I smiled, touched by his hopeful voice, and by his humility. "God willing."


THE SKY THAT NIGHT WAS lit by a defiant silvered moon, which threw tenuous light against the starless sky. I remember looking down across the moat from my chamber window and hearing the frenzied squeaking of bats circling the water, a sound all the more ominous because the colony of fierce beating wings was invisible.

I lay in bed, a favorite quilt pulled up around me, one hand resting on my swollen stomach, as I reflected on the day: the unnerving suspicions that my letters were being read, and then, my conversations with Agnes and Gallien.

The first conversation, with its revelation about Aiglantine and her abandoned child, had perturbed me. Of course—and I reminded myself of this more than once—there was no assurance that Agnes, known to revel in gossip, spoke the truth. The second conversation, with Gallien, should have reassured me. Hence it was the second conversation that I chose to dwell on—a shield against disquietude and inner confusion.

I was entranced by the man who had become my husband; I wanted only to think well of him; I even wanted him to love me. Indeed, I had come to another startling realization during his absence: I had greatly *missed* him, missed conversing with him. But this realization was twinned with another, more startling: I had missed his body, I missed our life in bed together.

So little had I been prepared for that realm that the initiation had come upon me as a thunderclap, as decisive in the way it defined the epochs of my life as the visit Nîmes had, years before. For that journey, at least, I had had some preparation, for Arnaut had long regaled me with stories of the city. That was not the case with matters of the heart, of sex. I had been hurled headlong into that alien world with no advance warning. What little I *had* been told by my mother and Hortense had been grim and cheerless: what I was to suffer in bed with my husband was a duty I was bound, by contract, to perform. An act to be soldiered through, dispatched. Nothing about that attitude seemed in the least extraordinary—that was in the previous century, after all! Like so many young women of my station, I had been schooled by family and church to defend myself against pleasure. Those pleasures I *had* seized—my delight in my cache of ancient objects or in the lulling recitation of stories and the incantatory rhythm of their verses—were more or less secret, private. They had been experienced alone.

Not so with carnal matters. The church had taught me that, in this domain, I might experience a certain kind of pleasure that was permissible *in so far as it helped produce a child.* But now I was with child. Even so, I felt no need to steel myself against the feelings which surged within me, not only in bed with my husband, but also when I sat with him, or watched him ride, or man his hawks. His own attitude had caught me off-guard, as well. I had assumed that much about the changing nature of my body—from sylph to this new, fuller creature of rounded belly—I had thought this would repel him. But no, my condition seemed to please him immeasurably. If anything, his wanting me, in that other way, redoubled. Nor with the fulfillment of conception had the waves of my own pleasure abated; quite the opposite. Worse, I had chosen not to defend myself against them. My mother had brought us up with the saying of Saint Paul, after all—"It is better to marry than to burn"—but still, I *burned.*

Would I be condemned by God for this? Was I really so sinful? In my heart I think I knew the answer, but at the time it was not easy—even for me, with my rebellious nature—to unlock the shackles of my upbringing. Nor, of course, did I ever discuss any of this with my husband. He belonged to the world of men; he had traveled; he had been to the East, he had been exposed to other influences. Some he had told me about; others, I suspected, were better left unspoken. No matter, in the end: his experiences captivated me, whether articulated by him or intuited by me.

In other ways I could not quite fathom he remained inscrutable. But *how*, and why, I was not certain; nor was I sure that these were not merely phantoms of my churning imagination.

A FEW HOURS PASSED. BY then it was midnight, but still I was too restless to sleep. It would be better to banish my nervous energy by composing a letter to Arnaut. I lit a taper and went to the table where I kept my writing implements. What bliss it was, in my new life, to be so profligate with parchment, ink, and quills! At home these things had been parceled out with painstaking care. But now, as the gilded wife of Gerard de Meurtaigne, they seemed to appear and to be replenished almost magically, like many of the other luxuries for which I had no small appetite and to which I had all too quickly grown accustomed: the lovely gowns of Damascene, the jeweled collars of rubies and pearls, and the delicious confections that routinely filled our heaping plates.

I took up the quill and wrote:

*From the Countess de Meurtaigne to Arnaut de Lapalisse, greetings—*

But there I stopped, staring at the taunting blank sheet, struggling to form the next sentence. Words seemed to congeal within a frozen part of my mind. I tried again, then again. But still *nothing* came, as if the words were buried as deeply as my ancient objects had been. Finally, admitting defeat, I climbed back into bed and drew the covers close. I would write Arnaut on the morrow.

I felt my dispirited mind relax; surely the letter could wait another day, even several. There was no rush to respond so quickly; he would not expect it. My thoughts continued to drift, and in those moments of half-sleep, half-awakening, I began to compose an imaginary letter in my mind, a letter that I knew I would never send:

CHERISHED BROTHER, IT BEGAN,

You were correct in observing that the voice of my last letter seemed to come from another being. I feel I have left girlhood and the world I knew with you far behind—our adventures, our pranks, our secret messages. I feel infinitely older. There is much about my marriage which has surpassed my expectations. My husband is an accomplished man who has seen the world in a way which we have only dreamed of, and he is not in the least unkindly. He lavishes me with presents, and he has given me a marvelous steed, Juno, as my very own.

I have not told you that I am with child: God willing, we will have a son next January. One would think, then, that all is well, but I must confess that a strange uneasiness often comes over me. I fear what will happen if this child is not a son; I fear my husband's displeasure. And if it is a son, he will be followed by another child, and then another. And then, having bred these creatures, I will have fulfilled my mission in life, or at least the mission which others have assigned to me.

Something within me fights against this. I miss the after-noons I shared with you and Grandfather, and the sound of his voice reciting our favorite tales. I miss our rides together. Most of all I miss freedom and privacy. It is for this reason partly that I suggest we begin to use our code. I cannot be sure that your last letter had not been opened and scrutinized; I do not feel entirely sure my own letters to you will arrive without having been read by one of my husband's minions. This may be more frightening to me than anything else.

Only you would ever understand this. You, who took me to Nîmes and who led me through the passage to the arena.

I send this letter to you with love and the hope that you will come to visit soon. And that after you do, you will embark on all the adventures which are forbidden to me, and which I know are your destiny.

*I remain, as ever, your loving sister, Isabelle*

## CHAPTER 6

The following day I was glad to see the morning light, for my sleep that night had been rent by bizarre, irretrievable dreams. I sat up in bed, my eyes drawn to the quill and the beckoning parchment for the letter to Arnaut.

I gathered the coverlet around me before I called for Berthe, the young girl who had taken Aiglantine's place during her absence and who reappeared, moments later, with a basin of water and a cup of hot milk. I splashed some water on my face: the cold was bracing, almost painful on my cheeks—my punishment, perhaps, for not having yet written my brother.

I walked to the window and saw that the weather had turned: hostile clouds had gathered in the sky, threatening rain.

I went to my writing table and took up the quill. But no words would come, and the few that did seemed stilted and belabored. Finally, I set the sheet of parchment aside and went again to the window.

A young page, Robert, knocked on the door. "There is someone who asks to see you, my lady," he said shyly, shifting from one foot to another. He had recently been given this position and was still unaccustomed to his braided tunic and to wearing proper shoes.

"What is the man's name?" I asked.

"I am not sure." He looked embarrassed. "It is a foreign name."

"No matter." I said, touched by his flustered face. "What brings him here, did he say?"

"He says to tell you that he sells relics. Fine ones, he said. He is a merchant, my lady."

I wondered if this was the same man whom my husband had mentioned—an agent of relics who also dealt in ancient artifacts.

"I will tell him to leave, my lady." He bowed and turned to leave.

"No," I said at once. "Tell him to wait. Fetch him some barley water and say that I shall see him shortly."

The thin dark-haired man who stood to one side of the great hall would have been good-looking save for an angry scar which cut across one cheek. He stood by himself, a bulging leather satchel on the ground near him. There was an air of shrewd alertness about him: I sensed he had already taken stock of the room, its furnishings, its inhabitants.

"My lady," he said, bowing with an exaggerated, almost mocking, flourish.

I bade him good morrow and asked what had brought him to our castle.

"My trade," he said, suppressing a smile at my fatuous question.

"Of course." I looked down, feeling slightly foolish, trying to avoid another glimpse of the scar. His accent was that of another land: Italian perhaps, for it seemed similar to that of a merchant from Amalfi who had once passed through my family's region. His eyes were almond-shaped, his nose narrow and long; his clothes were quite worn and of an older style, yet he wore them with an élan that made them almost seem fashionable.

"And you are called—"

"Bertuccio. I am from Naples. I came up through Genoa."

"And you trade in relics, they tell me."

"I do."

"And you have never been here before?"

"Only once," he replied, with a slight edge.

"You say that in such a way—" I stopped, wondering if this was the same man my husband had told me about. "I do not think my husband would be interested in your things," I said decisively. "Not in relics."

"But *you* might be."

I blushed, for he had quickly divined my secret: I was curious and bored. "I would be interested in *seeing* them," I said, affecting an off-handedness I did not feel, "but not in buying any. So perhaps it is not worth your time to show them to me."

"No matter to me. I have time enough, before I set off for Bordeaux."

"For Bordeaux, and then to?"

"Flanders. And from there across the Channel, to London. At least
that is my plan now. England has a strong market for relics."

"Why is that?"

He shrugged. "New churches. New royalty." He rubbed his fingers
together. "Great riches."

"You travel a great deal then."

"Yes. Only a few months ago I was in Milan, then in Venice."

The names of those faraway Italian cities alone fascinated me. Guy
had told me about Venice; so had my grandfather. "They are shrewd
traders, I am told, the Venetians."

"Shrewd, yes, and often not to be trusted. There is a saying in our
language—*Veneziani prima, poi cristiani.*"

"What does that mean?"

"'Venetians first, then Christians.' They are a people apart, the Venetians."

"And those from Naples?"

"Shrewd as well, but far more charming."

He smiled cagily; for the first time I caught sight of his decaying
yellow teeth. His expression should have made me slightly uncomfortable, I suppose, but his cocky mien and the idea of his travels intrigued
me too much to dismiss him.

All the while I kept stealing glances at the worn, lumpy leather
satchel at his feet. It looked strangely human, like an exhausted being
who had survived a foray to the underworld.

"Have you anything of Saint Radegonde?" I asked, still eyeing it.
"She is my favorite among women saints."

"Nothing now. But I could be *commissioned* to find something."

"That would not be necessary," I said at once, imagining how my
husband would scorn such a "commission." "And you trade *only* in
relics?"

"And in the objects which contain them. They, too, are in demand
among the Angevins." He knelt down and untied a long object wrapped
in cloth. "Like this reliquary, my lady." He unveiled a tall silver model

of a lower arm, its wrist studded with colored stones, carved seals, and curious oval stones incised with images of beetles. The fingers of the hand itself reached upward, toward the sky, as if beseeching heaven for a blessing.

"This is beautiful," I murmured, running my finger over the stones. "It must be very costly."

"It holds a relic. A relic. A very rare relic of a woman saint."

"Whose?"

"Saint Ursula. A piece of wrist bone."

I handed the vessel back to him with distaste: the martyred saint reminded me of my mother and the medal she had given me when we had parted. "I do not much like Saint Ursula," I told him. Our eyes met; in his, I gleaned the disappointment of a failed transaction. "But the hand reminds me of something else," I continued, "something I possess myself. Not at all the same kind of object. It is ancient, from the Roman people, or so my brother told me."

He feigned interest, though it was not lost on me that he saw this merely as a chance to prolong his stay, and hence the potential for a sale. "You might consider showing it to me, this object," he suggested, with an unctuous smile.

I drew back, for I had never shown anyone but my brother my secret things.

"I have some other wares here," he said, sensing my hesitation. "Some more, some less valuable. Some from Sicily. Norman work, much in demand. And I have a few other objects of value."

"Costly ones?"

"Some more, some less." He reached deep into the satchel and pulled out a large silk pouch. "This, for instance. Pieces for a chess set. Very fashionable among the court these days."

"They say Queen Eleanor is fond of chess," I said. My mother had told me this, though she disapproved not only of the game and its association with the queen's court, but also of its provenance. Chess had been introduced by the Infidels and had come to our lands through Spain. "Do show it to me. Though I should tell you"—I announced this rather proudly—"I have no need of it. My husband has promised to find me a set in Troyes."

"He may find you one there, but I doubt it will be as fine as *this!*" He unwrapped a long parcel that contained an ivory box with gilded mounts. When opened, it revealed an exquisite chessboard. "Beautiful, no? This is fine Norman work—the ivory, the copper mounts, the intricate carving of the pieces. The work of an Arab craftsman in Palermo. It will fetch a high price."

I turned one piece, then another, over in my hand. "This piece?" I asked.

"The queen."

"Of course," I murmured, examining the intricate carving of the crown, the gown, and the small crouching figures of preening courtiers at its base. "Have you ever seen Queen Eleanor?" I asked.

"Only once, years ago when I was a boy, when she passed through Rome. She was a young woman then, the Queen of France. Her husband Louis looked more like a lowly pilgrim than a king. They had recently returned from the Holy War, up the coast from Palermo. I saw her from afar. She was on horseback in all her finery. A graceful rider. They were on their way to see the pope, people said." He paused. "It is something I shall never forget."

"Because of her beauty, I suppose?"

"Only partly," he replied, furrowing his brow as he tried to recapture the memory: "More because of her *power.*"

"That does not surprise me," I replied. "The impression of her power. Perhaps—" But there I stopped, merely returning the piece to him.

He gave me an appraising look before he began to pack up his wares. "I cannot tempt you with anything, then?"

"I think not." Yet something within me resisted his leaving. "Wait," I heard myself say, "before you leave, I should like to show you the object I mentioned to you. It is bronze—not as valuable, of course, as the silver reliquary, but even so—" I stopped suddenly; servants in a far corner were watching us, and their prying eyes made me uneasy.

"I would like to see it," he said.

I asked him to wait while I fetched it, adding, "The sun has come out. It would be good to take some air. Wait here. Then we will go out into the garden."

I returned with the bronze hand, carefully wrapped in linen. "Come this way," I said, leading him to the garden, with its central quartet of quince trees. A pair of stone benches stood to one side; we sat down. I began to unwrap the bronze hand. "There," I said rather triumphantly, when the last bronze finger was revealed. "Surely this is Roman!"

He took it from me, examining the fingers, the fine geometric pattern of the bracelets, and the delicate rings. "It is much older than Roman," he pronounced. "We have things like this in my region, in Naples and the countryside beyond. This looks like the work of people to the north who were there long before the Romans. The most ancient people." Then, in a deprecating tone, "It is not worth much."

"Except to me," I returned rather fiercely.

A flash of his yellow teeth and a wily smile. "Of course."

"And the people who made these things, what do you know about them?"

"Their tombs are found in my land, and to the north. Not long before I began my journey here, I passed through a town to the west of Florence where farmers had just come across such a tomb. They had been digging by the side of a hillock when they struck something hard. It was the stone door of an entrance, an entrance to an ancient tomb. Inside—" He paused, tantalizingly, clearly savoring my rapt attention.

"Continue," I urged.

"After the men made their way inside, they found rooms built for the dead. The rooms held tombs and all the things in them were meant for the afterlife. Much had been plundered long ago, of course. Only a few lids of the tombs remained, the rest had been destroyed. But those tombs in stone—ah, they were frightening!"

"In what way?" I leaned closer.

"They were so *true to life*, you see! You almost expected them to rise and speak. Some tombs showed one person, others a man or woman reclining together. Only when the men returned with a priest to bless the chamber and rid it of pagan demons did they dare forage for anything else. Not much was found. Pots and vases in clay, some small utensils in bronze. In one place, they found small vials painted with weeping faces. The priest, who knew about such things, told us these were meant to hold tears. The tears of mourners."

Silence fell; I felt his canny, assessing eyes. But he quickly resumed the brisk tone of the trader.

"I have two bronze pieces," he said, stroking the side of his face close to the scar. "One is very old, one is recently made. But they are not the kind of pieces women would want."

"Show me even so."

He drew a heavy, bulbous shape swathed in ragged cloth from the satchel. "Look at this," he said as he uncovered a bronze helmet. "Greek most likely. From the Adriatic coast, not far from Brindisi."

"May I touch it?" I asked, though it was not really a question, for I had already taken the helmet in my hands. I turned it this way and that, mesmerized by the pair of long gaping slits in the front: through their vacant spaces a warrior's eyes had once stared in terror and rage. I ran my fingers across the smooth skull, which was aged to a lovely variegated green, the color of sunlit water. "Imagine," I said, almost to myself, "this could have been worn by a soldier from Troy."

He broke into my reverie and named the price—fifty Angevins. "I see," I said as I set it down. "You said you have something else to show me, did you not?"

He reached into the satchel once more. This time it was a Byzantine cross that emerged, and though also made of bronze, the cross seemed to have the delicacy of silver: it was chased with a design of spiraling ivy leaves around the central figure of a male saint. "From the Second Holy War," he said, placing it in my hands.

"Do you know where it came from? Whose it might have been?"

"Some poor wretch who did not survive the disaster, that is all I know." He gave a sigh. "So many had little to protect them, other than such a cross."

I thought of my brother and the plan we had once discussed, but never implemented: the notion of our using a Byzantine cross as a template for coded messages. This cross, with its secret life, would remind me of Arnaut and our secret life.

"My brother would like this," I said, gazing at the cross in my palms. "He has spoken of going to the Holy Land, and we have sometimes talked of——" I stopped myself, adding instead, "Perhaps this would bring him good fortune."

"God willing, it might," he said, in a lofty tone that even he must have realized was unconvincing.

"I would be interested in buying these two things from you—the helmet and the cross—but I have nothing to give you in exchange."

"*Nothing?* I doubt that, my lady." He tilted his head to one side, looking at me almost mockingly. "Nothing at all, nothing in silver, perhaps?"

I thought of the medal of Saint Ursula my mother had given me before my departure that morning in January. I never wore it and kept it hidden in the bottom of my trunk. "There might be *one* thing I could give you. A medal of Saint Ursula. But I have no idea what it is worth. I am told it is silver, and costly."

"Saint Ursula is popular in these parts," he said, mulling this over.

"So they tell me. Wait. I shall fetch it while you pack up your things."

I ran to my chamber and returned with the medal. He held it, mentally calculating its weight before taking a cloth from his pocket to rub the metal. "Yes, it is silver," he said, brandishing the blackened cloth. "And good quality, too."

"Take it in exchange then. I have no need of it."

"For the helmet?"

"For the helmet *and* the cross." A desire for the two objects, survivors of a mysterious past, had overtaken me, and with that desire, a vestige of my old self had returned—the self of my girlhood, the self I had left at my home, in the cave, before my marriage.

"My lady," he scoffed. "That would do for one, but not for both!"

"It is all I have to offer you," I replied, affecting nonchalance. *Never reveal how much you want something,* my husband had told me only recently, after I had observed him dealing with a merchant. Even so, my heart was pounding, so ardently did I want the objects.

"*Both* things for this medal?" Bertuccio repeated, shaking his head. "That is not possible, my lady."

"Very well, then." I indicated that he should depart; in that moment, a sickening feeling of loss swept over me, which battled another feeling, equally puissant: the reckless desire to purchase the things at any price.

He began to wrap up the two pieces, though he did not appear to be hurrying. By his feet lay the taunting leather satchel. "There is *nothing* else you can give me in exchange?" he asked, looking up as he fastened one strap of the satchel.

"Nothing of similar value," I replied, concealing my relief, for he was clearly reconsidering.

"The helmet is heavy," he said after a moment.

"Yes, I can imagine," I concurred, adding with calculated emphasis, "it must weigh upon you when you travel those long roads. A heavy burden for your journey."

His slanted green eyes narrowed, and one side of his face—the side with the scar—constricted in such an unpleasant way that I looked away. "*Nothing* else?" he asked again.

I thought quickly: a new gown had been made for me the previous week to accommodate my expanding waist; there remained some silk to spare. "I have a length of costly silk, silk threaded with gold, from a workshop in Constantinople," I said. "I could give you that as well."

"That will do," he said after a moment. "The medal *and* the silk in exchange for the cross and the helmet."

"Very well," I replied, trying to conceal my delight. "I shall fetch it for you."

I returned shortly: the silk was deep violet in color, a thick damask with a border of stylized leopards, which was a particular favorite of my husband. "Good," Bertuccio said, feeling the stuff between his fingers before folding it. "This will sell well in Antwerp."

"The helmet and the cross then," I said expectantly, holding out my hands. He handed them to me. I remember the weightiness of the helmet as I held it, and how, beside it, the cross seemed all the more fragile and ephemeral.

"You drive a hard bargain," he said, with an appraising smile.

I murmured "thank you," uncertain if this was the right response, before adding: "I would say the same of you, Bertuccio."

During our conversation, I had been quite oblivious to anything around me. I looked about suddenly with a start, relieved to find no servants lurking; no one had observed our exchange. Where I would stash the objects themselves was another matter, momentarily blotted out by the giddiness of acquisition.

"I must leave now," he said, taking up the satchel.

I escorted him outside, through the great hall and then to the main portal, and from there to the edge of the moat. His gaze took in the ramparts, the fertile fields beyond, and the escutcheon with the hawk's lure and the fleur-de-lis carved in the stone lintel. "A lucky woman," he observed, "to have all of this. And to be with child as well."

"Luckier still if the child turns out to be a son!" I exclaimed without thinking; I felt my cheeks reddening.

"There are those who can augur such things," he replied, looking at me so intently that I glanced away.

"So they say," I murmured. "But I do not believe it. Millicent, who attends me, tells me it is a boy because of the way I am carrying, all in the front. But I am not sure I trust her."

"You do not trust many people, I would say." At this I felt myself drawing away, as if we had ventured into dangerous territory.

We continued in silence until finally, stopping, he turned to me. "There is a healer and soothsayer not far from here," he said in a voice suddenly grown thoughtful, and, for the first time, without its edge and bravura. "A person who lives in the forest. Someone who can predict a child's sex. Someone, they say, who even knows ways to help conceive a son."

"What is her name?"

"Anthusis. It is an odd name. Some say it is Greek."

"A brave woman, surely, to live by herself in the forest!"

"I am not certain it *is* a woman." He paused; our eyes met. "Or, if it is, no ordinary woman." He swung the satchel over his shoulder. "But you will see," he added, with a knowing smile that made me uncomfortable.

When we came to the end of the drawbridge, he turned to me with an ingratiating bow. "I wish you Godspeed, my lady." Then, flippantly, "You will need it, especially now that you have given up the blessing of Saint Ursula."

"No matter," I retorted. "I do not need her. I never did." I turned and walked toward the gate, trying to pretend that his final salvo had not unsettled me.

AFTER SUPPER THAT EVENING, I went immediately back to my chamber. It was still light, for the days were longer then; the dark truncated afternoons of winter had vanished. Ordinarily I would have gone for a stroll in the garden, but not that evening: my new treasures, survivors of older eras and of adventures, beckoned.

I had placed the helmet and the cross carefully inside a corner of the small trunk, which had held my books and girlhood treasures. Now I took them out, marveling as I held one, then the other, in my hands: the helmet, which had protected a Greek warrior, and the cross, which had once been carried by a warrior to the Holy Land. How incredible that they had survived, and that now they were *mine*, and could join the lovely, yearning bronze hand from those early people he had described so vividly.

Was it the comfort I derived from them that seemed to have freed the words that had been trapped in mind? Suddenly I was able to compose the letter to my brother, which had hitherto seemed so daunting.

A sudden knocking at the door: it was Aiglantine, who had returned from her journey.

"Good evening, my lady," she said, bowing.

"Come nearer!" I exclaimed. "Oh, I am glad to see you!" I was indeed very glad, though I tried not to evince shock at her appearance. She had grown much thinner in the aftermath of her father's illness: her face looked gaunt, and the tendons of her long, thin neck were alarmingly visible. Her complexion had the opaque pallor of an ivory statuette.

I drew my shawl around me to conceal my belly, for Agnes's story about Aiglantine's abandoned child, and the silk that had been denied her, still haunted me. Now, in her presence, I felt strangely self-conscious, even slightly guilty. "Tell me what happened," I said, though it was already clear from the sadness in her eyes.

Her father had died four days ago, she told me, but it was "a good, peaceful death"—the priest had arrived in time for the cross to be placed in his hands and for him to hear the viaticum. She had been saving her wages to pay for his funeral and for the priest to offer prayers to Saint Martin in her father's memory. I had augmented this small fund by secretly giving her a few silver deniers I had set aside.

"I am so sorry," I said, embracing her. "But still it is good you were able to reach him in time." I beckoned her to sit beside me, but she chose to remain standing.

"Yes, I was there in time. You and Lord de Meurtaigne were very kind to let me go." She looked down, pulling at the sides of her apron.

"It is only human after all. Surely that is what God teaches us."

She looked hard at me, and in her gaze and delicate faded beauty, I saw the searing vestige of suffering. "Yes, only human," she repeated. "Some would say—"

"And to lose a parent is hard," I said, trying to console her. "I am fortunate. I still have my father and my grandfather, may God protect them."

"And your mother, too?"

"Yes," was all I replied. Then: "Go to the kitchen, fetch some bread and ale. It will do you good. Take one of my shawls. The wind has come up."

After the door closed, I made certain that the latch was fastened. Still sitting at the table, I lit a taper and watched as wax dripped to one side, pooling in the bottom of the glimmering brass holder. I was relieved to have Aiglantine's company again, and relieved, as well, that her words had reflected only gratitude to my husband. Even so, I could not quite banish Agnes's story from my mind. But then I chided myself: it was no doubt the sort of idle gossip that all too intrigued me, and ought to be dismissed as such. Yet what I could not dismiss so readily was the idea that my letter to my brother, and his to me, had most likely been read by someone else—a stranger whose eyes and fingers had pored over our words, our thoughts.

I turned to the actual letter I had written and reread it:

*Arnaut de Lapalisse, Greetings from his sister, Isabelle, Lady de Meurtaigne.*

Dearest brother, your words cheered me and brought me joy, for my husband and his men are at the fair at Troyes and I am here quite alone. Alas, I could not make the journey with them. I am with child, and God willing, will have a son in January. This seems to please my husband greatly, and pleasing him, I, too, am happy.

My life here is one of great comfort, and I have many things which I once only dreamed of. Lovely gowns and a beautiful steed called Juno, which my husband has given me. My husband is a generous man and has taught me much. Perhaps that is why you did not quite recognize the voice in my last letter. I feel much older, not at all like the silly girl I used to be.

I often remember how we used to listen to grandfather's tales of his journeys and adventures. Now it is my husband who tells me about such things, for he, too, has traveled to faraway places. He has been to Outremer, and even says there is much to be learned from the ways of the Infidels. Imagine how this would shock our mother!

Your own stories of Britain filled me with longing. How I would love to travel there one day! Of course I realize this is un-likely, but one can always imagine. I wonder if you still plan to go to the East as you mentioned. Please tell me that you will! It would be a great adventure, and you have always been destined for adventure. Indeed, I have found a Byzantine cross and will hold it when I pray for you.

I hope with all my heart that you will come to visit us before harvesttime. When you do, please bring some seeds from my favorite euphorbia bush, for I should like to plant some here to remind me of our home.

In the meantime, I commend myself to you and all our family.

*Your loving sister,*
*Isabelle*

I set down the quill, lost in thought. The sound of small light footsteps interrupted my reverie: it was Aiglantine, returning from the kitchen. Her eyes looked brighter, and a suggestion of a smile appeared on her wan, thin face.

"There is news—of the men," she told me, with excitement. "They will return from Troyes soon—the day after tomorrow, they say."

# CHAPTER 7

Days of feverish waiting followed.

The courtyard, the kitchen, the stables—all sprang back to life as the castle, hushed and cheerless during my husband's absence, prepared to honor his return. Silence gave way to a din of preparation, stillness to commotion. The piercing sound of blacksmiths' hammering rent the air, hounds bayed (as if they, too, sensed the imminent arrival of their master), smoke bellowed from the kitchen, and servants with furrowed brows rushed about, their arms laden with sheaves of wheat and fragrant boughs of flowering branches to adorn the great hall.

Each day, incessantly, I scanned the parapet for a signal from the watchmen—an upraised arm, a horn poised to trumpet. So unrelenting was my badgering—"When will they arrive? Have you heard?"—that I succeeded in exasperating even Aiglantine. "They will come, my lady!" she finally chided me. "And *soon* they say. But you must be patient."

Early one morning I walked once more to the gate tower and looked above: no sign from the men stationed along the parapet. A cool wind blew, though the murky clouds and hazy sky augured heat. Flocks of rooks wheeled past; my gaze followed their swooping path with fascination until they disappeared and all that remained was the sky itself—a milky blue, creatureless void.

I turned and began to walk toward the garden, only to stop after a few moments to look back at the parapet. From there, I would be able to see across the fields, and perhaps—if, by chance, it turned out to be the right moment—I would be able to catch sight of the men myself as they emerged from the edge of the forest. . . .

I began to walk quickly toward the staircase of the gate tower, intent on climbing to the top.

My foot had only reached the first step when I heard a voice: "There is no need for you to go there, my lady." I turned around: it was Raoul, a slight figure immaculately clothed in red, a sheaf of parchment coiled in his hand. "I will let you know, by and by, when the men arrive," he said, bowing slightly. "Rest assured, I will tell you at the first sign."

"I am sure you will," I replied, my skirt still in hand. "But I would like to go above, to the parapet, to see myself."

"That is not a good idea, my lady. Not in your condition. That would be—" He caught himself, for he was about to say "foolish." "That would be dangerous."

"Women in my condition have done things far more dangerous," I replied, irritated by his tone. "I am with child. I am not *ill*, after all."

"Of course, my lady," he replied, somewhat abashed. "And God be praised, you are well, and hearty. But it is not the custom here for the ladies of the house to climb to the parapet."

I glimpsed the scroll with a red seal he carried and thought of the letter from my brother, and wondered whether it was he, the ever-vigilant Raoul, who had opened it. And then I wondered whether he had been watching from afar when I had spoken with Bertuccio the trader.

"It is not the custom here for ladies—" he repeated emphatically.

"I come from a different region," I retorted. "With different customs."

Silently he bowed; I mounted.


AT LAST, ON THE SIXTH day, shortly before noon, the horns sounded. The men were in sight and would arrive in a few hours; we were to assemble in the courtyard when the signal was given.

I called for Aiglantine to help prepare me, for I must be bathed, my skin rubbed with lemon, my hair washed and then dried in the sun before it was plaited with gold ribbon. My best gown had long been readied and lay upon the bed. It was made of linen in a deep cornflower blue, the bodice threaded with silver, the skirt pleated in such a way that it emphasized my swelling stomach. I remember Aiglantine's nervous fingers as she fastened me into it, hook by hook, as Millicent, watching, told her to hurry.

And what do I remember of that moment, the moment when I first glimpsed my husband and his men? The vivid flashes of red and blue, the lusty shouts, the roar of pounding hooves; how the inner court-yard, until then peaceful and well tended, had been transformed in an instant into a raucous inferno of billowing clouds of dust; how the horses, panting and exhausted, foam dripping from their lips, pawed the ground, as if they balked at being suddenly reined in; and how my husband and his companions, their tunics caked with dust, their faces streaked with sweat and dirt, radiated the joy of a journey completed and the return to the known pleasures of home.

I would have hurled myself into his arms but had been told by Mil-licent that I must adhere to the custom of the household and wait to the side to welcome my husband: first with a low bow, then by offering him a cup of ale, which a page, next to me, would hold on a salver along with chunks of cheese and salted meat.

Gerard had barely glanced at me as he dismounted, while I had watched his every move, his every gesture, his every slight variance of ex-pression, as if he were almost, but not quite, a stranger. How robust he seemed, how elegant, even, in his soiled, worn clothes. I had forgotten the clipped edge of his Norman accent and the way he tilted his head back as he issued an order. I noted the offhand way he tossed his reins to Gallien and the brisk efficiency with which he pulled off his gloves and threw them to a waiting page.

Meantime Raoul, standing at attention, watched us from the side, slightly apart from the others, bowing as Gerard greeted him. They spoke quietly for a few minutes before Gerard finally returned to me.

Shyness overtook me as I bowed, welcomed him home, and offered him the goblet of ale. He finished it in a single gulp, set it down, wiped his mouth, looked at me intently, and murmured in the low voice one might almost use in confessing a sin: "I have missed you."

I felt my cheeks flush and stammered something in response.

"Come—it is too hot here," he said, wiping his brow before he took my hand and led me to the side, to the shade, away from the assembled group. He kissed me and then we stood together for a few moments, my hands in his as he looked at me intently. "You have grown much fuller, even in this time," he said, "and you are carrying all in front. That bodes well for a son, they say." He smiled.

"I pray it is a son. The midwife thinks it will be." I glanced down, then up at him, searching for reassurance. "But if it is not?"

"We will have another until it is." He smiled again, with a certain tenderness, my hands still in his as he kissed one, then the other. I remember how pristine and white mine looked against his, scraped and calloused from the journey.

"You have ridden very hard," I said with admiration; yet all the while, "We will have another until it is" continued to echo in my mind.

"I have ridden harder," came his dismissive reply. "But yes, hard enough. It is good to be home." Then: "Come. Best we go inside."

WITHIN THE GREAT HALL, THE air was cool and fragrant with the scent of apple blossoms and of rose petals, which had been scattered on fresh rush. To honor my husband's return, the benches had been covered with embroidered panels of linen, and gleaming bowls laden with fruit and sweetmeats were arrayed on the tables. Beyond, against the wall with the tapestry of the boar hunt, a row of pages waited.

"You are waiting for your presents," he said with a merry glance as we settled on bench.

The chess set and the book of poetry I had asked for. "So you were able to find them!" I exclaimed.

"Not quite. Something else." He opened the leather pouch strapped to his waist and drew from it a silver medal, encircled by green enamel, which was suspended upon a gold chain so finely woven it might have been a strand of silk.

I looked at the medal, puzzled, and tried to conceal my disappointment. Instead, this necklace with its shiny talisman—the medal bright, new and cold, etched with the face of a woman saint and a child.

"Saint Ann," he explained. And then, of course, I understood—Ann was the patron saint of pregnant women. He drew me close. "You must pray to her, it seems, for our wishes to be fulfilled. That we might have a son."

"The midwife tells me I must eat leeks, avoid parsley, press a stone of carnelian upon my left palm," I said, looking down as I turned the medal over in my hand.

"Do it then! All of it. Everything. I will find a carnelian for you."

"I thought you did not believe in such things," I replied slowly, puzzled. "In medals of saints, and votives. Things of that nature. Women saints are nothing but witches, you have said. And you do not believe in witches surely—" I ran my fingers across his cheek.

"No, I do not, though—" His tone had changed: it had not the fearsome adamancy I had anticipated. Fixing a wayward strand of my hair, he continued, "But when it comes to matters of great import, even *I* do not believe in tempting fate by ignoring such superstitions—" He stopped abruptly, only to add: "There is no reason not to do whatever possible to achieve an end."

He took the medal from me and placed it around my neck, smiling as he did so—indeed his expression was so loving that I felt ashamed the gift gave me so little pleasure. For I knew at once the implication of this token: it should replace the ancient coin with the crocodile and serpent that Arnaut had given me, and which Gerard had never ceased to comment upon—or, at the very least, to eye it in a way that made me uncomfortable. Many were the days when I wore a high-necked gown simply to conceal it. The coin had come to mean much to me; it was a symbol of my life before him, of my family and home, of girlhood freedom.

He had begun to loosen the clasp of the old necklace. I began to resist, gently pushing his hand away. "Can I not wear them both together?"

The unyielding expression of his eyes made it clear I could not.

Still, I persisted. "Perhaps one day I shall let the old one go. But not today." As he drew away, I continued, "Perhaps in the future, I shall take the old necklace off. When I have given you a son. But not now." Then, thinking quickly, I made up a story. "You see, this coin has always brought me luck," I began, the tenor of my voice enlivened by invention, "in my region, this is the coin women wear when they want to conceive a son. The crocodile is a symbol of fertility. I should not want to jeopardize that luck now—especially now."

This seemed to placate him. "As you like," he said, embracing me so hard that I felt the leather fastenings of his tunic pressed against my bodice. A kiss upon my forehead followed and with it, on my part, a flooding sensation of relief. "The old and the new," I murmured.

"If that pleases you," came his terse reply.

He pulled away; his voice assumed another cast, the imperious tone he used to bend others to his will. He motioned to the head page: "Tell Raoul to come at once."

In a few moments, Raoul stood before us and was told to have "a large parcel bound in red rope," which had been strapped to Gerard's saddle, brought to us.

Two pages returned with it shortly and placed it on the pavement before us.

"Open it," Gerard ordered them.

The next instant: the brandishing of knives and flashes of steel as the ropes were severed and the contents were unfurled: length upon length of cerulean blue silk undulating like a sea of gold upon the stone pavement, its design a shimmering wave of arabesques and interwoven peacocks. I had never seen fabric so spellbinding, and yet, at the same time, so disturbing—like a glistening body of water, enticing, but treacherous.

He had been observing me, watching my expression, and, no doubt, waiting for my approbation. But something had quelled my voice: during the unfurling I recalled Agnes's story about the silk he had denied Aiglantine for her infant, and was glad she was not there to witness this.

"You look as if the devil had just crossed your path," I heard him say.

I looked up, shaking my head vociferously, the way one does to conceal wayward thoughts. "A sudden dizziness, that is all. It is quite natural, the midwife tells me—" I bent down to touch the cloth. "It is beautiful," I said, looking up at him, still trying to banish those other thoughts.

"There is enough here for a robe and a matching cape for you. You will look like a young queen. My queen."

"Like Queen Eleanor, when she was young," I replied lightly.

"Yes. But more virtuous than Eleanor, let us hope!"

When I took his hand and stood up, I glimpsed Raoul nearby. He had been watching us intently.

"Bind up the cloth," Gerard told him, "and take it away." Raoul bowed and left with the others.

We sat there together, the first time we had been entirely alone.

"It has been lonely here without you," I told him.

"Good." He smiled and stroked my hair absentmindedly, his hand making its way along the length of my braid. . . .

"I hear there was a visitor," he said after a moment.

"A visitor?" I nervously smoothed the pleats of my skirt. "There was a man, a peddler, who passed through—"

"And you permitted him to enter?"

"I spoke with him outside. He was on his way to Flanders and seemed rather in a hurry."

"What was he selling?"

"Odd things. Relics," I replied, thinking fearfully of the things I had hidden. "He told me there was an ever-greater market now for such things, with the Angevins especially, and with those high up in the English court. For relics of Becket, and Saint Ursula, and things of that sort. For reliquaries, too, of a certain sort."

"That is a great deal to have learned from a man who merely passed through," he observed, a slight sharpness to his voice.

I realized I had revealed too much. "You know how I do like to ask questions. Once I begin, I find it hard to stop."

He pressed a finger against my lips. "Then you must learn more restraint."

I bit my lip and remained silent, resisting the impulse to add that restraint had never been my forte. "I shall do my best," I said quietly. "But I—"

From across the hall I heard someone suddenly enter—Raoul, who approached us. I looked away, suspicious that it was he who had told my husband about Bertuccio and his visit.

"Is there anything else you have need of, my lord?" Raoul inquired, rubbing his hands together obsequiously.

"Nothing. Everything seems in order. You may go."

I watched him leave, wondering what he had really been thinking.

Gerard stood up. "Now, for other matters," he said as he took my hand and led me to the winding stairs that led to our chamber.

# CHAPTER 8

Weeks passed; hot windless weather; more enforced idleness.

I could not ride my beloved Juno, for riding might jeopardize the baby; I could not bathe in the river, as I had done in summers past, for Millicent had told me that evil spirits resided in river water, and fairy goblins, too, and poisonous snakes that could smell a pregnant woman and wrest her to the bottom and strangle her. These stories frightened me, but then so much about being with child frightened me—the idea of this creature within me, with its fierce kicks and hidden life, this mysterious being who controlled my body and, it seemed, my destiny.

Morning walks across the meadows into the edge of the forest became my refuge from restriction, and from the searing heat and confinement of the castle. I remember the relief of entering that cool, green-tinged universe, with its towering canopy of oak and poplar branches, where the light was of another cast—lunar and hazy—and the ground yielding, damp and fragrant, its carpet woven of matted ferns, bits of feathers, and torn branches. No sounds, except those of foraging animals and of swooping eagles and ospreys.

To my delight, I was able to escape Millicent's surveillance while on these walks. Aiglantine would accompany me, as well as a young boy from the stables whom my husband had assigned to escort us. At first the boy—Hugo—kept so close behind us that Aiglantine and I could hardly speak freely together, but it happened that Hugo was an amiable sort and not unsusceptible to my own orders, especially if they were accompanied by an offer of sweetmeats and honey cakes produced from my pocket. Fueled by these treats—a bribe by any other name—he soon

learned to maintain a distance from us as Aiglantine and I ambled ahead
to joke and talk.

She had become much more than a servant to me by that time: she
had become a trusted friend. I often wondered how her life would have
been transformed if she had been born into other circumstances, or if
she had been taught to read. Stories about my own childhood seemed
to fascinate her. I told her about my grandfather—his library and the
books he had lent me—about my brothers and our trip to Nîmes, and
about Arnaut, whom I sorely missed.

Tell me more about him, she would say, as we ambled along. I told
her how Arnaut had taken me to see the splendid arena in Nîmes, how
we invented stories to pass the time, how we both loved adventure, how
we disobeyed our parents and were punished for it. I told her that Gallien reminded me somewhat of Arnaut in not only in his looks—the
freckled skin, the faraway yet intense look in his gray-blue eyes—but
in his fascination for birds; and that it was partly for that reason that I
wanted to help Gallien progress from stable hand to falcon keeper.

"He should be working in the mews, not in the stables," I told her
one day when, while returning from our walk, we glimpsed Gallien from
afar, leading a horse into the stables. "That is what he loves. What he
will do best."

"And have you spoken with Lord de Meurtaigne about this, on
Gallien's behalf?"

"Yes, many times! Too many!" I laughed, kicking some pebbles in
the path. "So many times that I think my lord is weary of it. About
Gallien and the mews. He said to me only yesterday 'Enough of this
hounding from you!' But he has been good-natured about it, and he
has promised to heed me. To move Gallien into the mews very soon,
perhaps even this season, before the hunt."

EVENTUALLY I EVEN TOLD AIGLANTINE about the things I had
bought from Bertuccio the trader; how I had hidden them in the wardrobe beneath some blankets; and how I feared my husband's disapproval
if he should discover them. Her eyes widened as I told her this—I

could tell she thought I was quite reckless—but even so curiosity got
the better of her, and when we returned later to the bedchamber, she
asked me if I would show them to her.

We locked the door. I unearthed the helmet and the cross from the
bottom of the trunk, and, after placing them in her hands, watched her
eyes grow in wonderment as she turned them this way and that. Then I
showed her my girlhood "secret treasures"—the bronze hand, the little
vessel of frosty blue glass. Long before, I had invented stories about
those treasures—where they had come from, who had worn them, how
they had survived and made their way to me. She loved these tales and
begged me to recount them while, at night, she brushed my hair and
helped me prepare for bed, or in the afternoon, while she swept the
floor and I sat by the window, embroidering.

The storytelling became a ritual between us, a way of transporting
us to another world, just as it had when I was a girl, sharing tales with
my brother. I do not know, looking back, who derived the most pleasure
from it: Aiglantine, listening raptly, or myself, luxuriating in the labyrinth of my imagination.

From the most mundane objects to the most luxurious—all were
fodder for me. I invented stories about the enameled griffins on the
lock of my bedchamber door, for instance—I told her they had come
from the shield of a Sicilian prince who had had them forged by a
slave in Palermo before he, the prince, set off for the Holy Wars; but
then he was killed by the Infidels, who wrenched the griffins from his
shield, and sold them to a trader from Constantinople who dealt in
such things. . . .

I made up an entire history of the Byzantine bracelets my husband
had given me, though I had not yet worked up the courage to ask the
one question that lurked in my mind whenever the cuffs were fastened
on my wrists: whether they had once belonged to my husband's late
wife. It seemed safer to take refuge in invention, to pretend that they
had come from a workshop that had crafted jewels for the wicked Empress Theodora; how she had worn them when she appeared at court,
or even in bed, when she was intent on seduction. . . .

This story tantalized, even shocked, Aiglantine, though she continued to listen and ask questions even so. ("Is it true what they say—that Theodora had been a circus dancer, a whore?") But then, many things I did seemed to scandalize her. I remember the day when I received a letter from my mother bristling with advice, and how I threw it into the fire, watching with spiteful delight as the flames devoured her hectoring words. Aiglantine, who adored her own mother, was horrified and thrust her hand into the fire to retrieve it.

"No," I told her, pushing her arm away, "let it burn."

THUS, VERY SLOWLY, PASSED THE summer of 1178—that summer of waiting and isolation, when I yearned for some freedom and for news of the outside world. I gleaned what I could from my husband after his journey to Troyes, and from the merchants and peddlers who passed through our land. Tell me, I would say, tell me what is happening beyond our castle, in other regions, and across the channel, in England. There were rumors that Joanna, Eleanor's daughter and the wife of King William of Sicily, was with child—"As you are" the same visitor had said to me, as if this royal pregnancy conferred upon my own a sense of privilege.

It was not lost on my husband that I hung on every word of those who passed through. He would watch me intently while I questioned them and would notice how subdued I became after the guests departed.

One night, after a feast in honor of merchants from Bordeaux, he promised that one day I should accompany him to one of the great fairs in Champagne, near Troyes.

"Next year—next spring?"

"Yes," came his response, sealed with a kiss. "When you are well recovered from the birth of our son."

*But if it is not a son?* This was the question that haunted me.

At such moments I would think incessantly of the healer Bertuccio had told me about—the woman in the forest who could tell me whether I would have a son or a daughter. Anthusis was her name, he had said; yet he did not seem to know what she was, man or woman. Sometimes

I would stare out the window or mount the parapet to look beyond, into the forest, trying to imagine where she lived. There were moments during my walks with Aiglantine when I would look down at the ground and see an undecipherable paw print and think—inexplicably—that this might be Anthusis's; or when I would hear the sudden sharp thwacking sound of vultures in flight and wonder if they, soaring above us, could see her lair.

BY THE FEAST OF THE Assumption in mid-August, the heat had turned so stifling that all activity in the castle would cease, come afternoon. The smell of leather, and dung, and horse manure, and fetid straw suffocated all which, earlier in the summer, had been refreshing and pleasant—the scent of apple branches, honeysuckle, freshly cut grass. The kitchen had become an inferno. I would see the women emerge at noontime in the scorching sun, and watch as they wiped their brows and splashed their faces from a bucket of cloudy rainwater, which I had passed earlier that morning, noticing that it was crawling with dead beetles and dragonflies.

One such afternoon I came upon Agnes, the talkative kitchen maid, fanning herself by the well. Seeing me, she stood up at once, and curtseyed: "You should take care with this heat, my lady."

"As you should, too," came my reply as I wiped my brow and stooped to pick up a branch from the bundle on the ground. I began to fan myself, shielding my eyes from the sun.

She shrugged. "We are used to this weather, all of us in the kitchen. And before long, autumn will come, then winter. And when it is winter, we will look back on these days and wish God would send us some of this heat!" A hearty laugh as she continued to fan herself, stopping occasionally to swat a fly.

"It seems there is hardly a soul here today. Even Raoul is nowhere to be found."

"I doubt that, my lady. You never know where he will turn up." Another swat. "Raoul Three Eye we call him." Then she seemed to catch herself. "But I reckon I should never have told you that, my lady!"

"Let us blame it on the heat and pretend you never told me," I said cavalierly enough; and then, looking at her intently, I posed a question to which I already knew the answer: "Why that name—Three Eye?"

"Because nothing is lost on him. That is what Millicent and the others say."

A succession of images flitted through my mind—Raoul, watching from afar; Raoul, with his soundless steps, surprising me that day when I was about to mount to the parapet. . . .

"He seems quite devoted to my lord, to my husband."

"He always was. Always will be. He will always be ready to do Lord de Meurtaigne's bidding, that is for sure."

"And he has been here long?"

"Longer than all of us, my lady. Except Millicent, of course." She broke off a stick from the bough and began to draw a circle in the ground. Then she looked up, her cheeks florid with heat, her perfect white teeth weirdly dainty against the broad expanse of flesh that made up her face. "The rest of us may come and go. But not Raoul. He's as much part of all of this as that stone wall"—she made a gesture, with the stick—"or the big oak tree at the edge of the orchard. He would die for his lordship. And his lordship knows it, I warrant."

"He does not seem unintelligent. I even venture"—here, thinking of the letter with the broken seal, I paused, weighing my words—"that he can read."

"Why, that he can!" she exclaimed. "And well, at that. Or so I am told. The monks at Saint Florent taught him. There was a time when he thought he would enter service there, but even the monks must have paused at the thought of Raoul. But in the end, he left the Lord's service and came to serve another lord. Ours here!" A ribald laugh.

"A fair exchange," came my wry reply.

"Some would say." She had taken out a small kitchen knife from her pocket and merrily began to whittle the stick.

Moments passed. The sun began to relent; a sudden breeze came up. I looked around the courtyard for a sign of life and then at the stables, beyond, hoping the wind would not cool her garrulousness.

"What of Gallien? My lord has spoken well of him. I think well of him, too."

"What of him? He is not one of ours. He is a Saxon. Keeps to himself. They say he is wellborn, for a Saxon at least, but then his family was punished by the Normans. Harshly they say, and who would doubt it? All their land taken, and Gallien forced to make his own way, little more than a slave. I hear he's angling to work in the mews." Then, after letting out a yawn, "If I were him, I would tell him to be mindful of Ragnar, I would."

"And why is that?"

"Why jealousy of course!" Her voice, lowering, took on a low confiding tone: "If you were Ragnar, would you want—" But then she stopped abruptly, for the baker had emerged from the kitchen and was calling for her sharply.

"I must return to my work, my lady."

And at that she stood up, stretched both arms high above her head, gave a great sigh, and left, leaving me with the whittled stick.

# CHAPTER 9

September's welcome weather, cooling breezes and less strident light, a clear deep blue sky, for the north wind had swept away the detritus of the long searing summer. Boar had been sighted: the men would leave soon for the hunt, and for hawking, and the forest would swallow them up for long stretches.

My energy had returned. The bouts of nausea had ceased, and I had begun to daydream about the creature who stirred within me. A boy, hopefully—a strong, heroic boy who would know an unbounded life, who would excel at tournaments, who would woo ladies with graceful songs—a young man who would return from travels and soaring adventures to regale us with his stories.

*And if a girl,* I would force myself to imagine, only to find that here, for once, my imagination, like a magic potion depleted of power, would fail me.

The idea of the woman in the forest—the healer, the augurer—had come to obsess me. Did she exist or was this Bertuccio's fabrication, a final deceitful salvo, meant only to disquiet me? And if she did live near our lands, did she really possess such powers?

And even if I could find her, and even if she could obliterate uncertainty, would it really be less daunting to know the future, or better to dwell in a cloud of unknowing?

I DID NOT FORGET WHAT Agnes had said about Ragnar and took care to avoid him when I could, all the while thinking of his devotion to my husband, and the suggestion that he would be jealous of Gallien if the latter were perceived as a favorite.

Yet I admit that part of me—the obdurate, willful part—had also taken this as a kind of challenge. If anything, I had redoubled my efforts to help Gallien, so determined was I that he should realize his dream: to work with the falcons, in the mews.

"Let him try, at least," I entreated Gerard one day, as I met him in the stables one afternoon when he had returned from a ride to the village. "I know you will not regret it!"

"I wonder why this means so much to you, my darling," he replied, his eyes scanning my face. "But if it pleases you, I shall consider it. I promise." He smiled, taking me into his arms.

"That is a real promise, then?" I asked.

"Yes, yes!" he replied, with an exasperated laugh. Then: "But what will I get in return for this good deed?"

"I shall think of something." I touched my finger to his lips.

"Good. I shall hold you to it. But not before you give me a kiss."

LATE SEPTEMBER IN THE WANING hours of the afternoon, a deep golden light, the lengthening shadows of towers and turrets, and the surface of the moat turned greenish-black, mirrorlike and fathomless. My husband and his men had left to supervise the beginning of the harvest; Millicent had gone to the village.

Aiglantine and I were alone in my chamber; I sat by the window, embroidering a shirt for the baby while she, across the room, sorted my dresses. Many were now too small for me, and new ampler ones, no less luxurious than their predecessors, had recently been fashioned. Guests from Saint Jean d'Angély were to come for the hunt the following month, and I, as the lady of the household, must look my best. ("Your most splendid," my husband had told me in a voice both loving and cautionary.)

Aiglantine looked almost beautiful that day, as if the veil of despondence had been lifted to reveal another radiant self. The expression of her eyes—those remarkable eyes, one blue, the other a gold-flecked brown—verged on the merry. Her ivory skin shone, her cheeks were rosy. I had given her some of my powder and had taught her how to conceal the purplish mark below her eye, so that it was nearly invisible.

Only her hands, with their calluses and ragged bitten nails, hinted at the other despairing self I had sensed from our first meeting.

I watched as, one by one, she folded the discarded gowns and placed them in an oak chest scented with little cloth bundles of dried rosemary, pine needles, and lavender: there the layers of linen and silk would remain, souvenirs of the earliest months of my marriage, only to be resurrected the following year, when I would be a mother. With a twinge of guilt, I thought of Agnes's story about Aiglantine and the scrap of silk, which my husband had denied her.

I sighed and resumed my sewing, secretly glad that Amélie and my mother were not there to criticize me and mock my embroidery, as they had my freckles, and much else. Then, suddenly, I pricked my finger on the needle, and cried out: a drop of blood spread upon the pristine linen, soiling the design of ivy I had embroidered.

"My lady!" cried Aiglantine, approaching me with a cloth napkin as I pressed the bleeding finger to my lip.

"It is nothing—a prick of the needle, that is all."

"I do not think your mind is on your needlework today, my lady."

"You know me well," I replied with a smile, holding the hoop away as I surveyed my woeful handiwork. "I doubt I shall ever be skilled at this, no matter how hard I try. I can hear my mother's voice as I stitch"—here, I imitated my mother's shrill voice—"'Isabelle, can you not do it *properly* for once?' It seemed I never could. My sister was always the paragon of stitchery. 'Isabelle,' she would say"—here, I aped Amélie's high, simpering voice—"'how *careless* you are, Isabelle, how do you manage to make such a mess of your sewing?' She would work for hours, bent over the hoop, producing masterpieces. But not I! I dreamed of walking outside in the meadows, or of listening to my grandfather read from his books. Anything but *this*." Sighing, I took up the hoop again and made a wretched attempt to continue, but the blot of blood upon the fabric had ruined it for me: it seemed to stare at me reprovingly, like a sin that even confession could not erase.

I tossed the hoop on the bench, stood up, and looked out the window, my eyes fixed on the edge of the forest.

"Is it true—" I said slowly, still facing the window, away from Aiglantine, "that there is someone who lives in the forest, a healer, who can tell me whether it is a son or a daughter I carry?" I turned to face her. "The trader who came that day—Bertuccio, the Italian," I continued, "it was he who told me about her. She lives in the forest, he said. Anthusis is her name. Surely someone here must know of this person," I added impatiently.

"I do not know," she murmured.

"Then you must ask for me, since I cannot. Find out where this woman dwells. She may be quite close, in which case I shall find a way to see her. And if far—well, that decides the matter, and I shall ask no more."

Still kneeling by the chest, a folded gown in her arms, Aiglantine looked up at me. "If there were such a woman, and she had those powers, what good would it be to know, my lady?"

"If I am to have a son, it would put my mind at rest. And if a daughter, I could prepare myself for disappointment."

"But if not a son *this* time, then surely the next time—"

"And the next, and the next . . ." I interjected; a despairing mood had suddenly engulfed me. "Perhaps you are right. Perhaps it would be useless knowledge—if there is such a thing."

"Or dangerous knowledge."

"Why *dangerous*? When can knowledge be dangerous, ever?"

She gave a distant, curved smile, which brought to mind that of the small stone head among my secret treasures. "Think not on these matters, my lady," she said. "By this time, surely, the soul has entered the baby. As God intended. All will be well."

"Will it?" I picked up a silk surcoat from the pile and tossed it almost angrily into the chest. "I cannot help but wonder. And how can *you* know how I feel, how I worry?" Then, almost immediately, I thought about the child Aiglantine had been compelled to abandon. "Forgive me," I said, taking her hands. "I know you only meant to comfort me. There is no reason for me to be so peevish."

She wrested her hands from mine and looked down at her apron, as if struggling with sadness. "Let us forget this conversation," I finally said.

She nodded and looked at me directly. "I will ask about the healer," she said after a moment. "About this woman."

"Thank you." Yet my harsh words to her still echoed in my mind; I only wanted to blot them out, to erase them, like the spot on the embroidery.

Wind had come up, fluttering the tapestry of the Annunciation on the wall in such a way that it seemed to bring it life: the Angel Gabriel, with his cryptic smile, alighting before the frozen, imperturbable Virgin. I turned away from it, only thinking of a way to banish Aiglantine's hurt. "I know—I shall tell you a story," I said brightly. "Another story to do with Theodora. Wait."

I went to my jewel coffer and opened the heavy, agate-studded lid: within lay a tray of beads in coral and amber meant to protect me in pregnancy and childbirth, and in another, the bracelets from Constantinople my husband had given me. "You must try these on," I told Aiglantine. "You must pretend you are a lady of high rank." I began to fasten the first bracelet on her wrist—

"Oh I can't, my lady—not these!" she protested. "They are much too fine for me. They are worth a king's ransom!"

"No matter—we are only pretending. But you are quite right, they are worth a king's ransom. Or a queen's, rather!" I stood back, assessing how she looked: the bracelets were much too big for her delicate wrists and looked incongruous with her plain servant's tunic, but the thrill of wearing them had brought the merriness back to her eyes and the color back to her cheeks.

I began to pace the room as I conjured up a story, thinking back on all I had been told as a girl about queens—about the ancient queen Radegonde; about the notorious Queen Eleanor, still imprisoned by her husband, in England.

"What was I saying—a queen's ransom—yes," I murmured; then, animated, I began in earnest: "Imagine these once belonged to the queen, to Eleanor. They were given to her by her uncle, Raymond of

Antioch, while she was on the Holy War with the old king, with her husband King Louis. 'You must look as fine as the Frankish noblewomen here in Outremer,' Raymond had told Eleanor. For this was the first time he had ever seen his niece: she had come all the way to the Holy Land, from France, with the king her husband. Nothing she had ever been given was as costly and dazzling as these bracelets, which her uncle had presented to her and which, he told her, had been made by the jeweler to the Empress Theodora."

I paused, thinking hard. "But the queen's husband, Louis, so pious, so meek, did not believe in such things, in such gaudy finery," I continued—slowly at first, then with relish. "They had joined the Holy War, after all, a holy mission! And when he first saw her wearing the gorgeous bracelets, when he heard they had been given to her by her uncle—her handsome uncle—King Louis was furious! For there had already been murmurings among his courtiers that Eleanor and Raymond were entirely too close."

Aiglantine stood by the hearth, listening raptly as she touched one gleaming bracelet, then the other. Even from a distance I could glimpse the milky pearl rosettes edged with glittering stones, and the vivid blue and green of enamel set off by bands of gold. Meantime I focused hard, straining to imagine what would come next.

Suddenly inspired, I recommenced, "And so the bracelets remained in Eleanor's possession for years to come. She brought them back to France with her, and after she divorced Louis and married Henry Plantagenet, and he became King of England, she wore them when she was crowned, and when she presided over great occasions. The bracelets were among her most precious possessions, though she never told the king of their provenance.

"But then years later, after she angered King Henry," I continued, "and he had her captured and taken to England and placed in captivity, the bracelets were lost to her. She had not the time nor the means to secure her all her treasures, and so the precious bracelets were left behind, in France, at her castle in Poitiers. The king had had it ransacked, and the bracelets, and all her treasure, were seized. But, of course, he never wanted to see these things again, for they reminded him of his rebellious wife. 'Sell them all!' he ordered his most trusted advisor. And so the bracelets were sold in Rouen by a famous dealer at a much lesser price than they might have commanded, for the dealer had been forbidden to reveal their imperial history.

"Now, let me see"—I furrowed my brow—"Ah, yes! A young knight bought them, thinking that he would save them for his lady love. And now let us pretend this valorous knight has given them to *you* as a token of his love. He has accompanied them with poems that praise your beauty, and he has put these poems to song. For he is not only a champion of the tournaments, but a lute player as well." At this, I beckoned to her, took her hands in mine, and together we began to dance around the room, cavorting and laughing, until suddenly—

"Take them off!" a deep voice commanded, startling us. We stopped, both of us breathless from dancing, and turned around: it was Gerard. "Take them off *now*," he repeated in a voice that frightened me, a deeper, strident voice I had never heard before.

"I can explain, my lord," I stammered, approaching him, the bracelets now clutched in my hands. "It is all my fault. It was *my* idea. It was never Aiglantine's. Blame me, my lord, but please not her—"

But he would not look at me: his eyes were fixed on Aiglantine. "Leave us," he ordered her.

"Yes, my lord," she stuttered, her face contorted by tears and humiliation, her hands trembling.

"This must never happen again. For you to lose sight of who you are, of your station."

"I promise, my lord."

"If ever this should happen, if ever you should forget decorum in such a way, you will leave this household, never to return here, never to find work in this region. I will make sure of it. And you know I will."

Within me, everything had congealed: words clutched in my throat, and every muscle tensed. Even the bracelets felt ice cold against my palms: disembodied from their invented history, and the root of this anguish, they were now merely two bands of chilly metal studded by stones wrenched from unsightly places. They no longer seemed beautiful or even desirable.

I watched Aiglantine leave, desperate to comfort her, but I dared not, for he was watching me.

Without a word I took the bracelets and placed them in the jewelry coffer. The thud of the heavy lid, closing.

I turned around, steeling myself to speak with Gerard—

But he was already gone.

LATER THAT NIGHT. COOL AUTUMN winds, the first intimation of winter. Inside the castle, tapers in twisting candelabra cast spidery patterns upon the walls as we dined in the great hall. I remember the glimmering goblets before us on the table, the hovering servants, the acrid smell of tallow. How welcome the wine was that night: I drank perhaps slightly too much, at one moment spilling some on the cloth, so that splotches of red meandered near my plate.

I had been very quiet since Gerard's harshness toward Aiglantine. I said little at dinner, merely picked at my food, and hardly even acknowledged the musicians whom he had commanded to entertain us. I remember wishing fiercely, rebelliously, that I were free, a girl again with my grandfather in his library, listening to tales of heroes and faraway journeys; a girl again, digging in the earth for buried treasures. . . .

Gerard stood up from the table, taking my hand: "It is time for us to retire."

"As you wish," I murmured, careful not to meet his eyes.

We began to walk to our chamber above: a slow, silent march along the gallery that led to our private stairway. Light flickered along the lavishly painted walls, each swirling with a separate story: a glimpse of Eve's slender arm brandishing an apple in the Garden of Eden; a grimacing horned creature prancing among the Seven Deadly Sins; the beatific gaze of Saint Margaret, calmly spearing the dragon.

We continued to walk until he stopped, suddenly, before the image of Saint Margaret. "Dinner displeased you," he remarked. Tapers illuminated his face, the gleam of his cheekbones, and the severity of his profile.

"It was not the dinner," I replied resentfully.

"You are tired then," he said, as if oblivious to my tone. His hand, caressing my hair. "You are tired after a long day. It is not surprising, given your condition."

"It was not right of you to blame Aiglantine!" I cried in a voice of passionate indignation. "If anyone was to have been blamed, it was I! I had given her the bracelets to try on. It was *my* idea. A bit of merry-making. That was all."

"She is your servant. She should have known better. And you are—"

"She is only human."

"She is a *servant*. You must not forget that. Ever."

His eyes were hard upon me as he added: "Let us forget this sorry episode. This mischief." The last word was uttered as one would pronounce something vile, like poison. "You will remember not to do it again, and I shall not hold it against her. I promise you that. And I shall allow you to tell her that on my behalf." His finger beneath my chin, forcing me to look at him. "Most of all, I ask you to understand the customs of our household. The rules, the decorum. Surely it is not too much to ask. I have given you everything you might desire in comfort, and in luxury. Things you never had before."

I did not reply but, rather, nervously fingered the coin from Nîmes around my neck, my habitual gesture against unease.

He noticed my tension: I felt him watching my finger on the ancient coin he had not given me. "You are not wearing the necklace I gave you," he observed. "The medal of Saint Ann." His voice was measured but edged with iciness. "Why is that?"

"I must have forgotten to put it on," I replied: this was a lie of course, uttered in a voice as smooth as I was able to muster.

He turned away for a moment, as if to gather his thoughts; then, returning to face me: "We must put this sorry incident behind us," he said in a different voice this time: softly, wooingly, the way he spoke to his falcons, to his doves.

"I shall try." Yet inwardly I still smarted and continued to avoid his eyes.

He took my hand, kissing it gently. "Come." We resumed walking to our chamber. He opened the door, and we entered. The windows were still open, but by then the sky was dark and starless: only the pearlescent reflection of the moon was visible on the inky surface of the moat.

The sudden harsh banging of loose shutters against the window rent the quiet, startling me. I watched as he walked over to latch them, only to glance away as he returned to me. "Come to bed now, my dove." His hand grazed my cheek as he turned my face to his and kissed me, still murmuring "my dove."

I pulled away. On top of the bed lay my linen night shift, a ghostly thing, like the vestment of a phantom who had long since fled. I began to undress quickly and carelessly, tossing my gown onto a bench, but it slipped to the floor, a chaotic mass of crimson silk, its lustrous waves caught by candlelight. He bent down to fetch it, folding it with what seemed to me exaggerated precision before placing it on top of a chest.

I donned the shift, jerking it over my head almost militantly, as if it would help preserve the protective mantle of my anger. And then I began to fasten the ties closely at the neck, a gesture that was not lost on him.

"No," he said gently but firmly, as he drew my hands away. "Leave it untied. For now."

Pride and anger warred against another part of me lulled by his voice, his endearments, the earthy scent of his skin, the strength of his arms pulling me close to him. All else began to recede: Aiglantine and her humiliation, his upbraiding me about the bracelets. . . .

His mouth, brushing the nape of my neck . . . I wondered that he wanted me so ardently. I, who had angered him earlier that day, I who was with child and whose body was distended and foreign.

"I fear—for the child," I murmured, perhaps disingenuously.

"But why? You have never mentioned this before."

"They say"—a nervous pause—"they say it is best for us to refrain now, when I am with child."

"Who says this?"

"The priest. The midwife. And I have always been told—by my mother, my sister. They told me—"

"They do not know of what they speak," he said sharply. And then intently, but with a semblance of gentleness: "What we do together, between us, does not apply to others. Or how they choose to live. It is up to us to forge our own rules."

I looked away, unsure what I felt surging through me: thrill, or fear.

Then: his arm tight around my waist, the other drawing my mouth to his as he murmured: "There is no need for fear. Not with me."

# CHAPTER 10

W ake up, my sweet," were the first words I heard the following morning. I turned to face him from the tumbled landscape of the bed. He was dressed, and I saw from his tunic and breeches and his flushed cheeks that he had already been out riding. It was not much past dawn.

I drew the coverlet about me and sat up, almost disoriented. The night had been tempest-tossed: I had lain awake a great part of it, my mind agitated, my thoughts skittering from one cause of vexation to another: the fear that it might not be a son I carried; the objects that I had hidden—what if Gerard should discover them, and what if he should also discover that I had traded them for costly silk that had been a gift from him? Lastly, and perhaps most piercingly, his cruelty to Aiglantine when he discovered her wearing the bracelets.

The balm of the soothing caresses and amorous rituals which I had succumbed to the previous evening had worn off. I was left with the brittle glare of the morning light.

He bent over to kiss me.

"Where have you been?" I asked.

"To the stables. To speak with Gallien and to tell him of my decision. I have told him I want him to work in the mews. He will replace Arnulf and will begin at once." His expression and voice radiated a certain expectation of approval from me, for he had, after all, fulfilled my wish that Gallien be granted a position as falconer. The news should have sparked only delight from me, yet now it seemed slightly tinged with the taint of the quid pro quo. I knew it was his way of mitigating his harshness to me the previous day. He would never admit this of course; he would address it obliquely. And so he had chosen this, he had chosen Gallien.

"I am glad you have given Gallien this chance," I told him. "And I am grateful to you, most grateful indeed."

I had managed to utter the words, yet how stilted they were, how formal! To my relief he did not seem to notice, and when he left the chamber, he was smiling.

I rose from bed, drew a shawl around me, and walked restlessly around the chamber. My gaze drifted to the spacious wall to the right of the window, which was painted with a scene of the Annunciation. The bright morning sun threw slanted rays across it, and the superimposition of wintry bluish light seemed to lend the Angel Gabriel and the Virgin another dimension of complexity. I looked at the image long and hard, studying it as if I were seeing each element for the first time: the long, strident feathers of Gabriel's wings and his tapered, upraised fingers; the sharp beak of the dove alighting on the Virgin. And the Virgin herself: her downcast eyes, her silent knowing mouth, her enviably calm acceptance of the inevitable . . .

My thoughts wound their way to the circumstances of the previous night, when I had gone to bed with my husband: how cavalierly he had treated the warnings of the midwives and Millicent! No carnal relations during confinement, they had told me: God in all his wisdom forbids it, lest you risk bringing forth a blind child, or a leper. Beware the stings of the flesh during this time, they had said, or God would inflict his punishment. Yet I, in weakness, and inflamed by desire, had given in to it, and to him, not only once, but other times as well. Hence the sin would lie with me, a sin for which there might be no expiation. And yet, and yet . . . was I so wrong to trust my husband? Was he not older than I, was he not wise and worldly?

I tried to lock these thoughts away, as I had the wares from Bertuccio, but my nervous, serpentine mind continued to wend this way and that. . . . Surely my husband would call my treasures "rubble"; and what if he should discover that I had traded them for the silk he had given me, silk threaded with gold and immensely valuable? I began to imagine his fury, I imagined the same frightening, implacable expression as I had seen when he discovered Aiglantine and me frolicking. And then—

for my thoughts continued to dart about—I realized that with Bertuccio, too, I had succumbed to another form of carnal desire: the desire for things of beauty, things with a mysterious history. Another kind of lust, but lust all the same.

"Guilt is sloth by another name"—a dictum written by Arnaut, when, years before, we had exchanged secret messages written in invisible ink. How well I remembered that moment when, by the heat of flames, those seven words had sprung to life! I repeated them to myself again and again, in an act of self-soothing as I tried to free myself from the iron fist of guilt.

It was still early morning. I was alone, for Aiglantine had not yet come to stoke the hearth. I walked to the chest where I had hidden my treasures. I opened the lid and felt deep inside beneath the layers of cloth for the helmet, the stone head, the bronze, and the cross: all were safely there, as enwombed as the baby within me. . . .

A knocking at the door interrupted my reverie. I hurriedly shut the lid, stood up, and asked who it was. It was Aiglantine; she entered carrying a tray with a water basin and a cup of milk. She looked deathly pale and in disarray: there was no concealing that she had spent a sleepless, tearful night.

"Come," I said gently as she set the tray down, "do not worry. I have told my husband it was all my fault. It was my idea, and you must *never* be blamed. He understands that now, and says he will not hold it against you." Then: "I give you my sacred oath I shall *never* let him hold it against you."

"Oh, my lady," she said, with touching fervor, "I thank you with all my heart."

"I am not worthy of thanks. It was my doing and my foolish mistake. Now we must put it aside." I sighed, absentmindedly running my hand across my rotund stomach. "Let us speak of something else." I forced a cheerful expression. "The guests! Yes, the guests. What of the preparations?"

"The great hall is being readied. They say the guests are grand people, well known in the region."

I smiled: "I suspect it may be from Agnes that you have heard this—"
She nodded.

"Of course! Agnes seems to know everything. She is indeed a gossip. What does she say?"

"Lord and Lady de Hauteclare are from Troyes. They say Lady de Hauteclare knows those in the court of the Countess of Champagne."

At this my curiosity was piqued. Troyes! A city I had heard so much about, with its fabled fairs, and towers, and troubadours, and poets. And then Marie, the Countess of Champagne herself: a daughter of Eleanor by her first husband, King Louis.

"And the Lord de Hauteclare? What of him?" I asked eagerly.

"A lord of the highest rank. Very powerful. That is all I have heard."

I reflected on this until I felt a sharp thrust within me: the baby, restless. "That was a fierce kick," I said, with a merry smile.

"That bodes well, for a boy."

"That is what I hope, and what I pray for every day." I walked to the table where Aiglantine had set down the basin and splashed my face with the icy water. She handed me a napkin to dry myself, and as I did so, the baby kicked again hard, almost furiously, as if it were protesting its confinement.

After dressing, I walked down to the courtyard to look for my husband, for I wanted to ask him about the guests, and the preparations, and what was expected of me.

I entered the stables first, but he was nowhere to be found. And then, still looking for him, I walked to the mews.

To my delight, there I found Gallien, a falcon perched on his wrist. The two pairs of eyes caught mine at the same time. The falcon's eyes were wary, but Gallien's radiated joy, the joy of someone in the midst of work he loves.

He gave a deep bow: "I am sure it is to you I owe thanks, my lady. For this position."

"Not at all!" I replied, then: "Though I do admit that I encouraged my husband to let you work here, in the mews."

"I am very grateful, my lady."

"I know that my lord will be pleased with the decision. And Ragnar, too, for he has missed the extra help here."

"That is my hope as well," he replied fervently, though the trace of uneasiness in his eyes caused me to wonder whether Ragnar had approved the decision.

"You will have much work to do, I assume, with the arrival of the guests."

"Yes. My lord is setting it all in place. The horses, the hounds, the hawks. All must be ready."

"And I have no doubt it *will!*"

The door opened suddenly: Ragnar, striding toward us, a supercilious look in his eyes. His face looked slightly swollen, puffy; I wondered once again if he had been drinking.

"Good morrow, my lady," he said, with a bow so belabored it was almost mocking.

I gave a crisp nod; then, in an imperious tone—my means of masking my sense of intimidation—I told him: "I came looking for my husband. And I was pleased to find Gallien here, and to have an opportunity to wish him well."

He was silent, yet his expression and clenched fists made his feelings all too evident. I murmured something in response and left, unsettled. For Gallien, most of all.

I WALKED ACROSS THE COURTYARD, up the steps, through the portal to the passageway that led to the great hall. Still, no sign of my husband. The chamber teemed with servants hard at work: everything bespoke a whirlwind of preparation, the likes of which I had never before witnessed. Fresh rush was being laid on the pavement; garlands of foliage and fruit had been looped across the top of each window and around each door. The great escutcheon of the falcon and the phoenix had been polished so assiduously that the gilded feathers shone to almost blinding brightness.

Raoul entered and walked toward me. "A messenger has arrived, my lady." I told him to show him in.

He returned in a few moments with a man who was so elegantly, even extravagantly, dressed that at first I almost doubted he *was* a messenger: his green scallop-edged cape was trimmed in marten, and his cap an elaborate confection of braid that sprouted so many plumes it seemed he might take flight. In his hand was a roll of parchment tied with a vivid red cord. Raoul commanded him to approach.

I had been hoping for a letter from my brother, or for some word of my family, but I knew that this brilliantly attired creature would not have been sent by them, but by a family of great means.

Raoul presented me to the messenger, who bowed with great panache before me. He told me he carried a message from the Lord and Lady de Hauteclare to the Lord de Meurtaigne.

"I see. It must be an important message indeed."

"No doubt it is, my lady," came his reply as he began to hand the letter to me.

Raoul, however, intervened and took the letter himself. "It is addressed to the Lord de Meurtaigne," he explained to me. "It is for me to give it to him."

"I believe it is for me, his wife, to decide who gives it to him," I told him as Raoul glanced awkwardly away. "I am the lady of the house. I shall find him and deliver it myself."

I DID SO, IN THE early hours of the afternoon, when Gerard returned to the castle. I ran down to meet him, the parchment roll in hand. The light was waning and tapers were being lit. Rush and pine lent the air a delicious bittersweet scent.

He unfurled the parchment, read it, and glanced at me. "It is a message from Hugh and Fastrada de Hauteclare. They will arrive later this autumn for the hunt."

I told him, with some excitement, that I had never seen preparations on this scale—all during the week, animals had been killed and flayed, the bakehouse was a whir of activity, and the great hall itself decked as for a royal wedding. "Our guests must be very dear friends to you," I remarked.

"Friendship has little to do with it," he replied. "Hugh could be useful to me. He controls the wine trade between Bordeaux and England. That is infinitely more valuable than mere friendship."

"But you are not involved in the trade of wine—"

"No. Not yet," he interrupted, in a clipped, assured voice. "But I could be. It has become an important business and is growing larger still. Since his marriage to Queen Eleanor, King Henry and his court have grown accustomed to French wine. The wine is shipped from here and stored in caves created for that purpose, in Southampton. I have seen them. They are impressive." He rolled up the parchment slowly and deliberately. "Hugh is close to the king. He has been generous to the Abbey of Grandmont, and to the Abbey of Fontevraud as well, places favored by the king and his family. And he is close to Prince Richard, the second son."

"And you?"

"It is the Young King, the eldest son, I know best."

"And Richard? You have no ties with him?" I felt at once that the question discomfited him, for his expression darkened.

"I have tried but have not met with success. Richard is a soldier to his core and keeps his counsel close. The men around him close. He favors those from Aquitaine, his mother's land. The Young King is a different matter. He has the luxury of being the heir. And he is in all ways easier."

"What do you mean—'easier'?"

"He has expensive tastes. He lives for tournaments, for the hunt. He requires money and those who can supply it—which I can, and have. Horses, hawks, armor." He tied the parchment roll with the cord, knotting it hard. "When the prince, Young Henry, becomes king, I will be well placed with him and his court. It is only a matter of time. The king is growing old. Eleanor and the sons have battered him with their feuds and lust for power—Richard most of all."

Gerard had never spoken with me so candidly about his relations with King Henry's court. I, who had rather dreaded the arrival of the guests, was now intrigued by this labyrinth of relationships and ambitions. "And the wife of Hugh de Hauteclare. What of her?"

"Fastrada? She comes from old Carolingian stock, from Troyes. She and her family, too, have been benefactors to Fontevraud. This was useful to Hugh when he married her. A convenient tie with the Angevins and the king. She came with a fortune, which he has expanded upon." He bent over to pick up a leaf that had fallen on the rush, and crushed it in his hand. "She is not a beauty by any means, but she is clever. A *belle laide*, I would say. A *belle laide* with a mind that works like a Flemish moneylender."

"She sounds rather fearsome," I remarked, before asking: "And how does a Flemish moneylender think?"

"Shrewdly, ruthlessly, and without any illusions."

"And the Lady de Hauteclare is without illusions?"

"Precisely. In all ways, including the way she views her marriage. She turns a blind eye to Hugh. His behavior."

"And is his behavior so unseemly?"

"Ah, my sweet, I hesitate to even tell you, so unsullied are you by the rough ways of the world." A slight deliberate pause, as if he were weighing his words. "Let us say that Hugh is a man of notorious appetites. He could people a town with his bastards. Plain or fair, no serving girl is safe within his sight. One glimpse of a bosom and he will grasp it." His voice radiated disdain. "I have nothing but contempt for such men—if he were not so useful, I would never have him here."

"Given what you have said, best I protect Aiglantine from him," I teased. "She is young and pretty."

"Hugh would never dare, not in my house. It is always Aiglantine you think of," he added, irritated. "Why is that?"

"She has been kind to me. And she is really quite intelligent. If she had been taught to read, to really think, her life might have taken a different path."

"What strange notions you have! I employ her to *serve* you, not to converse with you. And it is not your place, nor should it be within your way of thinking, to educate Aiglantine, nor to have preposterous thoughts about bettering her lot. She is a servant and must remain so."

His vehemence took me aback. Nonetheless I held my tongue and returned to a safer subject: the intrigues of the court, and King Henry's rebellious sons. "Is it not true," I asked, "that the Young King is close to

King Louis? That Louis helped him during the rebellion? My brothers told me so." Throughout my childhood in the south, I had heard the songs of the troubadours, the *sirventes*, who told of the Young King, the golden lad of the tournament circuit. Yet he, too, had plotted, with his brothers, against their father, the king. It was a famous story, and at the heart of it lay the queen, Eleanor, who had incited her sons to rebellion.

"Yes, it is quite true. The Young King used Louis, and Louis used him. And I am sure, of course, there was pleasure in this for Louis. After all, King Henry and Louis's wife, Eleanor, had cuckolded him. But Louis, too, is growing old. I doubt it will be long before the mantle passes to his son, Philippe. The dauphin."

"Do you know those in Louis's court?"

"Hardly at all. Remember, I am Norman. But Hugh and those in his circle know the French court, partly through his wife. I shall find out more from them. Philippe was crowned recently as the young king of France. It is strange, because he was meant to have been crowned earlier this summer. Yet I hear it took place only a week ago, at Reims." He paused, his eyes assessing the splendid decoration of the hall. "There is more to do here," he said, decisively. "But this is a good beginning."

Then, to me, as he extended his arm: "It is growing late. We must prepare for dinner."

AFTER DINNER THAT EVENING, I returned to my chamber while Gerard remained below to review the preparations with Raoul. As I began to undress, I asked Aiglantine if she had learned anything about the healer.

She shook her head. "I did see Agnes, though, my lady. She and the women in the kitchen were gossiping about the guests."

"Ah—what did they say?"

"Nothing about Lady de Hauteclare. Only about Lord de Hauteclare—"

"What did they say?" I prodded.

"Agnes told me he is known as 'The Rutter.'"

I t was mid-November, and a late afternoon of unseasonable, biting cold and bitter gusts. I sat by the window in my chamber, trying to sew, but so excited and preoccupied that even the thrusts of the baby within me went almost without my noticing. That morning we had learned by a messenger that the Hauteclares would likely arrive this day or the following.

The horns of the watchmen suddenly sounded from across the parapets. I threw down my hoop and knelt on the window seat, peering out to the ramparts. The flags had been raised, a sure signal of an approach. At last the Hauteclares and their entourage had been sighted!

Gerard appeared at the door moments later. "Come," he said, brusquely. "We must prepare to greet them. Where is the gown I chose for you?"

I gestured to a bench near the bed where the splendid red gown lay ready. "Dress quickly," he told me.

Shortly before the sun began to set, Hugh and Fastrada de Hauteclare and their entourage—a vortex of richly appareled servants and brilliantly caparisoned steeds—swept into the courtyard. Fastrada, tall and very slim, was draped in a rich mantle of fur which billowed in the winter wind as she dismounted. Her voice as she greeted my husband— "At last, my dear Gerard, how good to see you!"—had a beautiful, enchanting lilt. But after she doffed her hood, I saw that with her sharp aquiline nose, close-set dark eyes, and low forehead, she was a singularly ugly woman. And yet her ugliness, offset as it was by her confidence and poise, was of a memorable kind. She was indeed as my husband had described her: a *belle laide*, but of the most exalted sort.

Hugh de Hauteclare, stocky and far shorter than his wife, yet no less

powerful in impression, stood beside her, his eyes, with a certain prac-
ticed casualness, surveying Gerard, myself, and the assembled group. I
had already noticed that, contrary to custom, he had seemed perfectly
content to let his wife utter the first words of greeting to the host. Only
after she had spoken did Hugh himself address my husband with a few
jocular words, his voice robust and merry as he embraced him.

Next came a searching, yet slightly amused look in my direction:
"But what of the bride?" he asked. "It is about time, Gerard, that you
introduced us to her. Properly." Fastrada, still standing by his side,
smiled warmly. "Lovely, is she not, Hugh?"

Shyly I stepped forward as Gerard presented me. A deep curtsey before her first, then before her husband. As I did so, I noticed his rotund
middle, tightly bound by the ties of his leather vest, and caught a whiff
of his scent, redolent of musk and civet.

"I believe I met your brother once, in Troyes," said Hugh, training
his gaze on me. His eyes were blue, the color of faded cornflowers. "His
name is Guy de Lapalisse, is it not?"

"Yes," I replied.

"Good in the lists. Rather eager to meet me, as I recall."

"Yes, that would be my brother," I replied, inwardly cringing as I
imagined how aggressive and cloying Guy had probably been. "He has
told me about Troyes."

"Good things, I hope?"

"Very much so," I said, adding, "I long to visit one day."

"And so you shall," interjected Fastrada. "And we shall be your
hosts. And your guides. Your *vade mecum*, if you will. Unless"—she shot
Gerard a slightly mocking glance—"your loving husband thinks we
would be a bad influence." She took my hands in hers, her dark eyes
scanning my face. "You have found a beauty, Gerard! And she is with
child, I see! Fortune has blessed you both. And so soon." A pause as she
pulled up her hood, for it had grown even colder. "But I would expect
no less of you, Gerard." She smiled radiantly, her perfect, fine white
teeth at odds with the plainness of her face.

"Let us go inside," Gerard replied with a laugh. "If we are to talk, best we do so over wine."

He gestured to Raoul, who stood near us, carrying a lighted torch. "Show our guests inside," Gerard commanded him, and as Raoul escorted them inside, we followed.

A few moments later, we stood opposite our guests, inside the warmth of the great hall, for the ritual welcome. I bowed before them and offered boughs of evergreens. Servants passed goblets of warm wine, and platters with savory victuals. All the while I continued to watch the Hauteclares with fascination, as one might a rare species of bird or animal from a shimmering, exotic corner of the earth.

We stood before the fire, Hugh rubbing his cold hands together and speaking animatedly to my husband. Fastrada had doffed her fur mantle and, after handing it to Raoul, who stood near us, looked intently around the great hall. All the while she bantered with the men, and then with me, describing their long journey, or praising the wine, or extolling the fineness of the carpets and the strumming of the lute players, who performed in a corner. I was struck not only by Fastrada's quick, darting movements, vivacious eyes, and throaty laugh, but also by her clothes: her sleeves were so tight and so extravagantly long that the tasseled ends swept perilously close to the ground; her bodice so snugly fitted, and so intricately threaded with gold, that I wondered she could breathe. At her collarbone she wore a brooch of amethyst and gold so impressive that it seemed less a jewel than an emblem, very nearly a weapon. Her hands bore so many rings that each time she gestured the stones seemed to flutter through the air like tiny, sparkling birds of prey.

Meantime her eyes scanned the wall hangings, the linens, the silver plate, and the gleaming escutcheon above the portal. Finally, her gaze turned its focus on me.

"And the baby?" she asked. "When is the blessed date?"

"In mid-January, they tell me."

"So you will be ready to ride again, by the spring—"

"I hope so. I have missed riding very much."

"I know *I* did, during my confinements." She sipped some wine. "Wretched, is it not, to be so—" She searched for the word.

"Restricted?"

"Exactly," she said, lingering on the word to give it added emphasis. "I could never bear it. The midwives, with all their strictures. Harpies, really, do you not agree? I am glad to be done with all that."

I smiled to myself at her way of describing pregnancy as "all that." "How many children have you?"

"Three sons. Quite enough. For me at least."

"And they, too, are in Troyes?"

"No, alas, they are faraway. The eldest manages our estates in England. The second has settled in Outremer. And the third has taken the vows at Falaise. None resembles Hugh in the least—not even in his passion for hawking, alas!" She smiled somewhat ruefully. "A matter of some sadness to him, I must confess." Then she asked about my family, whether I missed them very much, and how the marriage with Gerard had come to pass. I was surprised how easy she was to converse with, not at all the cold, intimidating woman I had expected. Everything about her bespoke the cleverness and self-assurance of a woman who, having come to terms with the ugliness of her face, had learned to arrange herself in such an elevated way that the whole almost amounted to a form of beauty. I would learn later that her way of coping with her looks was only one of the ways she had unflinchingly embraced the realities of life.

As we spoke I glanced occasionally at Hugh, still deep in conversation with my husband. Whereas Fastrada was all angles, bones, and the reining in of appetite, her husband was the opposite. Everything about him spoke to embonpoint: the girth of his stomach, the roll of flesh that peeked over his collar, the fullness of his cheeks, which had long since overwhelmed his high cheekbones. Here was a worldly man, a man at ease with power, a man who had denied himself nothing. There was not, as of yet, any sign of rakishness: still, it did not take a sleight of mind to imagine him as lascivious.

Gerard had ordered benches be brought near the fire, and the Hauteclares and I sat down. Only Gerard, ever the vigilant host, continued to stand, glancing occasionally and rather sternly at Raoul, as if to make certain that the latter was properly attentive.

The wine had both relaxed me and quickened my curiosity. I asked about their journey and the route they had taken, from Troyes.

"Through Orléans, then Tours," replied Hugh.

"Nasty roads, some of them," Fastrada added, smoothing her skirt. "But the weather cleared by the time we reached Chinon. We stopped briefly, then spent the night nearby, at Fontevraud." She looked at me directly. "The abbey, perhaps you have heard of it?"

"I have, mostly in connection with the queen. Queen Eleanor."

"Of course," she said, nodding. "The noble prisoner."

"But Fontevraud is associated not only with the queen," added Hugh, somewhat pompously. "With King Henry, too, and all his family. It reeks of the Plantagenets, for better or worse. Prince John and his youngest sister, Joanna, were raised there."

"A splendid place," said Fastrada. "And the abbess is quite an extraordinary woman."

"In what way?" I asked.

"Strong, quite learned. It is she, you know, who rules over the abbey."

"Indeed," said Hugh. "She rules both the men and the women there. Fancy being a monk and having to report to the abbess!" He gave a mock shudder, raised one brow and mused, "Yes, the genial abbess and her women. And quite a collection of women it is."

I asked what he meant, but it was Fastrada, rather than Hugh, who answered, cavalierly, "From fallen women to noblewomen who have lost, or left, their husbands."

I noticed Gerard shoot her a disapproving look, but this did not seem to inhibit her. "Surely," she continued, "it is not surprising that Eleanor should be so fond of the abbey. But whether she will ever see it again, that is the question. The brutes have locked her up in England. Imagine! She, who had known the world. She who so loved adventure. And men—"

I was on the verge of asking if she had ever met the queen, when

Gerard interrupted. He was eager, I could tell, to swerve the conversation to a subject of greater interest to him. Addressing Hugh, he asked about the coronation of the dauphin, and why it had been delayed.

"Like most important things in life," said Hugh, with a wicked glance, "it had to do with hunting."

"What do you mean?" Gerard asked.

"The dauphin was boar hunting in early summer and lost his way in the forest. He was alone for days. No shelter, no food. Alone, and frightened. Remember, Prince Philippe is what—but sixteen? A hermit eventually found him and led him to safety. By that time the dauphin had fallen ill, was near death, in fact. Louis was beside himself, praying day and night for his son's recovery. Remember, after all, what it took him to beget that son! Louis was given a vial of Thomas Becket's blood they say, and it was on the following day that the fever broke, and the boy miraculously recovered. And so the coronation was postponed to November."

"So that explains Louis's visit to Canterbury this summer," said Gerard, mulling this over. "To give his thanks at the shrine of Becket."

"Exactly," concurred Hugh, taking a swig of wine.

"Ironic, is it not," added Fastrada, "that the spirit of King Henry's nemesis, the saintly Becket, should have cured his rival's son, the dauphin? I am sure the French court finds perfect justice in that!" She laughed heartily.

I was riveted by this story, and was eager to ask more questions, but once again Gerard interceded. He, too, wanted to know more, but it was not the Becket saga he was intent on.

"And the dauphin," he asked. "What sort of man is he?"

"It is too soon to tell," said Hugh.

"Give him more wine, Gerard," said Fastrada, with a laugh, "and my husband will give you his real impressions."

I was taken aback: I had never heard a wife, in company, speak to a husband this way. She had noticed my reaction, I think, for her eyes had a mischievous look as they met mine.

Gerard duly called for Berthe, the serving woman, to offer more wine. She was young and comely, and as she bent down to refill our goblets, I noticed Hugh's eyes taking in the line of her bodice.

Fastrada, either ignoring or not noticing Hugh's lascivious gaze, continued to bait him. "Now tell him, Hugh, what you *really* think of the dauphin," she said, her dark eyes flashing as she sipped her wine.

"As different a man from the father as fire to ice," Hugh replied.

"In what ways in particular?" asked Gerard.

"He is no monk, for one thing. And he is a plotter, I would venture." He took another swig of wine. "In that way, he may have more in common with Eleanor than with his father. They tell me he is no stranger to strategy, this dauphin."

"And what, pray tell, do they foresee of the dauphin's strategy?" asked Gerard.

"Divide and conquer. *Tout simple,*" Hugh added, with a malevolent twinkle in his eye: "Turn King Henry's sons against one another. And move in for the kill."

# CHAPTER 12

During the several weeks that followed, the visit of the Haute-clares proceeded, day by day, with its own ceremonies and panoply of order. My husband, intent on the perfection of each element—hour by hour, from sunup to darkest night—would scrutinize every detail, every task of each servant, with an intentness I found both admirable and unnerving. Many times, I thought to myself: woe to the page or falconer who disappoints him!

Each morning, several hours after dawn, the hunting party would assemble in the courtyard in a scene of ritualized commotion: the impatient snorting horses pawing the ground, their breath white in the frosty air; the nervous stable boys running to assist one rider, then another; and finally, the presentation of the prized hawks themselves, each poised on the wrist of a falconer. It was the deportment of the hawks I remember most keenly: their eyes were deadly alert, for they had not been fed recently and were, as my husband had told me with more than a little pride, fully in *yarak*. During the preceding weeks he had supervised their diet and feeding with great vigilance, intent that the hawks—his favorite, the eagle Féroce, especially—be hungry for the kill, which was crucial for the hunt's success. I mused to myself that never had so much seemed to rest on the wings of hawks—most of all my husband's *amour propre*.

In an act of seeming selflessness, Gerard had given Féroce to Hugh to man for the duration of the hunt. On the first morning Ragnar stood at the ready, Féroce tethered to his gloved hand, as he waited to hand the giant eagle to Hugh. I half expected Féroce to balk at being lent to another, yet Féroce seemed, for the first time, strangely compliant.

Heavily cloaked against the autumn cold, I would descend to the courtyard to watch the group depart each morning. I felt awkward and lumpish as I glimpsed Fastrada, taut and slim, her back arrow-straight as she sat astride. It might have been tempting to dismiss her apparel as merely superficial or frivolous, yet I sensed that it signified much more, that it was the reflection of a carefully constructed persona. I began to wonder what lay beneath the creation of this persona—what yearnings, appetites, and experiences.

Her outfit on the first day was particularly memorable in its vividness and complexity: a jacket of green suede piped with purple, the shoulders outlined with coiling gold thread, the waist nipped in by a leather belt studded with amethyst beads, and on her head a cap edged with purple braid, its peak topped with gray and white plumes so long they seemed to brush the sky. On another woman, with less confidence, the outfit would have been ludicrous, yet she wore it with aplomb.

It was not only her raiment that was singular, but also her manner. She sat with a certain offhand assurance on her mount, all the while gesturing in a spirited, coltish way as she addressed one person or another. "What a splendid troop we make!" she exclaimed to Gerard, in the lilting, girlish voice that continued to seem strangely at variance with her sharp aquiline features. "No wonder you are known far and wide as a host par excellence. You have even managed to bring out the sun for us!" Then, to me, with a wide admiring smile: "How is it possible you look so charming and fresh at this dreadfully early hour? When I was with child, I was such a hideous, dreary sight. Wasn't I, Hugh? It would have been better if they had simply locked me away for nine months!"

All the while, I stood by the side, feeling especially ungainly, and champing at the bit to join the hunting party, aware that if it were not for "all that"—as Fastrada had called my pregnancy—I would have been among them, astride my beloved Juno.

Fastrada suddenly loomed above me, her dainty gloved hands reining in her restive horse. "How I *wish* you could come with us, my dear!" she exclaimed, in a voice that seemed to brim with longing. "I would so have enjoyed having you as a companion. We will miss you!" As I responded to her with a smile and the pro forma "Oh, I shall be quite fine here, you must tell me all about it," the wind blew, and one of the plumes from her elaborate cap swept against her face. "Oh, what one does for fashion!" she exclaimed, laughing as she brushed it away.

She cast her eye beyond, on Hugh, a sturdy figure astride a powerful, black mount that tossed its mane and flashed huge white teeth. Hugh himself was deep in conversation with Gerard, astride his own mount.

"Oh my husband, he does look well on Champion, do you not think? The big black beast suits him."

"He does look very much at ease," I replied.

"He should be at ease. He adores the hunt. Loves nothing more." There was a slight pause before she added, with a knowing laugh and a chortle, "Well—*almost* nothing!"

I knew, of course, what Fastrada was alluding to—his reputation as The Rutter—but was taken aback by her bantering, by the playful way she alluded to a trait that would have mortified me had I been his wife. I finally said, "All men love such things. The chase, the hunt—"

"Yes, in *all* its forms," she interrupted, with an almost strident heartiness.

"I should go see them off," I said, slightly discomfited. I walked over to the men. Fastrada followed.

In his hunting apparel, as in so many other ways, Hugh de Hauteclare was the antithesis of his wife. His outfit looked ancient and worn, and his bulging stomach was such that the vest encasing it looked as if it might, at any moment, split its tight laces open. His boots—unlike the pristine, polished species worn by Fastrada—were old, dirty, and scuffed. Yet inherent in what he had chosen to wear there was, I surmised, as explicit a statement as that which lay behind his wife's clothes. What his outfit communicated was this: here was a man so powerful, so sure of his place in society, so conversant in a hunt of this august nature, that he had no need for grand clothes, nor for showy newness.

As for my husband: buoyed by the Hauteclares' compliments, he clearly delighted in the jostling tableau surrounding us—his hallowed guests, his expensive mounts, his expert band of accomplished falconers (for others had been recruited to help Ragnar and Gallien). His eyes, as he surveyed the scene, seemed to say: All this is my doing. And yet it is only a beginning. . . .

A few moments later, the hunting party set off; I watched until they vanished into the inky edge of the forest beyond. Then I drew my cloak around me and began to walk toward the interior of the castle, one hand upon my belly, for the baby had begun to kick. I continued to think about Fastrada and her quips, about Hugh and his cocky assurance, about my husband and his obvious pride in his household and falconers. Then my thoughts leaped to the hawks themselves—most of all to Féroce, the fierce eagle poised on the wrist of a stranger, a man who was not his master.

# CHAPTER 13

Early morning on the third day of the Hauteclares' visit, when I descended to the courtyard to see the hunting party off, to my surprise Fastrada was nowhere to be found. Without her vivid presence, the tableau seemed drained of color and savor, its elements merging into a cold, drab, murky whole. Even the sky, which on previous days had been a clarion blue, was now cloud strewn and moody.

Raoul stood to one side, officiously issuing orders to the harried servants. "Where is the Lady de Hauteclare?" I asked.

"She will not hunt today, my lady," he replied. "She asked that we might build a fire in the hall for her. She suggested that you might join her there."

I thanked him, lingering only a few moments to watch the men ride away, before I walked to the great hall. I found Fastrada standing at the far end of the chamber. Facing the hearth, she was a slim figure robed in deep blue with a surcoat emblazoned with a pattern of bold, stylized lilies. (This, I thought to myself, was her "interior" costume, as carefully conceived as her hunting clothes.) Her luxuriant dark hair, braided and intertwined with strands of pearls, wound down her back in such a way that, from a distance, it resembled a thick, black jeweled serpent.

Hearing my footsteps, she turned around, then beckoned me to join her. "I thought I might keep you company today," she said jauntily.

"I am glad to hear that!" I settled on the bench and picked up my hoop, which lay on the table beside me. I began to make one stitch, then another.

"I could never bear that," announced Fastrada, with a little gesture of her pointed chin in my direction. "Sewing, and the dreaded hoop.

Like a circle of eternity placed in one's lap to tinker with. Another sort of tyranny, at least I always thought so."

"I feel the same way!" I replied, with no little delight.

"I was fortunate to have a mother who did not press it upon me."

"Is your mother still alive?" I asked, half-heartedly continuing to sew.

"No, she died a few years ago. She was quite remarkable. She faced life—how can I say?—with great certitude, with no illusions."

"And she taught you to do the same?"

"Of course," came her brisk reply. She paused for a moment, the pointed toe of her shoe grazing the stone floor. "When I was just past girlhood, my mother said to me, 'Fastrada, you will never be a beauty. Therefore you must make something else of yourself. You are intelligent, you have spirit, you have a certain way of arranging yourself, all this is true. But it is not quite enough: you must learn to be resilient, and to be reliable.' She told me those qualities were, in the end, far more important than beauty. And you? What of your mother?"

"My mother was—is—the opposite."

"Tell me about her."

"She would say that beauty and correctness matter most. And in that regard, I suppose, I failed her." I looked down, trying to avoid her intent gaze and jabbed a few stitches; I was not accustomed to being so candid, and felt slightly uncomfortable in the face of Fastrada's directness.

"You certainly did not fail in terms of beauty," she remarked. "And if you think so, you are quite mistaken!"

"Oh, but my unruly hair, and my freckles!" I shook my head as I made another errant stitch. "My mother hates my freckles. She tried every sort of poultice on me to fade them."

"Both your hair and your freckles are charming. You have your own kind of beauty, and that is far more important than perfection. With your splendid coloring and your tawny green eyes"—she paused, studying my face—"you are *arresting*."

I smiled slightly, acknowledging, but not completely believing, her compliment. "My mother did not think so. And I was not obedient like my sister," I continued. "She is both pretty and dutiful. *I* was not dutiful, and I always wanted to escape. I was interested in other things, in adventures, in stories, reading, and being with my brothers and my grandfather. Much that my mother loathed, I loved." I made a few more desultory stitches and looked up. "I used to listen to all the stories about Queen Eleanor from my mother and her women. My mother thought the queen was scandalous. I thought she was fascinating."

I told her about my brothers, and about my grandfather, and his library and his garden. I told her how I would dig for ancient things in the earth when I was a girl, and how these unearthed treasures would keep me company. I told her about the secret messages I would exchange with Arnaut: how we would watch words etched in invisible ink spring to life when the parchment was held to a flame—

"It seems you were much closer to your brother than to the others in your family."

"Save my grandfather. Yes."

"It must have been difficult, then, for you to leave them and live far away."

I nodded and tried to focus on my sewing. She sat quite still, un-characteristically still, the lustrous colors of her many rings glimmering in the morning light.

"But tell me more about yourself," I said almost imploringly, eager to change the subject from myself. "Your family comes from Troyes, does it not?"

"From quite near Troyes, yes. Both my father's family, and my mother's, too—all from the region of Champagne."

"How old were you when you married Hugh?"

"Eighteen. Almost an old maid!"

I laughed. "It is hard to think of you as an old maid!"

"Oh, I am quite serious. I think my parents had begun to despair for me, though they tried hard not to show it. There had been talk of a nunnery. Imagine! For me!" She laughed heartily, shaking her head at the thought. "My sister, however, was later pledged and did go to an abbey. The life there, among the sisters, seems to suit her. "

"Where is she?"

"She is at Fontevraud."

"And that is why you stopped there on your way here?"

"Yes."

"Fontevraud—from what I have heard—is rather different from most nunneries. Not nearly as strict?"

"Yes. There are both monks and nuns there, of course. There is relative freedom. My sister brought her servant, her library, all the accoutrements of a civilized life. But, of course, it is a life of contemplation, rather than action, at least in great part.

"Eleanor and King Henry have been generous patrons. His aunt has been an abbess there, after all." She furrowed her brow in such a way that she looked quite homely; but when she began to speak, animation transmuted her face into something approaching attractiveness. "Some call Prince John the black sheep of the family," she said. "They say he is unruly and conniving, and without his elder brothers' discipline. Still, he is the king's favorite son."

"Because he did not join his brothers in fighting their father?"

"Precisely."

"John is his father's favorite, then, but not his mother's?"

"It has always been Richard she favored. He is a kindred spirit, and not only because she had him made Duke of Aquitaine. They are two of a kind, they say, two faces of the same coin. Both brave, ruthless, and lovers of music and poetry. In Richard's case, of course, he is a brutal soldier, too. Unusual that one so violent should also have this other artistic side."

"Have you ever met Richard?"

"No, never. It is his half-sister, Marie, whom I know."

"The Countess of Champagne? My brother Guy has been to Troyes and saw her once, from a distance, at a tournament. He told me what he had heard about her and her court. The poets who surround her, and the musicians. Is it true that the countess, too, is very much her mother's child?"

"In her love of poetry and thought, and her wisdom, yes she is. Not as daring as her mother, though. But then, who is?"

"And have you ever met the queen herself?"

"Twice. Once at Troyes, when I was very young, and once at Poitiers, years later. Both times unforgettable, I must say." She mused on this a moment, so deep in thought I did not dare to interject. "But let us talk of Troyes, since you have told me you long to visit."

"Yes, I would, very much."

She gave a disarming smile. "Then you must convince your husband to arrange a journey to see us."

"I hope to be able to."

"Hope?" She raised her brow. "*Hope* will achieve nothing, my dear! You must plan how you will accomplish this. It should not be so difficult. After all, Gerard seems very much under your spell." Her tone had softened. "Surely he would want to please you."

"I never think of my husband being under my spell," I replied, astonished by the suggestion.

"Then you underestimate yourself. And your power."

"If I give him a son, then perhaps I might have a chance to persuade him."

"But even if you do not, I believe he would still be"—she paused, searching for the right word—"receptive to the idea of taking you to Troyes."

"Only if it suited his own purposes," I replied quietly. "Not for my sake, only."

"So you are not without a sense of realism about men. That is good. At least *there* I am heartened."

"I do not think he really wants me to visit Troyes." Then, musing, almost to myself: "I am not certain why."

"Men like to keep young wives pregnant and in the country, away from the distractions and vices of the city. Surely you know that."

"I would not know. I was brought up in the country. I have only been to a city once, and that was to Nîmes, years ago, with my brothers."

"Surely Nîmes made an impression on you?"

"Yes, yes, it did. Very much so."

"Well then—imagine Troyes, with all its splendors and its rather—

shall we say—forward way of life?" She picked up my embroidery and glanced at the design of cherubs. "You are pretty, you are charming, you would be sought after in Troyes."

"By whom?" I asked incredulously.

"By members of the court. Ladies and young men. The witty young women in Marie de Champagne's court who love poetry and song. The young men who pursue them—"

"I doubt that very much!"

"Then you *are* naive indeed, as naive as those witless little cherubs on that linen you are stitching." She flicked her long braid so that it wound down her back again. "Who knows? You might be tempted to take a lover—"

"That would never occur to me! I could never betray my husband."

"If out of fear, yes, *that* I can understand. I would not want to cross Gerard. No one would! But if you would not take a lover out of lack of desire, or out of lack of curiosity, then no, I cannot understand."

Her tone had changed, was almost cutting, yet so accustomed was I by this time to her frankness, and so intrigued was I by her attitude, that I asked: "Have you a lover?"

"Why only one?" She laughed, shaking her head playfully. "I joke, of course."

I was not entirely sure she was joking.

"There was a time when I did dally, but not now," she admitted offhandedly. "This ring, for instance"—she pointed to a gold ring with the green stone—"This ring was given to me by a young man, a knight, who was quite enamored of me. Not such a bad thing, to be admired and sought after by someone other than one's husband." She held her hands away, studying the array of rings: a silver band with a sapphire, a gold ring with carnelian, another with garnet. Then, with a sigh, she said, "But the fever in the blood subsides with age, and one takes refuge in other things. . . ." She looked off into the distance, her expression uncharacteristically wistful.

"What other things?" I asked.

"Sport. Riding. The hunt, most of all. And fashion, I suppose."

"I have never seen clothes as beautiful and distinctive as yours."

"There is a certain pleasure in silk, and jewels, and tassels, is there not? And since I am not a beauty, it is a way I can create something memorable of myself." She leaned forward, looking at me intently. "And you? You are certainly exquisitely dressed."

"It matters a great deal to my husband, how I dress. He is very particular."

"That does not surprise me about Gerard. Not so with Hugh. How I dress matters little to him. His visual appetite tends to be focused elsewhere."

I looked awkwardly away, but she had already noticed my reaction.

"No need to be embarrassed, my dear!" she said, placing her hand reassuringly on mine. "My husband's habits are well known. Part of being a realist is to accommodate, after all."

"Yet it cannot help but hurt you. Or make you jealous—"

"In the beginning, yes. But not now. There are moments when I even find it"—she paused, searching for the right word—"*amusing*. To watch him and his adventures. Sometimes I try to guess whom he has set his sights on, and when he will pounce. It has become a kind of game to me."

"I cannot imagine that!"

"Stranger things have happened, I assure you. Wait until you are older. You will see."

I shook my head. "I cannot imagine reaching that point. The point of not caring."

She did not reply, a cryptic expression on her face as she began to walk slowly around the room, examining one embroidered hanging, or another. I resumed my sewing in silence, expecting a quip from her, or more banter, but to my surprise, perhaps even to my relief, she remained silent.

A few moments later came a welcome distraction: the sound of footsteps approaching. It was Aiglantine. She curtseyed deeply to Fastrada first, and then to me, bidding us good morning before inquiring whether we needed her to attend to us. She wore her best, most formal dress and looked particularly pretty that day: her cheeks were rosy, and her pale hair was plaited like a crown around her small, neat head. I thanked her, and told her we had no need of anything. Fastrada replied in kind.

"You are free to go," I told Aiglantine. I noticed how Fastrada watched her as she left.

"She is very pretty, that servant," Fastrada remarked after a moment.

"She attends to me. I am fond of her. *Too* fond, my husband says."

"Why would he say that?"

"I treat her almost as a friend. Sometimes I think she might have had a different sort of life, had she been given a chance."

"A novel way of thinking," she said, arching one brow. "I cannot imagine Gerard, with his sense of rectitude and decorum, subscribing to that idea."

"He says she was born a servant and must remain one. That is her lot."

"All men think such a girl has one place. Only one place, though perhaps different uses—" Her voice had assumed a dry, cynical edge. "And he can be rigid, Gerard, I am sure."

"But also very kind," I countered.

"Of course. When it suits him." She seemed to catch herself, adding with a shrug, "That is true of most men, of course." Then, settling next to me: "You rather worship him, don't you? You are still at that stage, how lovely."

"I hope more than anything to give him a son."

"You will, I have no doubt. And if not this time—"

"Then the next," I interrupted her, impatience edging my voice. "Yes, I know. I have been told that."

"I found it dreadful to be pregnant, I felt like an old sow half the time. With the last pregnancy, I decided, *finis*. Never again, I thought."

"Never again? But how is that possible, to deny one's husband?"

"It was not a question of denying him anything," she scoffed. "I merely took measures."

"What 'measures'?"

"I rode and rode. I kept very thin, for I found in doing so, I no longer had my monthly courses." She stopped, abruptly. "So you see, there *are* ways—"

"But surely, it is against God, it is a sin, it is against the laws of nature."

"I prefer my own laws," she retorted, "ones that are not ruled by the tyranny of conception." Then, passionately: "And what is *worse*, really, than to have a child who is not wanted? God knows the abbeys and the monasteries are full of them. Even Fontevraud has them, deposited at the gates during the night, by pathetic young women who have no other recourse." She shook her head, as one might in trying to dispel a bad dream. "During our journey here, we met destitute women on the road who begged us to take their newborn babies. Some wanted to sell them, some simply wanted us to take them. Is it fair, do you think, for God to subject a child to that? Or for a baby to be left in a basket, in the forest, to be eaten by wolves?"

Her words had unsettled me. I thought of Aiglantine and the baby she had given up, and what suffering this must have caused her. And then I thought of the healer I had been told about. . . .

A long, awkward silence followed that was finally broken by the sound of the chapel bells ringing. Two pages scurried in, with fresh logs and bundles of kindling. As they rebuilt the fire, I resumed my sewing, the needle piercing the linen stitch by stitch until I had completed the intricate wing of one little cherub. At last! I said to myself, breaking the strand of thread as I set aside the needle and put down the hoop.

"So you are finished then?" Fastrada asked.

"Not quite. But I am making progress."

She picked up the hoop. "Always cherubs and angels," she said, with a flamboyant sigh. "One would think that a few devils worked into the border might be more—"

"Interesting?" I suggested, with a teasing smile.

"Precisely." She tossed me the hoop and stood up, turning to warm her hands before the newly radiant fire, her dark eyes fixed on the high, hissing flames.

## Chapter 14

Not long afterward, I returned to my chamber, all the while reflecting on the talk with Fastrada; it had intrigued, amused, and unsettled me in equal measure. Never had I told anyone about the coded messages with my brother. Never had I been so candid to anyone save my grandfather about my feelings toward my mother. A wave of shame and distrust swept over me, as if I had confessed to a priest whose origins and credentials were unfamiliar, perhaps even spurious. Yet I felt a sense of cleansing and comfort, as well, in having voiced the painful and clandestine to a woman who had listened so intently, and who, despite her worldliness, seemed so sympathetic.

I moved to the window, looking for any sign of the men, but there was none: merely the lengthening shadows of lone, leafless trees in the meadow, and the black spiky edge of the forest. Finally I set down my hoop on the table beside the bed and turned to the wall nearby with the painting of the Annunciation. The scene did not appear as tranquil as it had in the past: the Virgin's expression, which had hitherto seemed so imperturbable, now looked almost uneasy, as if she were slightly threatened by the hovering Angel Gabriel, with his cryptic smile.

I turned away, still mulling over what Fastrada had told me. Much of what she had said shocked me, as if she had opened doors to rooms I had never known existed. I had never met a woman who was so frank and cynical about marriage. I had never met a woman who had not only taken a lover but also admitted to it almost cavalierly. Then there was her way of talking about pregnancy and childbirth, as if they were inconveniences to be endured, and dealt with by oneself, by taking action. Most of all it was startling to hear her assessment of my husband, her emphasis on his rigidity and imperiousness. Among all her observations, this last troubled me the most. What she had articulated was something I had already intuited: hearing it from her, however, gave it a certain reality. What she had meant merely as an observation fell upon me with all the ominousness of an admonition.

I looked down at the trunk before me: my ancient treasures were encased within it, the treasures I had traded surreptitiously for the costly fabric from my husband. Once more Fastrada's pronouncement came to mind: "I would not want to cross Gerard." Yet, by trading the silk, I had done just that.

Such fear suddenly came over me that I did not even open the trunk to uncover and touch the treasures, as I sometimes did when anxious. I took a deep breath instead, grasping my arms and walking to the opposite end of the chamber, to the wall painted with The Temptation of Adam and Eve. I had never really looked at it carefully before. My eyes went to Eve's arm wound around the tree, as sinuous as the snake coiling along the verdant branch above; then I glanced at her other hand, the hand that grasped the unblemished apple, with its lustrous leaves. A single apple, a single bite, a single transgression, and her world—their world—would change forever. . . .

JUST BEFORE EVENTIDE, I HEARD the sounds of the men returning and ran down to greet them. I suspected at once that something untoward had happened. Gerard looked angry, the falconers tense; even Hugh, customarily jovial, glowered.

Ragnar, with Gisela tethered to his wrist, passed me as he made his way to the mews, kicking the ground with tall muddy boots. He barely acknowledged me, looking up only an instant, time enough for me to catch the murderous expression of his eyes.

Gallien, manning Féroce, followed soon after. His brow was furrowed, his vest torn, and one side of his cheek was bleeding. He stopped to bow before me.

"What is wrong?" I asked him. "All the men look upset, as if something dreadful had happened. And you"—I motioned to his face—"you are hurt!"

"Not a good hunt today, my lady," he replied quietly, gazing down. "Féroce did not behave. He settled in a tree, and then in high hedges. Both times I tried to retrieve him from the brambles. That is how I cut my cheek. But he would not come. He would not hunt." Then, almost listlessly, he repeated, "He would not hunt."

"But surely this can happen—"

"It should not have, my master says," he replied, looking at me directly, his wistful gray-blue eyes so reminiscent of Arnaut's that I almost started. "Féroce should have been ready for the kill. Ragnar told me he took care to feed him just enough so that he would be in *yarak*. But he would not do Lord de Hauteclare's bidding. He would not even do the Lord de Meurtaigne's bidding. He caught nothing."

"Nothing?"

"Nothing." He shook his head, his eyes fixed on the ground.

I glanced at Féroce, his wings folded tight, his golden eyes opaque, his claws gripping Gallien's glove as if in supplication. He seemed defeated, with no vestige of his customary fierceness. So penitent did he look, in fact, that I almost wanted to comfort him by murmuring, "Féroce, do not fear. Next time you will make your master proud."

Instead I said in a steady, reassuring voice: "My lord told me that Féroce was in *yarak*. That he was ready. Quite ready."

"So we thought. But he would not obey, he would not fly. He rested on a tree and watched us."

"And there seemed to be no way to lure him down?"

"No. None." He shook his head, adding, "I must leave, my lady. Féroce must be returned to the mews—" Then, somewhat ominously: "To Ragnar."

I watched him leave before walking quickly toward Gerard, who approached. He was still astride.

"Gallien told me what happened," I said as I looked up at him.

"Did he then?" he replied almost sarcastically. "What did he tell you?"

"That Féroce would not hunt. That he would not obey."

"It was far worse than that." He gave a small, tense smile. "He flew hither and yon with no purpose, he did not follow us, he showed only indifference." He had pronounced "indifference" with contempt, as if it were something monstrous, evil.

"But you yourself have told me this can happen. That a hawk can be stubborn, can refuse to hunt. You said it is always a gamble, to hunt with a falcon."

"Within reason, yes. But in this case, there was no reason. Féroce had been fed very sparingly. He should have been in *yarak*." He paused, as if something had just occurred to him: "At least I do not think he had been fed much." He pulled his reins hard, so that the gleaming leather of his gloves stretched tightly across his fists. "I will get to the bottom of it, I assure you. I will have words with Ragnar. And with Gallien."

I felt a guilty pang at the thought of Gallien being questioned or chastised, for it was I who had encouraged him, and also encouraged my husband to assign him to the mews.

I bit my lip and glanced uneasily at Hugh, still astride, not far away. "Please," I entreated, returning to face my husband, my hand touching his leather trousers. "Do not make more of this than necessary. Surely Hugh understands."

"He may. But I do not. These are my falcons, this is my domain, and he is my guest." He dismounted in one swift movement; we stood face-to-face. "It will not do for Hugh to be dissatisfied with the performance of my hawks. It will not be good for me, for my relations with him. Nor for my purposes."

"I cannot believe—"

"You know nothing of these matters," he scoffed. "It is not a world you understand. He will tell others about it, trust me. He is a talker and will say my hawks are inferior. That my falconers are incompetent. It will reflect badly on me and my house."

"I do not think that is the case."

"Then you are sorely mistaken."

He turned in the direction of the mews, snapping his crop as he walked. I gathered my skirt and walked toward the great hall, nervously imagining the confrontation that would take place. Between my husband and his falconers. Between the falconers and the recalcitrant eagle, who would, no doubt, go without food that evening. . . .

I was fearful for Féroce, as one might be for a hapless child about to receive a harsh, unwarranted punishment. But most of all, as I remembered the brutal look in Ragnar's eyes, I was fearful for Gallien.

AN HOUR LATER, AT DUSK, as I sat in our chamber, I heard steps approaching—the slow, sonorous, methodical steps that I recognized as Gerard's.

He entered, clearly still angry. Yet his rage was so controlled that I doubt anyone but myself would have guessed it. There was a dense unpleasantness to his silence, which gave him away, as did his tense grip on his gloves, which he grasped in one hand. Most of all there was a certain cold, forbidding expression in his eyes.

I watched him take off his riding boots, almost wishing that he would fling them off, or slam the door, anything at all to expunge his anger. But that was not his way. Instead he remained silent and set his gloves on the chest near the bed. Then he sat down on a stool, pulling one tall black boot off, then the other, in slow, almost painstakingly controlled movements, afterward placing one boot, then its mate, next to each other with martial precision. He sat for many moments without acknowledging me, leaning forward, deep in thought, his clenched fists resting on his knees.

Finally I broke the silence: "I gather the discussion did not go well."

"What discussion?" he replied, without looking at me.

"The talk with Ragnar and Gallien."

"A 'discussion' is not what I would call it." He faced me now, his gaze at once stony and appraising.

"What would you call it then?" My tone was impatient, edgy, for his tone offended me.

"A reckoning is what I would call it. An investigation."

"That seems a harsh way to describe it—"

"Not harsh at all. Realistic."

I took a deep breath. "And what did you learn?"

"That someone failed to feed Féroce correctly."

"It was not Gallien. He told me it was Ragnar who last fed Féroce."

He flinched almost imperceptibly. "I am not sure I believe that."

"*I* do!"

"You would," came his sarcastic reply.

"Why do you say that?"

"Because you are naive. You have no idea what people are capable of, and what men will do to protect themselves. You have been very sheltered."

"That may be," I said slowly and quietly. "But I know Gallien, and he is not careless. And I do not think he would ever disobey your instructions, or that he would ever lie to you."

"And Ragnar?"

I dared not voice my suspicions about Ragnar's drinking, and whether this caused his moodiness. "Of Ragnar I am not so certain," was all I said.

"You are wrong in that," he said derisively. "But I am willing to hear you out."

"I think Ragnar is resentful of Gallien, and that he would do anything to discredit him. He has been this way since the day Gallien entered the mews."

"That speaks of competition and ill will on Ragnar's part. I have never seen signs of this."

"You do not tend to see such things."

"And you do?"

"Yes. I see it, and I feel it."

"*Feel* it?" he repeated, his voice mocking. "This is not an area where I would depend on feelings. This is a matter of following directions and my orders. That is all. You are making it far more complicated than it need be."

I let this go before asking: "What did each man say?"

"That each had followed instructions, and that Féroce had been fed very sparingly, enough so that he would fly, but not enough to lessen his appetite to kill. Ragnar said it was Gallien who last fed Féroce."

"And Gallien?"

"Gallien disputed this."

"You yourself have told me that there is chance involved in hawking. That the birds can be capricious. Even the best birds." He did not respond; I sensed, for a second, that my words may have penetrated. "And I know that Ragnar has worked for you a long time," I continued, softening my tone. "And that you trust him."

"As much as I trust anyone. Yes."

"You are wrong to do so."

"How dare you tell me that!" He stood up, enraged.

"I am telling you what I feel to be true," I continued with quiet conviction. I thought of Ragnar's moodiness, and the occasional afternoons when he would return from the village looking rather unkempt, and his face florid, as if he had been drinking. "Ragnar is not to be trusted."

"And I am telling you that you are wrong."

I shrugged, affecting a nonchalance that I did not feel: inwardly I burned with anger.

"You protect Gallien because you have some sort of affinity for him," he continued, beginning to pace the room. "Because he is young and unaccustomed to this world. As *you* are. And because you urged me to promote him, and now feel responsible for his welfare." He picked up his gloves and slapped them down on the chest. "Believe me when I tell you that Gallien will not succeed or fail in any measure because of you, and what you *feel*. He will succeed or fail because of his performance. Because he obeys my instructions. Just as Aiglantine, in her service, will do in kind. Do you understand that?"

I did not respond.

"Do you?" he repeated.

"Yes," I finally said, choking the word out.

"Good."

I turned away and walked to the window; daylight was almost extinguished. The lanterns above the gatepost had been lit and cast a ghostly light upon its whitewashed posts. I tried to propel my thoughts elsewhere, as I often did when trying to soothe or protect myself. I thought of riding Juno, I thought of the talk with Fastrada earlier that morning. . . .

A few moments later I felt his hand on the small of my back.

"Come," he said gently this time, as he turned me around to face him, "Come, my sweet. You think me harsh, I know." His hand stroked my cheek. "You must understand that all of this—my concerns, my worries that everything be right for our guests—all of this is for *us*. For our life together. Surely you understand that."

"I am not sure what I understand anymore."

"Then," he said, in the same gentle vein, "it is up to me to make these things clear. As your husband and your master. These things will become clear, I promise." He smiled, once more caressing my cheek with his finger, "It is only a matter of . . ."

"Time?"

"To some extent." He nodded. "But mostly experience, and your understanding of the world. Not the world you grew up in, but *my* world. It is hard for you at times, I know, to be thrust into a very different world, with different expectations."

I thought back on the morning. "Perhaps you would like it if I were more like Fastrada."

"Fastrada?" he replied, with an astonished laugh. "Whatever gave you that idea?"

"She has grown up in this world. In Troyes. She is accustomed to all of this in a way I am not."

"True. But it has also hardened her. And I would not want you to be that way."

"Perhaps it would be better. Easier. Not to feel so much."

"No," he said, shaking his head reassuringly, "not at all." He brushed a strand of hair from my forehead. "You must stay the way you are." Smiling almost imperceptibly, he added, "With some adjustments." He drew his arms around me and murmured: "You are dear to me, my dove. I only wish you were more"—he paused, looking away as he searched for the right word—"*receptive* to my way of thinking."

"I am not sure what you mean?"

"I need you to be more understanding of the demands of my world. And what may be required, at times, of me—and of you—to fulfill my ambitions."

"I shall try," I murmured, even as I allowed him to kiss me. Yet all the while I reflected on the moment when he had paused, searching for the right word, before finally alighting on *receptive*. I wondered if it was quite another word he had really meant: *subservient*.

# CHAPTER 15

The following morning, my husband and the Hauteclares set out earlier than usual for the hunt. All day I waited nervously for them to return; Gerard's displeasure the previous day, and the harsh words we had exchanged, still rankled. I had tried to suppress these feelings by absorbing myself in one task after another, but nothing seemed to quell my inner disquiet, which seemed vaguely linked to the conversation with Fastrada. I would suddenly recall the sting of Gerard's sarcasm, his distrust of Gallien, and his desire that I be more "receptive"—if that were the word he had really meant—to the demands of his ambitions.

When, at last, the hunting party returned in the late afternoon, I knew at once, with immense relief, that the excursion had been a triumph. The men looked exhausted but happy, and the air was thick with jubilation: merry shouts and the passing round of pitchers of foaming ale to riotous clamor, while packs of hounds raced around them. The falcons themselves looked satiated and victorious, sure signs they had gorged on prey. Indeed, cart after cart rumbled past piled high with fresh kill: at one instant, dismembered rabbit tumbled to the ground before me, only to be slung over the shoulder of a stable boy who scurried over to fetch them, whistling as he walked.

Féroce, manned by Ragnar, seemed to have reassumed his former august self: his golden eyes glittered with a diabolical fierceness, and his talons, which only the day before had gripped Gallien's glove in seeming supplication, now seemed to rest there lightly, even majestically, as if to say: "Today I have done my master proud."

Gerard and Hugh led the entourage: two victors returning from a battle, bantering between themselves as they entered the courtyard, still astride their formidable mounts. Seeing me approach, Hugh waved, a wide smile across his broad florid face, his eyes twinkling with satisfaction. Gerard blew me a kiss and beckoned me to come near. Both men, chafed and sunburned, smelled of sweat, pine, and leather.

"It was a good day, I gather," I said to Gerard with an eager smile, looking up at him. His gauntlet, strapped to his saddle, was gashed at the thumb and streaked with blood.

"A glorious day, my sweet," he replied, beaming with almost boyish pleasure. "The birds flew wonderfully well, like champions!" he boasted. "Nothing escaped them. Not a hare. Not a bird."

Fastrada followed not far behind, the long skirt of her fern-colored dress slung with insouciance to one side. "Hey ho!" she called to me, reining in her skittish gray mount. "A great success today. I doubt there is a creature left stirring in the forest! Gerard's birds and his men outdid themselves. How well the hawks flew! Nothing like a splendid kill to put Hugh in a merry mood. If only you could have been with us, my dear, it would have been perfection itself."

"I am so glad it went well! That the hawks made up for yesterday."

"Indeed they did. In spades. Look at him"—she gestured to her husband—"how thrilled he is! Like a child who has just devoured a huge morsel of honey cake. Nothing gives my husband greater pleasure than this—" She cast a sly glance in my direction, before adding, "Well, almost nothing!"

I blushed a bit, still discomfited by Fastrada's allusions to her husband's various appetites.

A stable boy helped her dismount. "Ah, terra firma," she said, with a jaunty hop. "How good it feels after all that jolting about. I am not certain I ever want to see another hare or hound in my life. Lots of blood and feathers. Quite enough for me."

"I am impressed that you could keep pace with them," I remarked as she smoothed her hair. "With the men."

"It was not easy, though I shall admit that only to you. But as a matter of pride, I compelled myself to keep up with them." Then, saucily: "Must not let the family honor down, that sort of thing." She glanced around the courtyard, taking in the bustling scene. "Next time you will be with us, let us hope. Would be infinitely more agreeable to have you for company! Not easy, being with those ruffians." She rubbed her hands together, then fixed the high, immaculate collar of her jacket. "Now I am famished, I must say."

"Good! Then you will enjoy the feast tonight all the more."

"How true. We will have much to celebrate. Our new friendship, and today's success."

A cart trundled past, loaded with still more kill—pheasants, venison, and hare. "The cooks will be pleased to see all these provisions," I remarked, smiling.

"I am glad we did our share, as your guests, to contribute. It is the least we could do, to repay your hospitality," she replied, taking off her gloves. "Of one thing I am certain," she said gaily, taking my arm, "no one will go away hungry tonight!"

I TOOK GREAT PAINS IN dressing that night, for Gerard had seemed inordinately concerned that I be properly attired for the celebratory dinner which fell, that year, on Saint Martin's day. Hours before the feast commenced, he asked to see the robe I had selected.

"Do you not trust me to choose one that is suitable?" I asked half-jokingly as we sat in our chamber together. Gerard, still aglow from the day's success, had been regaling me with the high points of the hunt.

"Of course I trust you," he said with a reassuring smile, adding, "though I admit I would feel more at ease if you showed it to me first."

"Then I shall. With pleasure." I took the very simplest gown from my wardrobe, one of a sober dark blue and devoid of any ornamentation.

A horrified look crossed his face. "You cannot possibly wear that!" he exclaimed, his expression darkening.

"I know," I said. "I was just teasing you. To see your reaction. And I succeeded—I fooled you, for once!"

"Not at all," he replied, with a slight shrug; then, with a conceding smile, "Yes, yes you did. I admit it. Checkmate."

He smiled, taking my hand and kissing it with such tenderness that I almost started: within the gesture there was simply no trace of the man who, only the day before, had harshly upbraided me. How relieved, even buoyant, I suddenly felt, as if that single kiss had erased all my earlier disquiet.

He drew me to him and engulfed me in his arms, my braid gathered in his hand as he kissed the nape of my neck.

"Show me what you will really wear," he murmured.

I reluctantly pulled away from the warmth of his embrace and fetched the gown. It was fashioned of a brilliant purple silk shot through with gold; a design of bold, interlaced laurel leaves made up the shimmering borders of its rich hem and sleeves. Gerard had given me the fabric months before: it had come from Damascus and had been woven, he told me, by artisans from Thebes.

I held it up before him. "Will this do?"

"Yes. It is perfect. And you will look beautiful in it."

"To the victor goes the laurel," I said, my finger running across the laurels embroidered in gold. "And today you were just that—the victor!"

"As I expect to be *every* day. Not just today." There was almost an imperceptible edge of reproof to his voice; whether it was directed at me, or at himself, I was not certain. His expression had grown thoughtful, his eyes cast down in such a way that I saw the shadow of his long lashes upon his cheek. Then, almost brusquely: "It is time to get ready. Millicent must come and help you dress."

"I have asked Aiglantine to help me, as well. She knows best how to arrange my hair. The way you like it."

"I am afraid you must make do with Millicent tonight. Aiglantine is needed at dinner. I have asked that she serve at our table."

"I see." I mulled this over and walked to the bed, laying down the gown.

He stood near the door, pausing with his hand upon the latch. "Remember your best jewels," he said, turning to face me. "The bracelets. You must them wear tonight."

"Of course," I replied, forcing a smile. The bracelets! So imbued were they with the bitter memories of the incident with Aiglantine that I had tucked them away in a coffer and had never once looked at them since.

"Do not forget," he reiterated, and then I heard the small sharp click of the latch as the door closed behind him.

A FEW HOURS LATER, THE glittering bracelets upon my wrists, Gerard and I entered the great hall together, arm in arm. The huge, vaulted room, thronged with guests, had never appeared quite so magical, so splendid—not even on the night of the first feast, before my marriage, when I had been a stranger to such grandeur and luxury. I would have gasped had I not felt the pressure, as the lady of the house, to conduct myself with dignity. Instead I pressed Gerard's hand and, still looking directly ahead, whispered: "How beautiful it looks," as I acknowledged one person or another.

The most prestigious local landowners and their wives had been invited, and as I turned this way and that to greet them, everything seemed to whir and pulse around me. Innumerable torches blazed with light, illuminating the hangings and murals and the legendary subjects they depicted: the Queen of Sheba, Adam and Eve, The Three Magi. One flickering figure after another, like a pageant resurrected from ages past to herald our arrival. Luxuriant, fragrant garlands of leaves and mistletoe were draped across all the portals; above the main entrance hung the great blazon of blue silk, its proud phoenix and triumphant falcon embroidered in gold. To one side of the hall, servants in livery stood at attention; at the far end, clusters of musicians waited, poised with their instruments.

Suddenly the troupes of minstrels, in deep green with vivid red slippers, began to stroll through the hall, weaving their way through the guests, their ballads and songs lilting and bittersweet: the rhythmic sensual music saturated the air and seemed to make any other sounds superfluous. Every so often the lutes and viols would pause: then one would hear the sound of silk rustling, of footsteps upon fresh rush, of laughter erupting in one corner or another. Meantime the fires blazed, their high flames like leaping tongues of riotous colors.

At the far end of the chamber, raised on a dais, stood the high table, our table, draped with heavy white linen embroidered with the swirling Meurtaigne crest. Behind it, on a covered bench, we would sit side by side with our honored guests on jewel-colored silken cushions, each embroidered with a golden M.

I could hardly believe that this was my house, and that I, as the Lady de Meurtaigne, was presiding over an evening of such opulence in honor of illustrious guests from Troyes. . . .

"My dove," I suddenly heard Gerard say, interrupting my reverie. "It is time to greet our guests of honor." A surge of shrill trumpet sounds announced the arrival of the Hauteclares. They entered through the great portal with an easy grace, walking with slow, measured steps, turning to one side, then another, as they acknowledged us and our guests.

Fastrada did not disappoint. She might have been a Byzantine empress, so dazzling did she appear in a robe of gold brocade that seemed to emit its own light. Crowning her dark, coiled hair was a diadem of gold and rock crystal; a collar studded with gems and pearls encircled her neck. The tight bodice of her gown, fastened with studs as bright as diamonds, emphasized her maiden-like slenderness: indeed, from afar, one would have thought her quite a young woman. It was only as she approached, as her face drew near, that the spell was broken: no amount of ravishing silk could obliterate her homeliness.

She stood quite erect, as still as a statue: not an iota of her usual friskiness. Her manner, as she greeted one guest, then another, including the bishop, was stately, even decorous. I realized this was her public face, the persona she adopted at grand occasions: that of the famous Lady de Hauteclare who hailed from Troyes.

Hugh was elegantly dressed in a red tunic, which, I suspected, had been selected by his wife, for its expert cut succeeded at making him look younger and leaner. A goblet of wine was already grasped in one of his hands and was just as quickly drunk, and refilled, by a hovering page.

Nearby stood Aiglantine: I caught her eyes and smiled, uncomfortably aware that I wore the bracelets that had caused her such humiliation. Clearly excited to be present at such an event, she smiled shyly in return as she curtseyed to me. She was dressed in the formal style of all the serving girls, yet she alone, among them, seemed to wear it with a certain grace: her long, pale neck rose from the low, snug blue bodice like the stem of a lily. Her appearance was not lost on Hugh: at one point I caught him watching her, his eyes moving from the curving lines of her hips to the laces of her rounded bodice, then to the rosy hollow of her neck and cheek. I turned away, relieved that Aiglantine herself had not seemed to notice.

The horns sounded once again, the signal that we must take our places. We mounted the steps to the long head table. Gerard presided at the center, with Fastrada on one side of him, and myself on the other. To my right sat Hugh, and near him, the Lord de Vanieres, one of the greatest landowners of the vicinity, an elderly, aimable man who listened to Hugh's stories of the hunt with the detached amusement of a jaded aristocrat. At the far end of the table presided the bishop, a pyramid of crimson silk with a catlike smile.

Gerard himself had never seemed more poised or impressive. How proud I felt to be his wife that night! And how handsome he looked: at moments light from tapers illuminated his high cheekbones, his profile, or the curve of his mouth.

Everyone had been seated. The music paused. Water in silver bowls was passed, so that we might wash our hands. Gerard took the ritual pinch of salt from the cellar before him; stewards poured the wine; the feast commenced. Once more the minstrels strummed, lullingly now, as if conversation and food dictated softer sounds and rhythms.

One course after another began to arrive, a progression of game, and fish, and savories, each rare, fragrant, and succulent. Savory veal pasties, hare stew, roasted rabbits, a confection of larks' tongues, joints of mutton, a quivering aspic of crayfish—all flavored with complex, costly spices, with saffron, and peppers, and rosemary and marjoram. Fastrada exclaimed at the variety and richness of the delicacies but ate very little. Occasionally her fingers would pick up a bit of meat, or fish, but then just as quickly she would wipe her fingers and take a small, neat sip of wine, her dark eyes darting this way and that as she spoke gaily to Gerard, occasionally punctuating their conversation with her throaty laugh. Clearly she amused him, for he seemed animated, immersed in their conversation.

Hugh, on the other hand, approached the meal with the ravenousness one expected of him—he ate greedily, passing up nothing, even as his goblet was filled, and refilled, with wine. Midway through the repast his napkin became so soiled from wiping his mouth and fingers that he summoned Raoul for fresh linen.

Raoul, gesturing to Aiglantine, commanded her: "Fresh linen, at once." She returned in a moment, bending over as she handed Hugh a pristine napkin. "Unfold it for me—here," he told her, with a crooked smile. She blushed as she spread the linen across his thighs, for he had ostentatiously spread his legs to accommodate the cloth. Then, the gaze of his gold-flecked eyes unwavering: "What is your name?"

"Aiglantine, my lord," she murmured, casting her eyes down.

"In service here, how long?"

"Five years, my lord."

He seemed to consider a moment as he savored more wine. "Stay here. I may need some more"—a long pause, and a small, ironic smile— "fresh linen." Once more I noticed his eyes taking in her bodice.

All the while I hoped that Raoul would direct her to serve elsewhere. But he did not: indeed, noticing that Hugh seemed to favor her, Raoul kept her even closer at hand. I tried to catch Gerard's eyes, thinking he might intervene by calling to Raoul himself, but his attention continued to be fixed on Fastrada, on his guests, on directing the minstrels and the stewards.

At last, the final course was passed: a panoply of sweets, among them a glistening custard anointed with delicate fruits and raisins, sugar-dusted honey cakes, and an exquisite compote decorated with candied lavender in the shape of a swirling M. But I had long lost all appetite.

Hugh, however, had not: he dipped into the compote, and then into the custard, with a huge spoon, relishing the delicacies with such gusto that pearly bits of custard clung to his lips. Throughout dinner he had made a pretense of conversing with me—recounting a few amusing details of the hunt, posing a few desultory questions about my family— but I knew his mind was focused elsewhere. Repeatedly he had sought out Aiglantine, inventing reasons for her to attend to him. Each time, as she approached, her eyes cast down, he ogled her.

The intent look in his gold-flecked eyes seemed eerily familiar to me, though I did not know exactly why. I glanced away, furrowing my brow in thought as I clutched my napkin. Then came a flash of recognition: his rapacious stare reminded me of Féroce in *yarak*.

But now the prey was Aiglantine.

# CHAPTER 16

The feast hurtled to its conclusion, the music mounting in crescendo and quickening in beat. The earlier songs of poignant longing and *princesses lointaines* had given way to witty, cynical ballads, a few laced with ribald verses that sparked tittering among the audience. Some guests had begun to dance; others stood to the side, listening to the strumming minstrels. Gerard and I remained in our seats: dancing had never been to his liking, and I was constrained by pregnancy.

How I yearned to join in that night as I watched the dancers and the red-slippered singers weaving their way through the crowd! All the while my feet tapped to the beat as I leaned forward, straining to catch the verses:

> *Lady of the stingy heart*
> *Tight with promises and gifts*
> *Since you do not want to bed me*
> *At least give me a kiss*

Fastrada, too, was listening intently, a rapturous expression on her face: "Ah, what marvelous songs!" she exclaimed, her beringed fingers lightly tapping the table. "Do forgive me if I get up," she suddenly announced to Gerard. "I can resist many things, but not music."

She sauntered to the troupe nearest us and began to lightly clap her hands, a tall animated figure in gold, like a queen from a tarot card, her long dark hair tumbling behind her. The minstrels, aware of her prominence and appreciative of her attention, formed a circle around her as they began their serenade. Fastrada beamed, basking in their attention;

I watched, wondering if she had noticed Hugh's ogling of Aiglantine during much of the dinner.

Fresh logs were thrown into the hearths. It grew very warm, almost stifling. The air was suffused with the scent of pine, roasted meat, and sweat. Bits of food and bones littered the ground, and the once pristine rush was splashed red in spots from spilled wine.

A sudden weariness overcame me. My eyes darted to Gerard, waiting for him to signal that the revelries had ended. All the while the rhythm of the songs pulsed with growing intensity as the final plates of sweets were passed.

At last, I turned to Gerard and said: "I am too tired to stay much longer."

He nodded and absentmindedly pressed my hand as he glanced here and there around the table, then around the hall, his eyes coolly assessing the throbbing scene. He had drunk only a modicum of wine: moderation was his wont, and discipline a quality he prized.

"We will retire soon," Gerard reassured me, his attention still fixed on his guests. He beckoned to Raoul: "More wine for the bishop," he ordered.

"And for the Lord de Hauteclare, as well, my lord?" asked Raoul, gesturing in Hugh's direction.

"Yes," Gerard replied tersely, watching Hugh. The latter's eyes were fixed on Aiglantine's bodice as she bent over to offer him a plate of sweets. She curtseyed as she was about to leave, but Hugh, once again, seemed to be concocting a reason for her to stay, for he was speaking to her, his mouth set in a lascivious smile.

Gerard looked away, withdrawing into silence for a moment, one hand tight around his goblet. "Hugh seems to be enjoying himself," he finally remarked to me, in a cold disapproving voice.

"Too much wine, I think."

"Wine?" he replied. "That is a charitable way to put it." Then, brusquely: "Come, I shall escort you upstairs. It is time you rest." He took my hand; we stood up together. The head minstrel, noticing this, signaled that the music stop.

"No—resume," Gerard commanded him. "Let our guests enjoy themselves. I shall return shortly."

We proceeded through the hall, arm in arm, as I bade good night to one person, then another. The throngs parted to let us pass as I held tight to Gerard, the enameled bracelets heavy on my wrists.

MILLICENT AWAITED ME IN OUR chamber, bent over her sewing as she hummed a little tune. "All well, my lady?" she asked, standing and curtseying as we entered.

"Yes, all went well. Very well. But now I am tired. I feel heavy to-night." I placed my hands on my stomach, for once again the baby had begun to kick.

"It is to be expected, my lady," she said, in a kindly voice, as she smoothed her apron. "You have done quite enough today."

She bade me sit down. Gerard kissed me on the forehead and left to rejoin the guests.

Millicent helped me undress, the glimmering bracelets first. As she began to unhook my gown, I held the bracelets in the palms of my hands, turning them over and over, reflecting on the web of memories they sparked; however beautiful, they remained all too imbued with an aura of hurt.

Overcome with sudden distaste, I set them down on the table. Still thinking of Aiglantine and how crudely Hugh had treated her at the dinner, I wondered what she was feeling, and what I would say to her— or not.

Millicent held up the robe with the weighty damask surcoat. The hem was soiled and slightly torn, and the dress itself had lost its triumphant aura: it, too, looked worn and tired.

"There," said Millicent as she came to the last hook; I stepped out of the robe. After she carried it to the wardrobe, she returned with my linen shift and said, "May your slumbers be peaceful tonight, my lady."

Shortly afterward I tumbled into a chaotic sleep, my dreams churning with grotesque creatures, some resembling griffins, others like grimacing hawks.

THE FOLLOWING MORNING, I AWOKE to find Gerard, already dressed, standing by the window, scanning the sky.

"I never heard you enter last night," I said to him, gathering the quilt around me in bed.

"I came in quietly. I did not want to wake you." He smiled, but seemed preoccupied, almost dispirited.

"What is wrong? Something *is* wrong, I know it."

"Yes. Something has happened. Something that has angered me." His voice was slow, somber, controlled.

"What is it?" I asked with concern.

"Hugh. He wants Aiglantine. To bed her." A small caustic smile crossed his face. "As a present. From lord to lord, he said. 'You are known to be generous with gifts,' he told me. 'Better a fresh girl than vintage wine.' Of course"—his hand tightened into a fist—"I know his reputation. But that he should make such a demand in *my* house, knowing how I feel about such things . . ."

I froze, horrified. Of course I had heard of lords who took servant girls as their right, but I had never dreamed that Hugh would demand such a thing *here*, of Gerard, his friend and host, and that he would ask for Aiglantine.

"And you?" I finally managed to ask. "What did you say?"

"I told him no. Absolutely no. What I refrained from saying was that he was behaving like a boor. No, I told him, I would not allow this, not in *my* household," he continued, with the contempt of one who saw lack of self-control as a pitiable weakness.

"How did he respond?"

"With anger. With indignation. Finally, he collected himself and was merely petulant, like a child denied a sweet."

I took his hands, kissing one palm, then the other, with a fervor born of relief and pride. "Thank you, my darling! I am so relieved. You know I am fond of Aiglantine. And if you had permitted this to happen"—I shuddered, as I imagined it—"it might have destroyed her. She would never have been the same."

"My dealings with Hugh may not be either," he said, with a dry laugh. "He did not take all of this lightly, let us say. It may put our dealings together at risk."

"Let him have something else then," I told him rather offhandedly.

"What?" he asked in an edgy voice.

"A splendid hawk?"

He laughed indulgently: a low, worldly laugh, one implying that these were men's matters, things I could not understand. "You *are* naive, my sweet," he remarked.

"Does Fastrada know about this?"

"I doubt it."

"They call him The Rutter, you know. The servants told me."

"At the very least then, he has lived up to his reputation," came his acerbic reply. "But now I must get ready for the hunt."

He kissed me quickly and turned to leave, pausing at the door to say: "Wish me—and Féroce—luck today."

"Of course," I replied with a warm, grateful smile. I blew him a kiss and called, *"Bonne chance!"*

# CHAPTER 17

Two days had passed since the night of the great feast, and Hugh had not shown an iota of anger vis-à-vis my husband's refusal to grant him the perverse "gift." With some relief, I said to Gerard: "Clearly Hugh has forgotten the whole incident. If anything, he seems even more jovial than usual."

"That does not surprise me. He is nothing if not resilient." He paused, adding, "And when he chooses to be, inscrutable. That is in no small measure a reason for his success."

I was surprised to hear him describe Hugh as inscrutable, for the latter's demeanor always seemed to project a certain candid bonhomie. I remarked as much to Gerard.

"More naivete, on your part, my darling! That bonhomie is a mask. Hugh is no buffoon. Believe me, he knows what is what—when it comes to the mechanisms of power, most of all. Who is ascending, who is descending. What compromises are necessary to achieve his own goals. Add to that, another crucial ability." He paused, as if reflecting on how best to define it. "He is a shrewd judge of character. Of strength. Of weakness. In that regard, there is no better negotiator than Hugh de Hauteclare."

"Then surely he must see his own—weaknesses, that is?"

"One would think so, if life were logical." He kissed my forehead tenderly. "But life seldom is."

ON THE FINAL DAY OF the hunt, Fastrada, pleading fatigue, remained at the castle. "I shall be much happier remaining here with you today," she told me, "especially with this nasty weather."

I greeted this news with some ambivalence. Though I had grown fond of Fastrada, I now felt slightly uncomfortable with her, knowing I was keeping a secret—if, indeed, I was. Had she not told me, in a manner that was stunningly cavalier, that Hugh's roving eye actually "amused" her?

That morning Fastrada and I watched the men set off, then walked together to the great hall. "It is far too cold and raw today for the likes of me," she told me, with a shudder. "Far better to let the men go and battle it out with the birds!" She took my arm and added affectionately, "And then the two of us have so little time left together. I shall miss you, my dear!"

"And I you," I replied with equal warmth, feeling a pang of guilt at my earlier hesitance to spend time alone with her.

The morning cold was damp and penetrating, the sort that seeps through the bones, so the roaring, crackling fire in the hall came as a welcome sight indeed. We sat together by the hearth, as we had done the previous time she had absented herself from the hunt.

"Let us roast some chestnuts," I suggested.

"Yes, that would be lovely!"

I summoned a page. He returned in a few moments carrying baskets piled high with plump, glossy chestnuts.

We had just begun to roast them when Millicent scurried in, brandishing my hoop. Fastrada, eyeing it, gave such a great sigh of ennui that I had to refrain from laughing aloud.

"I thought you might like your sewing," Millicent said, bowing, with her typical solicitousness. "Will you need anything more, my lady?"

"Nothing more."

"Are you sure, my lady?"

"I am *quite* sure, thank you. You may go."

"How tiresome that woman is," Fastrada commented once Millicent had left. "Like a little gray squirrel, always underfoot. What is her name?"

"Millicent."

"I should have known! A dreary name for a dreary woman."

I laughed. "Not so much dreary as conscientious. And"—I gave a small smile—"she is certainly pious."

"Then I am doubly relieved you have that sweet, pretty girl as well. She is young, and there is something touching and gentle about her."

"You mean Aiglantine," I replied warily, evading her eyes as I pretended to focus on the chestnuts. Nothing in Fastrada's demeanor indicated that she knew anything about Hugh's demand; yet I still wondered. "But Millicent, I am told, is most experienced in attending childbirth. No doubt she will be helpful when the baby is born," I added, with more conviction than I felt.

"I am glad you think so. I predict she will drive you mad with old wives' tales! Nothing like pregnancy and childbirth to bring out all those horror stories. I would ask to have her moved to another position."

"Gerard would never think of it. She has served his family for very many years and he is quite devoted to her. And besides"—I paused—"he does not think it is correct for me, as lady of the house, to have someone so young as my main attendant." To this I added, ruefully: "Let alone as a companion."

"He is really too rigid and protective. And all this emphasis on *correctness*," she replied, with an exasperated sigh. "One would almost think him jealous, in a strange way, that you should devote your attention to someone else." She paused, before continuing at a fast clip: "He cannot keep you always so secluded here. We are Franks, not Orientals, after all! He has spent too much time in Outremer, in my opinion. No, my dear, I shall speak with him about Aiglantine and encourage him to give her more responsibility. She will be far more comforting to you in the birthing chamber than that other, dreary woman."

"I do not think that is a good idea," I said at once, quite firmly, putting my hand on her shoulder. "It would be better if you do not. Leave it to me."

"Believe me, I know he can be headstrong, and—if I were to guess—quite jealous, too." She paused, twisting the familiar green and gold ring on her little finger as she seemed to study me. "Though I suspect that you too are not without stubbornness. Even fierceness."

I laughed. "I admit I can be quite stubborn."

"Yes," she replied as she nodded thoughtfully, her dark eyes narrowing. "I imagine that you are not unfamiliar with the siren call of the idée fixe. Nothing wrong in that, though at times these things are best kept under wraps. Especially for a woman." She drew her shawl closer around her shoulders and leaned back slightly, her arms folded, her glittering ringed fingers pressed upon the edge of her fur wrap. "You must marshal all your stubbornness to petition Gerard for the visit to Troyes. Promise me you will!"

"I promise," I answered fervently, relieved that the subject had swerved to Troyes, and hoping that she would refrain from bringing up Aiglantine again.

AN HOUR OR SO LATER, the men returned unexpectedly early from the hunt. A fierce storm had come up. One could hear the pounding of rain and hail; white, crackling spikes of lightning rent the darkened sky.

"Too treacherous out there today, even for us," said Gerard, striding toward us with Hugh. Both men were soaked, their vests wet, their boots leaving a trail of muddy footprints in the rush.

"What cowards!" cried Fastrada. "Usually Hugh will hunt in any condition. Never one to be put off the chase by a little rain and wind, my valiant husband. Isn't that right, Hugh?"

"If you say so, my dear." He shrugged, smiling as he took off his vest to dry it on a bench by the fire. "What are you two plotting?" he asked, blowing on his hands.

"No plots at all!" I replied with forced gaiety, fearing what Fastrada might bring up next. "We have simply been talking, and roasting chestnuts."

"What you call plots, I call plans," chirped Fastrada before she addressed Gerard directly: "I have told Isabelle you must both come to Troyes next year, during the fair. To visit us."

"We shall see," Gerard replied as he doffed his soaked vest.

"Far too tentative an answer, my dear Gerard. You must say *yes*, now! I insist upon it."

"Well then yes, yes, we will consider it," he answered tolerantly, brushing back his damp hair. "Next spring, God willing."

"I would rather this be placed in *your* hands than in God's. He can be unreliable. Any priest could tell you that."

We all laughed.

"And then there is another matter—" she continued in her sprightly way.

"What is that?" Gerard asked; I held my breath.

"Isabelle ought to have someone younger attend to her in child-birth," she announced to my consternation. "Not that ancient crone who trails her with the hoop! Why not that young woman, the pretty blonde I have seen? Isabelle tells me her name is Aiglantine." I noticed my husband bridle, but Fastrada, undaunted, continued to press him: "It would be far more comforting for her to have someone young and gentle with her. For the birth of the first child, especially."

I exchanged glances with Gerard, whose eyes had taken on a chilly remoteness. I realized with dismay that he might think I had put Fastrada up to this; then, with horror, that he might even think I had told her about Hugh wanting to bed Aiglantine. All the while Hugh seemed completely unperturbed, almost preternaturally relaxed as he gazed at his wife, then at me.

But Fastrada would not relent: "Why not this young woman, Gerard?" Then, turning to her husband: "Don't you agree with me, Hugh?" Then, with a certain shrill vehemence: "Surely you have noticed her? She is the pretty one, the one with the singular eyes, each a different color." He shook his head and replied dryly: "The choice of an attendant for Isabelle during childbirth is not something I have spent much time thinking about." His voice was steady, cool. "Surely it is up to Gerard to make these decisions."

"Up to Gerard *and* Isabelle, I should think," she retorted.

"As you wish, my dear."

"Well, then, Gerard?" she asked, turning to him.

"I will consider it," he answered unconvincingly. "As I will the possibility of our visit to Troyes."

"Promise me you will do more than merely consider it. Isabelle is so isolated here. She is far from her family—"

"As many young married women are," he interrupted, his tone now rather severe. "And she will have much else to occupy her in the next months. A baby, most of all. Our son, God willing. She will not be without companionship, I assure you."

"That is true, Fastrada," I chimed in. "I am not in the least lonely."

She smiled almost acquiescently, for I think even she realized that she had pushed Gerard far enough. She began to chatter about the preparations for their journey, about the route they would take home.

"Will you stop at Fontevraud, to see your sister?" I asked, immensely relieved for the change in subject, all the while avoiding Gerard's stony gaze. As for Hugh: he stood near us, tossing a few chestnuts from one hand to the other; he seemed so unperturbed there was simply no way of knowing whether he thought I knew about the Aiglantine matter.

"Fontevraud? Yes, I think we will spend a night there," she replied. "Shall we, Hugh?"

"I do not see why not," he said, handing her some chestnuts to roast. "It is en route after all."

"I told Fastrada how unlikely it seemed that she, of all people, should have a sister who is a nun," I remarked to Hugh.

"Clementia is no ordinary nun," he replied, with surprising gravity.

"In what way?" I asked, intrigued by his change in tone.

"She is immensely learned. A brilliant linguist." His voice was newly thoughtful, startlingly so, for he was still inextricably linked with his behavior at the feast—the leering eyes, the vulpine smile were still vivid in my mind.

"She sounds fascinating—like her elder sister!" I told him.

"Yes, fascinating, too, but in a different way. At least, some would say."

"And you—what would you say, Hugh?" I asked, recalling how Gerard had mentioned his aptitude in judging character.

"I would say"—he paused, measuring his words—"that Clementia, despite her gentleness, is a force to be reckoned with. The face of a Madonna. An almost Levantine cunning. Deeply private, and deeply loyal to those she loves and serves."

"A splendid description!" cried Fastrada, looking at her husband admiringly. "And suavely said. A papal legate could not have put it better." She turned to me: "It is quite true what Hugh says about Clementia. I should add that there is no one I trust more than my sister." Then, somewhat mischievously, to Hugh: "Well, *almost* no one."

"I am pleased to hear that, my dear," he replied with a wry smile.

"Do you not think Isabelle would like Clementia, Hugh?" Fastrada pressed him.

"Without question."

"Yes," she concluded, "it is decided. You must meet her one day."

"With pleasure," I replied. I turned to Gerard. He was facing the fire and had been silent during this last exchange.

"Do you not think that Clementia sounds fascinating, Gerard?" I asked.

He turned to look at us: "I would expect nothing less of Fastrada's sister." Yet there was a coldness in his chivalrous reply that made me uneasy.

# CHAPTER 18

A few hours later, when at last we were alone in our chamber, I turned to Gerard and said: "You are angry with me."

"Are you surprised that I should be angry with you?" he asked incredulously.

"Yes I am," I replied indignantly. "I have done nothing wrong."

"Why else would Fastrada have brought up Aiglantine, if you had not told her about the incident with Hugh?"

"I would never have done that," I told him vehemently. "*Ever.*"

"So it is a merely a coincidence? And do you think Hugh himself would believe that?"

"Yes! You know how Fastrada is. How willful and capricious she can be. She has become fond of me. And she wants to help me!"

"So you said nothing to her about Hugh's interest in Aiglantine?"

"Nothing. I swear to you."

"It seemed likely to me you had. And if you had, that would have been a betrayal to me, and humiliating to Hugh, whose goodwill I need. It is bad enough I had to deny him the girl." He began once more to pace. "You have a strange fondness for Aiglantine yourself, for some reason. I thought I had made myself clear in that regard. I have made a decision. Aiglantine must no longer be your principal serving maid. Millicent is more appropriate for a lady of your station. And I will not permit Aiglantine to be among those who attend you in the birthing room. It would not be appropriate."

I bit my lip. "I think you are being rather harsh."

"Not harsh. Merely *responsible*, as your husband." His expression softened. "Most of all I must know that I can trust you," he continued in a low, passionate voice, his vivid blue eyes searching mine. "If I cannot trust you, then whom can I trust? How can I confide in you, how can I share my private thoughts, if I cannot trust you, my wife?"

"But of course you can, my darling! I would never, ever betray your confidence!"

I took his hands in mine, kissing each finger, and then each palm.

"Good. I am relieved," he said, embracing me as he murmured: "Not to be able to trust you utterly, completely, would be terrible indeed."


TO MY RELIEF AND DELIGHT, Gerard told me late that same evening that his business dealings with Hugh had been happily concluded: Gerard would participate in the trade of wine to England, which he had coveted. He was in radiantly good humor that night, and made a gallant toast to Hugh and Fastrada at the end of the final dinner.

"To our lasting friendship, and partnership!" he declared, raising his glass as we smiled and joined him.

Aiglantine was nowhere to be found among the servants at the table: since the feast on Saint Martin's day, Millicent told me, she had been assigned to the kitchen.

All augured well the following morning at the departure of Hugh and Fastrada. The storm had cleared, leaving the landscape cleansed and fresh. The sun shone, the cold air was crisp but not bitter, and the sky a clarion blue. The entourage stood ready: the many loaded carts, the packhorses, the men at arms, and the band of liveried Hauteclare servants who accompanied them. Fastrada had not yet appeared, but Gerard and Hugh were conferring in a corner of the courtyard, their faces animated and jovial, while I watched and waited.

I heard Fastrada call my name and turned around. She approached, a regal, reedlike figure in a brown traveling costume with a purple feathered cap and matching gloves. "Oh my dear," she said, taking my arm, "how despondent I am to leave you!"

"I shall miss you, too, Fastrada. And our talks, as well."

"Will you?" she asked, with uncharacteristic earnestness. "There were moments when I thought—well, I thought perhaps I had said too much. But you must understand how fond I have become of you.

You must think of me as your older sister." She took my hands in hers, holding them tight as she added, even more vehemently, "I shall write you. And you must promise to write back!"

"Of course I shall!"

"And also promise that you will visit us in Troyes."

"If Gerard allows it."

"And Clementia—you must meet her one day!"

"Yes, I long to meet her!"

The stable boy approached with her elegant gray mount. Fastrada and I embraced and kissed each other's cheeks; I remember the whiff of her perfume—it was laced with lavender, reminiscent of my grandfather's scent. I looked down, holding back tears, thinking of the winter morning when I had left my family, and how it now seemed a century ago. . . .

The two of us stood face-to-face, our hands grasped together as we made our final farewells: I tried to memorize her features, as one might a page of text: the brilliant, hooded dark eyes, the wide pearly smile, the small determined chin. "Until the next time," she murmured, with tears in her eyes.

"Yes—yes," I reiterated as we embraced.

She mounted, her feet firmly in her stirrups, her braid tossed behind her back. "Imagine! The next time I see you, you will be a mother," she exclaimed, leaning down toward me. "Remember what I told you about those old wives' tales and horror stories. Pay no attention! All will be well."

"It will, I know." My voice choked; I tried not to cry.

Hugh approached and embraced me, adding warmly: "It gives me pleasure to see you and Gerard so happy together." He kissed my hand with such courtliness that I struggled to reconcile the man before me now with the boor from the feast.

"I shall never forget this visit. I have so enjoyed meeting you and Fastrada."

"As we have enjoyed meeting you. Next year you must come to Troyes."

He mounted in one swift, powerful movement and settled in his saddle, reins tight in hand.

Gerard and I stood arm in arm together and wished the entourage a safe journey.

"All ready?" called Hugh, looking back at the impressive train behind him.

"All ready, my lord!" affirmed his lead man.

"Set off," commanded Hugh.

"Until soon, I hope!" called Fastrada, blowing a kiss. She dug her heels into the flanks of her mount and cantered away, with a wave of one purple gloved hand.

# CHAPTER 19

In the days that followed, a terrible stillness descended upon the castle. What had been animated and enlivened by the presence of the Hauteclares now seemed possessed by an unnerving, claustral silence. Everything seemed haunted by the reminiscence of their visit, indeed the very word *reminiscence* seemed tinged with sadness and loss. Within me there was a profound shift, the nature of which I could not quite identify.

One morning I walked into the great hall, remembering how I had sat for hours before that very hearth talking with Fastrada: but now there was no crackling fire, only a mound of ashes, cold and deathly gray. I sat before the hearth for a long time that day, trying to temper disquiet in my customary way—by inwardly escaping to the elsewhere. I thought about Fastrada and what she had told me about Troyes; about her sister Clementia, at Fontevraud. I wondered if I should ever meet her; I wondered if I should ever go to Fontevraud. . . .

The child growing within me should have comforted me and filled me with a sense of joy and plentitude. That it did not only instilled me with guilt. Then I would chide myself: Had not God blessed me by granting me this pregnancy, and with a husband who had given me so much? But—here my nervousness quickened—what if I bore a daughter he did not really want?

Here, too, I paused and thought hard, forcing myself to search my own soul, only to find it far from spotless. Was it only my husband who was at fault here; or did I, too, share the same obsession? When I envisioned the child within my womb, it was never a daughter I imagined: it was a *boy* who would be free, who would master his own fate. He would not have to beg for a chess set, or spend his time sewing; he would not have to be decorous; he would not have to submit to *confinement* in all its guises.

But it was the idea of Gerard's disappointment I found most frightening. Every time I imagined it, I could not dispel the memories of the day when Féroce had failed to perform at the hunt: the terrifying look in my husband's eyes when he returned, and the barely veiled threat that this must never happen again. But then I would draw back, chide myself, and say: Féroce is merely a hawk, a primitive creature, not a woman, as I am, with her life before her—young, fertile, healthy. For a while this would soothe me: then I would touch my stomach, heartened by the movement of the baby within me, telling myself that the forceful kicks I was feeling could only be those of a strong, healthy son.

"The tyranny of conception" Fastrada had called it. She had spoken about these things as if they were not matters left necessarily to chance and as if one should not blindly accept them with a sense of resignation. What if there *were* a way to predict the baby's sex? Or a means—a potion, perhaps—that would help me conceive a boy in the future? Bertuccio had told me there *was* such a person; that she dwelt in the forest; Anthusis was her name. More than ever, I needed to know if she existed; and if she *did* exist, exactly where she dwelt.

First, it was necessary to seek out Aiglantine, for I would need her help. Since the feast and the incident with Hugh, Aiglantine had been working in the kitchen. I requested that she return to help me and Millicent with the preparations for the child. "There are many things she can do that Millicent cannot," I told Gerard. "Fastrada was right. It would comfort me to have her with me these next months." I added: "And since Hugh is no longer here, we need no longer keep Aiglantine away. Please, I beg you, my darling—"

I had carefully chosen the right moment to make this request. Gerard was absorbed in concluding the arrangements with Hugh for his share in exporting wine from Bordeaux to the Angevin court in England. At such times, he had little patience with household minutiae. "Very well, let her return, if that would help you," he told me, with an absent-minded kiss, before he added, "but you must promise to remember—"

"That I am the lady, and she is the servant?" I gave him my most winning smile.

"Yes."

"I shall! I promise," I answered, crossing my heart.

THE FOLLOWING MORNING, WHILE MILLICENT sat with me sewing, Aiglantine appeared at my chamber. Mindful of the older woman's possessive nature, I took care to restrain my delight in seeing the younger woman, and said, in a measured tone, "We are glad you have returned. Millicent has been working herself to the bone and will be relieved to have some help. Is that not so?" I gave the old woman a concerned smile.

"Of course," she replied, barely looking up.

"I am happy to be back. And to help," said Aiglantine.

"Good," I said. "Perhaps you should begin by stoking the fire. Millicent was just complaining of the cold."

"I will do it now."

After attending to the fire, Aiglantine began sweeping the hearth as we continued sewing. Looking up, I suddenly turned to Millicent. "Oh dear—I have forgotten to ask Raoul something important."

"What is that, my lady?" she asked.

"We must check our supply of linen. We will need more than ever in the coming months. For the baby clothes, and much else."

She looked puzzled. "Are you sure, my lady? I was certain we had an ample supply." (Little did she know that I had stashed part of it away.)

"You must have forgotten how much we have used recently," I told her disingenuously, for her memory had indeed become faulty of late. "Best we check. Imagine how upset Lord de Meurtaigne would be—"

"Of course. I will go see Raoul right now," she said, clearly disconcerted. She set down her sewing and excused herself.

Once the door was closed, I turned to face Aiglantine. "How good to have you back!" I cried, taking her hands. "It was not the same without you here."

She gave a bashful, appreciative smile. "I am so happy to be back. I was worried—"

"You must help me," I said at once.

"How, my lady?" she asked, clearly alarmed by the urgency in my voice.

"The healer I have heard about. I must find her."

"The woman, the strange woman, in the forest?"

"Yes."

"I have already asked about her."

"Whom have you asked?"

"Agnes. And she told me that Sybilla, who works in the kitchen, has seen this healer!"

"Ask Sybilla about the healer. Do not say why. Only say it is a private matter, not to be discussed with anyone else. Do your best."

"I will."

I took her hands in mine. "I know you will. You always do." I turned around to face the mirror. "Now we must finish my hair."

She began to brush my hair: long, rhythmic strokes that almost made me sleepy. I closed my eyes, only to sit up again suddenly: in that drifting moment I realized I had never spoken to Aiglantine about the night of the feast and Hugh's lecherous advances. How she must have suffered, how humiliated she must have been! But she was too private, too elegant in her own way, ever to have disclosed her own feelings to me.

"Aiglantine," I said, gently taking the brush from her hand as I turned to face her.

"Yes, my lady?"

"The night of the feast. The behavior of the Lord de Hauteclare. We have never talked about it."

She flushed with embarrassment, her eyes darting here and there, reluctant to meet mine. "There is little to say."

"I think there is a great deal to say. I saw your face. I saw how painful the situation was for you."

"Yes, I admit, I was embarrassed," she confessed in a low, quiet voice, shrugging her frail shoulders.

"Of course you were! But that this should have happened here, under our roof! With an honored guest at our table."

She was silent, yet her eyes spoke volumes: you are naive, my lady, they told me. You have been protected from the rough ways of the world, and of men.

"Has this happened before, elsewhere?" I finally asked.

She nodded, her mouth trembling. "Best we not talk about it, my lady." Her tone was definitive, firm. It did not invite me to probe further.

"Very well," I told her gently. "No more of this then. I only want you to know that I know what you were feeling. And that I do not want you to feel afraid in our house, ever again."

SEVERAL DAYS LATER, AIGLANTINE ASKED to see me. She told me she had spoken with Sybilla about Anthusis. "She has seen her, in the forest," Aiglantine said as I beckoned her to sit by me.

"But *where* in the forest?" I asked. "What part, and how far away?"

"Toward the eastern edge of the forest where people rarely venture, where there are ravens' nests, and vultures. Her lair is well hidden, Sybilla says."

"How does Sybilla know?"

"There is always talk about strangers. Sybilla has heard—" But here she hesitated.

"Has heard what?"

"People say that Anthusis is learned. That she can treat wounds that no one else can heal. That people go to her when ex-votos and prayer have failed them. They say she studied in foreign places. But nothing else about Anthusis is certain." She paused. "No one is even sure whether she is a man or woman."

I pondered this, then asked, "Are you certain Sybilla is to be trusted?"

She nodded. "She is a strange girl, but she is honest and strong. I am told she had the pox as a child, and she survived."

"Then she must be strong indeed! Perhaps it is best that I speak with her myself."

I saw a flicker of hurt cloud Aiglantine's eyes, as if I had implied her own word did not suffice. "Of course I trust you," I said reassuringly. "But I must be sure this girl will not betray me."

"I understand, my lady. There can be gossip here, in the household."

"From Agnes, I suspect, most of all—"

"Yes."

"I know *you* are not a gossip. And I suspect you are good at keeping secrets, are you not?"

She nodded slowly, solemnly.

"I, too, am good at keeping secrets," I reassured her, touching her hand. Then I stood up and said briskly, "Now—I must arrange to speak with Sybilla. But how? It will seem strange if I simply demand she see me. Raoul will be suspicious. There must be a good reason." I paused. "She works in the kitchen, you said?"

She bit her lip, thinking hard. "Yes. She works in the kitchen, but she has wanted to apprentice in the bakery. She loves to bake, and is good at it. She once brought me some of her own bread, and it was delicious. But Raoul has said no, she must remain in the kitchen. You could say you have heard she wants to work with the baker, that you have heard she has talent. You could invent a reason to speak with her about it."

I looked at Aiglantine in a new light: here was a craftiness I had never discerned in her before. "That is good," I said, "but in doing so I may risk making Raoul an enemy. He does not like me to intrude in these matters—"

"But you are the lady of the house."

"Even so." I took a deep breath. "I would not mind taking the risk for myself. But if he finds out *you* are involved, he will be angry with you. And that is a risk I will not take."

"You are right, my lady. I am grateful."

"We must find another way. It must be something I notice myself, so that you are never implicated." I stood up and began to walk to and fro. "What else can you tell me about her?"

"Her work is careful, very careful." Then, as an afterthought: "Though her own person is slovenly. The cook, Wilbertus, has often reprimanded her about this. But she works so hard her untidy appearance has never put her at risk."

"Good—I shall invent a reason to go to the kitchen when you confirm she is there. If she is indeed slovenly, I shall demand she come see me. But I must do it in such a way that Raoul does not find out."

"He will be away next week," Aiglantine said, excited, as if she were happy to be part of this conspiracy. "He is to visit his brother at the Abbey of Saint Florent."

"Let me know when he has left. Then I shall go to the kitchen myself."

THE FOLLOWING WEEK, AFTER RAOUL had left, I walked to the kitchen to speak with Wilbertus. A kindly man, he looked far older than his years, for he had lost most of his hair, and what little remained was gray and sparse. He was tall, fine-boned, and had an unfortunate way of blinking constantly, so that he looked perpetually perplexed; yet I had been told that when he was in the midst of cooking and supervising food, the blinking ceased. He was a fine cook known for his delicate way with spices, and he was always eager to please.

Aiglantine had confirmed that Sybilla would be working that day. My ostensible reason for the visit: to request a savory venison dish I suddenly longed for. "I have a craving for it," I told Wilbertus, moments after entering the cavernous, bustling kitchen, with its savory scents of spices and simmering fowl. He was clearly quite nervous and all the while blinked furiously.

"It is not unusual, my lady, that you should have cravings now, at this time."

"So they tell me," I replied, smiling.

I recognized Sybilla at once. Aiglantine had described her accurately: a tall, raw-boned young woman with a greasy, stained apron and a sallow face pitted by the pox. Strands of lank hair brushed her cheeks as she kneaded dough with strong, determined hands. Her forehead glistened with sweat.

"Who is that young woman?" I asked Wilbertus.

"That is Sybilla, my lady. A helper here. A good woman."

"Surely she should be wearing a clean apron," I remarked, watching her. "And her hair should not be falling into her face as she works."

"You are right, my lady." He looked embarrassed. "I will chide her."

"So you should. Has she been reprimanded for this before?"

"Yes. It is my fault I have let it go this time." Then, in a rather plead-ing voice: "But her work is very good. She made the chicken dish with prunes we served yesterday—"

"Indeed, it was delicious."

He looked relieved. "I am glad you thought so, my lady. She is a good worker, one of the best I have had."

"Her work may be satisfactory, but her appearance is not. Sloven-liness will not do, especially in the kitchen. The Lord de Meurtaigne would be appalled. I would like to speak with her."

"Of course, my lady."

"Tell her to meet me in the great hall, by the hearth, when the clock strikes eleven."

"She will be there, my lady." He bowed deeply.

"Good. That is all," I replied imperiously, gathering my skirt as I left.

A FEW HOURS LATER, AS I waited by the hearth in the silent, deserted hall, Sybilla entered. Her hair was pulled back from her brow, and her apron was now clean—no doubt the result of Wilbertus having scolded her.

She curtseyed clumsily before me, then stood up, shifting from one foot to the other in her clumsy wooden sabots.

"I am sure Wilbertus has told you why I asked to see you," I said, affecting an unaccustomed sternness (all the while reveling in the play-acting, I admit).

"Yes, my lady, he has told me why you asked to see me. I do apolo-gize for my appearance earlier. It will not happen again."

"I am glad to hear that. It is not appropriate to look so untidy in the kitchen. My lord, my husband, would not be pleased."

"I understand, my lady." Then, stammering: "It will not happen again."

"If it does, you will risk losing your job."

Her terrified eyes widened. "Please, my lady, please know that I will be very careful in the future." She rubbed her hands together nervously.

"In your favor, I do hear you are a hard worker."

"I like to think so, my lady." She looked relieved; her expression relaxed.

"And you like your job in the kitchen?"

"Yes. Though—" She paused, catching herself.

"Continue."

"I would like, one day, to work in the bakery."

"Ah. Why the bakery?"

"It pleases me to make bread. My bread is very fine, rich, and tasty. I would like my lady to try it one day."

"With pleasure. And if it is indeed so good—then, that is something I shall consider. Your working in the bakery, that is." I paused, fingering the long, braided sash of my robe. "I understand you know these lands well."

"I like to think so, my lady. My family has always lived here." She seemed a little more at ease.

"I have heard that you know the forest well—the eastern edge of the forest. The part frequented by few."

She looked puzzled at first, then slightly alarmed, as if she sensed the conversation was veering in a dangerous direction. She nodded warily, casting her eyes down.

"And I have also heard that you have seen a woman, a healer called Anthusis, who dwells in that part of the forest. Is that right?"

Moments passed before she answered with a barely audible "Yes."

"And it is a strange woman, I have been told—"

"A strange creature, I would say." She drew back, as if she had revealed too much.

"Go on—tell me what you have seen. And why you felt compelled to find out about this person."

"Oh, please, my lady, understand I meant no harm in this! I—" Her voice choked, and her face was contorted by tearfulness. "My father has been sick. He has a fearful shaking of the hands, he cannot control it, and I had heard that the healer had medicines to help. We have tried everything else. We prayed, we placed ex-votos in our church. Nothing has worked. God himself seems to have turned a blind eye," she lamented.

"So this need to see the healer, this was to help your father?"

She nodded.

"That is a good reason. You have no need whatsoever to be ashamed."

Relief flooded her face.

"I, too, have a family member I love and who needs help," I continued. "That is why I want to see this healer. But it is a secret, you understand, one that must remain between us."

She looked astonished. "My lady—"

"If you ever tell anyone about my questions, let me be clear that you will have no possibility of *ever* working in the bakery. What is more, you will lose your job here. Do you understand?"

She nodded vociferously. "Of course, my lady."

"Good. Now tell me everything you observed that day."

Sybilla repeated the details that Aiglantine had recounted about the area of the forest where Anthusis dwelled.

"What happened after you arrived?" I asked.

"At first, I saw her only from a distance. I hid behind the brambles for a long time, watching. Anthusis was carrying branches. She disappeared into her abode with these and then came back with a large copper pail in one hand. In her other hand were weird, tall blossoms, I do not know what kind. Then she went back into her dwelling."

"And then?"

"Soon after I saw someone approach. A woman in a dark cape. A noblewoman, by her dress. But I could not see her face."

"And that woman entered the dwelling?"

"After a moment, yes. She must have been known to Anthusis, for she did not come out for a good while."

"Continue—"

"I waited until the woman departed and the healer came out. I called to her. I told her I needed to see her, and that I had brought her bread I had baked myself." She paused, nervously twisting the edges of her apron.

"What was your first impression of her?"

"She looked like an old crone, like a hermit you would see in our parts. But then, when she approached, and fixed her eyes on me and began to speak, I was frightened. Those eyes, and her voice—" She shuddered and fell silent.

"What about them? Her voice and eyes?"

"They were strange and frightening. Like the picture of devilish creatures from my prayer book."

"What happened next?"

"I told her why I had come. My father, and his ailment. I told her I had nothing to pay her with, only the bread I baked. I expected her to turn me away. But she did not. She said it did not matter. That my bread would be enough, that she would give me potions for him to drink. She would make a poultice, which we should apply to his hands."

"And did she give you those things?"

"Yes. Yes, she did. She told me how to use them. 'Once you do, the shaking will stop,' she said, 'and he will begin to breathe more easily. But you must do as I say, very carefully.' I took the medicines back to my home and we used them. And we made the other remedies she had instructed us to brew."

"What other remedies?"

"The ground skin of a toad mixed with wine. A broth made of herbs and rabbit meat. We had Father drink them."

"And did these help him?"

She broke into a joyous smile. "Yes! Yes, they did. In a short time, my father's hands stopped shaking. And he began to breathe as he had before, easily. It seemed like—" She paused, preoccupied, as she searched for the right word. "A miracle."

Any hesitation I had harbored about seeking out Anthusis had vanished: it was only a question of when to see her, and how. I could not go alone, that much was certain. I required someone to accompany me, someone who would not gossip. It must be a man, for that sunless part of the forest was said to be perilous, with obscure paths frequented by very few, paths with thorny, even poisonous, vegetation and lurking boar. I could not place Gallien at risk by asking him; his position was already precarious enough. The stable boy Hugo, who had accompanied me and Aiglantine on other excursions, was certainly bribable, but I did not really trust him.

I called for Aiglantine and told her of my dilemma. "It must be someone"—I paused—"someone who will never speak of this to anyone. Most of all to Raoul, or Millicent."

"I can think of no one. Though—" She stopped, as if an idea had come to her. "There *is* a new boy who works in the laundry. He is strong and they say he is almost like an animal, so well does he know the forest. All the paths, the scents, the lairs of all the animals. And best of all"—she gave me a radiant smile—"he is a mute."

I looked at Aiglantine with renewed appreciation: here, once again, was an unexpected canniness and shrewdness. "A brilliant idea!" I exclaimed. "What is his name?"

"Corbus. They call him the Corbus the Simple."

"Is he so simple that he would not understand what I need of him?"

"He may be simple, but I think he will understand. In his own way, in his own language."

"That is heartening. And you are sure Raoul is still away?"

"Yes. For another week, they say."

"Good. Speak to Corbus when no one is watching. Tell him I want to see him. That I have a question about the forest."


I MET CORBUS THE FOLLOWING afternoon in a secluded place outside the laundry. He was of sturdy, medium build, with white-blond hair and ruddy cheeks. He was among the group of servants one never saw, for his work relegated him to the dark confines of the laundry. His clothes were tattered and his sandaled feet filthy, though it was obvious he had made an attempt to wash before seeing me, for he smelled of strong, acrid soap. He was heartrendingly pathetic, with all the trapped sadness of one whose tongue has been forever quelled. (To be con-

demned to voicelessness has always seemed to me the most infernal punishment God could mete out!)

"I know Aiglantine has explained to you that I have a question
about a place in the forest," I told him. "The eastern part."

He nodded, his watery blue eyes fixed to the ground.

"I understand you know the forest well. Very well, better than almost anyone else here."

He nodded again, this time with a hint of pridefulness.

"Good. I have asked you here because I need you to come with me
to a place in that part. I want to go there soon, in the next few days,
while the weather holds. There is someone who lives there, someone I
want to see. A healer." For the first time he glanced at me, and a gleam
of what I took to be recognition shone in his eyes. I wondered about
the mind within his silenced self, and if it was really as simple as people
assumed. The absence of a voice made it almost impossible to know, yet
there was an alertness about him, which made me think he had been un-
derestimated: that he had a subterranean intelligence, albeit of another
genus.

"I shall tell the head laundress that you are excused from work the
day you go with me," I continued. "I shall tell her I need you to help
me with something. She need not know the reason. And for this task, I
shall make sure you are well compensated, with extra food. With bread,
cheese, and special honey cakes for your family." He looked up for an
instant, his expression brightening. "Do you live with your family?" I
asked gently.

He gave a small, jerky nod.

"Then I shall make sure to give you plenty of food, enough for
everyone in your house." Suddenly, for the first time, he looked at me
directly; he gave me a grateful, touchingly childlike smile.

"Now I shall tell you what I have heard," I said, "and about the path
I have been told we should take."

THERE ARE MOMENTS IN LIFE when everything seems to augur well
for a journey or adventure: that week in November was among them.

Raoul was away. A messenger arrived, bearing a note from my husband, relaying the news that his return from La Rochelle would be delayed. Even the weather seemed to cooperate: it was unseasonably warm for November, as if God himself approved of my seeking out Anthusis.

It was only Millicent I had to reckon with; fortunately, she was gullible. I told her I was restless, that I yearned for fresh air and a long walk; that the midwives had told me that a walk in the meadows, by the edge of the forest, would be beneficial at this point in my pregnancy. "I wonder if this is the right moment for such exertion, my lady," she pleaded; but so convincing was I, and so determined, that she dared not contradict me.

I set off with Corbus shortly past daybreak two days after our first meeting. He carried a staff, a leather pouch with water, and a small bundle of food I had prepared. He could not read, of course, but he could make sense of a rudimentary map, which Sybilla had drawn for me on parchment, and for which I had compensated her handsomely, with sweetmeats and a silk ribbon.

A little way past the gatehouse, I turned to him and asked: "How many hours will it take for us to reach this place?"

He held two fingers.

"Two hours, then?"

He nodded.

"I am surprised it will not take more. Come, let us hurry."

Excitement and the idea of a goal had filled me with energy: for the first time in months, there was a lilt to my step, and everything about being outside, being free and far from the castle, seemed wondrous. I looked at the trees, the bushes, the acorns on the ground, as if I were seeing them for the first time.

Soon we entered the forest and veered to the right, along a path that was clear and sunlit at the outset but became increasingly rough and hard to navigate. We came to a place where a dense, leafy canopy of formidable trees loomed above us, obscuring the radiant morning light. Dead, torn branches randomly obstructed the path, as did errant logs and large, jagged stones. Yet Corbus did not hesitate as we proceeded: he strode with sure, faultless steps, as a deer or any stealthy forest creature might. His eyes remained fixed ahead and his demeanor was so confident that I, too, began to relax. All the while, during this long wordless walk, the forest itself teemed with its own vernacular of sounds—the cries of crickets, the sharp twangs of rooks, the hoots of owls. Even the crunching sounds of our footsteps seemed strangely magnified in this voiceless world.

We had walked about an hour when Corbus stopped suddenly and pointed far ahead in the landscape. I could hardly make out a distant outline, for it was enshrouded by mist. "But I cannot see anything there," I told him, struggling to glimpse what he clearly could.

He pointed again, urgently, a signal I now recognized as an admonishment: "Look closely, take heed." Indeed, we had come to a point in the journey where our positions were reversed: no longer the great lady issuing commands, I was subservient to him and to his strange, silent expertise. I had no choice but to trust him.

We continued to walk toward the distant goal he recognized and which I still could not. Here the path was almost completely hidden by fallen branches and pungent piles of leaves. Suddenly I smelled fire and burning charcoal: alarmed, I tapped his shoulder. He stopped, placing his finger on his lip, as if to say "be quiet." Then he pointed to smoke spiraling in the sky above distant trees.

"Ah, I see—" I murmured, though I did not really.

At this, he suddenly transformed himself into an old, contorted hunchback, like an actor in a pantomime imitating an ornery crone. What was he was trying to tell me? I struggled to understand. And then I realized: he was impersonating an old hermit, and he meant to convey that the fire came from a hermit's dwelling, and was nothing to fear.

We continued to walk, rather more slowly now; the light was scant and hazy with mist. I was becoming tired and edgy. "How much farther?" I asked once, then again, not much later.

He spread his fingers before him, as if to say, "You must be patient."

Soon after we came to a clearing in the middle of which stood a huge sycamore tree. There we paused, and he took out the map.

"Show me where we are," I said.

He pointed to a place quite close to where Sybilla had put an X.

"So we are not far then?"

His expression was maddeningly ambiguous: he took his staff and merely pointed ahead.

"Surely you can tell me how much longer we must walk?"

He shook his head.

I took a deep breath. "Well then, continue."

We had walked a little more than a quarter of an hour when the path, which had been relatively level, began to mount in steepness. In the distance, I could finally discern what he had spotted long before: a craggy hillside, most of it dense with brambles and thickets, other parts of rough-hewn rock.

"Is that where the healer dwells?" I asked, pointing in that direction.

He nodded in a manner that conveyed: "I told you I was familiar with the way. You had only to trust me."

He picked up the pace; I was almost breathless as I struggled to keep up. The hillside had seemed quite far away, yet only a short time later we were already approaching it. In the middle I glimpsed smoke rising, like a filmy white serpent edging into the sky.

I pointed to it. "Does the healer live there?"

He nodded.

The path, which had been treacherous and steep, now leveled out.

We continued to walk until we came to a copse of trees not far from the hillside itself. He bade me draw back so that we stood behind the trees, hiding from sight.

Suddenly, in the distance, we saw someone emerge from what appeared to be an opening in a crag: a woman in a flowing, wine-colored, hooded cape who carried a shining copper pail.

I clutched his arm and whispered: "That is she, is it not?"

He nodded, staring ahead.

I began to move forward quickly, but he pulled me back, forcibly, even roughly, as if to say: No, not now, you must wait for the right moment. We waited and watched. My heart pounded; any vestige of fatigue vanished.

Step by step, she came closer to us, so close that I feared she would spot us before Corbus deemed we were ready to emerge. I strained to catch sight of her face, but could not, for it was hidden by the ample folds of her hood. I could only glimpse her hands—one clutched at her throat, the other gripped the handle of the pail.

"Tell me when we can approach her," I whispered.

Once more he nodded, preoccupied, his eyes trained on the woman—if it was a woman—as she walked here and there with the pail, murmuring something to herself in a low, vibrant incantatory voice.

Suddenly she stood still, her face raised in the direction of the sun.

He grasped my arm and looked at me with an almost frightening intensity.

"Now?"

He took my arm, pulling me forward into the open.

# CHAPTER 20

I feared the eerie figure before us would be hostile; but to my surprise she was not. "You have returned," she said in a benevolent, precise voice, looking at Corbus. "I knew you would." The timbre was that of a woman younger than I had expected. Yet there was nothing about her demeanor that seemed young.

He remained impassive. I stood to his side, silent and fearful, yet excited, too, and afire with curiosity.

"Whom have you brought me?" she asked in that same measured, dignified tone as she nodded in my direction.

Corbus answered in a deft series of hand signals and gestures that seemed to convey in a few instants that I was a lady of high rank.

"Ah," she said, as if to appraise this and all its implications. "A lady. A noblewoman."

So august was she that I almost curtseyed before her; instead, rapt and silent, I merely nodded in acquiescence.

"What is your name?" she asked, drawing her cape more closely about her.

I hesitated to pronounce my name: indeed, it frightened me to do so. "No need for you to tell me," she said at once, her voice laced with condescension. "I already know your name." I looked down, discomfited by the realization that the question had only been meant as a test.

Then, brusquely, and in a much lower register, she commanded us: "Come."

We walked a little way to the steep hillside beyond. She stopped abruptly, pointing before her: "That is where I dwell."

I looked ahead intently, yet I could not see anything before us that resembled a dwelling. Tentacles of gnarled branches covered the place;

there did not appear to be an opening of any sort. I looked at Corbus for reassurance, but his eyes remained trained on her.

"You are thinking that there is nothing there," she observed, watching me. "Nothing ahead that resembles an abode. Is this true?" She almost looked amused.

I nodded sheepishly.

She faced me now in such a way that a ray of light caught her face. I started: it was gaunt, ghostly pale, a ravaged landscape of weathered skin and jutting bones. Never in my life had I seen a visage so wildly at variance with the clear, vibrant voice that issued from it—not at all the aged voice I had anticipated from Sybilla's description. I forced myself not to avert my eyes, for I sensed if I had, she would have despised me for it.

"That is good," she said, as if acknowledging the reining in of my revulsion. For the first time there was a hint of approval in her voice. "That is a first step."

"A first step, toward what end?" I asked, at last emerging from the speechlessness that hitherto had gripped me.

"It is up to you alone to decide what happens after the first step, and where it leads you. Surely you must know that."

"What is your name?"

"Now it is *you* who is asking what you already know," she told me with an ironic smile.

"I have been told your name is Anthusis."

"Of course."

We continued to walk until we reached the thicket she had indicated and which, from afar, had seemed quite impenetrable. Yet the next moment she drew the prickly branches apart easily, as if they were a veil of silk.

We stepped inside, into a low cave-like place with walls hewn of moth-colored rock. The serene, hospitable interior bore no resemblance to the wildness without. Even the scent here was disparate from that of the forest, for it was springlike and sweet. I looked about, taking deep breaths. To the left side stood a narrow bed covered with wheat-colored linen embroidered with a crimson border of interlaced ovals. To the other was a hearth with a glowing fire; before this, two rugged benches. The adjacent wall was hung with a multitude of iron cooking utensils arranged high, and in perfect order, from small to large. Below these, on shelves and on the ground, stood various copper pots polished to a dazzling luster.

In the right corner near the entrance stood more shelves, those on the bottom arrayed with transparent vessels in pale hues of blue, green, rose, and yellow; the top shelf held an array of elegant, shallow bowls carved of wood, stone, and clay, and, propped to one side, a number of large books. "You can read?" I asked, turning to her.

"That seems to surprise you." Her expression was unpleasant, scornful.

"I would have thought," I stammered, "because you—"

"Because I live in the forest, alone, that I am *ignorant?*" she scoffed.

"Not at all," I replied, though of course that had been my assumption. I collected myself, continued to look around, and took a few deep breaths of the rich, calming scent that infused the air. "It is lovely here," I said wondrously.

"That also seems to surprise you."

"It is true I did not expect it to be this way."

"So much the better, then."

I had been so absorbed that I had hardly paid any attention to Corbus: he remained by the entrance, standing there motionless and inscrutable, like a stone pillar. I bade him come closer.

"May we sit down?" I asked rather hesitantly, for I was suddenly a bit weary. "Is it permitted?"

"Yes," she said, gesturing to the bench. I sat down, hoping that Corbus would follow. But he shook his head and remained standing.

She turned from us, doffed her cape, and hung it on a hook by the bed. Now, uncloaked, she stood before me: a frail, thin creature in a long narrow tunic of deep green hemp, a thick twisted rope fastened about the waist with an intricate knot. Her tangled, thick hair was the color of straw, twisted and held up in back by a jagged wooden comb.

She was indeed remarkably ugly, but in the light of the cave her eyes had taken on a new brilliance: whereas previously they had seemed dim and careworn, they now shone a vivid, strangely youthful purply blue—the only alluring feature in an otherwise haggard face.

I took off my cape and placed it on the bench before I sat down.

"Tell me why you have come," she demanded.

"You knew my name. Then you must know the reason for my visit as well."

She settled on the bench opposite. "Ah—you expect too much of me, my dear," she said, with unexpected coyness.

"I doubt it."

"You are with child. Therein lies the reason, I suspect."

"You have guessed rightly."

"And this child is due in January," she pronounced with certitude.

"Yes," I replied, unsurprised, for I had expected her to divine this.

"You seem hearty and well. Therefore, what do you seek from me?"

"I want to know if it is a son I carry."

"To what purpose do you want to know this?"

"To prepare myself. For the comfort of knowing, that is all."

"I may be able to help you. But only if you are honest with me."

I felt my cheeks flush. "I assure you I am being honest."

She shook her head. "No, you are frightened. You fear that it may not be a son. It is *fear* that compels you here, in great part."

"Yes. That is true," I admitted. "It is for my husband's sake that I want to know the sex. He very much desires a son."

"I told you," she warned, glowering at me. "You must be honest with me."

"I do not understand," I murmured almost tearfully.

"Of course you do," she scoffed. "Else why would you avoid my eyes, and my question?" She leaned forward, closely. I felt the full scrutiny of her brilliant eyes as she intoned, "It is not only for your husband that you want to know. In part, yes. But it is really for yourself. You yourself do not really want a daughter, do you? Is that right?"

"Yes," I said, choking the word out.

"Tell me why you feel this. Expunge all guilt. It is useless here."

"A son would know the freedom I have not!" I cried.

"But he would also know dangers and challenges you have not known. That does not frighten you?"

"No," I said fiercely. "Better challenges and dangers than a stifled life. A life without adventure."

"Good. At last you are being forthcoming. That is the first step. Indeed, the first step toward knowledge of any kind." She paused, her eyes staring at the fire before she looked up at me again, with a searching look of the brilliant eyes: "If it is indeed knowledge you value."

"I do."

"I do not doubt that," she answered soothingly, her eyes fixed on mine.

"You told me that being honest was the first step. What is the second?"

"Come with me into the other room," she said with a shift in tone as she stood up; then, gesturing to Corbus: "The boy stays here."

I looked at Corbus imploringly, for I was suddenly quite frightened.

"The boy stays here," she repeated in such a way that I dared not challenge her.

I followed her to the back, which was curtained off with a panel of heavy red wool. She drew this away; I walked through into a low cave-like place.

Before us, to the left, was an elaborately carved bench covered with an ample red cushion. Opposite this stood a tall cabinet, the doors of which were loosely bound by a thick, twisted black cord with long, cha-otic silk tassels. Both doors were incised in bone: the intricate design, which I could barely make out, seemed to depict intertwined horned creatures. Nearby, against the wall, stood a small writing table appointed with a quill, a pot of ink, and pages of parchment, a manuscript per-haps; this was written in a language I did not understand, though I imagined it to be Greek.

"Sit down," she said, motioning to the bench.

She stood opposite, taking my chin in her hand as she examined my face, at one moment tracing a circle on each cheek.

"You are pale," she pronounced. "Your skin has little color."

"Is that important?" I asked anxiously.

"It is one element of many." She smiled inscrutably. "Now take off your dress, and your shift, so that I may see your bodice and your belly."

Her voice was gentle and reassuring, assuaging my terror. I unfastened my dress, hook by hook, until I sat in my undergarments.

"Your belly, first." She touched the left side, then the right, before she took a step back, still assessing me. "Your belly protrudes on the right."

"Tell me—"

"Let me finish," she interrupted. "Now your breasts." She gently touched the top of one breast, then the other. "They are both equally swollen," she pronounced.

"What does this mean?"

"Let me finish," she repeated harshly. "Now stand up. Walk to the curtain."

I did so as she watched. Then she said: "Now sit down."

"Tell me," I implored her, "what do you see? Is it a boy or a girl I carry?"

"There is a small chance it is a boy, but it is far from certain. Your belly protrudes on the right, which is a sign of a male. But your breasts are both the same size: if a male, the right would be larger. And you are pale, with little color in your skin. If you were carrying a boy, your complexion would be reddish."

"Why is that?"

"The nature of the male is hot, and this leads to good, warm blood, producing color in the skin."

"And so because I am pale," I said dejectedly, "you think it is most likely a girl?"

"I was inclined to think so. But then, when you stood and walked, you moved your *right* foot first. And that is a sign of a male."

"So you think it is most likely a boy?" I asked, elated.

"I cannot tell you for certain. After all, you have come to me too late," she added.

"Too late?" I repeated despairingly.

"Had you come to me much sooner, my ability to augur such things would have been far more accurate." She narrowed her eyes. "But you waited a long time to see me—out of *fear*, I assume." She had pronounced *fear* with contempt.

"Yes, that is true, I was afraid," I confessed.

"How foolish of you! Had you cast aside fear and sought my advice early," she continued, "I would have been in a better position to help you."

"But—"

"Let me finish. Had you come to me before the soul entered the baby's body, I might have had a chance to predict the sex more accurately. And had you been wise and brave enough to come to me *before* you conceived," she added in a disconcertingly silky voice, "I could have given you instructions and potions that would have influenced the sex."

"So there is nothing conclusive you can tell me now," I murmured with dismay.

"About *this* pregnancy—no." Then, as if something had just occurred to her, she commanded, "Give me your hands."

With one finger, she traced the pattern of the veins of each wrist, then those of each palm. "Hold your hands together in front of you, as if you were praying." As I did so, she studied the lengths of my fingers.

She raised her brow. "Ah—this is good—"

"Is it? What do you see?" I asked breathlessly.

"Your index fingers are long. You will not be unfruitful."

"That is heartening!" I exclaimed.

"Yes." She paused, ominously. "But on closer inspection, I also see death in the near future. A being of the female sex, someone dear to you, who dies."

"A child of mine? Pray, tell me this does not mean my child!"

She fixed her brilliant eyes upon me in that unnerving way, as if she were seeing, and yet not seeing me. "That is all I can tell you," she intoned.

I suddenly wished I had not come. Terror seized me; I wanted to leave at once. I began to dress, my shaking fingers frantically fastening each hook as she watched with infuriating serenity.

"You asked me for the truth," she remarked with maddening calm.

I did not answer.

"And now you only want to flee—"

"Yes!" I cried.

"Then go. Leave now. The boy will take you back."

I walked into the outer chamber, where Corbus waited. I gathered my cloak and told him as evenly as I could, "It is time for us to depart."

"Farewell," she said, watching as I hurriedly donned my cloak.

"Farewell."

I had only ventured past the threshold into the open when, suddenly flustered, I turned around to face her. "I have not paid you yet. Tell me what I owe you."

"In due time." She stood immobile, strands of ragged hair blowing across her face. "Now set off."

# CHAPTER 21

O h, Corbus," I cried, shortly after we left Anthusis. "I do not
know what to think, or who tells me the truth. If only you
could speak to me!"

At this he stopped abruptly. He began to gesture with his hands and
body; I strained to decipher what he wanted to tell me. "Be not afraid,"
he seemed to say. "Trust in her, trust in Anthusis."

"But can I really trust her? Are you certain?"

He nodded firmly.

I was suddenly exhausted and wanted only to return to the castle
as quickly as possible. I yearned for a warming fire and food, and to
speak with Aiglantine. We continued to walk, retracing the route we
had taken, though the journey back seemed infinitely longer. Each step
alternately echoed with the gravity of Anthusis's pronouncements, and
with my own growing sense of culpability and fear: that my husband
would discover I had lied, and that I had, without his consent, seen this
magical woman in the forest. This "witch," he would call her contemptuously.

As we approached Château Ravinour, I began to worry how I would
explain my long absence to Millicent. I took a deep breath, occasionally glancing at Corbus to seek reassurance. He stared straight ahead,
his staff making one thud, then another, on the wooden planks as we
crossed the moat. "What will I tell them, Corbus?" I asked him, in desperation. He stopped to face me, placing his fingers on both temples, as
if to say: "Think hard. Use your mind."

"You are right! I must invent something. I shall pretend."

We passed through the gatehouse—there, in the distance, I spotted
Aiglantine running toward us.

"My lady," she cried, approaching us, breathless. "I am relieved you are back!"

"I, too, am happy to be home."

We exchanged glances. "Millicent has been very worried," she said.

"That is not surprising. She is a worrier." I quickened my pace. "I shall go see her at once. You must come with me."

We began to walk toward the great hall. "Did you see the woman?" she asked.

"Yes."

"What did she say?"

"I shall explain later."

"Millicent is frantic. What will you tell her?"

"Leave it to me."

WHEN WE ENTERED MY BEDCHAMBER, Millicent leaped to her feet, so agitated that her hoop fell to the floor. "Oh, my lady, I have been so concerned about you!"

"Why, pray?" I took off my cape and tossed it on the bench. Brushing some loose strands of hair away, I smiled, looking at Millicent and then at Aiglantine, who stood next to her.

"You are so late, my lady!" Millicent continued. "We had no idea where you were. We feared you were lost, that something terrible had happened."

"Oh, Millicent," I said, feigning exasperation. "You really worry far too much. I had a lovely walk and feel so much better now, having had some fresh air and exercise. There was no need to worry, with Corbus by my side." I sighed contentedly, as one might in reflecting on a delightful memory. "Yes, it was a lovely day!"

"But my lady—you were gone for so very long." For the first time, there was a suggestion of suspicion in Millicent's voice. "Where did you go?"

"Far to the west. We found a lovely spot by a copse of beech trees. You cannot imagine how pretty it was, how peaceful! It was there we came upon a warren of rabbits. I would have thought they would have been frightened of us, but no, not at all. What a gift Corbus has with animals, like Gallien, but in a different way. We watched them for a long time, the mother with her babies, about five of them, all scampering about. They were looking for food. Corbus had brought some nuts and grains with him, and we fed the rabbits. Then a fawn approached us: he seemed to have lost his mother, and his front right leg was wounded. Corbus took some cloth and bound the leg, and I fed the deer with little bits of crusts." I paused, as if savoring the recollection of this idyllic scene. "Yes, it was a perfect afternoon, I feel quite restored!"

All the while, as I spun this tale, Aiglantine listened, her eyes widening in amazement.

"But you were away for so many hours," sputtered Millicent.

"Yes, I confess, we took more time than I had expected. But you know what they say about women who are with child—the mood changes from one moment to another! Suddenly I was full of vigor and only wanted to remain outside. I simply lost track of time." I stood by the fire, warming my hands, before turning to give her a cheery smile. "And now, I am back," I added exultantly, "and there is no need for your concern."

"I am so relieved, my lady."

"And I am glad I have put your mind at rest."

Aiglantine joined in: "Millicent has not eaten a bite all day, she has been so nervous."

"Oh, silly Millicent," I teased, taking her arm and chucking her under the chin. "All is well now. I am here safe and sound. I never meant to worry you so! Now, you must have something to eat," I said, addressing Millicent once more, before adding slyly, "I would give you a sip of wine, I think it would be good for you—"

She looked horrified at the suggestion. "No, no, my lady, I couldn't!"

"I knew you would say that," I said, chuckling. "But I thought I would try even so. I shall tell Wilbertus to prepare you something very hot and tasty, and very rich, to calm you." Then, in the commanding voice I used when I did not want to be questioned, I told her, "Now do go."

Aiglantine and I watched until Millicent walked through the door and was out of sight.

"What a story you invented!" marveled Aiglantine. "And how calmly you told it—"

"My brother always told me that when in doubt, or in great difficulty, you must invent. I only care that I fooled Millicent. Do you think I succeeded?"

She nodded, laughing. "Oh yes, without question."

"Good." I sat down, suddenly overcome by fatigue: the buoyancy of invention and my delight in duping Millicent had faded; I thought of Anthusis.

"Tell me what really happened," Aiglantine urged. "Did you meet the wisewoman?"

"Yes."

"What is she like? What did she tell you?"

"She said I had come too late for her to predict if it is a boy or a girl I carry. That I should have come earlier, before the soul had entered the body. She said the next time, before the next pregnancy, she would give me potions and tell me ways that would help to bring forth a son. I must come sooner."

"So it was too late?"

"Yes, this time, it was too late. *Too late.*" The last words resounded with a funereal echo.

"Are you glad you saw her?" Aiglantine asked.

"I do not know," I answered. "I cannot imagine *not* having taken the risk to see her, and yet—"

She looked at me searchingly. "And yet?"

"Yet there was no comfort in it. She seemed almost able to read my mind. She knew my name, though I never told her what it was."

"What else did she tell you?"

"'Expunge all guilt. It is useless here.'"

A few moments passed before Aiglantine asked, "Will you return to see her again?"

"Only if—" I paused, for everything in my mind still seemed in chaos. "I do not know." Then, longingly: "If only you had been able to come with me, Aiglantine!"

"But Corbus served you well. He got you there and back safely."

"Yes, I am indebted to him." I thought of how stalwart and confident Corbus had been on our journey. "They are wrong to call him Corbus the Simple. He is much more intelligent than people imagine."

"That is reassuring," she said, listening to this intently. "I often suspected it of him."

"He has a different *kind* of intelligence. He knows the forest and everything in it. The animals, their tracks, where to find water. There were times I was quite sure we were lost, but he knew how to follow the sun, the direction of the wind."

She smiled. "It sounds as if you made a new friend."

"Yes," I murmured, still gazing out; then, directly to her, in a clear, fervent voice: "But he could never be what you are to me! You are like the sister I always wished I had had."

Tears came to her eyes. "Oh, my lady—"

"Come," I said, clasping her hands in mine. "Let us be merry and celebrate our friendship!"

# CHAPTER 22

I hear you went away from the castle for a long time, a few days ago," said Gerard. It was evening; we were sitting before the fire in our chamber. He had returned that morning, two days after my journey to Anthusis.

"Yes, yes, I did take a walk," I replied with seeming lightheartedness as I tossed a few twigs into the hearth.

"Millicent was beside herself with worry, I am told," he said in a tense voice. I noticed a certain strain in the muscles by his temples, a sign that he was controlling anger.

"Who told you about this?" I asked.

"No matter who told me. The fact is you left the castle, which was in itself ill-advised, and you remained away for a long time."

"I longed for fresh air! I have been so constrained here, and I suddenly had a great burst of energy, and wanted only to take a walk."

"It was a foolish thing to do. It would have been foolish even if you had not been pregnant. But to do this while you are carrying our child! Your behavior shows a wanton disregard for prudence."

"Oh, but I did not go alone," I said. "Corbus, the young man who works in the laundry, came with me. Aiglantine had told me—" I paused, realizing I should not have brought Aiglantine into the discussion. "I was told he knew the environs well, the forest and the paths, and that he was a good sturdy sort. Indeed, he is a nice fellow—" I stopped, realizing I had chattered on in the way I sometimes did when nervous.

"Corbus? That simpleton, the mute?" He was incredulous. "What good would he be, in the forest, with you alone, if there were a difficulty?"

"I think you are underestimating him. He may not be able to speak, but he has—and this is what I discovered on the walk—his own sort of intelligence. His own language, you see."

He took a deep breath, stood up, and began to pace the room. "This is the second time that we have quarreled about your way of dealing with the servants," he said in a low, controlled voice. "First Aiglantine. Now Corbus. I begin to fear I have not made myself clear. You are *not* to consort with them. They are here to serve you, and that is all—"

"And is exactly what Corbus did! He served me well on this walk. We did not lose our way. And we returned safe and sound." My voice began to escalate in vehemence. "As for Millicent, I am fond of her, of course, but the truth is that everything frightens her. A sudden gust of wind outside. A mouse scurrying across the room sends her into fits. I cannot have my life ruled by her, I—"

"Who *does* rule your life, then?" he asked, his hands on my shoulders now, grasping them tight.

"*You* do, my lord," I said, bowing my head as I bit my lip.

"Do I? I wonder. There is much that goes on in your head that I do not understand." He took my chin and looked at me with grave intensity. "Sometimes I watch you, and I wonder what is really going through your mind. What you are thinking. You are so impressionable. And far too curious, sometimes, for your own good."

I felt a frisson of fear. "But curiosity, my lord, is not so dreadful a quality." My voice was now pleading, tremulous: "You yourself are no stranger to questions, and to questing."

"That is true. But I am a man."

A painful silence fell between us: for many moments I could not summon a word in response. I was startled and furious; my thoughts jolted here and there.

The sound of Gerard's voice wrenched me back to the present. "Even now, as I look at you," he said, beginning to pace once more, "I do not know what to make of your silence. What you are thinking. It is disconcerting to me to think you have another life."

"What other life?" I asked, the evenness of my voice masking my nervousness.

"A life apart, even if it is only in your mind."

"But surely no harm can come of *thoughts*—"

"Thoughts can have their own puissance," he replied, his expression darkening.

# CHAPTER 23

After Gerard had left the chamber, I felt alone, quite alone, my hands anxiously caressing my belly, as if seeking succor from the creature within me. Every so often I glanced at the door and its griffin handle, half-expecting, or hoping, rather, that Aiglantine or Millicent would enter. But no one did. Even the lively being within me seemed, for once, utterly still—as if, in having heard the conversation moments before, its spirit had been quelled.

"Thoughts have their own puissance," he had told me. If only it were solely my thoughts where I had trespassed, but it had also been in my actions! The objects I had traded, collected, and hidden; the journey to Anthusis; my deepening friendship with Aiglantine, all were tinged with the forbidden. I thought of these things again and again with mounting fear. If he should discover them, what would happen? Each was evidence of a furtive life.

Since childhood I had been no stranger to the clandestine: the secret hunts for buried objects, the codes devised with my brother, and, in a different way, the stories and histories recited to me by my grandfather. Suddenly I thought of my grandfather with an almost overpowering longing: the afternoons I shared with him in his library—his manuscripts with their gleaming letters, his ring carved with the profile of the Roman emperor. Had he said to me "Thoughts have their own puissance" those words would have been a heartening pronouncement, a dictum to cherish. Yet the same sentence uttered by my husband was redolent with disapproval, even menace. Gerard had meant it as a warning, as if my innermost thoughts were sins only waiting to be discovered.

THE FOLLOWING DAY WAS THE beginning of the Christmas season. On that day, a messenger from my family arrived, not the florid, extravagantly dressed creature sent by the Hauteclare household, but a weary young man with patched clothes on an aged, panting mount whose fetlocks were caked with mud. He carried a letter that I assumed was from my brother Arnaut. So great was my excitement that I had run to the courtyard to greet the messenger myself, and in my eagerness almost ripped the parchment from the man's hands.

To my disappointment, the letter was not from Arnaut, but from Guy. It read:

*To Isabelle, Lady de Meurtaigne, greetings from her brother Guy.*

I send you sad tidings that our mother passed from this world yesterday and will be buried with all holy rites this week. Her illness came upon her suddenly and progressed with such speed that there was no use in summoning you to come. At the onset, we were told that the disease was fatal: an affliction of the heart which stifled her breath and her will to live. She was bled and given all requisite herbs and remedies while we, her family, watched in agony as she suffered. Finally she was at peace, having relinquished herself unto the arms of our Lord. Take comfort in knowing that our family, including Amélie and her family, surrounded our mother as she drew her last breath.

She passed the final two days in a delirium, at several moments rallying herself to speak. At one such time, she asked to be remembered to you, for she knew that she would never see you again. She made me swear that I, Guy, would relay to you her blessings and her final words of advice. She asked that I transcribe these and that, upon her death, I convey them. This I do now, in respectful memory of our cherished mother.

"To Isabelle, my youngest daughter, before God takes me from this earth, my last words and counsel. Be mindful of your marriage, and grateful for everything your husband has given you. Without him, your life would have taken a different turn. We had not the means, nor you the prospects, to provide what you enjoy now. May you bring your husband sons and make him proud. May motherhood subdue the rebellious character which, in your childhood, caused us such anguish: prepare to make, as I did, the sacrifices necessary to be a worthy mother. Let the spirit of the martyr Saint Ursula guide you, dear daughter: hold close the medal with her image that I gave you upon your leave taking, and when you touch it, think of me and everything I taught you."

Father has been much affected by her death and is so overwhelmed with sorrow that he has asked me, the eldest, to impart this message to you. . . . .

The letter continued with details describing the funeral and burial, all of which I read quickly, even carelessly, for my mind surged with too much tumult and pain to focus on such things. It was not the loss of my mother that affected me, for I had never felt any love from her: if anything, her death came almost as a relief. I had long ago given away the cheerless keepsake, the medal of Saint Ursula, which had been her parting gift. No, what pained me most was the realization that my mother had not left this earth without hurling a wounding coda. Over and over again I read that single paragraph, mindful of its punitive implications (and wondering, as well, whether Guy had taken some delight in transcribing it). What she had really meant to say was this:

Be grateful for your marriage, for no one else would have wanted you. Now you are fortunate to have the means I never did, though you are hardly deserving of it: throughout your girlhood you caused us only suffering by your obstinance and willfulness. It is only by bringing your husband sons that you will make him and us proud: since I never valued girls, nor should you. Yet in motherhood I do not wish you joy: I wish that it wear you down as it did me, both in body and spirit, and that it exact from you the sacrifices that I was forced to make for my children. Think not on those wicked women you admired as a girl, but of Saint Ursula, the martyr, whose face is stamped on the medal I gave you as you left our home, and who should serve both as an exemplar to you, and a reminder of me and the successful marriage which, in my wisdom and charity, I arranged for you.

I turned in the direction of the great hall, longing only to go inside, mount the stairs, and escape into the privacy of my chamber. Suddenly I stopped abruptly: the augury of Anthusis! She had foretold the imminent death of a female close to me, and now, this news about my mother—

Her prediction, then, had come true! Anthusis was not a charlatan: she was indeed clairvoyant. The realization heartened me, for it confirmed I had been right in risking the journey to meet her. I took a deep breath and continued with buoyant steps to my chamber, my spirits and energy revived. Most of all I was relieved that it was my mother who had died, not the child within me.

WHAT WE CALLED "THE BLOOD month" of November passed: the sunless season when the animals were slaughtered, the time when everything in the environs of the castle—its fields, trees, and creatures— succumbed to slumber.

My mind, though, was not at rest. My relations with my husband had seemingly resumed a certain normalcy, yet I sensed, nervously, that something profound had shifted. I felt guarded, careful of each word and action, and increasingly suspicious of many around me. Who had told my husband about my journey to Anthusis? Millicent, with her seemingly guileless eyes? Had Ragnar heard about it, and told his master, out of spite? It could not have been Raoul, for he had been away during that time. . . . For days these suspicions preoccupied me and made me look at everyone around me, save for Aiglantine and Corbus, in a new light.

I yearned for company, for comfort. I thought of Fastrada: I wondered if I should ever see her again. I thought of our talks before the hearth—their warmth and merriment, her distinctive voice and witty sallies, her descriptions of Troyes and her thoughtful questions. Most of all I remembered how comforting it had been to have her companionship.

I longed, achingly, for my brother and grandfather as well. One morning, when rain mixed with snow fell in murky sheets outside, I picked up the casket that Arnaut had given me as a remembrance—the small casket of walnut, carved with our family shield and the motto "Courage above all else."

I ran my finger across the words of the motto and opened the box. Inside I kept Arnaut's last letter, along with several other keepsakes—my little doll of olive wood, a shell from my grandfather's pilgrimage to Santiago de Compostela, and a few small stones from my family's land. I held the smooth oval stones in my palm, thinking of all I had left behind that morning eleven months before.

How distant that moment and my girlhood now seemed! In a month, God willing, I would be a mother. If a son, my husband would have an heir at last, a boy to be named after him. If a daughter, the only solace for my husband would rest in her name: she would be called Editha, as a tribute to his late mother. I had long dreamed of another name for a daughter—Eleanor, after the queen. But I knew this was never to be: custom dictated that a girl, especially the first girl, be given a family name.

I walked to the window and looked out, a stone from my family's land still pressed in my palm.

THE SEASON OF ADVENT ARRIVED: the frosty, darkening weeks of December which slowly unfurled before us. For days, my husband and his companions hunted for wild boar, returning to the castle exhausted and triumphant with bloody, dismembered trophies trailing. Trees were felled, and huge logs dragged in to be kept alight during the twelve days between Christmas and Epiphany.

Unaccustomed to festal preparations of such opulence and magnitude, I watched with wonder and growing excitement. At my family's manor, the holiday had always been a humble celebration with scattered evergreen branches, roast goose, and pies flavored very sparingly with the costly spices of the Three Magi—cinnamon, clove, and nutmeg. Not so at Ravinour. My husband, never content with the ordinary, incorporated customs he had seen on his travels and others from royal Plantagenet circles into the festivities at our castle. Once, while traveling in Germany, he had seen great trees brought inside and decorated with apples, and stars cut out from parchment; thus he ordered huge pines to be decked with apples and silvered parchment and placed at each corner of the great hall. In the Holy Land, he had tasted confections made of an almond paste called *marzipan* and which, in expert hands, could be crafted into fanciful colored forms. Our confectioner was instructed to learn this technique and produced a wondrous *marzipan* Nativity scene, which was placed on a table by the entrance of the hall.

On the day before Christmas, when Gerard and I ventured into the kitchen to check the preparations for the feast, I was startled to see a gilded calf's head, its eyes studded with cherries, on a gleaming silver tray.

"I have never seen such a thing!" I exclaimed to him.

"A new delicacy which, I am told, is served at Young King Henry's court," he said with a proud smile. "Why should we not have such a dish, too?" He took my hands in his and kissed them. "All this is for you, my beloved, for our first Christmas together."

LATER THAT EVENING, BEFORE THE blazing yule log in the great hall, Gerard and I exchanged presents.

I gave Gerard a silk cushion with the embroidered cover I had been working on for months, with its design of angels and his crest. His gift to me was a wide silver girdle embedded with large agates which, according to tradition, would keep me safe in the time leading up to, and through, childbirth.

"Come," he said, drawing me close, "let me put it on you now." He fastened the girdle, then stood back to study the effect. "It is perfect. It suits you."

"Does it?" I asked, looking down and fingering the agates. Then, teasingly: "I thought you did not believe in such things. In magic. Or in talismans to ward against illness and evil—"

"But *you* do, my dove. And that is what is important, is it not?"

He kissed the top of my head and handed me a package tied with a braided silk ribbon stamped with an unfamiliar seal.

"What is this?" I asked.

"Open it."

It was a volume of poems from Fastrada—the very book I had longed for Gerard to bring to me months ago. The soft leather cover was exquisite, with my initials tooled in gold; within it was a blue silk place marker embroidered with my initials. The book was accompanied by this message from Fastrada:

"To Isabelle, Countess de Meurtaigne, loving wishes at Christmastime. We think of you with great affection and know that not long after this holiday, you will be a mother. May God bless you in all ways, and may you spend this first Christmas as a married woman in a state of joy and peace."

I touched the elaborate seal, with her swirling insignia, and reread her words several times before turning to Gerard: "I only wish I had thought to send a present to Fastrada!"

"Write to her after our son is born."


CHRISTMAS EVE: MIDNIGHT MASS IN our chapel. How vividly I recall that night—the moving, plangent cadence of the hymns, the banks of burning red candles, the inebriating smell of incense. Gerard and I stood together in the first pew: I in deep green velvet embroidered in gold, he in a silk waistcoat the color of garnet, with Sagesse, a particularly docile falcon, perched on his gloved wrist. Even the hood of the hawk had been carefully chosen for that night: crafted of bright red leather, it was crisscrossed with gold braid and topped with a cross of rock crystal.

Christmas Day dawned clear but damp, presaging snow. Inside the great hall that afternoon, however, all was warm and fragrant. The head table was draped in creamy linen and covered with garlands of evergreens, and the towering pine trees at each corner transformed the vast chamber into a fairyland.

Gerard had spared no expense for this feast. Ample cellars brimming with salt and pepper anointed the tables. He had pressed Wilbertus and his helpers to create their most elaborate concoctions. One immense table groaned with platters of roast goose, swan, stork, and peacock; in the center stood the gilded calf's head, looking almost disdainful of its neighbors. Another table was arrayed with a multitude of nut-studded breads, another with wobbling puddings dense with currants, and with cakes scented with saffron and cinnamon.

Throngs of guests began to enter—tenants, lesser lords of the region, and, lastly, the peasants who worked the major parcels of land. Many paused at the threshold to gaze in amazement; others stood before the crèche made of *marzipan*, marveling at its artistry, while still others gazed at the huge pines with their sparkling stars or warmed themselves before the blazing Yule logs. Bands of musicians roamed, for the solemn chants of Christmas Eve were now supplanted by the gaiety of carols and their merry vernacular of sounds: the beat of tambourines, the exuberant calls of horns, the lively strumming of lutes.

SNOW BEGAN TO FALL LATE Christmas Day, when everyone, sated and half delirious with wine and ale, had drifted into a festive stupor. Outside, all that had been gray and wizened turned ghostly white.

As the snow thickened and darkness fell, small bands of people began to pass through the gates into the courtyard. Gerard had told me it was the custom to keep the castle gates open for travelers, pilgrims, and needy laborers, all of whom were welcome to take refuge with us at the castle during Christmastime.

That night, at the very end of dinner, Gerard took me aside as our guests continued to revel.

"I know it is a nuisance," he told me, taking my arm, "but it is our custom on Christmas night that the lord or lady of the house makes the rounds of the visitors. Those to whom we have given shelter. It would please me that you do it. You need not spend too much time with them," he added, "just enough to make them think they are included in the celebration and treated with some consideration." He sipped some wine and brushed a few wayward strands of my hair back into place.

"I am happy to do this," I replied. "It is not a bother at all."

"Good. I shall call Raoul. He and a few pages will accompany you with some food and ale."

SOON AFTERWARD, I LEFT THE great hall and ventured into the dim outer corridor, where small groups of strangers huddled by low make-shift fires. The air was dense with smoke, and redolent of sweat, straw, and dung. Raoul hovered near me with a basket of food, while two pages carried pitchers of ale and wooden tumblers.

Slowly, and at first rather tentatively, I approached one group, then another. Most were very poor, in mean tattered clothes caked with ice and mud. Their voices hushed as I approached: some seemed fright-ened, others simply gaped at my velvet dress and jewels. A young woman about my age, nursing a baby, looked up at me with an expression of awe, fear, and curiosity as I greeted her and offered a spiced cake. As I continued to make the rounds, I became more at ease, and ventured to say more than merely "I wish you joy at Christmas," particularly to the travelers and pilgrims, for they interested me the most. I asked some how long they had been traveling; others about their homes and the family members they had left behind; still others about their destinations—Spain, it seemed, or Rome.

The neediest visitors seemed to have settled in the outer corridor by the great hall. One family—a father and mother with three young daughters—seemed particularly animated, though they looked so ill nourished, and the mother's face was so careworn and lined, that I won-dered how they could be so merry. The eldest two girls played a game of sticks and stones; the youngest, whose elfin face was smudged with soot, watched them, a doll made of twigs and rags clutched in one fist.

I stopped before them, offering sweet cakes, bread, and slices of pork, which they accepted with touching gratitude. I watched how tenderly the mother and father divided the food among the girls, making sure the children had the choicest morsels.

"How pretty your daughters are!" I said to the father, watching as the girls devoured the food.

"Yes, the fairest I know of. I am blessed to have such girls," he replied proudly.

"So you are indeed," I murmured.

"And you, my lady?" he ventured. "When is your baby due?"

"In a month or so."

"We wish you Godspeed," said his wife, shyly.

The youngest daughter stood up, cake in hand, and approached me; extending her other hand, she tried to touch the jeweled girdle around my hips.

"No, no! You mustn't!" admonished her mother, pulling her away from me.

I laughed and beckoned the little girl to come near. "It is quite all right, and if you would like, you may touch the stones. And may they bless you and your family, as they are meant to bless me."

The child did so, very gingerly, running her finger over one stone, then another. Then, giggling, she proudly joined her sisters who had been watching, astonished by her bravery.

"We must continue on our way, my lady," Raoul prodded me, for he and the page waited by my side.

I reluctantly bade the family goodbye, waving to the little girl, who watched me as she clutched her mother's skirt.

We walked to the far end of the corridor, which was almost, but not quite, immersed in darkness. A small group huddled together, including a figure draped in the color of deepest wine. "I wish you joy at Christmas," I said as the page passed the pitcher of ale, and Raoul the basket with food. One by one they drank until the last draped figure turned toward me: in that instant I caught a flash of piercing blue eyes amid a pale, haggard face: Anthusis! Frightened and stunned, I looked away.

The next instant, having regained my composure, I turned around—
only to find that the figure had vanished.

"We have finished, my lady," I heard Raoul say.

"Thank you for your help," I replied distractedly. "You may go.
Enjoy the rest of Christmas night."

He bowed. "Thank you, my lady. First I must see if my lord requires anything else from me." He and the pages left while I lingered for
a few moments before walking pensively back to the hall.

A tall, elegant figure stood within the archway: Gerard awaited me.
"You took a great deal of time," he observed. "Surely it should not have
taken so long to distribute a bit of food and drink."

"There were many people. And they were hungry."

"Of that I have no doubt." His gaze took on a certain remove. "But
it was not your place to converse with them at length. Certainly not to
let them touch you."

So Raoul had reported my words and actions to him, I realized
angrily, my cheeks burning with indignation.

"I did not want to offend the people by rushing," I replied carefully. "I did not think that would serve your name well. Or your reputation."

He smiled, as if heartened by my good judgment.

# CHAPTER 24

S hortly after Epiphany the birthing room was readied for my confinement. It lay in an upper wing on the eastern side of the castle
far from our own chamber. It was the custom of the household, I
was told, that the mother-to-be enter it only when confinement began. I
had found excuses to wander near it during the preceding weeks, watching as servants silently entered and exited, all under the scrupulous eye
of Raoul. Some carried pillows, others comforters, still others pitchers,
bowls, bundles of fresh rush, firewood and kindling.

"When will I be able to see the room?" I asked Millicent one snowy
afternoon in early January. We sat together in my chamber: she with
her sewing, I with the book of poems from Fastrada open on my lap,
though I was far too restless to concentrate on them.

"My lord wants everything to be in perfect order before you see it.
You must be patient, my lady." She gave me an almost maddening smile
of complacency.

"What will the room be like? Tell me!" I implored.

"Oh, you will be most comfortable, my lady," she assured me. "Of
course, the room must be kept very warm for you, and the fires stoked.
All the shutters will be closed, and the windows inside will be covered
with curtains, too. Everything inside will be covered—"

"Why must the windows inside be covered?" I interrupted, for this
seemed rather gloomy.

"To protect against evil spirits entering, and the devil himself!" She
announced this matter-of-factly, with a crisp smile and an air of disconcerting detachment.

"And this room," I asked in a tentative voice, "is it the same room
where the late Lady de Meurtaigne gave birth?"

Her brow furrowed as she looked down with exaggerated concentration at her sewing. "No," she replied slowly, avoiding my eyes. "It is not. That birth took place in another room, at the end of the corridor to the north. A room that is no longer used."

"The room at the end of the hall?" I had walked past this room many times, wondering why it was closed off. Its massive door was crisscrossed with strips of iron, and a lock, on a weighty chain, was suspended from the handle.

"Yes, that was the room," Millicent acknowledged; her pursed lips and stony expression did not invite me to probe further. I began to leaf through the poems but was too preoccupied to savor the verses: I was imagining the unhappy memories the chamber must hold for my husband.

At my family's manor, there had been no birthing chamber: babies were born in my parents' bedchamber. After the death of the last infant, who would have been my younger brother, that place had become forever imbued with the frightful memory of my mother's screams and the bushel of blood-drenched rags lugged away by Hortense, who had been told to burn them.

Trying to banish these thoughts, I turned once more to Millicent. "Who will attend me?"

"I will be there, of course," she announced proudly. "And you will have two midwives, the very best in the region. Lord de Meurtaigne has seen to that."

"And Aiglantine? Surely she will be with me, too?"

Her eyes narrowed a bit. "Oh, no, my lady!" She shook her head. "That is not Aiglantine's place. She is young and does not have the experience—"

"But I am told she herself had a child!" I blurted out.

"Yes," she replied warily, "or so they say. A baby who died. But that does not give her experience in attending at births. That is not her role in our household. That is *my* responsibility, and the work of the midwives, my lady. Lord de Meurtaigne has chosen your midwives with great care. He wants you to be comfortable." She looked up at me, announcing matter-of-factly: "Though scripture tells us that it is women's lot to suffer. It is part of our penance as women, for our role in creating sin. We are the descendants of Eve, after all."

The door swung open suddenly: Gerard entered. I knew at once from his strident steps and glowering expression that he was angry, though I had no idea why. Millicent stood up, flustered, her sewing tumbling to the floor. "My lord," she murmured, curtseying.

"What is this nonsense you are telling my wife?" His voice was furious, the deep harsh voice he used when he was crossed, or when he reprimanded servants. "You were saying that it is women's lot to suffer in childbirth, because of Eve and original sin?"

Her cheeks flushed and she stammered something unintelligible in response.

"Let me make this clear. I want my wife to suffer as little as possible. I have seen to that. I have asked the midwives for herbs and medicines to ease the pain."

"My lord," stammered Millicent, "please forgive me. I only told my lady what I have been taught."

"What you have been taught is nonsense. I do not want to hear such foolishness again. Now leave us."

She gathered her things and scurried out, her head bent and her sewing clutched in her hands.

"I do not think I have ever seen Millicent so frightened," I remarked in wonder, once she had left.

"I suspect that delights you!"

"I must confess it does," I replied, barely able to suppress my merriment.

"Come," he beckoned. He took me in his arms, holding me close, very close, so that I caught the scent of his skin, his hair, his leather vest. "Now it is time to forget the meddling Millicent and her ignorant notions. It is time for us to be together." He paused, gently kissing my eyelids and cheeks.

"I do not want you to be frightened, my darling," he told me with a new and passionate urgency, drawing me even more closely. He held me tightly now, so tightly that I could hardly breathe; my belly was pressed hard against him.

The baby moved, startling us both with a flurry of kicks. "There! Feel our child!" I cried.

"Our son."

"But if it is not a son?" I asked tremulously.

He placed his finger on my lips and murmured, "Do not think of that, my love. All will be well." He ran his hand across my belly tenderly, and kissed me slowly and purposefully, from forehead to lips. "It is only natural that you be anxious. I want you to know that I will do everything so that you suffer as little as possible. I have instructed the midwives myself. They will know what to do, they will have medicines—"

At that I thought of Anthusis and her cabinet with potions: how foolhardy I had been to surreptitiously seek her out, and then to have lied to him about it! I began to kiss him, kisses made all the more impassioned by guilt.

"You will want for nothing," he told me between caresses. "Whatever you desire to make you comfortable. Whatever you need from me. You have only to tell me, my dove." He had never spoken to me thus, with such tender concern and understanding; I felt a surge of love for him. It was as if, in that instant, that part of me I had kept protected from him, that part which had at times been wounded by him, now dissolved and flooded into an even deeper love. Dusk had fallen, and with it came a deep, grave silence, shattered only by the periodic howling of wolves. My head lay on his shoulder while he stroked my hair: I felt his breaths, and his heartbeat as he kissed my forehead and cheeks.

"There *is* something that would help me through this," I finally confessed.

"Tell me what it is. Anything."

"Allow Aiglantine to stay with me in the birthing room."

I felt his embrace slacken.

"Millicent told me Aiglantine would not be permitted to stay with me," I continued quickly, my hands pressed upon his shoulders. I searched his eyes, as if trying to will them back to their former warmth, for their sudden distance unnerved me. "But if I find it comforting to have Aiglantine with me, surely you will allow this, my darling? Oh do, please, I beg you. Having her with me would mean so much! I would rather have her with me than Millicent—" I stopped abruptly, my cheeks flushing.

He looked down, to the side, his mouth tensed. "A servant of Aiglantine's rank is never permitted in the birthing room," he told me firmly, though not harshly. "You must know that."

"I do know, that is what Millicent told me. But surely, just as you once said, you and I must make our own rules, do we not?"

He gave a wry smile, as if he were surprised, perhaps even rueful, that I should recall his own dictum. "I do not understand why you would find Aiglantine such a comfort."

"She is gentle and warm. And I have heard she had a child herself." I said no more, not daring to add what I really felt—that Aiglantine had become a friend, almost a sister to me.

"Hers was a child born of transgression. A child born in sin. That is very different."

"Yes, I know that. But still you permit her to work here, despite that transgression. And you are right to do so, to take pity on her, as a good Christian would."

"Even so, she belongs to another sphere."

"I know that—"

He took my hands, kissing them almost absentmindedly before he allowed: "But Millicent must stay with you as well—"

"Yes, of course," I conceded, delighted at my victory.

"Very well." He smiled indulgently. "I shall tell Millicent that Aiglantine may stay with you."

"Thank you, my darling! I am so relieved and grateful!" I kissed him again and again, fervently until he murmured, "Never could I have imagined—"

"What, my lord?"

"That Aiglantine would mean so much to you."

I looked down, nodding. "She does. I have sometimes felt very much alone here."

"Of course. You are young, and far from your family and home. I should have realized that. I should have known." He grasped my hands in his, his deep blue eyes scanning my face. "I never want you to be afraid," he said. "And I shall do anything, anything at all, to assuage your pain."

# CHAPTER 25

I moved into the birthing room several days later. The baby had begun to press down hard: a constant pressure, aching and urgent, deep within me.

For a long time, haunted by the memory of my mother's ordeals, I had dreaded seeing the birthing chamber. To my relief, it was utterly unlike my gloomy imaginings—a luxurious, even cossetting, place. The walls were covered in sinuous hangings, and its windows cloaked in brilliant silk panels, which shone like gems when the winter light filtered through. Against the long wall stood an ample bed with fine sheets, a high soft mattress, and a multitude of cushions. To its side loomed a tall cabinet arrayed with precious objects and vessels in gold, silver, and agate.

"Everything to delight your eye while you wait for our child," my husband had said when he ushered me into the room the first time. Two midwives awaited us there and were introduced: the elder a tall, handsome woman with lustrous black hair and a deeply lined face, whose every gesture radiated capability; and a much younger, rather heavyset woman, who seemed very shy.

IT WILL NOT BE LONG now," Aiglantine told me the next morning as she and Millicent helped me dress.

"You must take communion tomorrow, my lady," Millicent added as she began to braid my hair. "Best you be in a state of grace"—she paused portentously—"should there be any need."

"Of course," I replied, exchanging an anxious glance with Aiglantine.

"Have no fear, my lady," Aiglantine added reassuringly. "God will protect you, I am certain."

After the chastisement by my husband, Millicent seemed inordinately anxious to follow his dictates. She now professed nothing but approval for the medicines that were meant to calm me and placate pain. "Imagine, my lady," she said to me shortly after the confinement began, "the midwives are very learned. How *wise* Lord de Meurtaigne was to engage them!"

She had also accepted Aiglantine's presence in the birthing room, though she was quick to assign her the lowliest tasks—stoking the fires and sweeping the hearth.

Ensconced in this universe of women—Millicent, Aiglantine, and the two midwives—I waited and waited, chafing against isolation and longing to see my husband. At the beginning of my confinement, I asked incessantly for Gerard, only to be met with the same refrains: "This is not the place for men, my lady," or "It is not the custom of the household that men enter the birthing room during confinement." Twice I entreated Aiglantine to pass him a message from me: I missed him terribly, I wrote, and I missed his strength and support. Once, but only once, he sent a message in return which said:

"Fear not, my darling. Be strong for us and for our child."

I do not mean to imply that the midwives were at all unkindly. Quite to the contrary: they were gentle, quietly authoritative souls who told me with no little pride that they were familiar with the teachings of the famous Trotula, the healer and physician from Salerno. Thus several times a day, according to the Salernitan precepts, they anointed my forehead with mint, or rubbed my belly with a soothing elixir of olive oil and violets; occasionally they had me sip a potion of mugwort and rosemary meant to promote labor pains. All the while my back ached, and I felt at once exhausted and enormously restless, a strange creature bedecked in coral necklaces—talismans which, I was told, would help ensure a healthy birth.

A WEEK LATER, IN THE middle of the night, my body expelled a flood of warm, foreign fluid. "The time has come, my lady," said the elder midwife taking my hand as I struggled to my feet. She gestured to the younger midwife as she pointed above the bed: "Untie it now," she directed. The wide leather strap, fixed to the ceiling, was unfurled, so that I could, when the time came, hold it tight and brace myself against pain.

"But first you must walk about a bit," said the elder midwife, after helping me into a fresh shift. "This will encourage the labor pains to come, my lady." One hand on my belly, the other on my lower back, I walked from one end of the chamber to the other, all the while watching the other midwife as she solemnly mixed herbs and water in a bowl of black onyx, which, I was told, imparted soothing qualities to anything within it.

At last I lay down, for the pains had intensified and quickened; I tossed and turned, moaning and convulsed by pain.

"Open the cupboard and all its doors," commanded the elder midwife to Millicent as I heard the younger join in, "Yes, it is time, open them all, this will help the womb to open, my lady!"

"Do not leave me!" I begged Aiglantine as the cupboard doors were flung open. She took a seat on the bench by the bed and held my hand for a few moments before she mopped my brow. Millicent stood nearby, clutching her rosary beads.

"I want my husband!" I cried as another surge of pain overcame me.

"He cannot be here now, my lady," said the older midwife gently, but firmly. "This is not the place for men now. You will see him by and by." She then turned to Millicent: "Go and tell Lord de Meurtaigne that the labor has begun. We will let him know the moment the child is born."

What seized me afterward was pain so searing and obliterating that it seemed to transform me into an animal, with an animal's cries, grunts, and savage gestures. Morning passed in a delirium of pain; then the afternoon; then night.

At last, the midwives urged me to push, and push, and push again as I alternately held tight to them, or to the leather strap.

Finally, in the early hours of the morning, the baby slithered out so easily that it seemed inconceivable such anguish could have preceded its arrival. Suddenly, before me, was a tiny being with silken skin, bright startled eyes, long lashes, tufts of dark hair.

"It is a girl," said the midwife.

They washed her tongue with warm water—"So that she will speak properly"—and then anointed it with honey, "to give her appetite."

I begged them to let me hold the baby before she was swaddled.

"You may, but only for a moment, my lady," said the elder midwife. "The baby must be wrapped tight, to protect her."

Reluctantly I handed her back.

"My husband," I murmured, looking to one side as Aiglantine took my hand. "My husband—"

"You have done well, my lady. You are strong. The baby is very fair, a lovely baby girl, and of a good size and weight."

"But it is a girl," I murmured. "A girl. I promised him a son. It was to have been a son. What he will think?"

She took my hand and stroked it. "Have no fear. My lord will understand. Most of all he will be happy you are well, both you and the baby."

"Where is he?" I sat up, wiping my moist brow with the sheet. "Why is he not yet here?"

"Millicent has gone to fetch him, my lady. He will be here soon. Come, let me comb your hair."

She began to comb my hair, which was tangled from sweat. "What day is it?" I asked.

"It is the eighteenth of January, my lady."

"And the baby, where is my baby now?"

"She is sleeping soundly, my lady, in the cradle. Do not fret, she is right here, near you."

Moments later, Gerard arrived. The women curtseyed one by one as he walked slowly toward the bed—a composed, commanding figure who seemed strikingly at odds with this realm of pain and chaos.

"We have a daughter," I told him softly.

"Yes, Millicent has informed me," he said in a measured tone. He kissed my forehead and stroked my cheek.

"Bring us the baby," I told the midwife.

She did so. As she placed the baby in my arms, I felt a thrill of possessiveness and delight at this tiny warm creature who looked up at me with bewildered eyes.

"Our daughter," I entreated Gerard as I continued to gaze at her face. "Is she not beautiful?"

"Yes, she is. Like her mother." He held my hand but did not touch the child.

"I know that you had hoped—that we had hoped—"

He pressed his finger to my lips. "It is not the moment for that now."

I nodded, gazing down at the baby. "How pretty she is! And she is ours—our own little Editha."

He smiled, but his expression remained impassive. "Yes, Editha." His voice was muted. "It is time for you to rest, my love. You have been through a long ordeal. You have been brave. Most of all, I am happy that you came through this so well."

He gestured to the midwife. "Come and take the child."

"Not yet—" I implored.

"I must leave you now," he said, bending over to kiss me.

I began to cry, grasping for his hand.

"There is no need to be sad, my darling."

"I am not sad! I only worry—"

"Hush, it is best you be quiet now, and rest." He brushed away tears from my cheek; then, bending over to kiss me, he said softly: "Do not blame yourself. I know you did your best."

# CHAPTER 26

The wet nurse was a simple, full-cheeked girl with drowsy eyes and the mild, imperturbable nature necessary, I was told, for the ample production of milk. After each feeding, the baby would smile in sleepy contentment before she was given to me to hold, kiss, and caress. Nothing had prepared me for the joy I felt when I held her—this tiny, speechless being.

Aware that I had disappointed him by bearing him a daughter, I met each of Gerard's absences—to hunt, to meet with a breeder of falcons from Valkenswaard—with some unease. Yet I knew that his departures also freed me to luxuriate in the baby without constraint—to sing to her, to hold her and stroke her cheeks, or to simply marvel at her as she slept in her cradle nearby.

This was, in effect, the final phase of my confinement. For forty days, I had been told I could not enter church, nor could I have carnal relations with my husband; by doing so I would sin and risk the wrath of God's punishment.

One night three weeks after the baby's birth, Gerard came to me while I watched over the baby in our chamber. Taking me in his arms, he murmured coaxingly: "But surely time enough has passed—"

I pulled away, secretly grateful, this time, for the excuse of the church dicta, which gave me an excuse to forestall him. By then all my appetites in that realm—to touch, to hold, to feel, to kiss—had been transmuted onto the baby.

"It is not time yet," I said, gently trying to extricate myself from his embrace.

"As you like," he replied brusquely.

I bit my lip and looked aside, my hand brushing his shoulder. "Surely you would never want me to sin?" I asked, somewhat playfully.

"No," he replied unconvincingly. "But that is the last sort of sin I fear."

"I am surprised you fear any sins at all!"

His mouth formed a circumspect smile.

"We must wait until the end of February, until the twenty-seventh, when I bring my candle to church," I told him, taking his hand and kissing it. "Then we may"—I paused—"be together. I have counted the days."

"I have no doubt you have." He cast a brisk glance at the cradle, planted a kiss on my forehead, and pulled away, his lips set tensely. "Until then, I shall do my best to be patient."

ONE AFTERNOON IN EARLY FEBRUARY, Editha began to sneeze and was slightly feverish; I listened to her chest, alarmed by her deep, belabored breathing. Aiglantine and the wet nurse assured me all was well, that this often happened in the deep of winter. Even so, I remained uneasy: I stayed up all night praying, all the while watching as the baby's blanket rose and fell with each breath and resisting the impulse to keep my hand on top of her, lest I wake her.

Two days later, the illness subsided. She began to breathe easily, and color returned to her cheeks. I remember that morning, when Editha awoke, and how she looked at me with bright blinking eyes: the fever had vanished and her breathing was clear. I took her tiny warm fist in mine, kissing it again and again in gratitude.

Never in my life had I felt such intense relief. I knelt by my bed clutching my rosary, offering prayer after prayer of thanks to God.

ON THE EIGHTEENTH OF FEBRUARY, I awoke shortly past dawn. Editha was still sleeping peacefully; the wet nurse would arrive soon for the early feeding. I rose from bed, bundling myself in a wool shawl, for it was bitter cold that day and the fire barely glimmered. Outside all was white, black, and gray, yet I remember that the landscape seemed in no way sear, as if the pulsating fresh life within the chamber rescued it from bleakness.

I tiptoed to the cradle and placed my hand gently upon the little creature inside, as I had done each morning since her birth, to feel the rise and fall of each breath, the almost imperceptible fluttering of her lashes, each lazy movement of an arm or leg, as she slept.

But that morning, as I placed my hand upon her, I felt no movement. Her fist lay clenched, and her tiny mouth was open in an eerie expression, as if in protest at some strange fate. Terror seized me as I felt her again and again. "Editha!" I cried desperately as I took her into my arms. I was accustomed to her warmth and her sweet scent: not this tiny rigid bundle, frozen in my arms.

"Wake up! Wake up my darling!" I implored again and again, kissing her face and hair. But the face was unresponsive and cold, as cold as stone. I screamed for the wet nurse, then for Aiglantine, as I held the baby, rocking her and holding her tight, my own breathing wild and furious, as I frantically tried to will her to breathe again.

Moments later the wet nurse and Aiglantine arrived. "The baby! The baby!" I screamed, as they ran toward me.

The chamber came alive with our cries, and our weeping; but the baby, my baby, was dead.

IT WAS THE SLEEPING SICKNESS, an eminent physician who was summoned told me. He spoke gently, solemnly, as if this explanation might provide some comfort. But nothing was a comfort—nothing anyone could say, nothing anyone could do. Utter despair seized me, a wave of black and brutal thoughts: I wanted God to strike me dead. Day after day I stared at the empty cradle. I had forbidden them to take it from me, as I had the baby's blanket, which I wore tucked around my bodice, fearful that one day it would lose the last vestige of my baby, her scent.

We buried Editha on the twentieth of February: a clear day of tauntingly bright sun. I staggered step by step, sobbing, to the open grave. As the mother, I was expected to throw the first handful of earth upon the coffin before the ground was covered; but in my bitterness and despair I refused to do it, much to the consternation of the priest. That final grim task fell to my husband.

That "final task," I said. But there no finality to any of this—not even when the earth had swallowed up the coffin. Her face was the first image that came to me each morning; there was not a day when I was not haunted by the memory of the moment when I had touched her tiny body, only to find it cold as stone.

Nothing could assuage my pain. I shut myself in my room, alternately desolate, angry, and bitter at the God who had exacted this vengeance upon me. It was the same God, I knew, whom I had thanked so profusely after the baby had recovered from the first illness. But now He had forsaken me, and I began to search obsessively for the reasons why—what had I done to wrong Him? What act had I been guilty of? Would this have happened if I had borne a son, rather than a daughter?

More than once I flung open the windows of my chamber, looking down to the landscape below: at the moat, with its spidery pattern of frost, a frozen silvery pavement glistening in the unsparing winter sun. Transfixed, I would imagine how great the distance were I to jump; how terrible the pain; how swift the death.

The twenty-seventh of February came upon us, the date that was to mark forty days since the baby's birth, the date when I was allowed to reenter church. Aiglantine tried to coax me to bring a candle to the chapel, as was the custom, but I refused. I would not leave my chamber. My husband asked me to sup with him, but I refused any nourishment. From morning until night I sat before the cradle, clutching the baby's blanket upon my lap.

During those hideous weeks, Gerard's mourning was tempered, for he was a realist, after all. Babies were born, some babies died—this was the unspoken truth that lay between us and that he seemed to accept, while I fought it with every fiber of my being. I knew that some babies died—my infant brother had been stillborn, after all—but the loss of my own child seemed unendurable.

In my frantic need for comfort, I did seek relief from Gerard one night. I burrowed my face into his neck as he held me, wishing I could recover the pleasure and comfort I had once felt at the touch of his body. But it was not the feeling of his skin I wanted, nor his scent: it was hers, my baby's, I ached for. He would kiss my breasts, and the pleasure would be quelled the next instant when I thought of Editha being fed at the wet nurse's breast. Then it would take all my strength not to turn my body away, though my mind had already distanced itself.

Despair and sadness became my constant companions, gaping wounds no elixir could heal.

# CHAPTER 27

I hardly remember the months that followed, so clotted were they with grief, confusion, and a mounting sense of guilt, for the anger I had initially hurled against God now turned against myself.

An unceasing succession of questions pursued me, like arrows sprung from the devil's sheaf. Had I committed sins that might have cursed my baby's health? What prayers had I neglected, what offering to God had I failed to perform? Had I let the fire wane during the night, and because of my carelessness, had the baby caught cold? Had I chosen the wrong wet nurse, someone too young and untested, and had her milk been tainted? Or—and this was perhaps the deadliest of them all—was it the curse of Saint Ursula visited upon me for my having so cavalierly traded the medal with her image, the sacred medal that my own mother had given me, in exchange for the relics from Bertuccio?

For me, everything had changed and darkened; for Gerard, life seemed to proceed as it always had, with its customary rituals and duties. His measured response to my sadness often hurt and infuriated me, for at such moments I could not help but wonder: If we had lost a son, rather than a daughter, would he have maintained such composure?

"We will have another baby," he reassured me. But the very subject had come to fill me with dread and fear. That I might disappoint him by having another daughter. That I might have another child—boy or girl—who died, and thus have to endure another harrowing loss.

After the burial of the baby, Gerard waited several weeks before making it clear, with a certain courteous firmness, that it was time to resume our marital relations.

"But I am not ready yet, my lord," I told him, with an evasive glance.

He cleared his throat. "Surely your body is healed by now—"

"My *body* is healed—yes."

"Then surely—" he murmured, pulling me toward him.

"It is not my body I struggle with," I replied in a low, desperate voice. "It is my *spirit,* my thoughts, these demons, these black moods that intrude. I beg you to be patient with me!"

"And so I shall, as I always do," came his curt response, before he added with an edge of sternness: "But you, too, must do your part."

I looked at him uneasily, not sure what he meant.

"You must try to control those wayward thoughts. To cast them aside."

"I shall do my best," I replied tensely. Then, after collecting myself, I added, "But you yourself once told me that thoughts have their own puissance." I searched his expression for an acknowledgment. "Did you not?"

This seemed to catch him off guard; he hesitated before responding, his eyes cast down for a moment before he looked up at me directly. "Yes, it is true, those were my words. My very words." He paused, as if mulling this over. Then he continued in a slightly clipped voice: "But there comes a point when one must decide who is the master—those dark thoughts, or your own volition. There can only be one victor." He said this in such a way that I wondered if he, too, had ever struggled with such demons. I summoned up my courage and asked him as much.

He replied in a measured voice, the sort of voice one uses reluctantly, before a priest, in confession: "No thinking man, and certainly no man of accomplishment, is a stranger to such struggles."

"It heartens me to know that you, too, have known such things. Such dreadful moments." I took his hands and kissed them, noticing as I did so, that he looked almost abashed.

He drew away and walked to the table nearby, where he had left his gloves. I watched as he donned one, then the other, slowly and deliberately pulling the high, stiff gauntlets taut above his wrists, all the while his gaze at once faraway and immensely focused.

"One last word," he said decisively, turning toward me.

"Yes, my lord?"

"In this, as in all struggles, one thing is paramount."

"And what is that?"

"To win."

WEEKS AFTERWARD, ON AN AFTERNOON in March, I was suddenly overcome by a longing to unearth my hidden treasures—the idea of their survival had become a comfort, even an obsession for me, in the aftermath of Editha's death. Yet my fascination with them had also become tainted by the guilty terror that, in trading the holy medal for them, I might have unwittingly provoked God to punish me.

I sat by the table near the window, looking at one, then the other— the helmet, the cross, and then, lastly, a mystifying statuette I had unearthed near my family's home, in my girlhood—the idol of a woman, carved in stone. I studied her serene face, her collar incised with tiny darting creatures, the long braids running like twisting rivulets to each side of her neck, and the rows of plump, egg-shaped breasts that formed her chest.

I turned her this way and that, wondering what she had meant to the people who had worshipped her. Was she a kind of votive, much like our own images in beaten metal, that we placed on the walls of our churches? Everything about her spoke to fecundity, to the quiet confidence of ripeness. I ran my fingers from her arched headdress to her bound feet, wondering if young women like myself had once prayed to her with the hope of warding off barrenness.

A quick, light knocking at the door interrupted my reverie—it was Aiglantine, no doubt. My spirits lifted, for her presence was comforting, and she, alone among those in the household, knew about my secret objects and how I treasured them. "Come in," I said.

But it was not Aiglantine who entered: to my dismay it was Millicent, a basket of kindling in one hand.

"My lady," she said, curtseying, but not before eyeing the table and its array of objects. "I did not mean to disturb you."

"You are not disturbing me," I replied, thinking quickly, for I knew that asking her to leave would only pique her curiosity all the more.

"Your fire is low, I see. I have brought more kindling."

"Good. Set it down then." I turned away, and I began hurriedly to wrap the objects and return them to the trunk.

She busied herself in the chamber, folding a blanket before she began to sweep the sooty hearth. This last task annoyed her, I knew, for it was meant to be one of Aiglantine's responsibilities. While she swept, I went to the window and looked out beyond, my hands planted on the sill as I gave a sigh and exclaimed, "How I wish the sun would come out tomorrow!"

She put down her broom, her eyes fixed on me. "Oh, my lady, how I wish I could do something to help relieve you of your sadness!"

"There is nothing anyone can do," I retorted, trying to contain the bitterness in my voice. "They say that time brings peace, but I have found none."

"You must trust in God and in His wisdom, my lady. There is a reason for all His actions, even for the death of the child. It is part of our Lord's design." She made a step in my direction, pausing only when she saw me stiffen slightly. "You will have another baby. But you must continue to pray to Him, to ask His blessing." She smiled slightly, glancing from me to the chest where I had put my treasures, and back again, before pronouncing: "Healthy babies come from the virtuous, after all." There was something unnervingly pointed about her tone.

"What is it you mean, Millicent?" I asked. "Are you implying that I am *not* virtuous, and that is why my baby died?"

"Oh no, my lady," she protested. "I never meant that, oh no, not at all!" She paused, nervously rubbing her hands together. "There is no one *kinder* than my lady!"

I reflected on her reply—"kinder" she had said, not "virtuous"—before she stammered, as an afterthought, "And virtuous, too."

I tried to dismiss her prattling, but her words had pricked me. Perhaps it was not a coincidence that in the weeks that followed I redoubled my prayers and seldom let my rosary leave my hand.

ONE DAY AT THE END of March, Raoul came to see me while I was sitting before the fire in the great hall, trying to resume my sewing. He had been noticeably kind and solicitous to me since the death of the baby, an attitude that I met with some wariness. I had never forgotten Agnes's words about him—his wiliness, his all-seeing eye—and continued to wonder whether it was he who had opened letters addressed to me, perhaps even the letters I myself had sent.

"A letter has come for you, my lady."

"From whom?" I asked, hardly bothering to look up as I continued my stitching.

"The messenger is from the Hauteclare household, my lady."

I looked up at once, cheered by the thought. For the first time in months I felt a burst of excitement.

"Show him in at once and make sure he has been given some ale and something hearty to eat."

"I will, of course."

A few minutes later the same brilliantly appareled messenger who had brought the letter from the Hauteclares the previous autumn strode toward me. My heart leaped at the sight of him—not only because it meant the possibility of a letter from Fastrada, but also because his presence reminded me of a happier time. As he handed me a roll of parchment, I was heartened to see the familiar seal and red ribbon.

I was hungry for news of the world outside and asked him question after question, all of which he answered patiently—the roads were challenging but passable, the journey had taken six days, the Hauteclares fared well. "The Lady de Hauteclare asked that I be permitted to remain here until tomorrow, should you desire to send her a letter in return."

"I would be grateful if you would stay, so that I may entrust you with a letter. The steward will make provisions for you."

"Thank you, my lady." He bowed, the long plume of his florid cap sweeping the stone pavement as he did so.

"What is your name?" I asked, almost reluctant to see him leave.

"They call me LaFoi, my lady."

"In faith, it suits you well," I quipped, smiling.

"I have tried to live up to it," he replied with a sudden touching gravity.

"And I suspect you do."

He bowed before turning to leave.

"LaFoi—" I said, calling him back the next moment.

"Yes, my lady?" He turned to face me.

"When I said I would *entrust* my letter to you, I meant just that."

"*Sans la moindre question,*" he replied, and with another flourish of his feathered cap, he left.

# CHAPTER 28

I broke open the seal and read the letter at once:

*To Isabelle, Lady de Meurtaigne, warm greetings from Lady Fastrada de Hauteclare:*

Months have passed since our visit, but do not think I have not thought of you often, and with great fondness. I pray that all proceeded well with your confinement, and that you are now safely delivered of a healthy baby. Son or daughter, I long to know! I try to imagine you now, as a mother—a beautiful young mother, and a doting one, no doubt. Do please steal a few moments away to write me: indeed, I have asked our messenger, LaFoi, to stay the night, so that he might return with your letter in hand.

I ask—nay, almost demand—some word from you partly for this reason: I believe that, in those cloistered weeks before and after childbirth, it does the new mother's soul good to remember there is a world outside the nursery. To dote is natural; to erase any trace of one's own being or the needs of one's soul after childbirth is not sane, to my mind, certainly not for a woman of any wit. Will God frown on me for dispensing this advice? I doubt it, if my life is any example. I allowed my sons—and myself—no little freedom in those early days of their childhood, and they have never lacked for loving spirit, and boisterous good health. To this I shall add proudly that they seem to adore their willful mother!

The splendid tournaments will take place here in a few

months, with the advent of spring. I suspect it is too much to ask that you and Gerard come to visit us then. But surely, if not this spring, then perhaps this autumn? I have come to resign myself to the idea that I may not have the pleasure of your company, sadly, for a long time. In the meantime, I shall have to content myself with a visit from my sister Clementia, who hopes to journey north, to our region, in May, from Fontevraud.

When we returned from our stay with you last autumn, we sojourned at the abbey, as I had mentioned we would, and I told my sister all about you. I teased her—nun or not, younger sisters are born to be teased—and said I suspected that you and she are rather alike in spirit, with your seeming reserve, below which, no doubt, lurks a deep and enduring fierceness. I recounted some of your stories of growing up in Provence, and the secret messages you would exchange with your brother. This fascinated her, as I suspected it would: despite her angelic nature, she has a penchant for secrets and the like.

Here, within court circles, there have been rumblings of change: the dauphin, Philippe, has recently assumed his father's, King Louis's, powers. It is intriguing, is it not, to think that the dauphin's father, King Louis, was once married to Queen Eleanor—yet it seems that Philippe has far more of her penchant for cunning than his father ever did. Many say that Philippe will be crowned in the autumn. My husband hopes this will be true, for Hugh has come to know him and discerns the potential for greatness. Philippe is a strategic thinker, he says. "We have played at chess together," he told me, "and the prince outmaneuvered me every time." In matters of power, I defer to my husband. He is as exquisitely sensitive to the rise and fall of fortunes as I am to the subtle hue of a silk, or the cut of a sleeve.

In closing, I impart my loving wishes to you, dearest Isabelle, and to Gerard. We speak often of both of you, and of all your efforts during the hunt. There is no more genial or

generous host than your husband, and no one more deserving
of a loving young wife.

*Do write me, dear friend!*
*Fastrada*

How it cheered me to read Fastrada's words, and how happy I was to
be the recipient of her advice! Her letter in hand, I walked slowly in the
direction of my chamber. Once inside, I closed the door and went directly to the table that held my writing instruments—my quill, ink, and
parchment. I admit being grateful that Gerard was away so that I might
write Fastrada in peace. He had, of late, seemed immensely preoccupied
and more than usually detached—the consequence, I assumed, of my
own gloomy moods and sense of dejection.

I began to pen the letter:

*To the Lady Fastrada de Hauteclare, affectionate greetings from her friend, the
Lady Isabelle de Meurtaigne.*

I was grateful that you asked LaFoi to stay, so that he might
return with this letter for you. Your own letter cheered me to a
degree even you, dear friend, could not imagine possible. It has
been a terrible time here, replete with grief and loss, for the
baby girl I bore on the eighteenth of January died only weeks
later from the sleeping sickness. Even now, as I write this, my
hand falters, as if seeing those words upon this sheet of parchment confirms a reality too bitter to acknowledge.

Despair still tugs at my heart—alas, it has become my constant companion, an unwelcome guest I cannot seem to banish.
Yet as I read your letter, I experienced, perhaps for the first
time, a small measure of relief from sadness, as if your words
had stirred within me the possibility that one morning, I might
awaken without this black cloud hovering over my soul.

It is doubtful we will visit you this spring, though I will

entreat Gerard again to see if he might relent, if only as a way of lifting my spirits. I shall tell him about the news you imparted about the dauphin: I am certain this will interest him greatly. I smiled when you wrote of Hugh and his ability to discern the ways of power—which way the wind is blowing, so to speak.

I long to visit Troyes and to see you, and I cannot deny that I also long to visit Fontevraud. I would dearly like to meet your sister, the fabled Clementia (for in my mind, she is just that!). At moments, during the desolation of this last month, I have thought of you and her together, envying the closeness and affection you clearly share. Alas, I never knew that with my own sister.

Commend me warmly to Hugh, and know that I send you my deepest affection and my gratitude, as well, for your having written, and for your advice.

*In closing, I remain, as ever, your faithful friend,*
*Isabelle*

THE FOLLOWING MORNING, I DESCENDED to the great hall and summoned one of the pages stationed by the entrance. "Ask Raoul to come here, please," I told him.

I was warming my hands at the hearth when, shortly afterward, Raoul appeared.

"I hope my lady is feeling well this morning," he said, bowing.

"Yes, quite well." I turned to the side, almost irked by his question. Agnes's revelations about him the previous year had left a deep impression on me: I had long ago concluded that his concern was not genuine, and that it was born of his own self-interest. Thus I responded to him as I was wont to—coolly, and with a certain remove.

"I trust that LaFoi, the messenger, was given a comfortable place for the night."

"Yes, my lady."

"And that he was well provided for, in all ways? And that his mount is well provisioned for the journey back to Troyes?"

"I assure you, yes, my lady."

"Good." Then I added: "It would not reflect well on our household vis-à-vis that of Lord and Lady de Hauteclare that he be treated with anything but generosity and kindness."

I glimpsed a flicker of wounded pride in Raoul's eyes. "No guest of our household is treated in any other way, my lady," he replied in a quiet voice, "whether it be a master of falcons or a messenger. Nor does it matter whose household they belong to."

Smote by the well-deserved reproof, I quickly replied: "I am glad to hear that, Raoul. Thank you. Now, please tell LaFoi I would like to see him before he sets off."

"Of course." He bowed, and quickly left the great hall.

In a few minutes, LaFoi appeared, elegantly attired for his journey home.

"I hope you were able to rest," I said. "You have long days of riding ahead, and the weather does not look promising."

"I was generously provided for, my lady. Your steward was very kind to me, as was everyone else in the household."

"As we would expect them to be."

He smiled tentatively, his expression uncertain, as if he were hesitant to say something. Sensing this, I prodded: "Is there something else you would like to tell me, LaFoi?"

He took a deep breath before he began to speak haltingly. "Yes, yes there is, my lady. I wanted to express my sadness at the loss of your child. I did not know of this until your steward, Raoul, told me about it. He and others in the household have been concerned for you, as I know the Lady de Hauteclare will be, as well."

I was taken aback—not only by his own expression of condolence, but also by what he had disclosed about my household. "Thank you, LaFoi. It has been a terrible time." I looked away, my eyes welling with tears.

"These matters rest in God's hands. He will provide for you."

I collected myself and handed him the letter for Fastrada. "Take this to the Lady Fastrada. Commend me to her, and to the Lord de Hauteclare."

"It will be my honor to do so," he replied. He placed the letter carefully in his satchel before he bowed, and said "Adieu, my lady."

"Fare you well," I said with a grateful smile, thinking how perfectly his dignified manner suited his name. I watched as he turned to leave, the extravagant feather of his cap bending this way and that as he strode through the hall, in the direction of the stables.

# CHAPTER 29

I stood by the fire pensively for a while, looking up only when I heard the sharp, rhythmic sound of footsteps—footsteps I knew to be my husband's. I turned around: it was indeed Gerard, returning from Bordeaux. I ran toward him, eager for his embrace, for the letter from Fastrada had buoyed my spirits and I felt a surge of love and expansiveness.

He held me quickly, brushing my forehead with a kiss before letting me go. The desultory kiss disappointed me; I had hoped for a more ardent greeting. I drew back.

He stood before the fire, taking off his favorite gloves, which were drenched from the journey: I could see that the finger of one was badly ripped. "The journey must have been hard, with the rain," I remarked.

"Clearly. Yes." He threw the ripped glove down, his mouth set rather tensely. "This needs to be mended."

"I shall see that it is done."

"Good." He sat down on the bench, leaning forward to feel the warmth against his ruddy cheeks. "I see that the messenger from the Hauteclare household was here."

"Yes."

"For what purpose? A letter for me?"

"For me, actually. A letter from Fastrada, asking for my news. Asking about—" I paused, overcome by a wave of despondency.

"About the baby?"

"Yes."

He took a few sticks of kindling from the basket next to him and tossed them into the fire before asking me, "When did the messenger arrive?"

"Yesterday morning. Fastrada had asked him to remain here the night, so that he could return with a letter for her. That was thoughtful of her, was it not?"

"Practical, I would say, more than thoughtful."

I felt a twinge of anger at his cynical tone, but held this in check while I said softly, "Both practical *and* thoughtful, I would say. Very like Fastrada."

After a few moments of silence, he asked, still facing the fire, "And did she have any news? Word from Troyes?"

"Yes," I eagerly replied. "Fastrada mentioned that the dauphin has recently assumed many of his father's powers. That he may be crowned before too long. She said that Hugh is quite impressed with him, that he is shrewd, canny—rather like Queen Eleanor, in that regard. Ironic, is it not," I reflected, "since Queen Eleanor was the wife his father divorced?"

He did not respond and merely turned from the fire to look at me, though his gaze was inwardly absorbed. "I have heard reports of this nature about Philippe," he finally said, "and I cannot say they please me."

"Why should they displease you?"

He looked at me with some disparagement. "*Why*? What do you think?"

"I have no idea," I replied, feeling like a child who does not know the answer to a rudimentary question.

"Then you should begin to learn, my dove." He gave me a tight smile. "I will tell you why. My allegiance has never been to the father and even less to the son, whom I always thought ineffectual. A spoiled young man used to having everything his own way. Therefore, should the pretty prince"—he pronounced these last two words in a mocking way—"come to power, this will not be in my best interest." He tossed more kindling into the fire. "*Now* do you understand?"

I nodded and wondered whether the news about the dauphin was the reason for Gerard's ill temper the last several weeks. I had assumed it was my own dejection that had prompted his sour moods, but now I began to think I may have been wrong.

"Did things go well for you in Bordeaux?" I asked, perhaps too brightly, in an attempt to change the subject.

"Happily, yes."

I waited for a moment, thinking he might divulge the reason for his journey, but since he was not forthcoming, I asked, "Why did you go to Bordeaux? It is a long trip, especially in this weather."

"To meet a group of wine merchants, if you must know. I am seeking some partners. The trade is growing quickly—the shipments of wine from here to Southampton. The Angevin court has an appetite for our wine, it seems. Quite a hearty appetite."

"But I thought it was already decided that you and Hugh would be partners in this?"

"I had decided that. But now things have changed, particularly with the news of the young prince, who will want more control for himself over the lords in this region. It may be more advantageous for me to find another partner."

I froze, stunned both by his words and the cavalier way he had made this pronouncement. "Does Hugh know of this?"

"Not yet. But he will, soon enough. He is a grown man, and I expect him to understand."

"And it does not seem to you rather"—I searched for the correct word—"rather *disloyal* to announce this change, without having at least consulted with him?"

I sensed him keeping his temper in check. "Loyalty is one thing," he replied. "Profits are quite another. And if I am to choose one over the other, I will choose profits."

"But this will anger Hugh! And he is powerful, and may be perhaps more powerful in the future, if he becomes closer to Philippe, especially when he becomes King of France. Does that not concern you?"

"You know nothing of these things," he scoffed. "And I was wrong to even discuss them with you." He stood up, reached for his gloves, and handed them to me: "Remember, they need to be mended," he said, before kissing my forehead absentmindedly and announcing: "It is late, and I am hungry. Let us go into supper."

# CHAPTER 30

Sixty days had passed since the baby was born.

It had been the midwives' ritual to mark each day from Editha's birth on a small wax tablet they had reserved for this purpose. After her death, I forbade them to do away with the tablet, for it seemed the little crosses had become the last earthly vestige of Editha herself. Every morning I would incise a mark of precisely the same size and pressure at the end of each row—one of several rigid habits I had devised to soothe my unquiet mind.

That morning, the seventeenth of March, I asked Gerard to accompany me to Editha's grave, so that I might place some flowers there and offer a prayer. Until then I had not had the strength to do so: indeed, even the thought of seeing the tombstone filled me with such unutterable grief and dread I had hardly been able to sleep for days. Before we set off, I went into the garden and listlessly gathered a small bouquet: crocuses, snowdrops, gillyflowers, and forget-me-nots, the guileless posies of early spring. One by one, as I plucked them, I thought: these should have been the flowers I gathered for her baptism, not for her grave.

The sun was blindingly bright that day, with a bitter wind that lashed our faces as walked hand in hand, slowly and pensively. The cemetery lay a short distance from the keep, on the eastern side of our chapel—yet how long the walk seemed that day, how choked with sadness I felt, how leaden my feet!

I hung back as we finally approached the grave. There, at last, stood the tombstone: crisp, elegant, and white, with Editha's name so freshly chiseled its letters glittered in the sun. "Come," Gerard said gently, pulling me closer toward it.

He stood to the side as I placed the flowers on the ground, then knelt, my cape whipped by the wind and my hands clutching my rosary as I recited this prayer: "Know that you were beloved when you lived, however few the days. Forgive me for failing to save you, darling daughter, and know that my grief is fathomless. May God and all his angels keep you safely in heaven, as I could not, on earth."

I felt Gerard's hand upon my shoulder. "Come, my dove," he said tenderly, helping me as I struggled to my feet. "Now let us put this sad matter behind us." His voice was gentle, with no hint of irritation. I clung to his hand as we walked toward the castle, the sound of my sobs competing with that of the raucous wind.

At last we came to the inner courtyard and made our way into the great hall. "Come, let us sit here together," he said, gesturing to the bench before the blazing fire. He ordered the page to summon Raoul.

As Raoul entered, he glanced at Gerard and then at me with an expression of concern. "Might I bring a handkerchief for my lady?" he inquired gently.

"No. Bring us some mulled wine," Gerard told him rather gruffly.

Raoul reappeared shortly with two goblets of wine. I began to drink from mine eagerly, indeed so eagerly that the goblet was soon empty. I set it down, grateful for the wine's numbing warmth.

"Perhaps you would like some more wine, my lady?" Raoul asked at once.

"No," Gerard said firmly. "She has had enough. You may leave now."

The flames crackled and the wind howled as we continued to gaze at the leaping flames in silence while Gerard sipped his wine slowly and thoughtfully.

At last, setting down his goblet, he turned to me. "We must try anew to have a child. It would help you, I am certain."

"I do not know if I am ready yet."

"When *will* you know?" he asked.

"Soon, I hope."

"Do remember," he said, in the tone one would use to utter an admonishment, "you have obligations in this marriage. Obligations which, under God, you are bound to fulfill."

NOW I THOUGHT INCESSANTLY OF Anthusis and of our conversation that autumn afternoon. I had thought it was death of my mother she augured; but no, I realized now, it was my *daughter* she had meant! A being of the female sex, *dear* to me, she had said; it was the last, crucial part I had forgotten. If she was able to augur the death of my baby, then surely she was truly possessed of singular powers and real knowledge. She had told me I had come *too late*; she had also told me she knew ways to help me bear a son. It was imperative I see her again: but how, and when? I began to think of little else.

This was only one of the obsessions that gripped me, each promising a panacea. I had always delighted in fabrics and clothes, but not inordinately so. Now I rushed to these things with the fervor of the possessed, as if a certain rare silk would make all things right; or a gold and garnet necklace, the sort I had seen on the wife of a neighboring lord; or a new perfume. I began to powder my face; I colored my lips with an ointment used, it was said, by Saracen women: a blend of honey, red bryony, and rose water. My husband, eager to see the end of my grief, readily acquiesced to these whims, thinking that these novelties would soothe me. But in the end they were no more soothing than the little crosses I etched on the wax tablet.

A WEEK AFTER OUR CONVERSATION before the fire on the seventeenth of March, we resumed our marital relations.

In the past, I had sought pleasure with my husband simply for pleasure's sake and for the delight in his body, though of course I had been taught that carnal pleasure was permissible only in so far as it helped to bring about conception. But now purpose and intent intervened, quelling pleasure.

I wonder if the change was enough to have been noticed by Gerard. For me the shift was profound: the pressure to become pregnant felt like an iron shackle I could not loosen, so tightly did it bind my mind and every particle of my body. What I had once experienced so vividly with him now eluded me: it could not be willed back, it seemed, no matter how hard I tried. Often, at the end of our lovemaking, I would lie in bed, my thoughts lost in a labyrinth of rumination. Without those bursts of pleasure, I would never become pregnant. And if I should never become pregnant, what would happen to me?

Then I would imagine myself seeking out Anthusis—listening to her, following her instructions—and I would suddenly become calm and hopeful. Even so, I dared not make the journey yet, for I felt the servants' eyes upon me more than ever: most of all, those of Raoul. Although LaFoi had described him as having been genuinely concerned about me, I had dismissed this impression and refused to think of Raoul as anything but conniving.

AS SEVERAL MONTHS PASSED, GERARD'S moods were as variable as the spring winds—at times loving, at times diffident and remote. One day he would lose his temper with the servants and be almost scornful of me, referring to me as "the countess." The following day, he would be thoughtful and kind, complimenting my beauty, or even praising Gallien's work in the mews. "You no longer blame him for the incident with Féroce?" I asked one day. "Not a whit," he replied to my astonishment and relief.

Early one morning, as Gerard was about to depart for Bordeaux, I summoned my courage and asked whether I might be permitted to send a letter to Fastrada; it puzzled me that I had never had a response to my own letter telling her of Editha's death.

"It is not the right time," came his brusque reply when I asked his permission to write her.

"But surely, at some point, I might be able to—"

"We shall see how matters evolve," he said.

To my delight, two days later, while Gerard was still away, Raoul came to me and announced that a messenger from the Hauteclare household had just arrived. It was not LaFoi this time, but a younger man—amiable enough, but without the former's élan.

I assumed the letter was for my husband and that it came from Hugh himself. Indeed, as the letter was handed to me, my imaginings were already at fever pitch: Hugh had written because he was angry, he would accuse Gerard of disloyalty, he would denounce Gerard to others. . . .

But, to my delight, the letter was from Fastrada, and it was for me. She wrote:

I was utterly despondent when I received your letter with the sad news of your baby. How well can I imagine your despair during these months since the baby's death, and how I wish I might do something to comfort you.

I must tell you of a strange coincidence. Only the day after LaFoi returned with your letter, a letter from my sister Clementia arrived for me. It related her affairs at Fontevraud and the details of the visit she hopes to make to us early this summer. At the end, however, she told me that news of a sad nature had come to the abbey about young Queen Joanna, daughter of Eleanor and wife of King William of Sicily. It seems she has suffered a loss not unlike your own. Her infant son died after about a month, suddenly and in his sleep. The young queen is beside herself with sorrow, they say. She—like you—is quite alone. Perhaps even more alone than you, for she lives in that distant southern kingdom with its strange customs and exotic blood, far from her family, and far from her mother, the queen, who is still locked away in England by her father.

I tell you this so that you might take heart: the loss of a child, whether one is queen, countess, or peasant, is a dreadful thing for any woman. It is the primal loss. The heart needs time to mend. I pray that your pain will lessen as the months pass, and that you and Gerard will have another child very soon.

How grateful I was for Fastrada's heartening words, and her sympathy! I kept the letter with me night and day; before I went to sleep, I placed it under my pillow together with her first letter.

The following morning, I resolved to write her, for the messenger had stayed the night. Gerard, being absent, could not prevent me from sending a letter back with him.

And so I did write her, thanking her profusely for her loving words and reiterating how I longed to see her again and to meet her sister one day. I asked to speak with the messenger alone in my chamber, my letter for Fastrada in hand.

He came at once.

"You are ready for the journey back, I take it?" I asked him.

"Yes, my lady. All is well."

"I trust you were given all that you need?"

"That, and more. Your steward was very kind, as was everyone else in your household."

"I am glad to hear that." At this, I handed him my letter and asked that he deliver it to the Lady de Hauteclare, adding: "I trust you will not mention this to anyone in our household. It is a private matter."

He nodded gravely, my letter still in hand. "Of course, my lady."

I bade him safe travels and watched as he walked to the door. Millicent entered; he bowed to her and went on his way as she stood there for a moment, smoothing her apron. I saw that her curiosity had been piqued and hoped she had not seen my letter in his hand. "I did not mean to disturb you, my lady," she stammered.

"You did not disturb me," I replied, momentarily disconcerted by the expression in her eyes.

# CHAPTER 31

Two days later, while rereading Fastrada's letter in my chamber, I heard the piercing sound of horns upon the ramparts: Gerard had returned from his journey. I hurriedly folded the letter, placed it in my pocket, and ran down to the courtyard to greet him.

There, in the distance, by the well, I glimpsed Gerard deep in conversation with Raoul. I felt pangs of disquiet at once: surely Raoul would mention the messenger from the Hauteclare household and the letter from Fastrada.

I forced a smile and ran toward them, studiously avoiding Raoul's eyes. "Welcome home, my lord," I said, summoning a cheerful voice as I curtseyed before him.

Gerard took my hands in his, kissing each slowly, almost pensively. "It is good to be home," he told me with a warm smile, though he appeared rather distracted. He dismissed Raoul and told him to meet us in the hall.

As we walked into the great hall together, nervousness animated me: I began to prattle on about the weather, a spat between two servants, any trifle I could seize upon.

"I sense your spirits have improved," he said.

"They have, yes," I said softly, almost sheepishly, for I knew he felt my grief was almost inordinate.

"That is heartening." His tone was measured; his expression no longer seemed distant, but quite intent. "I was told that the messenger from the Hauteclare household was here a few days ago with a letter."

"I was about to tell you. But I see Raoul has already done so."

"I assume the letter was for me. Where is it?"

"It was not for you, my lord. It was for me, from Fastrada."

"Ah, I see." He unbuttoned his coat and tossed it on a bench. "I trust you did not answer her letter this time?" He posed the question in such a way that I felt he was testing me, to see whether I would tell him the truth.

"I *did* answer her letter, my lord."

"I thought we had already discussed this matter. I told you it was not appropriate to write her now." His eyes were unnervingly focused upon me.

I mustered my courage and replied resolutely, "I could not leave her letter unanswered. It did not seem right."

"Why is that?"

"Her letter was very warm, full of sympathy and kindness. It seemed impolite not to respond when she had made the effort to write me."

"There are more important issues than politesse. Loyalty to your husband, for one."

"This was not mere politesse on my part. Her letter touched me so deeply that I keep it with me all the time. My gratitude to her is profound."

"It seems incredible that a letter should mean that much to you!" He shook his head, as if in disbelief or exasperation.

"A letter from a friend is something I treasure. Especially now, after losing Editha."

His eyes, which had become cold and tense, scanned my face, but when he continued speaking, it was in a low, controlled tone. "Where is the letter? I want to read it."

"I have it here with me, in my pocket. But why must you read it? It was meant for me; it is a private letter between women."

"Why should we not share something that was so important and comforting to you? We are husband and wife, after all. Besides"—his tone shifted—"I find it hard to believe that Fastrada's words should be so—what did you say, 'touching'? Fastrada, of all people? She is hardly my idea of an angel of mercy."

"Do you think that Fastrada would have written something improper to me?" I asked indignantly.

"Why would that surprise you? She is no stranger to impropriety. And you are young and impressionable. In addition, I am not sure I trust her, as I have told you I am not sure I trust Hugh. Not after the way he deported himself here."

"I think you are wrong in imagining that of Fastrada, my lord. When you read the letter, you will see I am right." With trembling fingers, I took the letter from the pocket of my surcoat and handed it to him.

He began to read, slowly and carefully, as I anxiously watched his eyes scanning the parchment. "It is interesting that she received the news about the young queen, Joanna, in Sicily."

"Yes," I murmured, "and such sad news, like ours."

"More than sad, in the scheme of things. It is *important* news. The King of Sicily needs an heir. Much depends on this, for many."

I was startled and hurt that it was solely the political, rather than the personal, aspect of Fastrada's letter that preoccupied him.

"This is a blow to Henry, and to Eleanor as well," he explained with some relish. "They say that Joanna is very close to the queen, her mother."

"But the queen has been imprisoned for years," I said, forcing myself to follow his train of thought. "How could she, the queen, know any of this?"

"No doubt she does. Her spies are everywhere, and she has her own band of allies." He handed the letter back to me, before observing: "The king was right to lock her away. He had no choice. She and her sons conspired against him."

"Perhaps they had reason to conspire against him——" I interjected.

He looked at me in astonishment. "Against the king? Against Henry? No, it was foolhardy. Most of all for the Young King, for Young Henry. He had only to bide his time and be patient."

"Yet it is the queen who has most suffered, who has been punished."

"As well she should have been. She was the instigator." Then he reflected: "She may be imprisoned, but it should content her, at least, that her sons are free. And that the Young King has been forgiven and has emerged relatively unscathed."

"It is always the Young King you speak of," I ventured.

"He is the son I know best. He will succeed his father, God willing, and if he does, I shall be well placed in his circle. Very well placed, if I have my way." He walked to the window before turning to face me again. "But we have digressed. You have not told me what you said to Fastrada in your own letter."

"That I was grateful for her kindness, and that I hoped to be with child before long."

"If that is so, I am glad to hear it."

The subtly skeptical implication of his words was not lost on me. Even so, I managed a slight smile. I was still smarting from his forcing me to hand over Fastrada's letter, and by his obliviousness to the nature of its significance to me.

"Come here," I heard him say, in a newly gentle voice. He took me in his arms and kissed me tenderly. "You think me harsh, I know," he murmured, his hand stroking my hair. "You do not understand the game of life, how complicated it can be. These friendships and alliances. One day you will, though I would prefer you stay as you are—innocent, and untouched by harsh realities. Men do not have that luxury." I fought from acknowledging how relieved I was by his embrace, how inebriating his reassuring words were to me, how I longed for him to caress me.

Yet all the while, a feeling I could not quite identify chafed within me. It was only later that night, as I lay in bed, that I suddenly realized what it was. Husbands and wives do not have secrets, he had told me. . . . I thought of my clandestine visit to Anthusis, and my secret objects—what would he make of those, should he discover them? What would he say then, what would he do? A wave of guilt, and then of terror swept over me; but those feelings were eventually supplanted by something else equally as powerful—a surge of resolve. It was only much later, while pondering a course of action, that I finally fell asleep.

# CHAPTER 32

The conversation with Gerard had served as a warning for me, for it had made clear, as nothing had before, the danger of keeping secrets from him.

Henceforth I banished all thoughts of stealing away to visit Anthusis. When, on occasion, I was tempted to venture to her again, I would force myself to imagine the consequences of my husband's wrath. He would call her a witch, he would seek her out in the forest and have her dragged to the castle. As for me: I would be humiliated before Raoul, Millicent, and all the other servants. Never again would I recover Gerard's trust. Shaken by these imaginings, I would shudder and resolve to myself: no journey to Anthusis would be worth the risk of igniting his rage and likely destroying my marriage, no matter how tantalizing the promise of her potions and the solace of her knowledge,

But then the month of May arrived and with the reawakening of nature, and the lulling reviving rays of sun, the memory of the talk with Gerard that sear afternoon in March began, slowly, to recede. He had been warm and loving to me since; I had recovered the deep pleasure of our life in bed, and with this had come the desire to please him and the longing to bear his child.

The grief of losing Editha, while always present, gradually pierced me somewhat less: it became a dull ache that I was able, with force of will, to lock away in a chamber in my mind while I looked with faith toward the future. Many women lost babies: I was not the first, nor would I be the last. God had not meant me to have Editha, clearly; I would have another child.

But would that child be a *son*?

That was the question giving me pause, hurling me into an infernal realm where I recalled the pain and chaos of childbirth, the moment when I was told "It is a girl"; the coolness in Gerard's voice reflecting his disappointment in me and the child I had borne. Imagine how blissfully different it would have been, how relieved and proud I would have felt, if I had given him a son!

Such were the ruminations that chipped away at my ability to forswear Anthusis. At first there was just a fissure in the wall shielding me from temptation, but gradually the fissure became a crack, and then the crack a loose, gaping hole. I would think of Fastrada and what she might do when confronted by—what had she called it?—the "tyranny of conception." She would not cower, surely, she would take the matter into her own hands and secretly defy her husband: after all, it was for my marriage, and to give him a son, that I would be taking this risk. Gerard had never known about the first journey to Anthusis: Why would he discover a second? And even if he did, surely he would understand why I had ventured to her: it was for him, for *us*, that we might increase our chances of a son.

IN THE THIRD WEEK OF May, Gerard left for the tournament at Senlis, and I asked Aiglantine to secretly inquire if Corbus would accompany me once more to see Anthusis. The following day she told me he had agreed, though it was left to me to invent a reason for him to be excused from his chores. I instructed her to tell the laundry matron that I had the yearning for a long walk, since the weather had turned so fair, and that I needed a strong fellow to escort me. I had purposely chosen a time when Millicent would be away in the village.

That the journey might be dangerous should have made me fearful, but then I would reassure myself: I am doing this for Gerard, for *us*, in order to bear him a son. Hence the expedition became imbued with a certain nobility, even selflessness, of spirit.

But there would be an added complication to the visit this time: I would need money to pay Anthusis, and I had none of my own. The only money Gerard had given me were some marks to be used for alms: these were kept in a small coffer in our bedroom. So preoccupied was he with his own affairs, and the tournament, that surely he would never notice if a few were missing. And even if he did, was I not using the money for a worthy purpose, a purpose sacred to us, as man and wife? So I took out four coins, along with a silk ribbon of my own, and placed them in a small satchel.

Corbus and I set off the day after Gerard's departure. We seemed to take the same route to her lair, yet how much shorter it seemed this time, how much less daunting! Anthusis, too, had changed, or was it merely my recollection that played tricks upon me? No longer did she seem so spectral: her face looked less gaunt and her voice—that strangely youthful voice—was welcoming, even warm, as she greeted us.

"I see you have listened to me. And you have come in time," she remarked at once. "You are not with child yet, and your monthly bleeding has just ended."

"Yes," I replied, startled and blushing, "but how would you know this?"

"The color in your cheeks, and your scent." She looked at me intently. "You need not tell me why you have come. You had a daughter who died, and now you want to bear a son."

"You know that my daughter died—" I murmured, at once unsurprised and unsettled.

"Of course." Then, briskly, after a dismissive glance at Corbus: "Let the boy remain outside. Come with me."

She ushered me inside and commanded me to sit on the bench near the shelves, which held the familiar dizzying array of vials and canisters. Silently she took some powders from one, some purple liquid from another, a branch of spiky herbs from still another, and placed them in a mortar, then ground them with a pestle. She poured the murky red liquid into a vessel the shape of a gourd, and then, after pouring a small amount into a goblet, she ordered me, "Drink this."

I held the goblet in my trembling hands. She saw at once that I was fearful to sip from it; her expression was one of displeasure.

"How can I drink this, without knowing what it is?" I asked.

"Because you must *trust*. If you do not trust me, it is not worth your coming here." She leaned forward, wiping her hands on her apron, as she said, in a melodious voice: "I led you right before, did I not? I told you it was unlikely that you carried a son. I told you that a being of the female sex close to you would die. And then your mother and your daughter both died. Was that not proof enough—double proof—of my powers?"

So she knew this, too—that my mother had died! This startled, almost frightened, me, as nothing had before. "Who told you about my mother?" I asked, my nerves afire. I set the goblet down.

"It was not necessary for anyone to *tell* me," she replied caustically. "I simply know because I have the power to know. If you do not believe in my power, then leave." She shrugged. "Leave now, with the boy." She began to wipe down a vial and placed the top upon the open cannister.

I looked away, my hands slowly making their way back to the goblet. "I shall drink if you tell me what is in it, and what it is meant to do. But only then."

"It contains herbs and fluids that will cleanse your body and your blood. Males spring from those who are pure. The womb of a female is like a sewer in the middle of a town, the place where all the waste materials are gathered and from which they flow. This drink will purify that unclean place. It will also help lower the temperature of your womb— that, too, is important. Best the womb be cool, not hot, to receive and nourish the seed necessary to create a male. Now do you understand?" she asked, almost contemptuously.

"Yes." I took a deep breath and drank: the taste was bitter only at first, then a pleasant sweetness permeated my tongue. I set the goblet down.

"Good. But that is only the first step," she said with a disarming smile. "I will give you more of this potion to take with you. You must drink it each month—the moment you begin to bleed, and then the moment the bleeding stops." She poured some of the liquid into a smaller vessel and set it aside. "Each time, pour three thimbles full into a cup, and drink quickly." Then, lowering her voice, and with great deliberation, she continued: "There are other things you must also do."

I wiped the last drop of the potion from my lips and leaned forward, listening hard. "You must abstain from your husband every so often," she told me. "Yield to him in bed, at the very most, one out of four days. This will give your blood a chance to clear, and will encourage his own seed to be richer and more concentrated from abstinence. Spending his seed too frequently will only weaken it. Do you understand?"

I nodded.

"One last instruction," she said, turning to open a small box near her on the table and taking from the box a small sachet tied in violet ribbon. "Carry this with you, always. Touch it before you lie with your husband. Each time. Do not forget."

"What is inside?" I asked, taking it from her.

"A powder of my own making. Testicles of hare, a slice of bat wing, the sliver of a goat's hoof. Male creatures. All young and strong."

I placed the sachet in the inner pocket of my satchel; then, from the outer pocket, I dug out the coins I had brought as payment. I took them out awkwardly, along with the silk ribbon. "These are for you," I said, offering them, "as recompense."

She took them at once, silently, almost dismissively, before reminding me in a chastising tone: "You have almost forgotten this." She handed me the small vessel with the potion she had prepared for me, and which she had wrapped with a length of cotton. I murmured my thanks and placed it inside the satchel.

I turned to leave but stopped suddenly, for my gaze had settled on the strange dark cabinet incised with a design of horned creatures in bone, which I had noticed on my first visit. I gestured to it: "What do you keep in there, in that cabinet?"

"Ah," she replied. "Those drawers hold the most potent medicines of all. But they would not interest you. They are for women who do not want to bear a child." Her lips curled into a distasteful smile. "Such women exist, you know."

Her expression unsettled me. I wanted to leave at once and gathered my things frenziedly while she watched impassively.

She drew the dark red curtain open and led me outside. There Corbus, whittling some twigs, sat against a trunk of a tree. He stood up, bowing his head as we approached.

Turning to face me, she took my hands in hers—the first time she had touched me. "I have told you everything you need to do. The rest is up to you." She tilted her head back, narrowing her eyes as she surveyed us: "Leave with the boy now, while it is still light."

# CHAPTER 33

I was with child by early July.

How vastly different was this pregnancy from my first! I felt a new sense of freedom and confidence, a lack of apprehension, not an iota of ambivalence; nor did I experience much nausea, dizziness, or fatigue. My energy was all but boundless as the baby grew within my womb—this baby who, I was certain, was a boy.

As if to echo my lightheartedness, the summer of 1179—that summer of *salus et vita*—was resplendent with sun and a feeling of plentitude. It was a joyous season, with fertile crops and fruit trees so heavy with their yield that their branches seemed to nod almost drunkenly with every passing breeze. In early June, I asked Gerard for a plot of land of my own to the west of the bailey where I might plant quince trees, flowering bushes, and banks of fragrant roses. There were other plants I coveted for my garden as well, some simply for their names— lady's mantle, Cupid's-dart, foxglove, and Madonna lily—and others because they summoned happy memories: euphorbia, which reminded me of Arnaut, and lavender, whose pungent, bittersweet scent and vivid purple evoked my grandfather's garden in Provence.

There was no seed, no cutting, no transplanted bush that Gerard would not have fetched for me, no instruction he was not willing to issue to our gardeners on my behalf. Heartened by my pregnancy and newly revived cheerfulness, he was more affectionate and indulgent than he had ever been. "My darling" he would say as he swept me into his arms after returning from a ride; "my sweet dove" he would murmur as he drew his hand in wonder over my swelling belly as we lay in bed. And I was struck anew by the beauty and distinctive severity of his profile or the feeling of his skin and the marvelous strength of his embracing arms.

TWICE THAT SUMMER MILLICENT'S CURIOSITY unnerved me. One day she asked me what the little sachet contained, for I had rather carelessly left it on the table by my bed; another time I caught her looking askance at the vessel containing Anthusis's potion after she had entered my chamber unawares. The sachet was a good luck charm used in my home region, I told her, and the potion was meant to promote healthy blood flow during the early months of pregnancy. She seemed satisfied with these answers while I, confident of my cleverness, remained equally confident of my ability to dupe her.

One day when Millicent complained of an incident with Gallien—he had inadvertently taken some honey cakes that had been set aside for her by the baker—I simply ignored her. I would roll my eyes or chide her when, after this episode, she would find fault with Gallien for anything at all.

"That young man, Gallien, cannot hold a candle to Ragnar," she told me. "It is Ragnar who knows *everything* about hawks. Ragnar was to falconry born! His father and his grandfather were falconers. No one knows Gallien's family, or where they come from. He is nothing but a—" Here she stopped, her small gray eyes bright with malice, her long thin mouth twitching in such a way that the fine vertical lines above it seemed to assume a life of their own.

"He is nothing but a what?" I pressed her, almost amused by her rancorous vehemence.

"An ignorant *Saxon*," she replied, spitting out the last word as if it were a curse.

"That is quite enough, Millicent," I rebuked her. "I shall not hear any more of this talk." I added pointedly: "I admire Gallien. He has worked very hard to make something of himself. Tending Lord de Meurtaigne's falcons has become his life, his *raison d'être!*"

Afterward Millicent would seem quite repentant, even docile, and all would be peaceful.

I subsequently learned that Millicent had also had a falling-out with Raoul many years before. What had happened between the two servants remained veiled in mystery, yet it had created such rancor that everyone in the household, save myself it seemed, was aware of it. When I asked Aiglantine about the origin of the rift, she explained, "It seems that Millicent felt that Raoul had cheated her in some way. No one can even remember what it was, but she has continued to hold fast to her loathing of him!"

I asked Aiglantine—for she knew the history of the household as intricately as a royal chronicler might the workings of a court—why Millicent had been kept on, despite her maddening tendency to hold such grudges. "Do you not know?" she asked in astonishment. "Her family has been employed by the Lord de Meurtaigne's family for longer than anyone can remember. Millicent was his wet nurse, and also cared for him later, when he was a child. He promised take care of her, always. It was not in him to let her go. Then, or ever."

THOSE SUMMER MONTHS WERE MADE radiant by Gerard's successes in every realm. In late June, he returned jubilantly from the great tournament at Senlis and told me at once, barely able to suppress his pride, that he had greatly impressed the most powerful aristocrats surrounding the Young King Henry. Indeed, Gerard revealed that Henry had granted him several choice vineyards near Bordeaux and had virtually promised that he, Gerard, would be the lead importer of wine from the Aquitaine to the caves across the channel, in Southampton, when, one day, he assumed the crown.

Nor were Gerard's successes relegated to his relationship with the Angevin prince Henry. He confided to me that he had also made some strides with powerful members of the growing circle around the dauphin, young Philippe of France. He had made certain, he went on to say, that his triumph at Senlis had been communicated to Philippe by several esteemed knights close to the Young King. "I hear that Philippe is a young man who respects such things. Strength, most of all." To this he added: "The weak always do." I listened to Gerard's confidences raptly, though I could not help but be struck by his privately scathing words about the Young King. Gerard also revealed to me, almost boastingly, that he had refused to make any gesture of obeisance to Philippe at a moment when he had had the chance.

Not long afterward Gerard mentioned that Philippe had not only solidified his power with several lords of the Maine region, but that his chancellor had also negotiated a favorable trade agreement with the most important wool guild of Flanders. I ventured to ask: "If this is so, my lord, do you not think it is advisable to repair your friendship with Hugh—if Hugh himself is, as you have told me, becoming part of the dauphin's inner circle?"

"These are only fleeting triumphs for Philippe," he scoffed. "Mark my words. The dauphin is weak, like all long-wished-for sons coddled by aged fathers. He will come to nothing against the full might of Henry and his sons. Hugh will regret this alliance, I promise you."

About Gerard's own fractured alliance with Hugh nothing, alas, was further said; indeed the subject of Hugh and Fastrada had become a sensitive issue that I had learned to avoid. For a long time, I was distressed that I had not received a response to my letter to Fastrada. Yet even that sadness seemed to lessen as the days passed, so blissfully content was I.

Cheered by my pregnancy and his worldly successes, Gerard was noticeably expansive that summer. He addressed me with affection and praised Gallien's work; he enlarged the mews, and turned his attention with more than usual zeal to the acquisition of the finest falcons. One day he appeared before me in an especially merry mood: a costly white gyrfalcon, which he had purchased from the most famous dealer, in the Brabant, had just arrived for his inspection.

"Come, my love," he said, taking my hand, as we walked swiftly to the mews. "Let me show you. What a splendid fellow he is! They tell me this is a fearless bird, a great hunter, a creature fit for a king! I doubt there is a lord in this region who owns so exceptional a specimen."

"What will you call him?" I asked.

"Vainqueur."

"A perfect name, for such a champion!"

# CHAPTER 34

In late September, Gerard left for Bordeaux with Ragnar. They were to meet with a local breeder, for my husband was intent on acquiring more hawks before the hunting season. The two men departed shortly past dawn one windy morning.

By then I felt certain that the soul had entered my baby, and that the sex, too, had formed. Hence I began to watch, anxiously, for the indications that I carried a boy—the signs that Anthusis had enumerated. To my thrill, all signs seemed positive for a male: my cheeks were flooded with color; my belly protruded on the right side; and my right breast was far more swollen than the left. I began to test myself when I walked—did I step first with the right foot, or the left? Again and again I noted, with jubilation, I did so with the right—another promising sign!

Imagine, I thought to myself, how proud and happy Gerard will feel when I give him a son, a son whom he could teach to hawk!

Each day, compulsively, I would peer into the mirror to confirm the color in my cheeks, and to check my right breast for signs of swelling. At one such moment when I was in my chamber obsessively looking for signs auguring a male, I heard a knocking at the door. I hurriedly collected myself and asked who it was.

To my relief it was Aiglantine. "Raoul asked me to tell you that a messenger has arrived with a letter for you, my lady."

"Where is he?" I asked brightly, hoping that the letter came from Fastrada.

"He awaits you outside your chamber, at the end of the corridor."

"I shall go to him at once."

I spotted Raoul's slight, erect figure at the end of the hall; he gave a bow as I approached. "I hear that a letter has come for me," I said with excitement. "Is it from the Lady de Hauteclare?"

"No," he said, adding, "I knew at once that it was not."

"Why is that?" I asked, perplexed and almost irritated by his peremptory manner.

He hesitated before replying, "It is partly the way the messenger is dressed, my lady," he said, with the hauteur peculiar to upper echelon servants. "I would also say that his manner is not—" But here he hesitated again, his hands clasped, his expression slightly disdainful.

"His manner is not what?" I was becoming impatient. "Oh, do come out with it, please!"

"The messenger is an unkempt sort, my lady."

I restrained myself from smiling. "We cannot expect every messenger to be as elegant as LaFoi, can we, Raoul?"

He cleared his throat. "That is true, my lady."

"And you did not ask who sent him?"

"I did, but he told me that he had been instructed to speak only with you." His eyes narrowed as he repeated: "You, and only you."

Suddenly I was terrified that it was Anthusis who had sent this messenger. Raoul's description made me recall the forest and its rough denizen; that he had been instructed to speak only with me seemed an order very likely to have come from Anthusis.

"Where is he?" I asked, disquieted.

"He awaits you downstairs in the hall."

"I shall go to him at once," I told him, adding, "follow me, but wait outside in the corridor, while I greet him. If you are needed, I shall summon you."

The messenger was indeed a "scruffy sort" yet so amiable that what he lacked in elegance he made up for in jollity. He greeted me with a toothy smile and bowed before me, his pathetic, threadbare cap devoid of any LaFoi-esque feathers.

"Come this way," I said, leading him farther into the hall, before glancing around to make certain Raoul was nowhere in sight.

"Who has sent you?" I asked in a low voice.

"Your brother, Arnaut de Lapalisse."

"My brother?" I asked excitedly. "Where is he? From whence did this letter come?"

"From Syria. That is what I was told by the last messenger. He gave me the letter after completing the first leg of the journey."

Its seal was slightly cracked, and the parchment splotched with moisture. I took a deep breath of relief, overjoyed to have my brother's letter in hand.

"And you," I asked, "what is your name?"

"Milon, my lady."

"How far have you ridden?" His eyes were lively, but he looked thin and hungry.

"From Rome."

"A long way, indeed!" Then, gathering my skirt, I added: "Wait here while I fetch the steward. He will show you to the kitchen." I left him as I walked quickly to the corridor outside the hall to summon Raoul, who was waiting nearby. We returned to the hall together. "Raoul will make sure you are well provisioned," I told Milon, with a glance at Raoul, who stood to my side.

"I would be grateful, my lady, for some victuals," Milon replied cheerfully, before adding rather pointedly, "and they tell me the wine from this region is very good." He glanced around the hall, eyeing the lavish tapestries, the tasseled cushions on the benches, and the silken carpets. Finally his eyes lingered on a platter heaped with ripe pomegranates.

"Arnaut always loved pomegranates," I murmured almost to myself, following his gaze. Then, to Milon: "Have one."

"Might I? *Really,* my lady?"

I nodded. "Go ahead—taste it."

He bit into it, then winced. "Delicious! But so many crunchy seeds." After picking several from his teeth, he broke into a smile. "But you know what the good Lord tells us—"

"And what is that?" I asked.

"That there is no pleasure without some pain."

I gave a slight laugh. "You and Millicent would get along well." Raoul, looking down, tried to refrain from smiling.

"Who is Millicent?" asked Milon in his engaging way.

"No matter," I replied. "Now Raoul will show you to the kitchen."

THE LETTER FROM MY BROTHER, so long anticipated, was too precious for me to read anywhere but in the privacy of my chamber. I went upstairs and settled on the bench by the window before unfurling it:

*To the Lady Isabelle de Meurtaigne, by the grace of God, from her brother, Arnaut de Lapalisse*

Do not chastise me for my silence, dear sister. My life, while replete with adventure, has been lacking in the time and peace, even the implements, to pen a letter. Only now do I find the means to do so.

I was in Italy, in Apulia, when I last wrote you but returned home in haste during the final weeks of our mother's fatal illness. All of us—save yourself, of course—were with her at the end. I am well aware of your feelings toward our mother, though I would never fault you in that regard. She was a better mother to her sons, and to a daughter who was docile—Amélie—than she ever was to you.

A modicum of riches has not had a favorable effect on Amélie; she has become even more stout and, if anything, even more shrill. In addition, her patience is tried by her children. Our niece is the only one I am fond of; indeed, she reminds me something of you when you were a child. Thus it is not surprising that she irritates her own mother, for the little girl badgers her with questions.

I spent as little time as possible with Guy, for I find him increasingly insufferable: sanctimonious, stingy, and excessively impressed by rank and wealth. He has also become obsessed with his health and rattles on about the "precarious balance" of his humors. In addition, while he revels in his position as the eldest son, he never ceases to complain about the burdens it places upon him. He often loses patience with Father, who has become frail and who seems, at moments, disoriented without Mother's presence. "How is darling Isabelle?" he queried me more than once.

Grandfather remains a marvel of endurance, energy, and wisdom. His mind is still acute, his books and garden his greatest joys. His sight, however, has greatly worsened, and I am fearful of the day when he can no longer read; if that should happen, I doubt he will be able to sustain his will to live. One day when we were sitting together in his library, he showed me his ring with the intaglio of a Roman emperor. "When I am gone, I want Isabelle to have this," he told me. "But you are so strong," I replied. "I have no doubt you will outlive us all! Besides, the ring would be much too big for her—it is meant for a man of your fortitude." To this he replied, "She has her own kind of fortitude. One day it should be her talisman, as it has been mine."

After the month of mourning, I bade adieu to Guy, Father, and Grandfather and made my way back to Apulia, journeying southward from Bari to the port of Brindisi. Apulia is a remarkable region—in part Norman, Greek, and Arab. The Infidels there are different from my imaginings: many were learned in medicine, others were scribes, still others were musicians and poets of some repute. I was tempted to stay longer but chose, after some deliberation, to take a vessel to the port of Limassol in Cyprus: worldly Normans in Brindisi told me I might prosper in that city, for it teems with traders, pilgrims, and knights en route to Outremer. I thought of you as I traveled up the western coast of Cyprus and saw the remains of the cities built by the Romans: vast pagan palaces on the sea, the sort you and I imagined while we sat before the fire, inventing our stories. An old man took me to one place where, after brushing a thick

coating of sand from the pavement, he revealed a wondrous mo-
saic with a design of fantastical horses and sea creatures. How I
wish you could have seen it!

From Limassol I sailed to Syria. To take up the cross, I can
almost hear you ask—with alarm or, perhaps, with pride. I did
think of taking up the cross, I confess, but decided against it,
after hearing piteous stories from our kinsmen who survived
the last Holy War. Furthermore, the Normans in Apulia had
advised me I would do far better to make my fortune in the
region near Acre. They told me Frankish lords who have settled
there seek young knights for service and reward them with land
and other riches.

I am now at the fortress of Krak des Chevaliers—a marvel
of modern technique and architecture that draws knights from
all over the world. Some come from our region and others from
the Rhine, the Brabant, Venice, Palermo, and Rhodes.

I hope and pray that you are now delivered of your child,
and that you are content in your married life. By chance, while
in Cyprus, I encountered some Norman knights who, not long
ago, had participated in tournaments with your husband. Gerard
de Meurtaigne is well known as a formidable opponent, they
told me; indeed, they said there was no one fiercer on the field.
One year at Senlis, they recounted, he rode his mount so hard
that the beast, exhausted from the violent forays, broke a front
leg—an even more piteous calamity, as Tempete, a fearsome,
pure-blooded mount, was his prized favorite. Gerard made the
decision to put the creature to death; it was a terrible moment,
the knights recalled, when he drew his sword and plunged it
into the horse's heart. Yet even this did not make Gerard flinch:
he mounted another beast posthaste, entered the lists with renewed ferocity, and went on to vanquish his opponent.

The Normans, who were greatly impressed by this display
of sangfroid, went on to tell me about the dauphin, Philippe,
and his growing power. Some had even fought for him. They

told me he is formidable, but in his own way: not so much physically, they said, but formidable in mind and strategy. "He is canny, patient, and stealthy."

I hope to reach Acre in a few weeks, God willing, and will forward my address when I am settled. Please know, dearest sister, that this letter is meant to convey my love, and that I look forward to the day when I might receive word from you.

I set down the letter slowly, in a haze of preoccupation and deep concern. How very like Arnaut to mitigate the dangers of his journey, and to frame them in terms of adventure and excitement, as he set out in the world to make his fortune! He knew that I would fear for him in foreign lands, that I would fear him falling ill, or being taken by the enemy, or even—No, I dared not think of those things.

Yet I also knew that he had no choice but to take this course, both by dint of his position as younger son, and by his temperament. He did not have the security of inheriting our family's lands as Guy did, nor did he have Guy's timorous nature. Arnaut was a questing person: to deny him adventure, or to quash his ambitions, would have killed him. But I could not deny how agonizing it was to imagine him ever in harm's way. This, then, was the first source of my disquietude in reading the letter.

It was the part about Gerard, with its vivid depiction of his sangfroid, which unsettled me most profoundly. He had been able to kill the very creature he loved, and who had served him faithfully and well. Yes, the horse had been badly wounded, but even so, most men, most knights, would have left that dreadful act to someone else. Was this anecdote in itself as much a coded message as those in invisible ink that we exchanged as children? Did Arnaut really mean: Beware this man, your husband, for he is resolute and steely, and he will do anything to win? I tried to shove the troubling feelings aside and say to myself: surely I ought to admire a man who could be so tenacious, who could overcome the bitter loss of his favorite mount, only to take up the fight anew, with discipline and resolve?

But other feelings and uncertainties intruded. "I hope and pray all goes well in your married life" my brother had written. He had not said "I trust all goes well." Did he have doubts that I was well, and that I was content with my husband and my life? I knew he had had reservations about my husband from the beginning.

Then I turned to pondering what my brother had said about the dauphin, Philippe. It was striking how much his description of Philippe confirmed what others had said of the prince—qualities about which Gerard seemed remarkably cavalier. And then I wondered why Philippe seemed to rankle Gerard so. It may have been his disdain for a younger man who had assumed power by royal inheritance, and who had been spoiled by a doting father from the moment of his birth. Gerard had had to earn his place and his own fortune; earlier in his life, he had also had to overcome the contempt of his father, who had always favored the oldest son, Roger.

I carefully folded the letter and placed it in the little coffer where I kept other precious things, among them Fastrada's correspondence to me.

But later, during supper, and throughout the night, the words of the letter whirled through my mind like a tempest.

# CHAPTER 35

The following week, Gerard returned from the expedition with Vainqueur. "Never have Ragnar and I seen a falcon fly with such speed, and with such precision and endurance!" he exclaimed as I greeted him near the stables. Still astride, he was smiling broadly, boyishly; his cheeks were windburned, his gloves splotched with fresh blood and earth.

Resplendent in his master falconer's tunic of fine red cloth, the feedbag fastened on his belt, Ragnar stood a few paces away from us. Vainqueur loomed on his wrist, his huge dark yellow talons gripping Ragnar's glove, his eyes fixed upon me in such a piercing way that I moved even closer to Gerard.

"I will return Vainqueur to the mews, my lord," Ragnar said. "The day has been long—for us, and for him."

"That it has," Gerard replied as he dismounted. "And he has done us proud."

Ragnar gave Vainqueur a proprietary glance. "Yes, he performed well. But I knew he would."

"It is in no small part due to you and your skill, Ragnar."

"Thank you," he replied, bowing in his perfunctory way. Then: "Good evening, my lord." He paused, then murmured, "And my lady." He left us.

"What a wondrous bird Vainqueur is—more powerful than any I have ever owned!" Gerard marveled, his eyes following the creature. Then he turned to me, embracing me with such ardor that the stable boy, to whom he had given his reins, looked away.

As we walked together toward the great hall, I noticed a jauntiness to Gerard's step, and a buoyancy to his mood, the sort that comes from accomplishment and pride. It was a moment to savor, when life seemed to brim with radiance and promise—how wildly different from that unsettling moment when I had read Arnaut's searing description of Gerard in the tournament at Senlis! I had only wanted to seal away the rankling disquiet of that moment, whereas this was one I longed to capture and distill into an elixir, to imbibe at will.

"What are you thinking?" he asked playfully, squeezing my hand.

I paused for a moment, as I always did when he asked that question. "I am glad that Vainqueur did well, and that you are so happy with him," I replied.

"It was his success today which makes me happy. Not Vainqueur himself."

"I am not so certain. He is remarkable. The kind of hawk a king might possess!"

"Only a few kings, at that," he remarked, with an air of satisfaction. "I waited a long time for such a gyrfalcon. I owe Ragnar a great deal: he persisted with the dealers up north, he pursued them, and he told them I only wanted the very best."

"As you do in *all* things!"

"True." He smiled, and added rather teasingly: "Did I not choose you, as my wife?"

I laughed. "I am glad to think I am in the same exalted category!"

"Far higher," he replied, with a teasing smile. He drew me to him, kissing me hard before we continued on our way, walking hand in hand.

"You have great confidence in Ragnar," I reflected after a moment.

"I do. I am the envy of my peers. He is known far and wide for his expertise, as well as his ability to teach others. The young falconers who work with him are fortunate."

"They are indeed," I said, thinking of Gallien. I knew from members of the household that the young Saxon had become an accomplished falconer under Ragnar's exacting tutelage. It was then I thought again of my plan to ask Gerard if Gallien might be allowed a foray, on his own. It seemed the opportune moment to pose such a question, for Gerard was in an expansive mood. Besides, Gallien's devotion to my husband and adherence to Ragnar's instructions had long since helped to erase the ill feelings after the incident with Féroce.

"You are right," I reiterated, "that any young falconer taught by Ragnar is fortunate. I hear that Gallien has already learned so much from him." I paused, before adding, with seeming nonchalance: "I wonder whether you would let him take Vainqueur out, on his own, one day. It would be a good test, a way to show how much he has learned." Discerning a flicker of resistance in his eyes, I hastily went on: "Of course, I thought he might take out a few of the lesser prized birds first. And then, assuming he does well, as the final test—honor, really—he could try Vainqueur."

"When the time comes, yes, Ragnar and I will allow him."

"Surely it is really *your* decision—not Ragnar's!"

"It is true I have the final word. But it is for Ragnar to decide if Gallien needs more time."

"I would think that enough time has passed! They have been training Vainqueur together for months."

For a fleeting moment he looked askance, then almost amused. "Gallien, Gallien—always Gallien!" he teased. "I cannot quite understand why you favor him so. I am beginning to think you might be sweet on him—"

I laughed heartily, blushing a bit as well. "It is simply that I admire anyone with such passion for his work. Especially one who comes from a lowly situation and wants to better himself. And he does love your hawks! They are like children to him—as they are to you. And I suppose there may be something about Gallien that reminds me of Arnaut, as well," I mused. "You will see when you meet Arnaut one day. Before long, I hope. Arnaut, too, has a passion for hawks. How fascinated he would be by Vainqueur! Though of course he has never flown a gyrfalcon."

"Passion is one thing," he retorted. "Experience is quite another. That is what Ragnar has—years of experience, years of hawking. And, of course, the right instincts are also in his blood. The best falconers come from the North, as he does—from the Brabant, and from Norway."

As we reached the entrance to the great hall, he stopped and added in an affectionate, thoughtful voice: "But I want you to know I do listen to you, and I shall try to give Gallien more responsibility." He drew his finger across my cheek, then slowly traced it over my lips: "How hard it is for me to deny you anything!"

"Then do not deny me," I replied coquettishly, running my finger across his lips, "and I shall reward you!" He began to laugh; I embraced him and gave him a lingering kiss.

"I shall speak with Ragnar and Gallien tomorrow," he said.

"Do you promise?"

"I promise. And, since you devised this plan, you must come with me tomorrow to the mews." He took my hand and helped me up the steps, smiling roguishly as he added: "And then, my dove, I shall await my own reward."

EARLY THE FOLLOWING MORNING, GERARD and I walked to the mews together. It was quiet as we entered. Ragnar was sitting at the table in the back, mending a falcon hood; Gallien was sweeping the ground by Vainqueur's perch. Gallien stopped sweeping at once, and bowed deeply—first to Gerard, then to me. Ragnar stood up slowly, almost languidly. He seemed to take an inordinate amount of time to set things in order before he approached us.

"My lord," he said, before adding "my lady" almost inaudibly.

Gerard had walked to Vainqueur, who gazed at us fiercely with his vivid golden eyes, as if we were intruders.

"Was not Vainqueur a champion yesterday, Ragnar?" Gerard asked jovially.

"Indeed, my lord."

"How well he obeyed you—and me! I am still marveling at his performance."

"I have tried my best to train him well. To your standards."

"You have done more than well—you have done brilliantly."

"You do me honor, my lord."

"And it is because of that—because you have done so well at

training—that Lady Isabelle and I have come to see you. You"—he turned—"and Gallien, as well."

At that, Gallien's eyes quickened with curiosity.

"I believe it is important, as part of Gallien's training, that he be given more responsibility. That he be allowed a foray by himself, without your supervision. This is how a fledgling falconer learns, after all—just as a bird learns to fly on his own. Lady Isabelle has suggested that Gallien, having been so well schooled by you"—I forced myself to give Ragnar an ingratiating smile—"might have more responsibility. I suggested that he be entrusted with a few of the other prized birds, first, and then, as the final challenge, that he be given Vainqueur." At this, I saw Ragnar's brow furrow and an expression of displeasure in his eyes. "That is," Gerard added, with surprising deference, "when you are quite certain that he is ready."

"Gallien or Vainqueur?" asked Ragnar gruffly.

"Both."

I held my breath. "I am not sure Gallien is quite ready, my lord, for such responsibility," he replied.

"How long would it take, for him to be ready?"

"A few weeks, perhaps more."

"Good," Gerard replied. "Work with him for as long as is required." Next he turned to Gallien with a smile. "And now, what of you, Gallien? Are you ready to accept this challenge?"

"I would be most honored to, my lord."

"Vainqueur is fast, powerful, not easy to handle at times," Gerard said, in his brisk, assured way. "But once you succeed with a few birds of similar power, I expect you will do well. Lady Isabelle"—he glanced at me warmly—"certainly has confidence that you will."

"I am grateful to you and Lady Isabelle," said Gallien, "grateful for the chance. But I will leave it to Master Ragnar to make the decision."

Gerard looked delighted. "A proper response, would you not say, Ragnar? Then it is decided. Gallien will take practice with a few of our most prized birds first, and then, as the final test, Vainqueur. With a companion, of course, who can manage the hounds and carry the quarry."

Ragnar seemed to consider this long and hard before answering, "That young man from the stables, Haakon, would do well. He is a strong boy, a good sort. Not unfamiliar with hawks."

"Haakon—yes. He is nimble, a good runner, keen eyes. Good." He turned to address Gallien once more. "It is a great responsibility we are giving you."

"I am aware of that, my lord, and I am honored. Never would I want to disappoint you."

"A wise young man, indeed!" said Gerard, with a slight laugh. He took my hand in his and turned again to Ragnar. "I leave it to you to tell me when you are confident that Gallien is ready. A few weeks, you said—"

"More or less. If that pleases you, my lord."

"It does," he said decisively. Then, after a fond glance in my direction, he added, "And what is more, it will also greatly please Lady Isabelle. It is decided, then?"

"Yes, it is decided, my lord." Ragnar's tone was measured, his eyes inscrutable.

We turned and left the mews.

"Thank you with all my heart!" I exclaimed to Gerard. "I know Gallien will not disappoint you."

"Are you happy, my love?"

"Yes, very," I replied. Yet as we continued on our way, I could not dispel a certain uneasiness as I thought of the way Ragnar had replied "It is decided." For it seemed to me, within his voice, I had detected an undercurrent of bitterness.

# CHAPTER 36

Ragnar worked unceasingly with Gallien in the days that followed. Together, they ventured out in the fields and forest for hours—first, with several prized falcons less daunting than Vainqueur. Once Gallien proved he could handle these successfully, Ragnar accompanied him on forays with Vainqueur himself, the two men trailed by the lackey Haakon, a tall, rawboned lad with the fair skin, gruff accent, and the white-blond hair of people from the far north. (Gerard had told me he came from the same town in Norway as Ragnar, adding: "Their families have known each other for generations.")

Finally, a little over two weeks later, Ragnar announced that Gallien was ready. And so, on a brisk, clear Wednesday morning, Gerard and I walked toward the courtyard of the mews to see the young Saxon set out for the first time with Vainqueur. Trailed by a pack of baying hounds, Gallien approached us, his eyes shining with pride, Vainqueur perched imperiously on his glove; Haakon followed. Ragnar watched from a short distance, a coiled creance in one hand.

"All is prepared, then, Gallien?" Gerard asked as we stood outside.

"Yes, my lord."

"You have checked Vainqueur's keel?"

"Yes, my lord."

"The jess?"

"Yes, my lord. It is secure."

"And the feed bag?"

"Prepared."

"Then it is time for you to set off."

"I will, my lord."

"Good luck to you," Ragnar called out with surprising heartiness.

We watched for a long time as Gallien and Haakon made their way toward the forest.

"How excited and proud Gallien seemed," I said, turning to Gerard as they faded from view. "And how grateful I am to you, my lord, for granting him this opportunity. It is an honor he only dreamed of."

He kissed my forehead. "Now," he said, "it is all in Gallien's hands."

LATE THAT AFTERNOON, WHILE I was reading in my chamber, there came a frenzied knocking at the door. It was Aiglantine, pale, breathless, and agitated.

"What is it?" I asked, alarmed by her expression.

"Oh, my lady," she said, panting, her small hand pressing against her chest. "Something terrible. The hawk—" She stopped, almost too upset to continue.

"Vainqueur?" I asked, dreading what would come next.

"No one can find him. Lord de Meurtaigne is frantic."

I felt ill, my body afire with nerves and terror. I had set all of this in motion. Gallien would be blamed, and I would be blamed.

"I shall descend at once," I said, throwing a shawl over my gown. "Where are they now?"

"Beyond the gates. The men are searching the fields, the hedges, the forest."

"And Lord de Meurtaigne?"

"He is with them."

"And Gallien? Haakon?"

She shook her head in despair. "They are all out there searching. Gallien is distraught. Oh, my lady—"

I ran down the stairs, through the courtyard, toward the gates, to find the household in turmoil. In the stables, mounts were being hurriedly prepared for men setting out on the search. Above, on the ramparts, only one watchman remained: the others, no doubt, had left to join the hunt for Vainqueur. I could hear the echoing sounds of horns, and of the men's resounding, rhythmic calls for the falcon.

I ran through the gates. From a distance, I caught sight of Gerard, a tall, solitary figure advancing toward me through the tall grass of the desiccated fields. "They have told me about Vainqueur!" I cried out.

"I should never have let the boy take Vainqueur out by himself," he said, slapping a glove against his palm.

"Do not blame yourself," I pleaded, taking both his hands. "You know that gyrfalcons are capricious! And besides, it was *I* who asked you this—it was I who asked that you let Gallien take him out on his own."

He remained silent, almost unbearably silent, until he finally replied: "It is not your fault," in a low, controlled tone devoid of real conviction.

"It is not anyone's fault," I pleaded again. "I am sure that Gallien did everything properly. Ragnar said he was ready, did he not? I am certain he was very careful! This could have happened to anyone."

He did not respond.

"Go back inside," he told me. "There is nothing you can do. This is up to the men now. Ragnar is directing the search. He knows all the fields, the woods, all the places where Vainqueur might find refuge."

"Please—let me stay—I want to help!"

"You have done quite enough."

"But surely—"

"No, I told you. Best you go inside and remain with the women. Now."

I turned and walked listlessly back to the castle. As I passed the inner gate, I glimpsed Raoul stepping quickly toward me.

"My lady," he said, "what a terrible day!"

"Yes," I lamented. "Yes, it has been terrible. It is all the more terrible that this should have happened while Gallien was out alone with Vainqueur. The very first time!" I glanced at his face, wondering if he was secretly gloating that Vainqueur had been lost on Gallien's watch.

"Yes," he replied, with a surprisingly pained expression, "all the more terrible that it should happen to that boy."

I continued to look for signs that he was dissembling: yet everything about his demeanor reflected compassion—not an iota of the perverse delight I had anticipated.

"Poor Gallien," he repeated, looking at the ground as he shook his head. "That hawk was my lord's pride and joy. I only wish there was something I could do to help them."

"To help find Vainqueur, or to help Gallien?"

"Both, my lady," he said fervently, looking up at me.

"That is very kind of you, Raoul," I said. "Very kind indeed." I turned and continued on my way, all the while reflecting on Raoul's sympathetic words, for they had surprised and heartened me.

I arrived at the inner courtyard. All was still, save for the kitchen: smoke wafted defiantly from its chimneys, the sole sign of life in the preternaturally quiet household.

I came to the great hall, then to the staircase leading to the upper floor—how long and daunting the climb seemed that day! Once in my chamber, I walked to the window and looked out, straining to catch a glimpse of the search parties. I turned away and paced about, gazing out the window now and again, for I was too nervous to turn my attention to reading or sewing. I could not even bear to catch my reflection in the mirror, so distraught was I, so quick to lapse into self-loathing. Had not I, after all, willfully and stubbornly urged Gerard to let Gallien take Vainqueur out on his own?

When dusk began to fall, Aiglantine appeared, looking wan and nervous. "Nothing yet?" I asked.

She shook her head dejectedly. "No. Nothing, my lady. And it will be dark soon, and they will have to stop the search. At least, until to-morrow."

"Yes," I murmured, with a deep sigh, "until tomorrow—"

"I hear they will continue at dawn. That is what Millicent has told me."

"Where is Millicent?" I asked.

"She was near the gates when I saw her last. She was speaking with Ragnar."

Of course, I thought to myself. "Please find her. Tell her to come here."

The two returned together shortly afterward: Aiglantine, still visibly upset, and Millicent, whose eyes shone rather too brightly, as if she were enlivened by the emergency.

"My lady," she said, with an inordinately deep and mannered curtsey, "such terrible news about Vainqueur! How awful that this should happen to my lord's prized hawk."

"I hear you were talking with Ragnar." At this Millicent's eyes darted to Aiglantine's, then back to mine. "What did he tell you?"

"Very little, my lady," she replied, with a shrug. "I told him that the women in the kitchen have been making provisions for the men to take to them, while they search. Some barley water, and bread and cheese. He said that the search could last on a long time." Then she added, with a keen glance: "Such a pity, such a pity, about that poor boy."

"Do you mean Gallien?"

"Yes, such a shame, isn't it? I can imagine how angry my lord must be." She paused, then added: "Of course Lord de Meurtaigne has a right to be—"

"Why, a 'right'?" I inquired sharply.

"The boy did not have much experience. He is not like Ragnar, who was born to falconry. It is in Ragnar's blood. Gallien had none of that, did he?"

I looked away, for there was an unpleasant shrillness to her voice, and a malevolent gleam in her eyes I found distasteful; I dared not even look at Aiglantine, who stood near.

Still, I forced myself to address Millicent in a level voice. "These accidents can happen. And they can happen to anyone. It might have happened just as well under Ragnar's watch. And I am sure, Millicent," I told her, my gaze not wavering from her face, "that you, as a good Christian, would hope only the best for Gallien, would you not? Is that not the spirit of charity the Lord has taught us?"

She waited before answering me. The expression of her watery gray eyes was mild enough, yet a twitching of her thin mouth seemed to protest my implicit chastisement.

"Of course, my lady," she finally replied in a voice both ingratiating and strident. "I only hope the very best for the poor boy!" She dug into the pocket of her apron, producing her rosary beads before brandishing them rather ostentatiously at me, and then at Aiglantine: "I have spent the whole day praying for him."

# CHAPTER 37

The search for Vainqueur continued for several weeks, weeks during which I hardly saw my husband. At supper he would remain in the field with the men as they combed the forest by torchlight; at night he came to our bed long after I had fallen, however fitfully, to sleep.

I tried to occupy myself during that time as an antidote to nervousness and fear. I paced outside, I walked the lengths of my now-blossomless garden. So preoccupied and full of anxious energy was I that there were moments when I nearly forgot I was pregnant.

One morning, as Aiglantine brushed my hair, she seemed on the verge of speaking, but then hesitated, only to fall silent.

"What is it?" I prodded her.

She began to speak rather falteringly. "There are some who say if you make a wax model of a falcon and place it before a statue of the Virgin, and you pray to her, that the Virgin will listen, and the falcon will be found." With a shy smile, she added: "It is a custom of the region."

"And has the Virgin been known to respond?"

She nodded. "They say she does."

"Then let us make one together and offer it to her!" And so, that very afternoon, we worked together, melting wax from old tapers and molding it into a small figure of a falcon. We used a twig to delineate the shape of the wings, and a bit of blackened ash to mark its claws and beak. "Let us hope the Virgin takes pity on us, and on Gallien," I said to Aiglantine as we looked rather proudly at our handiwork.

"When will you take it to the chapel?" she asked.

"Tomorrow, very early."

The following morning I placed the falcon idol in the deep pocket of my cape and made my way through the inner gate, and toward the chapel, which stood by the edge of the outer courtyard, not far from the ramparts.

I had almost arrived at the chapel when I glimpsed Gallien approach—the first time I had seen him since the fateful expedition. He might have been a wounded bird himself, so injured and defeated did he look. And how gaunt he was, how pale, how harrowing the expression of his eyes! He walked feebly and with uncertainty, almost as an old man might.

I hurried over to his side, looking this way and that, for I did not know if it was prudent for us to be seen speaking together. His eyes looked haunted, the eyes of one who had not slept or eaten for days.

"I can only imagine what you are feeling," I said at once as he bowed before me.

"It is terrible, my lady—" he admitted, listlessly shaking his head.

"No doubt you did everything properly."

"I am sure I did, my lady."

"Do you have any idea what might have happened?"

"It was all going well at first. Vainqueur flew just as he had when I had been out with him and Ragnar. He went after a fox first, then some hare. We had not let him feed too much before our departure, and I knew he was hungry. But then, not long afterward, he appeared distracted—distracted by something in the distance. A sight, or a sound, I am not sure. Then he set off in that direction. Haakon ran after him—you know how fast he is—but when I finally caught up with him, he said there had been no sign of Vainqueur. No sound of his bells. Nothing, just silence. We called and called and looked at every place where he might have gone. The brambles, the sheltering trees. But he was nowhere to be found. Nowhere." He shook his head in despair. "I am sick at heart. My lord will never forgive me."

"But this might have happened to anyone! It is the chance one takes every time, when hunting with a falcon. And even more so with a gyrfalcon. You know that. And my husband knows that. "

"But it has never happened before with Vainqueur. He is fierce, but he is obedient. Very obedient. And I do not think—" Here he stopped, as if the thought were too painful to express.

"You do not think what?"

His cast eyes down, shaking his head. "I do not think Lord de Meurtaigne will ever forgive me."

"Of course he will! It is only human," I cried; yet even as I uttered those reassuring words I fought from acknowledging what I knew to be true: likely Gallien was right.

"I must return to the search now, my lady."

"Go on, then. And do not lose heart." I took the wax falcon from my pocket and showed it to him. "I shall place this in the chapel, before the Virgin, and offer prayers to her, beseeching her that Vainqueur return to us. Aiglantine suggested we do this. It is the custom in this region, she said."

"Thank you with all my heart, my lady."

"How I wish I could do more, much more! I feel a great responsibility in all of this."

"There is no need for you to, my lady. The responsibility was mine, and no one else's."

He turned to leave.

He was only a few paces away when Ragnar appeared, at a distance. I wondered if he had been watching me and Gallien from afar. Something in his demeanor led me to intuit he had.

"Good morrow, my lady." His bearing was slightly cocky, and his complexion had an unhealthy ruddiness about it; I wondered if he had been drinking.

I noticed him eyeing the wax falcon. "You are wondering what this is—"

"Yes," he said, his brow raised, his falconer's gloves clutched in one hand like a weapon.

"I am going to place it by the Virgin in our chapel and pray to her for Vainqueur's return. It is a custom in these lands, they tell me."

His thin lips were unpleasantly and skeptically set. "It is a custom I have not heard of," he remarked. "But then, in my country, it is not our custom to lose our falcons."

I felt my face flush. "I doubt that your countrymen have never lost a hawk. That is not possible."

He shrugged. "As you say, my lady."

"It is clear that Gallien did everything he could, just as you had trained him," I said with mounting indignation.

"That is true, insofar as he is able." He paused, adding, "Some things can be learned, others come only from instinct. From the right blood. He is not to falconry born." There was a subtly triumphant, sardonic edge to his voice.

I turned away, furious. Finally, having collected myself and facing him, I said, "Is that why you wanted Haakon to go with Gallien? Because he comes from your country, and has what you deem the right blood?"

"And if it were, my lady?"

I would not even dignify his riposte with an answer. "Good day, Ragnar," I said, turned, walked to the chapel, and entered.

What a relief to escape to its silence, its peace! I was grateful for the sheltering, beatific figure of the Virgin, grateful for the flickering lights of the banks of candles and the lingering scent of incense. After placing the little wax falcon by the Virgin, I knelt on the prie-dieu a long time, praying and thinking—trying, as well, to suppress the anger I felt toward Ragnar and, increasingly, toward Millicent.

At last I stood up to leave and walked pensively down the aisle.

It was only as I turned the handle of the door that I realized the root of my uneasiness: the words that Ragnar had used about Gallien— "The right blood. He is not to falconry born"—were almost the same words that Millicent had used, and which she had uttered in the same derisive tone.

THE SEARCH CONTINUED FOR THREE weeks. Vainqueur was never found.

My husband became increasingly distant from me. He did not

blame me outright for the loss of Vainqueur, yet I felt it, nevertheless, in his eyes, in his stance, and in the occasional insidious contemptuousness of his voice when he addressed me.

One evening, as we sat together silently after supper, he turned to me and announced icily: "Of course, Gallien must be punished. The only issue is how."

"I do not understand why he must be punished. He did nothing untoward."

"We do not know that for certain. Gallien may not have fed Vain-queur properly. In addition, he never confirmed with me, nor with Rag-nar, for that matter, whether he had checked the bewits."

"The bewits?" I asked.

"The leather bands attached to the hawk's feet to carry the bells," he answered in a condescending tone. "It is important the bewits be secure. In addition, I suspect Gallien may have given Vainqueur confusing sig-nals. All of this points to the fault being his, not the falcon's. Vainqueur always obeyed when the signals were clear."

"You yourself never mentioned the bewits before—to me, or to him, when he departed that day."

"That is not my role. As you are well aware."

"But it is Ragnar's, surely!" To this I added: "Perhaps he did not train Gallien as carefully as he might have."

"I refuse to believe that."

"Of course you do!" I retorted.

"I have heard quite enough"—he stood up angrily—"especially from you, of all people. If it had not been for your—" But here he stopped, fists clenched, and stared stonily ahead.

Then: "Give me your hand, my lady," he said with a trace of sar-casm. With a curt smile, and a nod to the attendants, he announced: "It is time that we retire."

We walked in utter silence to our bedchamber. All that while I tried to banish anger and sadness by remembering other moments when, after humiliation, I had found a way to soothe myself. In girlhood, had I not imagined myself as Helen of Troy, or Saint Radegonde, or even Queen Eleanor? Those women had never cowered. They would never let anger cloud their judgment; they would use the power of thought to their advantage. They would plan, they would devise a *strategy*—that word I had loved as a child, that word my grandfather had used so artfully, unveiling it as one would a jewel.

I had made a decision by the time we entered our bedchamber: angrily protesting would be a fruitless approach with my husband. Better I appear contrite, and appeal to his sense of reason and compassion.

As we entered our bedchamber, I turned to Gerard. Bowing deeply before him, I said: "I apologize with all my heart for anything I have done to offend you, my lord, and implore you not to be angry with me any longer."

This caught him unawares: his expression softened. "I am not angry. That is a useless emotion."

"If you are not angry with me, then why do you treat me so coldly and with such contempt?"

"It is Gallien who is the sole source of my displeasure. He was careless, clearly. His carelessness brought about the loss of a creature I cherished and respected. I have no tolerance for such carelessness."

"But Gallien is only human, and to make mistakes is only human. He never, ever, wanted to disappoint you." I went down on my knees before him, my hands together in supplication. "I beg you, my lord—punish *me*, but not Gallien! It is *I* who insisted on his going out alone with Vainqueur. I, who knows so little about such matters and who should never have intervened. I, who can be obstinate and ignorant. Punish me, but do not punish him!"

He did not respond.

"I entreat you, my lord. Reprimand him, yes! Deprive Gallien of caring for the hawks for a while—that will be punishment enough for him." I took his hand, with its heavy signet ring, and kissed it. "Promise you will consider what I say, my lord," I pleaded.

"Very well. I shall"—he paused—"consider it."

He offered his hand, and I stood up. "Come," he said genially enough, but I could not fathom what he was thinking.

WHEN I AWOKE THAT MORNING, it was very cold, but the late autumn sun shone with brilliant clarity, and the sky was faultless. The fire had already been lit in the chamber, its flames casting a soothing, rosy hue upon the brightly painted walls so that the room took on an incongruous air of merriment.

I sat up in bed, reflecting on the conversation with my husband the previous night, hopeful that he had listened to me, that he would reprimand Gallien, if need be, but that he would not exact a terrible punishment from him.

I gathered a heavy wool shawl about me, knelt by the side of the bed, and once again prayed to the Virgin to protect Gallien and help us find Vainqueur. Still preoccupied, I walked to the window and gazed at the frosty fields beyond.

A knocking at the door interrupted my reverie: it was Aiglantine.

"My lady," she said with great urgency, "Lord de Meurtaigne has told everyone in the household to assemble in the courtyard in an hour. He asked me to tell you. And to help get you ready."

"How was his"—I searched for the right word—"his manner?"

"He seemed very calm, my lady. More so, it seems to me, than he has been these last weeks."

"I am glad of it," I said with some relief. Then: "Come, help me prepare." I took a seat at my table as she began to brush my hair. "When will we know it is time for us to descend?" I asked.

"At the tolling of the bell."

THE ENTIRE HOUSEHOLD HAD ASSEMBLED when I entered the courtyard. There were no murmurings, none of the jostling one might have expected from such a large gathering. There was, rather, only a grave, eerie quiet. The wind had come up, and it was only with great difficulty that I kept my cape wrapped around me; my hair blew rather wildly, whipping about my face.

I walked to the front, toward Gerard, all the while shielding my eyes from the sun and trying to steady my shaking body. Now, regal and imposing, he loomed before me, as he had at our very first meeting: a tall broad-shouldered figure in a tunic of rich, dark blue cloth trimmed with extravagant passementerie. He greeted me formally, as was our wont on such occasions, as I curtseyed before him. Then he extended his hand; how massive his hand, with its rings of garnet and lapis, seemed against mine.

Fight fear, I thought as I rose to my feet and assumed my place beside him. I forced myself to look at members of the household, who stood in rows at a slight distance: Ragnar and Haakon, together and slightly apart from the rest, the former with a haughty expression, the latter awkwardly casting his eyes about. Next to them stood Raoul and Aiglantine, both profoundly sad and uneasy; Agnes biting her nails; and Millicent, craning her neck, distastefully curious.

Of Gallien himself, there was no sign.

Suddenly Gerard motioned to Raoul, commanding him: "Have them bring out the boy."

Gallien stumbled out before us moments later, led by two rough stable hands who seemed to have been given fresh tunics for this meeting, as they would have before attending an important feast. Gallien looked pale, weak, and ineffably weary. There was almost no vestige of his former self—the eager, spirited young boy with a passion for hawks, for animals. I cast my eyes down at the partly frozen ground, trying to distract myself by staring at the imprints of boots stamped upon it.

Next came the sound of Gerard's deep, unwavering voice. "You see before you a young man who has committed a grave transgression. He has overreached his place because of vanity and ambition, because he was not content with his position. He took on a responsibility he was not, in the end, equipped to fulfill, and he did this willfully, thoughtlessly. Pride goes before a fall, the Proverb tells us. So, too, he was guilty of the sins of pride and of vanity. He was too proud to admit that he did not have the ability, nor the knowledge, to fulfill the responsibility that he urged us to place upon him.

"I have no patience with such vanity, and even less patience for carelessness in the fulfillment of any task. His carelessness has brought about the loss of a precious and costly gyrfalcon, a hawk as dear to me as a member of my own family. But that is not all—his vanity has led him to commit a sin that is even worse: he will not confess to his fault. He will not admit he was wrong. He will not even admit having made mistakes. For that, above all, he deserves to be punished.

"And so, punished he will be. He will be placed in the dungeon for a length of time I have yet to decide upon, and which will depend, to a great extent, on his behavior. If he does not behave as he should, he will be whipped. And he will never again be permitted to care for my hawks, let alone to enter the mews."

Murmurs rippled through the crowd. "What have you to say, Gallien?" Gerard asked.

His reply was almost inaudible: "I can only ask your forgiveness, my lord."

"A worthy answer, but it comes too late. Too late for your redemption."

Gerard signaled to the two men at Gallien's side: "Take him away."

Then he beckoned to Raoul, who approached us, walking slowly and gravely, as one might for a funeral, his shoulders slumped, his eyes downcast.

Gerard drew Raoul aside to give him further instructions. After a few moments I heard Raoul ask: "How long is Gallien to remain in the dungeon, my lord?"

"Three days." There was a long pause before Gerard added, "But make him *believe* it will be longer. Much longer."

Those are the last words I remember, for suddenly a terrible dizziness overcame me and I felt myself spiraling, falling, falling; and then all was dark, and black, and silent.

# CHAPTER 38

S lowly and hazily I awoke, my eyelids so heavy they felt weighted with stones. I was lying down with a cushion propping up my head; above loomed a soaring ceiling with dark wooden beams that seemed to press down hard upon me. It appeared I was in the great hall: I had no idea why, or why I felt so strange and drowsy. Then I felt a hand, a cool, heavy hand, upon my forehead and heard Gerard's voice telling me: "All is well. Stay still. You must rest."

I turned my head to the right: it was indeed Gerard, sitting on a stool beside me. "Why am I here?" I asked.

"You swooned, and we could not awaken you."

"How long have I been lying here?"

"For a quarter of an hour, my love. You have been insensible all the while. We could not awaken you since the moment you fainted."

"I fainted? Where?"

"In the courtyard." His brow furrowed. "Do you not remember?"

I shook my head: only after a few moments did I succeed in retrieving a faint, resonant memory of being in the courtyard. Then came a succession of other flickering memories: the household assembled, the cold wind, the punishment being meted out to Gallien, and that brutal word *dungeon.* . . . I looked away, for the dawning recollections filled me with a vague terror that seemed allied with him, with Gerard. And then, of course, I realized why: it was he, my husband, who had imposed that dreadful punishment.

He stroked my cheek; I turned my head and looked away.

"Aiglantine is here with us now," he told me in the same level voice. "And Raoul is close by. It was Raoul who caught you when you fell."

"Raoul?"

"Yes."

"Then I owe him great thanks."

"I have thanked him already," he replied in his peremptory way. "But, of course, it is fitting that you thank him as well. In time."

"Where is Aiglantine?" I asked, glancing about.

"I am here, my lady," she said, coming forward and standing beside him.

"Take my place here," Gerard said, gesturing to the stool. "It will be a comfort for Lady Isabelle to have a woman with her."

I reached for her hand as she sat down; she took mine and stroked it gently, murmuring something indistinct. How soothing it was to see her and hear her voice! I was overcome by a childish longing for her to make things right, to blot out the bitter residue of memories that continued to flit through my mind.

"All of us were frightened, my lady," she told me, my hand still in hers. "It seemed you were insensible for an eternity. You looked like a statue when we brought you here! We could not rouse you."

"I feel quite all right now. I want to sit up," I announced as Gerard and Aiglantine exchanged anxious glances.

"Not yet. You must rest," said Gerard.

"I have no idea what happened to me."

"You were weak from lack of food or water, perhaps," Gerard suggested.

"No one can know for sure, my lady," added Aiglantine. "With your bodily humors, perhaps. I have heard they can be upset when you are with child. Or maybe it was an excess of heat in the womb which caused it. This happened to me once when I was—" Here she caught herself, color rushing into her cheeks.

"It does not matter what caused the fainting spell," Gerard interrupted, in the slightly irritated voice he used when anyone prattled on. "It matters only that we were able to revive Lady Isabelle."

"But how did you revive me?" I asked.

"We gave you a syrup of rose water, sugar, and cloves," Aiglantine explained. "I dripped the syrup into your mouth, spoonful by spoonful."

"Raoul suggested the syrup and had the kitchen make it," Gerard added. "He had heard it was a remedy for such things. For fainting."

"It seems to have worked!" I said. "Now I feel well enough to sit up—I promise you I do."

They helped me sit up; my feet were planted on the ground now, and I looked about the great hall. It was neither day nor evening, but that magical, nebulous hour in between. Candles flickered in the dusky light, lending the imposing space, with its vivid tapestries and swirling painted walls a strangely ethereal aspect. I caught sight of a slight figure in red, standing quite erect, to the side, not far from us: Raoul, no doubt.

I looked down: the ties of my bodice had been loosened, and my shoes had been placed near me, on the floor. I bade Aiglantine lace up my bodice and help me with my shoes.

"The color has come back to her cheeks, thank God," Gerard observed to Aiglantine, who was bending down as she slipped the second shoe on.

"Yes, my lord," she replied, glancing up at him. "She looks almost herself now." She stood up. "There, my lady," she said almost jubilantly, "now you are set to rights."

"I should like to thank Raoul," I said, turning to Gerard.

"By and by, of course."

"I should like to do so now," I said more insistently.

"Very well then." He turned to Aiglantine: "Tell Raoul to come here."

Aiglantine and Raoul returned together in a few moments. How relieved I was to see his slight, dignified figure and his small, pointed face! I extended my hand to him: only after a moment did he take it, and rather awkwardly at that, for it was not the custom in our household for servants to touch our hands. (Indeed, I discerned an expression of displeasure cross Gerard's face as I did so.)

Raoul took a few steps back, his hands clasped together with touching dignity as I addressed him. "I owe you great thanks, Raoul, for helping me as you did, and for saving me from falling. A fall, in my condition, might have been——" But here I stopped, as if the word were too dreadful to pronounce, only to add rather awkwardly, "And it was wise of you to think of the syrup to revive me."

"I only did what anyone would do at such a moment, my lady."

"I am deeply grateful," I repeated. At that, I looked at Gerard, Aiglantine, and Raoul standing together, an unaccustomed trio that only seemed to reiterate the strangeness of the scene that autumn afternoon. All this while Gerard had been gentle to me, and concerned; yet had he not been that other creature as well, the man in the courtyard I now recalled with a terrifying vividness, that man who had inflicted the punishment upon Gallien? Three days in the dungeon, three days in solitary darkness, he had decreed. And then the memory assailed me of him telling Raoul: "But make him believe it will be longer."

I jolted myself back to attention when Gerard began to speak. "I shall leave Lady Isabelle with you and Raoul now," he told Aiglantine. "I know she is in good hands."

"As you wish, my lord," said Raoul, bowing again. "I assure you that Aiglantine and I will take good care of her."

SHORTLY AFTERWARD, RAOUL AND AIGLANTINE helped me to my bedchamber. As we arrived at the door, I told Raoul: "There is no need for you to stay any longer. You have done more than enough! Aiglantine will come and fetch you if need be."

"Even so, my lady, I think it best if I wait at the end of the corridor."

"As you wish, but I do not think it is necessary."

He bowed and had only just turned to leave us, when I bade him return. "Raoul, I want you to know how grateful I am, as well, for your concern about Gallien. You have been kind in all ways. It is terrible to think of him in the dungeon." Had I been braver, I might have said more—that I had misjudged Raoul terribly, that I had foolishly believed gossip that had, no doubt, been spread by Millicent; and that my initial suspicions about him now made me feel quite ashamed.

He replied with his usual politesse—for politesse, I had begun to realize, was his bulwark against displaying the deep feelings he clearly possessed. "It is best we trust in Lord de Meurtaigne's wisdom," he pronounced. But then he added, in a low, poignant voice: "I will pray for Gallien, too, and pray that Vainqueur returns one day."

"Let us hope," I replied, touched.

"Yes. It is all in God's hands now."

The moment the door closed, I turned to Aiglantine. "I am worried most of all about the baby, that the fainting spell may have hurt it in some way."

"Babies are sturdy creatures, my lady," she replied. "Sturdier than you might think. Come, sit down, let me look at you."

I did so, my hands upon my belly, waiting for some sign of life. "I have not felt a thing," I said. "Not a bit of movement in the past few hours."

"Wait, be calm. You must trust in God, for He will protect your baby."

I tried to rein in my impatience: my eyes looked frantically about as I waited for an iota of movement within me. At last, I felt an infinitesimal thrust, a kick perhaps.

"There, I felt something!" I cried, with overwhelming relief. "The baby! I think all is well. I felt it move."

"Good! The baby is waking up, just as you woke up earlier. I do not think you need worry, my lady."

THE FOLLOWING MORNING, GERARD ANNOUNCED that the senior midwife would arrive that afternoon to examine me, for he, too, was concerned about my health, and that of the baby.

The midwife and I were alone, in my bedchamber, while Gerard waited outside. She was a woman who emanated capability and soundness, qualities Gerard revered. Having examined me, she pronounced that all seemed to be well, that I need not fear. My relief was immense.

I asked her if she had ever seen instances of this before—of a woman with child who had fainted and had lain insensible for such a long time.

"Ah, yes, it can happen," she replied in her brisk way. "The body in pregnancy goes through great changes, and the balance of humors is delicate. Of course it is possible you were simply very tired, or that you had eaten something that affected your blood, and your breathing."

"Perhaps," I murmured, trying to be heartened by her answer. Deep within me, however, I knew why I had fainted: it had nothing to do with fatigue, or lack of water, or an imbalance of humors. It was the shock of seeing Gallien condemned and utterly humiliated by a man he revered, it was the cruel, satisfied look in my husband's eyes as he pronounced the sentence, it was the thought of Gallien languishing in the dungeon, possibly even beaten; the thought of him deprived of the outdoors, of light, and of those fierce, soaring falcons he loved.

Within this skein of unraveling thoughts lay another, equally painful, realization that ate away at me: all of this had been my fault.

# CHAPTER 39

That night I was haunted by harrowing images of Gallien alone, abandoned, and in darkness, and of the expression in Gerard's eyes as he pronounced the hideous punishment upon him. My sleep was rent by savage dreams of Gallien in the dungeon—of him gasping for breath, encircled by voracious rats, pounding the door as he implored for help. . . .

I could not shake the sense of responsibility I felt for Gallien's fate and tried to lull myself into calm by repeating the dictum of Anthusis—"Expunge all guilt, it is useless here"—as one would a prayer, a soothing litany. But the guilt held firm, like a leering, multitentacled monster.

At dawn I felt Gerard stir in bed beside me before he rose and dressed. All the while I pretended to be sleeping, for I had no desire for him to touch me, nor for the amorous embraces customary for that hour. My body felt coiled and frozen as I lay beside him, the only succor the idea of the baby, warm and alive, growing within me.

I rose only after I was certain that Gerard had left the chamber. Indeed, I stood by the window for a long time, watching as he rode through the gates to make sure he had departed the castle itself. He was to ride to Limoges to meet with men who made barrels for wine; to my relief, he would be absent for several days.

Aiglantine would appear soon to light the early morning fire: only the anticipation of her arrival gave me a modicum of comfort. At last, I heard two quick knocks on the door.

Aiglantine bade me good morrow. I knew from her expression what she was thinking: I looked pale, tired, and sad.

"Gallien—" I murmured. "I hardly slept. I cannot stop thinking of him."

Aiglantine shook her head slowly, as one might in a trance, before saying, in a tremulous voice: "I, too, hardly slept." Then, her voice cracking: "He is given water, only water."

"Nothing to eat?"

She shook her head woefully.

I walked toward the window and looked out, though my mind was blanketed by such apprehension that I saw nothing. For many moments neither of us spoke.

Finally I heard her say: "It is time for you to dress, my lady."

"Yes, I suppose it is," I replied listlessly, turning to face her.

She helped me into a robe of a blue so deep it might almost have been mistaken for black. "A somber dress, for a somber day," I remarked ruefully.

She began to tie the laces of the robe—one, then another, as I stood rigidly immobile before her. After a few moments, I pulled away impatiently. "Let me be for a moment. I need to think," I said rather sharply, clutching my hands as I walked to and fro, the laces trailing.

I stopped before her: "Who brings Gallien water?"

"Raoul, they tell me. I have heard that Lord de Meurtaigne has asked him to look in on Gallien once a day." She paused, as if hesitant to continue, before adding, in an almost inaudible voice: "To make sure that Gallien is still alive."

"How terrified he must be," I lamented. "The darkness. The cold. The hunger."

I turned to address Aiglantine, with a new urgency. "You are certain it is Raoul who looks in on him?"

"Yes."

"Has he looked in on him today?"

"I do not think so. It is early, and he does so in the afternoon."

"Go and fetch Raoul. Tell him I need to see him. Tell him—" I paused, mulling over what I would invent. "Tell him I have a question about our supply of wool for the winter."

A tremor of fear crossed Aiglantine's face: she knew me well enough to know there was a plan afoot. "Are you sure, my lady," she said slowly, and with some trepidation, "that this—"

"Yes. Quite sure. Come, lace me up. Then go and fetch him."

When she was finished, I told her: "After you bring him to see me, I shall ask you to fetch something for me from the kitchen."

She looked puzzled.

"I do not want you to be privy to my conversation with Raoul. I would never want to place you in any danger."

Her eyes—those singular eyes, each a different color—met mine. I took her hands. "Do you understand, Aiglantine?"

She nodded gravely, then left, without a word, to fetch Raoul.

RAOUL RETURNED SHORTLY AFTERWARD, TRAILED by Aiglantine.

"You wish to see me, my lady?" he asked as Aiglantine stood behind him, by the door.

"Yes," I said, before turning to Aiglantine. "Please go to the kitchen, Aiglantine, and ask Wilbertus for some apples for me," I said in a light-hearted, capricious voice. "I have a sudden yearning for them. Have them peeled and cut, and bring them to me. It is odd, is it not, how women who are with child crave such things!"

I refrained from smiling as I noticed Raoul glance away, at the floor, as if he were embarrassed to hear this private chatter between women.

"I will go at once, my lady," she replied.

The door closed. I turned to Raoul and said directly, "I hear you look in on Gallien every day."

"Lord de Meurtaigne has asked me to," he answered, with some wariness. "Yes."

"How does Gallien fare?"

He paused for a moment, as if weighing how candid he should be. "He is desperate," he admitted. "With shame, most of all. And then, of course, the darkness must be unbearable for someone who is used to—"

"He is given nothing to eat, I understand?"

"That is correct, my lady," he replied.

"He must be hungry. Terrified."

"Yes."

"And if, Raoul, if I were to ask you to do something for him out of charity, out of kindness, out of your wish to be a good Christian, how do you think you would respond?"

His reply came swiftly and without hesitation: "I would try my best to help him, my lady."

I smiled to myself: he had answered unequivocally—not "it depends" or "I would consider it." He had said, without hesitation, that he would try to do his best to help.

"I am not surprised by your answer, Raoul."

"Why is that, my lady?" he asked unexpectedly.

"Because I have come to see that you are kind. You are a good man and a good Christian. And I—" I paused, for it was never easy for me to admit when I had made a mistake. "When I first arrived here, I was very alone and frightened. And perhaps, partly because of that, I misjudged you."

"No one, my lady, is faultless in judgment." He paused. "And you were—you are—very young."

"Thank you, Raoul, for your understanding. I would like you to bring Gallien a bit of food. Secretly, of course. Something from the kitchen—some bread, some cheese. Whatever you think possible and least likely to be discovered."

He pondered this a moment. "I understand."

"And I would also like you to bring him something else. A letter."

"A letter, my lady?" He looked alarmed.

"Yes, a letter from me. Which I shall write today and give to you."

His brow furrowed, and a tremor of tension crossed his small, neat mouth. "But my lady, a letter would be—"

"Dangerous? Yes, I know. But I have no choice. I feel responsible in great part for what has happened. I want him to know that."

"There is no need for you to feel a part in this, my lady. I can understand your concern, but no one in the household holds you responsible. I assure you of that."

I was tempted to tell him that Ragnar *did* blame me but refrained. "I am glad to hear that is so, and only wish that would assuage my pain. But it does not, so I must take action by helping him as best I can. I understand that Lord de Meurtaigne is away this evening? That he will return in two days?"

"Yes."

"I shall let you know when the letter is ready."

"I shall await word from you, my lady."

"When do you see Gallien?"

"At noon, my lady."

"That gives me a bit of time. Good. But now you should return to your duties."

He bowed, then turned to walk toward the door.

"And Raoul," I said, calling him back, "if anyone should ask why you were here, tell him—or her—that we were discussing the supply of wool, for the winter."

"Of course," he replied, with a complicit smile.

A FEW HOURS LATER, HAVING written the letter to Gallien, I asked Aiglantine to summon Raoul. When he arrived at my chamber, I asked her to wait outside the door.

"Here," I said, handing the letter to him. "Read him what I have written, and tell him, too, that you bring him food on my instruction. After you have read him the letter, destroy it."

"I shall do so, my lady. Exactly as you say."

"Of that I have no doubt." I stood before him in silence, absent-mindedly fingering my wedding ring.

"Best you leave now."

He bowed and walked toward the door—a slight, trim figure in red, my letter tucked in the pocket of his tunic.

"Raoul—" I said, having followed him to the door.

"Yes, my lady?" He turned to face me.

"Thank you."

He seemed touched; then he left me.

I watched as he walked down the corridor until he disappeared from view, all the while thinking of my message to Gallien and the words I had penned across that sheet of parchment, words that I now knew by heart: "Be not afraid. No one holds you responsible for the loss of Vainqueur, least of all myself. No one thinks you were careless or negligent. You will survive this and be the stronger for it. Hold fast to your faith and persevere through the darkness. Another day will come, I promise you: the sun will shine, and you will return to the world you love most: to a world of open skies, and light, and your cherished falcons. One day I know you will find a way to freedom."

# CHAPTER 40

I asked to take my meals in my chamber the following day and remained there, alone, relieved that Gerard was still in Limoges. I yearned to write Fastrada and tell her of Gallien's plight and my own guilt but dared not, fearing that a letter might secretly be opened and perused by my husband. I tried to read, without success, for my anxiety about Gallien and sense of responsibility for his plight fractured my concentration. Only my secret objects brought me a modicum of peace that somber autumn afternoon. I took the hidden things from the trunk and arranged them before me—cradling them, one by one, as I imagined their history and fantasized about their provenance.

While I was gazing at the objects, I heard a sharp, insistent knocking at the door. I leaped to my feet, hurriedly put the things away, and seized Fastrada's book of poetry, which I always kept near me. Book in hand, I took a seat on the bench and asked who it was: Millicent, to my dismay.

There was a slightly fevered look in her eye and a sprightliness to her step, signs I knew all too well: she had heard some titillating news, or some piquant gossip. After I bade her enter, I paid no attention as she began to sweep. The broom's bristles made a hard, rasping sound as they brushed against the stone floor.

All the while I sensed she was burning to tell me something. But I was nervous, and in no mood to accommodate her; instead I simply waited rather perversely, in silence, as I turned one page, then another.

Finally, she paused her sweeping and said: "There is something you might wish to know, my lady."

"Ah—and what is that?"

"I hear that Gallien is to be released soon."

I was uncomfortably aware that she was assessing my reaction; thus, I merely asked calmly, "Who has told you this?"

"Agnes. I saw her in the kitchen earlier, my lady."

Agnes, of course, I thought to myself. "There is little that Agnes does not seem to hear," I observed. "At least, that is my impression."

"She's a good, devout girl, Agnes is," retorted Millicent. "We are both from the same village." She began to sweep even more vociferously.

I did not voice what I was thinking: Millicent's beloved village also seemed to have bred two remarkably gossipy women. "But do tell me what Agnes has heard about Gallien," I said after a moment.

"There is some talk he will be released on the morrow."

"How did she learn this?" I asked with some skepticism, for it seemed more likely Raoul would have been apprised of this first.

"The boys in the stables told her. That is where Gallien will work now." Then, with a certain smugness: "That is what Lord de Meurtaigne has decided for him."

"I see," I murmured, before adding, with forced matter-of-factness: "That does not surprise me. Gallien worked in the stables before he began in the mews. I assume he will resume his old work—taking care of Lord de Meurtaigne's mount."

"That is not what I hear, my lady." There was an unnerving, slightly triumphant edge to her voice.

"Indeed?"

"He is to sweep out the stalls. Shovel manure." She paused, broom in hand, her eyes still intent upon me.

Despondence swept over me—the thought of Gallien forced to such lowly, degrading tasks! There was great cruelty in it. Many in the household, resentful of his aspirations, would mock him.

She resumed sweeping before venturing, "He is fortunate Lord de Meurtaigne is so generous."

"Generous?" I asked, struggling to conceal my incredulity.

"Gallien could have been told to leave, given all he has done. That costly hawk, lost forever! And all these troubles because——" She paused, her thin mouth set defiantly as she took up the broom again.

"Because of what, Millicent?" I asked, by then too irritated to let her disparaging words pass. "What were you about to say?"

She hesitated, carefully choosing her words: "Because Gallien was not ready to man such a great hawk." And then she repeated her customary litany: "He is not like Ragnar. He was not born with falconry in his blood!"

Our eyes met; color rose to her cheeks, and she looked away. I knew why, of course: this was not all she had intended to say. What she had fully intended was: And all these troubles because you, my lady, stubbornly promoted Gallien. Because you are young and naive and do not understand how a proper household works.

I set down my book and stood up, drawing myself up to my full height. Looking down at her with cold, restrained anger, I said, "We must put the Gallien matter behind us, Millicent. I do not want to discuss it ever again. Do you understand?"

"Yes, my lady." She looked almost frightened.

"I am glad of it. Now please leave me be."

She set down the broom and smoothed her tunic. "Is there anything else I can do for you, my lady?" she asked rather unctuously.

"Yes. Ask Raoul to come and see me."

RAOUL APPEARED AT MY DOOR later.

I bade him enter and told him to close the door. Then: "How does Gallien fare?"

"Poorly. He is starving"—he hesitated—"and he has been whipped."

Rage so overcame me that I could hardly speak. Finally I managed to ask, "Is it true that he will be released tomorrow?"

"There is some talk of this, yes. But it is far from certain. He was very grateful for your letter——"

"Which you have since destroyed?"

"Yes."

"I hear he is to work in the stables."

"That is true." He gave a deep sigh. "Doing the most menial work, I am afraid."

So Agnes's report was indeed accurate. "He will never, ever remain there," I told him vehemently.

## CHAPTER 41

At sunrise the following morning, when the stable boys awoke, Gallien was nowhere to be found. It seemed he had somehow managed to escape and had fled during the night.

When, a few hours later, Gerard returned and learned what had happened, he was enraged beyond all measure. "This is villainous behavior!" he exclaimed, his eyes afire with anger. "The boy fled, like a base criminal, during the night. If anything proves his guilt in losing Vainqueur, it is this."

"If you had disclosed your decision about Gallien to me, my lord," I ventured quietly, "I would have told you that he would never remain here under those circumstances. He would never have submitted to such a"—I deliberated for moments before I added—"humiliation."

"*Humiliation*, you call it?" he rejoined, with a scathing glance. "Anyone else would call my decision immensely generous." Then, sarcastically: "But not my wife, the countess, it seems."

"He is very proud."

"He is a Saxon," came his riposte, as if he had not really heard me.

"He is *human*."

"Where can he possibly go and not be found out? I will make certain his reputation is ruined." He mulled this over, seeming to savor the notion. "No one will dare hire him. And if someone does—then woe to him! That person, and anyone who helps him, will be considered a criminal. Criminals I will hunt down and punish."

I knew that it was a grave crime for a nobleman, or any accomplice, to lure a skilled falconer away from another's household; my brothers had told me chilling stories of falconers being subjected to hideous punishments, or even put to death, for disloyalty to their masters. Aflame with nervousness and terrified for Gallien, I could only stammer: "I am sure he meant no harm, that he simply could not bear the idea—"

"I have heard enough," he interrupted, infuriated. "And you have done—"

Enough, he was about to say, no doubt. I bowed my head and glanced away, before murmuring, in a low, tense voice: "I shall leave you be, my lord."

"Where are you going?"

"To my chamber."

"*Our* chamber."

I managed to nod, and left.

LATER, AT SUPPER, HIS CHOLER toward me seemed to have vanished. I wondered why, and whether it was due to the pacifying effect of wine. He took my hand as we sat at table, murmuring "my dove" and other endearments, as if nothing unpleasant had passed between us. He began to regale me with stories about the important men he had met in Limoges—producers of the oak barrels used to store the wine he shipped to England. "These are the men, the families, who make the best barrels, from the finest oak," he told me, as if he desired my approbation.

"And you only want the best—" I replied quietly, watching as he drank some wine.

"Yes," he said, setting his goblet down. "How well you know me." He kissed my hand; then he revealed he had a surprise for me and would show it to me afterward, in our chamber.

I smiled wanly: in the past I would have been excited about a present, but now a wave of ennui came over me.

"We must forget all about this," he continued, seemingly oblivious to my lack of curiosity.

"About what, my lord?"

"Losing Vainqueur. It was painful, yes, but I also know it amounts to comparatively little compared to other matters. In our life together."

He stood up, taking my hand as he helped me rise, before signaling to the servants that we had finished supping.

A heady, inebriating, and foreign scent wafted toward us as we approached our chamber later that night. "What is this perfume in the air?" I asked Gerard as we approached the door.

"It is part of my present," he said, with a mysterious smile.

We entered the chamber, illuminated by oil lamps and banks of flickering tapers. It was cold that night in November: the curtains had been partly drawn around the bed, and a fire blazed on the hearth. As the flames leaped and crackled, he told me: "Look for my gift."

It took a few moments before I glimpsed it: a glittering incense burner in the form of a life-size falcon, which gazed at us from a table in a far corner. I walked toward it. The "hawk" was fashioned in bronze, its haughty eyes of gleaming turquoise, its feathers delineated in vivid red, green, and blue enamel. Perfume, emanating from burning spices deep within, wafted through the intricate fretwork of the creature's breast: the scent was redolent of damask rose, frankincense, musk, and cloves, yet it was so layered and complex that it was impossible to discern which element predominated.

I assumed the object was a splendid creation of Limoges, from whence Gerard had just returned. I asked as much; he confirmed it was. "It reminds me of Vainqueur," I told him, tracing the outline of a feather with my finger.

"It does, does it not?" He smiled with pride. "I had it filled with dried herbs, rose, and incense. For you"—he embraced me—"who loves perfume."

I drew away, ostensibly to continue examining the object. "Where did you find it?" I asked.

"From a famous artisan in Limoges, a man who has created objects for me before. I had it commissioned months ago, not long after I purchased Vainqueur. It reminds me of incense burners I have seen in the Holy Land. They are used quite frequently to lend fragrance to rooms. There they are considered a great luxury."

"And the perfume itself, the herbs burning inside?"

"From a dealer in spices, from La Rochelle. I told him I wanted an ample supply, one that would last well into the winter. And that I wanted a rich, complex scent for my wife, who is herself"—he paused—"complex."

I closed my eyes as I drew in the intoxicating scent, wishing it would transport me to another place. In fact, the eerie creature only served as a haunting reminder of my own guilt, and of my part in the loss of Vainqueur and the humiliation of Gallien. I wondered, too, if Gerard felt any pangs of sadness as he glimpsed this reincarnation of his prized hawk. . . .

"What are you thinking?" he asked.

"That it is almost as if Vainqueur has been resurrected," I replied, instantly regretting my words.

"I am powerful—but not *that* powerful!" came his rueful reply. A fleeting expression of pain crossed his face before he forced a smile. "I am pleased you like it, my darling," he said, and kissed my forehead.

I murmured something indistinct, my hand upon his shoulder as I drew away. "It is late now. I am tired. And you, too, must be tired from your long journey."

Soon afterward, having said my prayers, I took my place in bed. I lay there silently, my head propped on the pillow, my belly high and mounded before me, swathed by blankets. He lay down beside me: I felt his hand grasp mine, before it wended its way to caress my stomach; he drew closer still, murmuring blandishments and professions of his love. In the past, at such moments—after rancor earlier in the day—I had managed to stave off lingering, angry thoughts, bolting them in an inner, inaccessible chamber while I rekindled others of a different nature—those that succeeded in promoting pleasure.

But that night, I could not.

# CHAPTER 42

With the advent of the Christmas season, the household came alive with all its customary rituals: the gathering of game, the feverish preparing of savories and cakes, the amassing of pine branches and berry-laden boughs to deck the great hall. I tried my best to assume a sort of jollity, but I did not feel it as I had the previous year, so beset was I with loneliness and agitation. I thought ceaselessly of my brother and grandfather, and of Fastrada, all of whom I sorely missed. And I worried about Gallien, wondering where he had gone and how he fared—if, indeed, he was still alive, for the forest and roads could be perilous.

Only the idea of the creature growing within me gave me comfort. I would feel my warm, swollen stomach, all the while imagining the baby's beating heart, and its tiny body, growing and stirring. My son, I would think, my son.

ONE EVENING DURING THAT TIME, Aiglantine came to my chamber to help me dress; men of high rank from Rochefort were arriving for a banquet that evening. "I know nothing of our guests tonight," I remarked as she helped me don my robe. "Only that they have had important dealings with my husband."

"Agnes told me a bit about them," she said, before adding, teasingly, "if her gossip would interest you."

"I think you know the answer," I replied with a smile.

"She told us that she had heard that one of them—the Lord of Noissy, from Rennes—had recently divorced his wife, a very highborn lady."

"Why?" I asked as she laced the ties of my bodice.

"The lady was barren. She had tried for years to become pregnant, and never could. Millicent told us there was good reason for it."

"What sort of reason?"

"She said the lady was not a virtuous sort, that there was talk about her being"—she paused—"wayward. Not God-fearing in her words and actions. It is because of her sinfulness, Millicent said, that the Lord cursed her with barrenness."

"And you," I asked, "do you believe that, Aiglantine?"

"I do not know what to think, my lady."

After she finished tying the last lace, I turned to face her. "Where will this lady go, now that her husband has cast her off?"

"To an abbey not far from here. At least, that is what Agnes has heard."


IN THOSE WEEKS BEFORE CHRISTMAS, the constraint of the castle, and of being with child, chafed at me as they never had before. I was possessed of a sudden fierce energy, a desire to move, and climb, and pace. I had little appetite. My sleep was fretful, and what dreams I managed to remember upon awakening were terrifying.

Despite the bitter cold, I walked to and fro across the bailey, and then, incessantly, along the borders of my slumbering garden. I would wait for moments when the guards at the ramparts were inattentive—then, surreptitiously, I would climb the high, narrow steps to the walkway along the battlements. From that lofty vantage point, the world, and all of nature, seemed to extend before me: a wintry universe, quiescent and sear, its palette one of white, and frosty gray, and stone.

As I walked along the battlements, starting occasionally at the cawing of rooks or the howling of wolves, I thought of my girlhood, and of all that had happened since leaving my home that frigid day in January; of my brothers and our trip to Nîmes; of the medal with the serpent and the crocodile my brother had given me and which I still held close, and of my beloved secret objects. I thought of my first glimpse of the falcons' lair with Gerard, and of the eerie bronze hawk whose eyes seemed to follow me whenever I entered my bedchamber. . . .

ON THE MONDAY AFTERNOON BEFORE Christmas, a strange calm came over me, a sudden unnerving stillness. Soon afterward I was overcome by dizziness, then by such ferocious cramping and bleeding that I could no longer stand nor speak. It was then, they later told me, that Gerard called for the physician.

The pain was searing, yet even in my delirium I knew it was not the sort that had accompanied Editha's birth. This was of a different order—a labyrinth of suffering through which there existed not an iota of light, nor a triumphant exit.

The baby was stillborn. They would not even let me see it, nor tell me its sex, before it was whisked away. To be buried, they said; where? I asked, weeping. Near the church yard but not within it, they told me firmly but gently, explaining that this was the fate of all unchristened creatures, no matter the sex or rank.

Finally, I succumbed to sleep. Hours later I awoke to find Gerard sitting by me.

"It was a boy," he said.

DARK, COLD MONTHS OF DESPONDENCE followed.

So frail did I become after the stillbirth, so listless with despair, that at times Gerard feared for my life. He ordered Aiglantine to minister to me; seldom did she leave my side. Raoul was allowed to come to my bedside as well, for my husband had come to realize I found his presence comforting.

As my body began to recover, guilt once more loomed large: Had my frantic activity in those weeks before Christmas—my incessant walking and climbing—brought about the stillbirth? Had I recklessly disregarded well-meaning advice in my compulsion to allay my restlessness? With these wrenching dark thoughts came self-loathing in various guises. That February I kept my hand mirror covered for weeks, unable to face my own reflection, for I had become terribly thin and looked much older.

It was only to Aiglantine that I expressed my deepest fears. One morning in early March, as we sat together in my chamber, I set down the book I had been trying in vain to read and asked, "Do you remember that day you helped in the kitchen, before Christmas, when you were working with Millicent and Agnes?"

"Yes, my lady."

"It was not long before I lost the baby."

"I believe so," she acknowledged, with the apprehensive look that always came into her eyes when I brought up the stillbirth.

"I was feeling very restless then. I walked a great deal and climbed to the ramparts. Do you think"—I paused—"Do you think this could have caused the stillbirth?"

"Oh, no, I do not think so! There are women who work and labor in the fields, and still they have healthy babies." She leaned forward and took my hand, pressing it gently to comfort me.

ONE MORNING EARLY THAT APRIL, while I sat in my garden on the feast of Saint Fulbert, a breeze wafted toward me infused with a warm, sweet scent of quince blossoms, laurel leaves, and grass. I breathed it in deeply, savoring the fragrance, for it was redolent of springtime at my grandfather's manor. Closing my eyes, I imagined him sitting at the table in his library—his wheat-colored linen tunic, and his fair, blue-veined hand with its Roman ring, poised upon a sheet of parchment. Most of all I tried to conjure up his elegant voice, at once clipped and sonorous, as he read stories aloud to me. . . .

A tremor of shame swept through me: how disappointed he would be to see me now, felled by sadness, despair, and slothful guilt! "This is not the spirited girl I know," he would say in a gentle, chiding voice. "Not the girl who loves stories of heroes who surmount misfortune, of queens who triumph over adversity." I stood up and began to walk quickly along the garden path, still thinking of my grandfather and the stories he had recounted to me. For he regarded stories with as much reverence as one did the scriptures, and had encouraged me to draw nourishment and strength from them.

These memories seemed to reawaken my former self, unshackling me from sadness, lethargy, and self-loathing. Little by little I returned to the things that always fortified me: I reread Fastrada's old letters and her book of poetry; I unearthed my secret objects, marveling, as I always did, at their survival; I took long walks with Aiglantine at my side.

IN THE FIRST WEEKS FOLLOWING the stillbirth, there were moments when I glimpsed Gerard fighting to conceal his sadness and pain—for these were emotions, after all, and he was a man who viewed emotions as opponents to be mastered. Only I, and perhaps Raoul, recognized how despondent he was: to the outside world my husband presented his customary disciplined, controlled exterior.

After the death of Editha, he had shown me a subdued compassion; after the stillbirth, he displayed an inscrutable politeness that was soon succeeded by an unnerving silence. As the days passed, it became clear that we were never to mention the loss of this baby, our son. The terrible event was dispatched much as the baby had been dispatched—swiftly, efficiently, into an unmarked grave no one acknowledged or visited. When, during this time, I asked Gerard whether it would not be better to voice his grief, he answered decisively, "There is no need. What is past is dead."

ONE EVENING IN EARLY APRIL, as Millicent was closing the shutters in our bedchamber, she turned to me and said, in the slightly querulous tone that usually bade ill: "I do not see your rosary beads, my lady, or the votive of the Virgin you usually keep here, on the table by your bed."

"I had them there this morning," I replied in a deliberately offhand fashion, "but I decided to put them away, for safekeeping." This was a lie, of course: I had tossed the rosary beads and votives into a cabinet. I still blamed God and the Virgin for deserting me, and felt no need to pray to them.

"But you must keep the rosary and votive near you, my lady!" she said. Then, with the slightest edge of insinuation: "All *virtuous* women do. Women who want to be with child, most of all. You must pray to God and the Virgin to help you, and to absolve you of all sin, so that you are ready—"

She stopped suddenly; Gerard had entered and stood silently watching us. "My lord," she said, with a flustered curtsey.

"Once again you are giving advice to Lady Isabelle, I see," he observed. She began to wring her bony hands as he continued to look at her, a slightly bemused expression on his face.

"I was only saying, my lord," she sputtered, "that God and the blessed Virgin reward virtuous women, and that my lady must always keep her rosary beads and votives near her. God blesses such women with pregnancy, and with healthy children." She added, with cloying meekness, "That is what the scriptures tell us."

I held my breath, waiting for him to mock her, as he always did when she spouted such pronouncements.

"Wise advice," he said instead, with a chilly look in my direction, "though I suspect Lady Isabelle has her own notions about the path to virtue."

DURING THESE MONTHS, WE HAD not engaged in carnal relations. The physician, and the midwives, had advised against them: my womb needed to mend and the humors of my body needed to reassume their balance after my terrible ordeal.

For once, I was glad to have the midwives' strictures as an excuse to forswear lovemaking, for I had become increasingly wary of my husband. The steeliness that I had once found rather fascinating—had even admired—now seemed frightening. I could not dispel certain images and memories—the cruel look in his eyes when he had pronounced the punishment upon Gallien; the story of his putting his favorite mount to death with such sangfroid; and the incident that Agnes had recounted about the swaddling cloth he had denied Aiglantine for her baby. These remembrances had once fluttered through my mind like evanescent moths; they now began to assume the power of monsters.

ONE AFTERNOON THAT APRIL, GERARD made it clear that our marital relations must resume.

"It is time we try again to have a child," he told me. His expression was pleasant enough, but there was an edge to his voice, a hardness, that unsettled me.

"And so we shall," I answered in a subdued voice. I bit my lip and picked up my sewing, which lay near me, and drew the needle through the cloth, trying to conceal my nervousness. The idea of another pregnancy, and all its implications, terrified me.

I felt his eyes upon me. Finally, he broke the silence: "I hope you will show more enthusiasm when it comes to the time."

SINCE GERARD HAD GIVEN IT to me, the bronze falcon had been kept alight day and night on a table near our bed, infusing our chamber with its dense, complex scent. In the evening, its turquoise eyes burned with piercing brightness, seeming to follow me wherever I went—to my table, to the window, to the bed. There were many times when I wanted to cover the object, as I had the mirror, but I dared not, fearing that doing so would offend and infuriate my husband. The bronze figure reminded him of loss, of the treasured falcon who had escaped, yet it did not haunt him as it did me: to me it was an emblem of failure, of guilt, of everything I had done wrong. After the stillbirth, there were moments when I could hardly bear to look at it; yet I dared not move it.

The creature's eyes and scent seemed to burn with special fierceness on the night we resumed lovemaking. It was a cold night in spring: rain beat against the shutters, and gusts of wind unsettled the tapestries so that they undulated against the walls. As darkness fell, the perfume emanating from the smoldering herbs was almost inebriating.

"We must try to have another child," he said not ungently as he helped me to undress. I felt myself draw back, inwardly struggling against the imposition of grim purpose and a host of troubling thoughts. He began to caress me as we lay together; all the while I strove to recapture the path to pleasure. "I am cold," I said, shivering slightly. He pulled the curtains around the bed: I remember the shrill sound of the drapery rings as the curtains slowly closed around us. I was grateful for those curtains, for they blocked the falcon's eyes from my sight.

# CHAPTER 43

The fear of pregnancy began to stalk me. Each time my monthly course arrived I felt immeasurable relief, as if the red splotches upon the napkin were emblems of freedom—from pain, from disappointment, from impending loss. From losing another Editha, or another baby son.

What I had once sought, I now only wanted to avoid. In the past I had welcomed carnal pleasure: now I fought to keep it at bay. I had been taught, after all, that conception was most likely to occur in that spasm of pleasure a wife experiences during carnal relations with her husband. If I resisted that moment, I thought to myself, if I prevented it from happening, then less was the likelihood of pregnancy.

At first this idea—this renunciation of that thrilling pleasure—was hard to contemplate, harder still to implement, for I longed for solace of any sort. Nor could I deny the spell of my husband's body, skin, and scent. But as my wariness of Gerard grew, and his obsession that I become pregnant superseded all else, my body seemed to follow my clenched mind, and it too girded itself against him.

I began to forestall him by pleading fatigue, or an upset stomach, or an aching back—relieved, and yet surprised, that he rarely questioned or challenged me when I did so. In this realm, the realm of feelings, Gerard did not have the courage to confront me directly: the arrows he directed took a far more insidious, circuitous route. He would respond to a request of mine with a caustic look or contradict me with stinging vehemence if I disagreed with him about even the most commonplace matter.

Often during this time I thought of Fastrada and our conversation before the fire that autumn morning. She had told me there were ways of keeping oneself from being with child, methods that she herself had tried: keeping oneself very thin so that one's monthly course ceased altogether, for instance, or riding a great deal. I would also think of that inner room in Anthusis's lair, where I had seen the cabinet that contained the potions for women who did not want to be with child. "Such women *do* exist, you know," she had told me. How her words had disconcerted me! To imbibe such things, to go against God, to risk mortal sin—even to think of it had made me shudder.

THE LONELY, TENSE SUMMER OF 1180 slowly passed. I grew accustomed to Gerard's behavior toward me: polite, even decorous when we were with others, chilly when we were alone together, except when we were in bed. Even there, however, he was not as amorous as he had once been: the consuming nature of his mission—that I become pregnant—had infected our lovemaking with a certain grim determination, a cheerlessness. All the while, I felt myself inwardly drawing further and further away, both in body and mind.

I returned to the solace of prayer, hoping that God and the Virgin, having hitherto deserted me, would take pity and answer my entreaties. I brought offerings to the altar of our chapel; I attended Mass with new fervor. And each night as I knelt by my bed, my head bowed in prayer, I asked Him and the Virgin to help me find my way.

ALL THAT SEASON WE HEARD rumors that King Louis was sickly, and that his son, the dauphin, Philippe, had assumed growing power. In late September came momentous news: King Louis had died at Saint Pont. One morning, not long after learning that Philippe had been crowned, Gerard told me gravely, "Let us hope Philippe uses his new power more shrewdly than his monkish father."

"But King Louis was a good man," I interjected, "and much beloved by the people, was he not? And we cannot really blame him for the failure of the last Holy War."

"He may have been the darling of priests and pious folk, but he was *weak*," he said with a look of contempt. "The King's greatest failing was in his dealings with Eleanor. He let her outmaneuver him at almost every turn. Imagine the humiliation of seeing her married to his rival, a younger man, Henry Plantagenet, and so soon after their divorce!"

"Imagine if King Louis and Eleanor had *not* divorced," I mused.

"He had no choice but to divorce her," came his swift reply. "He needed an heir, and she seemed incapable of providing one. The Pope was right to grant the divorce."

I felt a frisson of terror, yet he himself seemed to have no sense of the reverberating power of his observation. To my relief, moments later Raoul entered; he handed my husband a letter and left.

Glancing at the seal, Gerard gave a satisfied smile. "I have been awaiting this message. It is from Lord de Biozat, who resides near Saint Pont."

"Is that not where King Louis died?"

"Precisely."

His genial mood visibly changed as his eyes scanned the letter; the artery on one temple throbbed, and his expression became glacial. Once finished, he crumpled the parchment in his fist and ordered the messenger to wait in the stables.

"Come, it is late, let us go inside," he said brusquely, turning to me.

We walked quickly to the great hall where a young minstrel, in the corner, was tuning his lute. "Give us some music," Gerard commanded. The nervous young man began to strum as we settled on a bench. Gerard leant forward, his forearms digging into his thighs, his hands clutched.

After a few moments of silence, I quietly ventured, "I gather that the letter did not please you, my lord."

"No, it did not *please* me." He had enunciated "please" crisply, almost mockingly. "It seems that Philippe is basking in his new power. And not in a way beneficial to *me*, let us say. But do not worry, my dove, all will be well." With that, he kissed my hand and turned to the minstrel: "These songs are too melancholy. Give us something festive."

LATER THAT AUTUMN, A MESSENGER arrived: the same messenger who had brought word of my mother's death. His somber demeanor so alarmed me that I immediately conjectured, "My father is ill," as I nervously knit my hands together.

"No, my lady, not your father," he replied. There was a long awkward silence as he looked down, shuffling his feet. "I am sorry to be the bearer of bad tidings . . ."

"Oh, do tell me now, quickly, whatever it is!"

He bowed his head and then, looking up at me directly, announced with great sorrow: "Your grandfather has died."

"My grandfather?" I repeated, incredulously. My grandfather had always been the ballast of my life: he could not die, he was immortal!

"Alas, yes, my lady. He passed from this world but two weeks ago."

A frozen uncomprehending stupor seized me. I could not speak; I could not even cry.

He gently handed me two letters, explaining that one was from Guy, the other from my grandfather. "Your brother wanted you to have something else as well," he said, digging inside his large satchel. He produced a package covered in cloth and tied with string and bade me take it.

"No, I must read the letters first," I told him, shaking my head, still dazed.

The messenger, watching me with a pitying expression, waited a moment before he continued: "Guy asked that you begin with his letter, my lady."

I nodded numbly before walking toward a bench in a far corner; in my grief I craved quiet and privacy. I sat down and unfurled the first letter.

Guy's message was short and stoical to the point of callousness. It related the circumstances of Grandfather's death—a sudden illness that culminated in a seizure that quelled his heart. To the very end, however, Guy wrote that "Grandfather's mind was as keen as an arrow, as it had always been." It was my grandfather's dying wish, he wrote, that his letter and a few of his treasured possessions be delivered to me.

I set Guy's letter down and turned to the second letter, unfolding it slowly. It was penned in my grandfather's elegant hand with remarkable vigor and fluidity for a man of his venerable age.

*To Isabelle de Meurtaigne, my dearest granddaughter*

Greetings from her devoted grandfather. When you receive this, I shall no longer be present on this earth, and everything I once knew and cherished will be behind me. I cannot leave without professing that you, darling girl, have been the greatest joy of my life. To watch you grow and flourish, with your fine mind, and to share with you the books and stories I loved—these memories have sustained me during these last days. I ask, nay implore you, to remember our times together, not as idle remembrances, but as a kind of sustenance. Think of the stories we read, think of the magic and the rhythm of those words and thoughts—remember how the words of Virgil and the ancient poets lit those sparks that animated and enlivened your mind! Do not let your new life extinguish them.

I have asked Guy to send you a few of my dearest possessions: keep them with you always as you proceed through life. I know you will treasure them, as I treasured them, and as I treasured you.

Do not ever think of me as dead and buried, but as part of you. Let my spirit live within you, just as those stories and verses lived within you. Let them help guide you as you shoulder the duties of marriage and motherhood.

Remember me and our times together in my library, dearest Isabelle!

At that I wept as I had never wept before.

I heard footsteps approaching and looked up: Raoul. "A handkerchief for you, my lady," he said, coming to my side.

I daubed my eyes and inflamed cheeks with it, trying to collect myself.

"Best to let yourself cry, my lady," he said gently.

I nodded, biting my salty lips as I glanced at him. "Ask the messenger for the package," I finally managed to say. "I am ready to open it now." Then, pleadingly: "Stay with me, Raoul, while I open it, will you?"

"Of course, my lady."

He returned in a moment with the package. My fingers fumbled as I untied the string, so nervous and spent was I. Raoul, noticing this, loosened the tie for me; then he stepped away, a few paces to the side, as I unwrapped the contents of the package.

Enclosed were two books—a copy of the *The Aeneid*, and a volume of Cicero's writings. Together with these was a small linen pouch that contained something heavy. I opened it: inside was my grandfather's cherished ring with the green intaglio of the Roman emperor.

I held the ring in my palm, overcome by the memories that it evoked—of my grandfather, of those afternoons in his library. . . . "I shall wear this on a ribbon around my neck," I said, turning to address Raoul.

"May it bring you good fortune, my lady."

I set the ring down carefully and picked up one of the splendid volumes: the Cicero, first, a great favorite of my grandfather, who admired the Roman's stringent turn of mind and sober prose. I began to leaf through the well-worn pages. It was my grandfather's habit to mark his favorite passages by affixing a small oblong marker in parchment to the margin, where he would write *nota bene*. There were three such places in this volume.

I went to the first marked passage and read it softly aloud to myself: "*Animi cultus quasi quidam humanitatis cibus.*" Then I reread each word, translating as I did so: "Cultivation to the mind is as necessary as food to the body."

Next, to the second marked passage, which I recognized as one of grandfather's very favorites: "*Si hortum in bibliotheca habes, deerit nihil.*" How like him, I thought, smiling to myself as I recalled him repeating this very dictum: "If you have a garden and a library, you have everything."

I came to the third passage, which was unfamiliar and seemed to have been singled out among the others, for he had underscored *nota bene* with great emphasis on its parchment marker. It read: "*Quid est enim libertas? Potestas vivendi ut velis.*" I repeated the passage to myself, translating it slowly and carefully from the Latin: "What then is freedom? It is the power to live as one chooses."

## CHAPTER 44

In the days and weeks that followed, I struggled to contain my grief, most of all in the presence of my husband. He had greeted the news of my grandfather's death with a cursory politeness and showed hardly any interest in the things bequeathed to me. I took comfort in long walks with Aiglantine; I reread the marked passages from Cicero incessantly; I refused to abandon my somber mourning clothes, taking care to tuck the ancient ring deep within my bodice so Gerard would not see it. I had lost my desire for food, and supper became an ordeal.

At table one evening, Gerard, noticing I had barely touched my food, remarked: "Surely this has gone on long enough."

"I am still very sad," I replied in a muted voice.

"Why does this still affect you so?" he asked impatiently. "Your grandfather was an old man. You could hardly have expected him to live forever."

"Yes," I replied, stung by his riposte. "But he was my beloved grandfather even so."

"I understand that. Still, you must learn to manage your emotions. You cannot let them rule you."

"I am trying my best."

He remained silent, but his exasperated expression articulated what his voice had not: "Try harder," it said.

Only a few moments later, however, he took my hand gently: "My dove, time will heal your sadness. And so will your having a child. Of that I am certain."

I murmured something by way of assent.

"But until we have a child," he continued in the same lulling voice, "tell me, what would make you happy? You have only to ask."

"I would like to invite Fastrada for a visit," I replied at once, with a certain fierceness.

He withdrew his hand. "One day, perhaps," he said before continuing rather sternly, "but that would hardly be possible now."

"Why not?"

"The Hauteclares are making preparations for their hunt. It is not a moment when Fastrada would leave her husband or abandon her responsibilities. She may have her faults," he added, with a wry smile, "but she is, by all accounts, a good wife."

I should have expected such an answer—one both discouraging and implicitly critical. Hearing it, however, filled me with despair, though I did not have the spirit, that night, to challenge or contradict him. I forced myself to nod serenely.

He finished his wine and rose abruptly from the table. "Come, it is late," he said, taking my hand. "Let us retire."


I HAD COME TO DREAD our chamber at bedtime: the ritual of the curtains closing around the bed, the snuffing out of candles, the scent of the falcon's strange perfume and the piercing gaze of its eyes, which seemed to follow me, to follow us.

Here, at night, Gerard assumed another self—a wooing, seducing self. But I knew this sudden tenderness had an objective: I no longer trusted it and regarded it as one might a weapon.

One night in early October, after our lovemaking, I sat up in bed, drawing the linen sheet and woolen quilt around me. The curtains were drawn around us. Gerard had fallen asleep. All was silent.

I sat up and drew the curtain partly open, taking care not to wake my husband. For once I was grateful for the falcon on the table nearby, for its eyes shone brightly, providing some light.

I stepped out of bed and tiptoed to the window. One shutter was ajar. A brilliant full moon illumined the fields and the edge of the forest beyond—a camaïeu of gray-blue, black, and ivory, for long fragile clouds trailed across the sky. In the distance, to the left, past the ramparts, loomed a steep, craggy hill from which a tall spiky pine rose in-

congruously from the rocks. It was so bright that I could make out the
silhouettes of two wolves poised beneath the tree, their muzzles turned
to the sky.

I watched the wolves, waiting for them to move. When they do, I
thought to myself, that will be a signal, and I shall return to bed. But they
never stirred, and finally, impatient of waiting, I walked forlornly to
the table. There, beside the falcon, lay a candle: I picked it up, walked to
the still flickering fire, and lit it.

Nearby stood the chest where I kept my secret objects and now,
my grandfather's books as well. Candle in hand, I opened the chest and
took out the book on top—the Cicero. I held it tight, glad to have its
company, watching as the candlelight flickered across one page, then another. I reread the marked passages, and then, closing my eyes, repeated
my grandfather's final message to myself, almost as one would a prayer,
for I knew his letter by heart.

Suddenly I felt a hand on my shoulder: I started. It was Gerard,
standing beside me. "What are you doing?" he asked.

"I was reading, I could not sleep," I replied, my color heightening.
I closed the book, but kept my finger at one marked page, almost as a
measure of protection.

"Come back to bed," he said; then he paused, glancing at the book
in my lap, and added: "Show me what you are reading."

"It is the Cicero my grandfather sent me. The one I mentioned to
you. He marked it in certain places—his favorite passages." I stammered
as I told him this. To my relief, however, he did not seem irked—indeed,
he seemed intrigued.

"Show me what he marked," he urged. "Read the passages to me."

I smiled somewhat warily, at once longing and reluctant to share
them.

He noticed my hesitation. "Read them to me," he cajoled.

I turned to the first dictum about the garden and the library being all
one needed for happiness. And then to the second, about the cultivation
of the mind. Then I looked up, pausing as I came to the third, about
freedom. "Shall I continue?" I asked tentatively, looking up at him.

He shook his head and smiled indulgently, as one would smile at a child who had uttered something nonsensical. "What strange notions for a man of Cicero's shrewdness!" he said, shaking his head. "The ideas of a dreamer." There was a trace of contempt in his voice. I looked away, biting my lip.

He bent down and kissed my forehead. "Enough philosophy," he murmured. "Come to bed now. It is time to sleep."

We lay down, drawing the quilt over us. He quickly fell back to sleep; I did not. It felt much colder, for he had not drawn the curtain around my side of the bed, and I dared not wake him by closing it.

I looked past the open curtain, to my left, and caught the falcon's stare. For once I did not avert its gaze: I met its eyes and looked deep into them, my mind throbbing with questions and reflections. I thought of my marriage, and all the naive hope I had brought to it; I summoned up my first memories of meeting my husband—how dazzled I had been, how in love with him! Then loss, disappointment, and disillusionment had slowly encroached: he came to see me in a less pleasing way, and I, in turn, saw much about him that gave me pause, and which eventually made me feel hurt, even fearful.

I thought of the wolves, wondering if they were still there, poised on the craggy peak; and then of the full moon, which lit the sky outside the window. The same moon shone on Troyes, but Fastrada would not see it, no doubt she would be sleeping now. . . . I would never go to Troyes, that much was clear; I would never go to Fontevraud and meet Clementia. My life would be controlled by my husband until I was old, and weary, and all the curiosity to see the world had been extinguished from me.

I had read Gerard only the first two of the marked passages my grandfather had especially marked, pausing before I came to the third, my favorite, about freedom. I was grateful I had not read it to him, for I did not want to risk its being mocked. I closed my eyes and repeated it to myself, as I had countless times: "What then is freedom? It is the power to live as one chooses." How tantalizing was the idea of freedom! But I could never be free as long as I was married to Gerard. To be free I would have to leave him; I would have to abandon my marriage. But I would never have the courage to do so: How would I manage to live, afterward, stained by such disgrace? What would become of me? Then—for my mind was still afire—this idea came to me: What if it were *Gerard* who decided to leave me? What if he no longer saw me as a suitable wife? If I were never able to give him a child, he would give me up; that much was certain.

As she stood before her innermost cabinet, with its black griffins and secret potions, Anthusis had intimated that she could help women who did not wish to become pregnant. If I should venture there, to that terrifying place, and make the sinful decision to ask Anthusis for her help, would God forever condemn me, would my sinful act be irredeemable? Surely He would eventually forgive me! Had not the church taught me He was a merciful God? I would do penance, I would beg His forgiveness—perhaps I might even find a way to ask Clementia to help me.

I opened my eyes and once again caught the falcon's gaze: in that moment its eyes reminded me uncannily of Vainqueur's. I had always thought of Vainqueur as a villain, as the cause of Gallien's downfall and the source of my own guilt. In that instant I thought of Vainqueur in another light: a courageous creature who had wanted to escape, to be free, to fly untethered.

Was it not the time for me, too, to summon courage? Was that not the very message my grandfather had meant to convey, almost as a code, with the three marked passages?

If only the falcon could speak to me, I thought, if only it could advise me, as might a seer. My grandfather had told me stories about the ancients and how they sought the wisdom of oracles—some dwelt in temples, he had said, others in ravines, hilltops, and caves. The oracles would pronounce their judgments, and men, fearing the displeasure of the gods, would act upon them.

Tell me what to do, I whispered, as I stared at the falcon's brilliant eyes: tell me which road to take.

Be brave, the falcon seemed to say. Follow your heart, follow the path to freedom: follow Vainqueur.

# CHAPTER 45

I must see Corbus as soon as possible," I told Aiglantine with great urgency the following morning. "I must ask Anthusis for more medicines. Potions that would help me get with child. Months have passed, and still, I am not pregnant! I fear that my husband grows impatient with me. And perhaps"—I knit my hands together and added with more fervency—"perhaps Anthusis would give me remedies that would help me have a son, as she did before. I *did* bear a son, after all, when I followed her directions. Though the baby—" I looked away, my buoyant mood suddenly giving way to sadness.

Aiglantine took my hand, gently pressing it. "But surely, my lady, it would be safer for you to pray! To offer votives to the Virgin."

"That I will do, and more, I promise. Still, I must take every measure possible."

"Very well," she conceded, though I sensed an iota of hesitance. "I will ask Corbus to meet you. But where, and how? And what shall I tell him?"

"Find a time when he is alone, far from the others who work with him in the laundry. Tell him that I must see him, and that he must take a message to Anthusis for me. Last night my lord told me he must go to La Rochelle in two days' time, and that he will be away at least a fortnight. Best I see Corbus then, when Lord de Meurtaigne is away."

She nodded. "And Millicent? You know how she pries. She is always asking questions."

"I shall invent a reason for her to be sent to the village the day I see Corbus." I took both her hands and said with great assurance: "Have no fear. I shall make certain Millicent is away."

She quitted me thereafter, leaving me alone to ponder my strategy as I walked to and fro in my chamber. It was early morning on a bright day in late October. I had hardly slept that night, yet I did not feel in the least tired. Clarity had infused me with new vitality.

I approached the window: the sun shone, the tenuous clouds had vanished, and the pine rising upon the craggy peak had lost its sinister spiky aspect; the wolves were nowhere to be seen. When I turned from the window, the falcon's eyes seemed oddly benign, and the pungent fragrance emitted by its burning spices only barely lingered in the brisk autumn air.

I needed to compose the letter to Anthusis asking her for the potions and instructions to prevent me from pregnancy. Steeling myself, I sat down and took up the quill.

I had come to a decision. I would take the risk and write her: I was fearful for my health, fearful of another disastrous pregnancy, and would prefer to be barren rather than endanger my life. All the while I wondered whether Anthusis would surmise the truth—that this was, effectively, a way to end my marriage. At that instant, I set down the quill, overcome by the implication of the drastic, some might say reckless, steps I was taking—but then I thought of my grandfather's spirit, of the passage about freedom, and forced myself to resume writing. I ended the letter this way: "I ask you to give the boy the medicines I require, and with them, your written instructions: what I should do, and when. You know I am strong. You have seen me pregnant, and know which humors predominate in me. Most of all I swear you to secrecy and promise you more recompense if you send me what I need. I have sent the first payment here, which I trust will be sufficient."

I hesitated many moments before signing the letter with my initials; then I scanned the parchment, and took a deep breath. Suddenly I realized one aspect of this plan that I had neglected to consider: What would I send Anthusis as recompense? How would I pay her? It must be something small, transportable, and precious. I thought of the ring from my grandfather: no, I could not give that up, ever!

I stood up and began to pace. I had some fine silk thread, which I used for embroidery: that, together with a small brooch in horn, might do very well. I found both and sealed them in the letter.

TWO DAYS LATER, GERARD DEPARTED on his journey. I had dispatched Millicent to the village early that morning, having requested that she procure a few silver votives for me—"To offer to the Virgin," I had explained in an urgent, grave voice, my hands folded piously together. Once I was certain she had left, I called for Aiglantine: "Tell Corbus to attend me in my chamber as soon as possible," I told her.

"What should I tell the laundress?"

I thought quickly. "Tell her I have a desire for fresh mushrooms. And that I want him to gather some in the forest for me. She is a dim-witted woman and not in the least curious. She will not question you, I promise." To this I added: "As for Corbus—I know he will do whatever you ask him. He trusts you."

She blushed. "As he does you, my lady—"

"I hope so." I smiled. "But I think he trusts you more."

Corbus appeared soon thereafter. I had not seen him in a while, for I had been careful not to appear to favor him in any way. I was immensely glad to see him and, as always, touched by his eagerness to please and his ability to communicate despite his silenced voice. It was his simple dignity that affected me most of all: despite his lot, he had made his peace with life, and with God. This gave him a serenity—a serenity I knew I should never have had, if God had left me mute.

I handed him the letter and instructed him to venture to Anthusis on the morrow, leaving shortly past dawn. He would give my letter to her and wait to return with her letter for me. There would be a small parcel for me, no doubt, as well.

"Do you understand?" I asked. We stood face-to-face: he looked at me hard, nodding gravely as he took the letter. His large, pale, and nimble hands fascinated me, for they almost seemed to be those of a fantastical animal—a centaur, for instance, a mythical creature my grandfather had told me about.

I wished him a safe journey and accompanied him and Aiglantine to the door, watching as they proceeded slowly and silently down the corridor together.

# CHAPTER 46

The following morning dawned clear, the bright expectant sun auguring well for Corbus's journey. All that day I waited for him to return, my nerves at fever pitch.

The light had only just begun to fade when I heard Aiglantine's quick, light steps along the corridor. "Corbus has returned!" she said, rushing into my chamber. "I will meet him soon, behind the laundry. Then I will bring you whatever he has been given from"—she paused— "the woman in the forest."

I smiled to myself at Aiglantine's way of referring to Anthusis, as if she risked sinning merely by pronouncing the latter's name. "I am thankful all went well!" I said with immense relief. Then: "What of Millicent? Has she returned from the village?"

"I have not seen her yet. But I must admit I did take the liberty of telling her that you would not be vexed if she stayed the night in the village, with her sister's family. I thought it best to give Corbus as much time as possible."

"You were wise to do so," I replied, smiling to myself at her unexpected wiliness. "I would not want her to be suspicious."

"I do not think she is." Then, proudly: "I can be convincing, when I am set on it."

"I hope I have not been a bad influence on you!" I replied with a small laugh, touched by her willingness to be my accomplice. "I know you are not as accustomed to inventing as I am. And I realize, too, how concerned you are for Corbus." She looked away, blushing slightly as I added: "I also suspect you do not really trust Anthusis."

"But I trust *you*, my lady," she replied, with a poignant smile. "That is what matters, above all."

SHORTLY THEREAFTER AIGLANTINE RETURNED WITH the letter and basket that Anthusis had given to Corbus, as well as a small pouch with mushrooms he had gathered. "I was sure to tell him the excuse you had given the laundress for his journey," said Aiglantine with a complicit smile. "He remembered to bring these back, as well. He did not fail us."

"I never imagined Corbus would."

I took the basket and letter before asking: "Were you able to glean anything from Corbus about the journey, about Anthusis?" I knew she had evolved a way of communicating with him: she was able to read his gestures and expressions as one might read a text, or code.

"He seemed to indicate that the woman was not surprised to see him. That she did not seem surprised by your letter."

"By my sending it, or its contents?"

"Both."

A strange disquiet swept through me, as if someone had taken me unawares at an intensely private moment. I gazed at the letter in my hand, suddenly terrified to open it.

"My lady—" I heard Aiglantine say. I looked up, meeting her eyes.

"You seemed far away suddenly," she said. "Your face went so pale."

"It is only—" But there I stopped, forcing myself to assume a genial smile. "I am a bit weary, that is all."

"Then I will leave you to yourself, my lady."

She departed, leaving me alone to read the letter.

It was written on coarse, ragged parchment in a tall, spidery hand. There were great spaces between the letters—not chaotically so, however, for there was a definite cadence that governed the whole. Thick soaring loops distinguished the capital letters; the signature itself was comprised of a large, severe *A* underscored by a long, taillike flourish.

The letter began starkly, with no salutation:

I have included what you have requested and have marked all clearly. It is vital that you follow all my instructions and do this carefully. In one vial you will find juice of willow leaves. You must take a spoonful of this the day you have stopped

bleeding from your monthly course. In another vial is a mix of
Artemisia, fern root, and rue: infuse two spoonfuls of this in
a cup of liquid, and drink once a week. I urge that you drink
an infusion of sweet basil whenever possible, and that you eat
vegetables that cool the blood, spinach and lettuce first among
them. As soon as possible after carnal relations, eat green mint:
a little will suffice. Lastly, I have included a large amulet in jet.
Take this and place it under your mattress, in a place where no
one will see it. From there it will dispense its power to render
you barren.

She went on to reiterate that I must follow each instruction precisely, and that I risked "an unpleasing result" if I omitted any of her
"rules." Finally she told me to send "the boy" back in the spring, to
fetch more supplies from her.

I read the letter twice before setting it down. Its commanding tone
and the singular hand with which it was penned lent it startling vividness: I could hear Anthusis's voice and envision her face as I read each
line. Indeed, her voice echoed in my mind as I picked up the basket she
had sent, the top of which was covered by a thick, heavy brown cloth
with long, tangled fringe. I lifted the cloth and unearthed the contents:
each vial was marked in her eerie hand.

Nestled deep beneath these was the jet amulet—black, oval, and
shiny. I held it for many moments, trying to reassure myself: Corbus
had returned from the journey to Anthusis without incident, and now
I was in possession of the potions and instructions I required. But this
sense of satisfaction was fleeting, for the next instant a dreadful uneasiness came over me. How would I follow Anthusis's instructions without
arousing my husband's suspicion? Where to place the jet amulet so that
it would not be discovered? That I was about to venture into treacherous territory was terrifyingly clear: I was about to take steps for which
God Himself might smite me. I must not think of that, I told myself.
I must trust my plan, my decision. When the time came, I would do
penance, for I was young, and God would eventually take pity on me.

I forced myself to be resolute and walked to and fro, my eyes darting around the chamber. The chest that held my secret objects was, of course, the obvious spot. Even so, I hesitated, as if strangely reluctant for my treasures to risk exposure to Anthusis's sinful potions. But I had no choice: I placed the vials deep within the chest, making certain to cover them with linen rags.

I stood up, momentarily reassured, only to become anxious at the thought of the next task: placing the amulet beneath the mattress. How would I manage this?

I approached the bed, got down on my hands and knees, and slowly lifted up the mattress. To my relief, it was surprisingly light. I began to search for a hiding place beneath, only to become discouraged, for there was no way to conceal the amulet there. Then I began to examine each side of the wooden bed frame, thinking I might wedge the stone somewhere along it. I had almost given up when I suddenly glimpsed a thick crack along the frame below the head of the bed, where a piece of splintered wood had become slightly dislodged. I pried it loose: to my delight there was a niche where the amulet could be tucked—it would only be very slightly visible to the eye, for it was not much darker than the wood. This might do! I took the jet from my pocket and inserted it neatly within the niche; it was as if God Himself had created the hiding place. Surely this itself was a sign that augured well!

Somewhat reassured, I knelt by the bed and began to pray, imploring God and the Virgin again and again for their understanding and forgiveness.

# CHAPTER 47

As the winter passed, the unrelenting cold continued, and my restlessness and sense of confinement intensified. Our marriage had settled into rituals and routines bound by a glacial propriety. Even the festive customs of the Christmas season did not relieve me of this deadened feeling. At Mass on Christmas Eve, as was our wont, Gerard and I, splendidly attired in gold-threaded damask, proceeded arm in arm as we entered the nave. With each step, I found my eyes drawn to the marble tombs, which lined the aisles: gazing at the women's faces set in stone, their bodies encased in chiseled robes, I felt scarcely more alive than they. When the spring comes, I shall feel better, I said to myself that night, inhaling the wafting incense. But then winter passed, and spring arrived, and still my spirits remained unaltered, nor did they change with summer's sun.

All the while I followed Anthusis's instructions to the letter, watching with a secret, yet uneasy, satisfaction as my monthly courses continued unabated. Shortly after Easter and again in August, I sent Corbus to Anthusis for a fresh supply of potions. By then I was less anxious about his journeys being discovered, so inured to dissembling had I become, so adept at inventing ways of putting off Millicent.

Throughout this time, I performed my wifely duties faultlessly, if cheerlessly, for I had come to know what would arouse Gerard's ire and arranged my behavior accordingly. I avoided contradicting him, I never asked about writing Fastrada, I did not press him about his dealings with the Angevins. I wore the dresses he preferred and decked myself with the jewels he bestowed upon me. Whatever delight I had once felt in wearing these adornments was now transmuted into a sense of grim duty, for I knew the things were not given to me for my own pleasure, but for my husband's, who saw them as reflections of his own power, riches, and status.

Gerard did not seem to notice my change in attitude; he never seemed to wonder at the new, subdued self who scarcely resembled the young woman he had originally married. He seemed, if anything, pleased by my submissiveness. But to me, throughout that dreary winter, spring and summer, our marriage seemed a distant, diminished version of its earlier incarnation.

IT WAS ONLY IN THE autumn that year—the year of our Lord 1181— that I perceived a shift in Gerard, an irritated impatience with my inability to get with child. He made a point of curtailing his travels and insisted we lie together more frequently; as his demands increased, so did my concern that the potions would last through the winter. The dwindling supply made me increasingly desperate: I would need to send Corbus to Anthusis soon, before the onset of snow made the journey through the forest impossible. But when, and how, with my husband close by?

Late in October came my opportunity: I learned that Gerard was planning a lengthy sojourn to Poitiers and would depart in a matter of days. I immediately asked Aiglantine to speak with Corbus and arrange the excursion to Anthusis.

She returned soon afterward with the dismaying news that Corbus had only recently sprained his ankle. "There is no possibility of him making that journey, my lady," she said, disconsolate. "He can barely walk."

"Is there anyone else who could go to Anthusis for me?" I asked, trying to rein in my distress. "Is there anyone else I might trust?"

She pondered this a moment, finally looking up, her expression brightening. "There is someone, I believe. A boy, Sigibert, who works in the kitchen. You may have seen him—a swarthy fellow, a quiet sort. Wilbertus likes him and says that he is a good worker, steady and reliable. That he does not gossip."

"Is he known to my husband?"

"I doubt it," she replied, shaking her head. Then: "They say Sigibert knows the forest well. I will ask him—with your permission, of course."

"Tell him it is important, and that I will recompense him generously. Most of all you must tell him that he is not to discuss this with anyone. Anyone."

GERARD AND HIS MEN LEFT for Poitiers three days later; he would remain there for several weeks. There remained only the question of Millicent. This was resolved the following day, however, when I learned she had been afflicted with a stomach ailment. I urged her to rest and suggested that she spend the week with her younger sister in the village. Millicent greeted this offer with such effusive gratitude for my "compassion" that I almost felt ashamed. That did not deter me, however: I arranged for her to be transported to her sister's home and watched as the wagon carrying her made its way through the castle gates.

Immediately afterward I went to my chamber and penned the letter for Anthusis:

*To Anthusis, greetings from the Lady Isabelle*

> With the arrival of autumn, and with winter soon upon us, I ask you for more remedies, in greater supply and of even greater efficacy than those you have given me in the past. My husband becomes increasingly impatient with my delay in getting with child. I am pressed more frequently and vehemently to observe my wifely duties. Pray be generous in giving the boy what I require, for it may be long past Christmas when I am able to send him to you again. I have given him payment for you, which I trust will be sufficient.

The following day, shortly after sunrise, I met Aiglantine and Sigibert in a secluded spot behind the stables. He was quiet and earnest, with an engaging smile and a crop of hair as dark in color as Corbus's was light.

"My lady," he said, bowing rather clumsily as I greeted him. "I am glad to help you."

"And I am grateful for your service," I replied, touched by his eagerness. Then: "I am told you know where Anthusis dwells."

"Yes! I know the place well and how to reach it."

"Good." I handed him the letter. "Take this to her, then wait for her to give you something for me, a package. The moment you return, find Aiglantine."

"I will," he replied, tucking the letter inside his vest.

"There is one more matter," I added, observing him closely. "You must promise never to discuss this with anyone, nor to mention Anthusis. You must swear to secrecy. Do you understand?"

"Of course, my lady!"

I smiled, reassured by his fervency. "Then, set off—and good luck to you!"

With a quick bow, he strode away; Aiglantine and I watched until he disappeared from view.

It was a frosty autumnal morning, so cold that the fire had been laid in the great hall. I asked Aiglantine to join me by the hearth while I waited for Sigibert to return: "Fetch your mending," I told her, "and I shall fetch my embroidery." In my effort to placate Gerard and appear the dutiful wife, I had taken up the hoop again and was making my way through a belt intended as a present for him: an intricate design of lions and falcons within a border of ivy leaves.

From time to time I glanced at Aiglantine as she sewed, her cheeks slightly flushed by the heat of the fire. She drew the needle rhythmically in and out, pausing only occasionally when she looked up to cut or knot the thread. All the while we hardly spoke; we did not need to. I knew that she, too, was preoccupied with thoughts of Sigibert, and of his clandestine journey to the woman whose name she still avoided uttering.

My thoughts meandered to another autumn morning, several years before, when I had sat on the same bench, before a similar roaring fire, with Fastrada. How long ago that day seemed! How much I had changed, how much my life and my marriage had changed . . .

So immersed was I in these reflections that I had not noticed someone entering the hall moments before: but then I felt Aiglantine's hand upon my shoulder. "My lady, Raoul is here," she said. "And he asks to speak with you."

Raoul approached and stood before me, his face ashen. "I have had word that Lord de Meurtaigne approaches and will arrive soon," he announced in a low, urgent voice. "He means to see you at once."

"My lord, returned?" I answered with a tense smile. "But he was not expected back for several weeks!" I set down my hoop, exchanging a worried glance with Aiglantine.

"He has returned unexpectedly, my lady. And with him——" He paused. "He has Sigibert."

"Sigibert?" I stammered.

"My lord and his men came upon him in the forest."

"I am surprised that my lord knows Sigibert," I replied with a forced casualness. "He works in the kitchen, does he not?"

"Yes. But last year, he also worked in the mews awhile."

I looked skittishly about, trying to avoid Aiglantine's anxious gaze, my hands clasped so tightly they almost hurt. It was clear from Raoul's demeanor that Gerard was furious: he must have learned that I had sent Sigibert on a journey without his permission. There was no way of knowing how much else he had discovered. . . .

I turned to Raoul: "How long is it before my lord is expected?"

"Half an hour. Perhaps even less, I am told."

"When he arrives, tell him that I await him here."

"Yes, of course," he murmured, his eyes downcast; then he left us.

I turned to Aiglantine. "Go to the kitchen," I told her. "It is best you are not with me."

"But my lady——" she protested.

"Do as I say."

"But what will you *do*, my lady? What will you say?"

"I shall think of something," I replied with more conviction than I felt, my eyes darting to the fire. "I only pray that Sigibert did not mention Anthusis."

"He would never betray you!" she exclaimed, adding, "and if he did, it is *I* who am to blame—"

"We cannot think of such things now."

She hurriedly gathered her sewing. As she began to leave, I placed my hand upon her shoulder and told her: "Remember—you know *nothing* about this. Promise me."

"I promise. But, my lady—"

"*Go*, I say." She departed.

And so I waited, alone, the sound of the fire incongruously merry and crackling as I paced before it, one moment nervously smoothing my skirt, the next making the sign of the cross as I implored God to protect me. Bitter memories assaulted me—I thought of times in my girlhood when, having disobeyed my parents, I waited in dread for the punishment to fall upon me. All the while I struggled to calm my mind so that I could think clearly, so that I could decide what I would say to Gerard, the explanation I would invent. . . .

The strident call of trumpets arrested my thoughts: Gerard had arrived. Shortly thereafter came the sound of hard, determined footsteps advancing toward the hall: moments later Gerard entered and strode toward me, his face set grimly, in fury, resembling those harrowing masks I had seen carved on ancient columns. Following him was a new henchman, Dirck, a burly Breton, who pushed the stumbling Sigibert forward. They stopped suddenly, almost violently, before me—Sigibert disheveled, terrified, sniveling. He knelt on the floor, rocking slightly, back and forth, like a child trying to calm himself.

I bowed to my husband, trying to keep my hands from trembling. "My lord," I murmured as Gerard trained his dark blue eyes on mine. His jacket was torn in several places, as if it had been ripped by thorny branches; no doubt he had been riding at a ferocious speed.

He turned to Dirck, a glowering figure in a belted leather tunic, a dagger at his waist. "Leave us while I speak with Lady Isabelle. Wait over there with the boy"—Gerard gestured to the far doorway—"until I summon you."

They left us, the thudding of Dirck's footsteps punctuated by Sigibert's whimpers.

"What have you to say?" Gerard demanded. He stood rigidly still, his eyes never wavering from me.

"That I am pleased to see you, my lord."

"Is that all?"

"Why should it not be?" I asked with a tremulous smile.

"What about the boy?"

"He works in the kitchen, I believe."

"Obviously he was *not* in the kitchen when I found him," he retorted. "I came upon him in the forest. No doubt Raoul has told you that."

"Yes, he has, my lord."

"I recognized him and thought it strange to find him in the forest, when he should have been here working. When I asked him what he was about, he told me that you had sent him on an errand." He paused, barely able to rein in his fury. "Is that the truth?"

"Yes."

"You had no right to send him, or anyone else from our household, on such a journey without my consent."

"It seemed to me, since you were away—"

"Therefore my absence gave you this liberty? Is that what you are saying?"

"I suppose so." I lowered my head, admitting, "Yes, my lord."

"You did not have the right to take that liberty!" he berated me, pressing a clenched fist to his mouth. "But that is only partly why I am angry," he continued, his eyes fixed on me. "He also told me you had sent him to Anthusis. Did he speak the truth?"

"Yes," I said, struggling with the realization, the shock, that Sigibert had betrayed me.

"Therefore it seems you not only sent him without my authority on this journey, but what is even worse—you sent him to that witch!" He shook his head in disgust before resuming: "Why would you consort with such a person, a practitioner of black magic?"

I looked down, biding my time, trying not to let fear cloud my ability to think. Finally, looking up, I said, "I sought potions from her, remedies, to help me get with child. To help me bear a son."

"Am I to take comfort in that? In a wife who seeks out black magic? Only peasants, only ignorant folk, seek the help of such people!"

"I understand how foolish my actions may seem to you, my lord. I only did this out of desperation. After I lost the two babies—"

"You decided to take this action, this deceitful action, without consulting me, just as you sent the boy into the forest without my permission?"

"Yes."

"And in addition"—he threw back his head slightly, his eyes narrowing—"it appears that you gave him a letter for her." He produced a roll of parchment from his vest and brandished it before me, his mouth set in an unpleasant, almost triumphant expression. "A letter with your seal. You do not deny that this is yours?"

At this, feeling almost faint, I replied: "Yes, it is mine."

"Moreover, it is clear from this letter that you have been consorting with this witch for a period of time. This was not an isolated incident, nor a question of one letter, but an issue of several journeys, and several letters. You have deceived me, many times, it seems. Thus this was not an aberration, but a habit. A pattern of deceit!"

"I did this out of desperation," I reiterated plaintively. "You yourself have told me, when you want to achieve a goal, you must try every possible means—"

"Do not fabricate excuses!" Twisting my letter in his hands, he began to pace back and forth before me. "Who else knew of this? That you had sent that pathetic creature to that woman? Who else?"

"No one, my lord."

"Aiglantine?"

"No, my lord."

"Millicent?"

"Never."

"I shall speak with them both."

"Millicent is not here, my lord. She has gone to the village." I paused, knowing I had no choice but to explain. "I gave her leave to go. She had been ill, and I suggested she visit her sister."

"How kind of you to show her such largesse." He sneered. "How considerate. I assume that was to make sure Millicent did not witness the boy's mission, and your little plot. Thoughtful of you not to have involved the old woman. You are clever, of that there is no question." He paused, shaking his head in fury. "How I shall ever trust you again, I do not know!"

"Do with me what you will, but do not punish anyone else! All of this is my doing."

"The boy is a fool, a simpleton," he muttered. "The full measure of my anger is not directed to him, but to *you*, who involved him."

"Please understand—it is not Sigibert's fault. It is my fault, and my fault only!" With quiet, savage bitterness, I cried: "Punish me, but not him!"

"You will have no say in how I deal with Sigibert, just as you had no right to send him on this secret journey. *I* am the master here. *I* decide such matters!" He recommenced pacing, the sound of his footfalls echoing in the hall. "I would never punish the boy for your own foolishness," he said at last, before adding, in a voice edged with pride and wounded vanity: "You know full well I am not a vengeful man."

His pacing ceased; he stood quite still, ominously silent. Then he summoned Dirck.

The henchman rejoined us, dragging Sigibert with him—the latter collapsed on the ground, huddling before us. I could hardly bear to look at Sigibert, so woeful a sight was he.

"Take the boy back to the kitchen," Gerard commanded the henchman. "Tell Wilbertus he is not to eat today. No food until tomorrow."

Sigibert remained on the ground, trembling, as he cowered before the gloating Dirck; never once did he dare look at me. All the while Gerard had been watching Sigibert intently, a contemptuous expression on his face. Now he walked over to him and, squatting down on his haunches, fixed his gaze upon Sigibert's gaping eyes. "You are to go back to your place in the kitchen now," he told him menacingly. "You are never to see Lady Isabelle again. No one sends you on any errand from this house but *me*. Do you understand, boy?"

Sigibert nodded frantically, his eyes like a wild creature's, before he was compelled away.

A terrible quiet descended upon the hall. Gerard and I were alone.

I walked with uncertain steps toward the bench before the fire. I sat down, exhausted. I gathered my skirt about me and brushed some strands of hair from my face. A modicum of calm had descended upon me, just as it had in childhood at such moments when, after being caught in a transgression, I had decided upon an explanation, a strategy.

Gerard began to pace, his arms tightly folded before him. Stopping to face me, he asked in a subdued voice that was, in its own way, unsettling: "What can possibly excuse your foolish behavior?" Then, his voice escalating: "Your deceit?"

It seemed clear he was far from willing to abandon his inquisition. "I had heard that the woman, Anthusis—"

"The witch," he interrupted caustically.

"As I have told you, I had heard," I stammered, "that she had potions that would help me get with child. Remedies to help me bear a son. I was only trying to take whatever measures I could to please you." I paused, continuing in a pleading, almost pitiful voice: "I implore you to understand—it was not for me that I did this, but for *us*. For *us*."

I extended my hand to him; he did not take it, but his tone was less harsh when he returned: "Why this *witch* when I have provided you with the best midwives, the most experienced physicians, to help you?"

"It is true you have given me the best care. And for that, I am deeply grateful. Still, none of your experts succeeded in helping me." I continued, with even more vehemence: "Where else, and to whom, could I turn? It has broken my heart to lose two babies." I paused, heartened to see him listening intently. "When I heard about this woman, Anthusis, and that she had helped others, I sought her out. There seemed no harm in trying anything I possibly could, to help me bear a child. Hopefully, a son! I beg you, my lord—" I began to cry; I saw Gerard flinch, for he could never bear my tears. Little did he know what had prompted them—strain, terror, even artifice, rather than remorse.

"Do not make excuses," he replied, but his voice had lost its bitterness; my pleading, and my tears, had clearly affected him. "You did this for *us*, you say," he reflected after moments had passed. "For us." He walked over to the fireplace, deep in thought. Turning to me, he remarked, with more disappointment than anger: "Even so, there is no excuse for your actions."

"I did not feel I could discuss this matter with you. I know what you think about women like Anthusis."

"In that you are right," he acknowledged with some irony, one brow raised. "I have nothing but contempt for that sort of quackery."

Once more he began to pace, stopping to grab some sticks of kindling from a basket by the fire. He snapped one piece of wood, then another, tossing them to the ground as he continued in a pensive voice: "You say that this woman, Anthusis, has helped others to bear children. Is that true?"

"Yes."

"Many women?"

"So I have been told."

"Are you certain of this?"

"Yes!"

He seemed to mull this over. "And you say that she has helped others bear a son?"

"Yes."

He looked down, thinking hard as he recommenced pacing. "How long have you been taking these potions?" he asked, stopping to look at me.

"Almost a year."

"And you have been following this regimen carefully?"

"Yes. With great care."

"And still—" he mused. "Nothing has succeeded. The midwives could not help you. And neither—so it seems—could this woman, though you say she has had success with others. Many others." He came toward me, taking a handkerchief from his pocket. "Here," he said gently, "wipe your tears."

Watching me, he began to lament: "I have tried to give you everything. A life of comfort, of luxury. You had only to do one thing—bear my child, my son."

"And in that I have failed, my lord." He stood by the hearth, thinking hard, as if he were trying to assess the day's events, our conversation, and the tenor of our marriage. Yet I could not decipher his expression; I did not know whether to be frightened or heartened.

"Yes," he acknowledged, but without recrimination, "yes, you have." He began to nod, slowly, as if assessing the full extent of this failure. "You bore a daughter who died. And a son who arrived in this world stillborn. Yet even there, with these losses, I was patient. I tried my best to help. I was understanding." Then, almost pleadingly: "Was I not?"

I turned away and began to cry, this time with real sadness and hurt. Meantime the fire crackled and the long rays of noonday sun added a bizarrely festive aura to the vast chamber. At last I looked up, trying to dry my tears with the edge of my surcoat: "I never imagined things would take this turn," I murmured.

"Nor did I," he replied, his tone almost sorrowful.

Our eyes met: I sensed that something had shifted within him.

"Come," he said, helping me stand. "It has been a long and trying day. For both of us."

I smoothed my dress and wiped my cheeks with my palm, watching as he walked toward the hearth. He took more sticks of kindling and threw them into the fire, the flames crackling wildly, animating the vast, silent room.

He offered me his hand. As we began to walk across the hall, toward the doorway, I stole a glance at him. A sense of peace seemed to have descended upon him—his gait was relaxed, and his visage had relinquished its former tension. I knew him well enough to recognize what these signs meant: he had come to a decision.

# CHAPTER 48

I was at once soothed and unsettled by the opaque calm that seemed to have descended upon Gerard. My first concern was for Aiglantine: I knew he would lose no time in confronting her, and feared that she, like Sigibert, would never be able to withstand his interrogation.

For the remainder of the day I dared not seek her out, let alone ask her to attend me. When, late that night, while undressing, I heard the sound of her sprightly, distinctive footsteps along the corridor to my chamber, my heart leaped up. "I have been sick with worry," I told her as soon as she closed the door behind her.

"It is I who have been most worried, my lady!" she cried. "I feel I am to blame by recommending Sigibert. Never did I think—"

"No more of this," I interrupted. "You did your best. As for Sigibert—no one could have expected him to stand firm against my husband. I am sure he is mortified, poor fellow." I took her hands in mine. "I assume my husband questioned you?"

"Yes! He asked me many questions, and harshly, too. About Sigibert and his journey, and if I had known anything about it. No, I said, not a thing, as far as I knew Sigibert had been in the kitchen all day. And then he asked what I knew about Anthusis. He wanted to know if I had heard that she was known to help childless women. I told him that, yes, folk said she had a gift this way, that her potions worked miracles." She gave me an anxious, searching look. "I hope I did no wrong in telling him that!"

"Not at all," I reassured her, and indeed this was true, for I now realized it would be to my advantage for Gerard to believe in Anthusis's credibility and to conclude that I was not only beyond the help of the midwives, but hers as well. "How did he respond to what you told him about Anthusis?" I asked Aiglantine.

"He seemed very interested in hearing this."

"Are you sure he did not seem skeptical, that he was not sarcastic?"

"Yes, I am sure. He listened hard."

I was jubilant about his volte-face, though still it puzzled me how he had swerved from scorning Anthusis to fastening on her reputation for success in helping women beget children, even sons. "And you are also certain you convinced my husband you knew nothing about Sigibert's journey?"

"Yes," she replied, without hesitation.

"I am impressed you succeeded in convincing him," I said with no little admiration. I had expected her to crumble in the face of Gerard's relentless inquisition. Instead she had remained stalwart and unruffled; she had given away nothing. What a cool dissembler she had become!

She picked up a shawl that, earlier, I had tossed upon the bed. "You see, my lady," she said with a half-smile, deftly folding the silk, "you have taught me well."

I gave a small laugh. "I doubt God would count that as a laudable achievement—to have taught you how to lie."

"I would never betray you, my lady! Even if it meant I had to lie." Her expression clouded over. "Though I do feel I did disappoint you, by suggesting Sigibert for the journey. And he did betray you. Alas!"

"You must never blame yourself. A wise person once told me to expunge all guilt. You would do well to remember those words, whenever you are tempted to turn the cudgel against yourself."

"I will. Still—" She furrowed her brow, suddenly downcast. "If only Corbus, not Sigibert, had made the journey. Corbus would *never* have betrayed you!"

"It is useless to dwell on such things." I stopped, for I had heard some brisk footsteps along the corridor—it was Gerard approaching. I pressed my finger to my mouth and whispered: "He comes." Then I handed her my hairbrush. "Unplait my hair and begin to brush it."

NOTHING—NOT EVEN MY OWN IMAGININGS—HAD prepared me for Gerard's new stance toward me, the chilly politeness that informed his every gesture, his every word. "My lady, the countess," he would pronounce with scathing emphasis as he took my hand before we proceeded, step by step, into the great hall for dinner. His was a palpable, almost mocking coldness, unmistakable to visitors and everyone in the household. I held my head high, but it was hard, very hard, to withstand his chilly inscrutability. In bed, I had become accustomed to the satisfaction of his wanting me; if I had turned away from him in recent months—inwardly or physically—it had been my decision, and underlying it had remained the lingering pleasure of knowing I was still desired. Now this, too, had ended. At night we lay as two frozen creatures side by side in a catafalque; he never came close, he never touched me.

I felt a stranger amid the household. The servants scurried about, their glances at once curious, blaming, and evasive. They had heard, no doubt, as servants always do, that I had surreptitiously sent Sigibert to the witch in the forest, and that my husband was furious with me. I forced myself not to imagine the gossip in the kitchen, the laundry, the stables. Imagine, I thought, if they were to learn the real purpose of Anthusis's potions! What would they think of me then—a woman who, in taking these remedies, had committed a mortal sin?

I tried to banish these thoughts from my mind, just as I tried to banish the image of Sigibert, ostracized and humiliated. I avoided Millicent whenever possible, for I could not help but notice an even more pronounced smugness to her demeanor, as if recent events had proved what she had always insinuated—that I was not a "virtuous sort." I never ventured into the kitchen to speak with Wilbertus, as was my custom. As for Ragnar—whenever I passed him near the mews, he glared at me, his devious watery blue eyes aglow with a triumphant malevolence.

I took some comfort in knowing I had a few stalwart allies, Aiglantine and Raoul chief among them. The latter was in a difficult position: it would be dangerous for Raoul to show me any sympathy. One day I managed to tell him so. "I do not want you to be anything but polite to me," I cautioned. "Assume a distance, even a coldness toward me. It is better for you that way." He nodded reluctantly and replied gently, "I would find that very difficult, my lady." I told him I understood; nevertheless, I wanted him to follow my dictum.

I agonized that Aiglantine's closeness to me—long acknowledged within the household—would set her apart from the other servants and make her an object of scorn. "Do not stay with me too much," I advised her several times as she lingered in my chamber. "Best you keep a bit of distance from me, for your own good." But she was too loyal for my own misdeeds to affect her behavior, and remained my dainty, endearing defender. "I will behave to you as I always have," she told me more than once. "I cannot change."

Much of the time I withdrew from the household, sequestered in my chamber with the falcon burning, its eyes alight, while I tried to read or sew. So lonely was I that even the company of the eerie bronze creature now seemed welcome.

Late one such afternoon, with the falcon as my only companion, I decided to write my brother Arnaut: a fruitless plan, quite possibly, as a messenger would likely be denied me. Yet the act of writing itself—even if the letter were never sent—would surely be of solace.

I went to the table where I kept my writing implements and opened the deep, shallow drawer: to my astonishment and distress, the quills, parchment, and ink had disappeared. They must be somewhere here, I thought, frantically searching the back of the drawer, and then the smaller drawer below it.

But my writing implements were nowhere to be found. Someone had taken them away.

THE FOLLOWING WEEK, ONE AFTERNOON in late November, I stood by the window in my bedchamber. It had been a rainy autumn— the fields were muddy, and the drenched trees looked as if their soggy branches would break from their weight. Water lapped at the very top of the moat.

I heard a sudden knocking at the door. "It is Raoul," said the voice. I bade him enter.

"Lord de Meurtaigne requests to see you, my lady," he told me gravely.

"Where?" I asked, in a nervous, clipped way. "Here, in our chamber?"

"In the anteroom of the great hall, my lady."

"I see." Our eyes met; we both knew there was something unusual afoot. "Tell my lord I shall descend in a few minutes."

Gerard stood between two columns in the anteroom, a narrow, high-ceilinged chamber with a small hearth and, before it, two stately, richly carved chairs with blue silk cushions. The chairs were unfamiliar here; a narrow, homely bench customarily stood in their place. The sight of the empty, expectant seats, each facing the other, unsettled me.

I bowed before him. He was dressed formally, in a braided red tunic; over this was a heavy cape fastened by a formidable enameled brooch in blue and gold. I had a fleeting memory of my first glimpse of him—tall, solemn, dauntingly worldly—that snowy January afternoon long ago; he had awed me then, but he had not frightened me as he did now. . . .

"Come," he said, in a somber voice as he gestured to one chair. "Take this seat."

I did so, sitting up very straight, trying not to fidget with my hands, all the while my heart racing. He sat opposite, fixing his gaze on me so intently that I looked away, flustered, embarrassed that he should notice my nervousness.

"I have come to a decision," he announced. "It is clear, and certainly the events of the past weeks make it even more so, that we can no longer live this way together."

His words stunned me. Yet had I not *wanted* this outcome, had I not helped bring about this very decision? My strategy had succeeded, after all! Even so, suddenly I felt petrified; for many moments I sat utterly still, trying to reassure myself that all would be well. Finally, stalwartly, I said: "Then let us part, my lord," adding, "I have been nothing but a disappointment to you."

A fleeting look of consternation crossed his face. He glanced down, his long, dark brow furrowed, before he looked up at me anew. "And what have I been to you?" he asked, surprising me by his tone, which suggested genuine curiosity.

"A generous husband," I replied, choosing my words carefully.

"And a devoted one—"

"Yes."

"Have I not given you everything you could have wanted?"

"Yes."

"But still it was not enough."

In a quavering voice I replied, "I never meant—"

"Of course there was the immense disappointment of losing two children," he said, as if he had not heard me. "And then your inability to become pregnant again. But no, there was something else as well." He stood up and took a few paces away, then turned around to face me. "I simply could not make you *understand*."

"Understand what, my lord?"

"About life. The way it really *is*, not the way you imagine it should be. You have your own"—he searched for the right word—"notions of life." His tone had changed: for the first time there was an intimation of bitterness, though it was imbued with a certain bewilderment.

"Let me go, then!" I cried. "Let us part."

"Yes. It is best. I have made some inquiries, taken some steps. I shall ask for a divorce."

"And the reason—what will you give as the reason?" I asked anxiously.

"Have no concern," he replied with an ironic smile. "I shall not bring your Anthusis plot into this. I shall not mention your duplicity in seeking out her help without my permission. No, I shall cite your barrenness as cause. I shall say that the midwives could not help you. And that even this Anthusis could not help you. There is ample proof of your infertility. I shall issue a petition to the bishop."

"When do you intend to do this, my lord?"

"As soon as possible. I have already drafted a document. A formal request."

So this was a fait accompli—how swiftly and efficiently he had acted! "But where will I go—once this is done?" I asked fearfully. "What will happen to me?"

"That is up to me to decide."

"I suppose you will send me to an abbey," I ventured.

"Assuming an abbey would have you!" he retorted.

"Why would an abbey *not* have me?" I asked, disconcerted.

"You are not virtuous," he replied, in the voice one would use while addressing a naughty child. "You lie. You disobey. You are deceitful." He resumed his seat in the chair opposite, leaning forward with folded arms as he dug the heels of his boots into the stone floor. "You will return to your home," he finally said.

"To my home?" I asked, startled.

He raised one brow. "Yes, to your home. Your brother Guy is there, is he not? And your father?"

"Yes," I murmured. This was not what I had anticipated: I had always felt sure he would send me to an abbey. "I thought perhaps I might reside at Fontevraud—"

"Why Fontevraud?"

"I remember Lady Fastrada speaking of the abbey when she was here. Her sister Clementia resides there." Then, rapidly, nervously, "And I remember Hugh saying that the abbey is patronized by the Plantagenets—by King Henry's family, and by Queen Eleanor herself." I realized at once I had made a mistake—the mention of Queen Eleanor invariably prompted a contemptuous reaction from him, as it always had my mother.

"Eleanor? That hardly commends it! No," he said, "I shall simply write your family and explain what has happened. You will go *home.*"

"Let me write them first, I beg you—"

"No. It is my place to do so, not yours."

"I only ask that you let me know what you will tell them."

"The truth—what else is there to say? That I am intent on having children, and that it is clear you are barren. That I have grounds for divorce and intend to implement them."

"You will not mention the"—I hesitated—"incident with Anthusis?"

"No. There is no reason to. I do not act out of vengeance—not with a woman, certainly. There is no reason for others, especially your family, to learn of your wayward behavior. Nor would it give me any satisfaction to embarrass you." He gave a thin smile, asserting, "As I have told you before, I am not a vengeful man. Proud, perhaps, but not vengeful."

I fell silent, all the while thinking of the humiliation of returning home. A spurned wife, a failed wife, a young woman who no longer had a husband. . . .

"Never did I imagine this turn of events," he said. "Never did I imagine our marriage coming to this."

The sadness in his voice touched me. I began to cry. "Never did I either, my lord! Never did I think our marriage would come to this!" Memories assailed me—our rides together, my first visit to the mews, his tender concern about my being in pain, when I was in childbirth . . . I was seized by a sudden terror: Was I wrong, had I been reckless, in forcing the end of our marriage?

"And my name?" I asked. "Shall I retain my married name?"

"You will revert to your maiden name. It will make things"—he paused—"simpler. For the future. For both of us."

"I see," I murmured.

"I have begun to plan your journey home," he continued. "It is only a question of when you depart. Though, of course, it must be before Christmas. There are the roads to consider, the ease of travel. I shall send several of my men with you. They will look after you well."

"It will be a long journey," I murmured, unable to focus on the logistics he spoke of with such calm and clarity. I had imagined another life, not this journey backward, not the specter of a shameful confrontation with my brother and father.

I looked skittishly about, clutched my hands, then pulled a loose thread from my sleeve—nervous gestures that were not lost on him. "I hope you will consider what I say," he told me. "And that you will go quietly back to your home, so that we may put this all behind us."

I brushed an errant tear from my cheek. "I am prepared to follow your will, my lord."

# CHAPTER 49

What I had contrived to bring about—the end of my marriage—began to frighten me with new intensity. There were moments when I wondered whether Gerard might have spoken the truth: Were my notions of life misguided, and had these notions deluded me?

I had imagined a future of a certain freedom, a lofty life, a life devoted to reading and writing and good works—like Héloïse, like Clementia at Fontevraud, or at another such enlightened abbey. Instead I was to return home, to the very place, as a girl, I had yearned to escape. Where were my dreams now of emulating the independence of Saint Radegonde, of Queen Eleanor? The future seemed grim and confined. Even my holding up Clementia as a mentor seemed foolish, not to say ludicrous: I had never even met Clementia, and what I knew of her came only from her doting sister Fastrada's stories!

WHAT AWAITED ME, RATHER, WAS this: a return to my home not in triumph and prosperity, but as a woman spurned by her husband—a useless creature, with no role in life, with no real reason for existing. My grandfather would not be there to comfort me. My brother and father would hardly be able to mask their disappointment. My sister, Amélie, trailed by her flock of children, would gloat. The one comfort in this journey home—if a comfort existed—was that my mother was dead and would not be there to belittle or castigate me.

It was the beginning of December. I would set off in ten days; the preparations for my departure had begun. Two of Gerard's men would accompany me. One morning I passed him in the courtyard while he meticulously supervised the preparations—the wagons, mounts, and provisions. I watched with a certain detached fascination as he directed his minions: nowhere in his briskness or in the commands he uttered with such decisiveness did I sense a moment of regret or hesitation.

Elsewhere in the household, the preparations for the Christmas feast had begun. The kitchen and bakehouse bustled with activity; spicy scents wafted through the noonday air. But I would not be there to partake of the glorious results: I would not taste the delicious savories, the fattened goose, the cakes of marzipan and honey.

As for the servants: with what speed they seemed to have learned of the demise of my marriage! Many—Millicent among them—had already begun to treat me like a stranger. I studiously avoided the mews, dreading an encounter with a smug, triumphant Ragnar. Indeed, more than once my sleep was rent by nightmares in which I was pursued by a gigantic hawk whose plumage resembled Vainqueur's, but whose fierce, triumphant eyes were the same blue as Ragnar's.

There were others in our household I would greatly miss—Raoul, Wilbertus, and Corbus among them. But it was Aiglantine, naturally, whom I dreaded leaving. A piercing sadness came over me whenever I thought of the moment when we would utter our final goodbyes. Do not think of it now, I would tell myself at such moments, staving off a despair so wrenching it came upon me physically at times.

For her sake, I tried to be strong. During the first days I avoided speaking of my departure altogether, proceeding as if my leave-taking would occur in a dim, distant future. As the day grew nearer, however, I steeled myself and told her gently but firmly that it had come time to pack up my belongings.

"I want to give you some of my clothes," I said. "I have so many lovely things! At least you will have them to remember me by."

"They are much too fine for me. I cannot accept them, my lady—"

"But you *must!* And I insist you do. They will fit you, for we are not so different in size. I am only a little bit taller." To this I added wistfully: "I feel that you are the sister I always dreamed of having."

"Oh, my lady!" she cried, in a voice heavy with emotion.

"Besides, I shall have little need for these things in my"—I paused—

"in my new life." I realized she was on the verge of crying. Trying to distract her, I glanced about the room and said briskly: "But I do not see my trunk anywhere. I asked you a few days ago to have the men fetch it, did I not?"

"I forgot to ask them," she murmured.

"I see," I replied, knowing full well that avoidance, rather than forgetfulness, had prompted this lapse. "Go downstairs now and ask the men to bring it here," I told her. "And then tomorrow, when it is light, we will begin packing together."

THE FOLLOWING MORNING WE WENT to the anteroom where my wardrobe and personal belongings were stored. "Come," I said to Aiglantine, "we will go through the armoire first, then the cupboard." Before us, the immense trunk yawned open, like a hungry creature demanding silk and linen for nourishment.

I held up each robe, tunic, or cape, handing them to her to place inside the trunk, lingering over those I had worn on special occasions, for these were imbued with memories—some painful, some joyful, some bittersweet. Finally we came to the clothes I used for riding or travel—among them the robe, cape, and head cover I had worn the day I first ventured with Corbus to find Anthusis. I held up the dark green cape now, fingering its luxurious fur lining, then the lovely red passementerie around the collar and sleeves. These were the sumptuous clothes of a rich woman—the sort of clothes which, in my diminished new life, might appear almost ludicrous. Still, I felt a strange affection for this outfit, for it was associated with quests and journeys. "Set these aside," I instructed Aiglantine. "I shall wear them on the day I depart."

She glanced away sadly as she lay the clothes on a chair.

A wave of melancholy swept through me: the traveling clothes seemed to confirm the reality of my leaving as nothing else had. I thought of all I was leaving—my companions, the doves in the mews, my garden. . . . "Where is Corbus?" I asked after a moment, in an unnaturally cheerful voice, trying to deflect the sadness. "It has been such a long time since I have seen him."

"He is still working very hard in the laundry, my lady."

"Promise me he will be with you when I leave," I said, "so that I might say goodbye to him. Will you promise?"

Silently, and through tears, she nodded.

During this time, Gerard had never mentioned whether he had received a reply from my family—an acknowledgment that they knew I would return home, and why. Finally I forced myself to ask him if he had heard from Guy and my father.

"Yes," he replied. "I received a letter from Guy a few days ago."

"What did he say?" I asked nervously.

"He said—" But then he paused, reaching inside his jacket to produce a letter. "Here. You might as well look at it yourself. There is no reason for secrets."

He watched me intently as I read:

*To the most gracious Gerard, Lord de Meurtaigne, greetings from Guy de Lapalisse.*

My father and I acknowledge the receipt of your letter and admit that these developments have greatly dismayed us. The marriage was arranged in good faith, and with the expectation that Isabelle would please you in all ways; that she did not fills us with dreadful consternation. This untimely end to our agreement fills us with dishonor, for you know us to be a reputable family, from ancient stock. We beg you to excuse my sister and her failings.

I looked up and asked, "Is there not more?"

"No," he replied. "That is the extent of it."

"I see." I looked away, overcome by a torrent of emotions—sadness, anger, fear. The coldness of the letter both terrified and enraged me: my brother might as well have been discussing a dispute over an exchange of poultry, or lumber.

"And you may keep everything I gave you. It is all yours. You told me I had been a generous husband, and I intend to remain so, to the end." He smiled, and his expression took a different turn—it was considerably gentler, almost sad. "I gave you the bronze falcon as well, as a gift. You must take it with you."

"Oh—but I cannot!" I cried, at once reluctant to reject his act of generosity, and unwilling to tell him how ambivalent I was about the object itself. "It is so valuable," I finally said. "What use would it be to me?"

"Take it," he reiterated. "If it remains here, it will only remind me of you—" He caught himself, as if unwilling to reveal any evidence of weakness or emotion. "Now, let us discuss your journey home," he said, in his brisk, logistical voice. "The route the men will take, and which mount you will ride."

THE MORNING OF THE JOURNEY dawned. Aiglantine came to help me dress; I was standing by the window waiting for her, after a sleepless night. "It is time, my lady," she said, her face ravaged by sadness and fatigue.

I sat down at the table as she began to brush my hair. My hand trembled as I picked up the mirror: the face reflected in it was pale and weary. "You must help me look presentable," I said with a feeble smile as Aiglantine braided my hair.

My traveling clothes lay on the bed: how elegant and self-possessed they looked—the long robe, with its graceful sleeves fanned out, the luxurious cape lined in fur, the head cover with its intricate braid. Suddenly I felt absurdly grateful for these clothes, as if they would impart a strength to me, as if they were a defense against an uncertain future.

Shortly afterward I descended to the courtyard. The entire household was assembled: a motley blur of ruddy faces, rough brown wool clothes, cold, ungloved hands tucked into pockets. It was strangely quiet for such a large gathering: all was somber, still, and awkward.

It was cold, very cold, but the rising sun was radiant, imbuing the stone walls of Ravinour—and its turrets and ramparts—with a warm, mellow tint.

Gerard and Ragnar stood together, in front, slightly apart from the rest. I tried, unsuccessfully, to avoid Ragnar's eyes: they were just as I had imagined they would be—supercilious, cold, triumphant. Both men were dressed for hunting; Ragnar held the beautiful white falcon, Gisela, on one gloved wrist. I was glad Féroce had not been chosen that day—Féroce, with his menacing gold eyes; Féroce, who had always frightened me.

Gerard acknowledged me with a small, tense smile.

He walked toward me. I made a low curtsey before him and said, "I should like to say my goodbyes now, my lord. To the household."

"You may."

I walked first to those who stood at the far side: Wilbertus and Agnes among them. "I shall miss your treats, and especially your Christmas cakes," I told Wilbertus, who was nervously blinking. And then, to Agnes: "I shall miss your merry talk," I said, smiling as she curtseyed.

Near them, a few paces away, stood Millicent. "May the good Lord guide you as best He can, my lady," she said crisply, pointed and pious to the end. I managed a nod and turned away.

I took a deep breath to collect myself, for Raoul was next—how thin and diminished he looked, and yet how poignantly dignified. No longer constrained by Gerard's rigid etiquette, I took his hands and told him, "I shall miss you, Raoul. You have been so kind to me." He nodded, barely able to murmur: "You will be greatly missed, my lady."

Two final farewells remained, these the most painful of all: to Aiglantine and Corbus, who stood together.

I felt my strength ebbing away as I approached them. "Dear Corbus," I said, looking into his eyes, "I shall never forget you. Look after yourself, and look after"—here I paused—"look after your friends who remain here, with you." At this, he crossed his hands over his heart while I struggled not to cry.

I turned to Aiglantine and embraced her hard. "Dearest friend, I shall miss you with all my heart," I told her, weeping. "Remember all our times together, and the stories I told you! Keep them with you, always!"

"I shall, my lady, I shall, always!" For many moments we stood together, our arms around each other, sobbing. Finally I was able to choke out: "We will meet again, I promise!" Aiglantine nodded frantically, as if she were willing herself to believe this would be true, though we knew, in our hearts, that this would likely never come to pass.

I felt a hand upon my shoulder. "The men are ready," said Gerard, gently drawing me away. "It is time."

The young groom approached and helped me mount. Gerard stood close by, directing him: "Make certain the stirrups are properly adjusted," he said. "And that the saddle is comfortable. Lady Isabelle has a long ride ahead."

All was ready. I sat astride, reins clutched in hand. One final farewell remained. I leaned forward and said, in a tremulous voice, "May God protect you, Gerard. And may He grant all your wishes." He looked away, unable to respond—his expression sad, almost stricken.

Gerard signaled to the men. "Godspeed," he said, with a decisive nod. I took one last look—Aiglantine's head was bent; she was weeping, and Corbus was trying to comfort her.

I fixed my gaze straight ahead, not daring to look back for fear my strength would dissolve. It was still eerily quiet save for the slow, steady clip-clop of the horses' hooves as we proceeded toward the gate. We approached the portcullis. High above the ramparts, the blue banners with the Meurtaigne crest flew proudly above Ravinour. Shielding my eyes against the morning sun, I tried to make out the images of the falcon and the phoenix emblazoned upon them. Then a sharp gust blew, and the quiet was fractured by the crack of the banners flapping in the wind.

"Stop here a moment," I told the men. I turned around, seized by the desire to look one last time at the frozen tableau, the people and home I was leaving behind. Their faces, their clothes, the window of my chamber, visible in the distance. In the foreground stood the man who had been my husband—a tall, immobile figure with a white falcon poised on his shoulder.

I turned around and looked straight ahead. "Now, let us go," I told the two men flanking me.

"You are ready then, my lady?"

"Yes, yes I am." My hands trembled, but my voice was resolute. "Forward!"

# PART II

# CHAPTER 50

I arrived at my family's home ten days before Christmas. The men and I had maintained a brisk pace as we progressed south, toward the land of my forebears. Surely it will be warmer there, I kept thinking, trying to reassure myself. But memory was deceptive. I had quite forgotten the barren, dry cold of winter in Provence, the meager rasping wind, so different from the hearty gusts of the region I had left.

My childhood home seemed at once familiar, foreign, and diminished. It was an ancient structure in timber with a thatched roof that sat on a plot of land surrounded by a wooden palisade. Everything about it seemed gloomy, mean: no glint of stone, no brilliant, imperious banners buckling in the wind. Here, dwelling and land seemed to coalesce in shades of brown and wood and muddy earth.

Our arrival, at dusk, was greeted by the plaintive sound of a horn. The wizened watchman, having emerged from the gatehouse, then bade us enter, and the gate of the palisade creaked open. After some moments, two figures appeared in the distance and walked toward us: Guy, a tall thin figure with rigid bearing and an abstemious mouth, and my father—slighter than I had remembered him, his hair now sparse and white. I sensed at once they were disappointed in me, even vaguely hostile. Guy greeted me with a lackluster embrace; indeed, he seemed to welcome the two men who had accompanied me with greater warmth. Meantime Petru, my father's beloved dog, had bounded toward us. "Good Petru," I said, kneeling to pat him—heartened that the dog, at least, seemed happy to see me.

Rising, I faced my father. It was he I was most concerned about, for he had sustained the loss of my mother since I had last seen him. Theirs had been an often fractious marriage, to be sure—she the dominant figure and he the passive one—but one to which each had made a certain accommodation, arbitrated by many years of habit and companionship.

"How difficult this past year must have been for you, Father!" I told him at once, taking his hands in mine.

"Yes, yes," he replied, almost curtly. Perhaps he is angry with me, I thought; or his sadness in losing Mother is so intense, he simply does not want to discuss it.

We stood together in strained silence while Guy tended to my two companions with what seemed almost inordinate care. I felt him studying the accoutrements of the men, assessing the cost of their richly braided tunics, the high quality of their mounts, the value of their expensive saddles—all reflections of the exalted world which, in Guy's mind, I had cavalierly abandoned. I looked away, embarrassed.

At length the groom led the men away, for they would spend the night in the stable before departing on the morrow.

Guy turned to me and my father. "Let us go inside," he said.

We walked through a narrow passage before entering the main hall. Standing at its threshold, I looked in, gazing at the ponderous timbered ceiling, which seemed to bear down upon one; the threadbare tapestry of the crucifixion, its threads so faded that even Christ's wounds were no longer red; the dulled gray of the swords crisscrossed on the wall above the mantel. The room itself had not changed, yet I struggled to recover any sense of the comfort, even the comfort of familiarity, that I had once derived from it. There was nothing that reflected worldliness, curiosity, or expansiveness—no object that had wended its way here from a distant world, no fabric that had been woven in a foreign workshop. This was a shuttered room, a room for those who had made an accommodation with life.

I walked to the hearth; before it stood four high-backed chairs in exactly the same position as I had remembered them. The fire had long ago died down; dwindling flames struggled to assert themselves above the mound of blackened ashes.

Guy took a seat while my father and I stood by the fire, trying to warm our hands. "Perhaps we might ask for some more wood," I ventured.

"That is not necessary," returned Guy. "We will soon retire."

I bit my lip, chastised. Moments passed. My father assumed a seat before the fire, opposite Guy. "You must be hungry, daughter," my father said, turning to me. "Perhaps you would like some bread, some cheese."

I shook my head. "There is no need. We stopped to eat a few hours ago." In fact, on arrival I had been very hungry, but tension had since quelled my appetite. From time to time I glanced at Guy; his lips were pursed, and he made little attempt to conceal his displeasure with me.

"You had a good journey, I take it," said my father after a few moments.

"Yes. The men knew the route well, and Gerard had told them—"

"I am certain he directed them faultlessly," Guy interrupted. "It would be like your husband—" He paused, giving me a somewhat accusatory look. "It would be like Gerard to plan everything to the last detail. He is a generous and competent man."

I looked down. There was a long pause; a shutter banged. I heard the distant hooting of an owl.

"Guy lives at your grandfather's manor now," my father offered, trying to dispel the tension.

"How long have you lived there?" I asked, turning to Guy.

"Almost a year. I find it a far more salubrious location." He cleared his throat. "For my health."

"Arnaut did mention, in a letter, that you were concerned about an imbalance of humors, or something of that sort—"

"Indeed."

I was determined to pursue the subject, if only to goad him. "*Which* of your humors seems to be imbalanced?" I asked.

"It—uh—is not quite clear," he stammered, clearly irked. "What *is* clear is that the situation of Grandfather's manor has been most beneficial."

"It must be lovely to live there," I replied. "You must have all of Grandfather's books."

"We gave them to the monastery of Saint Sylvestre soon after he died," came his curt reply.

"Was that Grandfather's wish?" I asked, stunned. "I had hoped that his library would remain here. As part of his legacy."

"There have been benefits as the result of our donation," he replied, evading my glance, "and I have no doubt these would have pleased Grandfather."

After another awkward pause, I asked if there had been news of Arnaut.

"Not in many months," Father replied, rather mournfully. "He has reached the Holy Land, that much we do know. But little else."

Once again, a dreadful frosty silence fell among the three of us. Finally, unable to bear the tension which seemed to suffuse the atmosphere, I turned to Guy. "I know you are angry with me. That you do not understand what happened, and why my marriage ended."

"That is correct," he replied, adding, "I can only conclude you behaved foolishly."

"I did not seem to be able to bear a child. A healthy child. A son, most of all."

"Had you been a better wife, Gerard would have been more patient with you. I know him. I know how he thinks. And I know how you tend to behave."

"And how is that?" I asked, my voice rising in anger.

"You are stubborn. You are reckless. All of us saw how Mother wrestled with those qualities when you were a girl." He paused, his gray eyes fixed upon me. "You have not changed."

"You have no right—" I cried, defiantly.

"Please! No more of this, my children!" my father pleaded. "There is time to discuss these matters, but not now." He turned to Guy. "Your sister has had a long journey. Can you not see how tired she is?"

"Very well," said Guy, with a sour, resigned expression. He stood up. "Hortense can show Isabelle to her room. And then tomorrow, we will discuss Isabelle's future. Such as it is."

I remained standing by the fire, still agitated and trying in vain to warm my hands. I saw my father looking almost imploringly at Guy, only to be met by a frosty glare. I looked away, for it was painful for me to see how much the latter intimidated him. "It is time to retire," announced my father.

"Come, Father," said Guy. "Let us fetch Hortense and bid good night to Isabelle." The men stood up; my father gave me a distracted kiss. They left together.

A few minutes later, Hortense appeared, and I greeted her affectionately. I remembered her as a simple, warm-hearted young woman who often indulged my curiosity about household gossip; she had always been fond of my cat and tolerant of the escapades that so infuriated my mother. And yet how different Hortense seemed now! Rouge daubed her cheeks, and an impressive bunch of keys jangled at her waist; she wore a robe with a bright trim, which would never have been permitted while my mother lived. She did not seem particularly glad to see me. "We never expected you to return so soon," she remarked in a chilly tone, with a slightly raised brow. "And certainly not *alone*, and in these circumstances." Then she caught herself: "But you have come a long way," she added, with a forced smile. "You must be weary."

Casting my eyes about the room, I suddenly realized that I had not seen my cat's cushion: it had always lain near the hearth. "Where is Cachette?" I asked.

"Your mother got rid of her soon after you left," she clucked. "I will show you to your room." As I followed her I noticed a subtle change in the way she walked: swaying her hips slightly, she glanced here and there in an almost proprietary way, all the while the keys jangling.

We passed the small chamber with the portiere of deep red curtains where my mother had customarily sat. It was behind those curtains that I had huddled the night I overheard my parents discussing the arrangements for my marriage. I had crept to my bedchamber afterward, bewildered and frightened, curling up in bed with Cachette nestled beside me. In the days that followed, I managed to convince myself that my marriage would be an adventure—a way to escape my mother, most of all.

Now I had returned here, to this dismal house, alone and husband-less. Even my beloved Cachette was gone.

ONE MORNING, NOT LONG AFTER my arrival, I awoke before dawn and lay in bed shivering with cold, looking around me. This was the chamber I had always shared with Amélie. Nothing about it had changed—the same low ceiling and slit-like window, the same skimpy blanket, the same scratchy, lumpy mattress that made a crinkly, inhos-pitable sound whenever I stirred. What a contrast to the comforts of the bedchamber I had left—the silken comforter, the soothing mattress, the ample hearth. Today there would be no Aiglantine to greet me, no cheerful figure at my door, bearing a cup of milk and basin of warm water.

I forced myself to rise, dispiritedly donned the same dress I had worn the previous day, and contemplated the hours ahead. Late the previous evening Hortense had asked, unexpectedly, if I would like her help in unpacking my trunks; perhaps she is trying to make amends for her coldness, I had thought; perhaps this will signal the return of her former companionable self. It was true that her help would not be unwelcome, for I had come to dread opening the trunks. Looming phantoms of a past life, they had remained, virtually untouched, in the antechamber by the wardrobe.

Moments later came a knocking at the door; I bade Hortense enter. "Let us begin with my clothes first," I suggested, opening the largest trunk. She knelt on the floor, handing me the robes one by one as I put them in the armoire. All the while, she would finger the fabrics, the embroideries, the gilded buttons, and the fur trims, and exclaim: "Ah, such costly things!" or "Is this really Theban silk?" or "Never have I seen such damask!"

With each of her appraisals, I began to feel more and more uncom-fortable. Her willingness to help me, I soon realized, had been born of little more than a curiosity to examine the luxurious spoils of a discarded wife. I thought back, wistfully, on the day I had packed up my clothes with Aiglantine—Aiglantine, who had wanted nothing from me, and whose eyes had none of the covetousness, indeed the envy, I now saw in Hortense's.

We came to a silken purple shawl trimmed with tassels. "How beautiful!" cried Hortense, her hands running over the fabric. Then came the pointed aside: "And in my favorite color!"

I realized I could no longer bear going through the things with her. Putting my hand to my forehead, I feigned a headache. "Unfortunately, I am not feeling well enough to continue," I told her in a pained voice. "A sudden headache, I am afraid. You have already helped me so much. I can finish the rest by myself tomorrow."

She reluctantly put down the coveted shawl and left me to be alone.

THE LAST SUNDAY OF ADVENT fell two days later; we were due at the village church to attend Mass. As my father and I walked to the church together, I noticed a change in him: a new jauntiness to his step, a ready laugh. And what of his surcoat cut in the latest style, and the faint scent of sandalwood that clung to him?

Indeed, I began to wonder if it were possible that his reluctance to discuss my mother the previous day, and his seeming curtness, were born of something other than sadness. Could it be that he felt a sense of liberation? "I am relieved to see you looking so well, Father," I gingerly observed as we continued to walk. "I had thought—that is, with Mother's passing—"

"We have no choice but to continue our lives," he said with marked cheerfulness. "The good Lord teaches us that we must make the best of each day, does He not?"

"Yes, though—"

"Good," he interrupted, his eyes fixed ahead. "We are just in time." He scanned the portal of the small church, as if in expectation.

"Are you looking for someone, Father?" I asked.

He seemed caught off guard. "Oh yes—yes," he replied. "I was looking for Guy. Ah! He is there, ahead."

Guy was indeed ahead, conversing with the prelate, a diminutive man massively cloaked in brown and clinging to his staff. Nearby—

standing to the side—I caught sight of our servants: Andreu, the young, spindly groom; Clothilde, the rotund cook; Vincens, the aged manservant, and Hortense. "Good morrow to all!" my father cried, with almost inordinate jollity as they acknowledged him. He had always been a favorite with our household servants, for he was considerably kinder in his dealings with them than my mother, and much less demanding. But now his good cheer seemed, if anything, heightened.

We approached Guy, exchanged a few words with the obsequious prelate, and entered the church, our servants trailing behind us. As we walked through the nave, I noticed a certain jostling and exchanging of glances among those already seated. One woman nudged another, shooting a glance in my direction. I looked away, my cheeks flushing as I imagined them whispering: "There is the young lady of the house. The one spurned by her husband."

I was grateful when we reached the front pew, grateful to kneel and bury my head in prayer.

The Mass proceeded, rather austerely. There was hardly a whiff of incense; the decorations of the altar were rather crude; and the primitive crucifix bore no resemblance to the elaborate, gilded version of Gerard's family chapel.

The Mass came to an end. We slowly filed out of the church—we were the first to leave, for our family was of ancient name, and held large parcels of the surrounding land. As we passed the pews, I did my best to hold my head high, looking straight ahead, trying to avoid the stares of the curious villagers.

As we emerged, the sun shone brightly; a slight wind had come up. I drew my cape about me and began to look for my father so that we might walk back together. I looked here and there; finally I spotted him to the side of the church, at the edge of the graveyard. He was speaking intently to Hortense, whose back was turned to me. I walked toward them.

I approached and said, "Father, do come—" As Hortense turned around, they exchanged glances.

It was the nature of the glances that startled me—they bespoke a

kind of intimacy that shocked me. My father looked abashed, while
Hortense's smug expression verged on the distasteful.

"I was giving Hortense instructions," my father stammered, with a
sheepish smile. "About some provisions—"

"I see," I said, watching Hortense, who stood silently by. Then, to
my father: "I shall leave you then, and walk back with Guy. I did not
mean to interrupt." I waited a moment, expecting him to protest.

"Yes, best you go ahead, with Guy," he told me instead. "I shall
follow later."

# CHAPTER 51

When I learned from Guy that Amélie and her family would be joining us for the Christmas rituals and feast in a few days' time, I began to steel myself.

Amélie was six years my elder and was known in our family as "the beauty," I as "the clever one." With her golden curls, saucy eyes, and general air of fecundity, she was the daughter who had always inspired confidence in my parents: confidence about her future, her ability to marry well and lend our family luster. She was a paradigm of embonpoint—everything about her was soft, round, and plump, including her milk-white hands, of which she was inordinately proud (they had always rather reminded me of dumplings). With my father she had been obsequious, tending to him with an exaggerated care that disgusted me and Arnaut. She and Mother shared a love of frippery, mean-spirited gossip, and contempt for my "inventions"; often the two were united in conspiracy against me.

The day of Amélie's marriage to Balduin, a knight of middling rank, my mother had announced rather pointedly: "Amélie is my triumph!" My mother had always adored Balduin. He was appallingly boastful and crude, but he did have an unctuous way of praising my mother, and an ability to make her feel that she was a great lady and a most exalted *maîtresse de maison*. "Let us never forget," he would tell her with almost laughable solemnity, "what noble blood runs in your veins, my lady. After all, it flows from that of Charlemagne himself!" Whenever he came to visit, an endless stream of compliments about Mother assailed our ears. Her stitches and the designs of her embroideries were the most refined. Her recipe for rabbit stew the most savory. Our bread the most finely milled.

My mother would bask in the onslaught of his praise. "That Balduin!" she would say, after they departed. "What a charmer he is! Do you not think so, Isabelle?" To this, I would dutifully nod, then murmur, beneath my breath: "I would rather die than marry such a man."

Now I waited in trepidation as the day of Amélie and Balduin's arrival approached. It had been almost four years since I had last seen my sister and brother-in-law, who lived in the region slightly to the north, near the town of Albi. Guy had told me that they would bring their three children and several servants. To this he had added: "You should know that Amélie is with child." I felt his eyes upon me: "I realize this may not be easy for you. That is, to see Amélie happily married, with children, and with another on the way, God willing." He cleared his throat. "Given your own situation."

"Not at all," I replied, feeling color come to my cheeks—whether from anger or a sense of inadequacy that I dared not admit even to myself, I am not certain. But I was too proud to give my brother the pleasure of knowing he had aroused those feelings. I forced myself to smile and said: "I am very happy for her."

IN THE DAYS THAT PRECEDED my sister's arrival, I watched in wonder as the household assumed an atmosphere uncannily resembling one of gaiety. Everything was in a state of feverish excitement. Even the normally sullen Clothilde had taken on a cheerful air; indeed, she made a great show of announcing she was preparing Amélie's favorite dishes. Hortense bustled about, directing the servants as they readied the bedchambers with fresh rush and bed linens. "I have had all of Lady Amélie's linens washed with lavender. She is so particular about her linens," she told me, adding, "nothing must be wanting for Lady Amélie!" Part of me was amused by these frenzied preparations, while another part, admittedly, felt pricks of rivalry and deprivation. I had always known my sister was the prized daughter in the family: even so, the manifestations of that favor still rankled.

As for Hortense: since the awkward exchange of glances with my father that day at Mass, she had seemed bent on pretending that nothing untoward had happened between her and my father, yet there was a cold, defiant look in her eyes that did not escape me. Whenever she entered our presence, my father would avert his gaze from mine and his mouth would begin to twitch. I knew it was useless to broach the subject with him, nor had I any desire to castigate him. I had begun to realize that hearty, strong-willed Hortense was, in some measure, a substitute for the domineering wife he had lost and whom—if only out of habit—he missed.

ON THE MORNING OF THE twenty-third of December, while sitting in the main hall sewing, I heard the watchman's horn sound—the lengthy, sonorous signal indicating that the travelers had been sighted and would arrive imminently. I set down my hoop—reluctantly, for once—and donned my cape.

My father and Guy were already standing outside, by the entrance to the house—the former beaming, the latter unusually animated. "They will be here any minute!" exclaimed Guy, unable to conceal his delight, for he had always favored Amélie.

The pounding of hooves came next, followed by the rumble of wagons amid great whirling clouds of dust as the entourage entered. It was difficult to ascertain whether it was Amélie or her pregnant belly that appeared first, for my sister alighted from the wagon in such a way that the great mound protruding between the deferential folds of her fur cape seemed to precede her.

"Dear Father!" she squealed as they embraced. And then, to Guy, an equally effusive embrace and greeting.

Next, to me: "My dear Isabelle—" she said in a honeyed tone as she pecked my cheek, all the while grasping my hands so firmly it almost hurt. Her small blue eyes, thickly fringed with dark lashes, scanned my face, their expression one of condescension, pity, even triumph. She furrowed her brow in an attempt to simulate concern. "Poor sister, to have returned home, alone!" she lamented. "And in this way! No wonder you look so very weary. How long has it been since we have seen each other? Let me see—"

"About four years, I should think."

"Of course," she replied, unable to resist adding, with a less than genial glance: "You did not come for Mother's funeral a year ago. Oh, what a sad day that was!" She bowed her head slightly and seemed to brush away a tear, though when she looked up, there was no residual evidence of moisture.

As she spoke, her eldest child—a little boy, Walter—tugged at her with one hand and swung a wooden toy sword in the other.

"It is time to greet Lady Isabelle," Amélie told him. "You have not seen your aunt since you were very little."

The child looked at me petulantly, almost accusingly. "Who is she?" he asked, pointing to me with his sword.

"Why, your aunt!" she chirped. Then, coaxingly: "Lady Isabelle is my younger sister."

"Why is she *tall*, Mother?" he asked, peevishly. "And so thin? You are not tall! Grandpapa is not tall!"

"Not all sisters look alike, child." Amélie gave an uncomfortable laugh.

I knelt down. "Do you like stories?" I asked the child.

He nodded eagerly.

"If you are a good boy, I shall tell you some stories. Some fine ones, about goblins and strange sprites who dwell in the forest—"

He began to howl.

"Isabelle!" scolded Amélie as she comforted the bawling child. "Poor boy, you have frightened him!" She gave a deep sigh, patting her belly with plump, heavily beringed fingers before she continued sharply: "I had thought that with all that has happened"—here, an accusatory glance—"you might have changed. But no, you have not! Always going on about stories. What did you and Arnaut used to call them? 'Inventions.' Yes, that is it, your 'inventions.' No wonder your marriage—"

"Amélie!" interrupted Balduin, who had trundled over to us. "No more of that talk. It is not the time." Then: "We will discuss those matters by and by."

I greeted Balduin and the two younger children, who trailed him.

All had been given fashionable Norman names—the little girl was called Maude, and the middle brother, Fulk.

"Come, sister," Guy said, taking Amélie's hand. "Let us go inside." Then, to her, under his breath: "Never mind Isabelle." He shot me a withering glance.

The discussion about what Balduin had ominously referred to as "those matters"—my divorce, and the plan for my future—was what I dreaded most. I kept to myself as much as possible: I tried my best to join the family gatherings only when the children were about, for it seemed unlikely that Guy, Amélie, and Balduin would bring it up when they were present. (I had concluded that my father's role was relatively insignificant in the matter of my future, for Guy had clearly supplanted him as paterfamilias.)

On Christmas Eve, all the family attended Mass together, providing quite a spectacle—Amélie, a blooming vision in red damask and gold, walked with painstaking slowness through the nave, with one hand, weighted with massive rings of carnelian, poised on her swollen stomach as she acknowledged one familiar face or another in the pews with a regal nod. Every so often she would give an ostentatious sigh, as if acknowledging the preciousness of her nascent burden. At her side strode Balduin, rotund in green, with a yawning Walter tugging at one hand, and Fulk tugging at the other. Guy followed—a thin, austere figure in an elegant dark blue tunic which I recognized as having been my grandfather's.

My father and I came last, with Maude holding my hand. Of the children, Maude was the only one I really liked. She adored my stories and seemed enthralled by my tales of growing up—my escapades, my games with Arnaut. Indeed, her fascination with me had already become a source of competitiveness, even friction, for it was clear that her mother thought me a bad influence. ("Come along, Maude," Amélie would chide if she caught us playing together. "You must let Aunt Isabelle finish her mending.")

After Mass, the prelate scurried over to pay homage to Guy and my father, then to Amélie and Balduin. (I, on the other hand, was acknowledged with a barely perceptible nod.) After wishing them happy tidings of the season, the prelate turned to Guy. "We are most grateful to you and your family for your generous bequest to the monastery this year."

"It is our fervent hope that our contribution will be a useful addition to the monastery and its library," Guy intoned.

"I, too, was very much involved in this decision," interjected Amélie, for she was always one to seize an opportunity to play the beneficent great lady. "Was I not, Guy?"

"Without question, dear sister."

TO MY ASTONISHMENT, OUR FEAST on Christmas Eve managed to be festive. The presence of the children had propelled even the normally frugal Guy to engage some singers and lute players, which lent the ambiance a bit of merriment. The meal itself, while only a pallid version of what I had known with Gerard, was ample enough: the baker had even gone so far as to make the Thirteen Desserts that were part of our Provençale Christmas custom—one dessert representing each of the twelve apostles, and one for Christ. These concoctions, arrayed on a long table, delighted Amélie and Balduin quite as much as they did the children. "I must eat for the child," Amélie announced in a grave, self-sacrificing voice as she delved into a glistening custard. Balduin gave her a proud look as he sat back, his stomach almost as distended as hers, as he luxuriated in still another goblet of wine.

ON CHRISTMAS NIGHT, AFTER WE had supped, the family sat together by the hearth. Balduin regaled the men with stories, no doubt greatly exaggerated, of his hunting prowess. Amélie stitched an embroidery depicting the Madonna and child, both with mawkish expressions.

I stood by the fire, daydreaming, as I absentmindedly ate some honey cake. On the table beside me stood a small bowl of ground cinnamon, a costly Christmas treat that Guy, with uncharacteristic generosity, had provided us. I loved cinnamon and had just begun to douse the cake with a spoonful when I caught the eye of Amélie.

"You might think of saving some cinnamon for the *rest* of us, sister," she told me in a stinging voice, needle in hand. "Of course, your thoughtlessness is not surprising." Her eyes narrowed and her mouth assumed a sour expression I recognized all too well. "I am sure you did not need to think of such things, when you were married to Gerard de Meurtaigne."

"What 'things,' Amélie?" I asked, determined not to let her gibe pass.

"Practicing thrift. Using costly spices sparingly." She made a few more stitches before adding, "Guy has told us that Gerard de Meurtaigne's household is one of great luxury."

"So it is."

"Then it must be rather hard for you to return here, to this house. We have heard all about the grandeur of Château Ravinour. I am sure, while living there, you did not need to consider the cost of cinnamon, nutmeg, or pepper. I am sure those things were commonplace. No doubt you also had servants at your beck and call, and everything else you desired." She continued in this vein for many moments, and the more she railed, the more apparent was her jealousy—that I, not she, had made a splendid match. I was tempted to tell her as much; it was only for my father's sake, and my awareness of his aversion to contentious discussions, that I did not. Rather, I remained stonily silent. My silence seemed to infuriate her all the more.

"Tell me, Isabelle," she continued to goad. "Have you nothing to say?"

"Not to you," I retorted. "Though it does occur to me that—"

"I am sure Isabelle understands the change in her situation," interrupted my father, in a pleading voice.

"Perhaps you are sure that Isabelle understands, my dear Papa, but *I* am not!" she cried. "And I think Guy would agree with me. Would you not, Guy?"

"It is Christmas night, Amélie," he returned tensely. "Let us wait until tomorrow before we discuss these matters with Isabelle."

"Why?" she retorted. "What better time than when we are here, all of us together?"

"Amélie is quite right," I rejoined, wanting only to be done with the dreaded discussion. "Why not talk about these things now?" Then, facing her straight on: "Tell me, sister, what would you have me do?"

"Make yourself useful. So you are not a burden to Guy, and to Papa. A burden in all ways. You must recognize that you will have no time for your stories, your books, and your 'inventions,' as you call them. You must learn to act responsibly. For once!"

"And what do you have in mind for me?"

"That you take on all the tasks of the lady of the house, however tiresome they may seem to you. Keeping the accounts, taking over the sewing. All the work that our dear Mama did." She gave a great sigh, adding as an afterthought, "Though we can only thank the Lord that—" She paused, tendentiously.

"Thank the Lord for *what*, Amélie?" I pressed her.

"We can only thank the Lord that Mama is not alive to see how your marriage ended!" she cried in a spiteful voice, her cheeks reddening. "She had such hopes for you, Mama did. How hard she worked to secure your marriage! Why, I remember her talking about it—how worried she was that no one would ever want you. Sleepless nights she endured, just thinking about your future!" She shook her head woefully, as if pondering my mother's anguished nights. "And there you were," she continued, "married to Gerard de Meurtaigne. A wealthy man, a man of repute, a man close to the Young King and to so many of rank and title within the Norman nobility. You could have brought so much prestige to our family! But no, instead, you have brought us *shame!*"

"That is quite enough, Amélie!" rebuked Guy as my father looked away, burying his head in his hands. "This is not the time, on Christmas night—"

"Let her speak, Guy," I interjected. "I know this is what Amélie really feels. I knew it from the moment she arrived. It is better that she voices her anger, and that we be done with this."

There fell a long, painful silence. My father slumped back in his chair; Guy began to pace; Balduin slurped some wine. Amélie resumed her sewing, stabbing the needle through the cloth with each stitch.

Finally, I said, wearily, "It was never my intention to return home as I did. This was not how I had imagined it would be—not at all."

"What *did* you imagine then?" asked Amélie caustically.

"I had thought I might go to an abbey. To a place I have heard of—the abbey of Fontevraud."

"Fontevraud?" Amélie exchanged astonished glances with Guy. "Are you mad? How could you possibly expect we had the means to send you there? It would require an enormous donation."

"You know of the abbey, then?"

"Of course! I am not an ignorant provincial, sister. Our family is not in a position to send you to such a place," she added. "Why, it would require—"

"And if I were able, somehow, to find a way, by myself?"

She laughed sarcastically. "Then, go ahead, dear sister!" Another stab with her needle. "And even if you were to find a way, what would you do there? Take the veil?" she scoffed. "*You*, of all people?"

"I did not think of taking the veil, no," I replied in a slow, thoughtful voice, for I was determined not to take her bait. "I have heard of noblewomen who reside there as lay women, as conversas. Women who can read and write, and who do good works, and teach. Those are things I could do."

"Your head in the clouds, as always!" she retorted. "You are just like Arnaut—he is always wandering, always restless, always impractical." She made a great, heaving sigh. "Thank the Lord that Guy and I, at least, have been the sensible members of the family." She turned to her husband, slumped in a chair. "Am I not right, Balduin?"

He nodded hazily, red wine dribbling from his lips.

"Yes, I am so fortunate to have Balduin, and our life together, and our blessed children," she went on, with a simpering smile. Then, slyly: "And now, hopefully, Guy will follow me, with a very good match for himself." She noticed my surprise, then glanced expectantly at my brother. "Have you not mentioned your engagement to Isabelle, Guy?"

My brother looked slightly discomfited. "Not yet, no," he replied, shaking his head.

"Well, then, let me be the one to tell her!" She fairly gurgled with delight. "Guy will soon be engaged to Adelaide de Chabanel—a well-born, landed lady, who will provide him with a generous dowry."

"Good news indeed," I replied in a measured voice. "Chabanel is not a name familiar to me, though. She is not from our region?"

"No," exulted Amélie. "She is from a Norman family near Rouen, with land in England as well. We are told she is related to the *great knight*," she added portentously.

"The great knight?" I asked with seeming ingenuousness. I knew full well whom she meant but wanted to irritate her.

"William Marshal," she snapped, then went on, "King Henry has been generous to her family, as he has to Marshal's. The king has granted her family rich holdings in Anjou, and in the south of England."

"I am happy for you, Guy," I said, though I was happy most of all for the change of subject. "When will the marriage take place?"

"As soon as all the details are arranged with her family," he replied in a cheerless voice.

"I see," I replied, mulling this over. "Do you know her family well?"

"Well enough," he answered.

"Oh yes, she is most fair," chimed in Amélie, though Guy, notably, added nothing to confirm this. "It will be a wonderful occasion for our family, in all ways!" She resumed her sewing, smiling smugly. "I have no doubt that Guy will make a success of his marriage. And that you, Isabelle, will do your very best to welcome his wife into our family, when the time is appropriate." Her brow suddenly furrowed. "Though perhaps it is better that you not meet her right now. After all, your own situation does not cast our family in a good light."

I turned to look at Guy, then at my father, waiting for them to contradict Amélie's mean-spirited words. But that was not to be; both men remained silent.

THREE DAYS LATER CAME THE Feast of the Holy Innocents—the holiday when, according to custom, children were given license to play all manner of jokes. It had always been my favorite moment of the Christmas season when I was a child, for it was also the day when I, as the youngest, was granted the power to rule the household. Arnaut and I would spend days plotting our jokes. One year I had rubbed honey on the soles of Amélie's shoes, so that they stuck to the floor as she walked; another time I scattered dried peas on the stairs to make Guy slip. The only family member who escaped my pranks was my mother—I was simply never sure that I would be exempt from her retribution, even on Holy Innocents Day.

Before the bitter discussion on Christmas, I had looked forward to this day of gaiety and mischief: I had even imagined that I would help little Maude, who continued to trail me, in concocting some amusing pranks. Now, however, my spirits had descended to such a low ebb that I had no desire to participate at all, only managing to observe the children with a listless disinterest.

I should not have been surprised, I suppose, by their lack of imagination and courage. Little Walter seemed too terrified of his parents to attempt anything but a feeble joke: he hid Amélie's hoop beneath a bench yet made sure to keep the hem of the embroidery visible. Amélie made a great show of seeking far and wide for the hoop, though it was quite obvious all along she had already seen where it had been "hidden." Fulk, pathetically timid, meekly followed his sister. In the end, all the tricks the three children played were so meager, and so lacking in originality, that I wondered why they had bothered at all.

This lack of spirit, though, went unnoticed by their indulgent parents, who greeted their children's "antics" with exaggerated glee, marveling at their progeny's ingenuity.

To my relief, Amélie and her family departed several days later. I had no desire to linger over their leave-taking and fled the stable the instant Balduin mounted. I returned to my chamber at once, opened the shutters, and watched with a certain grim delight as the lumbering procession moved toward the gate. My gaze did not follow the entourage for long, however. All of a sudden, flocks of soaring birds appeared high, in the blanched white of the winter sky. Enthralled, I watched their flight as they circled again and again, until, at last, they disappeared from sight.

BY EARLY JANUARY, THE HOUSEHOLD had settled into a gloomy, rigid routine. My father would sit by the fire each morning while I sat near him, needle and hoop in hand, restless, and dreaming I were elsewhere. From time to time the silence would be broken by Hortense bustling about, or by Vincens attending intermittently to the fire.

Before Guy returned to my grandfather's manor, shortly after Amélie's departure, he had asked me pleasantly enough if I would like to visit him there, but I had demurred, knowing it would only fill me with sadness. It was unimaginable to see the house without my grandfather—his library devoid of his beloved books and manuscripts, his glorious, slightly unruly garden no doubt clipped and trimmed into stultified order by punctilious Guy.

As for my own belongings: I finished unpacking them myself, save for the small trunk with my secret objects. It was as if exposing them to my forlorn chamber would only confirm that this is where they, and I, would remain forever.

The only object I chose to display was the bronze falcon; curiously, it not only no longer seemed so fearsome but also gave me a strange comfort. To my delight, there still remained a supply of its aromatic herbs; I used them sparingly so that they would last as long as possible. After setting them alight, I would savor the pungent rich fragrance, which slowly permeated the small, cramped chamber. Meantime I would close my eyes and take long deep breaths, trying to lull myself to a distant, exotic land—the land of the elsewhere I had sought from girlhood.

Sparked by the heady scent, perhaps, vivid memories of my marriage drifted back to me: at first, a rush of happy recollections, which only propelled me to doubt myself. I would think: had I been mad, had I been reckless beyond all imagining, to destroy my marriage to Gerard? But the next instant, I would recall the darker times—when he had frightened or hurt me, his coldness when our daughter was born, the time he had punished Gallien so cruelly. Then a certain calm would descend upon me, but it was an uneasy calm, at best.

AS THE DREARY DAYS PASSED, I looked forward with more than usual eagerness to the celebration of Twelfth Night. Clothilde always made an especially splendid *galette des rois* decorated with crystallized fruit and topped by a fanciful paper crown. So bored had I become, so dispirited by the dull daily routine, that I prayed with almost childlike fervency that I might be the one to find the hidden "treasure"—the bean hidden within the cake—and thus be named the queen of the day.

Around the long table we sat that evening—my father and I, and, to my surprise, Hortense. Guy, too, had arrived for the festivities. After prayers, my father ceremoniously cut the cake and passed pieces to each of us. I gingerly bit into my own piece, hoping that I would find the bean. But it was Hortense who looked up, beaming. "Ah, here it is!" she squealed, brandishing the bean. "It is in *mine!*"

"To you goes the prize, then," said my father, visibly pleased as he lifted the crown from the cake and placed it on Hortense's head. I caught the two exchanging affectionate glances and looked away, overcome by awkwardness. "Now I am queen for the night," Hortense pronounced, as my father gazed at her proudly. She sat up very straight, almost regally, as she glanced at one person, then another; Guy, clearly discomfited, cleared his throat. When she looked at me, her mouth settled into a triumphant smile.

AS THE DAYS, AND THEN the weeks, passed, I grew slowly accustomed to the nights with little lamplight, to the silences, and to the tedium. Each morning, as I was sewing, I would think of Arnaut—I wondered where he was, and what adventures he had known. Perhaps, this day, we will hear from him, I would think to myself. But no message ever came.

One afternoon, however, Hortense rushed into my chamber in a state of great excitement. "Someone very grand has just arrived!" she exclaimed. "And he has asked to see you!"

"Who is it?" I asked apprehensively, afraid that it might be Gerard.

"He would not give his name until he sees you. Such clothes! He must be a nobleman, from the looks of him." She looked quite awestruck.

"Where is he now?" I asked, even more nervously.

"In the main hall. I offered him some wine." She looked both pleased with herself and apprehensive. "I hope the wine was good enough."

"I am sure it was," I replied, amused to see her so intimidated, but also frightened that it was Gerard who had arrived. Steeling myself, I told her, "I shall go down at once."

# CHAPTER 52

To my utter astonishment and delight, it was LaFoi who had come! He stood by the hearth like a gorgeous, otherworldly bird—a brilliant creature of gold braid and blue silk, his costume topped by an extravagant plumed cap which bore the swirling insignia of the Hauteclare household.

"LaFoi!" I cried, rushing toward him. It was all I could do not to embrace him. "How good to see you!"

He bowed with a flourish, and then gave me a gracious smile. "My lady."

"You have come with a message, I trust? From the Lady Fastrada?"

"I have, my lady."

"Such a long journey for you, to have ridden all the way from Troyes."

"I have been traveling for over a week."

"I am surprised it did not take you longer. The roads, being what they are, in winter."

"I was fortunate. There had been a thaw, in the north. And my mount is accustomed to such rides."

"You have been offered some wine, I know. Would you not like something to eat, as well?"

"Yes, I would, my lady."

"I shall fetch Hortense." As it turned out, there was no need to call for her: she had been hovering by the doorway. "Do come in, Hortense," I told her as she walked toward us with a sheepish expression.

"This is LaFoi, who has come with a message from a very dear friend, Lady de Hauteclare of Troyes."

She looked at him, and then back at me, in amazement. "He is the messenger of their household, then? And they are your *friends*, my lady?"

"Yes," I replied. Clearly my association with such an exalted family had elevated my own position in her mind. "He has ridden a very long way," I continued, "and it is likely that he will also spend the night here. Is that not so, LaFoi?"

He nodded. "Indeed, Lady Fastrada has ordered me to remain here until you have given me a letter to take back to her."

Now my curiosity was at a fever pitch: What could Fastrada have possibly written me, and why would my reply be so crucial? Still pre-occupied, I told Hortense: "Please see that he is given a chamber. And something to eat, at once."

"Of course, my lady," she replied, her gaze fixed on the splendidly accoutered LaFoi. Then, in a startlingly obsequious voice, one I had never heard from her before: "Is there anything else I might do, my lady? For you, my lady, or for your visitor?"

"No, that is all, Hortense, thank you," I replied, on the verge of laughter; this was the first time I had ever heard Hortense address me as "my lady" with such alacrity. "You may go."

Once I was certain she had left, I began to chuckle. "You seem to have made quite an impression on Hortense," I told LaFoi.

"I have encountered this before, my lady." He smiled. "In other provincial households."

"I am sure you have." But then I grew serious. "Now, LaFoi, do give me the letter! I long to read it."

He produced a roll of parchment from his satchel: how cheering it was to glimpse the familiar hand, and the florid Hauteclare seal! "Come," I said. "Let us get you something to eat and drink. Then I must retire, to read Lady Fastrada's letter."

HORTENSE NOT ONLY MADE CERTAIN LaFoi was given a proper supper but also waited on him with an attentiveness that continued to amuse me. Satisfied he was well tended, I walked quickly to my chamber, and once inside, unfurled the letter:

*To the Lady Isabelle de Meurtaigne, greetings from Lady Fastrada de Hauteclare*

My dear friend, I hardly know what to write, so astonished am I by this turn of events. In December, I sent LaFoi with a letter of Christmas greetings to you. He arrived shortly before Christmas Eve, only to be informed by Gerard that you were no longer there, that your marriage had ended, and that you had returned to your family's home. Imagine my shock when I learned this!

I am deeply worried for you. Instinct tells me that it cannot be good for a young woman of your spirited disposition to be thrust back, like a child, into the home you had left for your husband's. You, with your restless mind, and your curiosity— this cannot bode well. Moreover, I recall your talking about your home in a way that leads me to imagine it must be exceedingly difficult.

Therefore, I have a proposal for you. You remember the abbey of Fontevraud. As you know, my sister, Clementia, lives there now, as do other noblewomen—widows like her, or other women who have been cast aside by their husbands. It is a place where intelligent women can make a meaningful life for themselves. I think you would do splendidly there.

No doubt you will say that such a place is out of reach for you, that it would require a large donation, one that far exceeds your means. Please, let me help you! It would not be a hardship for me to make a contribution in your name. Think of this as a gift to *me*, if that makes my offer more palatable. It would give me such joy—indeed, it would comfort me—to know you would be there, with my beloved younger sister. I pray that you will accept my offer. If you do, I shall arrange for someone to accompany you there.

Write me at once, dear Isabelle, with your thoughts. I have instructed LaFoi to stay as long as he is needed. In fact, I

have told him he is permitted to return *only* if he bears a letter
from you.

> *With affection and concern, from your devoted friend,*
> *Fastrada*

I set the letter down, overcome by gratitude, astonishment, and—
yes, I admit—apprehension. This plan, my going to Fontevraud, was
what I had hoped for, what I had dreamed of—yet now it terrified me.
I paced my chamber for a long time, still wondering at this turn of
events. Gradually, however, another voice—a courageous voice—began
to emerge: a voice with no name, a voice without a persona, and yet a
clarion voice, one that pierced through the murkiness of my uneasiness.
It was this voice that spurred me on.

*Virtute omnibus supereminet,* the voice told me: "Courage above all
else"—the words that comprised the motto of my grandfather's family, and that Arnaut had carved on the box he had given me the day
I left my family's home. It had always been the artistry of the casket,
and the care my brother had taken in crafting it, that I had most cherished. But I now realized it was the motto itself that he had meant as
the real gift.

THE MOMENT THE SUN ROSE, I wrote Fastrada:

> My dear Fastrada, my gratitude to you is so profound that even
> now, hours after reading your letter, joy fills me when I think
> of the moment I saw LaFoi here and learned he had brought a
> message from you. It was as if the Lord himself, and the blessed
> Virgin, and all the holy saints, had listened to my prayers.
>
> The last year has been one of pain, loss, and confusion.
> Many times I wished I could have heard your voice or asked
> your advice. It is still unbearable for me to think of the loss of
> my babies—my little girl, and the baby who would have been

my son. Alas, alas, it was not to be. I do not blame Gerard for the demise of our marriage. I had disappointed him—not only in my inability to bear healthy children, but in the way I approached life. My turn of mind perplexed him.

When I first read your words, I was so stunned that I immediately thought—no, I cannot possibly entertain Fastrada's offer, it is asking too much of a friend to provide such an introduction as well as the donation that would make the plan possible. But through the night, as I pondered all of this, I realized that yes, I should accept, and accept with delight. And yes, I must and will be brave. Most of all, I should trust you and your instincts to know what would be best. You are a sensitive friend who has seen the wider world.

I shall speak with my father today, and to my brother Guy as soon as I am able. I fear, indeed I am certain, they will resist this plan—they will want me to remain here in this safe, plodding life. My father is growing old and takes solace in having my company. Guy also finds it comforting to have me here, minding our household, and caring for Father. But I am determined to go to Fontevraud no matter how hard they resist. I must make my own life and forge my own decision. It is time for me to take flight. . . .

I set down the quill and resolved to finish the letter later, all the while pondering how best to tell my father and Guy about Fastrada's offer and my decision.

# CHAPTER 53

I t was early morning; most likely Father would be sitting by the fire. I fetched my shawl and walked downstairs to find him.

There he sat, by the hearth, stroking Petru, who lay on the floor beside him. Father looked up as I approached.

"Good morrow," I said, kissing his forehead.

"You look especially well and rested this morning, daughter."

"That is strange!" I replied, with a laugh. "I hardly slept last night."

His brow furrowed. "I hope there is not something amiss in our household. I know that Vincens and Clothilde have been quarreling."

"They have, though I believe it has been patched up." I watched as he continued to pet the indolent dog. "But that was not the reason for my not sleeping."

He glanced about, preoccupied. "Where is Hortense?" he asked rather crossly. "She has made herself scarce."

"She may be with our visitor, Father."

"Ah yes—the messenger." He raised his brow. "A grand fellow, I must say. She told me he had a letter for you."

"Yes, he did. From a dear friend, the Lady de Hauteclare, from Troyes. And it is because of Lady Fastrada's letter that I wanted to talk with you. She has made an offer to me. A very interesting offer, and one I should like to accept."

"She is arranging a marriage for you, for the future?" he asked hopefully.

"No, Father, that is not what she is proposing! It is quite a different sort of arrangement she has in mind."

He looked crestfallen. "Ah—well, then, go on."

I steeled myself and said, "She has offered to help me reside at the Abbey of Fontevraud."

"Fontevraud? That is not possible!" He sat up quite straight, his expression wholly disapproving. "Amélie told you we do not have the means to send you to such an abbey. And certainly not to Fontevraud, of all places! That would require an immense sum."

"We would not need to make the donation. Lady Fastrada has offered to contribute to the abbey on my behalf."

"But why would a friend, a friend who lives far away, and whom you hardly see, make such a gesture?"

"I spent time with her when they came to our hunt. Afterward we exchanged letters. She grew fond of me, and I of her. She told me about her sister, Clementia, a nun at Fontevraud. She lives there and helps in the work of the abbey. Lady Fastrada thinks I would do well there and says it would give her comfort to know that I would be with her sister." My words did not seem to allay his skepticism, however; thus I continued even more fervently, "I realize, Father, that this may come as a surprise to you, and that you may think I am being impulsive. But I assure you I have thought of this with great seriousness and intentness and am certain that life at Fontevraud would be right for me." I added, firmly, "I would like very much to accept her offer."

He furrowed his brow and looked away, then down at Petru, stroking him again. "And what of *me*?" he asked petulantly. "How am *I* to manage, without your company, and your help? How are we to run the household with you far away?"

"You would not be without company, Father," I replied gently. "Guy lives nearby, after all. And as for household, there is—" I paused. "Hortense, of course."

He ignored my insinuation. "I cannot give you a decision now. I must speak with Guy. I suspect he will not approve this plan. He will want you to remain here, with me. With our family. He will not want you to accept the charity of these people."

"I understand your feelings, and of course, I shall speak with Guy. But I do believe this is my decision to make. It is my life, after all."

"But you are still my daughter."

"Then I should think you would want me to be happy! And if that means my living at Fontevraud, and helping with God's work, then, surely—"

He held up his hand. "No more of this, daughter! I shall send for Guy at once and we will discuss the matter together."

A FEW HOURS LATER, GUY appeared—pallid, composed, and dressed in another elegant but threadbare jacket I remembered as having been my grandfather's. Over this he wore an almost absurdly heavy wool vest. "Are you not dressed rather too warmly, brother?" I asked; the fire was roaring and, for once, the chamber seemed almost overheated.

"A measure of protection. As I told you, my health has been rather fragile." The expression of his watery gray eyes was circumspect, and his mouth was set in a priggish line as he stood by the fire near my father. "I have been told there is a matter to discuss with you, sister?" he asked.

"Yes."

"Tell me, then."

I repeated what I had related to my father—Fastrada's proposal, and my ardent desire to accept her offer to place me at Fontevraud—all the while girding myself for Guy's reply.

He did not answer at once but mulled over my words, all the while tapping the cold stone floor with his foot. The sharp, repetitive sound made me nervous. Guy would rebuff me, I knew, he would be harsh, he would tell me that the plan was out of the question: I was far more useful to him here, at home, tending the household.

"I do not think Isabelle's request untoward," he said at last, to my utter astonishment. "I am acquainted with the Hauteclare family." Then, with characteristic self-importance: "That is, I know Lord Hugh, from the tournaments, and I believe he has spoken well of me. And I know, too, that Lady Fastrada is well regarded. They are well landed, responsible, respected." To this he added: "And very rich."

"I am relieved to hear, Guy—" I said, still amazed.

"And what is more," he interjected, with a telling glance at my father, "they are an exceedingly well-placed family. They are close to King Henry, and are also close to the two eldest princes, Henry and Richard. In addition, the Hauteclare family has managed to maintain its ties with the French court. That, in itself, is a considerable accomplishment."

"What does this mean, then, my son?" my father asked in a piteous voice.

"It would be advantageous for us to be associated, even in this way, with the Hauteclare family," Guy replied. "It might be a help—to me, especially—to have Isabelle at Fontevraud with the Lady Fastrada's sister, and under her auspices. Yes, very helpful, indeed."

"I would have thought that you would have wanted Isabelle to remain here, with me. With us, her family. But to send her away—far away!" my father said in a querulous voice. "And what will I do, without her company? I have grown accustomed to having Isabelle here, minding the household!"

"Hortense is capable of running the household, as we all know," Guy returned, his tone now chilly. "As for companionship—you are hardly lacking in that, Father." Then, with a knowing glance: "At least, that is my impression. And Isabelle's, no doubt."

My father bit his lip. I held my breath, disturbed to hear Guy speak to my father in such a manner, as if he had usurped Father's place.

"Well, I suppose," said my father, after a few moments, "it would not be a terrible thing to have Isabelle placed at such a prestigious abbey. But to have her way paid for, by someone else"—he began to shake his head—"that does not seem proper."

"There is nothing shameful in this, Father," retorted Guy. "Quite to the contrary! We should think of Lady Fastrada's proposal as a great compliment to our family and accept her offer with gratitude. We must embrace this decision and wish my dear sister well." He turned to me with an almost repulsive smile: "What say you, Isabelle?"

"I am grateful to you, Guy, for your understanding," I replied, knowing that his enthusiasm had nothing to do with me, and everything to do with advancing his own prospects. I turned to my father, who suddenly looked rather small and diminished. "And I thank you, Father," I said gently, touching his hand, "for your understanding, as well."

Then I addressed them both. "I shall write Lady Fastrada this evening, and tell her that I gratefully accept her offer, and that I shall depart as soon as possible. LaFoi will set off with my letter to her tomorrow."

"Of course, we will send someone with you, when you depart for Fontevraud," said Guy. "Indeed, I am happy to go with you myself, sister."

"That is kind of you, Guy," I replied, all too aware of his ulterior motives: he was hoping to meet Clementia and possibly to encounter Fastrada herself. "But Lady Fastrada has insisted that she send someone from her household to accompany me, to spare us the expense and trouble." I gave him a bright, seemingly ingenuous smile. "Is that not thoughtful of her?"

"Indeed it is," replied Guy with faux heartiness, clearly chagrined that his plan had been thwarted. Even so, he managed a crisp, complacent smile as he announced, with rare bonhomie: "Now, we must celebrate this plan with some wine. I shall summon Hortense."

It did not take him much time to fetch Hortense: no doubt she had been lurking within earshot. The moment she entered, I observed that she seemed more than ordinarily cheerful.

"Bring us some wine at once, Hortense," Guy told her. "We have cause to celebrate, and celebrate we shall."

"Ah, what is it you are celebrating, my lord?" she asked, affecting such inordinate ignorance that I knew beyond doubt that she had overheard our discussion.

"The Lady Isabelle is soon to go to live at the Abbey of Fontevraud, near Saumur. Dear friends of hers—and of mine, I should add—have generously offered to sponsor her."

"Oh!" cried Hortense, her eyes radiant. "How wonderful!" Then, adjusting her expression, she added with patently concocted sorrow: "But, of course, this is very sad for us. How we will miss you here, my lady!" She gave a great sigh. "Oh yes, how we will miss you!" She took out a handkerchief and began to daub her eyes.

"Thank you, Hortense," I forced myself to say while my father, who had resumed stroking Petru, remained silent.

# CHAPTER 54

After having joined my father and brother in a celebratory goblet of wine, I left them and walked pensively to my chamber. How eagerly Guy had seized the opportunity for me to be used as a pawn for my family's ambitions! But I must dismiss all of this from my mind, I reminded myself. I must not be distracted by this hovering tristesse borne by my perpetual longing to be loved by my family in the way I had always yearned for: to be loved for myself, not for what I could do for them. Most of all, I must *act*: I must finish the letter to Fastrada.

LaFoi was ready to set off early the following morning with my letter. I had hoped to be alone while I said goodbye to him; alas, this was not to be, for Hortense, aware of his departure and insistent that she, too, bid him adieu, accompanied me to the courtyard outside the stable. There, assisted by the groom, LaFoi completed his preparations. I greeted him; Hortense remained a few steps behind. He made a final adjustment to the bridle before announcing decisively, "Good. All is ready." As I watched him mount, I imagined him in the days ahead—a brilliantly attired, solitary figure galloping along treacherous winter roads, and through forests frequented by robbers and other lawless people. I marveled at his calm and fearlessness.

"Are you never afraid, LaFoi, of these long journeys?" I could not resist asking. "And of traveling such distances, all alone?"

He shook his head. "There are moments when I am afraid, but I have learned how to conquer those fears, partly through experience and partly through God's help." Then, with touching gravity: "This is my duty, and I must fulfill it."

"That may be so, but you do it with grace and courage."

"Thank you, my lady." He replied in such a heartfelt way I knew my words had affected him.

He took up his reins; then, with a flourish of his plumed cap, he bade me adieu, and set off. "Godspeed!" I cried.

Hortense came forward, calling out, "Adieu, adieu!" again and again so histrionically that I glanced away in embarrassment.

We followed his progress until he disappeared past the gates. "Such an elegant man," she remarked, turning to me. "He must have noble blood. Do you not think so, my lady?"

"He has a noble *spirit*. And that is far more important."

IN THE DAYS THAT FOLLOWED, I began to pack up my possessions—alone, this time, for I now knew better than to ask meddling Hortense to assist me.

As I selected what to take, the words of Fastrada's letter came back to me. Thus I included things that gave me comfort and pleasure—my secret objects, the little box from Arnaut, and the bronze falcon (which, with the passing of time, had begun to seem oddly comforting). I did not deprive myself of my cloak lined in marten, nor of the lovely robes that Gerard had had fashioned for me. All the while, as I continued to place one thing, then another, in the trunk, I tried to imagine my new life; I had no idea what really lay ahead, which both excited and terrified me.

It became increasingly obvious that Hortense was keen for me to leave; once I departed, after all, she would become the actual lady of the household. Guy visited more frequently, ostensibly to keep us company, though it was clear, to me at least, that his real motives lay elsewhere. He not only wanted to make certain that I *did* leave for Fontevraud but seemed determined also to take part in my leave-taking—an opportunity, no doubt, for him to meet the Hauteclare emissary. "As soon as the representative arrives, send for me immediately!" he reminded me more than once.

I took a certain perverse delight in trying to dissuade him. "Oh, brother, it is too much trouble for you to ride all the way here, simply to wish me goodbye! There is really no need for such an effort."

"Oh, it is no trouble at all, sister!" he would reply. "It is the very least a devoted brother can do. How sad we will be, yes how very sad, when you are gone." To this he added: "And is it not proper for me, as the eldest son, to welcome the Hauteclare messenger myself?"

It was only my father who seemed saddened about my imminent departure. Indeed, during those weeks of waiting, he seemed to visibly age. He began to walk with a stoop; he seemed more than usually forgetful and would grow fretful if I left him even for a short time.

While we sat at table, he would look at me with harrowing sadness, as if he were thinking, Will I ever see my daughter again, once she leaves? He was newly impatient with the servants, and even with Hortense. "Where is my lap rug?" he snapped at her one morning as he settled into his chair. "Did you not hear me when I asked for it earlier?"

One afternoon, when Hortense had gone to the village, Father and I sat together by the hearth, Petru sprawled beside him, while I read aloud from my Psalter.

"Daughter—" he suddenly interrupted.

"Yes, Father?" I looked up.

"I have wanted to tell you . . ."

There was a lengthy pause. "Do continue, Father."

"If you do not find Fontevraud to your liking, you must not hesitate to return home. I do not want you ever to feel that I would be disappointed in you. I realize that Guy has endorsed this plan. But I wanted to make my own feelings clear."

"Thank you, Father. You do not need to—"

"I know I do not *need* to. I want you to know that this is what I *feel*. I know you can be stubborn." His lap rug had slipped; I arranged it over his knees while he reflected, "You were never an ordinary girl. There were times when your mother"—he made the sign of the cross— "when your behavior was not easy for her." The mention of my mother's displeasure with me rankled, but I held my tongue as he continued. "I know the abbey is reputed for its good works, and for the noblewomen of good character who live there, but even so—"

I leaned over, stroking his hand. "Remember, too, Father, that

Fontevraud is greatly favored by the Plantagenets, and by King Henry and Queen Eleanor—" I caught myself, aware that an endorsement by the notorious Eleanor would hardly assuage my father's fears.

"Queen Eleanor!" he retorted. "That is *hardly* a comfort, daughter." He gave me a sharp glance. "You know what your mother thought of her."

"I do," I replied ruefully. "But I must confess, Father, that I have never shared Mother's opinion of the queen. To me Queen Eleanor seems an admirable figure—brave, learned, and adventuresome. All qualities I admire." As his gaze wandered somewhat confusedly, I took his hands in mine and said, "Oh, Father, do not fear! If I do not feel at ease at Fontevraud, I promise, I shall find a way to let you know." I gave him a reassuring smile. "And then I shall come home and live with you here."

He looked immensely relieved. "Good," he said, kissing my forehead. "It pleases me to hear this, daughter." He sat up quite straight, as if his dignity had been restored. "Now, let us continue our reading."

FINALLY, ON THE LAST DAY of February, I heard the horns herald the arrival of a visitor. I raced down to the courtyard toward the palisade, my heart pounding.

I ran through the open gates and looked ahead, squinting in the noonday sun. There seemed to be a lone figure advancing toward us; and then—could it be?—I glimpsed a vivid flash of blue. Was it possible that Fastrada had sent LaFoi to accompany me to Fontevraud?

It *was* indeed LaFoi, resplendent in blue, who soon cantered toward me. A lovely gray steed fitted with an exquisite saddle followed behind.

LaFoi stopped before me. "My lady," he said as he doffed his plumed cap.

"Oh, LaFoi, I am overjoyed to see you!" I cried, unable to restrain myself. "It means so much that it is you who has returned, and that *you* will accompany me to Fontevraud."

"It is Lady Fastrada you must thank. She insisted that I come to fetch you. And it is also she who chose this mount for you to ride to Fontevraud." He gestured to the gray steed.

"What is her name?" I asked, stroking her mane.

"Folie."

I laughed. "I am not sure that bodes well!"

"Lady Fastrada seemed to think she would suit you," he replied with a wry glance. "She has also sent a letter for you, my lady." He reached into his saddlebag. "Here it is."

"I shall read it at once. But now, you must come with me." I could not resist adding: "I am sure Hortense will be delighted to see you."

Fastrada wrote me:

Your delight in receiving my letter, and in seeing LaFoi, was only matched by mine when I received your response. I should not have been surprised, I suppose, that you should have summoned your courage and accepted what might have seemed, at first glance, an unorthodox proposal.

I am overcome with joy that you might find a felicitous place at the abbey, that you and Clementia will finally meet, and that I shall have the pleasure, and the reassurance, of knowing you are both there together, two intelligent women occupied with worthy pursuits.

It will give you comfort to have someone familiar with you as you journey to the abbey. And there is no one steadier or more reliable than LaFoi.

Let me reiterate what I told you: you are not taking the veil, thus there is no need to deprive yourself of some fine clothes and other things you are fond of. The noblewomen live well at Fontevraud; indeed, some come with their own servants and libraries. But let me refrain from saying more. You will see for yourself, and, of course, Clementia will help you in any way she can. She is immensely resourceful.

I shall try my best to visit you both in the coming months, and, of course, I shall write to you.

> *With affection, and fervent wishes for a safe journey to Fontevraud,*
> *Fastrada*

My father and I decided that I would leave with LaFoi two days later, on the second day of March. Guy arrived at our house the moment he received word. He, like Hortense, seemed inordinately impressed by LaFoi: indeed, I had never seen Guy address a servant with such deference. When Guy learned, for instance, that LaFoi had been given a wine the former deemed inferior quality, he announced, "Oh no, that wine will not do! We must give our visitor the best vintage." One afternoon, Guy asked LaFoi: "Will Lord and Lady Hauteclare travel to Fontevraud themselves, to visit the sister of Lady Hauteclare, the good Sister Clementia? Early in the summer, perhaps? I myself have thought of visiting then. It would be fortuitous for us to meet. I should like to thank them for their generosity to my dear sister."

To this LaFoi merely replied, in his most formal manner, "I am not privy to their plans, my lord."

ON THE MORNING OF MY departure, the household assembled by the stable shortly past dawn. The sun was bright, but the sharp wind reminded me that spring was still far away.

My father held a handkerchief to his eyes and could not stop crying as I embraced him once, then again. It took all my force of will not to weep as well, for I would miss Father, despite his eccentricities.

Even Hortense looked somewhat somber—sensing, perhaps, that my absence might hasten my father's decline.

Guy was crisp and collected to the end. "Goodbye, sister dear," he told me, with a perfunctory kiss on each cheek. "Rest assured, I shall come to Fontevraud as soon as I am able." To this he added: "Perhaps you might write me, so that I might arrange my visit at a time when Lady de Hauteclare visits the good Sister Clementia?"

"Of course, Guy," I murmured.

Then I heard LaFoi say gently, but firmly: "We must not tarry, my lady. It is time."

I nodded, suppressing tears as I caught my father's eyes. "I am ready."

"Let us mount, then." LaFoi offered me his hand.

He mounted next; we stood astride together, my family standing expectantly nearby. My father walked over to me; I leaned over and pressed his hand in mine. "May God keep you safe, daughter," he said, with such fervent emotion that I could hardly refrain from sobbing. Hortense approached and tried to comfort him. Guy remained at a distance, gazing coolly at the scene.

"My lady—" I heard LaFoi say.

"Yes," I replied, trying to manage a smile. "Yes. Let us go."

We turned and proceeded slowly toward the gate. I glanced at LaFoi, whose gaze was resolutely fixed ahead.

We passed through the gate. Never once did I look back.

# Part III

# CHAPTER 55

Several weeks later, at dusk, we arrived at Fontevraud. Before us loomed two stone pillars reaching skyward, and, between them, a monumental portal crossed with bands of iron. The preternatural quiet, the breadth of the walls, the daunting door—all made me realize as nothing else had before: I was about to step into an insular world, a world of stillness and rules, locked away from the animated outer world I knew and loved.

"Who goes there?" a man called from within the gatehouse. LaFoi gave his name, and the voice replied, "You may enter." We heard the sound of inner latches being raised, then the opening of the lock; finally the great door inched open, and the gateman, a young man with shaggy dark hair and a jolting limp, appeared. "Come this way," he said, standing to the side and ushering us in.

Still astride, we stepped slowly inside a courtyard of graceful proportions edged by a low, meticulous border of boxwood, which emitted a fresh, sweet scent. My eyes took in the sober, yet felicitous mix of hues and textures—the bisque-colored stone walls of the elegant buildings beyond, the flinty gray of the high, gabled roofs, the magisterial outline of the bell tower. The ground had been recently swept, the rosebushes along the main path freshly pruned. There was an air of meticulousness and quiet surety about this space—as if everything here, guided by God's benevolence, had no risk of ever being infiltrated by disorder.

LaFoi dismounted, then helped me do the same. "This way," he said, after tying our horses to a post. We walked toward the right, to a tall door set within an arch. LaFoi knocked three times; the door swung open and a young woman, a novice with downcast eyes, silently ushered us in.

The next moment a substantial, older woman in a white habit appeared. Perched on her arm was a bird so riotous in color that it was brilliantly visible even in the dusky light. Suddenly the creature spoke: "*Bienvenu à Fontevraud!*" The high-pitched, rasping voice was weirdly human, yet not at all human.

"Good evening," the woman said. "I am Mother Gilles, the abbess."

I curtseyed before her, my eyes still fixed on the bird.

"You are surprised that this parrot, of all creatures, should greet you," she observed. "But Caprice is one of us, one of God's beings, is she not?"

I nodded, hesitant to admit that although I had heard people speak of parrots, I had never encountered one. It was a rare, exotic bird, the bird of kings, and noblemen.

The abbess was smiling broadly, if assessingly, now. "You are Lady Isabelle, I trust?"

"Yes. Yes, I am."

"Sister Clementia and I have been expecting you. And LaFoi, too"— she acknowledged him with a genial nod—"of course." The abbess had a rather wide, pleasant face, with a strong, square chin and eyes that suggested keen intelligence and authority.

"Come this way," she said. The parrot squawked: "Come this way! Come this way!"

"No more of that, Caprice!" she reprimanded, as one would a child; then, turning to me, she said, "She can be quite mischievous, I am afraid. There have been moments when I have threatened to take her to confession!" She gave a rather arch smile; I laughed and began to feel more at ease.

We entered a long, narrow room with a painted, vaulted ceiling— arch upon arch alive with tendrils, flowers, and doves. She pointed to a bench that ran the length of one wall. "Please take a seat. I shall return," she said with a reassuring smile, and left us.

A few minutes later she reappeared, accompanied by a younger, slender, very fair woman, with a graceful, if solemn, step, her hands serenely folded together. She brought to mind a statue come to life; yet her cornflower-blue eyes had none of the blankness of a statue's, for they were focused on me with great intentness. The perfect features of her oval face were, if anything, thrown into relief by the folds of her habit and the severity of the wimple. "The face of a Madonna," Hugh had told me: this, then, must be Clementia. . . .

"So, you are here at last," she said, her diction as precise and her intonation as aristocratic as her features and bearing. LaFoi bowed deeply before her, brushing the stone pavement with his cap in a manner that was almost exaggeratedly reverent. She seemed to expect the gesture, as one who had grown up with obeisances of this nature would. I continued to watch her in fascination: there was no seeming link between this ethereal creature—whose face recalled that of a *princesse lointaine* from a fable—and her *belle laide* sister, Fastrada.

As I curtseyed before her, she turned her gaze upon me. "I am Sister Clementia," she said. "And you, of course, are Lady Isabelle."

"I am honored to meet you, Sister Clementia."

"You have come a long way. Your journey was not too tiring, I hope?"

"With LaFoi as my guide, it was not difficult."

She glanced at him with warm approval. "It never is, with LaFoi." Then, to me: "Are you fond of journeys?"

"Yes, yes, I am."

"That does not surprise me."

"And you?" I asked impulsively; then I colored, realizing that the question, at first meeting, might be considered inappropriate.

"Yes," she replied, with no hint that my question had been untoward. "Although, of course, it depends on what kind of journey. One can travel far, after all, without taking a single step. That is, one can travel far *within one's mind*, even if the physical self is restricted. That is especially true here, in God's house." She turned to the abbess. "Is that not so, Mother Gilles?"

"Indeed it is," concurred the abbess genially. "One might even say it is our deepest purpose. Being able to journey inwardly in ways not conceivable to those outside our world. It is our hope that residing here will help you to more fully understand this. But now," she announced, "Sister Clementia will show you to your chamber. LaFoi, you will come with me."

I watched LaFoi and the abbess—her parrot quiet now—proceed down the corridor until they had vanished from sight.

"Do not be frightened, Isabelle," Clementia said, sensing my anxiousness at LaFoi's departure. "It is natural that all of this seems daunting at the beginning. But you will not be deprived of all freedoms, I assure you. You will be here as a lay sister, a conversa, after all. Come," she said, her hand grazing my arm, "let us walk together a bit."

We came to the end of the corridor and stood before a tall archway. "We will go into the cloister," she said. "It has a lovely garden. We are very proud of our gardens here," she told me as we made our way along the path. "In this we are very influenced by Hildegard."

"Hildegard?" I asked.

"The abbess of Bingen, in Germany. She believed in the healing powers of nature, and in deriving joy from music and beauty. She was against the conventional idea of separating the health of the body from that of the spirit. "

That she had said this with a certain admiration did not escape me. "There seems to be much about the abbey, about Fontevraud, that also goes against convention," I ventured.

"And does that intrigue you?"

"Yes," I replied, blushing slightly.

We walked a few steps, then passed through a generous archway into a small chapel, where we knelt together in prayer. I fought to keep my attention from wandering; more than once I stole glances at the grimacing heads depicted on the capitals, or at Clementia's chiseled profile, wondering if Fastrada had ever been jealous of her beauty. . . . She, by contrast, prayed so intently that I felt rather ashamed of my own lack of attention.

Suddenly Clementia made the sign of the cross, and stood up. "Now I shall show you to your chamber."

We walked down one passageway, then another, until we arrived at a different wing of the cloister. "This is where you will live. Not with the sisters, who have taken the veil, but with certain oblates and other conversas who help with the abbey's work. With our mission."

She took a key from her pocket and opened the door. The chamber was not much larger than my chamber at my family's home, but its windows were generous enough, and its ceiling surprisingly lofty. In the morning, I sensed, there would be ample light, for the room faced south and looked out on an orchard. The bed was simple but appeared comfortable; even the prie-dieu, with its plump linen cushion, looked inviting. A fire blazed in the hearth. As I looked about expectantly for my trunks, Clementia pointed to a narrow doorway. "Your luggage is in the anteroom."

To my delight, I spotted writing implements and parchment on a table in the far corner. I walked over to examine them and discovered there were several books as well, each of exquisite design. I took up the first—a Psalter with a white cover tooled in gold; then *Le Roman de Troie*, which intrigued me by its title alone; and finally, the third, a collection of stories including one called *Erec et Enide*.

"Fastrada sent those for you," Clementia told me as I leafed through a volume. "I suspect the quill and ink were not without an ulterior motive—I know she would delight in a letter from you." Clementia's expression was pleasingly girlish, as if the mention of her elder sister provoked her to a sense of playfulness at odds with her customarily stately self. Pointing to a small table before the far window, she said, "And she also sent *this* for you—"

I stepped quickly to the table; an exquisite ivory chess set was displayed upon it. Fingering one of the pawns, I turned to her and said, wonderingly, "I have longed for a chess set for years—"

"So I have been told, by my sister," she said with a soft laugh. "I promised her that I would introduce you to the game. She would not rest until she found a set for you."

"You, too, play chess?"

"That seems to surprise you."

"I would not have thought here, at the abbey, one would—"

"That one would indulge in such games here, among those who have taken the veil? You must discard your rigid notions of what it means to live at a convent, especially here, at Fontevraud. Many of our sisters come from families where one read, or was read to, and where one was acquainted with chess, and hawking, and such things. It is partly our background, our being acquainted with the world beyond these walls, that makes us effective in our work here. Indeed, the founder of the abbey was intent on choosing experienced women as his abbesses—widows who had already borne great responsibilities, for instance. Women who could manage properties and supplies. He thought it essential that they be capable."

The way she pronounced *capable* led me to believe this was a trait she greatly valued. I picked up the figure of the queen from the chess set, my finger tracing the line of its chiseled crown. "What of your own work here, Sister Clementia?"

"I oversee some of the work in the scriptorium. In addition, I supervise the messages that come into the abbey, by way of the *tour*. It is a rotating device, at the entrance, where things can be discreetly deposited without the messenger having to enter our private domain. Letters, small objects, and the like. Even babies left by unfortunate women who, for whatever reason—shame, poverty—cannot keep them."

"And the children are raised here?"

"Yes—very well raised, I might add." She took a few steps away from me, toward the window, which she proceeded to unlatch. "Good!" she said, taking a deep breath, "fresh air." She clasped her hands together, then turned to look at me intently. "You will meet one such child tomorrow, a little girl, Marie. It will be your responsibility to teach her. She is a bright child—lively, very intelligent, with a sprightly curiosity. She loves to learn, so I expect you will get on quite well with her."

"How did you know I love to learn?"

"Fastrada, of course! But even if she had not told me, I should have surmised it."

"What else did Fastrada tell you about me?"

"That when she met you, you seemed to love your husband very much."

"I did."

"And what happened?"

"Those feelings changed. Or perhaps it is I who changed."

"Surely the two are intertwined. And those changes would hardly be surprising, after all."

"Did you never dream of marrying?" I asked impetuously.

"As a little girl, of course," she replied serenely. "But then I chose another path. Doing God's work."

# CHAPTER 56

The vibrant morning sun flooded the little chamber with light—I had fallen asleep without even having undressed or said my prayers. I sat up in bed, the blanket drawn around me, waiting; yet I had no idea what to do, or what was expected of me. A memory of the first morning at Ravinour beset me: that morning, too, after awakening, I had waited anxiously. . . .

I rose quickly, smoothed my rumpled clothes, and had just begun to brush my hair when I heard a knocking at the door. It was Clementia, followed by an older servant in a tunic of a muddy color who walked with her head bowed and who carried a large wooden pitcher, plate, and cup. Clementia bade me good morrow. "We have brought you some warm milk, and some bread," she announced, before gesturing to the servant, who set the things down before me.

"This is Heraldis, Isabelle," Clementia announced as the woman curtseyed. "It is she who will attend you. You have only to tell her what you need. No doubt you would like her to help you unpack your belongings today." She turned to the woman: "But now you may wait outside, Heraldis, while I speak with Lady Isabelle."

Once we were alone, she said, with a touch of imperiousness, "It is time for us to discuss the day ahead. The Abbess will want to see you, of course. But before that, you will meet Marie."

"I am eager to meet her."

"She was deposited here as an infant," Clementia explained. "She has become something of a pet to us, the sisters, I must admit. We do know that she had been baptized, for among the few things left with her was a packet of salt. A fortuitous sign—"

"Why 'fortuitous'?"

"It is always comforting to know that a child was not left here in a state of sin. That the mother had cared enough to have her blessed. It would seem less likely, therefore, that this was not the baby"—she paused—"of a harlot, for instance."

"And if she had been?"

"That would not have mattered to me, but it might have mattered to other, older sisters here who are less tolerant in their thinking. It is our intention that she become a novice eventually and take her vows."

"You assume, then, that life in the abbey will suit her."

"Yes. There is no reason *not* to," she replied peremptorily. "Part of your work here will be to prepare her for such a life by teaching her and giving her lessons. She is already curious about letters, about reading— the signs of a quickening intelligence. She seems intrigued by the work of the sisters in the scriptorium."

"What have you told Marie about me?"

"That you were once married, but no longer. That God, in His wisdom, directed you here, to us." To this she added: "And that you know my sister, Fastrada. Marie adores Fastrada, as you can imagine!" She turned, gathering the folds of her robes about her, and walked toward the door. "I shall call Heraldis and ask her to bring your wash basin, and to help you dress."


I HAD ONLY JUST FINISHED dressing, when Clementia returned, this time with a little girl clutching her hand. The child had curly dark hair, sprightly blue eyes, and a delicate, elfin nose sprinkled with freckles. She held a rough-hewn wooden doll, which she cradled in one arm.

"Come, Marie," Clementia said, "let me introduce you to Lady Isabelle." Then she prodded her: "Remember what you must do now."

The little girl managed a curtsey.

"Well done!" said Clementia, leading the child closer.

"Sister Clementia has told me about you," I said gently, bending down to speak with her, all the while thinking what a pretty little creature she was.

Marie was silent, looking at me shyly, wonderingly, and then up, to

Clementia, as if for reassurance. "Tell her how old you are, Marie," said the latter, smiling.

The child held up her hand, all five fingers splayed.

"So you are five!" I said. "And next year you will be—"

"Six!" she exclaimed proudly.

"Very good!" I stood up, smiling, face-to-face with Clementia now.

"Best I leave and let the two of you become acquainted on your own," she told me. She pressed Marie's hand in hers and said, in a firm, yet tender, voice, "You must welcome Lady Isabelle here. She has come from far away to stay with us. Do you understand?" Marie nodded with touching, almost somber, acquiescence.

"I promise to return soon." Clementia left us, while Marie's eyes followed her until she disappeared from sight.

"Come," I said, "let us sit by the window together. When I was a little girl, my favorite place was the window seat of my chamber."

I helped her up and we settled on the cushions, Marie taking great care to prop up her doll beside her. "Where did you come from?" she asked, turning to me.

"From the south, from far away. With LaFoi, who has known Sister Clementia since she was a little girl. And Lady Fastrada, too."

"I wish Lady Fastrada would visit!" she exclaimed. "She always brings me treats." Then, as an afterthought: "It is hard to think of Sister Clementia as a little girl."

"Yes, we were all girls once! And one day you will no longer be little, but quite grown up. You may even wear a habit, and have a set of keys, like Sister Clementia. Would you like that?"

"Yes. I should like to have a big set of keys!"

"And what else would you like?"

"I would like to be able to draw. To use the quills, like the ones I see the sisters using here, in the—"

"The scriptorium?" She nodded. "Perhaps we will go there together, you and I. You can show me where it is."

"I can show you, but I cannot take you inside. Children are not allowed there," she said rather forlornly. She picked up her doll and cradled it in her arms.

Sensing her restlessness, and still trying to engage her, I asked, "Do you like birds?"

"Yes! Mother Gilles has a parrot, a clever bird who can talk. Did you meet Caprice?"

I smiled. "Yes. Caprice is a special bird, indeed. She almost frightened me, at first—"

"Caprice does not frighten *me!*" she announced proudly, adding, "I love all sorts of birds."

"What is it you like best about them?"

"They have pretty wings, and different colored beaks, and they can fly." She took the doll and held it high, above her, as if the doll were flying. "I should like to fly!"

"I should like to, as well," I replied, laughing. "But since we cannot, let me show you my falcon. He is beautiful, though he cannot fly."

"What good is he then?" she replied almost sulkily. "Can he sing?"

"No, I am afraid not. But he has lovely colored feathers, and he always keeps me company. Come," I said, taking her little hand. "We shall look at him together."

"But where is he?" she asked, casting her eyes about the chamber. "There is no falcon here."

"He is in my trunk, in the little room next to us. We will unlock it now, and I shall show you my falcon, and tell you some stories about him." At that, she took my hand eagerly, urging me forward as we walked into the anteroom. Before us stood the three trunks. "Try to guess which trunk holds the falcon," I said.

She looked searchingly from one to the other, her brow furrowed. "That one!" she exclaimed, pointing to the smallest trunk.

"Quite right! How did you guess?"

"The others look too big. A falcon might be lonely in them."

I laughed. "Do you think falcons become lonely?"

"Yes."

"Why?" I asked.

"They are all alone in the sky, and the sky is so big, and they must find their own food."

"That is true, but they can call to other birds and other creatures. They have their own language. And there are trees where they can rest."

"But when it rains, and thunders, how cold and afraid they must be!" She cradled her doll, then looked up. "I am not afraid. The sisters tell me I am brave!"

I smiled. "Why do they say that?"

"Because I am not afraid of the dark. And once, when I was ill, and had to take a medicine Sister Philippa gave me, I drank it at once and did not complain. Sister Clementia said she was proud of me. And the medicine tasted *awful*." She made a face.

"Then you are indeed very brave," I said as she beamed. "Do you think it is important to be brave?" I asked.

She nodded, before picking up her doll and stroking its hair.

"Sister Clementia tells me God wants me to be brave," she said, looking up. "And Lady Fastrada says it is important, too."

"You told me you like it when Lady Fastrada visits—"

"Oh yes! She wears lovely clothes. And she brings me pretty things. And she has told Sister Clementia that, one day, I must learn to ride."

"Lady Fastrada has sons, but never had a little girl. I am sure she loves to see you."

"She says I am her favorite," she boasted.

"Because you are brave?"

"Yes. And because I love her stories. She tells me about the ladies in Troyes, and the lists, and the men on their horses. And how splendid it is. And about the musicians!"

"Do you like music?"

She nodded, once more cradling her doll.

"What a pretty tunic your doll has," I said, leaning forward to touch it. "And it has such lovely blue flowers embroidered upon it. Do you know what kind they are?"

She shook her head.

"Forget-me-nots," I said. "They have always been one of my favorites." Then I asked: "What is your doll's name?"

She seemed to hesitate, as if almost unwilling to reveal this to a stranger. "Radegonde," she said in a low, shy voice.

An eerie sensation came over me as the little girl uttered the name of the Merovingian queen who had also fascinated me as a little girl. "Why did you choose 'Radegonde'?"

"Sister Clementia told me about her. She said she was a queen, and very brave."

"That is true. And then, later in her life, Radegonde pledged her life to God. Rather like Sister Clementia or Mother Gilles."

"I would rather be like Sister Clementia," she replied almost petulantly. "She is much prettier!"

"I cannot deny that," I replied, laughing. "But is that the only reason?"

"She has her own books and she knows stories." To this she added: "And it is she who meets the visitors who come here. She is always very busy." A fleeting sadness crossed her face. "Too busy, she says, to teach me to read."

"That is why she has asked *me* to teach you," I said gently. "Because she has other responsibilities." I took her hand in mine. "Let us fetch the falcon I told you about."

She watched expectantly as I took the key from my pocket and opened the lock to the trunk. "Come, sit by me here," I said, kneeling before it. She did so, her doll clutched in her hand as I slowly extricated the falcon from the layers of linen within. "Here it is!" I said, holding the falcon before her.

At first she seemed awestruck, but then I discerned a flicker of disappointment in her eyes. "It has no feathers," she said.

"You had expected *real* feathers?"

"Yes."

"Real feathers would be too fragile, I am afraid."

"But real feathers are strong enough when falcons fly in rain and storms!"

"That is true. But this is more of a falcon doll. It keeps me company, the way Radegonde keeps you company."

She seemed to accept this. "Where did you find the falcon?"

"It was a gift."

"Do you sing to your falcon?"

"No, but sometimes I ask it questions." This seemed to pique her curiosity. "I might ask what I should do now—whether I should go on a journey, for instance."

"Did it tell you to come here?"

"Yes," I replied, my voice almost faltering. "Yes, it did. Here," I said brightly. "Would you like to touch the falcon?"

"Yes!"

I watched as her small fingers ran along the falcon's painted wings, gilded beak, and shining eyes. Once or twice when she asked a question— "Where does the falcon sleep at night?"—I gave in to the impulse to stroke her hair, or touch her cheek. It was then I realized—suddenly, with piercing sadness—what lay at the root of my entrancement with the child, and my tenderness for her: had my own Editha lived, I might have experienced moments such as this.

Finally, her scrutiny complete, Marie turned to me, her brow slightly furrowed, her vivid blue eyes radiant with curiosity. "You told me the falcon was a gift," she said, clutching her doll. "Who gave it to you?"

I was seized by memories of Gerard and of the night he had placed the falcon on the table by our bed. . . .

"Who gave the falcon to you?" she asked again, insistently.

I hesitated before answering. "One day, when you are older, I shall tell you."

She was about to ask another question when, to my relief, there came a knock at the door: it was Clementia, who had come to fetch her.

# CHAPTER 57

C ome and see Lady Isabelle's falcon!" Marie exclaimed, taking Clementia's hand.

"Falcon?" she asked, astonished.

"Marie will show you," I interrupted, exchanging a conspiratorial glance with the little girl. We walked into the anteroom, Marie skipping ahead, her doll trailing in one hand.

"Here it is!" the child cried triumphantly, pointing to the bronze creature. "Lady Isabelle told me it keeps her company."

"Does it, then?" asked Clementia. "It is lovely indeed." She began to examine it, her finger tracing the outline of the feathers and gilded beak. "Such exquisite work!" she said, turning to me. "It is the work of Limoges, is it not?"

"Yes."

"It was a gift to Lady Isabelle," chimed in Marie. "And she says she sometimes asks it questions. She asked it whether she should come here, to live with us at the abbey. And it told her she should. And so she did!" The child beamed with pride at being privy to this information.

"It is a wise falcon, then, as well as a beautiful one," replied Clementia. "And are you glad, Marie, that Lady Isabelle came here, to the abbey?"

"Yes!" she cried, to my delight.

I WAS GRATEFUL FOR HERALDIS, however taciturn, and her help that morning. As we unpacked the trunks, I could not help but think of the last time I had done so—at my family's home, with chattering Hortense eyeing my possessions with barely concealed envy. I soon ascertained that the homely, diffident Heraldis was quite the opposite—

unburdened by other aspirations, she was a woman who had found her calling in serving others. I suspected she was not prone to gossip, which at once relieved and somewhat disappointed me.

We were still in the midst of putting things in order when a servant came to announce that the abbess and Sister Clementia awaited me for the midday meal. "Go ahead, my lady," said Heraldis, "and I will finish the rest."

THE FURNISHINGS OF ABBESS GILLES'S private dining room surprised me, for they bespoke a certain restrained, but unmistakable, luxury. The room itself was long and comfortably wide; its high, vaulted corners were painted with a design of lovely, if rather primitive, leafy branches, which made one feel almost embowered. At the far end, in the center of the wall, stood a painted wooden figure of the Virgin. Along the high sideboard to the left a few objects were arrayed—a small gold casket, a silver bowl, and a gem-studded crucifix among them.

Clementia and Abbess Gilles stood at the far end, quietly conversing as I entered. To my disappointment, there was no sign of the parrot, Caprice.

"I hear you had a productive morning," said the abbess in her deep, assured voice as they approached me. "Sister Clementia tells me your first meeting with little Marie was a great success."

"I hope so," I replied.

"She is being far too modest," gently chided Clementia, taking my arm. "The child was enchanted. I told Mother Gilles about your falcon, and how deftly you drew Marie in. I could hardly pry her away from you!"

"That augurs well—a sign the child will be receptive to your teaching," remarked the abbess. She glanced at the doorway: two women servants bearing platters, heaped with food, entered. "Now, let us sit and enjoy the food that God has granted us."

The abbess having said grace, I unfolded my napkin and looked about the table; it was covered with a finely woven cloth, its pristine white setting off the muted gleam of pewter plate. In the center stood several polished wooden bowls brimming with lemons and oranges, and, by each place, a strange metal implement with two long prongs. I picked this up tentatively, then set it down.

"You are wondering what to do with it," observed Clementia. "It is called a 'fork.' Mother Gilles was sent these by a relative in the Holy Land. They are the fashion there. One uses them instead of fingers to pick up food." She picked up her own. "Quite ingenious!" she marveled. "But then the Infidels are known for such ingenious accoutrements, as they are for all manner of luxuries."

"The man I was married to would agree with you," I replied, thinking of the cossetted life at Ravinour and Gerard's admiration for such things. "And what of the oranges and lemons? It is so rare to see them."

"The lemons were sent by Joanna, the Queen of Sicily," said the abbess, "and the oranges by her older sister Lenora, the Queen of Castile. Both women are generous to the abbey. As their mother has been."

"Their mother is Queen Eleanor," interjected Clementia.

"Of course," I murmured. "I remember Fastrada mentioning Queen Joanna in a letter to me."

"The casket there"—Clementia gestured to the sideboard—"was also a gift from Queen Joanna to the abbey. It, too, is the work of Limoges—like your falcon. And the lovely cross next to it was given to us by Queen Eleanor herself. 'The noble prisoner' my sister calls the queen. The unfortunate Eleanor is held in Salisbury tower now. Or so they say."

"She is indeed a prisoner," said the abbess, sighing deeply, "and for all these past years, sequestered in England. She will likely remain so for many more. Perhaps until the very end of her life, alas." She looked down, then up at us, with a determinedly cheerful expression. "But let us speak of something more agreeable."

"Marie told me she was looking forward to your lessons," Clementia said.

"She is a spirited little girl," I replied. "It is very hard, very painful, to think of the mother who had to give her up."

"It is a bitter fact of life to think of a woman forced to such desperate measures," said Clementia. "It is gratifying for us, at the abbey, to think we can help, in our own way."

I looked down with a pang of sadness, thinking of Aiglantine and all that she must have struggled with.

"Sister Clementia told me she will show you around the grounds today," the abbess announced. "And, when she deems fit, the scriptorium."

"I am eager to see it!" I replied, adding, "how many sisters work as scribes?"

"There are four now. Until last year, there were five," said Clementia. "But one was dismissed."

"Why was she dismissed?" I asked.

"The sin of pride," said the abbess.

"Pride?" I asked, my own conscience pricked, for my mother had often accused me of the same sin. "In what way did the sister—"

"Sister Aelith was gifted, and a hard worker," interjected the abbess. "Being a scribe *is* hard work and requires great fortitude. Not only mental fortitude, but *physical* as well, especially in winter, with the cold and the damp. But it was not physical hardship that defeated Sister Aelith. No, it was something else. She could not resist doing one thing for which we, and indeed God himself, has no tolerance—the sin of vanity. She was intent on leaving her mark."

"I do not understand—"

"We discovered that she had signed her name in the marginalia," Clementia told me. "Not only once, but repeatedly, in numerous volumes. And that is *never* permitted," she added icily.

"I see," I murmured somewhat uneasily, wondering what had become of the unfortunate Aelith, though I thought best not to pose that question. "Marie seems very curious about the scriptorium," I said.

"Yes, she is quite intrigued by it," said the abbess, "as she is by the act of writing. Even now she occupies herself by pretending to write her own 'messages' with childish symbols and scrawls on her tablet. She is quick—"

"Most of all, she is determined to learn," interposed Clementia. "And determination is everything, is it not?" She looked at me intently.

"Yes, yes, I suppose it is. I would not be here, after all, without Fastrada's determination."

"And without your own, as well," returned Clementia. "Though Marie said it was your bronze falcon who told you to come here," she added wryly.

The abbess rose. "I must leave now to continue my work," she announced. We bowed our heads in reverence as she departed; then Clementia, turning to me, said, "Come, let us walk together, and I shall show you the different parts of the abbey."

I followed her, and we began to walk briskly—past the kitchen first, a singular, rather whimsical building amid the elegant severity of the others, for it was shaped like a cluster of pointed, twisted cones, in stone. As we wended our way along the path that led to the verdant slope behind the abbey church, we came to an impressive, walled edifice: the infirmary and apothecary, Clementia explained, adding that these were the domain of Sister Philippa, an older, learned woman, who had studied with renowned physicians in Montpelier.

Not far from the infirmary lay a large, well-tended herb garden of which Clementia seemed particularly proud. "I had a garden at Ravinour," I said wistfully as we walked along the quadrants blooming with shrubs and flowers. I would have lingered longer to ask questions about this blossom or another, but chose not to, sensing that Clementia had no wish to dally. In the meantime, my attention had been diverted by a daunting structure in the distance with the forbidding, closed-off quality of a small fortress. "That is where the lepers are cared for," she said, following my gaze. "It is secluded from us, of course."

I was tempted to inquire about the courageous sisters who cared for those poor creatures, but Clementia's reserve caused me to refrain. As we turned and walked toward the apse of the church, I caught sight of an imposing building to the north. "And that?" I asked, pointing to it.

"La Madeline, where desperate women, many of whom had fallen into lives of sin, find sanctuary," Clementia said. I thought of my father's concern about my residing at the abbey—that I might be exposed to fallen women here.

"Many might call those women prostitutes," continued Clementia. "But here, in the spirit of our founder, we prefer to call them 'repentant daughters.'" As we resumed walking, the epithet echoed in my mind— had my mother not considered *me* an "unrepentant daughter"?

I was glad when we returned to the pristine peace of the cloister, where mellow sunlight flickered through the branches of the quince trees of the inner garden. "The abbess seems a remarkable woman," I observed as we walked past the entrance to her quarters.

"She is indeed. She took the veil as a very young woman, after she was widowed."

"How sad to be widowed so young!"

"Yes, but I think she has also rather enjoyed the freedom of widowhood. Just as she has enjoyed having responsibilities and power—power over the monks, as well."

I had never heard anyone refer to widowhood in that way, but merely remarked, "I have seen little evidence of the monks."

"As a rule, you will not, except in the scriptorium, when Father Riccardus comes to supervise the sisters who work there. The monks live at Saint Jean de l'Habit, slightly to the northeast, by the river. Our responsibilities and theirs are quite separate—it is one of the fathers who presides over Mass, over confession, for instance. The rules are extremely strict, and it is the responsibility of the abbess to enforce them. Only one of her responsibilities, I should add. She has expanded our activities here and is quite determined to broaden the influence of our order." To this she added: "She is intent on maintaining the link with our sister house in Amesbury, in England, as well. We often exchange goods—books from our library and from the scriptorium—with the sisters there. It is not far from Salisbury."

"Is that not where they say Queen Eleanor is being held—Salisbury?"

"Supposedly. Among other places."

"Have you ever met the queen?"

"No. But the abbess has. She says she is quite remarkable."

I was sorely tempted to ask more questions but thought better of it. Meantime we continued to walk, my gaze drawn to the handsome columns and their fanciful capitals: one carved with two wolf heads amid foliage, another with a weird, beaked creature. "This reminds me of Caprice," I said, pausing to look at it more closely. "I shall never forget the first time I saw her and heard her speak! Has the abbess always had a parrot?" I asked as we resumed walking.

"Only for the last few years. And before that, a cat. She is very fond of creatures. And rather good at taming them, I should add. Rather like my mother," she quipped.

"Your mother was fond of animals?"

"Yes, all sorts of wild creatures. Including her daughters." She smiled somewhat slyly.

I laughed softly. "I can imagine Fastrada as having been a naughty little girl—but not *you*, Sister Clementia."

"For once, you are lacking in imagination. Ask Fastrada when she comes and visits us."

"When will she visit?" I asked with great excitement.

"Within the next month after Easter, according to her last letter. But now I shall leave you to finish getting settled."

"But you have not yet shown me the scriptorium!"

"I shall, tomorrow. I know that you are eager to see it, but I must remind you, Isabelle, that your primary responsibility will be to teach Marie. She is eager to learn. And if, after your lessons with her, you should need advice, you may always—"

"Ask you—I assume?"

"No"—again, that mischievous glance that reminded me of Fastrada—"your falcon."

# CHAPTER 58

I returned to my chamber which, to my delight, Heraldis had arranged with surprising artfulness. She had positioned the falcon
on a small table near the window, so that the bird appeared to
have alighted from the outside. But it was her placement of my secret
treasures, my grandfather's books, and Arnaut's little casket, that most
pleased me. Freed from their long captivity in the trunk, they were now
arranged on a high table near the entrance.

When, that evening, Heraldis appeared to accompany me to the
evening meal, I tried as best I could to engage her in conversation.

"I very much enjoyed my meal with the abbess and Sister Clementia," I began. "Afterward Sister Clementia showed me the different parts of the abbey. And she will show me the scriptorium on the
morrow."

There fell a long pause. "Sister Clementia mentioned a Sister Aelith, who was dismissed. For the sin of pride, she said. Were there others
who were dismissed—because of pride?"

"Yes. And for other reasons."

She remained resolutely silent; no garrulous Agnes was she. "What
reasons?" I prodded.

"That is not for me to say, my lady," she replied in a peremptory
tone and which piqued my curiosity about those "other reasons" all the
more.

We then set off from the Sainte Marie residence, passed through
the small gate that led to the abbey proper, and arrived before a tall double door. "I will leave you here," she said. "This is where the conversas
and the pensionnaires like yourself enter the refectory. The sisters enter
through the other door." To this she added, "You must observe the rule

of silence here, of course." I thought back longingly on the convivial meal in the abbess's quarters.

"It can be hard for some," said Heraldis. "The silence, that is." I bade her good evening, and walked, with some trepidation, into the refectory.

There was a marked sense of delicacy about the long, vaulted chamber of bisque-colored stone, with its sequence of slender, arched ribs. This was a place meant only for women, it seemed to say. Iron crosses marking the stations of the Passion were set high, spaced in intervals along the stone walls. At the far end, facing us, stood the table for the abbess and other senior sisters, Clementia among them. Running the length of the room were numerous rough-hewn tables where all the others sat—nuns to one side, laywomen, like myself, to the other.

I took a seat at one such table, lowered my head, and listened to the abbess as she pronounced grace, then read the lesson. As we began, in silence, to eat the simple fare—smoked fish, barley, bread—I tried to stave off a mounting sense of disorientation and loss. It required a great effort of the will not to think of the teeming world outside the gates—the world I had left behind.

That night I struggled to fall asleep. The peace I had felt upon arriving at the abbey seemed to have vanished, replaced by loneliness and agitation. The silence of the evening meal, the somber tolling of the bell announcing holy offices that punctuated the day—I suddenly despaired that I should ever become accustomed to this strange, muted existence.

I had wanted to flee my former life. Yet I suddenly felt a terrifying sense of displacement—the aching yearning for the elsewhere I had experienced as a child and later, as a married woman. I had journeyed here, to the abbey, only to find myself adrift. Was I once again a useless creature, with no real purpose in life? I had neither the calling of the sisters here, and their devotion to God, nor the recompenses of my former worldly life. Was it better to be like Heraldis, whose work and position were clearly delineated, rather than a landed, childless woman like myself, whose temperament and education had ill-equipped her for a useful life?

I closed my eyes, trying to lull myself to sleep by recalling happy memories of my grandfather. I thought of his library, and the comforting scent of parchment, and the scratchy sound of his quill pen as he wrote. I thought of his stories, and how they had always soothed me; and then I wondered if the scriptorium would give me a modicum of solace.

I WAS ALREADY DRESSED WHEN Heraldis appeared at the door the following morning shortly past dawn.

"Have you been awake long, my lady?" she asked. "I was expecting to help you dress."

"The bell awoke me early. Sister Clementia will show me the scriptorium today, and I wanted to be ready."

A knocking at the door interrupted our conversation: Clementia, bidding me good morrow. Marie followed, a wax tablet in hand.

"I trust you have slept well," said Clementia to me. Then, to Marie: "Show Lady Isabelle your tablet, Marie, while I speak with Heraldis."

I took Marie's hand as Clementia drew Heraldis aside. "Sister Clementia and I are going to visit the scriptorium today," I said, kneeling down to speak with her.

"*Please* ask Sister Clementia to let me come!"

"When you are older, I promise, but not now." I stroked the top of her head. "Mother Gilles tells me you would like to learn to write. Perhaps you, too, will be a scribe one day. I see you have your own tablet."

"I already do my own writing!" she replied proudly, her expression brightening as she brandished the tablet. "Look!"

I studied the childish scrawls and the primitively formed letters: "Tell me what this says."

"It is the beginning of a story. About Radegonde and her adventures."

"Will you tell it to me one day?"

"If Radegonde will let me."

"Then you must indeed ask Radegonde's permission," I said with an understanding smile, recalling the secret stories and codes I had once shared with Arnaut.

"Come, it is time," interrupted Clementia, walking toward us. "Father Riccardus awaits us. It is always best to see the scriptorium in early morning, when the light is bright." She addressed Marie in her customary tone of gentle firmness: "You must stay here with Heraldis and practice your letters while we are gone."

AN HOUR OR SO LATER, as Clementia and I walked back to my chamber, I was absorbed in my teeming impressions of the scriptorium—a silent inner sanctum of contradictions, of opposites. How noiselessly, and with what discipline and intensity, the scribes worked, their backs hunched, their bent fingers moving painstakingly along the silky sheaves of vellum and parchment as Father Riccardus, a formidable German, moved slowly and watchfully among them. All the while, the pages and images they produced were often unruly, screaming and pulsing with life, with color, with glints of gold and black, with swirling lines possessed of almost demonic movement. And what of the drawings of huge, colored, capital letters the chillingly cerebral Riccardus had shown me—how alive they were, writhing with tiny creatures, flowers, and plants! He had come from a monastery near the Rhine, not far from the abbey made famous by Hildegard, Clementia had told me with admiration. He had pointed to the cabinets of books as a proud father might his children, and in his low, guttural accent, he had taken care to explain that the pages of manuscripts drying, on racks, would be bound into books, and then shipped to the sister abbey, at Amesbury. . . .

"You have been so deep in thought I dared not disturb you," I heard Clementia say; we had arrived at the hallway that led to my quarters.

"I was thinking what I will tell Marie about the scriptorium," I replied, and we entered my chamber.

Marie sat by the window, singing to her doll; Heraldis was sewing. Marie jumped up and skipped toward us as we entered.

"I have been waiting for you!" she cried. "Have you brought me the book you promised?" She glanced from Clementia to me, her expression becoming downcast when she saw we were empty-handed.

"I am afraid Father Riccardus had nothing suitable for a little girl,"

I explained gently. "He had only Psalters. But we have no need of those, since I have my own for us to use." I stroked the top of her head, adding, consolingly, "I shall think of something else that will interest you, I promise."

"Tell Marie about the scriptorium," Clementia encouraged. "About the work of the scribes. She has often asked me about them."

I began to tell Marie how one scribe pierced and lined the parchment, how another prepared the different colored inks, and how still another rubbed the parchment with pumice, to smooth it, and so on. "This is the preparation work," I explained, "the steps before the actual copying, and painting, begin." Then I described the lengthy, meticulous process, ending with the work of the scribe who adds the red ink for the headings and the beginnings of chapters. "He or she is called the rubricator," I told her.

"What do you think, Marie?" asked Clementia. "Did not Lady Isabelle bring the work in the scriptorium to life?"

"Yes, yes she did," chirped Marie. "But I would still like to see it myself one day!"

"I understand. But now, Marie," she said, kneeling down to address her, "you will stay here, with Lady Isabelle, while I tend to my work. It is time for you to put your doll aside and begin your own work. Mother Gilles and I expect you to do your best, as always."

Marie nodded with touching gravity; then, reluctantly, she set Radegonde down.

"Good. Lessons are no time for playthings." Clementia smiled in her genial, yet distant way before telling Heraldis, "We must leave Lady Isabelle and Marie to attend to their lesson."

The door closed behind them. "Come, Marie," I said. "Sit by me here, and bring your tablet."

"May I keep Radegonde with me?" she implored.

Aware of Clementia's dictum, I deliberated. "Yes," I relented, though with some apprehension. Smiling with relief—and triumph, perhaps—Marie, clutching her doll, happily settled beside me.

"I have an idea," I proposed. "Since we could not find a proper story for you in the library, perhaps we should make up our own."

She nodded, her eyes shining.

"But first we need a subject for our story. I shall let you decide what it will be."

"May I choose anything?"

"Why not? *You* decide the subject, and whether the story is happy, sad, mysterious, or scary. Perhaps a story with elves and goblins?" I suggested.

"No, I do not want a scary story today. Another day, but not today."

I smiled to myself, recalling how Amélie's son Walter had run to his mother when I had proposed telling him such a story.

"I would rather a happy one today." Her gaze turned to the table with my treasured objects. "Or maybe a story about one of the things on that table—"

"An excellent idea!" I concurred as she beamed. "Let us look at them, and you can select one as your subject."

We walked to the table together. "Where did these come from?" she asked, turning to me.

"I found several when I was a little girl—the little stone head of the maiden, and the hand. They were buried in the earth near my family's home. I bought the others—the helmet and the cross—from a man who traded in such things, years ago." I watched as she scrutinized each. "Which one do you choose for your story?"

She furrowed her brow, her eyes settling on one object, then another, until, at last, she announced: "The helmet!"

I smiled, delighted by her choice. "What is it you like about it?"

"It looks the most fearsome. And the soldier who wore it must have been brave. A warrior must always be brave! Sister Clementia told me that, too."

"Would you like to hold the helmet?" She nodded eagerly, and I placed it in her hands. "Now that you have decided on your subject," I said, watching as she examined it, "you must decide how the story will

begin, just as you did when you made up Radegonde's story. Close
your eyes now and let your thoughts wander."

A few moments later, she opened her eyes. "I cannot think of anything," she announced, folding her arms tightly across her chest, her
expression one of frustration.

"Perhaps we should try another way. I shall give you a first line, then
you will think of the next line. The rest will follow, I promise. You must
have faith that it will. And then, when we have finished, I shall transcribe the story for you. We will read it together, once you know your
letters. And now, for the first line: Once upon a time, there was a little
boy whose grandfather had returned from the Holy Land. . . ." I looked
at Marie. "Now it is your turn."

"He had brought a helmet back with him," she said slowly, "and he
had given it to the little boy as a gift. 'Where did you find this?' the little
boy asked. Now it is your turn."

"'It was given to me by a sorcerer,'" I began. "'A sorcerer I met in
Acre, after a long, frightful day, the day of a great battle against the Infidels. The man told me he possessed a helmet, the helmet of an ancient
warrior. A helmet with secret powers—'"

Later, when Heraldis came to announce the midday meal, Marie
and I had finished the story. She entitled it "The Tale of the Magical
Helmet."


DURING THE WEEKS THAT PASSED, I grew almost accustomed to
my new life—to the rules, the silence, the solemn tolling of the bell,
the processions of the sisters clad in their linen habits, their heads bent,
their hands folded as they made their way to holy offices. "Almost," I
say, because the world outside the abbey walls was never far from my
mind. Often, I would find myself imagining what was happening at
Ravinour—I would wonder about Raoul, and whether Vainqueur had
ever been found; I would think, longingly, of riding Juno, or of the
beauty and luxuries of my former life. But in the next instant I would
compel myself, as I had in girlhood, to cast things in a different light:
I would remind myself that I had escaped from a man who had caused

me much suffering; and that the life awaiting me, like Queen Eleanor's or Radegonde's, would now be determined not by *his* demands and ambitions, but by my own will and courage.

To my delight, Marie learned her letters quickly and began to read with astounding ease. Her own fears seemed to disappear as her confidence grew. She asked questions without inhibition; and she took pleasure in inventing her own stories, a process we came to call "the game of the first line."

Once Marie was fully at ease with her lessons, we began to study my Psalter, at first only with the pages that piqued her interest. One afternoon in mid-April, in the midst of studying the story of Saint Catherine, Clementia suddenly entered my chamber.

I HAVE WONDERFUL NEWS," SHE announced.

"What is it?" I asked, unaccustomed to seeing her in a state of excitement.

"Fastrada will arrive within the hour!"

# CHAPTER 59

I leaped to my feet. "Shall we go together and greet Fastrada?" I asked Marie. "We will finish your lesson tomorrow."

"Let us go!" cried the little girl.

"Then follow me," said Clementia, who began to walk so quickly that Marie and I quickened our pace to keep up with her. "She is longing to see both of you."

"Where is she?" I asked.

"Waiting in the reception room by the chapter house. The chamber in the guest hospice is being prepared for her now. You can imagine how particular my sister is. Fortunately, the servants know Fastrada and her habits, and since she is always so kind to them, they never mind accommodating her."

She spoke rapidly, with an almost girlish sense of excitement that seemed foreign to her customary restrained self. I realized that my longing to see Fastrada was now imbued with something else as well—a curiosity to see the two sisters, the beauty and the *belle laide*, together. One blond, the other dark, one content with the spiritual, secluded life of the abbey, the other the living embodiment of worldliness.

Perched on a bench in the somber reception chamber, Fastrada, in her traveling costume of peacock blue, her hands twinkling with rings, seemed a startlingly incongruous figure. Her hair was pulled back tightly, and two long black braids, wound with gold ribbon, fell to each side of her front bodice—a style which lent her the look of Esther, the biblical queen.

"Dear Isabelle!" she cried, darting toward me, her arms extended. I drew in her scent as we embraced—that blend of lavender, sandalwood, and lemon which seemed to transport me to the last time I had seen her.

"What joy to see you again, and to see you *here*, with Clementia and Marie!" She took Clementia's hand in hers, squeezing it affectionately while her younger sister glowed with obvious, if restrained, delight.

All the while Marie, hovering behind Clementia, observed the scene in fascination, her eyes fixed upon the exotic arrival. "Come, my child, let me greet you properly," said Fastrada, bending down to address the little girl. "Am I not—what did once you call me?—your honorary aunt?" She swept Marie into her arms as the child squealed with delight.

"I know it is a great treat to see Lady Fastrada again," Clementia remarked, after the two had embraced. "But even so, Marie," she gently admonished, "you must not forget to behave with due courtesy, as you would with any lady of rank."

Marie duly gave a deep curtsey.

"How proper you are, Clementia!" Fastrada teased, glancing at her sister.

"It is my responsibility that Marie learn the correct etiquette," Clementia replied. "And Isabelle's responsibility now, as well."

"Marie is fortunate to have such able teachers," replied Fastrada. "Though I have no doubt who will be the most exacting with etiquette."

"I doubt it will be me," I observed, smiling.

"Then she is fortunate to have Sister Clementia," she replied, shooting her sister a sly glance. "Without her, Marie might very well grow up to be a barbarian!"

Clementia shook her head in playful exasperation, as if long accustomed to her sister's affectionate barbs.

"You see, Isabelle, we have been forever thus," said Fastrada. "Clementia so very correct, and I, on the other hand, quite unruly. Indeed one might say *I* am the barbarian, compared to my saintly sister!" She knelt down, affectionately ruffling Marie's hair. "What do you think, Marie?" Fastrada affected a mock gravity. "Do you think I resemble a barbarian?"

"Oh no, not at all, my lady!" cried the little girl.

"Perhaps," Fastrada suggested, "a lady Infidel, then?"

"Really, Fastrada!" interrupted Clementia rather sternly, all the while suppressing a smile.

"But I have heard that some lady Infidels are very elegant!" continued Fastrada in the same teasing vein. "With my black hair and eyes, and my extravagant beak, perhaps I might be taken for one." She turned her profile to Marie. "What do you think, child—might I be a lady Infidel?"

"I would never take you for an Infidel!" replied Marie. "God would think me sinful if I said such a thing." She paused, adding with touching earnestness, "Even if I *thought* such a thing."

"Oh dear, is it sinful even to *think* such a thing?" Fastrada asked.

"Mother Gilles says it is," replied Marie.

"Yes, I hear that is the Church fathers' new thinking," said Fastrada, standing up. "One must be pure not only in action, but in *thought* as well. If this be the case, I shall certainly be doomed in God's eyes!"

"But the Lord always grants us forgiveness," said Marie. "That is what Sister Clementia tells me."

"Far be it from me to contradict my beloved sister!" Fastrada replied gaily. "Do you know, Marie, that there are Frankish ladies who go to the Holy Land, and who remain there—"

"That is quite enough," interrupted Clementia.

Fastrada stood up, her hand in Marie's. All the while the little girl's eyes took in every detail of Fastrada's costume—her lavish dress, dainty boots, and the pair of luxuriant braids wound with gold.

"May I touch them?" asked Marie, shyly pointing to the braids.

"Of course. It is the fashion now to wind braids with gold ribbon. Perhaps one day I shall braid your hair in the same way. Would you like that?"

Marie nodded eagerly; but then, discerning Clementia's disapproving expression, added, "I do not think Sister Clementia would permit it."

Fastrada smiled sympathetically, stroking Marie's curls as the child continued to inspect her dress—the embroidered bodice, with its jeweled buttons and its collar edged in marten. "I think you look like a great lady, with your splendid clothes," said the little girl admiringly.

"At least I have won Marie's approval, even if I have not my darling sister's!" exclaimed Fastrada with her lilting laugh.

Clementia shook her head in mock dismay while I, observing this exchange, continued to watch in wonderment. How quickly the two women had assumed what were, no doubt, their familiar roles: Clementia the epitome of propriety, Fastrada the saucy provoker. There was such palpable affection between the two sisters that I felt a sudden twinge of envy—theirs was the sort of loving closeness I had never known with my own sister.

"So you see, Isabelle, in our family some things never change," Fastrada went on to say, as if intuiting my train of thought. "The two of us still tease each other, as we have from time immemorial. My sister was, and will always be, the *comme il faut* member of our family. Always so proper, with or without wimple!"

"And you, Fastrada?" Clementia countered. "How should I describe you, with your flamboyant airs, and your way of descending upon us, like—" She paused, searching for the right epithet.

"An avenging angel?" said Fastrada.

"Precisely!" replied Clementia, as the three of us laughed.

"I am quite determined to be on my best behavior while I am here," continued Fastrada. "I do not want to give Mother Gilles and the good sisters a bad impression. I shall attend holy offices if you permit me. I have brought only my most demure clothes. Ones with the most pious colors and cuts. Scarcely a jewel or flourish in my trunk!"

"I find that difficult to believe," retorted Clementia, raising her brow.

"As do I, I must confess," I rejoined. "And if it is true you have forgone your lovely clothes for this visit, then you should disappoint us all!" I glanced at Marie, who had hardly stirred during this banter. "And I suspect you would disappoint Marie most of all." I turned to the little girl. "Am I right, Marie?"

She hesitated, as if she were not certain how much candor was permitted. Sensing this, Fastrada knelt down to address Marie, her skirt swirling in deep, silken folds on the floor around them. "Would you be disappointed if I did not bring my best clothes, Marie?" she asked. The child seemed reticent to answer. "You must have no fear of being honest with me," encouraged Fastrada. "That is part of the privilege of my being an honorary aunt."

"Yes," confessed Marie. "I would be disappointed."

"Then I shall make certain to wear clothes that are not of convent cloth and cut!" came Fastrada's delighted riposte. "Far more important for me not to disappoint *you*, Marie, than to bend to all this sobriety. Then—oh dear!—both of us will have to answer to Sister Clementia!" She kissed the top of Marie's head and stood up, fidgeting with her rings as she gazed about the room, her eyes taking in the somber furnishings. A sudden silence fell, as if the merry repartee had run its course.

"How good it is to be here, and to have such quiet, after the long journey," said Fastrada, with a contented sigh.

"How *was* your journey?" I asked, unable to resist inquiring. "Did LaFoi accompany you?"

"Alas, not this time. Another fellow, not nearly as companionable, though equally sturdy and trustworthy. And my maidservant, of course. It was not an uneventful journey. There is much fighting going on to the south, in the Limousin, we were told. Richard against Aimar of Limoges. Several times we came upon bands of mercenaries heading south, in that direction." She shuddered. "A terrifying bunch, from the Brabant."

"Who has engaged them?" I asked.

"Richard, of course," replied Clementia. "They are going to shore up his defenses. He is helping his father, the king, to take the fortresses of Aimar. One of the few times they are allied, *père et fils*, Henry and Richard. The alliance will not last long, no doubt. It never does."

"How much you know, dear sister!" observed Fastrada, mirroring my own thoughts.

Clementia's expression assumed that familiar detachment. "I simply know what most people know," she replied. "Surely it is general knowledge in this region. We are not so far from Limoges, after all."

"Even so, Clementia—" observed Fastrada. But then, sensing her sister's change of tone and unwillingness to expatiate, she turned her focus on me. "But enough talk of my journey! What of *you*, dear Isabelle? How are you faring? How is the adjustment to your new life?" She glanced at her sister proudly. "I am sure Clementia has been a splendid guide."

"Yes, she has," I replied. "She and the abbess have also given me work. I have been teaching Marie her letters. She has been a wonderful pupil and is learning to read quickly and well."

"Lady Isabelle has invented a game for us," interjected the little girl, as if emboldened by my praise.

"What game is that?" asked Fastrada.

"The game of the first line."

"And how do you play it?"

"Lady Isabelle gives me a line, and then asks me to continue with the next line, and so on, and we make up a story. She is helping me to write some of these down."

"All quite true," I added. "If we continue this way, we may have a little book of stories."

"How lovely!" cried Fastrada. "I wish my tutor had thought of such a thing. I was never much enthralled by prayer books. Rather boring, though I do remember liking the page with Daniel in the lion's den."

"Clementia has also shown me the scriptorium," I said. "I hope to be able to help there one day."

"The scriptorium, of course," replied Fastrada. "Very much Clementia's domain. I saw it during my last visit here. Impressive, indeed. Though I must admit, I would never have the patience for such work. For writing a letter, yes, though I much prefer to dictate. But to learn to *copy*, to set pen to parchment with such exactitude—no, never! I would make a mess of it, without question. Best I confine my love of color to my clothes, and my surroundings." She paused, her bejeweled hands smoothing the folds of her skirt. "But tell me more, Isabelle. About you, about your living arrangements. Did my sister follow my instructions, in the preparation of your chamber?"

I looked quizzically at Clementia.

"The chess set," she prodded.

"Oh yes, yes she did! It was there, in my chamber, the day I arrived. It was so generous and thoughtful of you to send it."

"Then I assume she has taught you to play?" asked Fastrada. "Clementia is a formidable player, I warn you. You could not have a better instructor."

"We have not played yet," I admitted.

"Pray, why not?" asked Fastrada, furrowing her brow.

"There are other things she must learn first," intervened Clementia. "Things more important."

Fastrada looked askance. "But surely—"

"It is not time yet," replied Clementia. "That is up to me to decide, Fastrada."

"I have had much to do these first weeks," I rejoined. "I am happy to wait to learn chess. It will be my—"

"Reward?" asked Fastrada.

"Yes."

"Very prudent, indeed," Fastrada replied with a hint of sarcasm. "And very like you, Clementia dear, to be so disciplined in your approach." She turned to me. "Strange, is it not, that my sister is younger than I? She has always seemed older, even when we were young. Always so sensible, always thinking a hundred steps ahead."

A knocking at the door interrupted us: it was Heraldis, informing Clementia that she was needed at the *tour.*

"Come with me, Marie," said Clementia. "We will go together while Lady Isabelle visits with Lady Fastrada."

Marie looked crestfallen but dutifully took Clementia's hand. "We will see you very soon," Fastrada assured the little girl. She and Clementia proceeded to leave, Marie giving us a lingering backward glance as they passed through the door.

# Chapter 60

Yes, how very like Clementia to decide when you will begin to learn chess!" observed Fastrada moments later. "She is nothing if not decisive, my sister. Some might even say rigid. Though even that does not really capture that quality of hers."

"I do not think that I have known anyone so insular," I mused. "I often have a feeling she has forged a plan to which only she is privy. Until, of course, she deigns to reveal it." To this I added, "She is not easy to know."

"You never will completely know her."

"What do you mean?"

"As much as I love her, as much as I am admiring of her, I also realize there is a part of my sister that is quite unknowable. One might as well try to guess the depth of the sea, or the size of a distant star."

She gave a sigh, her mouth curving into the incongruously sweet smile that seemed so at odds with her sharp features. Then she walked to the window, leaning out as her eyes scanned the orchard beyond.

"Come, let us sit down together and talk," she said, turning to me. "I have so often thought of those times when we sat together, by the hearth, during the hunt."

"I, too, have long thought of those times at Ravinour, and with great affection."

"You said very little about the end of your marriage, in your letter."

"I did not feel it was the time, or the right manner, in which to do so."

"But now that we are together, privately, here—surely you can tell me more?" She looked at me searchingly.

I glanced away, struggling with the sadness that still overcame me at the mention of my marriage. "I could not bear a healthy child," I replied, reverting to the safety of my usual refrain. "I proved a disappointment to Gerard."

"But what of him?" she asked. "Did *he* prove a disappointment to you?"

"Yes, I suppose so." I glanced away.

"You need say no more." She pressed my hand. "I can easily imagine what you felt. Even Hugh can imagine." A pause. "You know that they had a terrible dispute—"

"Yes. The wine trade—"

"Hugh vows he will never deal with him again. He will never trust his word. Gerard is brilliant, yet there are aspects of life he does not seem to understand, or want to understand, so overpowering are his ambitions and his need to have his way." She took my hand, pressing it gently. "I think you were brave to take the end of your marriage as you did, with calm acceptance."

"But after I returned home, to my family, I felt despairing. Until I received your letter."

"I am glad it cheered you. And that it cheered you to come here, to Fontevraud."

"It seems that you, too, had a plan. Perhaps you and Clementia have more in common than you realize."

"Yes, but my plans tend to be forged rather impetuously. Nor do I always consider all the implications as I plunge ahead. My plans spring from the heart, you see, hers from the head—that very beautiful head. You can only imagine," she reflected, tilting her head back slightly, "what it was to grow up with such a sister—and a younger one at that—who was not only the epitome of rectitude, but of beauty, as well." For the first time, melancholy tinged her voice and the expression of her striking face.

"Beauty fades," I said, trying to assuage her sadness, only to realize the next instant how unsatisfactory and prosaic my attempt.

"True," she replied. "But how lovely to have at least *experienced* it! I never did. Alas."

"You had other qualities—panache and wit."

"Poor substitutes, my dear!" She looked at me with a poignant wistfulness, seeming to take in my eyes, my coloring, my fair hair. "Only one who is a beauty would consider those attributes to be a comfort." Her dark, hooded eyes were fixed on mine, as if she were trying to fathom my innermost thoughts. "Marie is fortunate to have you here. You will provide a balance to my sister's"—she hesitated—"strictness. A little levity will do the child no harm."

"I hope so." I smiled. "Marie has a whimsical spirit. Clementia and Mother Gilles think she will be well suited to life here. They may be right. But I think it is far too early to tell. She is only a little girl, after all."

"And you?" she asked. "Do you think yourself well suited to life at the abbey?"

"I would like to think I am."

The cautiousness of my reply was not lost on Fastrada. "You are very different from Clementia," she finally said.

This took me aback. "Yet you always wanted us to meet. Therefore I assumed—"

"That I thought you twinned in spirit? No, not at all! You both have fine minds and a questing nature. But Clementia's path in life is easier than yours."

"In what way?"

"She is content merely to observe the world outside—at the very most, to participate in it from a distance. You are not. She is at peace with herself in this regard."

"And I am not?"

"That is up to you to find out. That is why I think your time here will be valuable. A way for you to contemplate, to explore. To see if a life of such serenity is really what you want." She leaned forward, gazing about the room, one hand fixing a dark strand of hair by her temple. "Tell me your impressions of life here."

I gave a few brief impressions before mentioning that I had greatly enjoyed, indeed been quite fascinated by, the scriptorium. I could not resist adding, "Sister Clementia told me the story of Sister Aelith, the scribe who was dismissed for the sin of pride."

"Ah yes, the unfortunate Aelith. It is often the most gifted who transgress."

"Like Héloïse," I murmured.

"True. Indeed—" She paused, her mouth slightly pursed as she reflected, "There are always those who cannot sustain a life of absolute virtue and abstinence. Six years or so ago, there was a nun, Sister Rosceline, the youngest and quite beautiful daughter of a noble family from Angers. It was discovered that she had been consorting with a monk, a certain Brother Marcel. Trysts by the river, that sort of thing. He got Sister Rosceline with child, and she was forced to return home in disgrace. Brother Marcel was compelled to leave as well, of course, though they say he has since joined some monastery of modest means in the Auvergne. As you can imagine, at the abbey, in the wake of this sorry episode, there was a redoubling of readings about the sin of lust." She gave a bemused smile.

"And the child?" I asked, my imagination ignited.

"Adopted by the wayward Rosceline family, it was assumed."

I thought of Marie, who was five years old, and how she often fantasized about her mother; was it possible that her mother had been a beautiful noblewoman, a noblewoman, like Clementia, who had taken the veil. . . .

"Your thoughts are wandering," remarked Fastrada. "We were talking about the abbey—your impressions."

I jolted myself back to the present and told her how I admired the selflessness and industry of Mother Gilles, and the devotion of the sisters; how I wished that I felt their sense of mission. "Something that would ignite my life, propel it, like an arrow to a deeper purpose. Clementia seems to think that I shall find my métier in teaching," I added.

"Does she? She has a role for you in mind, of that I am certain. She always thinks twenty steps ahead. She comes to a conclusion about a person's nature and then decides how he or she should proceed in life. Rather like my mother in that regard." To this she added, unexpectedly:

"And she has an idea of what you have been through, and of Gerard, as a man."

"From whom?"

"From my letters, and from hearing about him from others. She has a sense of his complexity, and of his punishing nature. Hugh has his faults, God knows, but he does not have *that*." She said this in a remarkably definitive way which startled me.

"It is true that Gerard could be punishing," I conceded, adding, "he could be cruel."

"That is a quality Clementia would abhor, you see. She may be strict, she may be exacting, but she is not *punishing*. She would not have been able to survive at the abbey if she were. She has seen too much of life in all its sadness and complexity here—children abandoned, women who have lost their way, and then, the most unfortunate of all, the lepers whom the sisters care for at Saint-Lazare priory—those poor, cursed creatures." She gave a sigh. "Clementia may have come to Fontevraud as a pampered noblewoman, but she has been quite unflinching in her ability to face the uglier aspects of life."

"She has never discussed any of this with me."

"Of course not. It is too soon. And she is far too private."

We heard the tolling of the bell. "It is the hour for nones," I said. "Should we go together?"

"No, let us remain here awhile. God will forgive us if we do not attend holy office today. Our tolerant prelate in Troyes told me long ago that God grants some latitude to weary travelers! A philosophy I have long subscribed to." She stood up and walked to the window, standing in profile, one hand poised against the sill. The thick black braids fell almost to her waist, like two uncoiled serpents against a sea of vivid blue silk.

I watched Fastrada's eyes moving from one corner of the chamber to the other, and wondered what she was thinking: how strange it was, perhaps, to see me here, in this simple place—how far removed from the luxury I had known at Ravinour.

She walked to a table and leafed through the pages of a large, open

Psalter that was propped on a bronze bookstand. The stand, with its handsome base of double eagles, was the only luxurious object in the room.

"This is a lovely thing," she said, looking closely at the double hawks. "It reminds me of the hunt—Gerard and his falcons. I shall always remember that day when his favorite falcon disappointed him."

"Féroce," I said. "And then, months afterward, his favorite falcon, Vainqueur, was lost. A terrible day. For all of us, but especially for the young falconer who was blamed. The falcon was never found."

"I know," she said. "I heard what happened."

"How?" I asked, startled.

"Because the boy, Gallien, works in *our* mews now! Hugh has engaged him. I was only waiting for the right time to tell you."

"But tell me," I said, astonished, "how did he—"

"The boy made his way to Troyes, seeking work at the fairs. He was emaciated and starving when Hugh first saw him, working in the stable of an inn. Hugh had never forgotten his face, and that bright red hair, and recognized his accent. He had always thought the boy gifted, and asked if he, Gallien, would help in our mews. This he has done, with much success. He will be the master falconer, once our own, who is quite aged now, retires."

"I am so happy for Gallien!" I cried, astonished and elated at this turn of events. But then a profound uneasiness overcame me—I feared for Gallien, and for Hugh, should Gerard learn of Gallien's new position. "Does Gerard know of this?"

"There is no reason to think he does."

"If he finds out, he will be very angry. After Gallien disappeared, he vowed that he would seek revenge on anyone who hired him. Anyone who 'stole him away.' Those were Gerard's very words."

"So be it then," she scoffed. "That will not frighten Hugh. After being betrayed by him, he has no liking for Gerard anymore."

"But Hugh must know that Gerard is capable of anything—of harming Gallien, certainly. Even of harming me."

Fastrada's expression darkened. "I shall tell Hugh what you said, though I know him well enough to guess his reply. He will say that Gerard does not have the power to harm Gallien—certainly not while he is under our aegis! And why would you enter into this contretemps at all? You had nothing to do with our hiring Gallien."

"Gerard will imagine that I did."

"Your imagination is getting the best of you, my dear," she said, with a slight smile.

I tried to convince myself that Fastrada was right. "You see, Gerard knows I was fond of Gallien," I explained, still uneasy. "And that I was horrified by the way he was treated."

"Yes, one of our falconers had noticed the scars on his back— the scars from the lashings—and mentioned it to Hugh. Hugh took it upon himself to find out what had happened."

"It was never Gallien's fault. If it was anyone's fault, it was in great part mine. But most of all," I added bitterly, "it was Ragnar's."

"The master falconer? It would not surprise me. He had the eyes of an executioner." She shuddered. "Gallien told us you were very kind to him."

"May I send a letter for him when you return? A letter, you might read to him?"

"Of course. With pleasure."

There was a knocking at the door; it was Heraldis once more.

She scuffled into the room, her eyes lowered, as if she could not bring herself to look at Fastrada in all her gaudy finery. "Mother Gilles requests that you and Lady Fastrada join her for the midday meal, in her apartment, my lady."

"Thank Mother Gilles," I said, "and tell her we will be there very shortly."

Heraldis exited without managing a single glance in Fastrada's direction.

"She attends to you?" asked Fastrada.

"Yes."

"Rather a contrast, I should say—"

"A contrast to what?"

"To the pretty servant you had. I remember her so well. The one you were fond of—"

"Aiglantine," I murmured, wondering whether Fastrada ever knew how Hugh had coveted her the night of the feast. But my drifting thoughts were wrenched back to the present when Fastrada took my arm. "Come along," she said jauntily. "Even *I* would not dare to be late for Mother Gilles!"

A t the abbey, it did not take long to ascertain how beloved a figure Fastrada had become. Despite her irreverence, she was a model guest—unfailingly kind and considerate as she participated in the duties and rituals of the sisters' life. I soon grew accustomed to seeing her strolling through the cloister galleries, or glimpsing her slender figure, dressed in vivid silk, genuflecting at the back of the nave during Mass.

What I had not completely anticipated was Fastrada's attachment to Marie. I had not imagined how much the little girl would entrance Fastrada—how tenderly and affectionately she would behave toward the little girl. She would praise her progress in reading, or delight the child by asking her unconventional, sometimes challenging questions. "Why do pilgrims to Santiago de Compostela bring back shells as remembrances?" "What do you think a halo is made of?" or "What would you do if you chanced upon a unicorn?"

One day I found them together in Fastrada's chamber; Fastrada had taken out her jewelry and was showing the glittering pieces to a wide-eyed Marie. Later that day, when we were alone, Fastrada told me: "What a darling child she is! It makes me realize how much I have missed in never having a daughter. How I longed for one! I adore my sons, of course, but it is not the same as a having a little girl whom one can spoil and chatter with."

She stopped abruptly, having noticed the sadness that had descended upon me. I was thinking, with despair, of my own little Editha. . . .

"Of course," she murmured, taking my hand in hers. "How could I have forgotten? Please forgive me. I can only imagine the sadness you must feel when you think of your baby girl. How terrible it must have been!"

"You cannot imagine how hideous that morning was," I said in a tremulous voice. "Waking up and finding Editha so still, frozen, in her cradle."

"You must have felt very alone."

"I did. Only Aiglantine really understood how much I suffered."

"And Gerard?"

"He had hoped for a son." Our eyes met. There was nothing more I need say.

"I should hope," said Fastrada slowly, "that it helps you to have Marie here, almost as a surrogate daughter. Clementia knows that you lost Editha. Perhaps that is why she decided that you become Marie's teacher—that you would find comfort having her with you."

"Yes," I murmured, trying to smile. "I do sometimes fantasize that Marie is my little girl. But still, it is not the same."

"Of course," she acknowledged, tenderly embracing me.

As we drew apart, I reflected, "I wonder whether Clementia feels any loss in her own life. In not having a husband or a child. I do not think she does."

"She places her energy elsewhere. And her emotions." Fastrada gave a slight laugh as a rare shadow spread across her angular face. "Such as they are. I never think of my sister in terms of emotion. To me she is all reason and logic."

FASTRADA'S TWO-WEEK SOJOURN AT THE abbey passed all too quickly; I was not alone in dreading the day of her departure. "I wish that Lady Fastrada lived here all the time!" Marie confessed one morning after Fastrada attended her lesson.

"What is it about Lady Fastrada you like most?" I asked.

"She says that one day I must learn to ride. May I, Lady Isabelle?" she implored.

"Yes! I agree you should. I shall discuss it with Sister Clementia."

"Promise me you will!" Heartened by my nod, she went on, "And she is not as strict as Sister Clementia, and she likes all my questions. She tells me stories about Troyes and the court. About the troubadours and their songs, and about the Countess Marie. She told me the countess is the daughter of Queen Eleanor."

"Yes, that is true. But the Countess Marie is Eleanor's daughter with the old king, with Louis. They say Eleanor has not seen Marie for many years. Since she was a little girl."

"That is sad," Marie said, casting her eyes down. She looked up with a poignant expression I shall never forget. "But at least the countess knows who her mother is!"

# CHAPTER 62

"Marie is very sad to think of your leaving," I told Fastrada the following evening as we walked together after vespers. "She told me she loved hearing your stories about Troyes and the Countess Marie. She will miss you terribly."

"And I shall miss her, and all of you, very much." Then, with a devilish glance, "I have told Clementia the child must learn to ride. Do you not agree, Isabelle?"

"I do," I replied, smiling.

"And I promised Marie to braid her hair with gold ribbon before I leave. A souvenir of my visit!"

After a moment, I asked, "Have you any idea about the circumstances of Marie's being left here?" I had never ceased imagining who might have been Marie's mother; and the story of the wayward Sister Rosceline continued to fascinate me more than I dared admit.

"Only that she was left by the *tour* as an infant, perhaps a month old. It is not so unusual, alas, for a baby to be abandoned this way. Marie was fortunate that she was left here, at Fontevraud." She paused. "It was Clementia who found her."

"Yes, she told me."

The sudden swoosh of birds in flight arrested our conversation. "How lovely they are!" Fastrada exclaimed as we looked up together.

"And how free!" I rejoined.

"You prize freedom, do you not?" asked Fastrada, turning to me. "Marriage to Gerard cannot have been easy for you. He is nothing if not controlling—whether of his wife or his falcons. I remember his anger when his favorite hawk would not perform."

"Féroce," I murmured, before adding, "and yet that was nothing compared to his fury when Vainqueur flew away. I only hope that Vainqueur is now free."

"Like Gallien—"

"Yes! At last Gallien is able to do what he loves most. That is the best kind of freedom, is it not?" As she nodded, I glanced at her: her eyes were fixed intently ahead, her profile, with its long, Byzantine nose, sharp as an arrow in the dusky light.

"I thought of what you said—about Gerard and Gallien," she reflected. "That Gerard would be furious, perhaps even vengeful, if he learned of Gallien's whereabouts."

"You believed I was overly concerned, that my fears were unwarranted—"

"And I still think they may be. But even so, I promise to tell Hugh what you said. That you fear for Gallien, and even for yourself. He will not take this lightly, believe me." She rubbed her hands together, for it had suddenly grown colder. "You must understand this about Hugh. He may appear jovial, the eternal bon vivant, but he is not someone one would want to cross. We have our differences, but Hugh is also profoundly loyal in his way. He would do anything to keep me safe, to keep his family and those he loves safe."

We had come to the doorway of the cloister. "You are lucky to feel that way about your husband," I told her rather wistfully. "And Gallien is lucky to work for him."

"Remember," she said, "you promised to give me a letter for Gallien before I leave."

THE SUN WAS BRIGHT THE next morning when I awoke. For once I did not rise at once but lay in bed for a while, gazing at the bronze falcon and thinking of the letter I must write to Gallien. Hearing of him from Fastrada had awakened many memories of my life with Gerard, and of the life at Ravinour I had left behind.

Finally I rose, and taking up the quill, I wrote:

*From the Lady Isabelle to Gallien, cordial greetings.*

It was with joy and relief that I heard from Lady Fastrada that you made your way to Troyes, and that you are now engaged as falconer by Lord de Hauteclare. God watched over you, indeed, as He has watched over me. I am now at the abbey of Fontevraud, and intend to make my life here...

I paused: Did I really intend to make my life here? Had I found my life's work, as Gallien clearly had? In my heart, I realized this was far from certain. I scratched out the sentence and closed the letter by writing:

I am now at the Abbey of Fontevraud—content, for the moment, to live among the sisters here, and to contribute what I am able. It has greatly cheered me to know that you are not only in the household of Lord and Lady de Hauteclare, but have also been entrusted with work that gives you joy.

*May God continue to protect you—*
*Lady Isabelle*

Shortly past sunrise, two days later, came the moment of Fastrada's departure. Her entourage was assembled: the woman servant who had accompanied her, and a young man who resembled a pallid version of LaFoi. Fastrada herself cut a startlingly flamboyant figure amid the somberly clad gathering—to the familiar traveling costume in peacock blue she had added a tall, matching headdress; a single braid, plaited with vivid blue ribbon, hung to her waist.

Clementia and Mother Gilles, serenely directing the servants, flanked me as we stood together by the stables. Marie clutched my hand as we watched the luggage being loaded.

Fastrada had indeed fulfilled her promise: the little girl's hair was now plaited with gold ribbon, much to the consternation of Clementia. In this matter, at least, I had succeeded in holding sway: "Let Marie keep the ribbons for a while," I insisted. "It will take away some of the sadness of Fastrada's leaving." Reluctantly Clementia had agreed.

One by one, we embraced Fastrada before she mounted, a tearful Marie last. "When will you return, Lady Fastrada?" she asked, tugging her hand.

"In the autumn, perhaps, before it grows too cold," she said gently, stroking her cheek. "In the meantime, you must promise to pay attention to your lessons with Lady Isabelle, and to make up more stories to tell me! Do you promise?"

She nodded solemnly.

"And I discussed the idea of your learning to ride, and both Sister Clementia and Lady Isabelle agree that you should." At this, Marie gave a rapturous smile. "And if you are a *very* good little girl," continued Fastrada, "I shall bring you a lovely treat from Troyes the next time."

"More ribbon for my hair?"

Fastrada smiled. "Of course! And something else as well. A surprise."

This seemed to assuage Marie, but only for a moment. Once Fastrada mounted, the little girl looked quite dejected: she lowered her head, scuffing the ground with her shoe almost angrily. "Come," I said, "you must look up now, and we must bid Lady Fastrada goodbye."

"I do not like goodbyes," sulked Marie, her eyes still cast down.

"Nor do I. But that does not mean we can ignore them," I said. "They are important."

Fastrada had been watching us from a slight distance. "Look!" I said. "Lady Fastrada is waiting for us to wave goodbye."

We did so. Fastrada responded in kind before she cantered away—a slender, jaunty figure in peacock blue, astride her gleaming dark mount.

DURING THE DAYS THAT FOLLOWED, I felt as I had after Fastrada's departure from Gerard's castle, years before. The same melancholy and loneliness descended upon me—this time even more painfully, for I no longer had Aiglantine. Marie seemed even more affected—so glum and distracted that she could scarcely concentrate on her lessons. I tried various ruses, attempting to engage her.

"Come," I coaxed her one morning, shortly after Fastrada's departure. "Let us play the game of the first line. But this time, *you* must provide the first line."

"Must I?"

"Yes."

She gave a sigh. "I cannot think of anything."

"I do not believe that for a moment. You were thinking of something just now, were you not?"

She nodded.

"Begin with that thought, then."

She glanced at me almost warily. "There was once a beautiful young girl, who lived with a family in Troyes," she began slowly. "One night she dreamed that she would finally learn of the mother who had left her long ago—

"Now it is your turn, Lady Isabelle," she said.

"The next morning, a messenger arrived with a letter for her," I continued. "A letter with the splendid seal of a noble house. . . ."

THE FOLLOWING DAY, WHEN HERALDIS appeared at my door, she announced that she had a letter for me. Her grim little eyes were alight with curiosity.

She handed the letter to me.

"Ahh, from Guy," I murmured, noticing the seal. "Thank you, Heraldis," I said as she lingered. "You may go."

The moment the door closed, I began to read:

*From Guy de la Palisse, greetings to his sister, Lady Isabelle, at the Abbey of Fontevraud*

I trust you are well settled, and that you are finding great fulfillment in helping the good sisters, and in doing God's noble work. Both Amélie and I hope that you find comfort in your new life after the failure of your marriage—a failure that pained us as much as it did you.

Perhaps you recall, before your departure, that I voiced my intention to journey to Fontevraud for a visit with you come springtime—a proposal that seemed to cheer you as you struggled with the sadness of separating from your devoted family. The absence of a letter from you in the intervening months has prompted me to surmise that you have not wanted to burden me by entreating me to embark on the expense and effort of such a visit. One can only admire this new spirit of self-abnegation, dear sister! It is heartening to think that you are learning to emulate the pious ways of the nuns.

I have taken it upon myself, therefore, to divest you of these inordinately considerate feelings: I have decided to venture to Fontevraud. Indeed, by the time you receive this missive, I shall have departed. Assuming all goes well, I should arrive at the abbey in about ten days, by the middle of May.

It is my hope that my visit will coincide with that of the Lady Fastrada. For I learned this winter, from acquaintances in Troyes, that she habitually came to the abbey about this time in May to see her sister, Lady Clementia. I was also told, by those same distinguished acquaintances, that I had favorably impressed Lord and Lady de Hauteclare years ago when I met them at the lists, in Troyes. Modesty inhibits me from divulging more: suffice it to say that what I learned leads me to conclude that my presence at the abbey during Lady Fastrada's sojourn would be most warmly welcomed.

It also seems appropriate that I thank the Lady Fastrada in person for her role in your new life. I do not only mean her monetary generosity: given your history, it was surely helpful that you reside at Fontevraud under the Lady Fastrada's distinguished auspices.

Please know that you need make no special arrangements for my stay. When one is among the holy sisters, one must adhere to their regimen and customs, though the reputation of Fontevraud is such that I assume a certain level of comfort and a

servant will be provided for me, a man of rank. As for my diet—
you know that my stomach tends to be delicate, and therefore
hope that meat will be provided for me, rather than fish.

I should add that I very much look forward to making the
acquaintance of Sister Clementia, whose noble character is
known to many, far and wide. I imagine that she will find some
comfort in the company of one like myself who is similarly
contemplative, who eschews worldly pleasures, and who always
strives to do what is best in God's eyes.

Father is pleased I shall soon see you and joins me in relaying his greetings. He fares well, though his bodily strength
has declined, and there are often moments when he experiences
forgetfulness and becomes befuddled. Alas, Hortense seems,
increasingly, to dominate him, and I must often reprimand her
for overreaching when she presumes to be the mistress of the
house. Despite my admonishments, she seems to quickly revert
to her inordinately familiar behavior.

From Arnaut we have had no word. The absence of a letter
from him distresses Father; Amélie and I have long become
accustomed to his errant behavior—behavior which you, dear
sister, have always all too readily excused. It was only by chance
that we learned of his whereabouts recently, from several
knights who had returned from the Holy Land. They had met
Arnaut in Aleppo and told us that he has pledged service to a
Norman knight in that region.

I have entrusted this letter—at great expense, I should
add—to a most reliable messenger, and hope it reaches you in
timely fashion. I commend myself to you, dear sister, and look
forward to seeing you before long.

Below Guy's signature came a postscript:

Lastly, I should mention that I am no longer betrothed to Adelaide de Chabanel. Shortly before we were to be wed, I discovered

certain shocking things about her life and family that led me to believe she would not be a suitable wife for a man of my position. Please know that I shall not object if you discreetly mention this development to the Lady Fastrada and Sister Clementia.

I put the letter aside and sat down on the bed, my head in my hands, not knowing whether to laugh or cry. I wondered what Guy's motives really were. To see Fastrada again, of course, with a view to currying her favor and eliciting an invitation to the famed Hauteclare hunt, perhaps. Despite what he had said, I suspected there were other reasons for his fractured betrothal to the much-vaunted Lady de Chabanel: perhaps her dowry had not met his expectations, or her family had decided against the marriage. They may have had reservations about Guy or our own family: it cannot have pleased them to learn that our father now consorted with a servant.

With the change in his circumstances, it was possible Guy thought Fastrada might eventually introduce him to new prospects for a wife— some rich, landed woman from Troyes, or a plain, but wealthy widow. It was well known that many women, particularly in the region of Champagne, of which Troyes was part, had lost their spouses during the perilous expeditions to the Holy Land.

And then another idea even more mortifying, indeed stupefying, occurred to me: Was it possible that he entertained the thought of his courting *Clementia*? I told myself this was preposterous: Clementia had pledged herself to God, she had taken the veil. There were, of course, instances of women who had forsworn the holy life to marry. But this was very rare, and Clementia, of all people, was an unlikely candidate for such a swerve.

There was only one aspect of Guy's upcoming visit that made me gleeful: I longed for the moment when I would tell him that Fastrada had left the abbey weeks before—oh, the perverse delight of witnessing his disappointment!

THE FOLLOWING MORNING, WHEN I saw Clementia in the cloister, I bade her good morrow, then told her: "I received a letter yesterday—"

"I hear it was from your brother."

"Yes," I said, adding, "he will visit me here soon."

"I assume, by your expression, that you are not overjoyed at the thought of seeing him."

"No, I am not." I gave a sigh, adding rather gloomily, "But you will see for yourself, when Guy arrives."

"Perhaps his visit will be better than you expect, and you will be pleasantly surprised."

We began to walk toward the refectory. "When will your brother arrive?" Clementia asked.

"Very soon, I imagine. He mentioned he would be here in mid-May." The more I had reflected on Guy's letter, the more irritated and resentful I had become. Indeed, I was tempted to ignore his requests for certain privileges and comforts, and to impose austerity upon him instead—the very austerity he purported to espouse.

"I shall have a chamber prepared for him," said Clementia. "In the appropriate part of the guest hospice, of course. I assure you he will be most comfortable there."

"Oh, we need not go through much trouble for him," I said, increasingly excited about the idea of a ruse. "My brother has become quite abstemious. He told me he was intent on adhering to the rules and the customs here. A room with a pallet and a prie-dieu will suffice—a place for meditation and prayer."

"In that case, we will give him the simplest room. Even so, he will need someone to wait on him."

"I doubt it," I replied, barely able to suppress a smile. "I am sure he will be content to manage on his own."

"Perhaps, but it is the custom here for a man of his rank to have a servant. Mother Gilles insists upon it. I have already assigned someone to him—Symon, whom you have met." Symon was a beloved figure at the abbey: an orphan, born with a deformed arm, and now, alas, almost hunchbacked, he had served the sisters devotedly for many years.

"Symon would be most suitable," I replied at once. Little did Clementia know that Guy harbored an aversion to any sort of deformity or physical defect.

A FEW DAYS LATER, HERALDIS came to tell me that Guy had arrived and awaited me in the chapter house. As I approached, I saw Mother Gilles outside, Caprice perched on her shoulder. "It is only fitting I come with you to greet your brother," she said, and we entered together.

Guy stood before a bench, gazing intently at the tapestry above— assessing its value, most likely. I was struck, at once, by the severity of his raiment: his dark gray tunic of rough wool had nary a braid or embellishment—what I imagined an anchorite would wear.

Glimpsing Caprice, he visibly flinched but quickly regained his composure as we approached—bowing solemnly before the abbess as she introduced herself, then embracing me with inordinate fervor. "Dear sister," he intoned, "it is a joy indeed to see you here, at Fontevraud, surrounded by the worthy sisters, and to meet the esteemed abbess." He lowered his head slightly, as if overwhelmed by emotion.

"*Bienvenu à Fontevraud!*" Caprice squawked; Guy fairly jumped. "What an unusual"—here a long, searching pause—"and *eloquent* creature!" he exclaimed, feigning delight as I struggled not to laugh.

"We, like our beloved parrot, are delighted to welcome you," said Mother Gilles; sensing Guy's revulsion, she smiled serenely and added, "He, too, is one of God's creatures."

"And all the more fortunate to be *here*, in God's house!" He made the sign of the cross. "And does this blessed creature have a name?" he asked cloyingly.

"Caprice," said the abbess. "And he, like everyone here, has grown very fond of your sister. All of us must thank you for permitting her to join us here," she added, glancing at me warmly. "Lady Isabelle has worked hard and has already contributed a great deal."

"How heartening to hear this!" he exclaimed in a way that implied that her praise had surprised him. "I might have imagined—"

"Your journey went well?" I interrupted.

"Very well. The weather was temperate, and I encountered no difficulties along the roads. Clearly God, knowing my mission, blessed each step of the way." He glanced meaningfully at the abbess and made the sign of the cross, as I wondered what he construed as his "mission."

"You were fortunate indeed to have God's blessing," she said with a slight smile. Then, turning to me: "I have sent Heraldis to fetch Sister Clementia. I know she will be delighted to meet your brother. I shall leave you both now, as I am sure you have much to discuss."

"I am eager to meet Sister Clementia," interjected Guy. "And of course, the Lady Fastrada as well—"

"Lady Fastrada?" asked the abbess, puzzled.

"My brother was under the impression that Lady Fastrada would be visiting at this time," I explained. I turned to Guy. "You see, dear brother, Lady Fastrada was here recently but left several weeks ago."

I saw him blanch, then struggle to contain his disappointment; tempted to laugh, I looked away.

"Perhaps she will be here when I visit again," he said, after clearing his throat and rearranging his expression. "I greatly enjoyed the time I spent with her and the Lord de Hauteclare, at Troyes—at their celebrated hunt, I should add."

"I see," returned the abbess with a patient smile. "And now I am afraid I must leave you, for I have much to attend to today." She bade us goodbye, and Guy bowed deeply. Once she was out of earshot, I said, "I was distressed to hear what happened with Adelaide de Chabanel."

"A sorry matter," he said bitterly. "Though it was better, of course, to learn the truth when I did. Before taking our vows, that is."

"It all seems quite strange," I said, "Amélie told me that she and her family were quite distinguished. 'Faultless in lineage and character' was the way she described them."

"The devil works in many ways," he said, clearly reluctant to pursue the subject.

"How long do you intend to stay, brother?" I asked, after an awkward pause.

"A week or so. Longer, of course, should there be any contributions I might be able to make."

"What contributions have you in mind?"

"I trust the abbess to guide me. And Sister Clementia, too, of course."

"I doubt the work available to you here will be to your liking."

"You know full well that I am willing to do anything to serve God, dear sister." He gave a self-satisfied smile.

"There *is* work in the hospice where the lepers are cared for," I said. "It is not easy work, of course, but—"

I saw a flicker of alarm in his eyes. "Ah," he said mournfully, "that, I am afraid, would not do. You know my constitution—"

The arrival of Clementia, however, prevented him from expatiating. He bowed deeply and rather ostentatiously before her; I knew from his radiant expression that her beauty had surpassed his expectations.

"It is an honor to meet you, Sister Clementia," he said. "The Lady Fastrada, whom I have met, at the lists in Troyes I should add, has told me much about you. I have long admired your decision to devote yourself to God. It is not many women of title who, having been raised with worldly riches, have decided to reject a life of such vanities, and to create another, more exalted way of living. A life of simplicity, a worthy life, devoid of so much that is corrupt, and ungodly."

As I listened, cringing, I wondered how long Guy had rehearsed this speech: I suspected the same thought had already occurred to Clementia. "I hardly think I am worthy of such praise, my lord," she said, raising one brow.

"You see," I interjected in a somber tone, "my brother is quite pious. Nothing pleases him more than to think he will be living here in great simplicity, among us." I turned to him and asked brightly, "Is that not so, Guy?"

"My dear sister, I could not have expressed it as well myself!"

"With that in mind," said Clementia, "we have assigned you a simple room in the part of the hospice reserved for pilgrims. It has everything you should need—a pallet, a few candles, and a prie-dieu."

"Excellent," he said, but his eyes looked perplexed and his lackluster tone reflected a lack of enthusiasm. "I suppose, though," he added gingerly, "that it would not be untoward on my part to ask to be provided with a servant——"

"I was under the impression that you would prefer to manage on your own, brother," I could not resist interjecting. "As a holy pilgrim might."

"Ordinarily I would,"——I could see his thoughts racing——"but recently I have had some troubles with my health. I must not exert myself too much."

"You need have no concern. Naturally, I have arranged someone to wait on you," said Clementia, with a chiding glance in my direction. "Symon should be here at any moment and will escort you to your chamber." Guy's expression visibly brightened.

We continued to converse——Clementia asked about his journey, the condition of the roads——until we heard a knocking at the door. Clementia bade Symon enter, and he shuffled toward us——a squat, crabbed figure whose physical state did not prevent him, touchingly, from smiling and attempting a bow as he stood before us.

I noticed Guy flinch; had Clementia not been with us, I suspect his lip would have curled in revulsion.

"Lord Guy has had a long journey," Clementia told Symon. "I am sure he would like to see his chamber. Please escort him there now."

A FEW HOURS LATER, CLEMENTIA, Guy, and I gathered in the abbess's dining room before the midday meal. The array of precious objects on the sideboard immediately caught Guy's eye. "Such artistry perfectly reflects the glory of God!" he exclaimed, examining the splendid crucifix. "I have never seen a cross with such gems——such rubies, sapphires, and rock crystal!" To this he added, in a less lofty tone, "I can only imagine their value——"

"There is another cross, with even more exquisite craftsmanship, that is kept at the altar of our church," said Clementia, watching him intently. "I shall ask Symon to show it to you."

"Oh, there is no need, Sister," he quickly replied—partly, I suspected, to avoid an unnecessary foray with Symon. "I am not one to be impressed by such things. It is solely the *spirit* of the craftsmen that moves me—the notion of these objects created as tributes to our Lord." He gave his version of a beatific smile.

"Come, let us sit," she announced, moving to the table.

"Should we not wait for the abbess?" Guy asked, looking expectantly about. I knew he was eager to become more acquainted with Mother Gilles, who belonged to an illustrious family closely related to the Plantagenets.

"I am afraid Mother Gilles will not be able to join us today," Clementia said, taking her seat. "She has been called to Saumur to visit a family whose child is quite ill."

"I am very sorry to hear that," he intoned, though I felt sure it was the abbess's absence, not the family's plight, which most concerned him. "No doubt it will cheer them to have the blessings of such an august figure of God's community." He paused, knitting his hands together. "May I know the family's name, Sister?"

"I believe they are called Bonace," replied Clementia, clearly puzzled that he should ask.

"I intend to remember them in my prayers this evening," he said reverently. After sitting down, he added, "I do hope it will not be too long before I see the abbess again."

Clementia smiled noncommittally and proceeded to say grace, after which a servant appeared, bearing the first dish—a platter of cod.

Recalling what Guy had written me—his preference for meat, rather than what he deemed "less digestible" fish—I was curious to see his reaction. His thin mouth pursed as he was served, but even so, he took a generous portion and set to with gusto. "How delicately this is seasoned!" he exclaimed. "Spices that are most unusual must have been used on this excellent fish. Coriander, perhaps, or cumin?"

"I very much doubt either," said Clementia. "We seldom use expensive spices here." She took a bite. "I am quite sure it is parsley," she said, glancing up.

"Ah," he said, "undoubtedly parsley, cultivated here, in the blessed earth of the abbey, has far more savor than ordinary parsley."

"A novel idea," she replied drily. "And one which our cooks would find heartening."

As the meal proceeded Guy ate with relish, despite his previous claims of a "delicate stomach" and "easily imbalanced humors." All the while I tried to steer the conversation, not always successfully, for Guy seemed intent on brandishing his scanty knowledge of liturgical matters, for instance, or on making observations of certain famous figures he assumed that Clementia, like himself, disapproved of: Hildegard of Bingen and Héloïse, among them. In most cases, he was able to extricate himself from potentially awkward moments with some adroitness: once he sensed that Clementia did not share his opinions, he adjusted his comments so that they appeared to mirror hers.

And then he broached another subject: the circumstances of my coming to Fontevraud.

"Our family is so grateful to yours, Sister Clementia, for helping my dearly beloved sister to find her way," he said, gazing at me soulfully. "It was hard for all of us, very hard, when her marriage failed," he added, in a melodramatic voice.

"Hardest for *her*, I should think," Clementia said calmly, but firmly.

"Of course, yes of course!" he said. "But we shared her pain, you see, and her abject sense of failure. We took it very much to heart."

There was a long, awkward pause. "I have never felt that ascribing blame is particularly helpful," replied Clementia. "Nor have I—nor has Lady Fastrada—construed Lady Isabelle's situation as a 'failure.'" She looked at him coolly.

He delved into his food and then, undaunted, continued. "In light of all this, I do want to thank you, and your sister, Lady Fastrada most especially, for your generosity in allowing my sister to reside here. It was not only your financial largesse that we so appreciated, but your largesse of *spirit*. It must be admitted that my sister's situation might have given others pause."

"I am not certain what you mean," said Clementia, furrowing her brow.

"That is to say, given the fact that Isabelle is divorced—culpable, therefore, of having broken one of God's holiest sacraments—Lady Fastrada was exceedingly charitable to support her."

"I think you should know, Lord Guy, that Lady Fastrada and I had no hesitation in endorsing Lady Isabelle's desire to reside here. Lady Fastrada is immensely fond of your sister. Indeed, I had heard about Lady Isabelle long before the possibility of her coming to Fontevraud was ever broached. Your sister is not the first woman to become divorced, after all. The queen herself—Queen Eleanor—is divorced."

"That is true, of course," he replied, "though, surely, we would not want to place my beloved sister in *her* company."

"The queen is much beloved, here, Lord Guy," she replied in a frosty tone. "She has been immensely generous to Fontevraud. We have always admired her intelligence and spirit, indeed her courage. Perhaps you do not know that her youngest children—John and Joanna—were raised here."

"Of course, I understand," he rejoined rather unctuously. "One must never decry one's patrons." Then, with an unpleasant, almost conspiratorial look: "You need say no more."

Clementia looked stonily at him, her hand tight around her goblet as she sipped from it. Trying to assuage the growing tension, I changed the subject. "I do want you to know, brother, that I have no doubt I made the right decision to come here, and to embark on a different kind of life."

"That cheers me, sister," he said unconvincingly. "Life must proceed apace, through all its vicissitudes—that is certainly what the Lord instructs us." He paused, delicately wiping his fingers with his napkin. "As one might expect, your former husband has also continued his own life. You may not know that he has remarried. Naturally I thought it best to wait until we were together to impart this news. I am told he and his wife—a great beauty, they say—are very happy."

I glanced away, pricked by the hint of triumph in his voice. "I wish them well, brother," I said. "I hope you know that."

"Of course, of course," he replied, his dismissiveness making it clear he did not.

Clementia had remained silent during this exchange. I looked down, feeling her eyes upon me and wondering what she was thinking. A custard was being passed, providing a welcome caesura.

"I know that Sister Clementia asked Symon to show you the grounds and the different wings of the abbey," I ventured, turning to Guy. "I trust he did?"

"Yes. The good man showed me each part of this splendid establishment. The noble abbatial church, the delightful gardens, the refectory—"

"There is no better guide to the abbey than Symon," said Clementia. "He has lived here for years and knows each corner intimately."

"I told the good man that I would remember him in my prayers," continued Guy. "I also said I considered him truly *blessed*. God blesses those most whom He afflicts most. Is that not what the scriptures teach us, Sister?" He looked expectantly at Clementia.

"It is indeed," she replied briskly.

"I offered to place a votive in our chapel, our family chapel, I should add, and told him I would pray for God to bless him. Most of all I assured him that he need never feel any sense of shame or embarrassment for his"—he paused—"*affliction*. He seemed most grateful for my concern."

"None of us has ever felt that Symon should be *ashamed* of his condition," retorted Clementia so sharply that I drew in my breath. "Nor has it *ever* been suggested that he should feel embarrassed by the burden God has placed upon him. Quite to the contrary. We respect him all the more for bearing his lot uncomplainingly, and with dignity."

"I did not mean to imply that I myself should think of him in that way," replied Guy quickly, for even he had realized he had committed a terrible gaffe. "It is simply that one cannot help but be aware there are others—others in our woefully imperfect world—who are less charitable in their thinking."

"One can only hope that such ignorant folk will learn by the example of those who follow the precepts of the Lord," came her stern riposte. "Those who emulate the humility of Christ. Here, at Fontevraud, we aspire to provide such an example."

For once, Guy had no response: he looked down, twisting his hands together. A knocking at the door mercifully broke the strained silence: it was Symon. Clementia bade him enter.

"You have arrived at the perfect moment, Symon," said Clementia, standing up. "We have just finished dining. You may show Lord Guy back to his chamber." Then, to Guy: "Unless of course you would like Symon to show you the holy vessels in our church. The crucifix I mentioned earlier—"

"Thank you, Sister Clementia, but that will not be necessary," he mumbled. "I shall go directly to my chamber. I must devote time to prayer."

"An excellent idea," she returned.

He bowed and left, Symon scuttling behind him. Once they had disappeared from sight, I turned to Clementia. "I can only apologize—"

"You need say nothing more," she interrupted, her hand gently upon my shoulder. "It is *I* who should apologize. I was wrong to dismiss your apprehension about the arrival of your brother." She gave a sigh. "Now I perfectly understand why you were not looking forward to his visit."

# CHAPTER 63

Even Guy, with his staggering obtuseness, seemed to have realized that his first significant encounter with Clementia had been little short of a disaster. During the next day, he kept himself to himself, claiming he was deep at prayer or meditating upon the scriptures. The following day, however, Symon appeared at my door with a message from Guy requesting that we meet as soon as possible for a walk in the cloister.

"Lord Guy asked that I return with your reply," said Symon.

The seeming urgency of Guy's message made me uneasy. "Perhaps it is best I go with you and speak with him myself," I said.

We left at once, with Symon accompanying me to Guy's chamber. After greeting him, I said, "I was concerned that something might be amiss, brother."

"No, not at all, sister dear! I merely wanted to spend some contemplative time with you, a few moments for us to meditate upon God's beneficence. Let us go walk together."

Shortly afterward, as we came to the end of one passage in the cloister, I noticed him furtively looking about.

"Is something wrong, brother?" I asked.

"Oh no, nothing at all." Then, somewhat uneasily: "I have not seen Sister Clementia today." I looked at him closely, unable to decide whether he was trying to avoid Clementia or to engage her, in an attempt to make amends.

"She is away," I said. "She has joined the abbess in Saumur."

"Ah, ministering to the good family Bonace, of course! I found Sister Clementia to be most intelligent and *sound* in her thinking." Then, pointedly: "An excellent mentor for you particularly, sister."

"She is most impressive," I replied, annoyed by his implied slight.

"Indeed." He cleared his throat, which usually presaged a pronounce-ment. "Inspired by Sister Clementia, I have decided to forgo the service of Symon. While I am here, I intend to live in all simplicity, as a monk might."

"That is laudable of you, brother." I refrained from smiling, certain that his decision had nothing to do with a longing for austerity, but with his physical aversion to Symon.

"I do hope, when the moment is appropriate, that you will inform Sister Clementia of my decision."

His smug expression irked me. "Perhaps it is more appropriate you tell her yourself," I suggested.

"Hopefully I shall see her again very soon," he replied, "so that we may continue our last conversation."

AS GUY AND I LEFT Mass the following morning, we glimpsed Cle-mentia standing outside the church. He strutted up to her at once.

"How very good to see you, Sister," he exclaimed. "I would like to tell you that I have reflected on our last, substantive dialogue, one that I found profoundly inspiring. Indeed, I would like you to know that, during my stay, I have decided to live in utter simplicity, as a pilgrim or a monk might. Thus I shall forgo the services of Symon."

"I see," was all she replied, to Guy's visible disappointment.

There was a long, awkward pause. I turned to Clementia. "I do hope your visit to Saumur yesterday went well—"

"No doubt the good family Bonace took great comfort in your presence, and the abbess's," interjected Guy.

"We tried our best in very sad circumstances," said Clementia in a tremulous voice. "The child died yesterday afternoon."

"I am so sorry to hear this," I said. "It must have been a dreadful day."

She gave a weary sigh, her delicate face pale and grave. "It was a day when one felt that God had forsaken us. Perhaps that is why I felt es-pecially glad for Mass this morning—to see the sun streaming through the windows, and to feel God's presence again. But now, if you will excuse me, I must go and speak with Mother Gilles."

Guy and I hardly saw Clementia or Mother Gilles during the subsequent days. Mother Gilles was continually immersed in the affairs of
the abbey, and Clementia had much pressing work at the *tour* and the
scriptorium—grateful, I suspected, to have excuses to avoid Guy.

With each passing day, Guy seemed to grow more disenchanted
with his visit. Every aspect of his sojourn had proven disappointing to
him: Fastrada was absent; Clementia and the abbess were not available
for another "substantive dialogue"; the abbey cuisine was far from his
liking; and, without a servant, he was left to fend for himself.

After a week of failed attempts to see Clementia, and unattended by
a servant, he was looking noticeably unkempt and haggard. "You have
lost weight," I said to him one morning as we walked to lauds.

"Ah, dear sister," he replied. "When one is nourished by the life of
the spirit, food seems almost immaterial, does it not?"

Given his dashed expectations, I was not surprised when, the following day, he announced he was cutting short his visit and would depart on the morrow.

"I do hope there is nothing wrong," I said with an exaggerated concern that masked my relief.

"I fear there may very well be something amiss." Then, ominously:
"If one is to trust the presentiments of Saint Martin."

"What does Saint Martin have to do with your leaving?"

"He appeared to me in a vision last night," he replied, with near comic
seriousness. "Saint Martin told me that all was not well at our home. He
intimated that Father was ill, and urged me to depart as soon as possible."

"This is very worrisome indeed," I said, suppressing a smile.

"So now you understand why I must leave," he proclaimed in a
portentous tone. "Never before has Saint Martin spoken so clearly and
eloquently to me." Then, lowering his voice dramatically, "You have my
permission to tell Sister Clementia. She will attribute this vision to this
intense period of meditation and prayer, I am certain."

"Of course," I murmured, though I could not resist asking: "I did
not know that Saint Martin has appeared to you before. This is the first
time you have ever mentioned visions."

"I am a deeply private man—not one to brandish my religious fervor, sister."

"Do tell me about this vision," I urged, intent on making him squirm. "I am very interested to hear all the details. Indeed, I am sure Sister Clementia will be eager to know about them as well. Where did Saint Martin appear, in what setting?"

At first he seemed taken aback, then began to think fast. "In an olive grove," he announced. "Yes, in a rather desolate olive grove."

"Strange, because Saint Martin is from Tours, after all, rather close by. And this is a region very far from olive groves."

"It was a grove of *some* sort, sister, I know not which kind," he replied with some impatience. "The light was exceedingly dim, you see. All very grim."

"What was he wearing?"

"A toga of some sort. A very pale blue."

"It is fascinating, brother, that you should remember the color so vividly when, as you said, it was all so dim."

"It was merely a *suggestion* of blue." He cleared his throat. "Really, sister, let us speak of something else. Do you not comprehend how disturbing the vision was? I do not wish to discuss it any longer. Indeed, I shall go pray to Saint Martin now. I must ask his blessings before I embark on the journey home."

Guy departed the next day, shortly past dawn. The abbess and I saw him off; Symon was there as well, for he was entrusted with helping to pack Guy's trunk and making certain he had adequate provisions. Clementia claimed she was indisposed, and asked me to relay her wishes to Guy for a safe journey. To his abject disappointment, he had never been able to relate the details of his "vision" to her.

Had the abbess not been present, I suspect Guy would have treated Symon perfunctorily, at best. As it was, he repeatedly addressed him as "my good man" in such an unctuous way that I was more relieved than ever to watch Guy pass through the abbey gates—a weary, gangling figure on an ancient gray mount.

# CHAPTER 64

The moment Guy departed, my spirits lifted and everything seemed brighter. That morning I could hardly refrain from humming snatches of ballads as I threw crumbs at the pigeons sauntering on the lawn by the abbey church.

Now that he was gone, I realized how much energy Guy's visit had demanded from me. There had not been a conversation in which I had not needed to intervene for fear that he would embarrass himself or me. Yet the visit had also been heartening, for it had made me appreciate how fortunate I was to live at Fontevraud, and how miserable I would have been at home. I felt doubly grateful to Fastrada and Clementia for the opportunity they had provided me.

Guy's visit also subtly changed my relationship with Clementia: no doubt it gave her an appreciation of my earlier life and my struggles with my family. All of this remained unspoken between us, of course, for Clementia was far too elegant and private to express such feelings. Still, I began to notice a greater sensitivity on her part, a certain change in the tenor of her glances and in her warm, if restrained, concern.

Though I had, by then, become slightly more accustomed to my new life, I continued to long for word of events beyond the abbey walls. In this regard, as in so many others, I depended upon Clementia. It was she who greeted the travelers, pilgrims, and messengers who arrived at the gatehouse, providing us with news—of feuds between rival lords, of rumors about Queen Eleanor, and of the bitter battles between the Plantagenet princes and their father. These snatches always enticed me, for they were a reminder of the outside world, the world I still found enticing.

ONE AFTERNOON IN MID-SEPTEMBER, AS I was in the midst of
teaching Marie a psalm, Clementia abruptly entered. "Forgive me," she
said, hurrying in. "I was tending to a stranger who arrived at the *tour*
earlier. The woman was terribly weak and ill. Heraldis and I helped her
to the hospital. Sister Philippa is with her now."

"Then at least the poor woman is in good hands," I said reassuringly. Sister Philippa was known as an exemplary teacher and nurse, a
learned practitioner of Galen's theories.

Clementia seemed pensive, preoccupied. "I would like you to come
with me to the hospital and see this woman," she said. Then, in a more
urgent tone, "It is possible you know her. She says she was a servant at
the castle of your former husband."

"At Ravinour? Then she has come a long way indeed!" I said, taken
aback. "It is possible I have met her, I suppose. Though we had so many
servants there, not all of whom I knew. "

"Of course. But let us see, just the same."

I asked Marie to continue her reading and left with Clementia. As
we walked the short distance to the hospital, she said, "I must prepare
you. I do not think the woman has long to live. She has a disease of the
lungs. Scrofula, I fear."

"Do you not fear that the air around her is corrupted?"

"We know that God protects us here."

"But surely—"

"To live here is to submit to His design," she replied with radiant
certitude as we entered the vestibule of the hospital.

We came to the long, vaulted chamber where the patients lay. Sick
pilgrims, peasants, and women who had had perilous childbirths were
often cared for here, but only a few beds were occupied that day. The air
was suffused by the slightly acrid scent of cleansing herbs, and shafts of
mote-flecked light streamed like arrows through high, slender windows.

Sister Philippa, a tall, rather rotund woman of immense dignity,
stood at the end, before the only bed around which the curtains were
drawn—the sign of a critically ill patient. After greeting us, she said, "I
gave the woman a tisane to soothe the cough, and some broth, and told

her to try to sleep. Rest is what she needs most. And God's grace, if she is to live." She gave a heavy sigh. "It is scrofula, alas, of that I am quite sure. Now that you are here, I shall go to the apothecary and prepare some medicines. There is no time to waste," she added gravely, and left.

"Let me see if our patient is still sleeping," whispered Clementia, pulling the curtain aside and peeking within. "Come," she said, gesturing to me. "Her eyes are open. She is awake." She slowly drew open the panels.

"It is I, Sister Clementia," she said softly. The woman's head was turned to the side, her hair matted with sweat, her breathing belabored. "And I have brought someone to see you." The pallid face turned ever so slowly, listlessly, to face us, as her eyes slowly opened.

I started; I froze; this spectral being was no "stranger." This was *Aiglantine* who stared at me, *Aiglantine* whose gaunt face lay upon the pillow. I stared, incredulous, at the ghostly, aged face.

"She is—" I gasped.

"You know her, then?" Clementia asked, but no sooner had she uttered those words than Aiglantine, her eyes fully open now, struggled to sit up. "Lady Isabelle? Is it you?"

"Yes!" I cried, taking her wasted hands in mine. "Indeed, it is I!"

"How is it you are *here*? Not at your home, my lady?" So terrible was her coughing that she had barely been able to eke this out.

"I came here last year. Lady Fastrada helped arrange for me to live at the abbey. But how is it *you* have come here?"

"I have come to see my family in Montreuil-Bellay. My mother and sisters, before I die." There fell a long pause during which the heaving cough overtook her again; then she managed to gasp, "And there is something else I must do, something I never told you about—"

"Of course," I comforted her. "And you *will*. But now you must rest." Her head fell back against the pillow.

"You seem to know her well," said Clementia, drawing me aside. "Perhaps it is best I leave you to speak with her alone."

"She is the servant who attended me, and with whom I shared so much. She might as well be my sister. We must do whatever we can to help her!"

Clementia pressed my hand, her brow knitted in concern. "I shall confer with Sister Philippa and see what she advises." She nodded gravely and left.

I drew up a stool to the bed and sat down. "My dear Aiglantine, what has befallen you?" I stroked her emaciated hand, its veins vivid blue against the blanched flesh. "How long have you been ill?"

"Months." She made an effort to sit up; I helped her, propping up the pillow as her eyes, with their sickly brilliance, seemed to devour my face. "I know I am going to die—"

"No! You are not!"

She nodded, coughed, and then smiled grimly. "I shall die content if I see my family once more."

"You will! We will make sure you do."

"And then I must see if my child still lives!" she cried; I leaned forward, trying to catch her words, for they were almost inaudible through the wracking coughs. "My daughter." She reached for my hand and held it tight. "I had a baby once, a baby I abandoned, may God forgive me!"

"I did hear a story to that effect when I was at Ravinour, dear Aiglantine," I said, stroking her hand. "But now that you are here, and we are together, you need have no fear, no shame, with me. Tell me about the child," I said, trying to pacify her.

"I left her here, long ago."

"*Here?* At the abbey?"

"Yes! I came home, to my village, for her birth. I knew that by depositing her here she might have a chance to survive."

"How many years ago was this?"

"A little over five."

"There are many children who are deposited here, and almost all of them leave to live elsewhere. The sisters give them to families to adopt. There is only one little girl here, and she is being brought up as an oblate."

"Perhaps she is mine!" Again, the dreadful cough.

I waited for her to rest a moment before asking, "Did you leave anything with the baby, a birth token of some sort?"

"Yes. A little wooden cross tucked into her swaddling clothes."

"Ah, my dear Aiglantine, there is scarcely a baby who is not left here with a cross!" I cried with despair, wiping some sweat from her brow. "Was there *something* that might distinguish her? A birthmark, like yours?"

She shook her head. "No, she had none. She was perfect."

Then, suddenly, her eyes brightened with excitement. "I *did* leave something special with her that might have been kept."

"What was that?" I asked eagerly.

"A little tunic I made for her to wear when she was a bit older. I tucked this into the basket with her. I embroidered the tunic with a border of forget-me-nots."

"What color were the forget-me-nots?" I asked with surging excitement.

"Blue with yellow centers."

One thought after another raced through my mind: Marie and the little tunic with which she dressed her doll, Radegonde; the forget-me-nots with yellow stamens. "Pity the mother who took such care to embroider this for a baby she could not keep," Clementia had said. "This is the only thing I have of my mother," Marie had told me so poignantly. Marie was five, the very age Aiglantine's child would have been. Was it possible, I thought, stupefied; and yet, in my pounding heart, I knew—as if a riddle had been solved—that it *was* true. "Dearest Aiglantine," I cried, taking her hands in mine, "I believe we have your daughter *here*—and she is safe, and well!"

"Can this be true?" she asked, her eyes wild with incredulity, then joy. "Is it true?" she asked again, between tears of relief and happiness, and wracking coughs.

"She is called Marie," I said, holding her hand tight. "And I have been her teacher."

"I must see her now!"

"You will, soon, I promise! But first you must sleep a little and gather your strength. For your sake, and Marie's. And I must speak with Sister Clementia."

"And I must thank Sister Clementia, with all my heart!"

"Yes, of course. But now—we must think how to prepare Marie. How to explain all of this to her."

"You are afraid, because you know I will die soon."

"No," I lied.

"My only wish is to tell her I loved her. That I never wanted to give her up."

"I know, I always knew that!" I replied passionately. "But you must be reassured. Your little girl has been well loved. By Sister Clementia, and by all of us!" I paused, still trying to grasp the complexity of the discovery and its effect upon Clementia, let alone Marie. "You see, it was Sister Clementia who found your baby. She has been her—" I had almost said "mother" but caught myself. "Her protector."

For the first time, she smiled—a seraphic smile that momentarily transformed her ghostly visage. But then an expression of anguish crossed her face. "You must promise that my family never learns about the child. My mother would die if she knew. Her granddaughter, a child born in sin! Marie must remain here, at the abbey." She took both my hands in hers. "Swear to me, Isabelle!"

"I swear," I said, crossing my heart.

Spent, she lay back upon the pillow, struggling to keep her eyes open.

"Sleep now," I told her softly. "I shall go and speak with Sister Clementia. We will discuss what to tell Marie. And then, very soon, you will meet her." She nodded, and drifted off to sleep.

I stood up, and as I walked down the hall, past the other patients, I glimpsed Clementia entering. "You are leaving her?" she asked, alarmed.

"She has fallen asleep." I took her arm. "Come. We must speak. There is something astounding I have learned."

We went into the antechamber. I told Clementia the story detail by detail as she listened, astonished.

"Can it be?" she asked. "It seems so improbable. And yet, the child is five, and there is no question about the tunic with the forget-me-nots. I shall never forget the moment when I found it in her basket!"

She spoke quickly, almost uncomprehendingly, as if she were trying to convince herself that all of this could be true. "Who was the father?" she finally asked.

"The son of a serf, they say."

"Of course. A story as old as time." She nervously fingered the crucifix suspended from her neck. "We must prepare the child. A dreadful thing for her to meet her mother now, in this state."

"Aiglantine knows she has not long to live. But perhaps seeing her child will help restore her! Such miracles *do* happen." I looked at her beseechingly. "Do they not? Tell me that they do, Clementia!"

"They do, but far too seldom, even here in God's house," came her mournful reply. "We can only pray, and hope that the Lord takes pity on her. That He grants her some form of peace."

"I shall place offerings for her in the chapel."

"Yes, yes, of course," she replied distractedly. "But first you and I must meet with Sister Philippa and tell her what has happened. And then we must decide how to tell Marie."

"*What* to tell Marie about Aiglantine is my paramount concern. How will we explain Aiglantine's plight, and why she was forced to abandon Marie? And what to say about the man who fathered her?"

"Let me think on it," Clementia replied wearily. "Most importantly, we cannot dissemble about the gravity of the illness. That Aiglantine has little time to live."

"Unless there is a miracle—"

"Yes, a miracle . . ." Her voice trailed off. "I shall fetch Sister Philippa now," she announced. "Best we ask her counsel, not only in her assessment of Aiglantine's physical condition, and when Marie should meet her, but how to explain these things to the child." To this she added, "Philippa is wise, and has seen a great deal of the world, for better or worse."

# CHAPTER 65

The two women joined me shortly thereafter. "Sister Clementia has told me the story," Sister Philippa said to me. "It is extraordinary that the young woman was able to travel such a distance in her pitiable condition. She is terribly frail and has great difficulty breathing. Her lungs are warm, and there is blood in her phlegm. The poultice seems to have helped her cough, thankfully. And I have given her some figs steeped in a wine, and a syrup of goat's thorn and ginger." She paused, before adding more somberly, "But I do not want you to have any illusions. I treated a similar case last year, and I do not have much hope."

"Then we must not waste any time," I said, exchanging glances with Clementia. "Marie must be told tomorrow."

"Yes, that is what I recommend," said Philippa. "Let the child absorb the news. And then, as soon as I deem Aiglantine strong enough, we will bring the child to her."

"And you do not fear contagion, Sister?" I asked.

"Once several days have passed and the corrupt air around Aiglantine has been purified, and the humoral imbalance addressed, there should be nothing to fear. As for Marie—since you are the two closest to her, I assume you will speak with her together."

"The question is what to tell Marie," Clementia said. "And how much to tell her."

"I think it is best to be completely forthright," advised Philippa at once. "In my experience, children always surmise the truth. It is obfuscation that causes them disquietude."

"Wise counsel, Sister," I murmured.

"Aiglantine will need all His wisdom and help in the coming days," added Sister Philippa. "As she will our prayers." She lowered her head and made the sign of the cross. "Now, if you will excuse me, I shall see if Aiglantine has awakened. If she has, I shall administer the first dose of theriac."

"Theriac?" I asked.

"A panacea, but so costly we rarely use it. I have spent the last hour mixing the ingredients—viper's flesh, cinnamon, gum Arabic. We are privileged here, to have such medicines. And to have patrons who are willing to provide them. But now"—she clasped her hands—"I must return to our patient."

I VISITED AIGLANTINE LATER THAT night and was relieved to find her in better spirits. Her cough had slightly abated: it was without the frighteningly deep rumble that had so alarmed me earlier. I told her I would come see her as soon as possible in the morning, after Clementia and I had spoken with Marie, and then bade her good night. Exhausted, bewildered, and anxious about the impending discussion with the little girl, I returned to my chamber and fell into a fitful sleep.

I was awakened early the next morning by a knocking at the door. Clementia and Marie entered, the former looking rather pale and strained, the latter bright-eyed and buoyant.

I bade them good morrow. "Come, let us sit together by the fire," I said to Marie, who was holding her doll.

"But that is not where we usually have our lesson," said Marie, casting her eyes about.

"We are not going to have a lesson today, Marie," I said softly.

"But why not?" she asked, perplexed, almost petulant, for she adored her lessons.

"Lady Isabelle and I have something we need to tell you," said Clementia. "Come, let us sit together."

Clementia and I drew up a small bench, then a stool for Marie.

"I see that you have dressed Radegonde in her special tunic," I said, glancing at the forget-me-nots.

"I thought she might be cold," she replied, adding proudly, "and I must be a good mother to her."

I smiled gently; then, with a deep breath, I leaned forward, and began. "A dear friend of mine has arrived here unexpectedly. She is very ill. Sister Philippa is taking care of her."

"I like Sister Philippa," Marie said. "She always gives me treats. Licorice drops. But if this woman is very ill, we must pray for her. What is her name?"

"Aiglantine."

"You said she is your friend. How is it you know her?"

"She was my servant in the household of my husband. She was dear to me. Far more like a friend, even a sister, than a servant."

"I always wanted a sister!" said Marie longingly.

I smiled, leaning forward to stroke her hair. "Aiglantine traveled a very long way to come here. It was a wretched journey. She walked most of the way, and only rode in a cart when people took pity on her. She wanted to reach Fontevraud very, very much."

Marie was listening intently. "Aiglantine wanted to see someone who might live here, at Fontevraud," I continued. "Someone she loved deeply." I leant forward, toward Marie. "Imagine *how* much, for her to have taken this journey, all alone! And struggling all the while. She took a great risk to come here."

"She must care about this person very much," surmised Marie.

"Yes, Marie. Very much indeed."

"Who is the person she wanted to see?" Marie asked.

Clementia and I exchanged glances. "She wanted to see if *you* were here, Marie," she said.

"Why? I do not know her."

"But she knows *you*, Marie," I said. And then, taking her hands in mine, I said: "You see, Marie, she is your mother."

"My mother?" Marie's eyes opened wide, uncomprehendingly, as they darted from me to Clementia.

"Yes," I said. "She is your mother. It is she who made the little tunic for your doll. The tunic with the forget-me-nots. She left it in the basket when she deposited you here. You were a tiny baby."

Marie looked up at me, then at Clementia, but remained unnervingly silent.

"And now, you see," Clementia began, "she has returned to see you, because she fears this illness."

"She is afraid she will die," said Marie softly.

"Yes," I said, knowing it was fruitless to dissemble.

"And she wanted to see me, and to know I was well," continued Marie pensively, slowly, deliberately.

"Yes," I said. "Though all this time, she always thought of you, and loved you."

She pondered this; then asked, angrily, "Why did she leave me here, then?"

"She knew she could not give you the life you deserved. The life she wanted for you. She did not want you to be starving and poor. She did not want to go begging with you, and to be at the mercy of others. We have seen such unfortunate people here, have we not?"

She nodded, still stunned, confused. Moments passed before she asked, "But I am already five, and she has never come before." Her expression darkened almost imperceptibly. "Why did she never come to see me before?"

"She was afraid you might be ashamed of her," I replied.

"If she loved me so much, I would *never* have been ashamed!"

"Ah, Marie, if only life were so simple!" I cried. "We know how good you are, how kind, and that you would not have been ashamed. But she did not have that confidence. And perhaps she was fearful that you would be angry with her. But I told Aiglantine that I did not think you would be angry. That I know you would do your best to understand these complicated and difficult things."

The little girl looked down, stroking Radegonde's thatch of wool hair.

"Do you know why Lady Isabelle and I are confident you will not be angry?" asked Clementia softly. "Because it is in your nature, Marie, and also because it is what we have taught you. Think of the stories in the scriptures, Marie, and the parables you love. What do they teach us, most of all?"

"To forgive," she said almost inaudibly, her finger tracing the forget-me-nots again and again. "So she never really forgot me, then," she finally murmured, looking up.

"That is right," I said, smiling through my tears. "All her life she wanted to return to you." I knelt down on the ground beside her and took her hand in mine. "It will make her so happy to see you now, Marie, and to know not only that you are safe. But to see also how much you have learned, how intelligent you are! She will be proud to know that you can read, and even write. No one ever taught Aiglantine these things, you see."

"Does she like stories?" Marie asked after a moment.

"Yes. Very much!" I replied. "She used to love mine."

Her eyes brightened. "Do you think she would like it if I read a story to her? While she is resting, and trying to get well?"

"I think she would like that very much," I replied. "Shall we choose one together for her?"

"Yes," replied Marie, adding, "but it must have a happy ending."

# CHAPTER 66

Two days later, I brought Marie to meet her mother. As we walked hand in hand to the hospital, she glanced up at me nervously once or twice, as if to ask a question, only to remain silent. She had dressed Radegonde in the forget-me-not tunic and held her tight.

When we arrived, Aiglantine was sitting up in bed. Her hair had been carefully brushed, and she was wearing a nightgown I had lent her the night before. The anticipation of seeing her daughter, and Sister Philippa's skillful care, seemed to have greatly improved her condition. Her cheeks had lost much of their pallor; her cough had diminished. She almost resembled the Aiglantine of old.

After one tentative moment of awed silence, she and Marie fell into each other's arms with unforgettable fervor. It was as if Aiglantine had summoned every iota of strength to embrace her lost daughter. I stood to the side, smiling through my tears.

My concern that Marie would feel awkward or nervous was soon quelled as the little girl began merrily chattering: "You must meet Radegonde, too. Look!" she cried, brandishing the doll. "She is wearing the tunic you made. It is her favorite."

"How happy that makes me!" exclaimed Aiglantine.

"Yes, Radegonde likes it when I dress her in the tunic. It keeps her warm, and the posies make it pretty. She also likes to listen to my stories. Lady Isabelle told me that you love stories, too."

Aiglantine was utterly entranced by the little girl. Her eyes followed Marie's every gesture—the expressive way she used her hands, or her habit of tilting her dimpled chin upward as she laughed. "Tell that to me again, Marie!" Aiglantine would say, her attention fastened on each utterance. Or, "Repeat the word you used to describe the stories Rade-gonde likes."

Marie fussed over Aiglantine with the same touching concern and loving kindness she had always shown her doll. She would fix Aiglan-tine's pillow or blanket or ask if she needed some tisane or a spoonful of hyssop syrup.

Shortly before an hour had elapsed, I suggested that I leave the two alone for a little while. "Would you like that, Marie?"

She nodded happily. "I shall take good care of Aiglantine, I prom-ise," she said.

FOR THE NEXT WEEK, AS Aiglantine slowly gained strength, she and Marie spent part of each day together. Marie would read to her, or re-count stories about her life at the abbey. Aiglantine told her about her family, and how she came to work at the castle of Gerard; about first meeting me, and how our friendship grew. She told Marie about the mews, and the falcons, and about Raoul and Corbus. Marie loved hear-ing about Corbus most of all: the notion that he could "speak" with animals and knew each twist and turn of the forest.

After her visits with Aiglantine, Marie would arrive for her lesson even more animated than usual. But after about five days or so, when she appeared, she seemed rather serious and quiet.

"Is there something troubling you, Marie?" I asked.

"Do you think it would be proper—" she began, before stopping abruptly.

"Go on."

"Do you think it would be proper if I asked Aiglantine today if I might call her 'Maman'?"

"Why, of course! I am sure nothing in the world would make her happier."

The joy of reuniting with her daughter, together with rest and nourishment, seemed to help Aiglantine immensely. To our delight, lit-tle by little she was able to stand, then to walk about. "I am feeling so much better!" she said one afternoon as we proceeded slowly through the outer hall together. "Surely it is time to fetch my family. I know I am strong enough to see them now."

"I believe you are strong enough. I shall discuss it with Sister Philippa and see if she agrees."

She smiled gratefully, but then her expression changed. "Remember what you promised me," she said, somberly, taking my hand in hers. "My family must never know about Marie! My mother especially would be so ashamed to discover I had a child born in sin."

I reassured her that the secret would remain with me, as it would with Clementia and Philippa.

Later that day, I met Philippa at the hospital before she made her rounds. I told her I had seen Aiglantine earlier and thought her well enough to see her family. "She is better," she concurred, after examining her. "We will send a message to her family tomorrow morning saying that her condition has improved. That they should come soon."

Early the following afternoon, however, Sister Philippa came to my chamber looking grim. "I have just seen Aiglantine. The cough has returned. It is deeper and more ominous."

"But she has seemed so much stronger!" I protested.

"Until now, yes. But alas, this is what I feared—that she would not be able to sustain such a marked improvement."

"Please, let me go to her now!"

"I should not permit it," she replied, sighing deeply. "But I shall, knowing you will brook no opposition. Come—we shall go together."

We walked quickly to the hospital. The moment I saw Aiglantine, ashen white and listless, I knew that she had taken a turn for the worse.

By nightfall, a harrowing fever took hold: she tossed and turned, almost delirious, as if her body were on fire. She was bled, she was given more theriac, but still the fever raged.

Later that night Sister Philippa and I watched as Aiglantine, now deathly pale, fought for each breath. Her head tossed feverishly, incessantly, upon the pillow; the cough became frightening; she began to spit up blood.

"Perhaps this is her way of expunging the evil elements that make her ill," I said imploringly to Philippa.

"We can only entreat God to vanquish the ills that have overtaken her," she replied, making the sign of the cross. "Come, let us kneel and pray for her."

A few hours past midnight, Aiglantine, struggling to sit up, called my name.

"I am here!" I said, clutching my rosary as I drew closer.

She looked up, her eyes luminous, almost otherworldly. "It is time," she murmured. "He calls me." Her head fell gently back upon the pillow.

Tears streamed down my cheeks. I turned my face away, unwilling for her to see me weep—an irrational gesture born out of shock and grief. I wiped away the tears and turned back to comfort her.

But Aiglantine was no more.

## Chapter 67

It fell to me to tell Marie, and later, Aiglantine's family, the terrible news. The little girl was stunned and inconsolable, even, at moments, angry. "Why did God take her away from me?" she tearfully protested. It became heartbreakingly clear that dear little Marie had almost felt she could *will* her mother to health and long life.

Familiar as they were to privation and death, and sustained by faith in God, Aiglantine's mother, brother, and sister, however disconsolate, were far more accepting. "During her final days, she expressed her love for all of you," I told them. "Her greatest hope was that she might see you again."

I never mentioned the existence of Marie. My promises to Aiglantine—that her mother should never know of a granddaughter born in sin, and that Marie should be raised at the abbey—remained engraven on my heart; I was relieved that the abbess and the sisters had agreed to honor Aiglantine's final request.

The abbess, in her kindness, granted Aiglantine, an unwed mother, all proper funeral rites, and the permission to be buried in the abbey's cemetery. This touched and gratified me: I knew it was as much a tribute to me and my feelings for Aiglantine as it was out of deference to Marie.

IN THE WAKE OF THE funeral, I replayed Aiglantine's final days in my mind, anguishing over what we might have done differently.

"We did all we possibly could!" Clementia comforted me one morning as we sat in the cloister. "As did Sister Philippa."

"But perhaps we did not give the theriac soon enough," I agonized. "Perhaps it was wrong of me to encourage her to rise from bed, to walk about a little—"

"Nonsense!" interjected Clementia. "You must stop this. And most of all, you must be strong for her daughter. It will not help Marie to see you this way."

"I have told her she need not have her lessons this week. Let the child rest and play with her doll."

"That is hardly what I would recommend! It is more important than ever that Marie adhere to her normal regimen. Do you not see? She loves her lessons. They will distract her—and perhaps you as well—from sadness." Clementia took my hand. "We all wanted Aiglantine to live, but we knew from the beginning there was little chance. The reunion with Marie was joyous, yes, but was it not also tinged with sadness from the start? None of us thought her mother would survive long."

I nodded numbly. "Yes, I suppose you are right."

"God chose to give Marie the joy of meeting her mother. And then, in His wisdom, He chose to take her mother away."

"Why 'in His *wisdom*'?" I asked bitterly.

"Because I believe it is part of God's design that children not be deprived of suffering." She added gently, "You see, Isabelle, I trust in Him in a way that you have yet to achieve. Come," she said, standing up. "Let us take Marie for a walk in the garden. Then, later today, promise you will resume her lessons."

"What shall I tell her?"

"Tell her to remember how proud her mother was that she could read and write. And that her mother watches over her now, from heaven."

I soon saw the wisdom of Clementia's advice. The resumption of lessons and of learning seemed to help assuage not only Marie's sadness, but also my own. Not once, however, did she mention her mother's name. This concerned me; I felt it was better for her to voice her grief.

One morning when Marie appeared for her lesson, I ventured, "I see that Radegonde has not been wearing the tunic Aiglantine made."

"It is too soon for her to wear it. She is in mourning."

"I see," I murmured. "And when will mourning end?"

"When I tell her."

"Quite right," I said, embracing her. "It must be your decision."

THE FOLLOWING MORNING, WHILE I was giving Marie her lesson, Heraldis burst through the door.

"Sister Clementia asks that you come to the *tour*, my lady," she said, her ruddy face alight with curiosity.

"What has happened?" I asked.

"Someone has just arrived with a letter for you. From your family, I believe."

"Oh dear," I murmured, fearing the worst—that my father was ill, or that he had passed away. "I shall come at once." I stood up and turned to Marie. She looked anxious. "Stay here with Heraldis and continue practicing your letters. If I cannot return shortly, I shall let you know."

I donned my cape, walking so quickly that I arrived at the *tour* out of breath. There stood the same messenger whom Guy had dispatched months earlier: a scruffy young fellow on a shriveled mount. As soon as I approached, he handed me a slightly bulky package.

After thanking him, I instructed him to go to the stable for fresh provisions. He managed a clumsy bow and left.

I went into a small antechamber near the *tour*, settled on the bench, and untied the package. A letter addressed to me in my brother's hand lay within; it was loosely secured to a small, but slightly weighty packet wrapped in a linen pouch and tied with a silken cord.

The letter read:

*To the Lady Isabelle, from her brother, Guy de Lapalisse*

It is my fervent hope that this missive finds you well, and that you are continuing to thrive in the blessed atmosphere of the abbey. I hope, as well, that you will send my warm regards to Sister Clementia, whom I greatly admire, as you know, and who seemed such an exemplary mentor when I last saw you. No doubt she has been enquiring when I shall return for another visit. Tell her to have no fear! I fully intend to make my way north early next spring, when I venture to the fair at Troyes.

When I do, I would like to spend some contemplative time at Fontevraud and also resume the immensely illuminating discussions with Sister Clementia I remember so fondly.

I should tell you about our family before discoursing on other matters. Father has become rather deaf, a condition commensurate with his age, of course, but unfortunate nonetheless. This has allowed Hortense to exert even more influence. She has become increasingly familiar with him as well, despite my attempts to discipline her. Arnaut continues, predictably, to remain irresponsible and elusive. We have had no word from him. There is a rumor he is in Syria.

Amélie, Balduin, and their children, by contrast, remain constant, delightful presences in our lives. Amélie is with child once more: you can imagine how this blessed news has pleased Father, especially in light of your own situation.

Recounting these domestic concerns in extenso, however, is not the purpose of my writing you. I enclose herewith a letter for you—a small package, rather—which was delivered by a messenger from your former husband's domain only yesterday. Anyone else must have been tempted to open the letter and the package before sending it on to you. But, as you know, I am far too honorable a man to commit such an indiscretion.

I did, naturally, try to inquire what this package might include, and the nature of the contents. But the messenger resolutely would not say: he was instructed to say they were meant for only you. I informed him that you no longer resided with us but had retired to an abbey in the Loire Valley. A very prominent abbey patronized by the Plantagenets, I did add. Once again, discretion forbade me to say anything more, and certainly not to a lowly messenger. Rather, I asked that he remain overnight, so that I might give him a letter to take to the Lord de Meurtaigne the following day acknowledging the receipt of the package, and assuring him that I would forward it to you. To this generous offer, the messenger was most grateful. He

also informed me that the Lord de Meurtaigne would be traveling by the time I received this—an urgent trip to Marseilles
to resolve a disputed claim to property he recently purchased.
Therefore it was doubtful he would read my letter until after his
return in a month or so.

I trust you will concur that I felt it only right to send a
proper letter to your former husband. It has always seemed to
me expedient not to make an enemy of him. In addition, the
tenets of courtoisie, of which I am known to be an exemplar,
also demand that I address him with the respect due a nobleman of his rank.

Thus, in my letter, I mentioned that I had seen you in the
spring, and that you seemed to be thriving at the Abbey of
Fontevraud. I thought it prudent—indeed, humane, as a good
Christian—to assure him that you were quite recovered from
the travails of your divorce. That you were devoting yourself to
penitence and the work of Our Lord, even if you had not yet
taken the veil. *Nota bene* that I say "yet," always hoping that this
hovers as a possibility, dear sister.

I also mentioned that you had come to the abbey under
the auspices of the Lady Fastrada, and that you were working
quite closely with her sister, the good Sister Clementia. Surely
you will agree it is best he know that we are no strangers to the
exalted noblesse of Troyes.

Lastly, do not trouble yourself with the expense incurred by
my sending a messenger such a great distance. Though it might
behoove you, on the part of our family, to mention our reputation for largesse to Sister Clementia.

I relay my warmest wishes to you, dear sister, and with them
the hope that I shall see you again in the spring.

A postscript followed his signature:

If you feel it would be helpful to discuss the contents of the letter I am forwarding, please do not hesitate to write me. Suffice it to say I am always ready to impart the sage advice that only an older brother can provide.

I set Guy's letter aside and looked uneasily at the parcel from Gerard. I picked it up and hastily untied the cord: inside lay a letter, and with it, a small, sealed wooden box. I held the box, wondering what it contained—a gift, perhaps? Yet that seemed unlikely.

The letter was stamped with the Meurtaigne crest. The thick, ragged impression appeared to have been done hurriedly, for there were errant drops of red wax scattered over the surface of the heavy parchment.

A sense of foreboding came over me as I broke open the seal and began to read:

*From Gerard, Lord de Meurtaigne, to the Lady Isabelle*

Several years have passed since we parted, during which time we have exchanged no word. I suspect that the arrival of my letter has surprised, perhaps even unsettled you. Why "unsettled"? one might ask. Did we not part in good faith, and wish each other well? I thought we had. Or so it seemed.

I have remarried: my wife is a noblewoman, like yourself, though of a different character—patient and selfless. Indeed, her patience extended to Aiglantine, whom she continued to employ, despite the latter's increasing moodiness. Recently, however, when illness made it impossible for Aiglantine to work, my wife was forced to engage a new servant.

The servant approached her duties with refreshing diligence and meticulousness; part of her regimen included a thorough cleaning of our bedchamber. While doing so, she turned over the mattress and discovered something strange, something which had to have been placed there during my marriage to you: an object tucked between the mattress and the bed frame.

The object in question was an amulet of jet. But this should come as no surprise, for it was *you*, no doubt, who secretly placed it there. About your intent there can be no question. Everyone knows this insidious black stone is meant to prevent a woman from conception.

And so, Isabelle, I have concluded this: during a great part of our marriage, and with remarkable cunning, you deceived me. You pretended to take measures to encourage pregnancy, whereas, all the while, you were doing the opposite. No doubt Anthusis played her part in this monstrous scheme. Who, then, was the greater witch? That hideous creature you frequented in the forest, or *you*?

Had your ruse merely affected the years we were married, I might have a more measured reaction. But in leaving the talisman behind, you perpetuated its spell. My wife has been unable to conceive. Now I know why.

I wonder how you will greet this news: whether you will repent your twisted actions. It matters not a whit. Your intent was clear.

Know this above all: I will have retribution. It is merely a question of how, and when.

His signature followed: a phalanx of tall, jagged letters, the first and last penned with such force the nib had perforated the page. The bold vertical strokes, and the thick blotches of ink, only seemed to invest the final menacing salvo—"I will have retribution. It is merely a question of how, and when"—with even more brutality. Trembling, I set the letter down; then I bent over, my arms clutched around me.

Moments passed before I realized, with still more apprehension, that one unopened item remained: the little box, which lay on my lap. But each time my fingers ventured to break the seal, I found myself drawing back. Finally, I forced myself to open it. There, within, lay the jet amulet—black, insidious, and glimmering, it stared at me as if it contained all the evidence of my sins and guilt.

At that moment, terror transmuted itself into self-loathing; I began to berate myself. How could I have been so careless? I had been scrupulous about everything else around my leave-taking—the parceling out of my clothes, the packing up of my secret objects—and had neglected to address the most crucial element of all: the object I had hidden beneath the mattress.

How long I remained on the bench I am not certain. Eventually I placed the smooth, oval stone back into its box, and the box into the linen pouch, together with Gerard's letter. I knew I must discard the jet and burn the letter; that no one must ever, ever see what Gerard had disclosed, no one must ever discover the sins against God I had committed—not Clementia, not Marie. I forced myself to think clearly, to decide what, in fact, to reveal to Clementia. She was due to arrive at any moment, and I would need her help, if I was to survive.

I heard a knocking at the door; as Clementia entered, I stood up, unsteadily. "I have been concerned," she said, hastening toward me. "Did you receive bad news? You are deathly pale. What is wrong?"

"Come," I said, taking her arm. "Let us go to my chamber. I shall tell you what has happened."

# CHAPTER 68

When we arrived at my chamber, I drew up a small bench for her by the hearth and took a seat opposite. Then, slowly and carefully, I described the essence of the letter—its menacing tone, its final threat. "Gerard rages that I have ruined his life," I told her. "That my barrenness, somehow, has cast a spell upon him and his new wife, and her ability to conceive. He is a vengeful man, as you know, and quick to punish when things do not go his way. He will never rest until he finds retribution."

All the while Clementia sat utterly still, her hands folded in her lap, her calm azure eyes never wavering from my face. "'Vengeance is mine, I will repay,'" she murmured, slowly shaking her head. She stood up and began to walk silently back and forth before the window. "One thing is certain," she announced, stopping to face me. "You must leave at once. It is only a matter of time before he finds you here. And I am not sure even *we* could protect you. Even abbeys are not always safe places—not when they are confronted by a man like Gerard. No, you must go far away. You must leave the country." Then, decisively: "You will go to England."

"To England?" I asked, stupefied.

"You will go to the queen at Salisbury," she replied. "Only recently, she requested a companion—someone to read to her, to converse with her, to take her dictation, and to play chess. It must be a young woman connected with Fontevraud. Queen Eleanor insists upon it, and the king, whose family also has connections with the abbey, has agreed to it." She added wryly, "That in itself is a triumph."

"But are you quite *sure*, Clementia?" I stammered. For a moment I thought I had misunderstood the import of her words. I could not believe this thrilling idea to be true—that I should actually meet Queen Eleanor. "Are you quite sure that I would be suitable? As companion to the queen? After all—"

"I have no doubt whatsoever. Even you—who do not trust in God as fully as I do—can only conclude that He must have had a part in this plan. Is it not strange that we should need someone to go to England, just when it is necessary for you to leave the country? And at the root of this"—she shook her head slowly, reflectively—"another coincidence of sorts: two women punished, each in a different way, by a vengeful husband!"

"Yes, it is almost uncanny," I replied with a rueful laugh, only to be assailed the next moment by the danger and enormity of the undertaking. It would be immeasurably exciting to meet the queen, and to journey to England; but once again I would be forced to abandon all that was familiar for life with strangers in a foreign place. I would leave the abbey, I would leave France, and I would leave Marie.

"You look rather somber," she remarked. "What are you thinking, Isabelle?"

"How wrenching it will be to leave the abbey. To leave all of you. Most of all, to leave Marie!" My eyes filled with tears. "She has just lost her mother, and now she will also lose me."

"That is true, but you must also remember you are very fortunate," she replied in a firm, almost reprimanding tone. "*You* have a means to escape. Most women do not. And I have seen firsthand the terrible things such women have endured."

"You are right, Clementia," I replied, chastened. "If I were to remain here, I would have no peace. I would live each moment in terror. One day, surely, Gerard would find me here, and then"—I shuddered, remembering how savagely he had punished Gallien—"it would be terrible. So I am very fortunate indeed to be able to escape." As I spoke, my spirits began to lift, as if I had truly just begun to grasp the reality of the adventure that lay ahead: I would cross the Channel and see England. And I would meet Queen Eleanor herself, the queen who had captivated me since childhood!

My palpable change of mood seemed to content her, for her expression softened. "Yes," she nodded, "you will be safe in England, ensconced with the queen. Even Gerard de Meurtaigne could never reach you, or harm you, there." She placed her hand gently upon my shoulder. "And who knows? Perhaps, one day, you might be able to return to us. Perhaps his wife will finally bear a child, an heir, and his appetite for revenge will wane. We must all pray for that." She continued with new fervency, "Just as we pray that one day King Henry will release Eleanor. That she will be able to return to France, at last, perhaps even to Fontevraud." She touched the cross that lay beneath her wimple. "One man above all is hoping for this," she added in a low, wistful voice, "and doing all he can to achieve his mother's freedom."

"Who is that?"

"The queen's son Prince Richard, of course. He is her greatest ally, and his father the king's greatest foe." She stood up. "But that is another matter. You have absorbed quite enough for one day. Come, let us walk together and discuss what you will tell Marie about your departure."

# CHAPTER 69

The next morning, with an aching heart, I told Marie that I had been entrusted to carry out an urgent journey involving the sister abbey at Amesbury; and that I would leave in several days for England.

"It cannot be!" she cried.

"Alas, it must. I have no choice, my darling."

"What about our lessons? Who will teach me? Who will keep me company?"

"Sister Clementia will be here with you. And Mother Gilles, and all of the sisters who are your family here." She had begun to cry. "I know this is especially hard, since you have just lost your mother. I know!" I took her into my arms. "We all know. But God sometimes asks us to do difficult things."

She burst out sobbing. Still I held her tight, trying to comfort her as I stroked the silky dark hair on the back of her head, and drew in her sweet girlish scent. "But now you must be brave. You must think of our stories! Think of my stories about the queen, and how brave she has always been."

"But you *must* return here," she implored through tears, "please say you *will!*"

"I hope to, dearest," I replied gently, knowing all too well that if I ever were to return, it would be years henceforth.

"No, 'hope to' is not good enough! Swear on my medal of the Virgin that you will return as soon as you are able!"

I touched the little medal she wore around her neck. "But now *you*, too, must promise me something, Marie. You must promise to be brave, and to continue your lessons with Sister Clementia."

"I shall. But it will not be the same. I shall miss your stories! Sister Clementia does not know stories, as you do."

"I shall leave some for her to read to you. And perhaps you will invent some on your own. You can write very well now, and I shall ask Sister Clementia that you be given some parchment and all you need to set your stories down."

"As much parchment as I want?"

"Yes," I said, brushing some tears from her cheek. "As much as you want. I shall ask Sister Perpetua to show you how to bind your stories into a little book. And there is something else I shall ask—"

"What is that?" she asked, both wary and curious.

"I shall ask Sister Clementia that you learn to ride." I chucked her lightly under the chin as I asked, "You would like that, would you not?"

She gave a tentative nod. "But you must leave something of your own here, with me," she insisted. "Something precious of *yours* here, so that I know you will return for it."

"Tell me, and I shall leave it for you."

She planted her chin on her fist, thinking hard. Finally she looked up. "The bronze falcon! Yes, you must leave it here to keep me company. And to remind me of you."

"And so I shall," I said, kissing her forehead. "So I shall."

DURING THE FOLLOWING FRANTIC DAYS, terror, the necessity to flee, and most of all, the thrill of the adventure ahead energized me and somewhat mitigated my sadness in leaving Fontevraud. In England, I reassured myself incessantly, I would be safe, I would be protected by the queen; even if Gerard were to discover my whereabouts, he could never hurt me there!

The day before my leave-taking, Clementia requested to speak with me privately—"To give you some instructions about the journey, and about the queen," she added. I admit that the notion I would meet Queen Eleanor still seemed almost ludicrous: there were moments when I had to pinch myself to believe this would shortly come to pass. Clementia described what I might expect of the week-long journey to Barfleur, the trip across the Channel, and how I would be brought to the queen.

"When you arrive at Salisbury, you will need to tell the man who greets you a password. I shall give it to you shortly. I suggest you record it somewhere—you will be nervous, no doubt." With a teasing smile, she added, "Perhaps you should record the password in a code?"

"That had already occurred to me," I replied, returning her smile.

"Excellent thinking." She gave me the password. "I shall ask you to repeat it just before you leave." Her expression suddenly softened as she asked, gravely, "How are your spirits, Isabelle?"

"I am a bit frightened," I admitted. "And I shall be so relieved, most of all, when I am on my way and settled in a place where Gerard cannot reach me! I know it would only be a question of time before he found me here. But, of course, I am excited to think of being a companion to the queen—"

"It is a strange twist of fate, is it not, Isabelle," she mused, "that you will actually *meet* the queen, who has fascinated you for so many years?"

"Yes, without question!" I walked over to the falcon and touched its enameled feathers. "Marie asked me to leave something of my own with her," I said, turning to Clementia. "Something I would return here for. She asked for this falcon. Will you place it in her chamber after I leave?"

"Of course!"

My hand still resting upon the bronze creature, I reflected, "It is strange, Clementia. When my husband gave me this, I was rather wary of it. There were moments when I avoided its eyes. But now I feel quite differently, as if the falcon were an old, sometimes perplexing, friend. Perhaps seeing it through Marie's eyes has changed my feelings."

"That would not surprise me," she replied. "Children often teach us as much as we teach them. And then there is another factor, of course—"

"And what is that?"

"The passage of time. Time alters perspective."

"'The passage of time,'" I repeated, overcome by a wave of despair. "Who knows how much time will pass before I am to return here, if I ever do?"

"You must trust that you are in God's hands, Isabelle dear. We can only pray for Him to guide and protect you."

At dawn the following morning, the abbess, Clementia, and Marie, clutching Radegonde, gathered together in the courtyard by the *tour*. To the side stood Pierre, the simple, taciturn young fellow who would accompany me to Barfleur; behind him, at a slight distance, the groom managing the packhorse awaited.

The moment Marie glimpsed me, she wrested herself from Clementia's grasp and ran to me. "You cannot leave!" she wailed, tugging again and again at my hem. "I shall not let you!"

I knelt down and embraced her. "I know how terribly hard this is, dear Marie," I said. "It is very hard for me, too. But you promised me you would be a brave girl, did you not—and you would never want to break a promise to me, would you?"

"*This* time I might!"

"Dearest Marie"—I tenderly stroked her hair—"that does not sound like you. Not the brave little girl I know, the Marie I am proud of. Promise me to be brave!" I glanced at her doll, which she held tight. "I am sure Radegonde wants you to be brave, does she not?"

She nodded reluctantly, then wiped her eyes with her fist. "Did you leave the falcon for me?"

"Yes. It will be in your chamber. I promised you, did I not? Just as I promised to return. And I would never *ever* break a promise. Now you, too, must keep your word. Will you?"

Finally, and ever so reluctantly, she nodded. "You *promise* to return to me and your falcon?"

"I promise to do my very best," I said, my voice choking up as I kissed the top of her head. "Come now," I said, taking her hand as we walked to Clementia and the abbess.

"Come, Marie," said Clementia, extending her hand to the little girl.

"Not yet!" Marie protested fiercely. "Lady Isabelle has not left yet!"

"Very well," conceded Clementia. "But have you not forgotten something?"

At that, Marie walked to a basket set on the ground nearby; reaching inside, she drew out a small bouquet of flowers, then a little book.

"These are for you," she said, offering the bouquet to me. "The last flowers of autumn. I gathered them myself."

"How lovely!" I exclaimed, fighting tears as I fingered the petals. "Roses, pinks, rosemary, and myrtle. And lavender, too!"

"Sister Clementia said you should place the flowers by the statue of the Virgin at the crossroad and say a prayer for your safe journey."

"I shall, darling Marie," I said, embracing her. "And I shall say another prayer to the Virgin, as well, that she watch over you, my dearest."

She smiled tentatively. "And I have something else to give you," she said, handing me the book. "I have written two poems and a story for you." Then, proudly, "And inside the cover, look!"

She had pressed dried forget-me-nots onto the frontispiece. I looked up, unable to arrest my tears, and hugged her with all my strength. "Of course I shall never forget you, *ever!* And I shall keep this book with me always."

"Come now, Marie," said Clementia, trying to take her by the hand.

"No! I want to stay by Lady Isabelle until the very last moment!" she replied defiantly.

"Let her," I said gently.

"You must not tarry, Isabelle," admonished Clementia. As the two of us embraced, she whispered: "Tell me the password."

I did so. "Good," she murmured. As we stood face-to-face, she added, "Remember, Isabelle. You must try to trust in the ways of our Lord."

"I shall try. But most of all I trust *you.*"

She smiled wistfully, her eyes cast down in such a way I noticed the glistening of tears on her thick, blond lashes.

I came to the abbess next; Caprice was perched on her shoulder—a sprightly, even ludicrous, touch on that sad whirlwind of a day. "May the Lord guide you, in all ways," she said, making the sign of the cross. "Adieu, my child," she added, embracing me. "Adieu, my child!" came the raucous echo from Caprice. "Adieu, Caprice," I murmured, with a sad smile.

Finally, I turned to Marie. "The time has come, dear Marie. I must mount now."

"No!" She began to sob.

"Remember your promise to me—"

Clementia took Marie firmly by the hand. "Marie will not disappoint you," she said gently, bending down to wipe the little girl's face with her handkerchief. "She will be brave, and make us proud."

I wiped my own tears with my gloved hand and mounted with Pierre's help. The gates were slowly opened by Lothar, the man with the limp who had greeted me and LaFoi upon our arrival. The sun shone; the wind was mild; everything about the day itself was beneficent, as if God himself had orchestrated the journey.

"Set off!" signaled Pierre.

I turned to wave goodbye, trying to manage a smile, but then I glimpsed Marie sobbing, and quickly faced forward again. My heart was heavy; even the fear that propelled me, and my love of adventure, did not seem to protect me from the stabbing loneliness I felt the moment the gates of the abbey closed behind us.

We arrived shortly afterward at the statue of the Virgin by the crossroad. The base was bare of flowers, and I was glad to have Marie's bouquet to leave as an offering. I knelt, uttered a fervent prayer, and remounted.

THE FINE WEATHER HELD; THE journey was swift and uneventful. Little by little, the relief of escaping Gerard's reach, and the thrill of travel, began to lift my spirits. Soon I shall see the sea! I thought to myself as we passed into Normandy and came closer to the coast. I tried to imagine Duke William and his men gathering here centuries before, as they prepared to cross the Channel in advance of the great battle at Hastings.

On a Tuesday at noon, we arrived at Barfleur—a dazzling sight! The chaos of tall, conflicting masts, of billowing sails and foreign flags; and beyond, a tranquil, gleaming green sea that seemed at odds with the tumult of the port.

As we approached the docks we dismounted and began to slowly weave our way through the teeming crowd, with its mélange of strident scents and noise, merchants hawking cloth and furs, cocky sailors ambling among haughty noblemen, swarthy women in exotic costumes babbling in foreign tongues. One moment, a legate from Rome sauntered through, leading a mount splendidly caparisoned in scarlet and white; I had seen such an emissary years ago, during my visit to Nîmes with my brothers. I gazed at him, overcome with memories of that first, momentous journey.

Pierre negotiated my passage with a boat—the *Bête Bleue*—and we took rooms at an inn nearby for the night. I barely slept, yet the following morning I brimmed with energy.

My luggage had already been loaded on the boat. The captain, a gruff, leathery little man, extended his hand and helped me board. "First time across the Channel?"

"Yes."

"You are lucky, my lady. The weather has held. It will be a swift crossing."

"How long will it take?"

"Six hours. More or less."

We set sail. As I watched the harbor slowly recede from view, my fears slowly receded as well, and my thoughts turned to the adventure ahead in the country I had so long imagined—England.

*Incipit vita nova.*

# PART IV

# CHAPTER 70

I spent my first sea voyage in misery, fighting nausea. From time to time the kindly young boatman descended to administer a remedy of quince and chervil to me, alas, to no effect.

I had suffered a similar disorienting queasiness when I had been with child. As the boat pitched and swayed, my mind began to toss and turn with memories of my two pregnancies and the babies I had lost—Editha, especially. And then I thought of Gerard's discovery of the jet amulet; terror swept through me. As the hours passed, I struggled as much with inner tumult as I did with a roiling stomach.

At last, to my immense relief, the boatman informed me that we were nearing Southampton. The motion of the waves began to subside; my condition mercifully improved, and so did my spirits. Somewhat unsteadily, I made my way up to the deck, shielding myself from a light rain just as we approached the great port.

We docked and I disembarked, grateful to set foot on terra firma. The light was dismal; all was devoid of any color other than brown and gray. People rushed to and fro, as one boat, then another, was unloaded.

The captain stood beside me as I looked ahead, scanning the crowd. "I was told someone would be here to meet me," I said somewhat nervously.

"Someone will, by and by, my lady."

"What is this quay called?"

"West Quay. Castle Quay, over there, to the north"—he gestured in that direction—"is only used for the king's affairs."

My energy revived, I took in the chaotic scene: traders shouted to each other in a strange, guttural language; rowdy men hoisted huge wine barrels onto carts; others loaded wagons with bundles of wool or unruly stacks of sheepskin. Two men with scabbards strapped to their waists filed past, their faces so disfigured by scars that I flinched. "Mercenaries," the captain muttered. "Flemish, I reckon."

I turned around, startled by a sudden, fierce squawk; a man carrying a cage with a hooded white falcon had appeared. I thought of Gerard, and the day when the breeder from Valkenswaard had arrived with Vainqueur. How long ago that seemed . . .

A tall, bearded man with reddish hair and a trim leather tunic strode toward us. There was a strikingly purposeful, authoritative air about him; I noticed how the crowds parted as he passed. After greeting the captain, he turned to me with a quick, penetrating glance. "You are Lady Isabelle, I assume?"

"Yes."

"The password?"

I uttered it.

He nodded, introduced himself as Tancred de Bernay, and said he had been sent to escort me to Salisbury. "Where is your baggage?" he asked.

"Over there."

"Good. All is in order, then. The boy will load the things." He spoke with great decisiveness in a fine, but not noble, Norman accent. "Our mounts are ahead," he said. "Come this way."

I bade goodbye to the captain and followed Tancred. We came to our mounts: mine was gleaming, sleek and black. "What is its name?" I asked, stroking its flank.

"Vitesse."

I smiled. "Let us hope he lives up to his name."

"He will, my lady," came his decisive reply. "I assure you."

"How long will the journey to Salisbury take?"

"Two hours, perhaps slightly more. The boy will follow with your baggage." He gestured to a young man with a packhorse who stood to the side, at a slight distance.

We wove our way through the teeming street, passing through the great tollgate to the north. As we set forth on the open road, Tancred maintained a fast pace; there was not a moment to linger, nor for me to pause and ask questions about this rough, alien land.

After a short time, we came to a smaller port. A band of shackled, emaciated men was being herded onto a boat—Saxon slaves, no doubt. With their grim, shuffling gait and filthy, ragged clothes, they looked like beings about to cross the River Styx; I could not even bear to look at them. Gallien had been part of such a Saxon "cargo" once. I thought of him and of all he had suffered as we continued on our way.

We progressed through villages and forbidding forests, past crossroads marked with crude stone monuments incised with primitive circular insignias. As we galloped, the wind beating against my cheeks, I thought fleetingly of the rides I had once so enjoyed with Gerard; then I began to imagine, with mounting excitement, the adventure ahead. Was it really possible that I would soon meet the queen? The queen I had admired since childhood, the queen my mother had scorned, calling her "sinful," "unwomanly," and "born of a line of devils." I thought of Bertuccio, the trader, and how he had described the queen, and "the aura of power" she radiated. But it was Fastrada's words that echoed most insistently in my mind as we rode toward Salisbury: "Eleanor is drawn to intrigue as a hawk to a hare."

MIDWAY THROUGH THE RIDE, WE came upon a statue of the Virgin by the side of the road, a few withered blossoms at her feet. Her features were rather pinched, her expression forlorn; she seemed only distantly related to her rosy-cheeked French peers. With a pang I thought of Marie and the bouquet she had given me, and of the prayers I had offered at the crossroad upon leaving Fontevraud.

The sun was setting when we approached the outskirts of Salisbury. "There," said Tancred, pointing ahead. "Salisbury tower. We have made good time."

I gazed in wonder at the citadel—the most formidable stronghold I had ever seen. We galloped to the edge of the moat. Brilliant red banners with lions rampant flew above us, snapping in the wind. It began to rain hard; I drew my hood closer.

Tancred sounded his horn—once, then twice, then once again. The watchmen above the ramparts returned the signal, and the drawbridge began to descend. "Come ahead," Tancred ordered me. As we rode slowly across, I felt my eyes drawn to one side, then the other, of the vast, impregnable moat. Darkness was falling. Soon the water would no longer be mirrorlike and steely gray, but black and pitiless. I felt a tremor of fear.

Two guards, their long shining swords crisscrossing the portcullis, manned the gate. Tancred exchanged a few words with them; the men bade us enter; the portcullis opened; and then, ever so slowly, we rode inside.

We guided our mounts carefully up a long, steep ramp, its cobblestones gleaming from the rain; the slippery stones made each step precarious. Flames from massive torches flickered high against the walls; our figures cast huge, looming shadows upon them, making it seem we had been transformed into giants.

Two grooms, young and fair, awaited us in an inner courtyard and helped us to dismount. "This way," ordered Tancred.

We walked through several more torchlit corridors, and then through a series of stone arches and narrow vaulted halls until we came to a winding staircase. We mounted one flight, then another, until, at last, we reached the top, where a tall doorway, inset with a motif of lions in wrought iron, loomed before us. Two guards of startling height stood at attention: their features were rough-hewn, their eyes watery blue, their hair white-blond. They reminded me of Ragnar; I shivered.

Tancred turned to me. "Now we enter the queen's domain."

"Wait!" I whispered. "You have given me no instructions. Am I allowed to look straight ahead, or must I keep my head bowed as I approach the queen?"

"Straight ahead. 'No deflected faces.' The queen's commands."

We stepped into a lofty octagonal room, its walls bare of decoration. Flames leaped from a monumental stone hearth, their raucous crackles mingling with the monotonous sound of rain beating against the shutters. The air here was pleasantly warm and infused with an unfamiliar scent, both bittersweet and spicy.

At a slight distance, between two tall arched windows, in a throne-like chair, sat the queen. She wore a robe of dark red, which fell to the ground in swirling folds, and stroked a small black-and-white creature nestled in her lap. A chess set stood on the table to her right.

Her eyes were cast down; she had not moved since I entered—indeed I had the impression she had not noticed me at all. Therefore I was startled when she beckoned me to approach. "Come, girl," she said, in a rich, melodic voice. "I may appear an aged monument. But rest assured—I still live and breathe."

I came as close as I felt permissible.

She looked at me rather wearily, all the while stroking her pet, a sleek little ermine. "This is the girl?" the queen asked.

"Yes," Tancred replied. "The countess. From Fontevraud."

I made a low curtsey before her.

"Come closer," she commanded, severing the air with one impatient gesture of her ringed hand.

Never before had I seen a woman who was old (she must have been about sixty) yet alluring. Her fair skin was wrinkled, but her vivid dark eyes, framed by a luxuriant expanse of brow, were still beautiful and bespoke an undaunted spirit. Her wide gold belt fell just below a waist that had remained youthfully slender, and the bodice of her red samite gown was tightly laced. Her hands, however, looked aged: no number of rings—a large amethyst, another with a cameo—could mask the bony, speckled fingers.

"You came by way of Southampton?" she asked, all the while stroking the ermine. Her voice was distinctive, and her elegant accent familiar to me, for it was not unlike my grandfather's.

"Yes, Your Majesty."

"You are tired after the voyage, no doubt." This was uttered as an observation, with no hint of sympathy.

"I am not tired in the least," I said, determined to hold my ground.

"Why not?"

"The journey was an adventure. Adventures are never tiring—they fill me with energy."

"I am glad it seemed an adventure to you," she replied, a note of approval in her voice.

She looked down, her long fingers caressing the ermine. "Was this your first journey across the Channel?" she asked, without looking up.

"Yes."

"Your first outside France?"

"Yes."

"It must have seemed rather daunting, then—not only to make the journey, but to make it alone as well."

"Only at the beginning, when I left Fontevraud."

"And then?" She raised one brow.

"I began to enjoy it," I replied. "I was excited to see new places. To see Barfleur. I imagined Duke William and his men setting off from that coast—" I stopped abruptly, realizing I was prattling on out of nervousness.

"What was it"—the queen tilted her head back—"that you particularly enjoyed?"

"Seeing this new land. England."

"An unimaginative answer," she retorted.

Color rose to my cheeks. I tried again: "As we rode from the coast, I thought of other peoples who had come here long before. Romans, the Northmen. I thought of those who had survived. And those who had not."

"Tell me your impressions of 'this land,' as you call it."

After I gave my impressions, she turned to Tancred. "She likes to describe. That is useful." Then, to me: "What have you been told about your role here?"

"That I am to be a companion. That I am to read to you."

"Who taught you to read?"

"My grandfather," I replied, adding proudly, "He also taught me to write."

"An unusual grandfather who educates a girl. He must have been enlightened."

"He was."

"Then that is something we share. My grandfather, too, was enlightened."

I waited, hoping she would say more about her grandfather, William IX, Duke of Aquitaine, notorious adventurer and poet. My own grandfather had told me stories about him and had even read me a few of his verses. But, to my disappointment, she turned to Tancred. "Where is Jeannette?" she asked testily. "I requested that she be here."

He glanced at the door. "She comes now, Your Majesty."

A young woman entered. She had lustrous dark hair, pert features, and wore a fine robe of vivid green silk. She curtseyed before the queen and, after exchanging a charged glance with Tancred, took a place at his side.

"This is Jeannette," the queen informed me. "She will show you to your chamber. We shall continue our discussion tomorrow. And then you can commence your duties." She went on to muse, "It is odd to reach a point in one's life when companionship must be assigned to a stranger." She looked down, brushing the top of the ermine's head with her lips before she resumed stroking its sleek, pointed snout. I remember how, at that instant, their eyes—the queen's, and the creature's—resembled each other as they glanced at me.

I curtseyed, and then followed Jeannette to the door.

"Wait!" called the queen, startling me. She watched intently as I returned.

"How uncivilized I have been!" she exclaimed rather sardonically. "It seems I have lost all my manners while here in captivity. I have not inquired whether there are questions *you* would like to pose. Well, then?"

"Yes. I do have a question, Your Majesty."

"Tell me."

"What is the name of your ermine?"

She seemed almost amused. "Are you fond of ermines?" she asked.

"I have never seen one before. Not a live one, that is."

"I have seen both—dead and alive. I prefer them living." She stroked the creature again. "His name is Paris."

"I imagine you must miss Paris, Your Majesty," I ventured.

"Not at all!" she retorted. "Paris holds no fond memories for me. A dreary little place, compared to the lovely cities of my Aquitaine. No, my ermine is named after the hero in *The Trojan War*."

"But Paris was not fortunate in his fate," I returned.

"It is the rare person who is." At that, she dismissed me.

I turned and followed Jeannette to the door. Tancred signaled to the guards; one, who held a massive set of keys, unfastened the lock; the other raised the iron latch. "Come," said Jeannette, gesturing to me. The men let us pass, and the door of the queen's domain closed, resoundingly, behind us.

# CHAPTER 71

I followed Jeannette through one hall, then another. There was a certain sauciness about her and the undulating way she walked; once or twice she glanced back at me, a vivacious glint in her eye.

We descended the stairwell and came to a chamber on the floor below the queen's reception room. "This is where you will stay, my lady," said Jeannette as she opened the door.

The room was small but comfortably furnished; through a narrow hallway to the right was an antechamber where my baggage had been placed. A fire had been lit; tapers burned on a table to the side. One wall was dominated by a hanging depicting a regal woman on horseback, holding a hawk. Eyeing me studying it, Jeannette said, "The queen jokes that it is meant to be her."

"The queen must miss her freedom very much," I observed. "And France, of course."

"The Aquitaine, more than France. It is very difficult for her here, as you can imagine. To be locked up, when she has traveled the world."

"How long have you served her?" I asked, hopeful that Jeannette would prove a garrulous sort.

"Several years. I came from France. From Coutances. The king wants Normans here—and he is wary of anyone from the Aquitaine, of course," she went on. "The Poitevins, most of all. He does not trust their loyalty." She arranged the tassels of her sleeves almost pridefully.

"Your dress is lovely," I remarked.

"The queen insists that those who serve her are—what were her words?— 'pleasing to the eye.'"

I smiled at this. "And the king allows her to exercise this fancy?"

"Why should he not? He cares little as long as she is here, under lock and key, and supervised by his men."

"Tancred is one of the King's men, I assume?"

"Yes."

"Are they all from King Henry's inner circle?" I asked, hoping she would elaborate.

"I am not certain," was all she replied, to my disappointment. "I should help you unpack."

"That can wait until tomorrow. I can manage myself tonight."

"Then I shall leave you now to get settled. You must be hungry. I shall ask the kitchen to prepare some supper and have it brought to you."

"What should I expect tomorrow?"

"You should be ready early. Not long past sunrise. Most likely you will accompany the queen for her morning walk. She is allowed to walk outside several times a day, when the weather permits."

"And the rest of the day?"

"She will decide. She is fond of chess."

"Is she a skillful player?"

"So they say," she replied. "Though, of course," she added with a sly smile, "the women attending to her have always let her win."

I considered this. "Is there anything the queen dislikes?"

"Cowards. She likes to test people."

"She tests everyone around her?"

"In different ways, yes. You passed the first one quite well today. You did not seem intimidated. Most are."

"I was nervous, but I was also determined not to show it. But then curiosity and fascination overtook me. I have heard so much about the queen all my life—it seemed inconceivable that I was actually meeting her!" After a pause, I added, "I know that I shall be expected to read to the queen. Was she allowed to bring her library with her?"

"A small one. And sometimes books arrive from the abbey at Amesbury. Those will be your responsibility."

"In what way?"

"You will decide which among them will most interest the queen. Her tastes are particular."

"I can imagine," I replied. "Is there anything else I ought to know?"

"She is allowed visitors occasionally."

"Who is permitted?"

"It varies, according to the king's orders. I should attend to your supper."

I thanked her and told her that I looked forward to unpacking with her the next day.

"You do not have much baggage," she observed. "I was surprised there was not more." She sounded almost disappointed, as if she had expected a countess to arrive with grander accoutrements.

"I left in a great hurry. And I had been living at the abbey, at Fontevraud. I did not need much there, among the sisters."

"Was it your decision to live at the abbey?" I sensed that she did not find the idea of residing at a convent appealing.

"Yes. Why do you ask?"

"We have met other women from Fontevraud or Amesbury here. You seem quite different."

I smiled. "Am I to take that as a compliment?"

"That is for you to decide, my lady." At that, she curtseyed, and departed.

AFTER JEANNETTE LEFT, I LAY down; my body felt exhausted, but my mind was oddly exhilarated and resistant to repose.

I had met the fabled queen, and she did not frighten me. I was in a bleak, foreign land, far from France, and yet I, who reveled in freedom, did not feel confined. It was because of the queen, of course: she seemed to carry a wide world around her, a tantalizing nimbus of experience and personal history about which I was intensely curious. It did not seem a sacrifice to give up physical freedom to be in the company of such a personage.

The shutter was slightly ajar; I caught a glimpse of iron bars outside the window frame. Strangely, I now found the feeling of being sealed off against the world comforting: Gerard could never gain access to this place. Even if he were to learn my whereabouts, the queen and the King's men would protect me. I felt a rush of gratitude to Clementia, who had so deftly helped me escape.

I closed my eyes, my thoughts darting to Jeannette and the intimate glance she had exchanged with Tancred when we stood before the queen. He was a lesser knight, clearly; I wondered where his real allegiance lay—to the queen, or to King Henry?

Hopefully the weather would be clear tomorrow, when I accompanied the queen on her walk. I would ask her questions. And if she should ask me, later, to play chess? To choose books for her? These would all be tests, but now they intrigued rather than intimidated me.

I heard a knock at the door and sat up abruptly. A serving woman entered, carrying a tray with supper. I thanked her; she left. Only when I unfolded the napkin and took my first sip of wine did I realize how hungry I was. There was a good joint of beef, and some potatoes in a savory sauce. I ate quickly, ravenously, and drank the wine greedily, happy to feel its warmth coursing through my veins. It was from Bordeaux: it tasted of French earth, there was smoothness about it. I thought of Gerard, and his exporting wine to England for the Angevins. It was a lucrative trade, he had told me; it had helped make him an even greater fortune. I recalled his describing the wine caves that King Henry had created at the port of Southampton. Were they hidden there, cut out of the cliffs, at the King's Quay? And were those barrels of wine I had seen destined to be stored there?

Perhaps those vessels held Gerard's wine, the wine that had caused his bitter conflict with Hugh. I thought of Hugh and Fastrada. Gallien was their falcon keeper now. How was he faring? Had Gerard discovered they had taken him in, after his brutal dismissal? If so, his rage would know no bounds.

I realized that the wine had made me sleepy, so I lay down on my bed. I never rose to undress or say my prayers that night, but fell, instead, into a profound and dreamless sleep.

# CHAPTER 72

I heard a voice urging, "My lady, it is time to wake! To prepare!" I drowsily opened my eyes, struggling to emerge from sleep and momentarily uncertain where I was. Jeannette stood by the bed. "The queen has risen early today and is almost ready for her walk. You must make haste!"

"I was very tired last night," I said, rubbing my eyes as I came to my feet. "The voyage, the ride, the excitement."

She saw that I had fallen asleep in my traveling costume. "You cannot appear before the queen in those rumpled clothes. Come, I shall help you dress. And I have brought you some milk and bread."

I splashed icy water on my face from the basin on a table, then sipped some milk and took a few bites of bread.

"Quickly—we must unpack a few things for you," said Jeannette.

We went into an antechamber, and I helped Jeannette draw a few robes from my trunk. She held up one, then another, examining the cut, the fabric, and the trim of each. "Is there nothing else you have?" she asked, clearly surprised, even somewhat dismayed, by their lack of richness.

"Nothing else that would be suitable for day, and for this damp climate. I packed hurriedly when I left Fontevraud," I explained, without mentioning that I had given away most of my finery in the aftermath of leaving Gerard.

"Very well." She sighed. "Then we must pick the best among them. The queen is particular about the way her women are dressed."

"Your own clothes are very fine," I remarked as she helped me dress.

"A gift from the queen. She can be generous," she said, fastening my collar. "Now, for your hair. Come, sit here, before the mirror, and I shall brush it."

It had been a long time since I had looked into a mirror, for the sisters had viewed them as vain, even sinful extravagances. I took a seat and peered into the glass with some trepidation, as if almost uncertain what I would discover. That I was pale and a bit thinner did not surprise me; it was the contours of my face, and the expression in my eyes, that had changed. They seemed to belong to a different self—chastened, more thoughtful, older.

"Where am I to meet the queen?" I asked, standing up.

"In the courtyard, by the edge of the garden. That is where she walks. She has given a name to the place."

"What does she call it?" I asked as she helped me with my cape.

"The Queen's Promenade," she replied, with a sly smile.

A tall, cloaked figure in dark purple stood at a distance on a narrow, paved walk that bordered a spacious interior courtyard. I realized why Jeannette had smiled so slyly: there was nothing of a "promenade" about this spot, nor was there anything remotely grand or queenly about it. Above, along the ramparts, guards watched us, their lances pointing against the glum sky.

The queen bade me good morrow. "I have been waiting for you," she announced imperiously.

I nervously made my apologies for being late.

"Come," she ordered, glancing at the sundial along the path. "There is no time to waste. These times, these walks, are precious to me."

This was the first time the queen had stood before me. She was tall, about my height, and walked quickly, nimbly; from her gait, one would have thought her a much younger woman. As we set off, I caught a whiff of her perfume—Damascene rose laced with frankincense.

"You are settled in your chamber?" she asked.

"Yes, Your Majesty."

"It is well appointed, I trust?"

"Yes. It is quite comfortable. The wall hanging is lovely—the lady hawking on horseback."

"I like it as well," she said, adding, "I was fond of the hunt, when I was younger."

"Was it the chase, or the capture that you most enjoyed, Your Majesty?"

"A bold, even rather forward question." There was not a whit of disapproval in her tone, however—indeed, to my relief, quite the opposite. "I most enjoyed the chase, especially when the capture was achieved. And you? How would you answer that question?"

"The thrill of the chase."

"You hunted as a girl?"

"Yes, with my brothers. And my husband, too, was keen on the hunt."

"I understand you are divorced."

"Yes," I replied, discomfited. Wanting only to deflect the conversation from my divorce, I said, "It was at a hunt years ago that I met Sister Clementia's sister, Lady Fastrada. It was she who helped me secure a place at Fontevraud."

She raised one brow, drawing in her cheeks and tilting her head back as she reflected. "Lady Fastrada? She is a friend of my daughter Marie, in Troyes, I believe. Yes, I remember her distinctly. Ugly, spirited, exquisitely dressed?" She shot me a wry glance. "You are smiling."

"Only because you described Lady Fastrada so accurately, Majesty."

"You are divorced, you resided at Fontevraud, and you did not take the veil," she observed. "I find it curious that you were chosen for this position. The rest"—this, almost deprecatingly—"were proper nuns. You, clearly, do not have that sort of temperament."

"Why 'clearly,' Your Majesty?" I asked, unsure whether this was intended as a compliment or criticism.

"You yourself told me that you loved adventure, after all. I cannot imagine you now, at your young age, being sequestered at an abbey—even at my beloved Fontevraud. Well, then? Is my observation accurate?"

I smiled. "Yes. You are quite right."

"Why were you chosen, then, to come here as my companion?"

"I was free. I had no attachments. And I could read and write."

"Those are not the only reasons. I suspect there was another."

I knew it was futile to dissemble. "It was necessary for me to leave France."

"Why?"

"To escape the man who had been my husband."

"Let us hope you are more successful in escaping yours than I was in escaping mine," came her mordant response. "Who was he?"

"Gerard de Meurtaigne."

"Ah, I have heard of him."

I was not surprised that Gerard's name was familiar to her. He himself had proudly told me he was known to the Plantagenet court, and in particular, to the coterie of Prince Henry, the Young King.

"What are you thinking?" I heard the queen ask, jolting me from my reverie.

"I was wondering about your life here," I lied, "and how long it has been since you have seen your children. You must miss them."

"It depends on the child. I miss some more than others."

"Few parents would dare to admit that," I replied, with a smile. My initial nervousness had abated, and I began to feel more at ease.

"Since I am deprived of so much here, in confinement, I might at least have the freedom of utter candor. It is Richard and Joanna I miss most." She fixed her eyes upon me. "You rather remind me of Joanna. She has the same coloring, and a similar manner. The same inquisitive spirit."

"I take that as a great compliment."

"You should," she said crisply.

"How long has it been since you saw her?"

"Five years—since she left me here, to be married in Sicily. She was twelve." Her voice was replete with sorrow; she looked away, as if reluctant for me to see her eyes.

"How old would she be now?"

"Seventeen. I think of it every day. I count the days, the years." She gave a brave, strained smile.

"I remember seeing the lemons from Sicily that Joanna sent to Fontevraud, as a gift. The abbess mentioned them to me proudly."

"It would be like Joanna to make such a thoughtful gesture. She is devoted to Fontevraud. She spent much of her early childhood there, as did my son John. The nuns did well with my two youngest children."

"Queen Joanna must preside over a splendid court in Palermo."

"Splendid and strange."

"In what way, 'strange'?"

"The influence of the Infidel, for better or worse. Sometimes for better—the gardens, the luxury, the poetry and music. But it is also a place of harems, eunuchs, spies. As for the intrigues of that court—even I fear to think of them! There is a certain snakelike insidiousness to the plots of the Infidels. I witnessed this myself when I made a journey to the Holy Land."

"That was a famous journey, Your Majesty."

"Yes. And there is nothing about it I regret. Except, of course, the disastrous outcome. That fault did not rest with me, however, but with my husband, Louis. The monk." I repressed a smile. "We could not convince Louis to attack Aleppo," she continued. "He was intent on making the pilgrimage to Jerusalem instead. A mistake for which we all suffered." She pulled her cape tightly around her as she strode forward.

"Do you play chess?" she suddenly asked, turning to me.

"Yes. Sister Clementia taught me, though I cannot pretend I play very well," I replied, adding, "I asked my husband for a chess set once, but he never gave me one."

"That cannot have augured well."

"I do not think the game interested him."

"Do you believe that was the real reason?"

"No," I said, before admitting, "I do not think he wanted me to learn a game for which he had no expertise."

"I am glad you are able to face the truth." She gave a small, satisfied smile. "It takes some courage to do so."

We had been walking awhile. "Come, let us sit and enjoy the sun," she said, gesturing to a long stone bench by the edge of the path. "There is so little sun in this infernal, gray country."

As we settled on the bench, I tilted my face toward the sky. Grateful for the first rays of sunlight since my arrival, I closed my eyes, savoring the warmth and quiet, and the momentary respite from conversation.

"Enough silence," she announced, startling me. "The ebb and flow of conversation is among the things I crave. I always have, but here, especially, with so little else to entertain me. You will find I have no tolerance for boredom. You seem to have no dearth of questions. Go on. Ask me one now."

My initial nervousness returned as I thought, frantically. "You have talked very fondly of Fontevraud, Your Majesty," I said. "When did you first visit the abbey?"

"It was in the springtime of the year I married Henry Plantagenet. 1152. I was thirty, he was nineteen. He was a young, able warrior when I met him—not yet a strategist, let alone King of England. I had been Queen of France and had already seen the world. It was I who schooled him in statecraft." To this assertion, uttered with startling fierceness, she added ruefully, "Perhaps too well!" She placed her gloves in her lap, stretching the leather taut.

"His aunt, Mathilda Plantagenet, was the abbess then," she continued. "An impressive woman, subtle in the way she wielded power. Henry was eager that I see the abbey and meet her. His family had great affection for Fontevraud, and my own family had long had ties to it, as well. I had always been intrigued by the stories my grandfather and father had told me about its founder, and its community of accomplished women. And indeed, that first visit made a profound impression on me. I shall return to Fontevraud one day, God willing."

She looked up at the sky: flocks of birds flew in great circles above us. "If only I might have their freedom!" She sighed, before adding, passionately, "When I think what I could do now if I were free—help my children, help my sons succeed!"

I heard the sound of strident footsteps and turned around: one of the fearsome guards from the queen's chamber was approaching us.

"It is time to return, Majesty," he said gruffly, but not disrespect-fully.

The queen rose to her full height, glancing at him coquettishly. "Surely you might allow us to spend a little more time here—" she wheedled in a honeyed voice.

A big blond brute whom she had almost, but not quite, succeeded in taming, he looked flustered, almost sheepish. "I cannot grant you more time, Majesty. I have my orders."

We returned to the castle, made our way through corridors, and then up the stairwell to her reception room. As we stepped inside, I heard the door close behind us, then the sharp, weighty sound of the iron latch descending. Unlike the previous evening, it was preternatu-rally quiet. The room's heady fragrance remained the same, however. I took some deep breaths, savoring its strange, exotic richness. "What is this scent?" I asked the queen.

"It is among the few luxuries I am afforded here—a special mix of herbs and flowers, which Joanna sends to me from Palermo. I keep it burning in the braziers day and night." She walked to the window and looked out, before turning to face me, her expression wistful. "It re-minds me of Byzantium."

# CHAPTER 73

M oments later, Jeannette entered with Paris, the ermine, trailing on a leash. "Ah, my little creature," said the queen, her eyes shining with delight.

Jeannette made a deep curtsey before us. "Shall I unleash Paris, Your Majesty?"

"Of course," replied the queen. "He is never to be kept on a leash while he is with me. He always follows my commands."

"I only ask because he is not accustomed to Lady Isabelle yet," she replied, abashed. "He can be unruly with strangers."

"That may be so. Nonetheless, I want him to be free."

"Of course, Your Majesty," murmured Jeannette as she untied the leash.

"Tell the men to have the fire lit," the queen said. "And then you may go." Jeannette curtseyed to me and the queen, spoke to the guard at the door, and departed.

"Come to me, my precious," the queen coaxed Paris in a low, beguiling voice. "Come."

Paris loped up to her. "My sweet, my comfort," she murmured as he crept onto her lap. I watched her hand, with its globe of amethyst, stroking the top of the ermine's head. "Let us sit together now." Addressing Paris in the lulling voice one would use with a child, she said, "It is time you become acquainted with Lady Isabelle." She gestured for me to approach. "Come, now you must pet him."

I did so; Paris turned his dark, inquiring eyes up to me in an oddly human way.

"He likes you," said the queen approvingly. "That bodes well. Ordinarily it takes longer for him to trust a stranger."

I wondered how long it took her to trust, if she ever did. "I had a cat once," I replied. "A cat I loved." I thought of my girlhood, and the comfort of having my little cat during lonely times; how sad I had been, on my dismal return home, when Hortense had informed me so cavalierly that Cachette was gone.

"This was in Provence?"

"Yes, Your Majesty," I replied, adding, "I did not realize you knew I was from Provence."

"I know everything. And even if I had not been told, it would not have been hard to discern."

"Why is that?"

"Your accent, of course. And your"—she paused—"*sensibility.*"

I wondered what she meant; there were so many questions I yearned to ask, but I would have to bide my time. "You have trained Paris very well, Your Majesty."

"It is one of the things I am good at. Taming creatures. I was less successful with my husband," she added wryly.

A servant shuffled in with a basket of kindling; after bowing before us, he proceeded to light the fire. The queen closed her eyes and seemed to withdraw within herself. I took the opportunity to study her profile: the long, straight nose, the defiant chin, the high, proud forehead. Suddenly she opened her eyes, looking at me in the particularly intense, expectant way, which I now recognized as a signal: she expected me to pose a question.

"Where do you keep your library, Your Majesty?" I asked.

"Such as it is," she replied dismissively. "It is kept in another chamber—our version of a scriptorium, where you will also find parchment and writing implements. That is where I shall dictate to you when the time comes. And where you will copy documents and letters for me."

"Are you"—I was about to say "allowed" and caught myself. "Do you receive many letters here?"

"Not nearly as many as I have been accustomed to, alas. And all must pass the scrutiny of Tancred and the king's men." Her finger ran along the top of Paris's snout. "Letters have always meant a great deal to me. I have been diligent about keeping copies of the most important ones."

"Of your own letters, Your Majesty? Or letters written to you?"

"Both," came her curt reply.

She sat up very straight, as if she had just come to a decision. "Let us play chess," she announced, glancing at the chessboard nearby. "Draw up the table, and a chair for yourself."

I did so, my nervousness returning, for I was all too aware I would be no match for the queen.

"You seem nervous," she observed.

"I am sure I am far less experienced than the opponents you are accustomed to."

"I suspect you judge yourself too harshly. By admitting your lack of confidence, however, you have given me an opportunity to teach you the first, crucial lesson. Never show anything but confidence. Reveal fear or confusion, and you are doomed. Affect bravado, come what may. That is a most important aspect of this game." She settled back in her seat. "Not only in this game, but in the larger, most important game."

"And what is that?"

"The game of life. Come, let us set up the pieces."

I picked up one ivory piece, then another, marveling at the beauty and intricacy of the carving. I thought of the set made by Muslim craftsmen in Palermo that Bertuccio had shown me that day long ago; however fine, it was not comparable to the queen's. "I have never seen a chess set quite as lovely as this," I told her.

"And I doubt you will again. I brought it with me when I left Chinon to come to England. It came from Antioch. My uncle Raymond gave it to me—it was he who taught me chess. Among other things."

I finished setting the pieces carefully in place. "Other than affecting confidence," I ventured, "what would be your advice to me before we begin?"

"Try to imagine how your opponent's mind works. Is he or she impetuous or deliberate? Patient or overeager? Which move will tempt him, and which will not? You must take all of these things into consideration and trust your instincts. You must learn to *think well.* Impulsiveness is the surest path to defeat. Come, let us begin."

After playing for an hour, she remarked, "You have the makings of a fine player. And you will improve under my tutelage."

"I should have thought you might prefer me to remain an indifferent player, Your Majesty. So that you would always win."

"That would hardly be amusing!" she scoffed. "You will come to realize that I find more satisfaction in a strong opponent than in one less worthy. There is little joy in an easy victory. It is those victories that take time, toil, and sacrifice which matter most. I have taught that to my sons. To the prince, especially."

I wondered which of her four sons she meant. "The Prince?" I asked, assuming that she meant her eldest, Henry, the Young King.

"Richard," she replied, as if the question were hardly worth posing. "Come, let us sit by the fire." Then, to Paris, "Come, my sweet." The ermine followed her to the bench before the hearth.

"That is a rather dreary dress you are wearing," said the queen, scrutinizing me from top to toe. "Surely you have something better."

"It is the best dress for daytime I brought. I did not think I would need anything finer, since you are"—I was about to say "exiled," but thought better of it—"away from court life here."

"I find that rather insulting! I am still Queen of England, after all." But her tone was amused, rather than critical, and her mouth had curved into a teasing smile. "I shall discuss your wardrobe with Jeannette. It is gloomy enough here without having my companion dressed like a penitent."

"I have no desire to look like a penitent, Your Majesty," I said, restraining a smile.

"That is heartening. I am suspicious of women who have no vanity. It connotes a cheerless, martyr's spirit—and I have had enough martyrs in my day, I assure you. We must find something more suitable for you to wear. Something in a lovely fabric and less somber color. Yes," she mused, as she continued to study me, "you ought to have a narrower cut, and tapered sleeves, less antiquated in style."

Jeannette entered, followed by Tancred, who announced, "The midday meal is served, Your Majesty."

"Ah, my captors deign to feed us," said the queen with some sarcasm. "I do hope the wine will be better than yesterday's. The least the king can do is to provide me with good wine from the region that I bestowed on him as my dowry."

She turned to me. "Come, Isabelle, it is time for us to dine."

# CHAPTER 74

We followed Tancred out of the queen's chamber and turned onto a long, dim passageway that ran along the western edge of the castle, the sound of our steps accompanied by that of the fierce, whipping wind. "Ah, the wind of Salisbury," said the queen ruefully. "Rough and constant. They say one becomes accustomed to it. But I have yet to reach that blissful state."

After thirty paces or so, I began to discern the sound of men's voices—muffled at first, then slowly growing more distinct as we approached the great oak doors that loomed at the end of the corridor; this, then, was the entrance to the great hall.

As the burly guards stepped aside to let us enter, I looked about in wonder. The hall was richly, even riotously, decorated with scenes depicting battles between good and evil: men fighting devils, knights subjugating pagans, princes and kings towering over the vanquished. An immense screen, painted to resemble stone, separated one end of the chamber from the dining area near us. Servants stood at attention along the wall behind the long, narrow table, which was raised on a dais. Silk cushions covered the benches before it; one sole, intimidating chair, placed in the center of the far side, was clearly designated for the queen.

A small group of men, who had been standing to the side, proceeded toward us. After they made their obeisances to her, they were introduced to me—the chaplain, the constable, and Ralph FitzStephen, who wore the heavy key of royal chamberlain with élan.

"Come," the queen announced to the group with a beneficent smile. "Let us dine before the food grows cold." FitzStephen took her hand

and escorted her to the table, where she was placed between him and the chaplain.

Tancred led me to my seat, almost opposite the queen, before he took his own place, to my right. After unfolding my napkin, I glanced across the table: the queen majestically surveyed the scene, her hands resting on the arms of the chair, the ends of which were carved like lions' heads, in ivory.

The chaplain said grace; then the service of the meal commenced. Accustomed as I was to the considerably simpler fare of the abbey, with its emphasis on fish, I savored each dish—aubergines with almonds, venison with a gem-colored jelly, beef braised in red wine. It was not only the exotic spices and seasonings that fascinated me, but also the unusual combination of dishes and their artful presentation.

At one point, as we were passed a thick white broth, Tancred interjected, "Beware—this is Saracen broth. It is highly spiced. The queen has a fondness for it. As she does *this* dish"—he indicated the meat confection being presented to me—"which they call Turk's Head."

"What is in it?" I asked, not knowing whether to be amused or horrified.

"Ground pork and chicken, flavored with sage and served in a pastry. If it is done well, it is decorated in such a way that it looks swarthy."

I sipped the broth, and then bit into the meat pastry. "It is delicious, despite its name. Does the queen dictate the cuisine here?"

"Very much. The cook comes from Normandy, though it is not hard to see the influence of the queen's travels as well." He seemed to hesitate before adding, almost under his breath, "The kitchen is one area where the king grants the queen sway. It is a harmless way to indulge her fondness for luxury."

As a platter of roast quail, vividly garnished with delicate vegetables, was offered to me, I glanced at the queen, who was deep in conversation with FitzStephen. "I assume it is FitzStephen who oversees the men here."

"Only partly. It is Ranulf de Glanvill, the king's justiciar, who has the final say. Over us all."

I looked about. "Is he here?"

"He comes often but is not here now. An admirable man. You will see. The queen respects him. As she does FitzStephen."

We continued to dine, though mostly in silence. To my disappointment, Tancred seemed to focus his attention elsewhere—on his food and on the conversations of the other men. This freed me, however, to observe the queen, and also, I confess, to glean snatches of her conversation.

I was not surprised, given her reputation as an intellectual, by the lofty tenor of the talk. There was a discussion about the nature of dreams, for instance, and whether these were influenced more by the body, or the mind. With FitzStephen, she debated whether poetry was a superior form of art to music. (She thought it was; he did not.) Of all that was mentioned, one subject seemed to be studiously left untouched: anything to do with court politics or matters relating to her sons, the king, and the Plantagenets.

Sweets were passed—stewed pears, marzipan in the form of oak leaves, and apples baked in a glistening custard fragrant with cinnamon. It was then that the queen looked across the table and addressed me. "I have told FitzStephen about you," she said as the others listened intently. "That you have come from Fontevraud, and that this is your first time across the Channel. Your first time here, in England."

"Yes," I replied. "I was eager to see England. I had heard about the country from my grandfather and brother, both of whom have traveled here."

"To London?" FitzStephen asked, in a kindly tone that encouraged me to expatiate.

"Yes, and to the north, to Northumberland, and the eastern coast, as well. My brother has been to Canterbury and sent me a long letter about it once. It sounded like a splendid place. He told me about the pilgrims who had come there from all over the world. One day, I should love to see the cathedral." The moment I uttered those words, I felt color rising to my cheeks. That I should want to see the cathedral where Thomas Becket had been murdered—most likely at the instigation of the king—was an appalling gaffe. FitzStephen looked down; Tancred gulped some wine; one of the men coughed.

It was the queen who broke the silence. "One can only admire Lady Isabelle's spirit of adventure," she said. "And her sense of history." At that she rose; the others followed, and the meal came to an end.


AFTER WE RETURNED TO THE queen's chamber, I asked the queen if I might be excused for a short while to attend to my things. "Jeannette has offered to help me," I said.

"You may," she replied and gestured to Tancred, who stood to the side. "Tell Jeannette I want to see her."

"She has been awaiting your instructions, Your Majesty," he said. "I believe she is outside, in the hall." He left, returning moments later with Jeannette, who was trailed by Paris.

"Lady Isabelle needs your assistance," the queen told her as Paris crept onto her lap.

Jeannette nodded. "Of course, Your Majesty."

"I understand she has only brought rather *plain* clothes. Perhaps we might be able to find something more appropriate to her position. She is meant to be my companion, not a visiting martyr."

Jeannette stifled a smile. "I understand, Your Majesty. I indicated as much to Lady Isabelle earlier when we were choosing something for her to wear."

"Good. Tell Tancred I would like the tailor called and some fabrics brought here for me to select. Make it clear that the new dress need not be elaborate, but it must be of an appealing color, one that would suit Lady Isabelle's complexion." She turned to scrutinize me. "A vibrant blue, I should think. Or a lovely green. Nothing *somber.*"

"You have good taste, Jeannette," continued the queen, "and a keen sense of color and cut. Tell the tailor the style should be narrower over-all, and the sleeves longer, far more ample."

The queen turned to me. "He is English, alas, not Norman, and will need some guidance."

I thanked the queen and left with Jeannette.

AFTER WE ARRIVED AT MY chamber and Jeannette began to set my things in order, she asked, "Did you enjoy the meal?"

"Yes. The food was delicious."

"The queen sets store by such things."

"And there was no lack of luxury in the dining chamber, to be sure," I remarked. "It was not what I had expected."

"Tancred says that the king has no wish for the queen to suffer. He wants to prevent her from stirring up trouble with her sons, most of all. The king thinks she is a dangerous influence."

"And you? What do you think?"

"I think the queen will do anything to keep the Aquitaine from being—what was the word she used?—'devoured' by the Angevins. And anything to assure her sons' victory against their father."

When we had nearly finished arranging my things, it began to rain hard. "The queen will be disappointed not to take another walk," said Jeannette, closing the shutter. "She cherishes those times—being outside, having some freedom. I could tell that she enjoyed the walk with you."

"I am glad to hear that."

"She did not find the last women sent here satisfactory. 'Boring and tiresome' she called them. They were afraid to ask her questions. The queen enjoys lively conversation."

"She said as much to me."

"And you passed the chess test," she added. "That augurs well."

"How do you know that I passed it? We were alone."

"The queen is never completely alone here. That should not come as a surprise."

I thought of the curtained passages, the slits cut into the stone walls, then of the screen that divided the great hall in two. "So you were watching us?"

"No." She smiled smugly. "Tancred told me."

"I see," I murmured. As she resumed working I recalled my first glimpse of Tancred at the quay. I had been too tired, stupefied by the rigors of the sea voyage, to study him closely then. He was a commanding presence, to be sure, though he seemed to temper this in the queen's presence, as if he thought it prudent to appear more acquiescent. I suspected he was an ambitious younger son who had come to make his way and his fortune, here, among other enterprising Normans.

"Tancred seems to wield much power here," I observed to Jeannette, who was folding a shawl. "Power to enforce the rules, and the queen's schedule."

"That he does," she said, pausing. "Though the queen is good at working around him, I assure you. But he is aware of that. He is one of the few here who is. The rest"—she stood back, her eyes narrowing as she surveyed the clothes she had arranged in the armoire—"are easily manipulated."

"By the queen?"

"Yes."

I wondered whether Jeannette's alertness to such things sprang from her own modus operandi; I suspected that she herself was no stranger to manipulation. I thought of the glance she and Tancred had exchanged and wondered if she saw him as the means to her ascendance—not only here, in the circle around the queen, but also in the wider Plantagenet court.

"I shall be done soon," said Jeannette, adding, "you did not bring very much with you, my lady." Again, that disappointment, even an iota of pity, in her voice.

"It was kind of the queen to ask that the tailor be called on my behalf."

"I told you the queen can be generous. She has done that for others here, but not for any of her companions. You are the first."

She had finished putting my things away and stood back, assessing her handiwork. "Your clothes are in good order." She eyed the small locked trunk, which stood in a corner and contained my private effects. "I should unpack that one now for you, my lady."

"I can manage it myself later, thank you."

"If you wish," she replied with some reluctance. "I shall see if the queen needs you now and will return shortly."

After the door shut, I walked to the window and closed my eyes, listening to the sound of the rain. Alas, there would not be another walk with the queen that day; not an opportunity to talk privately, and to ask more questions while we were outside, distanced from the watchful eyes and attentive ears of the king's men. There was so much I wondered about, so much I burned to ask. The queen had never even mentioned her third son, Geoffrey, and had only fleetingly referred to her youngest, John; I wondered what she thought of them and of her eldest, the Young King, Prince Henry. She had made it quite clear that Richard and Joanna were her favorites.

It was curious, yet a relief to me, that she had never asked the circumstances of my divorce; yet she had implied she knew Gerard's name. This had not surprised me: Gerard himself had often mentioned the Young King to me. The prince loved the lists, he said, and he always needed money—Gerard's money, no doubt. And then I recalled Gerard's discomfiture at the mention of Prince Richard; I had always sensed that there had been a rupture of some sort between them, that Gerard had failed to be successful in gaining access to him, and that this gnawed at him, as if it impeded his ambitions vis-a-vis the Plantagenet hierarchy.

The rain continued; it was growing dark. I looked around the chamber: how bare it seemed without the bronze falcon! I had become accustomed to the company of that fanciful creature, with its chameleon-like gaze—sometimes questioning, at other times oracular or admonishing. Now it kept Marie company at the abbey. I smiled as I thought of her, overcome by a sudden longing to feel her small, eager arms around me, to hear her sprightly voice asking one of her searching questions.

I walked to the wall with the hanging of the regal woman hawking on horseback followed by a girl and a falconer. As I drew closer, I realized that the jeweled band encircling the woman's headdress resembled a crown; perhaps that was why the queen joked it was meant to portray her.

These musings were interrupted when I heard a knocking at the door—Jeannette had returned.

"The queen asked me to tell you that you may rest until the evening meal, since it is not possible for you to walk together in this weather. And there is something else I was asked to tell you."

"By the queen?"

"By Tancred. He wants to inform you that some books for the queen should arrive next week, hopefully. From Amesbury. Perhaps there will be some volumes of poetry," she added. "The queen is fond of poetry."

"And you, Jeannette—are you also fond of verses?"

"Yes! Especially the verses of ballads." She sighed. "But there is almost never music here. The queen longs for music, she says." She paused, toying with a tassel on her sleeve. "And I am fond of the romances, too."

"Ah, so you can read—"

"Yes, well enough," she replied proudly. "The queen and her court set store by such things. Tancred can read very well. All the king's men do. King Henry is insistent upon it, Tancred says. He tells me the king and his counselors are very learned." Once again she eyed the small locked trunk. "I should help you unpack that last one now," she said, gesturing to it.

"Thank you for all your help, but I am happy to do it myself, later," I replied. In truth, I was tired, and also slightly wary of her questions about my private possessions.

"As you wish," she said, looking rather crestfallen. "Then I shall go and attend to other things."

# CHAPTER 75

"Where are the queen's books kept?" I asked Jeannette early the following morning as she plaited my hair before the mirror.

"Just below this chamber, my lady. The library was once in another part of the castle, but the king had it moved. There used to be a few scribes working there as well, Tancred says. But after the king decided to keep the queen here, he assigned them to the abbey at Reading."

"I see," I murmured. She was in a good mood that morning, and unusually talkative.

"He was determined that she have no means of communicating," she continued. "The king allows her many luxuries here. Rich clothes, furs, fine food. But scribes, no. Tancred says the king is afraid of her power to convince."

"To convince?"

"To convince them to write messages on her behalf."

"But surely she is allowed to write her children—"

"I suppose that her daughters are not considered as being so dangerous. But the queen's *sons!* That is another matter." She had lowered her voice, and her eyes had taken on an eager, confiding look. "Richard and the Young King have been in league together all this past summer, they say. Her middle son Geoffrey, too, is wily and married to a woman the queen greatly dislikes—Constance, a noblewoman from Brittany. A savage bunch, the Bretons! We Normans have never trusted them. And then there's the youngest son, John. Tancred tells me he is very greedy. 'Covetous of his older brothers' domains,' that is what he says." She sighed as she secured the plait with a ribbon, pulling it so tightly that I almost cried out in pain. "Each maneuvers for power, and for riches," she went on. "The king must be ever watchful. Especially in the last year, since—"

"Since what, Jeannette?"

"You promise *never* to mention what I am going to tell you to anyone else?"

"Of course."

"A few years ago, she connived somehow to pass messages to her daughter, the Countess Marie. Since then, she has been under stricter surveillance."

"The Countess Marie, from Troyes?"

"Yes."

"That is strange. I did not think that the queen had maintained a relationship with Marie," I replied. "I remember my mother telling me long ago that the queen abandoned Marie and her younger sister, Alix, after the divorce, when they were little girls."

"True, but blood is blood, and a mother is still a mother. King Louis sent those two girls away to be married not long afterward, when they were very young. They did not grow up with him at his court. And what is more"—she had begun to fasten the other plait—"Marie's husband, Count Henri, came to the aid of the kings' sons during their rebellion." Reveling in my attention, she paused, tantalizingly. "And I would expect the queen hears from Alix. She is the Countess of Blois, after all."

"Go on—" I prodded.

"Ah, yes, the queen has long been known to be crafty. Tancred says that very soon after she was divorced from King Louis, she sent a messenger secretly to Henry Plantagenet with news that she was free to marry. Just weeks afterward. *Imagine!*" She paused, looking at me hard, as if trying to elicit a reaction.

"I had never heard that before," was all I said, without admitting that the story fascinated me.

"They say she will do *anything* to achieve her ends. Most of all those of her sons." I caught Jeannette's expression in the mirror: despite the contempt in her voice, her eyes shone with admiration for the queen.

"I am impressed with how much you know!" I remarked, turning to face her.

She seemed pleased by the compliment. "The men talk to me, Tancred especially. He hears a great deal from the men here, and from the men who pass through, from the king's court. From other parts of England, or from France. But you must promise not to mention that I have told you these things."

"Of course I promise."

"There!" She took a few steps back, scrutinizing me. "You are quite ready now. The queen expects you within the hour."

A knocking at the door interrupted us—a young page, with a letter he handed to Jeannette.

"For you, my lady," she said, giving it to me.

"It is from Sister Clementia at the abbey," I said, noticing her eyeing the seal. "Now you may depart, Jeannette."

I waited for the door to close and began to read. Clementia began with a cursory sentence saying she and Marie fared well, and that she hoped I had made my way to England without difficulty. But then, in an alarmingly different tone, she continued:

Now to less pleasant matters. Only a week after you departed, Gerard de Meurtaigne came to Fontevraud, determined to find you. His manner was menacing. I told him you had left, and that I had no idea where you had gone. That life in the abbey did not seem to suit you, and that your plans seemed vague. I had the impression, I told him, that you intended to return to your family's home. The meeting with him left me shaken. That he is very angry is evident; that he is obsessed with finding you is clear. What he intends, I cannot fathom—indeed, I hesitate to imagine.

Given this, it seems clear that we were correct in sending you to England. Meeting him made it unequivocally clear that even the sanctity of the abbey, the power of the abbess, and the stone walls of Fontevraud, could not succeed in protecting you from this man. His anger knows no bounds, and he has friends in high places. Do not despair, Isabelle. Time, hopefully, will assuage his rage. In the meantime, you are protected by the queen and her men. Remember the words of the Proverb: "the name of the Lord is a strong tower." Lean on Him for strength; carry Him in your heart.

Rest assured of the place you hold in my affections, and that you are constantly in my thoughts and prayers, as you are in Marie's.

*Clementia*

I set down Clementia's letter with a trembling hand. Here, then, was the punishment that Gerard, and perhaps God Himself, were intent on inflicting upon me. Gerard's rage was born of his discovery of having been duped, in having had his ambitions thwarted. God raged against me for other reasons—for having sinned, for having sought the help of a healer with wicked potions and magic stones. All so that I might prevent myself from having a child with a man I feared.

I paced to and fro, trying not to cry. I could not dispel my indignation at the cruelty of this sentence—a banishment meaning that I must, for a long time, perhaps forever, forgo returning to Fontevraud. Years might pass before I would see Marie again: if and when I did, she would no longer be a little girl. In the meantime, Gerard, intent on revenge, would hunt me down. Yes, he would hunt me down in his relentless way, just as he had Gallien; just as he had any person who had crossed him, any creature who had escaped his control. I thought of the expression he would use about his falcons' eyes at the onset of the hunt: he wanted them *in yarak*, he would say, "alert to kill." With a shudder I thought of his own eyes and how, at certain moments, they, too, had shown that same cruel, glittering gaze. But Gerard's eyes were not flecked with gold like the falcons': they were deep blue, the color of the Northern Sea.

I took deep breaths and walked to and fro, my thoughts dark, my mind convulsed by fear. I felt like a hare wriggling in a trap, biding my time for the huntsmen to discover me. I closed my eyes, imagining this so vividly that I could almost hear the triumphant barking of hounds, the shrill call of the huntsmen's horns, and then the greatest terror of all—the sound of pounding hoofbeats signaling the advance of the master himself, the man who had once been my husband.

One element of the letter, and one element alone, gave me a modicum of relief: Gerard had no idea where I was. Still, I knew it would only be a matter of time before Gerard, with his web of cronies, and his friendship with the Young King, would discover I was here, in Salisbury.

I took up the letter again, examining it carefully: the original seal had been broken, but then resealed so artfully that few would ever have suspected it. Tancred, no doubt, had read Clementia's words. Would he ever admit to this? And if he did, what, if anything, would he say? I knew Clementia well enough to know that she must have intended the King's men, and the queen, to know of Gerard's fury toward me; to know that he was intent on revenge. This was as much a part of her message as the words she had written.

After I set the letter down, I walked to the window, planted my hands on the cold, rough sill, and forced myself to look beyond, at the sky; for the first time since my arrival, the sun was shining. "A sign from God," I murmured, "to remind myself to give thanks that I am *here*, safe from Gerard, far away in England. That I was right to escape when I did." I gathered my cloak, shut the door, and walked, pensively, toward the place where I was to meet the queen.

# CHAPTER 76

Despite my initial sense of relief and gratitude in being far from Gerard's reach, Clementia's description of the encounter with him continued to haunt me. Sleep often became difficult, and my dreams would teem with hideous creatures from whom I fled in terror.

About a week later, after an especially restless night, Tancred came to see me. Partly as a way to lift my spirits, I had donned the lovely new bright blue robe which the queen's tailor had made for me.

"You look pale and tired," he remarked, to my annoyance.

"If the queen and I were given more time outside, to walk, my sleep might be less fitful," I prevaricated. "I am not accustomed to being so confined."

"There will be even *less* time to walk today," he replied. "The books have arrived. The queen is eager to peruse them, and for you to read to her. I shall show you to the library."

"Are there many?" I asked him.

"No more than usual. Come."

I followed him down the stairwell one flight. We came to a door on the landing—modest in size, but with a formidable lock. Tancred opened it, and we entered.

The library was hexagonal, with a low, beamed ceiling that gave it a slightly oppressive feeling. I wondered what the chamber had been previously used for: a waiting room, perhaps, for the king's men. There was a small cabinet arrayed with a row of books, and to one side, a trestle table where the newly arrived volumes, I assumed, had been arranged. A small stack, to the right, had been set to one side.

"These three have been chosen for her," he explained, handing me those to the right. "We always look through them first, to make sure the material is both appropriate and to the queen's taste. She is particular, as you can imagine."

"Is there anything else I should know?" I asked, clutching the books.

"Not at this time. Come, then," he said. "The queen awaits you. She is impatient."

He led me to the reception room which, to my surprise, was empty, save for the guards at the door. "But where is the queen?" I asked Tancred.

"In there," he replied, pointing to an archway to the side, which was partly covered by a vivid green damask portière emblazoned with lions rampant. "Her reading chamber."

He drew open the portière, and I stepped inside.

A stately figure in deep blue, the queen stood near the window seat, Paris curled at her feet. Two chairs sat before the crackling fire—the queen's, and another, considerably less majestic. Between them stood a small table arrayed with several objects. Again, that pervasive, heady fragrance in the air—the scent of Byzantium.

She gestured to me, the heavy gem-studded bracelets at her wrists glinting in the morning light as we approached. I noticed she looked rather weary. "You are wearing your new robe," she said, casting her eyes over me in such a way I felt slightly uneasy. "A vast improvement. The penitential look did not suit you."

I resisted the impulse to laugh, and curtseyed. "I am glad you approve, Your Majesty."

"I see Tancred has given you the books."

"Yes, Your Majesty. These three."

"Good. I need something to enliven my mind. Now, take your place there," she said, gesturing to the smaller chair.

I did so, the books resting in my lap. As she settled in her own seat, I could not resist craning my neck to look at the items on the table: a splendid hourglass, and a small gold and enamel casket.

"You seem quite intent on those objects," she remarked while I, sheepish, sat bolt upright. "Do such things interest you?"

"Yes. They do, I confess—very much."

"Why 'confess'? It is hardly a sin to admire beautiful things."

"Many in the Church would say it is."

"Then they are foolish. Anyone truly civilized has a longing for luxury, for beauty. It is an eternal human hunger." She looked down, touching her amethyst ring. "I, for instance, have always had a fascination for gems. It is as much their *properties* as their colors that draw me. This amethyst for instance"—she held out the beringed hand—"was thought to be the stone of Aphrodite. Some say that it also protects you from the devil. Garnets are for healing, or so my father told me that the ancients said. And as for rubies, which I am also fond of—they are imperial stones," she mused, "the stone of monarchs. The stone of power. The stone that most resembles the color of blood." She looked at me directly. "And you? Are you drawn to gems? Some women are, some women are not."

"I only had occasion to become acquainted with such things when I was married, Your Majesty. My husband was fond of precious stones. It delighted him to see me arrayed in jewels." I glanced at her bracelets. "He once gave me a pair of bracelets that came from Byzantium. Not so different in style from those you are wearing. The same beautiful gold filigree. But mine was also set with sapphires, and pale blue stones whose name I cannot remember."

"Chalcedony, perhaps?"

"Yes. Precisely." As I gazed at her bracelets, my thoughts roamed to my marriage and the moment when Gerard had discovered Aiglantine cavorting with my splendid bracelets; and then, with a pang of fear, to Gerard's menacing visit to the abbey.

"Is something wrong?" she asked. "You suddenly looked in distress."

"I was thinking of my bracelets," I replied, "and how they came to be associated with sadness, and with the punishment of someone I was greatly fond of—the young woman who served me. And so, after that, never again did I take much delight in wearing them, no matter how exquisite they were. It was always the idea of where they had been made, and their provenance, that lent them their fascination for me—more, perhaps, than their actual beauty and craftsmanship." I smiled. "I told Gerard that I wondered whether they had been made for the Empress Theodora!"

"Or," she interjected, "the beautiful Queen Melisende. I knew her, you know. In Jerusalem, on my journey to the Holy Land. This hourglass"—she gestured to the object on the table—"was her gift to me."

"May I hold it?" I ventured.

"You may."

I picked it up with great care. "How lovely!" I exclaimed, examining the facetted rock crystal top and base, both studded with multicolored gems and intaglios. "I can imagine how you must treasure it."

"Yes," she replied, with a slightly mournful expression, "as much as one might treasure anything that marks the passage of time. I cherish its beauty, but I also cherish it for another reason, one which you, clearly, will understand—for its associations. Some pleasant, some bittersweet, as is so much in life. Most of all I treasure it because it reminds me of Melisende, who greatly influenced me during that journey to Jerusalem—not only as a woman, but also in the way she served as queen. She was drawn to art and beauty, and she also wielded great power. Not in the strident way I had already seen my mother-in-law, Mathilda, wield power. No, Melisende was far more subtle, and she possessed a far more"—she paused—"*luxurious* spirit. She opened up a world of possibilities to me, as well—a certain way of facing life."

"In what way, Your Majesty?" I ventured.

"She was never daunted when confronted by constraint, or convention. There have been many times, in the years that followed, when I have thought of her. When I have had to take control, on my own. When I have had to make decisions that customarily fall beyond the realm of women." A certain expression had come upon her face—at once intense, faraway, and slightly melancholy. "And then there was her sense of history. Of dynasty. Of blood. Of the continuation of rule through her sons. She also knew how to employ beauty, poetry, and art to perpetuate a dynasty. In that regard"—she paused —"I have often thought of the tombs we saw—not only in Jerusalem and Antioch, but in those desolate places in the desert as well.

"The Abbot Suger understood the power of art and beauty, as well," she continued to reflect. "I came to appreciate that quality of his a few years later, on my return to France. But the Outremer of Melisende was of another intensity entirely! The dazzling nature of the churches, and the court, with its scholars and poets. Yes, as I look back on that journey, I often think of Melisende. And of others there." Her expression abruptly changed. "But I have diverted us from our mission today," she announced.

"Our mission?"

"Yes. Our reading together. The stories in the books."

"I do not think we have deviated from our 'mission,' Your Majesty. We have merely provided a prelude to it."

"A prelude?"

"Yes. Our *own* stories have served as the prelude, have they not? I told you the story of my bracelets, and you told me the story of your hourglass, about Melisende and Jerusalem."

She looked at me wistfully. "It is strange how much you remind me of my daughter, of Joanna. Now, let us get to the stories at hand," she continued in the brisk tone of one keeping emotion at bay. "Tell me the titles."

"One is a book of three ballads—*Lanval, Yonec,* and *Laüstic.*"

"Ah, the *lais* of the famous and rather mysterious balladeer Marie de France. Her works are much in fashion at the court," she added.

"Why 'mysterious'?"

"No one is quite certain who she is. Some whisper that she may be Henry's half-sister—a half-sister born in sin, I should add. A rumor that has piqued much gossip, as you can imagine." She smiled slyly. "I am well acquainted with the first tale—indeed, it is one of my favorites—but not the other two. Tales of unrequited love and of the *mal marié,* no doubt. Stories all too familiar to me." Then, wryly, "And to you, as well, no doubt."

Smiling slightly, I replied, "I am surprised that the sisters should send literature that is not of a sacred nature. I had expected only Psalters and the like."

"It should not have surprised you. Amesbury is akin to Fontevraud. The same order, the same ethos. Noble women like yourself live there, women who have not taken vows. Thus they have access to other sorts of books. Histories, and the latest works from France."

"Tell me the titles of the others," she commanded.

"*A Life of Saint Radegonde.* And *The Romance of Alexander.*"

"Ah, those are much too somber," she said. "Let us begin with the *lais.*" I read *Yonec* first, then *Laüstic*—melancholy tales of women kept in check, and ultimately punished, by their husbands. When I came to the end, the queen asked, "What do you think of the tales?"

"Artfully told, but terribly sad. Stories of women struggling to be free, in one way or another—" But there I stopped, unwilling to admit how deeply the theme had affected me. "I cannot help but wonder—"

"Wonder what?"

I felt my cheeks flush. "It is not my place to say, Your Majesty."

"I command that you *do* say. Tell me."

"I think it odd," I ventured awkwardly, "that stories of imprisoned women should have been chosen for you."

"Odd?" She gave a hearty laugh. "It is not 'odd' at all! No doubt it is meant to be a message, to remind me of my own situation, and of Henry's power over me. It is not the first time such a veiled, if poetic, reminder has been sent. And it will not be the last, I assure you. But let us stop now. That is enough for today." Again, the imperious tilt of her head, which usually signaled a new train of thought. "You are an able reader," she said, "not a compliment I have given many. You have managed in this short time to transport me to another world."

"I sense you find great solace in stories, Your Majesty," I remarked, closing the book.

"Yes, that is quite true. Even the king knows how much literature means to me. As a pleasure, as a comfort. For him to deprive me of books—no, there is a limit to his cruelty, even if that limit is partly motivated by pragmatism. It would not help him if my sons knew I was suffering unnecessarily. It would only spur them on to greater action. And that is the last thing that Henry wants."

She bent down and drew Paris to her lap. "You may tell Tancred we have finished," she announced. "We will continue reading tomorrow."

I glanced at the other objects on the table beside her. "May I ask a question before I leave, Your Majesty?"

"You may."

"You told me the story about the hourglass. What of the other object—the gold casket? Does it have a story as well?"

"It does. The casket was given to me by my son Richard, when we were together, in France." She turned it so the front panel, with its scene of slashing swords, was visible. "If you look closely you will see that it depicts the murder of Becket. It, too, has a message: to remind me what the king—my husband, and Richard's father—is capable of."

# CHAPTER 77

Thus it was in her library, and through the medium of stories, that I truly came to know the queen. Sometimes, as we sat together, I would close my eyes and recall those cherished afternoons of reading with my grandfather. Yet there was a difference in the nature of the two experiences: my grandfather's tales had provided an escape from the dreariness of daily life, a respite from the censure of my parents, some solace in the aftermath of punishments. Reading with the queen became a way to excavate her life, her history, her character. Often I would find a way to pose an important question obliquely, through stories. In this fashion I began to glean much about her—whom she liked and whom she detested; whom she admired and whom she scorned; whom she trusted and whom she did not.

As we read of the Trojan War, I learned of the queen's fascination with the legend of Helen of Troy: as we read of King Arthur and his knights, I recognized her alertness to legacy—her own, and that of her family. A saga featuring fractious children would cause her to stop and reflect upon her sons and their struggles with their father; a tale about a girl wrenched from her family would spark wistful reminiscences of her own daughters' departures to foreign lands when they were children— Lenora to Spain, Joanna to Sicily, Mathilda to Saxony. The tale of a celebrated knight who had betrayed his wife with another woman prompted her to bitterly recall the king's flagrantly public liaison, years before, with Rosamund Clifford, a beautiful young Englishwoman.

History, poetry, and philosophy also elicited reactions that provided a window to her inner self. Among the most illuminating in that regard were the letters of Seneca. The titles of a few favorites: "On groundless fears," "On worldliness and retirement," "On the futility of halfway

measures," and "On travel as a cure for discontent." The last included a
passage that she asked me to read aloud twice: "Though you may cross
vast spaces of sea, your faults will follow you whithersoever you travel.
Do you ask why such flight does not help you? It is because you flee
along with yourself."

After I had read this aloud, she reflected, "Earlier in my life, I would
never have appreciated the wisdom of such an idea. It is only after
being shut in here that I am able to understand it."

Such conversations also helped me to discern the shifting landscapes
of the queen's mind—her moods, pleasures, and foibles. I quickly discerned that there was not one self, but several: the private woman—wife
and mother—and the imperial persona, the Queen of England and
fabled Duchess of Aquitaine (the latter employed, to great effect, de-
pending on her purpose).

Only very occasionally were there glimpses of the impulsive young
woman she professed once to have been. It was clear, as time passed, that
she had, with her formidable will, learned to accept with grace what the
Fates had decreed for her. "As one who has always been accustomed to
acting in media res, and who is now a bystander, I have had to learn
a different set of skills. A different kind of discipline. I have learned
to wait and be patient." I came to realize that captivity had not only
chastened her, but also had forged her into a wiser and more responsible woman. It was her stalwartness, discipline, and courage I came to
admire above all; I daresay it was those very qualities that had also won
the respect of the men guarding her.

But even my absorption in my new life, and my growing friendship
with the queen, could not erase my longing for word of the world I
had left behind. When, on occasion, I received letters from Clementia,
I fell upon them hungrily (albeit not without a first anxious glance to
ascertain if there were more ominous news of Gerard). No matter that
their language was guarded, and that their contents had, without doubt,
already been perused by Tancred: they were a connection to the world
of the abbey, and, most of all, to Marie.

Clementia had warned me, before my departure, about the constrained nature of any letters we would exchange. "All correspondence is reviewed by the king's men," she had told me. "Do not be surprised if you find seals broken before my letters are given to you." The lack of privacy was most vexing, at first, when I would respond to Clementia: I found scant pleasure in writing when I was obligated to measure each word. Gradually, however, I grew accustomed even to this, and found satisfying, if indirect ways, to express myself. Soon, in what became something of a ritual, I began to share Clementia's letters with the queen. As I read them aloud, I was struck by her attentiveness to even the most prosaic details—word of a new land grant to the abbey, for instance, or repairs to a mill. To my delight, descriptions of Marie—her love of stories, her progress with Latin—also seemed to intrigue her.

It quickly became clear, however, that these necessarily measured descriptions of abbey life were never quite enough to satisfy the queen's lively mind. Thus I began to augment Clementia's anecdotes with my own recollections of life at Fontevraud. It amused the queen to hear of priggish Guy's visit and his clumsy attempts to win over Clementia, for instance, or of Fastrada descending upon the abbey like an "avenging angel." I told the queen more about Marie, as well—her fascination with the bronze falcon, and how I had left it with her "almost as a talisman."

Occasionally, after I had recounted these stories of my past, a certain melancholy would engulf me. I would begin to wonder when I would see Marie and Clementia again; when, if ever, I would see Fastrada, or my father, or beloved Arnaut, whose absence and silence filled me with despair.

What would life hold for me in the years to come? Would I ever marry again, or have a child? Sometimes, as I observed Jeannette's coquetry with Tancred, I would feel uncomfortable, almost envious: not of her actual liaison with Tancred, but of the idea of it. I was a young woman, after all, and far from immune to romantic longings. At such moments, I would think of the bronze falcon I had left behind, and how, in the past, I would gaze into his enameled eyes, seeking guidance. But here, faraway from France in my solitary chamber, the rough English wind buffeting the stone walls, I had no such oracle.

ONE MORNING, JEANNETTE ARRIVED AT my chamber in a notably merry mood. Her eyes had a certain gleam, which I knew by now meant one of two things: she had been consorting with Tancred, or a letter had arrived from France.

"My lady," she said. "This"—she brandished a roll of parchment—"has arrived for you. From Fontevraud!"

"Go and inform the queen that I have just received a letter from Sister Clementia," I told her. "You know how precise she is about time. Explain that I shall be a bit late, and that I ask her understanding."

Intent on lingering, she nodded somewhat reluctantly; then, more brightly, "And then should I return to fetch you, my lady?"

"Yes." Always aware of her nibbling curiosity, I added, with a patient smile, "And then I promise to tell you if there is any news."

The moment she left, I broke open the seal and cast my eyes upon Clementia's letter. My delight in seeing her signature—tall, elegant, controlled—was tempered when I discovered another letter contained within hers: a letter in my brother's hand. I set his aside uneasily and began to read hers. It began auspiciously enough—life at the abbey was peaceful, the abbess had been tending to another unfortunate family in Saumur, the crops looked promising, etc. I came to the final page:

You will find another letter enclosed here, and which arrived only yesterday. It is from your brother Guy. I told the bearer that you had left in a great hurry with the intention of helping a friend, and that I was uncertain of your whereabouts. I instructed him to tell Guy that, should I discover where you had settled, I would do my utmost to ensure that his message made its way to you.

The abbess and I have no doubt you continue to be a pleasant and able companion to the queen. And we trust that our sisters at Amesbury also continue to provide you with books to enrich and edify your life, and that of the queen.

We savored your last letter and your descriptions of life in the English realm, and do hope you will write us soon. Until then, I send my God's blessings, dear Isabelle, as I do my affectionate thoughts—

*Clementia*

After finishing her letter, I reluctantly picked up Guy's, which was penned in the crabbed hand I knew all too well:

*To the Countess Isabelle, greetings from her brother, Guy de Lapalisse*

Let me not tarry in conveying the details of the misfortune that has befallen our family; to expend unnecessary words, and to indulge in the elaborate locutions which some would employ in imparting such somber developments is not, as you know, my modus operandi. Therefore, I shall be brief. Word reached us yesterday that our brother, Arnaut, has passed from this world—drowned, yes drowned, on his return from the Holy Land. Those fortunate few whom God elected to survive apprised us of this tragedy upon their return home. They told us they had taken ship at Tyre, and that the vessel was unable to withstand a storm that raged along the coast of the Adriatic.

While struggling to recover from distress, I forced myself to inquire what, if anything, the men knew of our brother's state of affairs on his departure. (Even you, dear sister, cannot deny that Arnaut had been appallingly negligent in informing his family of his circumstances, material or otherwise.) They informed me that our brother had acquired a considerable land grant from the wealthy Norman knight he had served in the region of Tripoli, and that it had been Arnaut's intention to make a new life in Apulia. Again, and despite my great sadness, I forced myself to inquire if they knew whether the land bequeathed to him would pass to our family, in the event of his demise. The men, who seemed familiar with the tenets of the grant, did not think it would. (I hesitate to mention, in the light of his plight, what seems all too evident: Arnaut's considerable, though admittedly woefully characteristic, lack of judgment in forging the statutes of this agreement.)

It has required all my strength, as you can well imagine, to shepherd our family through this tragedy. Father is distraught and has hardly been able to eat or speak. Even Hortense cannot coax him to consume a single morsel. I, as the eldest, and the de facto head of the family, do not have the luxury of indulging in such behavior. I must conduct myself as is my wont—by summoning the strength of Hercules, and the faith of Abraham, in my efforts to ease our family's pain. In this I have been ably aided by Amélie, who has displayed the dignity and composure one has long come to expect of her. I should add that wise, steadfast Balduin has been a source of great support to us: how fortunate your sister is to have made such a marriage, and to have a husband who exemplifies such devotion and compassion! I realize, of course, that you have not had the good fortune of your sister's marital situation—still, it is my fervent hope that you will at least emulate her worthy example in this regard, as you grieve, and that you will comport yourself in a manner befitting our family and rank.

My sole consolation amid this sadness is the knowledge that you will receive my letter while you are in the holy community of Fontevraud. It comforts me to know that while you are in mourning, the prayers of the good sisters will reinforce your own.

I would not be surprised should Sister Clementia, in her effort to assuage your sadness, also suggest that I return to visit you at the abbey. After all, who other than myself, your devoted brother, would be able to provide you comfort at such a time? I give you my leave to inform her that I would readily consider making the journey north, if only to be at your side. In addition, I must confess that prayers presided over by the nuns in that hallowed setting would provide me great solace as I, too, grieve; so, too, would the wise counsel and serene presence of the noble Sister Clementia. I shall await word from you in this regard. If she deems it expedient, I could set forth to Fontevraud within the month.

Lastly, I counsel you to withstand the temptation to indulge yourself in sorrow so inordinate that it verges on unseemliness. God wills when we are born; God wills when we will die. Let me remind you that the reserve of human grief, unlike that of His love, is not infinite. In my own sorrow I have found it helpful to recall a passage from Virgil often cited by our grandfather: *Dabit deus his quoque finem.*

I shall await your response. Until then, fare you well, sister.

*Guy*

I stood in stunned silence; then I began to sob. After the deaths of my babies, I had feared the death of my brother more than anything else. Now that, too, had happened—and it had happened far away, in a churning foreign sea, without my ever being able to say goodbye. He had not even known a good death, with family around him and a priest to administer holy rites. No prayers, no solace of human touch, no loving goodbyes! I held my head in my hands, trying to annihilate my horrifying imaginings of his final moments—the moments when, submerged by relentless waves and choking in black, fathomless water, he knew he had expended his last breath, and that the sea would devour him.

I thought of our games, our merriment, and our secrets, and all they had meant to me. With Arnaut gone, my last connection to all I had cherished in my childhood had vanished. It seemed yet another cruel trick that God had played upon me: He had taken away the brother I adored and left me with two siblings I neither loved nor trusted.

Finally, exhausted from sobbing, I wiped my hot, swollen face. Then I closed my eyes and began taking deep breaths, trying to calm myself— alas, to no avail.

I heard a knocking at the door, and Jeannette entered. I wiped my face once more and struggled to gain my composure.

"My lady!" she said, hurrying toward me. "What has happened?"

"My brother has died. Arnaut. He has drowned in a shipwreck. Drowned—" I repeated the word again, as if still trying to comprehend its meaning.

"Oh, my lady, how sad I am for you!" She stood close by, awkwardly extending her hand, as if she did not quite know the proper way to console me. "I shall tell the queen you are indisposed," she said. "Should I also tell her about your loss?"

"I must tell her myself. It is only right." I took a handkerchief from my pocket, wiped my eyes, and hastened to the queen's reading chamber.

The guards tried to bar me from entering—she and Tancred were conferring, they gruffly informed me—but that did not deter me. "I *must* speak with the queen now," I announced so fiercely that even the blond brute reluctantly drew aside his lance and let me pass. Deep in conversation, the queen and Tancred looked up, startled, as I burst into the room. After performing a hasty curtsey, I said, "I must have a private word with you, Your Majesty."

"At this very moment?" She looked puzzled, then almost alarmed, by my sense of urgency, as Tancred, at her side, scowled at me.

"It is not proper that you should disrupt the queen this way, Lady Isabelle," he reprimanded. He had become rather wary of my increasing closeness to the queen—indeed, there were moments when he seemed suspicious of the increasing time I spent with her.

"I cannot wait," I told him as he tried to hold me back. "It concerns the letter I have just received."

"You have gone quite pale," interjected the queen, beckoning to me. "What can it possibly be? Not bad news concerning Marie—"

"No. Something else. Something I must tell you in private."

"I see," said the queen. She turned to Tancred: "Best you leave me now to speak with Lady Isabelle. We shall resume our conversation later. I shall call for you."

"Very well, Your Majesty." At that he bowed, and after a curt, even furious, nod in my direction, departed.

"Something terrible has happened," she said, beckoning to come close. "Tell me, Isabelle—"

I walked toward the chair opposite her as a sleepwalker might— uncertainly, hazily, as if the ground might give way with each step. Then I let the dreadful story tumble forth—what I just learned, and how Arnaut had died. Holding my face in my hands, I began to weep.

"Oh, dear Isabelle," she lamented, "I know how much you loved your brother, and how painful it must be to think of him dying this way!"

"I am sorry to trouble you with this, Your Majesty," I murmured. "To burden you with my sadness."

"It is hardly a burden! Far better to give vent to your feelings, and to your sorrow, than to let those emotions destroy you. It is only the foolish who find courage in masking grief." She extended her arms to me. "Come, pull your chair closer."

I did so; she took my hand in her lap and began to stroke it gently. "I promise you, Isabelle, that the pain will eventually subside. Little by little, day by day. I have lost so many loved ones, you know! My mother, my father, and my brother when I was a girl. Later, my beloved uncle Raymond, killed in battle. Then Petronilla, my younger sister, whom I adored, and my eldest child, William, when he was but three." She smiled forlornly. "I can only tell you that the spirits of loved ones eventually become woven into the warp and woof of one's life. You will come to see this." She took a handkerchief from her pocket and gave it to me. "In the meantime, cry until you can cry no more."

I continued to weep until at last, looking up wearily, I said, "I have shed all the tears I can."

She took the handkerchief from me and wiped my cheeks with it. "Perhaps a story of my own would help you," she said. "Shall I tell it?"

"Yes," I murmured.

"Long ago, I was told of the German nun Hildegard, and her way of using plants and even gemstones and music, as agents of healing. Both of the spirit and the body. She was a woman whose learning and intellect greatly intrigued me, and whom I longed to meet. But how? It was not possible then for me to travel to Regensburg, where she resided. Then, at a fateful moment, a moment when I sorely needed guidance, I decided to send her a letter.

"It was during that terrible year when my world was in disarray—the year before the murder of Thomas Becket. The nobles in my lands, in Aquitaine, were in a state of rebellion. Several had already betrayed me—the Lusignans, among them. I had never trusted them, of course, but even so I had not imagined their genius for deceit. Then, in our English realm, Henry refused to heed my advice in his battle with Becket. I had counseled him to exercise restraint. But *no*—driven by rage, he would not cede ground. It did not help that his knights, all too eager to take the matter into their own hands, goaded him to act. Meanwhile my sons chafed under their father's iron hand. And as for Henry himself—I had been able to ignore the bastards born of servant girls and wenches. It was harder to endure when the mothers were women of rank. Women I knew, such as the daughter of Roger de Tosny." She looked down, sighing deeply. "Yes, that year when every aspect of life was thrown into chaos. It was then I wrote Hildegard."

"Did she reply?" I asked.

"She did, and her words gave me great comfort. They still do. I repeat them to myself at moments of despair. 'Your mind is like a wall battered by a storm,' she wrote. 'You look all around, and you find no rest. Stay calm, and stand firm, relying on God, and God will aid you in all your tribulations.'" She stroked my hand again. "Repeat those words to yourself, Isabelle, whenever you need strength."

DURING THAT TIME OF MOURNING, I grew even closer to the queen. I began not only to confide in her, but also to recount stories of my past life even more freely. These seemed to captivate her; sometimes, to my delight, they even made her laugh (anecdotes about Amélie's pretentions and Millicent's tiresome "piety"). I told her about my family—my beloved grandfather and the lessons he had taught me, and about the secrets I had shared with Arnaut, and our indelible journey to Nîmes. I told her how I loved the lands of my girlhood and the buried treasures of the ancient peoples I had found there—treasures I had kept, secretly, and which gave me a strange sort of solace.

Eventually, and most importantly, I began to tell her about my life with Gerard: how intoxicating the first six months had been; about his passion for his falcons and the unforgettable day I first visited the mews. But gradually, I said, the tenor of my married life had darkened. I recounted my grief in losing little Editha and my baby son, and the pressures I had felt; how scathing Gerard had been about my closeness to Aiglantine. Finally I told her about the last year of my marriage and why, in the end, I had found it unendurable. I even told her the story of Gallien, and how brutally Gerard had punished him for the loss of Vainqueur.

And then, one day in late winter, as we sat in her reading chamber, I finally told her what I had learned from Clementia's letter—that Gerard had come to the abbey, searching for me. "He is still angry with me, angry for leaving him," I said. "And I fear that his rage against me will never abate. That he will blame me for any misfortune which befalls him. Above all, I fear his capacity for revenge. That is, of course, in great part why I came here. Why Clementia thought it best I leave Fontevraud for England."

"Nothing you have said surprises me," she replied. "It is what I would have surmised."

"How?" I asked, astonished. "Did you know Gerard?"

"After we met," she began slowly, "and we took our first walk together, you mentioned your husband's name, and I told you I had heard of him. I said nothing more at the time, thinking it was neither germane nor appropriate. But now you have almost become another daughter to me. There are things I know about your husband that I can no longer withhold from you."

"Tell me what you have heard," I urged uneasily.

"It has to do with my son Richard. He told me that, years ago,

Gerard de Meurtaigne had tried to ingratiate himself to him and those in his circle. At first, impressed by his various successes, as well as his valor and resolve, he entrusted him with several important missions. But then he began to see certain traits that greatly troubled him—aspects of his character that made him uneasy."

I thought of Gerard's reticence and discomfiture whenever Richard's name had been mentioned; he did not know him well, he had told me, adding that it was the Young King, rather, with whom he maintained an allegiance. . . .

"This occurred at a time," continued the queen, "when Richard was charged with quelling the rebellion of the most intransigent Poitevin lords. There was one among them, Lord de Choiseul, who was among the rebels—a man Richard knew well and whose courage and shrewdness he admired, despite his recent acts of disloyalty. He also knew that winning over Choiseul would be key to subduing the other rebels in the region, notably Aimar de Limoges. This Choiseul was a revered leader in the region; Richard knew the others would follow his example.

"The Poitevins were effectively subdued, and your husband was given the responsibility of rounding them up, and then of dealing with those of highest rank. In a misguided attempt to curry favor perhaps, he decided on the terms of the punishment himself. Some rebels were maimed; several were executed in the most hideous way—Choiseul among them. When he learned of this, Richard was furious. With this course of action, your husband had only succeeded in engendering a legacy of hate—a destructive legacy that continues to this day.

"It was then Richard became aware of certain dangerous aspects of Gerard de Meurtaigne's character—the impetuousness, as well as the arrogance and self-regard that had deluded him into thinking he had no need to consult his superiors. Richard also discerned his quickness to punish, and to punish brutally, even if it would be far from advantageous to do so. It was *these* qualities that caused Richard to distance himself from your husband."

"Yes," I said. "I observed those same traits in my husband—his tendency to be punitive, to rush to judgment. Yet he always prided himself on being a politic man, a man skilled in strategy. Does this not seem contradictory, in light of his actions?"

"Only in one who lacks self-knowledge," came her unnerving reply. She looked down, her expression pensive. "After that episode, your husband, aware that he had destroyed any chance of allying himself with Richard, focused his energies instead on Henry, the Young King. No doubt it seemed most expedient for your husband to ally himself with the eldest prince—it is Henry, not Richard, who is next in line to the throne. It was not difficult for Gerard de Meurtaigne to win over Young Henry—with money, of course. My eldest son is as profligate as he is impulsive. It is equally true of John, my youngest, alas." She shook her head in dismay. "These traits are a dangerous combination, but most of all, in a future king!

"But the story does not end there," she resumed. "It seems that only recently Gerard de Meurtaigne has encouraged the Young King to plot against Richard, as my two sons maneuver against their father. In this, your husband has made a grave mistake. Richard is not someone who countenances this sort of deceit. He, too, remembers the past and those who cross him. Richard is the Duke of Aquitaine, after all: there is a certain passion and also steeliness in his blood that my eldest son, however charming and handsome, however *popular*"—she pronounced the last word with disdain—"lacks. I am a mother, of course," she continued, "but even more importantly, I am a queen. It is my responsibility to assess my children, and especially my sons, dispassionately—to recognize their faults as well as their strengths. It is my sons who will inherit the mantle of power, and who will preserve the empire Henry and I have created—*his* England and Normandy, with *my* Aquitaine. Therefore I must see them for who they are—not what I *hoped* they would be. That is one great difference between myself and my own husband. For all his brilliance as an administrator and strategist, Henry is woefully lacking in astuteness with regard to his sons."

But it was, of course, what she had revealed about Gerard that I fastened on. "I had no idea you knew so much about my husband—"

She smiled in an almost playful way. "Then, clearly, you did not listen to me! Months ago, I told you I know *everything*." Her tone resumed its previous gravity. "So now you know that when the time came for your husband to reveal his true self, he did, and in a way that made a profound impression on Richard. It is also through these incidents that I came to understand your husband's character. He is ruthless. Ruthless, determined, ambitious, and punitive. You have a right to be frightened." She leaned forward, taking my hand in hers. "Fortunately, you are here, with me, and well protected," she added reassuringly. "Your husband will never be able to reach you here!"

"But if I should leave England, Your Majesty?" I asked anxiously. "If I should ever return to France, to Fontevraud, if only to see Marie and Clementia?"

"Ah, then, I cannot know for certain. If I resided at Fontevraud as well, it would of course be another matter. Then I could protect you. Even he would not dare to go against the queen. But if I were *not* there—alas, we know from recent history that even being in a holy place does not necessarily shield one from harm. From plots. From those who seek revenge. Becket's murder made that all too clear. Indeed, one could almost say his death marked a new era: we now live in a world where a cathedral is no longer sacrosanct. Not even for its archbishop. Why would we think that an abbey, then, would protect a nun?

"And you, Isabelle, you are not a holy sister after all," she continued. "You have not taken vows. And if I am correct—and I believe I am— you do not intend to do so. You have many wonderful qualities, but I do not envision you taking the veil." She smiled almost mischievously. "Am I correct?"

"You are. I cannot deny that."

"Then you must be resigned to remain here, with me. I must admit, selfishly, that this does not displease me. I would miss you if you left."

"And I would miss you, Your Majesty. But there are other pulls—"

"Of course. Marie. You need say no more. Come, Isabelle," she said, embracing me. "Do not think of yourself as having been banished from France, but as being *safe*, and far from Gerard and his vengefulness. Above all you must hold strong," she exhorted. "You must gird your mind, and your considerable will, as you always have. You must be canny, and you must not cower." She pressed my hand. "And you must also remember the words Hildegard wrote me: let them sustain you, as they have sustained me. Repeat them to yourself as you might a prayer to the Virgin. Pray to God and ask Him to guide you."

"I still struggle to achieve that kind of faith. I told Sister Clementia as much," I said, adding, "there have been too many times when I have felt that God has deserted me." I glanced away, haunted by the memory of the moment when I had discovered Editha in her cradle, as cold and still as stone; the moment when I had learned that Arnaut had drowned.

"I, too, felt that way when I was younger," she replied, glancing at the hourglass, which stood on the table by her side. "But the passage of years, and of learning to accept what once seemed unfathomable, changes you. It is only then you reach some sort of peace." She touched my hand again. "Mark my words. There will come a day when you will realize that I am right." She ran her finger along the rim of the hour-glass. "The passing years have taught me there is a certain grace, even a virtue, in resignation."

# CHAPTER 78

One morning, in late spring, I noticed that the queen seemed unusually distracted. "Is there something wrong, Your Majesty?" I asked before we commenced reading.

She glanced at the doorway, which was only partly covered by the portière. "Draw the portière," she said.

I walked to the doorway and pulled the heavy curtain closed. "Come nearer," she instructed me, after I returned to her.

"There is chaos in France," she began in a low, urgent voice. "The king and Richard fighting my son Henry. There are rumors of depredations, of the looting of holy places. I do not know exactly where, and by whom. If only I could find out!" She looked down, wringing her hands.

"Perhaps I can find out," I murmured.

"How?"

"I am sure that Tancred and the men have heard. Recently I have seen them huddling together, speaking with great urgency. When I came near, they abruptly ceased. Is it not likely that they were discussing the situation in France?"

"Even if they were, they would hardly tell you."

"True," I replied, with a conspiratorial smile. "But it is not unlikely that Tancred would tell Jeannette."

LATER THAT NIGHT, AS JEANNETTE was brushing my hair, I told her: "I have seen the men talking together in quite an urgent way recently. They look so intent, as if something quite serious had happened."

"Is that so, my lady?" she asked.

"Yes. I could not help but wonder what they might be discussing."

I yawned, then sighed. "Life is so tedious here, is it not, Jeannette? The ennui of being so confined. How I dream of returning to France!"

"To France?" She looked alarmed. "Oh, you must not, my lady! The queen would miss you. We would all miss you. But the queen especially. She has been in much better spirits since your arrival. You have made life here much easier for us. I know you have for me! I have more freedom now because you occupy the queen so well."

"That gladdens me to hear," I replied; then, almost petulantly, "I only wish I might occasionally have word of what is happening beyond these walls. What is happening across the Channel. I assume that Tancred and the men must hear news quite regularly."

"Oh yes," she replied, with surprising matter-of-factness as she grasped my hair and began to plait it.

"I suppose it may simply be my imagination," I continued, "but I cannot help but think that something important must have happened. The way the men have been convening."

"Well," she said rather coyly, "I *have* heard a few things."

"Do tell me, Jeannette! Otherwise I shall die of boredom here, and I shall ask Ralph FitzStephen to allow me to return home!"

I held my breath, watching as she deliberated. "But you cannot tell the queen!" she said at last. "Tancred would be angry. And I would be in great trouble. Not only with him, but with the others, should they ever find out."

"I feel rather insulted that you should ever think I would do such a thing!" I exclaimed. "The abbey has entrusted me with responsibilities and a code of honor. You yourself said I was trustworthy."

"Oh no, my lady, I did not mean to suggest otherwise." She hesitated, and then, leaning forward, began to speak softly. "The men say there is much fighting in France. King Henry and Prince Richard have reconciled and are in league together. But the Young King, Prince Henry, has somehow allied himself with the King of France."

"With Philippe?"

"Yes! The men here call Philippe 'crafty.' That was the word they used. And it also seems that the Young King, in desperation—they say he always needs money—has done some terrible things." She shook her head in dismay. "Yes—*terrible!*"

"What has he done?"

"Best I not say, my lady," she replied, tying the plait. "I have already told you too much."

I refrained from replying and merely stood up, trying to think of a way to spur her on. My eyes alighted on a red shawl of Alexandrian silk, which lay on the bed; Jeannette had long admired it.

"Ah—I forgot to put this back into the cupboard!" I said, picking it up. Then I draped it around my shoulders, parading before her as an elegant court lady might.

"Oh, how lovely you look in that, my lady!" she said admiringly.

"It *is* a splendid color, is it not? Here." I took it off and placed it around her shoulders. "Look how well it suits you!" The shawl did indeed enhance her coloring, for it made her eyes look very green.

I held the mirror up, watching as she gazed at her reflection, and said, "It would make me happy to give the shawl to you—"

"Oh, my lady!" she cried with delight, turning to me.

"I only ask one thing."

"What, my lady?"

"Tell me what you hear from the men—what is happening in France. What the Young King has done."

"Oh, my lady, I cannot!" she protested, but—I noticed—somewhat mildly.

"Well, then"—I sighed, taking the shawl from her—"I suppose I must resign myself to boredom."

"Perhaps I *could* tell you a few things," she said, eyeing the shawl.

"Think how lovely you will look in it! You yourself told me that the queen likes her attendants to dress well. Finish telling me what is happening in France, and it is yours," I said, before adding, "you said that the Young King has done some terrible things—"

"Yes," she said, lowering her voice. "He has stolen from churches. He has looted the shrine of Rocamadour, can you imagine! God will smite him for that. The people in the countryside and towns are cursing him. They say he is following the path of Satan. Most of all, he has made enemies of his father, the king, and his brother Richard. The men say his father will never forgive him."

"This is frightful news, Jeannette." Then, with concerted casualness, I asked, "Do you know whether the king and Richard have succeeded in holding their lands against him?"

"The men say they have. And that the king and Prince Richard are in close pursuit of one of the most important rebels—one of the ringleaders, they told me."

"Do you know the rebel's name?" I asked.

She shrugged. "They did not tell me."

"Perhaps you can manage to get more information." I handed her the shawl, which she took with reassuring alacrity.

"It is late," Jeannette exclaimed. "I must leave and attend to other things." I bade her good night.

As she approached the door, I called, "Jeannette—do not forget!"

"What, my lady?"

"Try to find out the name of that rebel."

She gave a quick nod and left, the shawl trailing behind her.

PREOCCUPIED WITH WHAT JEANNETTE HAD revealed, I hardly slept. It pained me to think of telling the queen that two of her sons had turned against each other; most of all that her eldest had not only forged an alliance with the King of France but had also desecrated holy shrines. But these were only a few reasons for my disquiet: I wondered about the implications of these developments with regard to Gerard, and whether he had played a role in pitting the Young King against his father and brother.

As we set off on our walk the next morning, I told the queen all I had learned. That the Young King had allied himself with the King of France did not surprise her quite as much as it had me. "Philippe is his brother-in-law," said the queen. "Henry is married to Marguerite, Philippe's sister. But that will matter little in the long term. My son has made a great mistake, one he will come to rue. Philippe is merely using him as a pawn against my husband."

The Young King's looting of Rocadamour, however, truly horrified her. "To desecrate a pilgrimage place—no, that I cannot countenance! It brings shame upon our family. He must indeed be desperate." She shook her head in despair. "He will lose support among the people if he continues on this path."

"I remember my husband saying that the Young King always needed money," I murmured.

"Yes. For the lists he loves, and all the reckless spending that requires. For the mounts, the equipment." She gave a deep sigh. "As for your husband," she added, "it cannot bode well. Mark my words."

"And, assuming it does not," I asked, "what do you foresee happening?"

"A dangerous situation. My son Richard's anger toward your husband, and his distrust of him, will only become more intense. That will make his life more difficult. But that is not all I predict."

I looked at her anxiously. "What do you mean?"

"Your husband will find a way to blame you for these failures. Such men always do."

"But why would he blame *me*?" I asked, stunned. "I had nothing to do with this!"

"It is in his nature. He cannot admit to having made mistakes. He will find a way to ascribe blame, I assure you. And his rage will know no bounds."

We continued to walk in silence, the queen walking quickly, as was her custom, her gaze fixed ahead. Suddenly she turned to me. "Yes, it is good you are here with me, in England. I shudder to think what might happen if you were discoverable, in France. I am not even sure my son and his men could protect you."

THE QUEEN'S SOBERING WORDS THAT day deeply affected me. Though I had, by that time, become accustomed to life in England, I had always harbored the hope that I would, one day, be able to return to France. (With the queen, perhaps, I would think in a sanguine moment.) But the conversation about the implications of turmoil in

France, vis-à-vis Gerard, quelled those hopes; nor did the subsequent weeks of interminable late spring rain help to lift my gloomy, fearful mood. Under the tutelage of the queen, I had, admittedly, become more skilled at concealing these emotions: I doubt that Tancred and the men, or even Jeannette, ever suspected what surged within me.

With the queen, however, it was impossible to dissemble. She could discern my disposition by the slightest inflection in my voice or by the way I carried myself. She tried with unceasing, almost touching, determination to create distractions for me—reading, chess, long walks during which she told stories of her own past (the last, by far the most effective).

One rainy afternoon in early June when I was feeling particularly disheartened, she made an effort to divert me: first, with reading some lighthearted tales, then with a game of chess. After I had made an especially deft sacrifice, she observed, "Your game has definitely improved. Alas, I fear your spirits have not."

"It enrages me that Gerard now effectively controls my life—where I live, where I may travel. And while I have treasured my time here with you, Your Majesty, it galls me that I cannot return to Fontevraud anytime soon. If only for a short visit, to see Marie! Has God not punished me enough?"

"I am surprised it is not the 'ruthless gods'—or so your favorite Roman poet called them—whom you blame," she replied, adding, "self-pity is highly unproductive, and quite unworthy of you, Isabelle."

I looked down, feeling my cheeks color.

"You are thinking too much," she continued, her tone somewhat gentler. "And projecting far too much into the future. The future is not a wall one comes up against, but something infinitely more mysterious, with unforeseen twists and turns. Think of the labyrinths of the ancient peoples who fascinate you."

"What else can my future hold but darkness, with Gerard lying in wait, intent on revenge?" I asked with some bitterness.

"You have no choice but to embrace the future bravely, whatever it holds," she went on, tilting her head back in a way that usually signaled an idea had come to her. "Perhaps we should put chess aside and try another game. One that might help divine the future." She picked up her treasured copy of *The Aeneid*, which lay on the table next to her, and handed it to me. "A game having to do with your treasured Virgil."

"A game?"

"Yes. Close your eyes and let the pages fall open where they may," she instructed. "Then place your finger upon a passage, open your eyes, and read it aloud. We will see what it augurs."

"And if it does not augur well—what then?" I asked, only partly in jest.

"That it will fall to *me*, as Duchess of Aquitaine and Queen of England"—this, in a theatrically regal voice—"to interpret it. Good! You are smiling. The Sortes has already lifted your spirits. Now go ahead."

I closed my eyes and followed her instructions; my finger still resting upon a page, I looked up.

"Read it," she said.

"'Since Fortune is victor, let us follow and turn our course whither she calls.' From the fifth book." My hand still lingering on the page, I gave a sigh of discontent.

"One of my favorite passages," she remarked. "But not *yours*, clearly."

"I had hoped for something more decisive. Something *clear*, something comforting."

"If only Aeneas' journey—and life—were so simple, dear Isabelle!"

JEANNETTE, MEANTIME, SEEMED TO TAKE her information-gathering assignment with a seriousness that almost amused me (whether motivated by the thought of another trinket, or merely because the task enhanced her sense of self-importance, I was not certain). A week after I had given her the scarf, she came to my chamber. "I have something to tell you, my lady," she announced with excitement. Then, in a low confiding voice, "From the men."

"Best to close the door," I said.

She had learned the name of the rebel whom the king and Richard were pursuing: Bertrand de Born. "A famous troubadour, and an evil man, the men say," she added. "They told me he has been stirring up trouble for years, using his songs and poems to rouse the people against the king. That he has been in league with Young Henry. They are closing in on him. The men say it is only a question of time before they capture his castle."

"That is very interesting," I replied, already planning when I would tell the queen. I untied a ribbon from my hair and handed it to her. "This would look lovely on you," I said, adding, "a little gift, for your efforts."

"Oh, thank you, my lady!" she replied, her eyes shining with delight.

LATER THAT DAY, WHEN I was alone with the queen, I told her what I had learned.

"Bertrand de Born?" Her tone was alarmed, her expression anguished. "Ah, if Henry and Richard are closing in on de Born, and if they capture him, that bodes ill for Young Henry." She shook her head. "Very ill."

"Is he such an important figure?"

She nodded. "A crucial ringleader. He was always a bad influence on Young Henry. One of those who, in his own quest for power, flattered my son, convincing him that he had the right, and a strong enough following, to go against his father."

She walked to the window, gazing outside, her hands planted on the sill. Finally, she turned to me and said, "If only I had been able to help my sons set things right! To counsel them all this time. As it is"—she paused—"I can only ask God to guide them. Come, Isabelle, let us say a prayer together." She approached the prie-dieu, which stood in the corner, and beckoned me to join her. As I knelt beside her, she said, "I have learned, in captivity, to find more solace in God. Let us pray that He hears me now—if not as a queen, then, as a mother."

TWO WEEKS LATER, IN THE middle of June, as I sat in my chamber penning one of my carefully worded letters to Clementia, I heard a frantic knocking. After setting down my quill, I hastened to the door. It was Jeannette, her face ashen.

"What has happened?" I asked.

"Terrible news from France, my lady. The Young King is dead! Tancred asked me to tell you. The queen is distraught."

I stood up, shocked. "Do you know how he died? And where?"

"No," she said, shaking her head. "Come with me now. The queen asks to see you."

As we entered the great reception chamber, I glimpsed Tancred and another man, a stranger, deep in conversation before the side entrance to the queen's reading chamber. The man was tall and white-haired, elegant in mien. I knew from the rich stuff and costly trim of his cloak that he was a nobleman of high rank.

"Who is that gentleman?" I whispered to Jeannette.

"The emissary sent by the king, from France."

Tancred beckoned me to approach. As I did so, accompanied by Jeannette, he gave a vehement signal that she should stay back. She looked away, so visibly abashed that I almost pitied her. There was an unpleasant smugness about him—the smugness of one who has been entrusted with sharing important intelligence.

"Let me present Thomas of Early," he announced rather pompously. "The king has sent him from France with the bad tidings."

I curtseyed before de Early, whose craggy face was taut and emotionless.

"I am greatly saddened by the news," I said.

"It is indeed a tragedy," he replied in a voice disconcertingly even.

"The queen awaits you," interjected Tancred. "You may enter her chamber."

The queen stood by the window, her back toward me, Paris curled at her feet.

"Your Majesty," I said.

She turned to face me, her cheeks glistening with tears, a ghostly white handkerchief crumpled in her hand. In the harsh noon light of summer her eyes looked ancient, and the lines of her face cruelly deep.

"You have heard, then?" she asked wearily.

"Yes. My heart breaks for you." I did not dare to embrace her; grief seemed to have made her even less approachable than usual.

"But you do not know how the Young King died?" she asked with that terrible, quizzical weariness.

"No, Your Majesty," I replied, lowering my head.

"Come and sit with me." She gave a small, despairing smile. "With me and Paris." The ermine, as if sensing his mistress's sorrow, crawled into her lap.

"He did not die fighting," she began, stroking the creature's fur. "My greatest fear was that he would be killed by his father or brother in battle. God has spared me that pain, at least. No, it was illness— dysentery. At Martel. The people will say that God finally caught up with him—punishing him for having defiled His sacred places. And they may very well be right." She looked down, still stroking Paris, tears running down her cheeks. "He was a beautiful little boy! And so promising as a young man. If only he had listened to the wisest men around him. To William Marshal, whom he loved, and who trained him as a knight. But no, he was too fond of diversions, and all too easily distracted by the sycophants who people royal courts. They must have deluded him into thinking that he was a match for his father and Richard. Alas! My only comfort is that they say he died a good death." She looked at me almost imploringly.

"What do you know of his last moments?" I asked, leaning forward.

"De Early said he repented of his sins and asked to be buried at Rouen as a monk—in a sackcloth, surrounded by ashes in the shape of a cross."

"Was de Early there, with him?"

She shook her head. "No. My son was surrounded by a few of his own men. Henry learned these details from his own emissary, whom he had sent with a token—his sapphire ring. My son had implored his father to come to his deathbed, but Henry would not, thinking it possibly a ruse." With quiet bitterness she added, "I am told my son took the ring as a sign of his father's forgiveness." She looked up, her eyes fixed mournfully inward, as she added, "They say he bequeathed the cloak he had chosen for the Holy War, to William Marshal."

"I did not know that the Young King had ever gone to the Holy Land—"

"He did not. He had merely *hoped* to." She sighed deeply, before repeating, "'Hoped to.' Those can be fatal words. The words of one who chooses easy paths—wishing and plotting, over the rigor of strategy, sacrifice, and action. One can always"—her voice took on an almost caustic tone—"*hope to.*" She looked at me directly. "I am glad you are here with me, Isabelle," she said, with sudden, touching warmth.

I stood up and embraced her. But the moment we drew apart, she quickly brushed her face of tears. "But I cannot permit myself to luxuriate in grief. It would be—I was about to say 'unseemly.' But it is only partly that. No, I must force myself to look ahead. To fix my attention on the future."

"But surely, Your Majesty, you may permit yourself a time of proper mourning."

"I may—as long as it does not affect the focus on my capital concern."

"And what is that?"

"Richard and his new status as eldest son. His role in the realm." Her expression brightened almost imperceptibly, and her hand, which had been stroking Paris, suddenly dropped to her side. She drew her shoulders back, assuming her customary queenly bearing. "With Young Henry gone, it is Richard—*my* Richard—who will succeed his father," she continued in a clear, unwavering voice. "Richard, who will next be king."

I looked down, uncertain how to respond, for the note of triumph in her voice had taken me aback.

"Yes," she said, seemingly lost in thought. "This will signal change. Great change." She looked up decisively. "Was de Early waiting outside, with Tancred?"

"Yes."

"See if he is still there. Tell him I want to see him."

"And if he is not?"

"Tell Tancred to find him at once."

# CHAPTER 79

The death of the Young King seemed to free the flow of information, and it was no longer necessary to resort to subterfuge to obtain news for the queen. This came as something of a disappointment to Jeannette, who had clearly come to savor her exalted role as intelligence-gatherer, particularly in the wake of Tancred's rebuff in the presence of de Early. (Indeed, there was a notable new coolness between them: Tancred's attempts to soothe her wounded pride after de Early's departure seemed to have met with little success.)

Through various, lesser emissaries, we learned that the castle of Bertrand de Born had been taken, that the key insurgents in league with Young Henry had been captured, and that the king and Prince Richard emerged victorious. One envoy brought us poignant details of Young Henry's final hours: on his deathbed, the prince had dictated a letter imploring his father to grant his mother more freedom. Upon hearing this, the queen finally broke down before me and wept. "Long ago, I said I would give anything for more freedom," she told me. "But for it to have come about *this* way"—she shook her head in despair—"no, that was never what I desired!"

Soon the restrictions imposed upon her for the past decade began to loosen—a welcome, if bittersweet development for the queen, who found scant pleasure in her new liberties at first. "They are tinged by my son's death," she said, adding, "they have come at too great a cost."

"But you yourself once told me that everything comes at a price, Your Majesty," I returned gently.

"Alas," she conceded, "that is all too true. I suppose it is foolish, and perhaps even disrespectful of my son, for me to reject the privileges he sought for me."

"The king himself must want you to avail yourself of those privileges. Your son's entreaty must have greatly moved him, as well, or he never would have acceded to it."

"I doubt pity was behind this," she scoffed. "Henry's 'generosity' is never without an ulterior motive. Anyone who deals with him knows this." Her tone was mordant, her expression caustic. "I have heard, for instance, that many now call him generous for having granted a sizable pension to my son's widow. But Henry did this only in exchange for the borderland, which had been her dowry—the Vexin, which is crucial to his ambitions. Never let sentiment muddle your judgment, Isabelle," she cautioned, adding, "and never forget—true generosity is unknown to the ruthless."

We quickly embraced our new liberties and began to take more extensive walks. Soon we were also permitted to ride beyond the citadel walls—always escorted, of course, by the king's henchmen—and to make a sojourn to Waltham, in Essex. It filled me with delight to accompany the queen on horseback—she was a strong, graceful rider—and, for the first time, to experience with her the world outside Salisbury's forbidding ramparts.

My pleasure in this new freedom was tempered, however, by my enduring fears vis-à-vis Gerard: How would the death of the Young King affect his situation and, hence, my own future? We had learned that many associated with Young Henry had escaped to foreign soil; others, such as Bertrand de Born and Aimar de Limoges, had been punished severely and stripped of their domains. A few, like William Marshal ("the miraculous survivor," the queen fondly called him) had so impressed Richard by their valor that they went on to serve him.

"I should think that Gerard being in great disfavor would fill you with relief," the queen said one afternoon in August while we were playing chess.

"I only wish it did! Instead, it makes me even more uneasy. Gerard will not accept losing power and prestige. He will bridle against it—it may even drive him to recklessness." To this I added resignedly, "I find nothing reassuring about being left in limbo."

"I will do my best to find out what has happened to him and will ask FitzStephen to ask his sources. He is the only one here I trust." She moved her pawn. "In as much as I trust anyone."

"It will not be easy to find out. I suspect Gerard has gone into hiding or has already tried to escape. He can be cunning."

She shot me a rather wicked smile. "And what am I—if not cunning?"

The queen did indeed ask FitzStephen to inquire about Gerard, but even his sources came up with nothing conclusive. "There has been no word of him."

"And that is all they have been able to surmise?"

She nodded. "In the meantime, I suggest you cast all thoughts of him from your mind. Think to the future. Let us hope that Gerard has fled to another, distant country—Cyprus or Sicily, perhaps—and that his departure will grant you the freedom and clarity you crave. I pray it does." She made the sign of the cross.

# CHAPTER 80

One morning in early October, Jeannette came to the door and, in an excited voice, announced: "A letter has arrived for you, my lady! And the messenger who has brought it has asked to see you."

"The messenger? That is unusual."

"At least that is what Tancred calls him. But my lady"—she paused, her eyes aglow—"*never* have I seen such a splendid messenger. His beautiful blue cape!" she continued to rhapsodize, "and his cap—with not only one, but *three* white plumes! And the way it is trimmed, with a beautiful gold crest! Even the men say they have never seen anything like it."

I set down my quill. "Can it possibly be," I wondered with mounting excitement, "that it is LaFoi who has come?"

To my rapture, it was indeed LaFoi—an older, slightly thinner La-Foi, but still gorgeously appareled in blue and seemingly unscathed by the long journey. Curious, I thought, that Fastrada had dispatched him all the way from Troyes with a letter; but then, she was well known to be extravagant.

"LaFoi!" I cried, extending my arms to him.

"My lady," he replied, warmth breaking through his customary reserve.

I glanced at Jeannette, who stood to the side, agape; next to her was Tancred, who looked astonished and disapproving at my disregard of etiquette. LaFoi, after all, was merely a messenger to Tancred, who possessed all the snobbery of the arriviste.

"You are well? The journey was not too difficult?" I asked LaFoi.

"Yes. An easy crossing, happily." He reached into his sack and drew out a letter. "And I have brought you this, from the Lady Fastrada."

"Nothing could please me more!" I replied, taking it. "How does she fare?"

"Very well, my lady. She asked me to convey her heartfelt greetings. She also asked that I return with a message from you. If you permit me, I will stay the night, and await your letter."

"Of course! You shall stay, and I shall write her at once. But in the meantime, we must give you a place for repose." I turned to Tancred. "Please find a chamber for LaFoi and make certain he has all the provisions he has need of."

"I will escort him to the stables," he replied stiffly. "There should be a place there, above the stalls."

"I meant a *chamber*, Tancred. Not a place in the stalls." I glanced at Jeannette, who could hardly mask her delight in my countermanding Tancred.

"The stables are where those of his kind"—Tancred cleared his throat —"are given shelter, my lady."

"But not in *this* case, Tancred. I gladly take all responsibility."

"Very well," he said coldly. "But then I will leave it to you to answer to FitzStephen and the queen."

"I am happy to do so." I glanced at LaFoi, who remained completely at ease, all the while observing this interchange with amusement and disdain. "My only concern is that LaFoi be made comfortable. Perhaps Jeannette should accompany him," I added, just to irk Tancred even more, "to make certain he has everything he needs."

"As you like, my lady," he said gruffly, turning to LaFoi. "Come this way," he ordered.

"Do go with them," I told Jeannette, who proceeded to them with quick, eager steps. Once the men had passed through the door leading to the interior, she turned and shot me a triumphant, complicit smile.

I returned to my chamber at once and began to read Fastrada's letter.

*To the Countess Isabelle, loving greetings from the Lady Fastrada*

I shall waste no time in telling you the somber news. We have learned that Gerard has died—killed in a fire that destroyed him, all his falcons, and his mews.

A neighboring lord acquainted with your husband—and a kinsman of Hugh's—learned this from Gerard's former master falconer, when the two met, by chance, in Ypres, where each had come to meet with a breeder. Ragnar told Lord de Croies that Gerard, upon his return home from travel in Flanders, had been deeply despondent, indeed very bitter, about his disgraced circumstances. He knew he was in peril, and that the king and Richard were intent on finding a way to punish him. Increasingly he sought solace in drink, it seemed; his wife, and all the household, had been increasingly concerned. He was spending more and more time alone in the new mews he had built, far from the castle itself.

One evening, before Ragnar left for the village, Gerard asked him to see him. He told Ragnar that he wanted to spend the night in the mews, and that no one be permitted to disturb him. "I want to be alone with my hawks," Gerard said. "They are the only beings who have not disappointed me." It was clear he had been drinking.

In the deep of night, a fire must have erupted—a fire that was only discovered after it was too late, and his splendid mews was razed to the ground. It is thought that Gerard, drunk, had fallen asleep, and that oil lamps near his customary seat set off the blaze. I do not know all the details—Hugh is trying to obtain more information—only that almost nothing survived. The poor birds, tethered to their perches, died a dreadful death, and so, of course, did Gerard. His charred bones and his signet ring were discovered among the detritus.

His young widow, the Lady Gerlotte, has nearly been driven mad by the thought of her husband dying in this frightful way.

I should also tell you that there have been whispers on the part of Gerard's enemies, no doubt, that he might have taken his own life. In the aftermath of the Young King's death, they say, Gerard had become resentful and melancholy, and had simply surrendered to despair. He knew his position among men of high rank was in great peril, given the part he had played in Prince Henry's benighted decisions. And there were credible reports, as well, that the king would imminently seize his property and treasure. Thus, they conjecture, Gerard chose to avoid this ignominy by ending his life.

The Lady Gerlotte resolutely refuses to entertain the idea of her husband choosing a shameful, un-Christian death, as do all of us who knew him. He was far too proud and resilient ever to have taken that step, nor can anyone imagine him electing to have his precious hawks perish that way.

I can imagine the host of complicated feelings that you must be experiencing as you learn of Gerard's death. Immense relief, of course; perhaps a glimmer of sadness, too, as you remember the happy times with him. But mostly, utter relief— Gerard held rageful feelings toward you and was intent on revenge. Clementia and I have been desperately worried about your welfare; there are few things more poisonous than the resentment of those who have either been spurned, or who feel, somehow, that they have been cheated of their rights, or of reaching their ambitions. Gerard, alas, seemed to have succumbed to all those deadly impulses. I had always intuited that seed of anger within him but had hoped that the marriage to you would somehow stifle it.

The blessed aspect of this shocking development is that you are now free to live your life without fear! To return to France, and to Fontevraud, as soon as you like. I know, of course, about your situation now, and that you are with the queen. I imagine that it has been a fascinating time for you—to be in the queen's august company, despite the restrictions of her life at Salisbury.

But know, dear Isabelle, that Fontevraud will always welcome you with open arms!

I wrote Clementia only yesterday to tell her what we learned about Gerard. She will have received the news by the time you receive this letter and will, no doubt, feel enormous relief for you as well.

I end this somber missive with an entreaty that you write while LaFoi is there, so that he may return with your letter. I shall devour every morsel of news you can provide, as I know Clementia will, as well, when you write her. I often think of the first time we met—those long talks before the hearth. How darling and perceptive you were, and how eager to make a success of your marriage. To think it has come to this! How well I can imagine your tumultuous feelings now, upon finishing my letter.

Hugh joins me in sending all heartfelt wishes, and the hope that God will keep you well, and safe, and that we will see you before long, in France.

*Fastrada*


I set down the letter—stunned, horrified, almost disbelieving. Of course, I felt relief—enormous relief—and yet this was mitigated by the hideous images that stalked my imagination. Gerard, despondent and drunk, and all his birds, his beautiful birds, condemned to death by fire! I suddenly remembered the nightmarish day long ago when Arnaut and I, on a foray, had come upon a heretic condemned to be burned at the stake just outside the gates of the village. A gloating man, flaming torch in hand, stood ready to ignite the pyre. I told Arnaut we must leave at once—I could not bear to witness such a thing—but even so, as we made our way through the gates, we could not avoid hearing the screams, those heartrending screams, as the smoke snaked into the sky. I remember clapping my hands over my ears, and almost vomiting from the stench of burning flesh.

I pressed my palms against my face, trying to blot out imaginings of

Gerard's terrifying last moments. Had he been so drunk, and in such an oblivion of sleep, that he awakened, only too late, to find himself and all the winged creatures around him ablaze? Too late, too late—the fatal death knell of those two words. And what of his hawks—his beloved falcons, and his lovely white doves, so gentle and trusting? I thought of the falcon's eyes—those golden eyes, the color of fire itself—and how they, too, must have burned in protest and agony as the fire raged. I could not rid myself of the image of those desperate creatures fastened to their perches, their terrible screams rending the night as flames engulfed them—

I forced myself to sit, trying to calm my mind, as I thought of Fastrada's description of his death and the theories it had sparked. It was inconceivable to me, as it was to her and Hugh, that Gerard would have taken his own life. To give up, and to inflict such a death upon himself and his beloved hawks—no, that was simply not possible. Those rumors spoke to other issues: he had enemies, clearly, who reveled in his descent from grace and who would ascribe to him a shameful death; perhaps these same men hoped that the king and Richard would strip him of his land and treasure—riches that they coveted.

No, Gerard would *never* have taken his own life! And yet, was it possible that the shock of failure, and the loss of status, would have transformed him into a different man? No longer the man who disdained those who drowned their sorrows in drink, the man of daunting fortitude and resilience, the man who approached life with immense discipline and rigor.

I paced to and fro before picking up the letter again. My initial shock having slightly abated, I began to reread it, feeling a fresh rush of gratitude for this flurry of Fastrada, if only on parchment—her distinctive voice, the loops and flourishes of her florid hand, the heartening touches of warmth and concern. But it was, of course, the opening of the letter, and the idea that Gerard was dead, that I fixed upon. I still could not quite believe the news was true: Gerard was no more.

I sat down, resting my head upon the table. The shutters of the windows banged, as if they were echoing the clanging confusion of my mind. . . . And what of Gerard's household, and those I knew so well—Raoul, Corbus, Millicent, Wilbertus, Agnes, and the others? Had they remained to help his widow? Given the tragic circumstances, would the king permit her to retain the castle and its land? And what of Ragnar—for whom was he working now, as master falconer? Shuddering, I thought of him—his menacing blue eyes, as glacial as those of the falcons were fiery.

At last, I stood up and, filled with a new resolve, walked to the window, gazing at the vast, undulating lands beyond the ramparts as if I were seeing them for the first time. It was only then I truly realized the turn my life had taken: from this moment on, I would never have to fear Gerard again. I would never have to dread his retribution, his hunting me down, his fathomless rage.

Freedom from those anxieties meant the dawning of new possibilities. I could return to France to see Clementia and Marie—for a short time, or perhaps, forever. But what of my work here, with the queen? That is what had given me a purpose; I had been able to play a part in the larger world—the world of the court, which had always intrigued me. And only because of my mission and its impetus had I come to know the woman who had fascinated me since childhood—Eleanor, Duchess of Aquitaine, Queen of England.

I sat down at the writing table: I must reply to Fastrada at once. But then I thought—*no*, first I must tell the queen. I threw a shawl about my shoulders and hastened to find her.

# CHAPTER 81

The queen greeted the news of Gerard's demise with unmiti-gated relief. "Most of all I am happy that this gives you the freedom and sense of clarity you longed for," she said as we sat together in her private chamber. "It is a terrible thing, to live as you have been forced to live—like a creature being hunted down. And how strange," she mused, "that your new liberty should not only follow, but be intertwined with, the same events that influenced my own circum-stances. Of course, I am not completely free, as you now are—but at least my situation is not as confining as it was."

"It is a strange turn of events, indeed," I murmured.

"One might be tempted to see the hand of God in this—He has chosen to protect you."

Her hand reached out to mine. "Yes, it is a terrible thing to contem-plate," she said, her eyes fixed upon me. "I do not know Lady Fastrada well, but I can imagine, from what I surmise of her, that she, too, must have been shaken by this dreadful story. I assume you will write her soon?"

"Yes. At once. Her messenger awaits my reply. He will spend the night here. I would like you to meet him—LaFoi is his name. I am greatly fond of him. A rather extraordinary figure, you will see." I smiled—the first time I had smiled since reading the letter. "Tancred seemed rather shocked when I insisted we give a mere messenger a chamber."

She gave a small laugh. "I hardly find that surprising. It is always those strivers, insecure of their own positions, who most begrudge granting privileges to those of lesser status." Her expression turned quite serious. "But enough talk of the messenger. What will you tell Lady Fastrada?"

"That I am shocked, but also immensely relieved. That I agree that Gerard would never have taken his own life, that it must have been a hideous accident. And that I hope to return to Fontevraud as soon as I am able. It is strange, Your Majesty," I added quietly, "that the idea of leaving no longer fills me with pure delight. I have grown so accustomed to being here and being in your company. But, of course, I long to see Clementia and Marie again—and my father, too, God willing."

"And not your brother and sister?" she asked, mischief in her voice.

I laughed outright. "I think I have rather successfully cast those two from my mind!" Then, in a thoughtful voice, I added, "When I think of my arrival here—how nervous and intimidated I was—and now, how differently I feel. I have come to have such affection for you, Your Majesty." I glanced at her fleetingly, hoping I had not overstepped my bounds.

Her smile and expression returned my own with warmth. "I once told you that you reminded me of my Joanna. Indeed, I now think of you as a surrogate daughter," she said. "And having you here has brightened many gloomy days."

"Thank you, Your Majesty! I shall always think of our talks, and all I have learned from you, with enormous gratitude—they have meant so much to me!"

I WROTE FASTRADA THAT NIGHT, and the following morning, letter in hand, I called for Jeannette. "Tell the queen I shall join her soon. Then tell Tancred to escort LaFoi to the queen's private chamber. I shall meet them there and will have the letter ready for him. LaFoi should depart as soon possible for France."

"But my lady—" She looked aghast. "To the queen's *private chamber?*"

"Yes." I raised my brow. "Why ever not?"

"I know LaFoi is not the *usual* sort of messenger we have seen here, but even so, is it proper—"

"I assure you the queen will not find it untoward in the least. As for Tancred"—I smiled devilishly—"that is quite another matter. Go and tell him."

The queen was indeed delighted at the idea of meeting LaFoi. "What you have said about him has piqued my curiosity," she said, with a glint in her eyes.

"I know he will be honored to meet you, Your Majesty."

LaFoi, resplendent in blue and gold, appeared soon thereafter, escorted by a singularly peeved-looking Tancred. A wide-eyed Jeannette, trailing behind with skittish steps, looked as if she were holding her breath, anticipating disaster.

"Approach," the queen ordered LaFoi, who proceeded to bow before her with such extraordinary, swooping panache that even I was taken aback. "You have come on the part of the Lady Fastrada, I understand," the queen said.

"Yes, Your Majesty," he replied. That he appeared quite nonchalant seemed to irritate Tancred all the more.

"Your mistress is a gallant, gifted woman. And most spirited in the hunt, they say."

"She is indeed, Your Majesty," he said, with evident pride.

"I trust we provided for you well last night?" the queen inquired. "I realize this is not France, after all. The customs are different here in this chilly country. I hope you were given a proper chamber?"

"Yes. And a very comfortable one it was."

"I am glad of it. I would have been mortified," she continued, "if you had not been shown all due respect." At this, I could not resist glancing at Tancred: his cheeks had turned red, and his mouth was set in an expression of cold displeasure. No doubt he was already planning his revenge upon me.

"You have brought important news with your letter," said the queen, continuing to address LaFoi. "News that has been especially important to Lady Isabelle. For that I am deeply grateful, as I know she is. We ask that you convey our warm wishes to the Lady Fastrada. We know that Lady Isabelle's letter is in good hands. And now," she continued briskly, "you must be on your way, LaFoi. We wish you safe travels." Then, to Tancred: "Escort LaFoi and Lady Isabelle to the stables. I am certain she will want to wish him Godspeed."

I WROTE CLEMENTIA THE FOLLOWING day that I hoped to return to Fontevraud as soon as weather augured well and proper arrangements could be made for my journey. Shortly thereafter, the queen and I decided the time was right for my departure. "But only if you promise me first," she said, "that you will come visit me here, before too long." I duly promised, adding that I hoped one day she, too, would be able to return to France. I was heartened that her daughter Mathilda would visit in the spring—the first time in many years they would see one another.

Despite my longing to see Clementia and Marie, sadness weighed upon me as I prepared to leave England. I would miss the queen—her inspiring presence and her counsel. In the weeks preceding my departure, I began to record my recollections of our conversations—her stories, her observations, her words of wisdom. I kept those precious pages locked inside the trunk I had brought from Fontevraud and guarded them as zealously as I had my secret objects. I sensed that the queen, customarily so stalwart, was sad, as well, at the idea of my leaving.

On the eve of my departure, I joined the queen in her private chamber; she had suggested that we read together. "Something fanciful," she said, "that will distract me from dwelling on your departure—and perhaps help lift your spirits, as well."

After choosing a whimsical tale set in the time of King Arthur, I began to read aloud. But it did not take long for the queen to notice a certain strained quality to my voice. "You are not reading with your customary verve," she interjected. "Your mind is elsewhere."

"Yes, you are right." I sighed. "I try to imagine the future, and what will happen to me. How will Fontevraud seem, after being here, with you?"

"One must face the future resolutely. One can only persevere." She paused, her dark eyes fixed upon me as her hand touched mine. On her middle finger glimmered the great amethyst, which I remembered so vividly from our first meeting.

"Let us play a round of the Sortes," she suggested. "Perhaps it is time for Virgil to guide you." She gestured to her copy of *The Aeneid*, which lay on a table near us.

I picked it up and reassumed my seat. "Now," she said, "let us see where chance, and your favorite poet, take you."

I closed my eyes, let the book fall open, and placed my finger upon a page.

"Go on—" she said. "Read it."

"There is nothing to read, alas. It is a page with an *illustration*, from Book Six. And a gloomy one at that—Aeneas and the sibyl, in the underworld. An awful scene of monsters and writhing creatures in cauldrons." I closed the book. "I hope that does not bode ill."

"Since you chanced upon an *image*, not a passage, it falls to me to supply one from the same book."

"I was not aware that was a rule of the Sortes—"

"As queen, I make my *own* rules," she interjected, and we exchanged smiles. Then her expression changed; she fell silent, deep in thought. At last, her eyes fixed upon me, she began to recite this passage:

"Easy is the descent to Avernus; night and day the door of gloomy Dis stands open; but to recall one's steps and pass out to the upper air, this is the task, this the toil!"

# PART V

# CHAPTER 82

I departed Salisbury on a bleak, misty November morning. The queen's demeanor was all the more touching in its stoicism; after bidding me adieu, she turned her face away, brushing tears from her cheek. Jeannette, by contrast, was histrionically weepy—as if she were losing the sole friend and confidante she had ever known. Flanking the two women stood Tancred, observing the scene with cool detachment and palpable relief as he hurried me along.

The journey was uneventful. I was escorted by a somewhat dour, but experienced, squire, Wadard, selected by Tancred to accompany me. What Wadard lacked in conviviality—no LaFoi was he—he made up in his conversation with the roads and his skill in guiding the horses. We arrived at the outskirts of Fontevraud several days earlier than I had anticipated, on a brilliant morning in late November.

How delighted Lothar, the gateman, was to see me! "Lady Isabelle!" the poor lame creature cried, hobbling toward me before grasping my reins. "We were not expecting you for several days." (This, after a suspicious glance at my companion, whose accent and raiment were clearly not only those of an outsider, but also English.)

I told him how happy I was to be back, before asking, "Where might I find Marie? And Sister Clementia?"

"I expect they are in Sister Clementia's chamber, my lady. It is usually about this time that Marie has her lessons."

As Lothar attended to Wadard, I walked quickly toward the cloister. Outwardly nothing had changed; and yet, after the worldliness of the queen's English court, everything at the abbey seemed startlingly different—the quiet more enveloping and intense, the colors and light more austere.

I came to the door of Clementia's chamber and knocked. "Come in," said a hazy, preoccupied voice.

Marie, who had been sitting by the table, leaped to her feet and ran toward me. "Lady Isabelle!" she squealed, embracing me so hard that I could scarcely breathe. Tears came to my eyes; never, ever shall I forget the feeling of her warm, sturdy arms and the scent of her thick, dark hair as we held each other. Clementia stood behind her, radiant and composed. "Oh, how we have missed you, dear Isabelle!" she said, in a voice of restrained joy.

"Come, let me look at you two!" I said, laughing slightly as I drew apart. First, to Marie: "How you have grown! How tall you have become!"

"Yes!" said Marie. "Sister Clementia says I am quite tall for seven! I hope one day I shall be as tall as you, Lady Isabelle! Can you imagine?"

"Perhaps—but to me you will *always* be a little girl!" I kissed her cheeks and forehead, before addressing Clementia. "But you, Clementia, you have not changed a whit!"

"You flatter me, I am afraid," she replied, with an almost shy smile.

"Have you had any word from Fastrada?"

"Yes!" replied Clementia. "She said she had received your letter from England. She was overjoyed to hear that you would return to Fontevraud, and is longing to hear about your time with the queen. She spoke of visiting us in the early spring."

"What good news!" I replied, smiling, before I returned to Marie. "Tell me about your reading. And how your penmanship is coming along," I said, ruffling her hair. "I hear you have become quite a scholar."

"You must not flatter her too much," chided Clementia half-jokingly. "She will have a swollen head—"

"And then"—Marie sighed—"I shall have to go to an additional confession. And I do not much like confession!"

"Neither did I, at your age!" I chimed in, laughing.

"Come, my books and exercises are here," said Marie. "To show you."

"Penmanship first," I told her.

"Here," she said, leading me to the table. "I have just completed these pages. Look!"

I turned one page, then another. She had indeed made great strides—her hand was remarkably fluid and distinctive for a girl her age. "I am quite impressed, Marie. You have done very, very well under Sister Clementia's tutelage."

"Each time I picked up the quill to practice, I thought of you, Lady Isabelle," she replied, beaming. "I wanted you to be proud of me."

"As I am indeed, and always shall be, dear Marie." I kissed the top of her head, struggling to restrain my tears.

"Come," interjected Clementia. "Let us go together to the abbess. She will be delighted to see you. And, of course, all of us long to hear about your life in England."

"But first I must take Lady Isabelle to see her falcon," chimed in Marie, tugging my arm. "I told him that she would return to us, and that when she did, she would tell us stories about England. And about the queen!"

DESPITE MY DELIGHT IN REUNITING with Marie and Clementia, it required some time to reaccustom myself to the life of the abbey. Although it was a relief to inhabit a world devoid of the subterfuges and tensions of a royal court, there were moments when I would reflect longingly on the excitement not only of being with the queen, albeit in exile, but also of being exposed to the intrigues of her inner circle.

It did not take long, however, for intrigues of another nature to intervene. Shortly thereafter a letter arrived, transported by the familiar threadbare messenger—it was a letter from Guy. After arranging provisions for the pitiable emissary and his sorry mount, I tore open the letter and began to read:

*From Guy de La Palisse to the Lady Isabelle, now residing at the Abbey of Fontevraud*

Heartening it is, indeed, dear sister, to have received your letter and to know that you have returned to the hallowed peace of the abbey after the tragedy that has rent your life—the death of your former husband, and in such a hideous way. It gives me im-measurable comfort, as you can imagine, to know you are once again ensconced in the Lord's house at Fontevraud, receiving so-lace from prayer and from the worthy Sister Clementia, who has, in the past, provided such an exemplary example for you.

Even I, with my gift for description, cannot express the hor-ror that I felt when I learned of Gerard's frightful demise. For him, and all of his beloved (and dare I say costly) creatures to have burned to death! And to have perished in the mews, which he had constructed with such care, and at such considerable expense—I shudder each time I think of it!

I suspect, alas, that certain dreadful gossip may have wended its way to you—*id est,* the whisperings that Gerard may have taken his own life. Only a malicious, witless person could think this could possibly be true. A man of Gerard's charac-ter, rank—and considerable means, I should add—would never have taken such a reckless, sinful, and ignoble step! I fear that these vicious stories will not only impugn Gerard's reputation, but that of our noble family as well: they associate us, through your marriage, to a man believed to have elected to die as only a depraved, un-Christian would. Do everything in your power to dispel those slanderous stories, dear sister! Trust that I shall do the same.

Needless to say, my own innate sense of Christian charity and compassion has compelled me to inquire about the welfare of his bereaved widow, the Lady Gerlotte, in her hour of need. (I should add that she, like you, hails from a family of no-ble blood—the Lacrancières. Surely you have heard of them.) I have endeavored to provide her solace with the sensitivity and grace that are, as you know, second nature to me. My only wish, as I have told the gentle widow, is to console her, and to provide her with comfort and guidance at this delicate moment.

I do not mean, in this missive, to dwell solely on the death of Gerard, but wish to relate news of our family as well. Alas,

Father has greatly declined. He has lost most of his ability to see and is physically quite feeble. Most of his days are spent sitting with vacant eyes before the fire, with Petru as companion. (Would that Hortense were as attentive as Father's faithful hound! She has become increasingly negligent in her duties, and imperious in manner, and it is only because of our father's fondness for her that I have chosen not to expel her from our manor.)

Amélie and Balduin's family continues to blossom. They have lately been blessed with another son, whom they have called Roland, after the hero of old. Balduin has recently come into a great deal of land, after the death of both parents. But do not let this diminish your own sense of worth, dear sister, as you reflect on the path your own life has taken! It is not every woman who is blessed with Amélie's child-bearing capacity, as well as the good sense and fortitude to make a happy, advantageous marriage. I have no doubt you, too, will succeed in your own way, if only by doing God's work at the abbey, with Sister Clementia.

I end this somber missive with a bit of good cheer for you, dear sister: I fully intend to venture to Fontevraud again—propelled by a sense of brotherly responsibility, as well as a deep yearning for contemplation and prayer. I shall likely come this spring. Do not hesitate to mention the possibility of my visiting to the good Sister Clementia, if only as a way to buoy her spirits. I should add that if the timing of my sojourn coincides with that of Lady Fastrada's, I would not be displeased. I suspect that she would greatly appreciate meeting me at last and am sure, moreover, that she would be gratified to be apprised of the help I have given to the bereaved Lady Gerlotte. I have learned only recently that these two exemplary women have long been acquainted—not surprising, given their noble lineage and reputation for grace, charity, and virtue.

Fare you well, dear Isabelle. I hope you will derive comfort in knowing that, God willing, we will see each other again before long.

*Your devoted brother,*
*Guy*

Guy's letters had often irked me; sometimes, riddled as they were with pretentiousness and lack of self-knowledge, they had almost amused me. This letter, however, simply incensed me. I began to walk from the stables to the cloister, my anger-fueled gait quick and decisive. With each step, I thought of Guy's transparently self-serving implications and motivations. His first concern about the manner of Gerard's death was, of course, how it might be viewed as a reflection on our family. I also knew that the horror of the falcons burning to death, and the destruction of the mews, had, in Guy's eyes, as much to do with their costliness than anything else. But the worst aspect of all was Guy's conniving to meet Gerard's widow—vulnerable in the aftermath of her husband's cruel death. I closed my eyes, imagining Guy's unctuous efforts to ingratiate himself to her, all in the guise of "comfort."

Equally dreadful was the notion that my brother intended to visit, and his delusion that he actually thought we would greet this news with delight. Shaking my head in disbelief, I entered the cloister, intent on finding Clementia.

I came upon her as she was walking toward her chamber.

"What has happened?" she asked. "You have a frightful, almost murderous look in your eye!"

"I have just received a letter from Guy—"

"Ah—no wonder then!" Sighing, she opened the door to her chamber. "Come in. Tell me what he said."

After we took a seat, I handed her the letter. "Best you read it yourself."

I watched as she perused the pages. Once or twice her mouth curved into a slight smile; at another moment, she laughed outright. "You must confess he never disappoints!" she said, returning the letter. "He is as leaden and transparently conniving as ever."

"But what to do?" I moaned. "How can we avoid having him visit?"

"Let me see," she pondered, fingering her weighty silver pendant cross. Then, brightly: "I suppose there is little chance that we could convince him to join the Holy War?"

I began to laugh. "His delicate stomach would never survive the voyage!"

"Well, then"—her lovely blue eyes were as mischievous as I had ever seen them—"perhaps you might convince him to set off on pilgrimage? The road to Santiago would certainly allow him ample time for the contemplation he craves."

"Please, Clementia, be serious! I am desperate to think of a way to stave him off."

"I fear there is little we can do"—she paused, her mouth curving into a sly smile—"except pray that the noble widow Gerlotte finds Guy's company such a 'comfort' that she is loath for him to leave her side."

# CHAPTER 83

The hallowed weeks of Advent arrived. After the luxury of the queen's court, the abbey's celebration of the holiday rituals seemed strikingly sober and restrained. But in mid-December, we received a sumptuous gift—an elaborately carved and painted crate containing fresh lemons from the queen's daughter, Joanna of Sicily. Shortly thereafter Clementia informed me that a messenger was being sent to the abbey of Amesbury with some needed writing supplies and asked if I would like him to carry a message conveying our Christmas wishes to the queen. I penned a letter at once, describing my reunion with Marie and Clementia and my work at the abbey; I also included a rather acerbic description of the recent letter from Guy.

To my delight, a letter from the queen, accompanied by a small package, arrived for me shortly after Christmas. It was transported by, of all people, the blond brute from the Salisbury fortress who had always frightened me; without his lance and the panoply of royal accoutrements, however, he was not nearly as fearsome as I had remembered. Indeed, he seemed awed by the ambiance of the abbey and utterly cowed by Clementia's beauty. After handing me the letter, he watched her, transfixed, as she asked about needed provisions for his return journey; doffing his cap, he ventured a few words in his best Norman French so meekly, and with such deference, that I could only conclude my intuition was right: he was enamored of her.

After he departed for the stables, I turned to Clementia. "I think you have found another admirer!" I teased.

"Another?" she turned to me, one brow raised. "What do you mean?"

"First Guy"—at this reminder, she winced—"and now, this fellow! He seemed quite entranced by you."

"Proof that he has been sequestered at Salisbury far too long," she returned drily.

"I hardly think that is the reason, my dear Clementia," I replied with a smile, glancing at her exquisite profile as we continued on our way. I was always struck by Clementia's insouciance about her own beauty: it was as if she viewed it as an inconvenient attribute, one that was an impediment to her larger purpose.

The moment I reached my chamber, I untied the roll of parchment, which was stamped with the queen's glorious seal:

*Eleanor, queen of England, and Duchess of Aquitaine, to the Lady Isabelle, residing at the Abbey of Fontevraud*

I think of you often, dear Isabelle. Your absence has been keenly felt by me; thus the arrival of your letter gave me special delight, as did the descriptions of your life at the abbey, and of your reunion with little Marie and Sister Clementia. To the latter, I send my salutations.

Only recently I suffered a great loss—that of my beloved ermine, Paris, faithful companion throughout these past several years of turmoil and seclusion. There has been talk of finding another creature for me, but I have not insisted upon it; at least, not yet. Paris seemed to have a singular instinct as to my moods and wishes; he will not be easily replaced.

I have been told I shall move to the castle of Windsor come spring, and Mathilda will join me with her husband and children there.

Herewith I enclose for you a few gifts—things of my own which, at this advanced stage of my life, I scarcely have use for. I suspect they may be rather frowned upon at the abbey: I hope this will not diminish your pleasure in them. When and if you choose to wear them, think of our times together in England, and of the life that stretches before you—a life without the fear that originally propelled you to us at Salisbury.

I send you my affectionate wishes, and also profess the hope
that it will not be long before we meet again.

Following this was her swooping, formidable signature; I gazed at it
for many moments, trying to imagine her dictating this letter and then,
at the end, taking the quill in her own hand, the globe of her amethyst
ring moving slowly and rhythmically above the parchment as she in-
scribed her name.

I set down the letter and began to untie the package; two small silk
pouches lay within. The first contained a pearl necklace from which an
ancient intaglio was suspended: it was carved with a helmeted, winged
goddess in a chariot drawn by two owls. The pearls themselves were lustrous and slightly rose-tinged, but it was the pendant, with its depiction
of Athena, that most captivated me. So precious did the necklace seem,
and so imbued with the spirit of the queen, that I hesitated to fasten it
around my neck; but after a moment I did so, trying to catch my reflection in the crude piece of brass that passed, at the abbey, for a mirror.

In the smaller pouch lay a gold ring with an intaglio depicting another goddess, Persephone; a wreath of flowers encircled her head, and,
in one hand, was a pomegranate split open to reveal its seeds. I studied
the exquisite carving and then slipped the ring on my finger; it fit perfectly. Still gazing at it, I thought of the queen's fingers, now thickened
and gnarled, and imagined her as a young woman wearing this ring on
her slender hand.

Slowly and contemplatively, I took off the necklace—as the queen
had rightly surmised, it was too lavish for the abbey—and held it in the
palm of my hand, stroking the smooth, perfect pearls before reluctantly
enclosing it in the pouch. But I could not bear to forgo the wondrous
ring: it would remain on my finger forever after.

I WORE THE RING WITH some apprehension, knowing that it would
not meet with Clementia's approval. It did not take long, however, for it
to be noticed. A few days later, Marie and Clementia arrived unexpectedly at my chamber, and the little girl noticed it at once.

"What is that ring upon your finger!" she exclaimed. "How pretty it is! Where did it come from?"

"It was a present from the queen," I said, catching Clementia's disapproving glance.

"From the queen!" asked Marie. "Let me see!"

I extended my hand, watching as she studied the intaglio. "Who is this lady?" she asked.

"It is the goddess Persephone. Look at her symbols—'attributes' they are called—the pomegranate, and the wreath about her head. Do you not remember when I told you her story?"

She shook her head. "Tell me again."

I suddenly realized why she had forgotten—I had told her the story in the sorrowful aftermath of Aiglantine's death. "I told you that Persephone was destined to spend part of the year in the underworld," I began, "and she was only reunited with her mother after a very long time, and only for a short while." I stroked her dark curls. "I said *you* were a little like Persephone, for you, too, were only able to see your mother fleetingly—an experience of joy, but also of sadness."

Marie nodded slowly and thoughtfully. "Yes, now I remember," she murmured, her expression clouding over.

"Perhaps this ring will be yours one day when I can no longer wear it." Wishing to dispel her sudden sadness, I joked, "When I am old and stout, and my fingers are no longer this slender!"

"That will *never* happen to you, Lady Isabelle!" Marie cried, with a smile.

Clementia, who had been listening intently, finally interposed. "It was a lovely gesture indeed for the queen to send this token to Lady Isabelle," she said with some stiffness. "We should appreciate it most of all, not as a vain ornament, but as a token of the queen's regard for Lady Isabelle. Is that not so?"

I nodded, and then added, "But I also think that the queen would be pleased that the ring has prompted Marie's questions about Persephone. Perhaps that was even part of her intention! The queen would want us to introduce Marie to the tales of the ancient poets—to read about their myths, goddesses, and heroes. Surely you would agree, Clementia—"

"I shall try to think of it that way," she replied with a gentle, if not entirely convincing, smile.

THE WEEKS, AND THEN THE months, wore on—"Wore on," I say, because the winter of the year 1184, despite the companionship of Marie, Clementia, and the sisters, seemed particularly long, cold, and isolated. But to my thrill, in late March, a letter to us from Fastrada arrived (it was delivered not by LaFoi, alas, but by a disappointingly nondescript underling). Oh, the joy of glimpsing her florid, oversize signature upon the parchment! And then of reading these words: "I intend to visit the abbey quite soon—in a matter of a few weeks, God willing! I cannot tell you how much it raises my spirits to think I shall be reunited with my favorite trio. I must warn you, however, that I intend to be as corrupting an influence as possible upon darling Marie." More details followed, including a reference to Guy. "I have some interesting news of your brother Guy, as well, but I shall wait to share this with you when we are together." At that, I turned to Clementia and groaned, "What on earth could this be?"

She shook her head slowly, adding with a sigh, "I expect we shall find out soon enough."

# Chapter 84

What an unforgettable moment when Fastrada arrived! First, the creaking open of the massive gates, then great billows of dust, and finally, this dazzling apparition—a willowy figure in brilliant green astride a dark mount, the tall plumes of her jaunty purple cap swaying in the breeze. "*Me voici!* And in such good time!" she exclaimed, dismounting with the speed and grace of a woman decades younger, afterward whisking some dust from her costume with a few dramatic flourishes before striding toward us.

"My *dear* Isabelle!" she cried, in that memorably emphatic way of hers as she stood facing me, her eyes moist with emotion, and her hands, outstretched and vividly beringed, holding mine. "How well you look! Each time I think what you have been through, I simply shudder. But you seem to have weathered it all with your customary grace."

Next, to Clementia. "Sister dear," she cried, embracing her. "I have missed you dreadfully—even your annoying little chidings about my extravagance."

Finally, she came to Marie, who stood at my side fairly hopping with excitement, her eyes wide and adoring. "Can this be *Marie?*" Fastrada exclaimed with mock disbelief. "How tall you are! And what a little beauty!" After ruffling the little girl's hair, she looked disapprovingly at the child's robe. "Thank goodness I have come," she intoned, with theatrical gravity. "We must have another costume made for you immediately! This one looks far too worn, and such a dreary color! Clearly, your honorary aunt has arrived just in time!" At this Marie simply beamed but then added, with shy consternation, "But, Lady Fastrada, I do not know if Sister Clementia and the abbess will permit me to have a new costume."

Fastrada knelt down, whispering in her ear. As the "honorary aunt" stood up, Marie, awed, asked, "Really?" To which Fastrada merely replied by pressing one finger to her lips.

With mock annoyance, Clementia said, "We shall have to have a talk, dear sister."

"That is right, dear Clementia! And I, as the eldest, will prevail. But you must admit I always keep my word," added Fastrada, merrily linking her arm in her sister's and then in mine. "Did I not promise you to be a corrupting influence on Marie?"

At that, laughing, and with Marie skipping behind, we made our way to the cloister.

LATER THAT DAY, CLEMENTIA, FASTRADA, and I ventured outside for a stroll. The radiant spring sun lent the abbey grounds a paradisal feeling—the roses had begun to bloom, and the mélange of plants in the extensive herb garden infused the air with a subtle, soothing scent.

"You have brought such blissful weather," I said to Fastrada. "Until now it has been quite damp and gloomy."

"I always bring the sun!" she jested. "It is part of my *modus operandi*. Even Hugh admits that—in his generous moments, of course."

All the while it was the mention of Guy, in Fastrada's earlier letter, that had been weighing most on my mind. "Tell us what you know of my brother," I prompted her.

"I was saving that for a little savory to offer up later. I do not like to parcel out all the good gossip at once."

"Please, Fastrada, *do* tell!" urged Clementia, with a smile. "It is cruel to keep us in suspense!"

"You must first know," began Fastrada, in a dramatic tone, "that Gerard's widow has been left with a sizable fortune. All his lands, Ravinour, and his considerable holdings elsewhere in France. In the south of England, too, we are told. The widow—Gerlotte by name—hails from a *very* distinguished family. Almost as old as yours, dear Isabelle. One would have expected nothing less from Gerard, after all. Was he not obsessed with noble bloodlines? It appears that your brother," she continued, "made his way to Ravinour in order to be a comfort and adviser to her. Apparently he emphasized his relationship to Gerard by way of your marriage." She nodded in my direction. "Can you imagine?"

"No doubt he was eager to win her good graces," I interjected. "He is as besotted with noble name and position as Gerard was with bloodlines."

"If only that were *all!*" exclaimed Fastrada.

"What do you mean?"

She fixed her eyes upon me. "He was intent on *courting* her, my dear!"

"*Courting* her?" Clementia and I asked in astonished unison.

"Yes! Do you not see? Despite what Guy has told you—that it was he who broke off the engagement to the Lady de Chabanel—everyone knows that he had been roundly rejected, in the end, by *her*. But let me continue. Guy and his shabby retinue made their way to the castle on the pretext of helping the grieving Lady Gerlotte with her affairs and bolstering her protection. It did not go well—after a few days, he was on his way home."

"What happened?" I asked.

"It was quite simple—she simply could not bear him! 'Never in my life have I encountered such a pretentious, silly, tedious man,' she reported to a cousin of mine. 'I was counting the hours to his departure!' To this she apparently added, 'I would rather be abducted by the Infidels and sold into slavery than be married to that man!'"

"A wise woman, clearly," quipped Clementia.

But given still another instance of Guy's maladroit conniving, I was in no mood to laugh. "Oh no, how mortifying," I lamented, my head in my hands. "What a disgrace upon my family, to have Guy shaming himself this way!"

"All of us have family members we would happily disown," chimed in Fastrada. "Our family has its own black sheep—do we not, Clementia?" she asked, turning to her sister, who replied with a nod. "Yes," she continued, "that second cousin of ours who professed to being a desert martyr of old, and who then proceeded to strap himself to a tree deep in the forest, denying himself of food and water for days at a time, in a misguided attempt to emulate the spirit of Saint Simeon. So you see, Isabelle," she added reassuringly, "you are not the only one with a family member who has caused some shame!"

"But I have the distinct privilege of being the only one with a brother intent on courting the widow of a family member's former spouse. And I am the only one with a spouse who perished in such a hideous way."

"And in a *questionable* way," murmured Fastrada darkly.

"I know that you find it inconceivable, as I do, that Gerard would have taken his own life."

"At first, Hugh and I roundly dismissed the idea," she began in an uncharacteristically slow, deliberate cadence. "Why would a man of Gerard's wealth, power, and rank commit such a heinous, sinful act? But as time passed, and certain things became clearer, we were not so quick to reject the idea. After all, Gerard had made some very powerful enemies indeed, Prince Richard principal among them. Had he lived, he would have been in a perilous position, a position of shame, one he would *never* have withstood.

"Hugh says it is questionable as to what would have happened with his fortune," she expatiated. "Many say it is remarkably charitable on the king's part that he did not divest Gerard's widow of all she had inherited from Gerard. Were she not from such an important family— one crucial to the king's ambitions in Normandy—Hugh thinks the situation would be vastly different."

"But, Fastrada," I interjected, "it is not only the idea of Gerard's taking his *own* life. But those of all his glorious hawks and doves as well—they were so precious to him, as precious as children. Never, *ever* would he have committed them to such a death!"

"Yes," Fastrada conceded, with a deep sigh. "You are right. And that, finally, is why I suppose we can only conclude that his death must have been a hideous accident."

"I shall *never* believe that Gerard took his own life," I said. "Indeed, this is one instance when I might even give my brother's own theory some credence. He says these stories are meant not only to sully Gerard's name, but that of our family's, by association, as well." To this I added: "I am sure that is one of the reasons why Guy intends to visit here soon—to put these rumors to rest by trumpeting his views to both of you, whom he considers so distinguished and important."

"You never mentioned that Guy might visit," Fastrada said, her eyes lighting up. "This could be quite amusing!"

"Only one who has never met him could *possibly* say that," returned Clementia.

"All too true!" I lamented. "I simply dread the idea of his descending upon us again." Then, ruefully, "And he has been longing to meet *you*, Fastrada, most of all."

"Then I hope I shall be here when he makes his way through the gates," Fastrada replied, adding archly, "I promise I shall be on my very best behavior."

"This is *one* time, dear sister, when I would *not* want you to be on your best behavior," said Clementia drily. "I would want you to be as wicked as possible, so that Guy becomes disillusioned and cuts his visit short."

"I am shocked, Clementia, to hear you speak so uncharitably!" Fastrada teased.

"The two of you may joke about this, but I, as his long-suffering sister, find nothing in the least amusing about seeing him again. We must find a way to prevent him visiting, at all cost." Then, plaintively, "But *how*?"

"If the abbey were not known to be situated in such a salubrious location, I would suggest telling him we had been struck by the pox," Clementia ventured, as Fastrada and I laughed. "I remember how sensitive he was to all matters of health—"

"Alas, I do not think even the plague would deter him from meeting Fastrada." I groaned. "Therefore I suppose we must be resigned to seeing him here. At least we shall have time to steel ourselves before his arrival—he promised to write, confirming his plans."

"Oh, let us talk of something other than your irksome brother," said Fastrada. "Your ring, for instance!" She took my hand and began to examine the intaglio. "How exquisite it is! You have never worn it before, have you? I hesitate to ask if it came from Gerard—it looks rather like his taste."

"No," I replied. "It was a present from the queen." Clementia remained notably silent.

"A marvelous present, and one that she would not give out of mere cordiality," observed Fastrada. "She must value you greatly."

"It pleases me to think so," I answered. "I treasure the ring, as I do the time I spent with the queen. And I love the image of Persephone upon it."

"I suspect that it, too, has something of a message to it," said Fastrada. "Did it never occur to you that the queen might associate *you* with Persephone?" she asked, her dark eyes fixed upon me. "You, too, have endured a world of sorrow and shadow. And you, too, have survived, and have entered a new world, one of light." She placed her hand upon my shoulder and gave me a smile replete with affection.

"That never occurred to me," interposed Clementia, visibly touched. "You may be right, Fastrada."

"Even so, dear Clementia, I know you do not really approve of my wearing it here," I remarked. "That many here may see it as something vain and ornamental—"

"And what if they do?" Fastrada piped up at once. "You have never taken vows, my dear Isabelle. And even if you had, I would not hold you to that kind of cheerlessness. We certainly know of nuns who live in luxury."

"There is still the matter of setting an example, and of adhering to abbey decorum, after all," said Clementia with some sharpness.

"*Decorum!*" cried Fastrada, rolling her eyes. "Oh, what a dreary word! I have never wanted *decorum* to guide my life." She glanced at me, before turning, with exasperation, to Clementia. "And I sense that Isabelle does not either, sister dear. That is probably why the queen became so fond of her. The two are kindred spirits."

"An interesting, and not implausible theory," Clementia replied with a small, resigned smile before announcing, "in any event, it is time for me to meet with the abbess."

After she left, Fastrada turned to me with a certain victorious gaiety. "Do not mind my sister. Clementia has these little pockets of rigidity—even as child, she tended to rules, and I to pleasure. Strange, is it not, how wildly different siblings can be! And yet, of course, we still love each other deeply." She took my arm. "Come, let us find a place to sit down together. I adore my sister, but sometimes it is a relief to be able to talk freely, without her hovering righteousness."

We settled on a long stone bench, carved with acanthus leaves, which stood near a pair of flowering quince trees—a favorite spot of mine, especially in springtime. As we sat down I noticed how carefully she arranged her robe, the skirt of which fell in generous folds of lustrous green silk trimmed in saffron-colored passementerie. "Even the queen has heard of your elegance, and your flair for fashion," I told her.

"Really?" She fluttered her thick dark lashes, looking immensely pleased.

I nodded, smiling, before turning my face to the rays of sun.

"I long to hear about your time with the queen," said Fastrada after a moment.

I began to give my impressions of the queen and her court in exile, and shared a few anecdotes about Jeannette and Tancred. But it was the queen's own stories of her life that I dwelt upon.

"How fascinating to be a witness to her life in captivity in England, and also to hear her recollections of her past!" Fastrada exclaimed. "You must keep a record of those discussions. For yourself, but also for posterity."

"I intend to."

"Yes, you *must*," she replied emphatically. Then, turning to me with a wistful smile, she said, "How distant your old life with Gerard must now seem—how remote and foreign. Yes, how well I remember first meeting you," she began to muse, "how eager you were to please, how in awe of Gerard, and yet how *questing*. I still think of you as 'questing,' but in so many other ways you seem quite a different woman." She paused, looking at me searchingly. "Do you not feel that way?"

"I do. But most of all I try to think of the happy times with Gerard and try to banish the sad memories. He gave me something which I have bequeathed to Marie," I reflected. "An enameled falcon in bronze. Whenever I see it, so much rushes back to me—life with Gerard, his castle, and all those I knew then—Aiglantine, Raoul, and Gallien, of course—"

"Ah, dear Gallien! He is quite devoted to Hugh, almost as a son would be. Hugh says he is the envy of his peers, to have such a gifted master falconer."

"Strange to think that it was Gerard, and that dreadful Ragnar, who taught Gallien so much," I murmured.

"Ragnar, how well I remember him!" She shivered. "Tall, blond, and with that cruel blue gaze. But let us swerve from the wicked Ragnar to jollier things," she went on. "Gallien is to be married!"

"Married?" I exclaimed. "To whom?"

"To one of the maidens who attends me—Douceline. She adores him and seems to share his fascination with hawks."

"I am so happy for him! To think that his life has come full circle—from Saxon slave to master falconer, and now to be married to a maiden who serves one of the most distinguished families of France." I looked up, smiling at the brilliant sky as I continued to marvel at the news. "When is the wedding to take place?"

"This summer—late July. Hugh and I have offered them a parcel of land nearby our domain, as their wedding gift, and have offered to host the nuptials. You *must* come."

"Do you really think—"

"Yes! We know how grateful Gallien is to you for all you did to help him. And he has also spoken of inviting others from Gerard's household. There is a steward, Raoul, whom he has spoken about, and another fellow"—she furrowed her brow, straining to remember—"Corlus, could that be his name?"

"Corbus!" I cried. It was the idea of seeing Corbus, and Raoul, as well as Gallien, that decided the matter. "Yes, I must come! I shall discuss it with Clementia. I suspect she will be concerned about my being away from Marie."

"There is no need for you to be away from Marie," she replied at
once. "Marie must come with you. It will be good for her to see Troyes
in all its glory. We will discuss it with Clementia *together*," she asserted,
fluttering her beringed hands. "My sister would never dare say no, once
she knows my mind is set upon it!"

# CHAPTER 85

As the days passed, Fastrada continued to enliven life at the abbey with her gaiety, splendid clothes, and wit. The joy of her presence was only partly clouded by my constant worry about the imminent arrival of Guy. "Perhaps he will choose not to come," I tried to convince myself. "Perhaps something will happen, something that will prevent him from coming." I admit that several times I sequestered myself in the abbey church, imploring God to grant me this wish. (Once I even lit an entire bank of votive candles, in an attempt to summon the Virgin's help, as well.)

Finally, however, my fear was realized: while I was strolling in the garden with Fastrada, Clementia rushed toward us, a letter in hand.

"From Guy?" I asked, dejected.

"Yes. I am afraid so."

"Come, best we take a seat and hear the news together," I told them.

We came to the bench near the quince trees and sat down. I unfolded the letter and began to read it aloud:

*To the Lady Isabelle, at the abbey of Fontevraud*

I write in haste, and in joy, dear sister, to convey word that will, no doubt, delight you quite as much as it has delighted me! I am betrothed to a most exceptional woman—a woman of beauty, of piety, of grace; even, I dare say, of considerable intellect. She is known to many, for her family, which hails from Orléans, is of the most noble stock, an ancient Frankish family with holdings far and wide. Her name? you will ask. Ermengarde de Vieupin Saugière. She is a widow, having been married once before to a nobleman of high rank and of even greater valor; alas, he died young, tragically young, not long after their first year of marriage.

That I have found this paragon of virtue—this gentle, demure spirit—fills me, as you can imagine, with ineffable happiness. At last, I will be able to share my life, and to dispel the loneliness that has hitherto filled it, with this incomparable woman! She has convinced me to take up residence with her at her castle near Bourges, which has been recently and, I am told, brilliantly, constructed according to the most modern precepts. As you can imagine, my betrothed—reputed far and wide for her thoughtfulness and charity—is greatly preoccupied with my delicate health, and has reassured me that the air and purity of the water near her idyllic abode will prove a boon to my fragile constitution.

The only disconcerting aspect of my betrothal is the fact that I shall not, alas, be able to venture to Fontevraud, due to the preparations necessary for the wedding. Please know that this pains me just as deeply as it must pain you and the noble Sister Clementia; and I suspect it will be, as well, a crushing blow to the distinguished Lady Fastrada, who has no doubt been eagerly awaiting my arrival. Do apologize to Lady Fastrada on my behalf, and assure her that, when she deems fit, my future wife and I shall be delighted to visit her and the Lord de Hauteclare at their own establishment. I should add that Lady Ermengarde distinctly remembers making the acquaintance of the Lady Fastrada in the not-so-distant past, and also professes to be greatly fond of Troyes.

Father and Amélie are overjoyed at my news, and look forward to welcoming Lady Ermengarde into our illustrious family. Indeed, it was blessed Amélie, with all her perspicacity, who introduced me to my cherished betrothed, thus setting into action this felicitous turn of events.

I send you loving greetings, dear sister, in addition to the

fervent hope that you will meet your new sister-in-law before
the end of summer,

I set down the letter, thrilled and astonished. "God has answered
my prayers!" I cried.

"Prayers?" the two women asked.

"I prayed that he would not come, that something would happen
to prevent it," I admitted somewhat sheepishly. "And the good Lord
listened!" I slapped the letter down on the bench, smiling broadly as I
looked up at the cloudless sky.

"God may have answered your prayers, but—trust me—it is doubtful He has answered Guy's," said Fastrada; her tone was ominous, her
dark eyes sparkling with mischief.

"What do you mean?" I asked.

"As he mentioned, I have indeed made the acquaintance of Lady
Ermengarde," she replied. There fell a long, and tantalizingly dramatic,
pause. "And she is hardly the paragon he describes."

"Oh, do tell," urged Clementia in a remarkably gossipy tone. (I had
come to realize that Guy, and perhaps only Guy, provoked her to a certain, welcome, girlishness.)

"Ah, yes, I remember the woman very well," began Fastrada, flicking
a bit of dust from her skirt. "How could I not? She is simply one of the
most hideous women I have encountered—dazzlingly ugly, for one, and
with a voice so piercing one could very well forfeit use of a horn and
employ her instead. As I recall, much talk preceded her visit to Troyes.
Her family had long despaired of finding a husband for her—"

"But Guy indicated she was a widow," I interjected. "Therefore—"

"Precisely! She had been married once, to a knight of lower station
from a family of diminishing fortune. Hugh happened to know him
slightly—Aimeric by name, one of five sons. The very youngest of these
was destined for the priesthood. As the second youngest, Aimeric was
faced with two choices: marry a landed heiress, or set sail for the Holy
Land in search of opportunity. To his everlasting regret, he elected marriage to Ermengarde. Before his death, he was reputed to have moaned,

'Would I had chosen the siege of Damascus rather than life with this woman!'"

"Poor man!" cried Clementia, while I struggled to restrain tears of laughter.

"So you see," Fastrada continued with the confident sprightliness of one who has an audience in thrall, "Guy must be either blind, dumb, or deaf—"

"Or desperate and deluded—" I suggested.

"Indeed." Fastrada nodded. "Let us just say that the demure, saintly woman he describes bears no resemblance to the woeful reality. Struck by her churlish personality, not to mention her shrill voice and considerable girth, I remember subsequently making inquiries after our meeting in Troyes. I was told she was a harridan, and that she had driven her husband to an early death by her shrewish, selfish behavior. And that, despite her wealth—the wealth that enabled her to attract a husband—she was a renowned miser. 'The food at her table is appalling,' I was told. 'And her wine diluted by water. If her servants obey her, it is only out of fear.'"

"And yet," I said, dumbfounded, "Guy mentions her castle as being the epitome of modern construction—"

"Modern it may be," retorted Fastrada, "but that hardly rescues it from its dismal location. Her obsession with saving money led Lady Ermengarde, and her late, beleaguered husband, to settle on the cheapest, and hence the least desirable, land possible for the site of this"—she paused, her brow raised—"how did Guy describe it, Isabelle?"

I picked up the letter. "'Idyllic abode,'" I quoted.

"Yes, quite—this 'idyllic abode' is, Hugh and I have heard, utterly pestilent. Rancid water, malodorous air—a place of bat droppings and stunted vegetation." She fixed her eyes upon us with an incongruously radiant expression as Clementia and I cried "Oh dear!" in unison.

"Now I am almost beginning to feel sorry for my brother," I added with a sigh. "His new home alone may doom him to an early death."

"It appears that he will hardly need worry about the effect of the castle's situation," remarked Clementia cavalierly.

"What do you mean?" I asked.

"It seems far more likely that marriage to Lady Ermengarde will kill him first," she retorted, in a tone so mordant that even Fastrada seemed taken aback.

"Clementia!" she exclaimed. "Never have I heard you—"

"You have never met *Guy,* dear sister."

# CHAPTER 86

A s Fastrada's departure drew nearer, my spirits were buoyed by the thought of attending Gallien's wedding in Troyes later that summer. "Even better," I told her, "Clementia has agreed to let Marie come with me. She was beside herself with excitement."

Fastrada's smile vanished. "There is one matter we have completely neglected discussing." She turned to me with a look so grave I was almost alarmed. "What will both of you *wear*?" she asked. "We must order new clothes for you and Marie, at once! I shall call for the tailor—"

"Oh, Fastrada!" I laughed, shaking my head as we continued on our way.

THE FOLLOWING DAY, A LETTER from Hugh arrived for Fastrada. "A letter from my husband?" she asked. "A rare treat indeed!" Fastrada's tone, though slightly sarcastic, was not without affection. She proceeded to read the letter quickly, afterward looking up at me and Clementia with a bright, satisfied expression.

"Well?" I asked expectantly. "What does he say?"

"Typical Hugh mélange. What it lacks in artfulness, it makes up for in quantity of information." Scanning the letter, she began to give a running commentary: "Gallien's farmhouse is finished, on the land that Hugh bestowed to him. And now the stable is being constructed! Hugh seems quite pleased about this—did I not tell you that he treated Gallien as another son? Then, let me see. . . ." She furrowed her brow, as she resumed reading. "He says our servants are wildly excited at the upcoming nuptials 'partly because Gallien is so beloved.' And Hugh hopes that I have invited *you* to come, Isabelle!" She glanced at me with

a broad smile. "Lastly, some word of the court and the latest machinations. Philippe is stirring up trouble with King Henry. *Plus ça change,
plus c'est la même chose!* And there are rumors—ah, this will interest you,
Isabelle—that the queen may be permitted to attend Christmas court
this year, at Winchester."

"That *is* important news indeed," I remarked, wondering what the
king intended by this hitherto forbidden privilege. "And does he indicate whether their sons will also attend?"

"Yes," she replied. "It is expected that Richard, Geoffrey, and John
will be there—an attempt for a rapprochement between *père et fils,* no
doubt."

"Even if a rapprochement is achieved, it will never last," observed
Clementia quietly.

"No doubt you are right," I replied, adding, "I am certain the king
is merely using the queen as a way to exert pressure on her sons."

"*Exactly,* Isabelle," concurred Fastrada. "Clearly your time with the
queen has sharpened your insight into royal machinations." Folding the
parchment, she added almost absentmindedly, "Ah, I forgot to tell you
the last bit of good news—Hugh is sending LaFoi to fetch me for the
journey home!"

LAFOI ARRIVED A WEEK LATER—FESTOONED with a bright cap, he
was a vivid sight on a gloomy afternoon in April. It touched me to see
how warmly LaFoi greeted Marie, and with what earnestness he conversed with her. For the rest of that day, she seized every opportunity
to seek him out.

The following morning, decked in a traveling costume of purple
serge, Fastrada departed with her customary flurry—an absurd number of trunks for a relatively short visit, effusive thanks to her sister,
promises of delicacies to be sent from Troyes to the abbey, and, lastly,
confirmation that the wedding apparel, which had been ordered for me
and Marie, would be completed to her specifications.

Her final farewell was to Marie, who had hung about her with special urgency those last several days. "My darling girl," said Fastrada,

embracing the tearful child. "Please do not cry! I shall see you soon enough, this summer, at the wedding of Gallien! And then you will meet my husband, and others whom Isabelle knew years ago, in her other life." She knelt down, tenderly adding, "And they will tell you about your mother, and what a dear, beloved creature she was." At that, she stood up, kissed Marie several times on the top of her head, and, with LaFoi's help, mounted.

"And will I see LaFoi again, in Troyes, too?" entreated Marie, her hand by the stirrup, looking up at Fastrada.

Fastrada glanced at LaFoi, splendid in blue livery, with affectionate benevolence. "*Of course* you will! All of us—including Gallien—could not imagine the wedding without him."

At that, LaFoi, coloring slightly and smiling in quiet appreciation, mounted, and the two set off.

MAY BROUGHT THE ARRIVAL OF the clothes that Fastrada had ordered—several ornate, yet charming frocks for Marie and others, of splendid quality and great elegance, for me. "Are these really *mine*?" Marie cried, then, breathlessly, jumping up and down: "May I try them on?"

I assented and helped hook her into each robe. Around and around she twirled, ecstatic. "Come now, Marie, let me see a proper curtsey," I finally said, after which she executed one perfectly. "You *do* look very pretty indeed," I told her. "Like a proper little damsel, or a little princess!"

It was then that Clementia entered. "The porter told me that the tailor was here earlier," she announced in a decidedly frosty voice. "I wanted to see the confections which my sister ordered for you," Clementia continued. "And now that I *do* see them—"

"You must admit that they are *lovely*," I rejoined firmly, determined not to let Clementia ruin the child's pleasure. "Marie looks like a little angel in her frock—"

"A rather *gaudy* angel—"

"But an *angel*, nevertheless. For her *spirit* is like an angel's, is it not, dear Clementia? And surely that is what truly matters?" All the while Marie, standing between us, never moved an iota. "It would be dreadful not to appreciate these dresses for what they are," I continued cajolingly, "generous gifts from Fastrada, and emblems of her affection and spirit. I assure you that Marie knows they are meant for the wedding, and for Troyes, only. Do you not, Marie?" I looked at her directly.

The little girl nodded with inordinate, almost comical alacrity.

"Very well, then," said Clementia after a moment. "But while Marie is here, those things are to remain in the trunk."

"Of course," I replied. "Marie and I will fold them and put them into her trunk at once."

At that, Clementia turned and peremptorily left.

"Oh, Lady Isabelle, *thank you!*" cried Marie, hugging me tight. "For a moment I thought—"

"Yes, I know you feared their being taken away from you." As I began to unhook her robe, I added, "Even I had no idea how luxurious and costly these clothes would be. But you know Lady Fastrada, and her taste! She does not *skimp*, unlike—" But I caught myself; I had been thinking of Lady Ermengarde and Fastrada's contempt for her parsimony.

"Unlike *who*, Lady Isabelle?" Marie asked; like most children, she perked up at the mention of anyone's peccadilloes.

"Oh, a stranger, someone I have merely heard about." Then, as I helped her out of the dress: "But these clothes must remain in the trunk, dear Marie. You must be mindful of Sister Clementia's rules." I chucked her under the chin. "Do you understand?"

She nodded eagerly.

In the weeks that followed, I came upon her peeking into the trunk several times; and once, when I entered, I discovered her sitting on a bench, stroking the robe in her lap as one would a doll, or a kitten.

"Marie!" I admonished.

"Please, Lady Isabelle!" She leaped to her feet and pleaded, "Oh please, do not tell Sister Clementia!"

I knelt down, taking her hands in mine as I looked searchingly into her eyes. "Do you think I shall?"

She deliberated for many moments. "No," she finally replied, with a slow, tenuous smile.

"You are right," I replied, gently laughing at myself as much as at her. I stood up. "But *do* put the robe away at once, lest we both get into a great deal of trouble."

AT LAST, ON A DAY in late June with a sky almost as brilliant a blue as his elaborate cap, LaFoi arrived to fetch us, in a livery even more elaborate than usual. A lovely, docile mount had been chosen for Marie, whose skill as a rider did not yet match her enthusiasm. I felt inordinately stylish in the traveling costume that Fastrada had commissioned for me—a slim confection in wheat-colored linen piped in crimson. ("I cannot have you and Marie arrive looking like two stragglers from purgatory," she had declared.)

After we had mounted—Marie picturesque in forest green embroidered in white—LaFoi turned to address her. "Listen to me carefully, Marie," he began as she leaned forward, her worshipful eyes fixed upon him. "As we proceed, it is important that you follow my instructions. I shall warn you if the road becomes steep, or if there is a slippery descent. Most of all, you must try to stay right behind me. Do you understand?" To this, she nodded so solemnly, all the while evincing such palpable excitement, that tears almost came to my eyes.

The journey confirmed what I had already intuited—Marie loved adventure, and she loved the outside world. There was no aspect of our travels, no matter how paltry or unpleasant, she did not find delightful. The straw pallets on which we slept, at the inns, she pronounced "wonderfully comfortable"; the barley water at a tavern near Orléans "the most delicious" she had ever tasted; the landscape we traversed "the most beautiful" she had ever seen.

I tried to imagine her later in life, as a young woman, wondering whether the self she was truly meant to be coincided with the one Clementia so firmly intended for her. I thought of Aiglantine and how proud she would have been of her spirited daughter—as I was, as well.

ON A GLORIOUS SUMMER MORNING, we caught sight of Troyes's surrounding walls; not long thereafter, we approached the principal gate. "Look!" I cried to Marie, pointing to the splendid pennants waving proudly, almost arrogantly, above the high, graceful turrets. "Can you make out the design on the pennants? Your eyes are better than mine—yours are like a little hawk's!"

She nodded, her eyes fixed ahead. "Yes! I can see," she replied. "On the top, a row of fleur-de-lis, and then broad bands of white and blue."

LaFoi, watching his two transfixed companions, prodded, "Come! No time to lose. We must make our way through the gate, and then north to my lord and lady's domain, before darkness falls."

Once at the gate, LaFoi dismounted while we waited for him to obtain permission to enter (Marie quite agog, all the while, at the reverence with which the gatekeeper greeted him). LaFoi having remounted, we passed through—savoring a bit of welcome shade afforded by the passageway under the ramparts—and made our way through the winding, clamorous streets. What a sight, what a cosmopolitan jumble! One moment we were jostled by men carrying great bolts of silk and damask; another we crossed paths with a fellow carrying a set of scales on a balance beam. After the sober camaïeu of the abbey, I felt almost drunk from the onslaught of vivid colors, scents, and textures.

As we progressed, I could not help but think of my journey to Nîmes, at an age only slightly older than Marie's. Now it was she who imbibed every new sight, sense, and sound: not only what was beautiful—the cathedral, the richly appointed shops, the handsome, half-timbered houses—but also what was not: the scabrous, filthy travelers who huddled in doorways, the maimed beggars, and other beings, equally wretched, who bore the evidence of scourge. Not once, I distinctly noted, did she avert her eyes.

WE CAME TO THE OUTSKIRTS of the Hauteclare citadel by late day; LaFoi, coming to a halt, pointed ahead. "Do you see those high towers? Those red banners?"

We nodded.

"That is the castle of my lord and lady." He gave an almost proprietary smile. "Come, let us gallop, and we will arrive all the sooner! I suspect the watchmen may have already sighted us."

Indeed, that must have been the case, for the drawbridge seemed to descend magically just as we approached; then came the slow, welcome creaking sound of the gates opening. From a distance, we heard that unmistakable throaty voice—Fastrada's—and glimpsed a tall figure in a saffron-colored robe striding toward us, one extravagant sleeve flapping like a banner. The next instant, having flung our reins to the waiting pages, we fairly leaped from our mounts, and embraced her.

"How *exciting* this is!" she cried, glancing from me to Marie and back again. "And the journey?"

"Wonderful!" we cried in unison.

"How could it *not* be, with LaFoi as your guide?" (At this LaFoi, after making a deep bow, beamed.) "Come, let me look at you both. I must see the costumes I ordered." Her eyes narrowed slightly, as she studied us. "Yes, both are perfect! What a difference it makes to have Marie in something other than *dispiriting* colors."

"Mine is so pretty!" she cried. "May I keep it?"

"Of course, darling girl! And you must wear it again, as long as it fits you."

"But Sister Clementia said—" Marie's face clouded over.

"Oh," Fastrada scoffed. "You are with *me* now, child, in my home. We do not need to think about such tedious matters *here*. This is a time to forsake all dreariness." The little girl nodded enthusiastically.

"Where is Hugh?" I asked, eager to change the subject.

"Inside, awaiting us," said Fastrada, taking Marie's hand and my arm. "Come!"

# CHAPTER 87

Hugh was quite different in aspect from the rakish man I had remembered: his hair had thinned and gone quite gray, and his stomach had evolved into a decided paunch. It was in this new persona, as jolly paterfamilias, that he greeted us. "So this is the little angel I have heard about!" he said upon meeting Marie. "I shall show you the mews tomorrow," he added, bringing himself down to her level before asking jauntily, "what do you say?"

"Yes!" replied Marie with a huge smile. "I would like that very much. Will Gallien be there?"

"Gallien?" Hugh glanced at me, smiling, as he came to his feet. "So you have told her about him—"

"Of course," I replied. "Will he be there? I long to see him!"

"Hopefully he will have returned from his mission."

"Mission?"

"He rode north to purchase a hawk for his bride. It will be his nuptial gift to her. My idea." He smiled broadly, immensely pleased with himself.

"Her own hawk?" piped up Marie.

"Yes! Her very own," he replied. "And one day, when you are older, you will have one, too. What do you say to that?"

"Oh, Hugh, really," I interjected as Marie trilled with delight. "You are going to spoil her. Remember—"

"Yes, yes, I know," he replied, rolling his eyes. "The abbey, Clementia. But as my beloved wife would say"—at this, a prideful glance at Fastrada, who stood nearby in a corner, directing some pages—"This is not a nunnery. Come, Marie, let us get you something to drink. You have had a long journey."

As they went off hand in hand, I began to look about: not since my marriage had I found myself in a great hall of such splendor. I had a sudden, vivid recollection of my arrival at Ravinour, and the first grand dinner. There had been a certain tension about Gerard's largesse—a nervous, often rigid, perfectionism. I was struck by the markedly different ambiance here: my hosts radiated a marvelous sense of ease, a palpable delight in the true pleasure in giving.

I had thought Fastrada might seem slightly diminished, less larger-than-life than she appeared amid the austerity of the abbey. But no, in fact, she seemed even more magisterial and striking—a commanding, resplendent central figure in an extraordinarily vivid tapestry. "Look at Hugh and Marie—she has made a new friend, clearly!" she exclaimed, beaming, as she walked toward me. "And what a treat for Hugh, who has known only sons, to have a little girl about. It will do Marie good to be among men like Hugh. The only men the poor child has known are monks."

"She has met Guy," I interposed with a sly smile.

"That hardly counts—"

"Oh dear," I replied, laughing almost despite myself, "how mortified Guy would be to hear you say that!"

She took my arm gaily before calling out to Hugh, "Come, it is time to dine."

We approached the long, gloriously appointed table. Draped in a heavy linen cloth with a deep embroidered border, it was arrayed with silver trenchers and goblets, swan-necked pitchers of wine, enameled water vessels shaped like fanciful animals, and numerous lustrous small bowls, heaped with spices and artfully placed in groups, along the center of the table. Hugh sat at the center, flanked by myself and Fastrada; and to her left, Marie.

"As your honorary aunt," Fastrada announced to her as the meal commenced, "I am entitled to have you beside me, am I not?" Marie, visibly thrilled, broke into a wide smile as I watched with pride. The combination of the splendid setting and her new raiment seemed to have affected her deportment: sitting uncharacteristically still, with her back ramrod straight, she had the air of a little princess.

As Hugh and I chatted in a measured way, I noticed that Fastrada and Marie barely took a breath between words. I overheard Fastrada regaling Marie with stories of the famous lists at Troyes, about Marie de Champagne and her poets, about the great fairs. Intermittently she took care to describe the food being passed, most of which, being rich and highly spiced, was unfamiliar to a child raised on abbey cuisine. "I am sure you have never tasted lampreys," Fastrada said as a platter of this rare dish was being presented. Or, "You must taste this," she urged, with a dramatic emphasis of a beringed hand, as a timbale of rice, fragrant with nutmeg and studded with nuts, was proffered. How astonished Aiglantine would be, I thought, to see her daughter here, in this noble setting, seated next to Fastrada at such a splendidly decorated table.

As the meal came to an end, the dessert appeared—a glistening, molded pudding ornamented with a design of fleur-de-lis in currants and accompanied by a sauce served in a silver tureen fashioned like a centaur. Marie was given the honor of taking the first portion. "Children should never have to wait for sweets," proclaimed Fastrada (still another dictum that would have provoked displeasure from Clementia).

"It looks almost too pretty to eat," exclaimed Marie, before taking a tiny bite and setting her spoon down.

"Come now, Marie," Fastrada chided, "you must eat this lovely sweet, or my cook will be quite insulted. And then the cook will tell LaFoi, and how upset he will be to hear this." She leaned forward and said, theatrically, "And you do not want that to happen, do you?"

"HOW MANY QUESTIONS MAY I ask Gallien?" Marie asked me the following morning, as we followed Hugh to the mews. It was an idyllic summer morning—a morning of sun, birdsong, and the sweet scent of fertile fields.

"As many questions as you like. Do you mean questions about hawks, and the mews, or other questions, Marie? About your mother, perhaps?"

"Yes," she confessed softly. "About my mother, too."

"I am sure he will be very happy to tell you what he remembers

about her. And at the wedding you will meet others who knew Aiglantine as well. They will be overjoyed to meet you." How strange that after
all these years, I would again see Gallien, Raoul, and Corbus, and in
this setting.

"Here we are!" cried Hugh, pointing ahead to the mews—a large,
handsome structure that more than equaled Gerard's mews in size and
impressiveness. Presently we came to a tall door emblazoned with the
Hauteclare escutcheon, and Hugh ushered us in. As we stood at the entrance, Marie's head swiveled this way and that while the birds greeted
us with their chorus of shrill, hoarse calls.

"What sounds all of them make, together," said Marie, her eyes
wide with wonder. "I wonder what they are trying to say?"

"That they are very pleased to meet you," replied Hugh heartily.

A tall, red-haired fellow in falconer's garb strode toward us—so
vigorous was he, and so assured, that I had to jolt myself to imagine,
Could this be Gallien?

"My lady," Gallien said, his voice quivering with emotion as he
bowed deeply before me. I struggled meanwhile to reconcile my last
memory of him with this poised, confident young man who stood before me now.

"Come, enough ceremony!" I exclaimed, tears in my eyes as I extended my hands to him. "How good to see you looking so well." And
indeed, I marveled to see what he had become—a glowing, dignified
figure in his slim, elegantly cut falconer's tunic; only his ingenuous expression and the freckles scattered across his nose and cheeks made me
recall the young, uncertain boy I remembered so well from our first
encounter in the stables long ago.

I felt Marie gently tugging at me. "I would like you to meet Marie,
Aiglantine's daughter," I said as she stepped forward, curtseying before
him. "She has heard all about you and has been so excited for this moment."

He knelt down to speak with her. "And I have heard about you,
Marie, from Lady Fastrada. My lady has great affection for you."

"She is my honorary aunt," she replied with pride. Then she

marveled, "I have never met a master falconer before. And I have never seen so many falcons, and a great eagle, too!"

As Gallien, smiling, stood up, Hugh interposed, "And, Marie, I venture you will never meet as fine a falconer as our Gallien." He gave him a warm, fatherly glance.

"It is you who have taught me what I know, my lord," Gallien returned. Meantime I listened to this repartee in fascination, reflecting how different it was in tenor from the exchanges between Gerard and Ragnar.

"Marie and I are honored to be invited to your wedding, Gallien," I said. "And we so look forward to meeting Douceline. Lady Fastrada told me she is winsome, and that she shares your love of hawks."

"She does indeed," he proudly replied. "And of much else. You will see, Lady Isabelle, she will make me a fine wife, and will be a fine mother."

"As you will make a fine husband," I replied. "But come, I would like you to show Marie around. She has questions to ask you about your work." I paused. "And about her mother, too."

"Lady Isabelle said I may ask as many questions as I like," piped up Marie.

"And, as usual, Lady Isabelle is right," Gallien returned. "But since Lady Isabelle already knows quite a bit about hawks, perhaps it is best I show you about, and we discuss them on our own."

She nodded eagerly.

"Let us begin at the back, and I will show you where I work," Gallien said. "And then I will tell you about the birds, and how we train and take care of them. Each has its personality, you see——" I watched them go off together, Gallien's hand in hers as they walked to the back of the mews, where his worktable and equipment stood.

"She is a winning child," said Hugh, who stood with me watching them.

"That she is," I replied. "Her life has been both sad and wondrous." Having noticed that Marie was absorbed in talking with Gallien, I took the opportunity to broach a subject that had been weighing on me. "It is so strange, and so tragic, about Gerard's death."

"It stunned me. But others, closer than I am to the inner royal circle, thought it was quite plausible that he took his own life. They said he would have been disgraced, stripped of his lands and much of his wealth, had he lived. He had broken promises—as he had to me once—and had made bargains with the devil. He had also become isolated, I hear, and had taken to drink."

I gave a deep sigh, then murmured sadly, "To think of him, of all people, ending his life that way—"

"But enough of Gerard and his demise," he interjected. "Gallien bids us join them."

We stood up and walked toward them. "Gallien has told me all about the birds," Marie began to chatter. "Imagine, each has its own special hood, in his own color, and he told me how he feeds them—just enough, so they are ready to hunt, and that is called being in *yarak*. Is that right, Gallien?" She turned, her sparkling eyes fixed upon him.

"Exactly right," said Gallien. "A good student you are, like Lady Isabelle."

"And Gallien has told me about my mother, too," said Marie, "and how he and Raoul and Corbus were so fond of her, and always tried to help her."

I nodded. "Yes, she was dear to all of us," I rejoined, feeling my eyes tear up.

Hugh, who was never completely at ease with any display of emotion, intervened. "Come, Marie, let us take a hawk outside. We will choose one together, and then I will show you how to make him fly, and then return to you. I suspect that is a lesson you will enjoy!"

The little girl gave a rapturous nod. "And that will also give Lady Isabelle and Gallien a chance to talk."

Marie took Hugh's hand and they left together—Hugh with a falcon on his wrist, Marie, at his side, beaming.

"Marie will never forget this visit, nor will she ever forget your wedding," I said to Gallien. "It was kind of you to invite Raoul and Corbus, too."

"If all goes well, they will be here on the morrow, or the day after. I owe them so much," he added.

"Those days after Vainqueur escaped—what a dreadful time that was! I never thought you would be able to escape—"

"I was only able to do so with Raoul's help. He gave me money so I could travel north. He told me that I should try to make my way to Lord and Lady de Hauteclare. He was confident that they would help me."

"I never knew this," I said, thinking how wrong I had been not to have trusted Raoul at first.

Just then we heard Hugh calling to us. "Come outside," he cried. "It is a glorious day, and we must give Marie a chance to fly a hawk by herself."

# CHAPTER 88

Hugh's pride in Gallien and his hawks was matched only by Fastrada's in her garden and orchard. "Enough of hawks and the chase," she quipped when Marie and I returned from the mews. "Now it is time for flowers and fruit trees." She led us to the orchard in the southeast corner of the castle ward; there, after we duly admired her bounteous apple and medlar trees, she began to regale me and Marie with details of the wedding. "I oversaw the design of the gown Douceline will wear. You will see how exquisite it is," she exclaimed. "I believe it will strike just the right note—both celebratory and simple."

"What color is it, Lady Fastrada?" asked Marie.

"I cannot tell you that, dear child. It must be a surprise. And I have lent Douceline the ceinture she will wear. It was my grandmother's, and mine, and now, hopefully, it will bring her and Gallien good fortune as well."

"I am sure it is exquisite," I rejoined.

"Of course. But that is only part of it. Most of all, it has the proper stones—agate to guard against illness, sardonyx to ensure a stable marriage, and amethyst for fertility."

"Did *you* wear such a ceinture, Lady Isabelle, when you were married?" asked Marie.

"Alas, I did not," I replied quietly. The mention of "amethyst" had unsettled me—a reminder that it was not amethyst, with its life-giving properties I had eventually sought during my marriage, but its antithesis, jet. "We had nothing of that nature, or splendor, in my family," I went on. "I *did* wear a robe trimmed with pearls, a gift from my husband—"

"Pearls?" asked Fastrada. "They are meant to bring freedom and the ability to foresee the future," she returned, looping her arm through mine. "And since you have achieved your freedom," she continued, "we must assume that the pearls were at least partly effective. As for being able to augur the future—"

"That would be a wonderful thing, would it not, Lady Isabelle?" interjected Marie, with a child's poignant optimism.

"Of course," I replied, though I was far from certain that was true.

"And what do you foresee for *me*?" asked Marie.

"Many years of happiness and accomplishment," I replied, with a tender smile, trying to imagine her as a young woman.

"'Accomplishment'?" asked Fastrada. "That speaks to lofty ambitions, does it not?"

"It does indeed," I rejoined. "Clementia and I have great faith in Marie and her abilities."

"And I shall try my very best never to disappoint you!" cried Marie with such fervency that tears came to my eyes, and to Fastrada's.

AT NOON ON THE DAY of the wedding, Marie and I assembled at the stables, where Hugh and Fastrada, strikingly elegant in their finery, awaited us for the departure to the village church. Fastrada looked at us with her intent, appraising gaze. "How charming both of you look! There is just one thing awry. We must arrange your braid properly, Marie." After adjusting the wayward braid, Fastrada stepped back to assess me. "Exquisite," she proclaimed.

"It is *Fastrada* who is the vision!" I interjected, for she was indeed resplendent: her robe, in samite cloth of a violet hue, artfully laced at the bodice in gold, and trimmed at the hem and sleeves with shimmering gilt ribbon, was unlike any I had ever seen. Coupled with a cascading gold necklace and long, glittering earrings, the attire lent her the look of an eccentric Greek empress.

"I would *never* insult Gallien and his friends by appearing at his wedding in some humdrum costume without my best jewels," Fastrada exclaimed. "What would they think? They expect me to be the great lady I am, and I would never *dream* of disappointing them."

"You are quite right, Fastrada," I returned. "You will dazzle them."

"You may even out-dazzle the bride," Hugh teased.

"*That* would not be possible," she returned. "She is young and beautiful. I am of a certain—shall we say—less-than-ripe age"—her lips formed a wry smile—"and must rely on artifice. Therein lies an unbreachable difference." She looked about impatiently. "But where is LaFoi?"

He appeared the next instant, followed by cluster of grooms leading a parade of gorgeously caparisoned mounts. They had been fitted with festal saddles, the gilt trim of which seemed to glow in the sun; ornate badges with the Hauteclare coat of arms dangled from their bridles. The most beautiful among them was Fastrada's—a long-legged chestnut steed whose expression seemed almost human in its haughtiness. Clearly LaFoi had also been given Fastrada's directives as well: he was decked in his grandest livery and wore an especially ornate cap topped with towering white plumes. He bowed, bade us good day, and made such a special point of greeting Marie that she broke into a huge smile.

Shortly afterward, our courtly entourage set off. As the ancient, domed structure, nestled in the valley, came into sight, we saw that a large crowd had already assembled. The road narrowed; we came to a slow trot as we filed along the path to the church itself; and a sudden hush fell upon the motley throng massed near its entrance. Necks craned to glimpse us; a few boisterous young men elbowed to the front to get a better view; I heard the murmur of "Hauteclare" through the crowd.

"Let us stop here, LaFoi," Hugh directed. "Best we dismount and let you and the men take care of the horses. I will escort the ladies to the portico."

"Come," said Fastrada, taking my arm. "You will see, it is a simple little church, but a lovely one. Such fond memories it holds for us—so many family rituals. It was, how long ago?"—she paused—"ten years ago, almost to this day, that my eldest son, Nicolas, was married here."

A merry, jostling multitude awaited the wedding—country folk in their best finery, peasants leaning on staffs, ragged mendicants, all of them mingling with the many servants from the Hauteclare household. The crowd parted as we made our way to the front; men bowed, women and girls curtseyed as Fastrada and Hugh, hand in hand, made their way past, looking to one side, then the other, with stately nods and smiles. As Marie and I followed, my eyes searched the crowd for Raoul and Corbus.

"We should not enter the church yet," Fastrada told us, as we came to the portal. "We must wait here to watch the bridal procession. Marie must not miss it."

"Indeed, she must not," rejoined Hugh, glancing fondly at an enthralled Marie.

The priest—short, stout, and disconcertingly cross-eyed—emerged to greet us. It was clear, from his nervous, almost slavish manner, that the Hauteclares rarely graced his little church. "What a great honor, my lord and lady," he intoned again and again until Hugh, partly as a way to interrupt him, introduced myself and Marie.

As I looked back to the narrow, dusty path that led to the church, I spotted two figures in the distance: one rather slight, and another, stockier, whose distinctive, steady gait I recognized at once as Corbus's.

I told Hugh and Fastrada that I had just sighted them. "Go and see them," Fastrada urged. "We will await you here."

"Come with me, Marie!" I said, seizing her hand as we made our way back through the crowd. The two of us dashed down the path— Marie's scampering steps keeping pace with my long, quick strides. I waved and waved until, at last, the two men, having glimpsed me, returned my wave, and rushed toward us.

Now I stood face-to-face with them—two cherished friends, whom I had never, ever thought I would see again. I grasped Raoul's hands tightly in mine, and then Corbus's, as I exclaimed "how good to see you" over and over. Even as I rejoiced in our reunion, I was startled to see how the intervening years and the change of setting had altered them. Raoul appeared thin and worn, and, without his livery, quite devoid of his customary air of authority. Standing before me now—in his very best attire, no doubt—he looked like an aged, dignified denizen of the village. As for Corbus: his wide, fair face was deeply lined, making him appear older than he probably was, and his flaxen hair was now interspersed with strands of gray.

"It is hard to believe it is *you*, Lady Isabelle," said Raoul in wonder as Corbus, his pale eyes fixed upon me, nodded his assent.

"Yes, it is indeed wondrous to meet again, Raoul! I am so grateful to both of you for making the long journey from Ravinour. Most of all I am grateful that we are here, together, to celebrate Gallien's nuptials. Did you ever think—"

"No," he interrupted quietly. "I prayed for him, and gave him what guidance I could, but I was never sure he would survive."

"He has not only survived but *flourished*! But now you must meet Marie, Aiglantine's daughter." The child stepped forward, curtseying before the two men. "I know Gallien has mentioned her to you," I added. "She has heard how fond you were of her mother."

"We were indeed," said Raoul. "Imagine Aiglantine's joy, were she here to see us all together."

"Sister Clementia tells me that she *does* see us, from heaven," said Marie. "She may be watching us now."

"I am sure she is," I murmured. Raoul, touched, looked down; Corbus wiped his eye with his sleeve.

"Do you hear music?" I asked, grateful for a touch of levity. "The bridal procession must be approaching. Come, we must walk quickly back to the church."

THE SOUND OF PIPES, AND jangling tambourines, and raucous cheers, became more insistent; and then, almost magically, the procession made its way toward us—Douceline, fair, blond, and sprightly, in a tight-bodiced dress of fine green linen embroidered with golden sheaves of wheat, her filmy matching veil held in place by a delicate wreath of white flowers, her thick braid falling to the waist. There was a graceful vivacity to her looks, and to her step; her hips, encircled by the wide, gem-studded ceinture, swayed slightly as she walked. Six or seven maidens, in their best finery, followed her; and behind them, alone, strode Gallien, handsome and proud in the tunic of the master falconer.

As she came before Fastrada and Hugh, Douceline murmured "my lady" in a tremulous voice and began to curtsey. "No! Not today," intervened Fastrada, extending her hand and entreating her to rise. "This day is *yours*, Douceline," announced Fastrada. "You are the honored bride—today it is *I* who must offer you deference." She made a deep, measured curtsey while the throng, spellbound, watched. Then I too curtseyed before Douceline, and so, without my having to prompt her, did Marie.

Hugh stepped forward to address the crowd in a voice at once powerful and heartfelt. "Before we enter God's sacred house, Lady Fastrada and I wish to beseech Him that He may grant every blessing to the marriage of Gallien and Douceline." With a murmur of "amen," the assembly made the sign of the cross in unison.

"Come," cried Fastrada, shaking off solemnity as she exhorted the bride and groom, "now lead the procession inside—we, and all your friends, will follow."

I doubt that the damp, musty interior, with its primitive, faded frescoes, jagged stone floor, and shabby pews, had ever been as richly adorned or as radiantly lit as it was that day. Summer flowers massed the interior—roses, lilies, long branches of fragrant apple blossoms. Banks of tall, flickering candles illuminated the altar and transepts. The unaccustomed grandeur of these touches, combined with the presence of the Hauteclares, seemed to have so unnerved the poor priest that he stumbled several times during the Mass (while reciting the Agnus Dei, he transposed one line, and completely forgot another). None of this mattered a whit, however, least of all to the radiant young couple who stood before the altar and who shone with transfixing happiness. From time to time I glanced at Marie, who was utterly, and touchingly, rapt.

Watching the couple exchange vows, I was moved, but my emotions were also tinged with sadness—even at moments, I must admit, with envy. This unadulterated joy in being wed, this sense of warmth and surety, this is what I did not know with Gerard, I reflected, only to realize, with a pang, This I shall most likely *never* know.

At last, the ceremony having concluded, we followed the wedding couple, who led the procession as we made our way down the aisle. "Look, there is LaFoi!" Marie nudged me, adding, "I almost did not recognize him without his feathers." Indeed, having doffed his fabled cap, LaFoi did look quite different, even rather diminished. He was seated near Raoul and Corbus, in the back; next to them sat the sweet young chambermaid who swept our floor every morning.

From the dank, cool church we made our way into the luminous summer sun. There, outside the threshold, the priest bestowed his final blessing on the couple; then came the cheers, the roars of delight, the clapping, and the chaos of the crowd. Fastrada wiped tears of happiness from her eyes; Hugh embraced Gallien and gave him a hearty "Well done!" Meantime Marie, hopping up and down, tugged my hand and asked, "What is next, Lady Isabelle?"

"We must present Raoul and Corbus to Lady Fastrada and Lord de Hauteclare. Then we will ride to Gallien's home for the wedding feast."

GALLIEN'S DWELLING LAY CLOSE BY—HALF a league away, through fields of wheat and meadows with grazing cattle and flocks of sheep. The house and its stable, barn, and granary were set near the banks of a rippling stream shaded by stands of poplars. There was a sturdy, simple friendliness and openness about the abode and its setting—a perfect reflection of Gallien himself.

"What a lovely site," I exclaimed, looking about the peaceful landscape, which abounded with flowering hawthorn trees—the plant of fairy legends, of brides, of hope, I wistfully remembered.

"I helped him select the land," said Hugh with pride, as I dismounted.

"Look at those, over there!" exclaimed Marie, pointing to two white tents with red peaks, which stood at a slight distance, in the middle of the adjoining field.

"Those are the tents where we will sup and where the dancing will take place," said Fastrada, shielding her eyes from the afternoon sun. "It gives me and Hugh pleasure to provide the fête. When we think of Gallien's life, and the turn it might have taken . . ." Her expression clouded over, but just as quickly resumed its former joyfulness. "Come," she said to me and Marie, "let us walk over there and check the preparations."

Not far from the tents, calf and sheep were roasting on spits; nearby stood great barrels and bubbling cauldrons, tended to by servants. "Ah, the scents of pepper and juniper," said Fastrada, taking a deep breath. "The welcome sign of a wedding feast!"

In the first tent stood long trestle tables looped with greenery; minstrels and jongleurs roamed about, lightly strumming and singing as the guests awaited the bride and groom. Presently they arrived, to clapping and cheers—Gallien driving a wagon garlanded in berry-laden branches, with Douceline, one hand holding tight to her coronet of flowers, smiling beside him.

I spotted Corbus and Raoul among those following the wagon. There was now an almost palpable pride in Raoul's step—no doubt he was still basking in the moment when, earlier, Fastrada had mentioned she clearly remembered meeting him at Ravinour.

"When may I ask Raoul about my mother?" whispered Marie as the two approached.

"Why not now, before supper?"

"And may I ask Corbus, too?"

"Of course. But remember, he cannot speak. He has his *own* language." I knelt down to her level. "Shall I stay with you, or would you rather speak with them alone?"

"Please stay," she entreated softly.

I beckoned to Raoul and Corbus. "Let us find a quiet place to talk before the revelry begins. Over there, perhaps?" I pointed to some benches nearby.

The four of us sat down, Marie in the center next to Raoul. "It seems like an eternity since I have seen you and Corbus," I began. "When I think of first meeting you, Raoul, when I arrived at the castle that night"—I gave a wistful smile—"how nervous I was, how frightened—"

"I cannot imagine *you* ever being frightened, Lady Isabelle!" Marie chimed in. Glancing at Raoul, who was the very picture of gentleness, she added, "And certainly not of *Raoul*."

"I am glad to hear you say that Marie," he replied, somewhat amused. "And I am also glad that Lady Isabelle seems to have taught you to speak your mind."

"Lady Isabelle has taught me *many* things," the little girl said proudly. "And Sister Clementia, too. I am lucky to have them, especially since"— her expression clouded over—"especially since I never really knew my mother. Lady Isabelle has told me that you knew my mother well."

"I did," Raoul replied, "and was greatly fond of her. She was a fine, gentle soul. I am sure there was not a single moment when she did not think of you, Marie, and pray to God that the good sisters of Fontevraud were caring for you."

Marie, her head bent, seemed to ponder this; then she glanced up at Corbus, who had been listening attentively, his chin resting in his hand. "Did Corbus know her well, too?" she asked.

"Yes," I replied. "Your mother had great affection for Corbus." At this, Corbus gave a smile of unsurpassable radiance; no words could ever have equaled its eloquence. "He and Raoul helped me," I went on, "and they helped Gallien, too, when he had"—I paused—"difficulties."

"How did they help *you?*" asked Marie, plainly bewildered at the idea of my ever needing guidance.

"They gave me confidence," I replied, "and a strong sense of friendship. Without them, I would have been lost, and even lonelier—" I caught myself, knowing it was neither the time nor the occasion to discuss my troubled marriage.

To my relief, Marie turned to Corbus. "Lady Isabelle says you know all the paths of the forest, and that you can talk to animals. Is that really true?"

He gave a wide, assenting grin. "Can you talk to *them?*" Marie asked, pointing to some rabbits scampering beneath a nearby oak.

He gave a merry nod. "Show me how you do it!" she exclaimed. Corbus gestured her to follow him; Raoul and I watched, smiling, as the two set off hand in hand.

"Lady Fastrada told us in a letter about Aiglantine's final journey to Fontevraud," Raoul remarked.

"You cannot imagine how frail and dreadfully ill she was."

"Alas, I can. Lord de Meurtaigne was cruel and threatening to her after you departed. I overheard him say to Ragnar, 'The girl must leave.

I cannot tolerate the presence of anyone who was in league with my wife.' With each passing day, Aiglantine grew weaker and weaker and more frightened."

"How awful for Aiglantine," I said, shaking my head in sorrow. "I have heard the rumors about Gerard's death—that he may have taken his own life. Do you think that possible?"

"Yes," he replied, to my surprise. "He had changed a great deal after the Young King was defeated. He had become bitter, especially after King Richard assumed greater powers. Even his marriage to Lady Gerlotte, which seemed, at first, to have brought him some happiness, did not lift his spirits."

"A sad ending indeed," I murmured, my voice drifting off. "I hear my brother traveled to Ravinour," I resumed, "to pay his respects to Lady Gerlotte."

"Yes, he did. It was a very"—he cleared his throat—"short stay."

"So I heard!" I replied with a laugh. "How does Lady Gerlotte fare?"

"She has not been in good health."

"I am told she is quite beautiful," I ventured, affecting nonchalance, "and well landed, herself."

"Both may be true, Lady Isabelle, but she has not your *heart*. And in that way, she was, perhaps, a better match for Lord de Meurtaigne."

We exchanged glances; he knew his words had touched me. "What of the others in the household?" I asked. "Millicent and Agnes?"

"Millicent died shortly after we buried the little that remained of Lord de Meurtaigne. I wager that the shock of his death, but most of all the *manner* of his death, killed her. After his funeral, she wandered from chamber to chamber, murmuring 'But for my good lord to have died *in a state of mortal sin*' again and again. Agnes is now crippled and helps as best she can with menial work in the kitchen."

"I am sorry to hear it," I rejoined. "And Anthusis—what of her?"

"After you left, Lord de Meurtaigne was intent on finding her and punishing her. 'That witch who consorted with my wife' he would rant. Fortunately, Corbus was able to get word to Anthusis in time for her to escape. Some say she now lives in Brittany, others in Ireland."

"Wild places, both," I reflected.

Marie and Corbus returned. "Corbus can make himself understood to all the animals!" she exclaimed. "No wonder he and Gallien are such good friends."

"You must tell Gallien that yourself," I rejoined, smiling as I stroked her cheek. "Come, it is time to join the others."

Within the tent, the scene already brimmed with merriment and music. As we made our way to the high table, Marie nudged me. "Do you think I might sit at that *other* table"—she pointed to the side— "with Corbus and Raoul and LaFoi?"

"Not tonight, Marie," I replied. "We must sit with Lady Fastrada, who is our hostess, and with the bride and groom."

"Are you *certain* I must?" she asked plaintively.

"Come now, Marie," I chided as I knelt to speak with her. "I am very glad you have made new friends, but we are the guests of Lady Fastrada, after all. And remember"—Fastrada's tactic had just come to mind—"LaFoi would expect you to be here, seated with us."

At that, she smiled acquiescently and took my hand.

The priest offered grace. Once wine was poured, the feast truly commenced, and commenced with gusto—a long, increasingly boisterous meal featuring platter after platter of meat, and other special savory dishes of game and poultry. Midway through the meal, I asked Fastrada if I might see how Raoul and Corbus were faring—they were among strangers, after all—and ventured over to their table. Any concerns I might have had were quickly quashed: I had never seen those two exemplars of protocol, Raoul and LaFoi, quite so voluble and exuberant. As for Corbus: he was seated next to our sweet young chambermaid, who, if her gleaming eyes were any indication, was utterly entranced.

As light began to wane, supper came to an end and Fastrada stood up from the table. "Come," she said, beckoning to Hugh, me, and Marie. "Let us go to the other tent, for the dancing!"

When we arrived, Hugh called to the famous minstrel Marius, who awaited. "Give us something spirited," he commanded, "a tune to set our guests dancing!"

Marius began to play a rousing song of desire, of partings, of long-lost lovers triumphant. The crowd began to shout and stamp its feet; and then the maidens, in their country finery, joined hands in a circle and began to dance—their youthful arms raised, their shoes stepping lightly to the beat. In the center frolicked the bride—perspiring, elated, her braid now loosened, her eyes glittering with joy. Finally, Gallien, partly propelled by the crowd, entered the circle and grasped Douceline's hand; then, to whoops of delight, the two danced together.

Marie had scarcely moved as she watched; she had never seen such dancing, after all, nor ever heard music that was not intended for church. "What are you thinking?" I asked, bending over to smooth her hair.

"I was thinking that it was better that Sister Clementia did not come with us," she said with a slightly guilty look.

Laughing, I replied, "Yes, it is hard to imagine her here," without admitting that the same thought had already occurred to me many times.

Now the men had begun to dance while the women watched; and so the celebration, escalating in noise and rowdiness, continued with dance, and song, and flowing drink. Some folk became raucous; others, drunk, fell into a stupor; still others, exhausted from the revelry, curled up on the ground and slept, only to erupt from time to time with startlingly loud snores.

Darkness had just begun to fall when LaFoi, having recovered both his cap and his courtly self, came to fetch us. "We must leave soon, Lord and Lady," he said to Fastrada and Hugh, "before it becomes too late. We are fortunate tonight to have the full moon."

As we awaited our mounts, Fastrada glanced at Marie, who was leaning against me and struggling to keep her eyes open. "The poor child is sleepy," said Fastrada. "We cannot let her ride back on her own."

"Oh yes, I can, Lady Fastrada," protested Marie, suddenly alert. "I am not the least bit tired."

"I am afraid you may *not*," she replied sternly. "You must ride with Lady Isabelle." She exchanged glances with me, then smiled rather craftily. "Or better yet, with LaFoi! How does that sound, Marie?" The little girl nodded enthusiastically, and we set off.

# CHAPTER 89

After we entered our chambers, I closed the shutters and helped Marie prepare for bed. As she watched me fold what she called her "Fastrada gown," she asked, "Do you think I shall ever wear it again, Lady Isabelle?"

"By the time there is another opportunity, it will probably be too small for you," I replied, knowing full well it was unlikely another such occasion would arise. "Come, it is time for your prayers," I said, taking her hand and leading her to the prie-dieu. She knelt, recited her prayers, and climbed into bed.

As I kissed her forehead, she said, "Stay with me a moment, please."

I took a seat by the bed, expecting her to fall asleep at once; instead, she lay there quite alert, her eyes fixed on the ceiling. "I know it was an exciting day, Marie," I finally told her, "but now it is time for sleep. Try to close your eyes." After she did so, I began to gently stroke her forehead and hair.

After a few moments, she opened her eyes again. "Do you think they are still dancing at the wedding?"

"They might very well be."

"Corbus and Raoul, too?"

"Perhaps."

"When do they leave?"

"On the morrow, very early, they told me."

"How beautiful Douceline looked! *You* must have been a beautiful bride, Lady Isabelle."

"All brides are beautiful. I do remember I was very nervous. I did not know my husband at all. My wedding"—I hesitated—"was very different from Gallien and Douceline's."

"You never speak of it."

"One day I shall tell you more. But not tonight."

"If I stay at the abbey, I shall never be a bride, will I?"

"You will be a different kind of bride," I replied carefully. "You will have your own sort of ceremony, lovely in its own way."

"But no dancing, no music?" she reflected, her expression verging on melancholy.

"A different kind of music," I replied softly. "Come now, time for sleep, my little Marie." I began to sing a favorite lullaby until, at last, after her lids had closed, I spread the coverlet over her and tiptoed into my own chamber.

But her poignant, searching questions lingered in my mind. I thought of the sequestered world of the abbey, and of Clementia's adamantine vision of Marie's future; and then what I had witnessed during the visit here—Marie's delight in worldly things, her love of adventure, her fascination with the earthy gaiety of Gallien's nuptials. As I closed the door, I wondered uneasily whether it had been wise for me to have brought Marie to the wedding, and to the glittering world of Troyes.

SEVERAL DAYS LATER, AS FASTRADA and I strolled in the herb garden, she asked, "Where is Marie? I expected her to join us here."

"She is in the mews. Gallien had promised to show her how he tends to the hawks. She is quite fascinated."

"By the hawks, or by Gallien?" she asked, her broad, thin mouth curving into a droll smile.

"Both!" Then, after a moment, "I suspect it will be hard for Marie to return to the abbey"—I looked about the lovely garden, and at the brilliant pennants fluttering above the ramparts—"and leave all of this. And I, too, will miss being here."

"But you *will* return." She looked at me intently. "Come, now, Isabelle, there is something else that is troubling you. Tell me."

"It is Marie's future I worry about," I admitted. "Clementia has very distinct notions of what she should be. And I am not sure they will coincide with Marie's."

"I agree it will not be easy for Marie to carve her own path, whether she remains at the abbey or not. Either way, she will have to contend with Clementia. And as much as I love my sister, I also know she can be rigid."

"Much can happen in the interim," I replied, taking her arm. "It is much too soon to tell."

"Yes! Look at your own life, Isabelle. How very different it is from anything you might have imagined. Marie has not the advantages of your name and parentage, of course. Her prospects are limited, but that does not mean she cannot create her own life, even at the abbey."

A robust voice calling from a distance interrupted us: to our surprise it was Hugh, who had left for Troyes two days earlier.

"I thought Hugh was returning from Troyes *tomorrow*," I said to Fastrada as he approached.

"He was. Perhaps he was lovesick for his darling wife"—she smiled mischievously—"or perhaps he concluded his affairs early." Then, wryly: "I suspect the latter."

"I have been looking all over for you, dear wife," he said in a jolly voice as he embraced her.

"All went well in Troyes?" I asked.

"Yes. It is always invigorating to be there—the bustle, the trading. And, of course, the gossip one hears."

"Do tell," urged Fastrada, whose attention always quickened by the mention of such things.

"Not precisely *your* kind of gossip, Fastrada," he returned good-naturedly. "News of the court. Of Queen Eleanor."

"That will do very well," I returned eagerly.

"Indeed," chimed in Fastrada. "Come, the two of us will sit over there, while Hugh serenades us with the latest reports."

She led me to a long, handsome stone bench that stood prominently at the far end of the garden. "Look!" said Fastrada, pointing to a date, *22 May Anno Domini 1155*, carved in the center, flanked by the letters *F* and *H*. "This was a wedding gift from Hugh," said Fastrada proudly, as we took our seats. "Now, for the news, dear husband—"

"For Isabelle's sake, I shall begin with the queen," he began. "Her daughter Mathilda and her family are thought to be with her now at Woodstock—a place that cannot hold pleasant associations for Eleanor. That was where the king kept his mistress Rosamund Clifford, for many years. Therefore," he continued, "I suspect the visit of Mathilda will not be without some sense of humiliation for a woman as proud as the queen."

"Continue, Hugh," prodded Fastrada.

"And there has been a great fire at the abbey of Glastonbury. The chapel, and many manuscripts destroyed. Ralph FitzStephen has been sent to supervise the rebuilding."

"Ah, FitzStephen," I mused, thinking of my time in England. "He is a fine man, and one of the queen's favorites."

"So they say," murmured Hugh, adding, "I am surprised that has not worked against him. There is also talk that the queen will be reunited with her sons this Christmas, at Windsor. If so, that is an important signal that the king has clinched a bargain with her. Grant her a bit of freedom, then *use* her to negotiate with their sons for his advantage. It would not surprise me if she were allowed, next, to come to France."

"France!" I exclaimed. "And perhaps even to Fontevraud."

"A happy thought indeed," said Fastrada, rising, "especially for you, Isabelle. And for Marie—imagine her being able to meet the queen! Which reminds me," she went on briskly, "I promised Marie to show her around my garden today. Alas, she seems to have forsaken me for Gallien." She feigned a sulky pout.

"I doubt even you, and your charming garden, would be able to compete with Gallien and the hawks for Marie's attention," said Hugh playfully, taking her arm, then mine. "Come, ladies, let us to the mews and see what Gallien, and my precious birds, have taught her."

DURING THE DAYS PRECEDING OUR departure, Marie spent as much time as possible with Hugh, flying a hawk, and followed Fastrada about so persistently that the latter began to call her "my little shadow."

When it came time for me to prepare our trunk, Marie begged me not to pack her "Fastrada dress" until the last moment; she clung to it the same way she clung to her doll. Finally, on the eve of our departure, I told her gently but firmly, "We must put the dress in the trunk now, Marie. We leave very early in the morning, and all must be ready."

"May I keep it near me, in my chamber, at the abbey?" she asked.

"As a keepsake?"

She nodded. "I do not see why not," I replied; but then, thinking better of it, I added, "As long as Sister Clementia allows it."

She looked crestfallen. "Must I ask her?"

"Yes."

"She will *never* allow it," she remonstrated. "She will want it put away. She will say it is 'a vain thing' that belongs to Lady Fastrada's world, not to the abbey's."

In my heart, I knew this was true. "If I promise you that I shall discuss it with her, and ask for a bit of lenience, will you cheer up a bit?"

She gave a tentative smile and nodded; I took her hands in mine. "You know Sister Clementia can be strict, but she loves you dearly." I kissed the top of her head. "Now it is time to sleep. We have a long day ahead."

THE SUN ALREADY BURNED BRIGHT the following morning when Fastrada, Hugh, Gallien, and the household gathered at the stables to bid us adieu. Cocks crowed, dogs barked; our restive mounts pawed the earth as stable boys strapped the trunk into the cart. Never was I so grateful for stalwart LaFoi—an elegant, composed figure standing to the side as we made our final goodbyes, one by one.

"Might I fly a *real* falcon next time, not just a hawk?" Marie asked Gallien as we came to him and Douceline.

"If Lord Hugh agrees, then I do not see why not," he replied with a broad, indulgent smile, as Marie beamed with delight.

"Dear Gallien," I said fervently, "it has been one of the joys of my life to see you again, and to attend your wedding." I took his hand, and then Douceline's, in mine. "May God bless you both, and your marriage."

"And your hawks!" piped up Marie.

"And yes, your hawks, as well," I added, with a soft laugh.

Finally, we came to Hugh and Fastrada, both of whom enveloped us in their embraces. "I shall come to Fontevraud to visit you," she promised as she and I drew apart.

"When?" asked Marie, her eyes lighting up.

"Later in the summer, God willing—perhaps at the time of the Assumption. It is always lovely at the abbey then."

LaFoi approached Marie. "Come, my little lady," he said, "it is time I help you mount." After Fastrada embraced her once again, he took Marie's hand and led her away.

"Here is a letter for Clementia," said Fastrada, handing me a sheaf of parchment. She took my arm, pressing it tight. "I wrote that she should be very proud of Marie, and entreated her to give the child some latitude. I included some other advice as well"—she shrugged—"but whether she will heed it, I have no idea."

"I shall do my best to explain my own feelings about Marie to her," I said, adding, "but we may learn that Clementia is not nearly as obdurate as we imagine her. She has surprised me before, many times. And I have never known her to be without compassion."

"Yes." She nodded thoughtfully. "You are right, Isabelle."

"We must keep hope in our hearts," I said. I looked about at the bustling scene, and at Marie, now mounted, who was smiling with the special eagerness of one about to embark on an adventure. I felt a sudden rush of possibility. I thought of the queen, and her new freedom, and of the prospect, which had once seemed so improbable, that I might one day see her again, in France.

And so, it was with a welcome inner peace and hopefulness that I mounted, waved goodbye, and set off for the journey back to Fontevraud.

# PART VI

CHAPTER 90

As she grew up, Marie began to show great promise as an artist. Few things thrilled her as much as the arrival of a box of fresh pigments—often supplied by Fastrada—or the permission to try her hand at decorating some sheaves of especially fine parchment. Her drawings of animals and birds were immensely accomplished, and her vivid, almost hallucinatory depictions of fanciful creatures and scenes were even more remarkable. Indeed, her talent was so prodigious that she was given permission, earlier than customary, to apprentice in the scriptorium. She would work for hours there, even in the depth of winter, when the cold and dark made the effort daunting.

From time to time I had to assuage Clementia's fear that Marie seemed far more devoted to her lessons in the scriptorium than to her religious duties. "This does not bode well for her future as a novice," Clementia told me one day when Marie, immersed in drawing, was once again late for Mass. "She does not seem to be taking her holy obligations as seriously as she ought—she is often late for confession and daydreams during catechism lessons. I may have to be far more stringent with her. She is quite undisciplined."

"She is *very* disciplined in the scriptorium," I interjected. "As for becoming a proper nun—it will do no good for us to *compel* Marie to take vows. That calling must come from within, as you yourself know. Pressuring her may even provoke her to become rebellious, or angry. Perhaps she is not destined to take vows, but to remain here as a lay sister—as I do. But that must be *her* decision," I added firmly.

I was acutely aware of Marie's fascination with the world beyond our walls, and her poignant questions at Gallien's wedding had prompted other questions within me as well. Yet I also knew that she had no prospects outside the abbey—she was an orphan with no dowry and no "family" other than myself and the sisters. At most, she would be able to obtain work as a servant or laborer, and, as such, be subjected to the hardships those lives could entail.

As she matured, I increasingly recognized a crucial side of her—the solitary, tenacious figure who seemed most at peace, and most joyful, in her work in the scriptorium, and who flourished amid the disciplined, contemplative world of the abbey.

FONTEVRAUD HAD BECOME MY REAL home, and Clementia and Marie my real family. Exchanges with my own kin were little more than pro forma and increasingly infrequent. But that June, I received a letter from Guy advising me that Father was failing; he urged me to come see him as soon as possible. Clementia arranged for me to be accompanied by an accomplished horseman, Eudes; we set out a day or so later. All the journey, I prayed, "Please God, let me see Father before he dies." Finally, about ten days later, on a hot, humid afternoon, we arrived at my father's home.

"As usual, sister, you are too late," said Amélie the moment I crossed the threshold. She shot me an exasperated glance. "Father died yesterday afternoon."

Overcome with grief, I burst into tears. "All during the journey I prayed I would be in time to see him! I only hope Father did not suffer."

"Not *too* much," replied Amélie. She had grown immensely stout in the eight years since I had last seen her; her features, which, in her prime, might have been called pert, now appeared porcine. "You should know that he asked for you many times," she continued in a castigating tone. "'When will Isabelle be here?' he said. 'Why has she not come to see me?' Naturally, it fell to me and Guy to care for Father in his final days and hours," she went on, "but that is not surprising, after all. Mother always said *we* were the responsible ones. You and Arnaut were never to be counted upon." She gave a great sigh that set her multiple chins wobbling.

Trying to ignore her gibes, I turned to Balduin, who leaned pathetically on a cane. "Have you hurt your leg?" I asked with concern.

"I have—"

"Gout," Amélie interjected sharply. "And let us pray this is the last time that tiresome subject is mentioned. It is all he talks about these days." Balduin looked away silently before meekly settling on a stool.

"Where is Guy?" I asked.

"He and his wife are at the chapel with our children," she replied, adding pointedly, "you may remember you have a *niece* and three *nephews.* They are all faring well, thank you for inquiring."

"And Hortense?"

"Hortense"—she fairly hissed the name—"is also with them." Disapproval of Hortense and the power she had come to wield over Father was one of the few things that Amélie and I had ever shared. "Guy and the Lady Ermengarde are making arrangements for the funeral tomorrow. You will see them later, at supper."

"And Father?" I asked. "Where is he? I want to sit with him awhile and pray for him."

"Very well," she replied, in the same tone she would have used if I had asked her to show me a new mare. "Follow me."

LATER THAT EVENING IN THE main hall, I was struck that everything was exactly as I had remembered: the threadbare hangings, the chipped vessels of pottery arrayed along the sideboard, and the long, scuffed trestle table, which summoned memories of many tense family meals. But my first glimpse of Guy shocked me: he had grown almost spectrally thin and pale; there was a beleaguered look about his eyes, like that of a hunted hare. "How good to see you, sister," he said, before introducing me to the woman he had eventually married—the short, stocky, scowling Lady Ermengarde. Even Fastrada's description had not quite prepared me for her ugliness. "Go fetch my shawl," she told him shortly before we took our seats. Once the shawl was fetched, she caviled, "This is not the right one, husband. I told you I wanted the *green* one—the one with embroidery. When will you learn to listen?"

It did not surprise me that she and Amélie seemed to enjoy a certain rapport.

My nephew Walter, a sallow, swaggering young man with a spotty complexion, greeted me rather coolly; his sister, Maude, with shy deference. The former resembled his mother in looks and arrogance, the latter, to my dismay, seemed to have had the spirit stamped out of her. The lively, inquisitive little girl I fondly remembered had grown into a young woman of almost painful reticence. To her mother's annoyance, Maude still seemed rather in awe of me, as did Fulk. The youngest, plump little Roland, a diminutive version of Balduin, seemed to interest his mother little. ("Go and mind him now," was Amélie's constant, irritated refrain to his older siblings.)

We said grace, and dinner commenced; that the food looked rather unappetizing mattered not a whit, for I had lost all appetite. The others dug in with gusto—Balduin, sauce dripping down his chin, kept calling for more wine, which provoked Amélie to more aspersions. ("The physician says wine is not good for your gout! But no, you never listen to me.")

Struggling to make conversation, I began to describe life at the abbey to Maude. Overhearing us, Amélie piped up: "Do not put any untoward ideas into her head about Fontevraud, Isabelle! Unlike you, she has no desire to be locked away in a convent. She is to be *married*."

"To whom?" I asked brightly.

"It has yet to be decided," Amélie replied as Maude sheepishly looked down at her trencher. "My daughter has many suitors. As you can well imagine."

"Of course," I murmured, glancing sympathetically at my niece.

Meanwhile, the grieving Hortense, having been denied a place at the table by Amélie, hovered in the back hall, the sounds of her sobs intermittently interrupting the conversation. Finally, I turned to Guy and Amélie. "Should we not ask Hortense to join us? It only seems right, and human. She always sat at the table when father was alive. Surely—"

"But now he is *dead*," interrupted Amélie. "And life has changed. She must *adjust*."

I tried, then, to swerve the talk to Father and our memories of him, but to little avail; the others were intent on discussing his will and the provisions of his estate. Guy, as the eldest, would, of course, stand to inherit what little was left. ("It is about time he brought *something* to this marriage," I overheard his wife mutter to Amélie.) Among the group, Amélie seemed to be most intent on parsing the details of the will. "Of course," she said, addressing me, "since Guy has no heir as of yet, should he pass from this world"—she closed her small eyes tightly and made the sign of the cross, as if she were trying to banish this grievous thought—"then his inheritance would fall to my children." She leaned forward toward Guy, who sat across from her, and asked in a honeyed voice that was not without a threatening undercurrent, "Is that not correct, brother dear?"

"Of course, sister," he mumbled, after exchanging uneasy glances with his wife.

Only after this matter had been broached did Amélie, who had liberally partaken of wine, address me in a tone that simulated civility. "Guy has told me that you spent time in England, Isabelle," she said unctuously, leaning forward, goblet in hand, "and that you came to know the queen."

"Yes. That is true."

"Come, now, sister," she said, leaning forward, goblet in hand, "surely there is something you can tell us about her. Is the queen as scheming and dangerous as they say?" She took a large bite of pork, then looked at me intently. "Mother, as you may recall, reviled her."

"Mother was influenced by hearsay," I replied, trying to rein in my annoyance, "and hearsay can be dangerous and inaccurate. The queen is protective of her sons, as any mother would be. That is quite different from being scheming."

"A fine thing for *you*, of all people, to say," retorted Amélie. "How can *you* possibly know what a mother would do?"

At that, I folded my napkin and stood up. "That was quite unnecessary, Amélie. Perhaps it is best I retire now."

ON THE MORNING OF THE funeral, the sun was so scorching and the air so oppressive that, for once, the chill of the dank, dark little church seemed welcome. Although it was summer, and our garden in full flower, the altar was adorned with little more than a few wilting lilies carelessly tossed in a vase. The Mass itself was merely perfunctory. Throughout it, Amélie heaved great sobs and wiped her eyes with a dramatically long handkerchief, more than once brushing off Balduin as he attempted to comfort her. Lady Ermengarde looked bored; several times I caught Walter and Fulk stifling yawns; Maude dutifully tried to quiet the petulant, squirming Roland. Hortense had been relegated to the far side of the back pew.

Later, at the burial site, I took my place in front with Guy and Amélie, the latter weeping histrionically as the priest intoned the final blessing. Hortense stood in back, crying softly. Of those present, other than myself, I had no doubt that it was she, who had cared for my father in his final years, who was most affected. In fact, she seemed so genuinely bereft that I felt ashamed of myself for having misjudged her.

As we filed past the grave, and began to depart, I sought out Hortense and embraced her. "We are grateful for all you did to care for Father," I told her.

"Thank you, my lady. He was a good man, and always so kind to me." She began to cry, covering her swollen red face with her hands. Finally, she looked up. "What will become of me now, my lady?"

"We will help you. Has Guy spoken with you about finding work?"

She shook her head. "No. No one has."

"Then I promise to take the matter up with him before I leave tomorrow morning."

Although Guy had promised to be at the stables that morning to see me off, I thought there was little chance that he would actually appear. Since there had been no appropriate moment to discuss Hortense

the previous day—his hectoring wife had never left his side—I had prepared a letter for him to read after my departure.

To my surprise, however, he was waiting at the stables when I arrived. "All is nearly ready," he said, standing by my mount.

I took Guy's arm. "Let us sit for a moment, brother, before we say
goodbye." We settled on a bench under the eaves. "We have not yet discussed Hortense," I began.

"I did not realize there was something to discuss."

"She was a loyal servant and took good care of Father. We must
help find her some work."

"Of course that had occurred to me," he replied unconvincingly.
"I intended to ask my wife whether a place in our household might be
found for her."

Not wishing that fate upon anyone, I replied, "Very generous of
you, brother, but I am sure Hortense would prefer to stay close to *this*
region. The Abbey of Pont Séverin is nearby," I suggested. "Perhaps we
could inquire if there might be a position for her there. And that would
have an advantage," I added. "The abbey would pay her wages, and you
and your wife would not have to take her on as an added expense."

"Excellent thinking, sister!" he replied enthusiastically. "I shall venture to the abbey myself and make inquiries before we depart." He
paused, clearing his throat. "Naturally, I would have made provisions
for her, even if you had not brought it up."

"Of course," I murmured.

We sat in silence for a moment.

"You have a long ride to Fontevraud ahead," he observed.

"It will seem much shorter than the ride here. The journey home
always does."

"I gather you consider Fontevraud your real home now?" he said,
echoing my own thoughts.

"Yes. Very much."

He seemed to consider this. "And the good Sister Clementia—how
does she fare?"

"Very well. As angelic and competent as ever."

"And Marie?"

"She brings me great joy."

"I would imagine that, given——" But then, rather awkwardly, he stopped. "And the Lady Fastrada?"

"She visits us several times a year. She is a remarkable woman."

"Pity," he said, brushing some dust from his sleeve, "that I was never able to see her when I came to the abbey. Now, of course, that I am married, and have all the attendant responsibilities, there is hardly a moment to spare for journeys of that nature. My wife, as you have no doubt surmised, is an immensely capable woman, and beloved by many. She takes so much upon herself, perhaps *too* much, I often tell her. But I doubt that surprises you—I am sure you have noticed how caring she is. Yes"—he gave a sigh —"We do indeed have a productive and satisfying life together. Though I do hope, one day, we will be able to visit you at Fontevraud," he added.

"I am glad you are happy, brother," I replied.

"Yes, I could not be more fortunate in my marriage," he said, with forced heartiness. "*Very* fortunate indeed——" But then his voice drifted off and his expression dissolved into one of melancholy, as if the mask had dropped. For the first time, I pitied him.

A certain nostalgia came over me as I thought back on our early life. "Do you remember, Guy," I began to reflect, "when we were children, and we went to Nîmes together, with Arnaut?"

He smiled. "Yes. The two of you disappeared, as I recall."

"He took me to see the ancient arena," I replied wistfully.

"You and Arnaut were always so close. You must miss him——"

"I do. I try not to think of him too much—it makes me so sad, sad to think that we never saw him again after he left. That we were never even able to bury him." Holding back tears, I continued to reminisce. "And then, do you remember when you accompanied me, that cold winter day, to the castle of Gerard?"

"You were very frightened, as I recall."

"Yes, *very.*"

Eudes approached. "All is ready, my lady," he said cheerfully.

Guy walked me to my horse. Just as I prepared to mount, I felt his hand upon my shoulder. "I have something to give you, sister," he said as I turned to him. "Something for your journey."

He placed a small, worn medal in my palm. "Saint Christopher," I said, surprised by his thoughtfulness. "Is it yours?"

"It was Father's. I know he would have wanted you to have had it." Clearing his throat, he added somewhat awkwardly, "To protect you on your journey."

"Thank you with all my heart." After we embraced, I said, "I do hope I shall see you again one day, brother."

"At Fontevraud, perhaps?" he asked with touching jauntiness. "I may even come alone, if I should find myself in the north. The fairs, and so forth."

"Of course," I said, knowing full well that this would probably never happen. I felt the sudden need to embrace him again, and did so, with special fervency. "Goodbye, brother," I murmured, tears welling in my eyes as he helped me into the saddle.

Eudes and I made our way slowly to the gate. There I stopped, turning around to wave at Guy; I had sensed, rightly, that he would still be watching. As the gate closed, I looked ahead at the road, which stretched before us. My heart felt heavy, as if it were laden with weighty, tangled strands of sadness: sadness at the death of my father, sadness for Guy, sadness that, in leaving my family's home—most likely, forever—I felt immense relief.

# CHAPTER 91

I returned to the abbey with renewed appreciation of my own life—my work with Marie, as well as my friendships with Clementia and Fastrada, whose periodic visits continued to delight us. With her visits, and her letters, also came news of Gallien and his flourishing family. All the while, his renown as a master falconer had continued to grow, his ambitions nurtured by Hugh. One day, a letter from Fastrada arrived which, to my astonishment, included a short letter penned by Gallien himself; "Lord Hugh," he explained, was having him taught to read and write. Six months later, when Fastrada arrived, she brought another missive from Gallien—this, more advanced in style and penmanship—in which he informed me that Corbus had come to work for the Hauteclare household, and that "Lord de Hauteclare has hired him to care for his hounds." The thought of these young men working together for a family of such humaneness and generosity cheered me immeasurably.

As for that *other* household, so radically different in spirit—Gerard's—I had only occasional reports, and these primarily from Fastrada. It seemed that Gerard's widow, who was known to suffer from fragile health, had come to a sorry end: devastated by her husband's untimely death, and tormented by the fear that he had died in sin, she had lost her will to live. After her demise, the entire Meurtaigne household had been disbanded: Agnes had left to live with relatives, and Raoul to serve at another, lesser, household in the region. Hearing of this turn of events filled me, at first, with sadness and bewilderment—to think that the splendid world of Ravinour had come to such a dismal end! I could not help but think what a contrast it was to my own rewarding life—one I had chosen, and created for myself.

And what of the world beyond the Channel, and of the Plantagenets, with which, however briefly, I had been acquainted? In the years after Gallien's wedding, the queen was granted increasingly more freedom and was also permitted to see her children from time to time when this suited King Henry's purposes. But the king was growing old, and weary; and his sons, whose fractiousness and resentment were never far from the surface, soon resumed their hostilities. Richard, as always, was at the helm, his younger brothers following his lead—conniving Geoffrey of Brittany, the middle son the Queen seldom mentioned, and greedy, impetuous John, who had been made Count of Ireland.

Then, in early July of the year 1189, the world as we knew it vastly changed: ailing King Henry, under siege, died at nearby Chinon. A day later, we received word that his body would be brought to Fontevraud for burial. "The royal agents told me the king died a bitter man, deserted by his sons," Clementia said as she hastened to make the arrangements. "Not even his final wish, to be buried at the Abbey of Grandmont, will be granted."

"Why?" I asked, walking quickly beside her.

"The journey would take too long—his body would never survive this sweltering heat. He will arrive here as a pauper might," she lamented. "The men told me his body has been stripped of regalia, his best clothes filched."

A few afternoons later, led by king's renowned and still loyal knight, William Marshal, the royal "entourage" arrived—the corpse enclosed in a rickety cart drawn by weary henchmen on sweaty mounts. As they made their way through the gate, I remember how the courtyard erupted in suffocating whorls of dust, and how harshly the sunlight glinted from the massive breastplate of Marshal's armor.

With the ascension of Richard as king, the queen was immediately released. Whereas, in the past decade, reports of her actions and whereabouts had been shadowy and sporadic, now they were explicit and frequent. Word of her activities in England came to us from our sister abbey at Amesbury; at other times from Hugh, with his connections to the royal circle in Troyes; very occasionally, and thrillingly, from the queen herself. In one of her early letters that first autumn, she wrote of Richard's splendid coronation at Westminster; later, of her travels throughout England as she tried to redress ills that had been inflicted upon the populace during her late husband's reign. Of her son Geoffrey, whose death had preceded his father's by several years, she related noticeably little.

My letters in reply were rather tentative at first—surely, I thought, life at Fontevraud would seem rather dull to a queen grappling with momentous matters of state. To my delight, however, she seemed eager to receive my accounts. It was I who informed her of the death of Mother Gilles, and the ascension of Mathilda of Flanders, another formidable, canny noblewoman, as abbess. Anecdotes about Marie—her work in the scriptorium, and her passion for drawing—seemed to particularly interest her. In one later letter I confided:

> Sister Clementia has always assumed that Marie would take the veil. I feel that Marie would best be suited to remain here as a lay scribe, rather than as a nun: in this way, she would have a modicum of the freedom she thrives upon, but also the nurturing safety of abbey life. I fear that the duties of a wholly religious life would stifle her spirit. I intend to tell Clementia that whether Marie takes vows makes little difference, as long as her gifts are devoted to His service.

Early one morning, shortly before Easter of the year 1191, an excited Clementia sought us out. "Come at once," she urged. "An infant, a baby girl, has been found at the *tour* this morning."

As we hastened to the gatehouse, I asked, "Is the baby in good health?"

"It appears so," replied Clementia.

"Was anything left with her?" asked Marie.

"Only a small wooden cross. The baby was wrapped in little more than rags, I am afraid. We found some swaddling and have fed her."

We arrived at the gatehouse where Clementia's servant, Grecia, stood, gently rocking a small bundle.

"Let us see her!" cried Marie.

Grecia drew apart the swaddling, and we glimpsed the baby's tiny face. As I gazed at her vivid blue eyes, I felt a sudden piercing sadness at the memory of my lost little Editha. "A bonny baby," I murmured.

"May I hold her?" Marie asked. Grecia handed her the baby. "We must raise her," said Marie, looking up at us as she held the baby tight.

I exchanged glances with Clementia; both of us had recognized the special poignancy of the foundling for Marie. "Yes, of course we shall bring her up," replied Clementia. "God has protected her—and now we must follow His example." After making the sign of the cross, she added, "She is His gift to us at Easter time."

"What shall we call her?" I asked. "Marie, *you* must name her!"

She thought hard. "Aiglette," she finally pronounced, with a tender smile. "In memory of my mother."

"Yes, that is perfect, Marie," I said, thinking how touched Aiglantine would have been to learn that her own daughter had not only embraced an abandoned baby, but also had chosen to name that baby in her honor.

AIGLETTE GREW INTO A DELICATE, reserved child—very much like Aiglantine, in fact. She was a docile little thing—more like a sparrow than an "eaglet," and without the falcon-like fierceness or tenacity of Marie at the same age. What the two *did* share, however, was a love of stories, and of images. Marie would sit with her for hours, inventing new tales about the bronze falcon, or telling other stories that I had once told her. She created a little book with pictures of animals and birds for Aiglette; there were many times I would glimpse the pair—Marie with her dark and Aiglette with her blond curls—bent over its pages. Marie seemed to find much that Aiglette did something of a marvel—her first word, her first step, her first recitation of a proper prayer.

Both Clementia and I—she absorbed in her duties, and I with the children—had little sense of life beyond the abbey during that peaceful time. Indeed, my English sojourn seemed ever more remote, even dreamlike, as did my relations with the queen, partly because her letters were not only infrequent, but less personal—the messages of an acting monarch, as it were.

It was not long, however, before the outside world encroached upon us—after 1190, when King Richard fulfilled his vow to try to recapture Jerusalem. From neighboring towns and villages, men of all ranks departed for the Holy Land, leaving behind families who, often desperate, would turn to us for help—for food, for protection, the solace of prayer. All the while, confused reports trickled to us of battles, deaths, occasional victories, and catastrophes. After two years, to our bitter disappointment, Jerusalem was not won. King Richard, having secured little more than a precarious peace from Saladin, had left Outremer and departed for France.

With his anticipated return, we fervently hoped the queen would return to France as well, perhaps even come to Fontevraud. But that was not to be: one winter morning, early in 1192, Clementia and I received a letter with somber news from Fastrada. We sat together as I read part of it aloud:

> One tragedy has followed another here, in Troyes, and throughout our region, throughout Champagne. So many men have perished! All around us, mothers—rich and poor—tend to orphans.
>
> But that is not the extent of the misfortunes. Alas, we have learned that the king has been taken prisoner by the Holy Roman Emperor and languishes in a prison—somewhere north of Vienna, in a place called Dürnstein. There are rumors that an enormous ransom has been demanded.

"It cannot be!" cried Clementia as I set the letter down. "Mark my words—there will be terrible consequences. Without Richard, the queen and her counselors will struggle to maintain peace, and to protect their Norman lands from Philippe."

I knew that Clementia, with her political astuteness, was right. "That is why the queen will not rest until Richard is freed," I added. "No efforts, no ransom, will be too great for her to raise."

"And then there is John," rejoined Clementia, shaking her head. "With his brother absent, he will seize the opportunity to make mischief. No, it does not bode well at all."

Clementia's predictions were borne out. The years of Richard's imprisonment grew dark and desolate; we despaired he would ever return. Meantime, as John connived with Philippe, we heard rumors of old alliances being shattered, of castles seized and borders redrawn. Our sisters in Amesbury wrote to us of new lawlessness, famine, and disorder in England.

Under the stewardship of the abbess and Clementia, life within Fontevraud, however, remained relatively peaceful, if notably more austere. I continued to give Aiglette her lessons and to assist Marie, and sometimes Clementia, in the scriptorium. Often, as I walked along the lovely allées, or watched Marie and Aiglette reading together in the garden, I thought how unlikely, even ludicrous, it seemed that much of the world outside the abbey walls teemed with turmoil.

Meantime the bond between Marie and Aiglette had only become more steadfast. The latter had evolved into a sweet, diligent little girl, as delicate, blond, and shy as the former was spirited, dark, and tenacious. With quiet delight, I would watch as they walked together hand in hand along the halls of the cloister; or I would listen, rapt, at the door of their chamber before bedtime, touched by how tenderly and patiently Marie would help Aiglette say her prayers and recite her rosary.

I was especially grateful for Marie's help with the little girl, as my own attention was very much centered on assisting, sometimes even nursing, Clementia, whose health had begun to founder. Her lungs had never been strong, and her considerable discipline did not extend to taking adequate care of herself. She worked incessantly and had become quite frail. One day, watching her stifle a rasping cough, I told her, "Dear Clementia, it concerns me, and all of us, to see you so weak, and suffering. You must go and rest."

She looked at me with a loving, wan smile and said, "Thank you, Isabelle."

"You have always been *my* protector," I said, gently taking her arm. "Now you must let me be yours."

EARLY IN 1194, AFTER TWO years of turmoil and uncertainty, we learned that the queen had won a great victory: she had succeeded in raising the stupendous ransom for King Richard's release and had departed for Germany to reunite with him. I dispatched a letter at once to Fastrada, hoping for more details; Clementia and I duly received a reply a month later. I read it aloud as we sat together one winter morning:

> Only a woman of the queen's power and persistence could possibly have succeeded in raising such a ransom! Hugh fears there will be repercussions, however—he hears the English barons are furious about the monies exacted from them. Nor has the English church forfeited its gold and silver treasures without resentment.
>
> The queen arrived in Mainz not long ago, and we have learned that Richard is to be freed shortly. The emperor struck a hard bargain, it seems; word has come to us that the queen convinced her son to swear homage to him for the English kingdom. A bitter end, indeed! Still, all of us here, in Troyes, have confidence in Richard and his ability to restore peace. No doubt one person who is not greeting this development with joy is John. It now remains to be seen what will happen between the two competing brothers. Hugh wagers that Richard will forgive him; I do not. Let us see how this family drama unfolds.
>
> As for the queen—I suspect she is your capital concern, dear Isabelle—there are reports that she will pass through Normandy on her return from Germany. And there is even a strong suggestion that she will soon retire at Fontevraud.

I can scarcely describe my joy as I came upon those last words, for it had long been my dream to see the queen again. "Might this be true?" I asked Clementia.

"Let us hope it is. Come," she said, smiling as she rose. "We must tell the abbess at once."

# CHAPTER 92

Fastrada's report was subsequently confirmed: the queen would retire to Fontevraud in the late spring. The news sent a surge of excitement, but also of nervousness, through the abbey. Many seemed intimidated by the thought of the queen's arrival; others feared that her august presence would disrupt our peaceful life. Even the abbess and Clementia, both normally imperturbable, seemed rather anxious as they oversaw arrangements in the wing she would inhabit. My own delight was tinged with apprehension, but of a different kind: it had been nearly a decade since I had last seen the queen; she was a very old woman now, a woman at the end of her seventh decade. The death of King Henry five years before had granted her freedom, to be sure, but also grave, unrelenting responsibilities. It would not be surprising if she were exhausted, even failing; moreover, I worried that she and I might not enjoy the same closeness we had shared during her captive time in England.

ONE SUNDAY, AS WE WERE walking from Mass, Marie, always attuned to my moods, asked, "Is there something preoccupying you, Lady Isabelle?" Meantime Aiglette skipped merrily beside us, kicking some pebbles along the path.

"I have been thinking about the queen," I admitted, touching the ring with the intaglio, which the queen had given me. "I was only slightly older than you when I first met her. You cannot imagine how terrified I was."

"*You?* Terrified?"

"Yes! But slowly I came to know her, and to have a great deal of affection, and—most of all—respect for her. You will see. I know she will like you, and what is more, *appreciate* you, very much."

"What about *me*, Lady Isabelle?" piped up Aiglette, who had been listening intently to the last part of the conversation.

"She will like *you* too!" I said, ruffling her blond curls. "But you must be a very good little girl and follow Marie's directions when you are presented."

"Marie is teaching me a proper curtsey," Aiglette said proudly. "She says mine are very good."

"Yes, but not quite *perfect*," replied Marie.

ONE MORNING IN LATE MAY—THE lilacs were in full flower, and the earliest roses had just begun to bloom—word came that the royal entourage had been sighted. The entire household hurried to assemble at the gatehouse. Clementia insisted that Marie, Aiglette, and I stand close by her and the abbess, in front; behind us, like a flock of doves, stood the nuns and novices.

The queen was hardly the weary woman I had envisioned, but a vigorous, upright figure poised on a mount whose gilded saddle glinted in the sun. A hush descended as she and her gloriously caparisoned procession came to a halt; in unison, we curtseyed; the horses neighed almost regally, as if to acknowledge our obeisance. The queen turned her head slowly from one side to the other as her gaze encompassed the scene; and then I heard her voice—that rich voice of clarion distinctiveness—exclaim: "I have long dreamed of returning here, and of passing through these gates!" At that, assisted by the royal steward, she gracefully dismounted.

The abbess stepped forward to greet her first; and then, Clementia.

"Ah, Sister Clementia," said the queen, with warm emphasis. "It is to *you* I owe special thanks. It is you, and your fellow sisters at Reading and Amesbury, who provided such succor when my life was more"—she paused—"*restricted*. Most of all, you had the prescience to send Lady Isabelle to me, in England."

Clementia acknowledged her thanks and bowed her head, before beckoning me to come forward.

"Your Majesty," I said, with a deep curtsey.

"Rise, dear Isabelle!" she gently ordered. "Let us embrace, as we did in the past." As we did so, I caught a whiff of her perfume—the mingling of rose and frankincense which seemed to instantly evoke our time together in England. Now, smiling, we stood face-to-face. Her dark eyes had retained their liveliness, and her complexion was so flushed with exertion that she had no need of the rouge that had been applied, rather inexpertly, it seemed, on her cheeks. Although there were deeper furrows above her brow and at each corner of her mouth, there was an even greater sense of vivacity about her than I had remembered.

"Your travels do not seem to have exhausted you, Your Majesty."

"When one has been constrained for so many years, travel is the greatest delight of all." She glanced behind at Marie and Aiglette. "Have your companions step forward." I beckoned to the girls.

"This must be Marie," said the queen.

"It is indeed," I replied, glancing with pride at Marie, who stepped forward and performed a deep curtsey. "Your Majesty," she said.

"How lovely she is! Just as you described her in your letters. Though I did not expect her to be quite so tall." Then she addressed Marie: "Lady Isabelle has told me about your work in the scriptorium. I would like to see your creations."

"I would be honored, Your Majesty."

The queen was looking at her intently—the same, almost unnervingly assessing, even challenging, gaze I remembered so vividly from first meeting her in England. "Scribes have told me, on occasion, that certain images become their favorites to depict," she said. "Their specialty, as it were. And yours?"

Undaunted, Marie immediately replied, "I would say the Archangel Michael, Your Majesty." To this she added, with a charming smile, "Partly because I am fond of depicting dragons."

"And I am quite fond of slaying them," returned the queen. "So I suspect we will get on quite well together." She glanced at Aiglette, who was now clinging to my hand. "And the little girl?"

"This is Aiglette," I replied. "She has become part of our family here." I prodded Aiglette, who stepped forward and managed her best curtsey.

"A graceful little sprite," observed the queen. "How old are you, child?"

Aiglette held up three fingers.

"I imagine *you* prefer dolls to dragons," said the queen. "Even *I* did, at your age. Am I right, Aiglette?"

The little girl nodded.

"How heartening to be surrounded by the young," the queen mused, almost to herself. "It is good for the soul. Just as it is good for the soul to be here, at Fontevraud." She looked at me warmly, almost wistfully, and then at Marie and Aiglette. "Quite a lovely trio you make!"

# CHAPTER 93

We gradually grew accustomed to the queen's presence, as we did the coming and going of many others who passed through, seeking her attention: royal emissaries, foreign envoys, as well as purveyors of luxury goods (silk merchants from Julfa, Russian fur traders). In addition, there was her considerable retinue, including her chaplain, steward, and clerk—the punctilious, slightly pompous, Rupert de Saint-Julian. Although her position as dowager queen dictated a level of formality I had not been accustomed to in England, it did not take long for that formality, at least privately, to dissipate and our closeness to reestablish itself. Indeed, she seemed eager not only to recount the progress of her own life in the intervening years, but also that of those from her English court. Tancred had remained in Salisbury, his rank and holdings enhanced by his loyalty to King Richard; Jeannette, having reconciled herself to Tancred's failure of interest in her, had married an affluent wool merchant from Nottingham.

Of her favorite daughter, Joanna, the young widow of William, King of Sicily, who had died five years before, she spoke often and lovingly. "Fate has not been kind to my youngest daughter," she said. "Her only child, a son, stillborn years ago, and then William's life cut short. She was forced to flee Palermo in the tumult after his death. Her brother Richard, despite his affection for her, would then have married her to the brother of Saladin," she added. "Imagine!" She shook her head in despair.

ONE DAY, UPON ENTERING THE queen's chamber, I noticed that a desk arrayed with writing implements had been placed by the window.

"Your very own scriptorium," she said, pointing proudly to it. "You must let me know if anything is lacking."

I took a seat at the bench; its height was perfect, the ink and quill of excellent quality; the silky parchment fine and velvety. "Thank you, Your Majesty! I have everything necessary. But tell me—why have you done this?"

"I have an assignment in mind, one that will require us to work privately together." There was an enticing pause. "I would like you to record certain vignettes of my life."

My initial thrill gave way to some apprehension. "But would not Rupert be better suited to such work? He is your official clerk, and surely it would be appropriate—"

"As loyal and meticulous as he is, Rupert would *not* be appropriate," she interrupted. "He is a master of the pro forma—official texts such as writs, charters, and the like." She gave a brisk, dismissive gesture. "This is a more delicate, intimate, task which requires a certain finesse. It must be implemented by someone I completely trust. Equally crucial—someone adept at telling stories. *You* meet those criteria."

"You honor me, Your Majesty," I replied, basking in pride, and secretly triumphant that I, rather than the proprietary Rupert, had been chosen. But then, aware of the tensions the assignment might provoke, I added, "I am concerned that Rupert will take offense."

"He need never know. I said we would work *privately*. I trust you understand."

I nodded, only partly reassured by her avowal of secrecy; then another question occurred to me. "Is this not unusual, Your Majesty? A queen recording her own story?"

"Yes, I am aware that some may find it unusual. But I have never followed convention and do not intend to start now. I have no wish for my own history to be recounted by Louis's sycophants or Henry's slavish chroniclers. Many of them hate me and would distort important aspects of my life." She took a seat and beckoned me to do the same. I took up my quill and looked at her expectantly.

"Let us start with my recent life—my meeting early this winter in Mainz."

"It would be helpful if you would give me a sense of the people, and the setting, before we begin," I suggested.

"Very well. I had come to meet the Emperor Henry, the dreadful German, and his Hohenstaufen cronies, to free my son," she began. "I forfeited the enormous ransom and dealt with him cordially enough. But trust me"—there was an almost murderous look in her eyes—"the day will come when Henry pays the price for his endless machinations against us, and for his designs on the kingdom of Sicily." After a pause, she muttered, "I pity the poor Norman princess who was forced to marry him. Henry is a cold, stony monster. Gaunt, dour, scant of beard, with lightless eyes under a massive brow."

Her chilling description made me shudder. "And his wife is a Norman, you say—"

"Yes. Constance. She is older than the German by ten years—as I was to Henry, you may recall. Her father was King Roger of Sicily. I met her in Lodi three years ago. She is charming and gentle. And, happily for our purposes, *childless*." Her eyes narrowed slightly. "Quite different from the other Constance."

"The 'other Constance'?"

"My daughter-in-law. Constance of Brittany—the widow of my son Geoffrey. Henry obligated him to marry her for tactical reasons. I never liked nor trusted her, nor did it surprise me that her scheming intensified after Geoffrey's untimely death."

It was evident from the stony look in her eyes that she had no wish to pursue the subject of her elusive middle son; I had always intuited she never considered him a kindred spirit. "Yes, Constance, too, has designs, but for her young son, my grandson Arthur." Then she sat up quite straight, her hands clasped. "But come, time passes. We must continue."

DESPITE THE QUEEN'S ENDURING RANCOR toward Henry VI—
"The German"—and Constance, I sensed a new inner tranquility about

her, a tendency to reflect, even to forgive. More than once I discovered
her in prayer in the chapel, alone, or walking slowly and meditatively
along the path that led to the garden.

One sparkling day, late that June, I found her sitting in the garden,
an open book in her lap, and her face, eyes closed, turned toward the
sun. Hearing my steps, she looked up; I colored, embarrassed that I had
intruded on a private moment.

"I did not mean to disturb you, Your Majesty."

"You are not disturbing me. I was merely savoring the peace, and
the warmth of the sun." She looked down briefly, her beringed hand
resting upon the book. "I rarely had either when we were together in
England." She gave a wistful smile.

"With all you have achieved, and with Richard now king, you de-
serve this peace."

She nodded, though not altogether convincingly. "Alas, I suspect
the peace will be as fleeting as the English sun."

As she continued to dictate her story, she would occasionally pause,
preoccupied by the continuing friction between her sons. "While he was
abroad, John made concessions, far too many. Concessions that will come
to haunt us." She gave a heavy sigh. "It was a dreadful thing to have my
sons pitted against each other in years past. Dreadful, and unproductive."

The characteristic addition of "unproductive" nearly brought a
smile to my lips. "Fortunately, the strife between your sons has ended,"
I replied. "Surely, with Richard and John now allied, Philippe will tread
carefully."

"*He* may tread carefully, but I assure you, my Richard will not. The
loss of those Norman territories—of the Vexin—chafes him. He is
only biding his time before he confronts Philippe. He has already spoken of constructing a great fortress in the Seine Valley," she added.

"Where?"

"Just south of Rouen. 'A fortress rising from the rocks' he dubs it.
I know my son—he will not rest until it is built." She sighed wearily
as she rose. "Let us visit Marie in the scriptorium," she said. "It would
cheer me to see her. What an unusual young woman she is. There is an

*intentness* about her; she is that rare and wonderful thing, an artist, of that there is no question."

"Fortunate most of all in her mother, who was remarkable, and in her own way, very brave."

"That is not what I mean," returned the queen with the slight sharpness that often characterized her assertions. "She is fortunate to have discovered what gives her joy. A métier. A purpose in life."

"No one has had greater purpose than you, Your Majesty."

"A misguided purpose, to many. One that has brought me many enemies."

"That does not seem to concern you greatly."

"I have never known an interesting or ambitious person who does *not* have enemies. Indeed, I have instilled that credo in my sons."

"They seem have taken it to heart," I returned with a wry smile.

THE QUEEN'S WORDS PROVED CLAIRVOYANT: several weeks later, in early July, word came to us that the king had routed Philippe to the northeast, at Fréteval, only eighty leagues away. The French king—the son of the queen's first husband—had been roundly humiliated.

The queen, savoring her son's victory, eagerly awaited news from Richard himself. One morning, while I was reading to Aiglette, her servant sought me out. "The queen requests you come to her at once," she said.

"Stay here, with Aiglette, while I go to the queen," I told her. Then, quickly, I walked to the reception chamber, where the queen sat alone. It was ample and comfortably furnished—by far the most luxurious chamber of the abbey—with a high, vaulted ceiling and walls painted with scenes from the life of the Virgin. She sat close to the window in a chair whose scale dwarfed the others in the chamber; on the small table beside her sat the enamel casket with the scene of Becket's murder, an object that unfailingly reminded me of the days in England. A letter lay in her lap.

"Come," she said, gesturing to the bench opposite her. "I have just received a letter from the king."

"With good news, I hope?"

"Good news. But also *sobering* news. News that has caused me to reflect."

"About the victory?"

"About the *nature* of the victory. It seems that Richard captured Philippe's archives—his seal, his letters, and other crucial documents, many of them secret. The names of his spies, and of his agents in the Aquitaine. The names of the Angevins here, in our region, who have deserted to the French. A priceless trove of intelligence! One that will come to haunt Philippe in the future."

"The archives are in safekeeping with the king and his men?"

"They are too precious to remain here, with Richard and his court constantly on the move. My son says the documents will be taken by ship, to London, and safeguarded there. Philippe must be enraged." She gave a small, satisfied smile.

"A great victory indeed, Your Majesty," I considered, before adding, "but you say the news has caused you to reflect."

"The gains of Fréteval may or may not endure. But the archives *will.* It is a lesson to us all—to my sons, and to myself. These spoils, this intelligence, are as valuable as any coffer filled with gold. Promise me, Isabelle, when I die, that you will keep all my letters and private papers safe. Never let them fall into hostile hands. Better you burn them first!"

"You need *never* fear, Your Majesty," I replied, unsettled as I always was, by the mere thought of her dying. "I assure you I shall guard them with my life." I took her hands in mine and held them tight as I fought back tears. "But surely," I continued, "your present fears are quite un-grounded. Your son is the king, and we have always been quite protected here, at Fontevraud."

"I have lived long enough to know that one can *never* be certain of anything—of the twists and turns of time, and fate." Glancing at the Becket casket, she added drolly, "In a world where my husband the king walked barefoot in penance to Canterbury, to pray at his enemy's tomb—*anything* is possible." She looked down, fingering the letter. "And remember, Isabelle, I have *two* sons," she went on, "Richard still has no heir, and John has proven less than trustworthy." Then, gravely, even fiercely, she reiterated, "Promise me that you will always keep my papers, and my letters, safe!"

I gave her my hand and placed the other on my heart. "I swear to you, and before God, that I will always keep them safe, Your Majesty."

THE SAFEKEEPING OF HER LETTERS and the records of her life story were not the only aspects of the queen's intense preoccupation with her own, and her family's, legacy. That autumn, she turned her mind to the decoration of her late husband's tomb. "That he died ignobly, stripped of his raiment and crown, like a pauper, haunts me," she confessed one day. "He was a king, and for my sons' sake, for all our sake, he must be depicted as such, for eternity."

On occasion I would accompany her to the crypt. There, kneeling before Henry's tomb, her gnarled, beringed fingers clasped together, she would pray, as I, beside her, inwardly marveled that her animosity toward him seemed to have dissipated. On one such occasion, as we left the church, I turned to her. "How strange to think that a king of his power, of his restlessness and energy, should now be trapped in stone, within a crypt."

"None of us escapes that fate, dear Isabelle," she replied drily, "whether one is born with a scepter or a scythe. Years ago, on my travels, I encountered a sage, a Spaniard, who told me an adage: 'Everyone dies in darkness—even the man who sells the candles.' Alas, how true, how very true." She smiled ruefully. "One can only hope that my late husband enjoys a less tumultuous afterlife than the life he knew here, on earth. I daresay I had many moments when I cursed him." She sighed. "I do not feel that same degree of hatred now."

She had begun, in a strange sense, to reinvent him—to craft his legend in the way she wanted—not for her private self or pride, I came to believe, but for that of her sons, her family—most of all, for posterity's. Always mindful of the court chroniclers who, in recording history, created legends, she was now intent on crafting her own. In his death, at least, Henry would be subjugated to her will.

THE GOLDEN MONTHS OF SUMMER slipped away, then the burnished, meditative autumn; when Advent arrived, it hardly seemed possible that the queen had already resided among us seven months —months in which she had continued to dictate her life story to me. Of late, she had also been greatly preoccupied by the latest maneuvers of "the German": Henry VI had seized control of Sicily. I was sitting with her on a gray, frigid morning weeks later, at the end of Epiphany, when a letter from the king's chamberlain arrived. After reading it, she looked up, clearly vexed.

"What is it, Your Majesty?" I asked.

"Constance, the wife of the German, has borne him a son. It seems she was not only miraculously fertile for a woman of forty, but also clever. She bore the child in the middle of the marketplace, and showed her swollen breasts afterward to quell any gossip that the baby did not come from her womb. She has named him Frederick." She set the letter down. "That Henry now has an heir will greatly complicate our position in Sicily. I must write my son at once and tell him this does not augur well. No"—she shook her head—"not well at all."

# CHAPTER 94

The machinations of "the German," and the threat he posed to Norman Sicily, continued to preoccupy the queen throughout that long, dark winter. Thus, I was particularly happy when I arrived at her chamber one morning in early spring to find her in an unusually lighthearted mood. "I have just learned that Joanna will visit us next month," she announced, springing to her feet, a letter in hand. "How happy this makes me!"

"How long has it been since you have seen her?"

"Four years, and then only too fleetingly—the spring when Berengaria was betrothed to Richard, and I had accompanied her to Sicily." She paused, looking at me intently. "It gratifies me to think that you will finally meet Joanna. I suspect you will like each other—I told you long ago that you rather remind me of her." Her expression became pensive. "It is remarkable that she has remained so resilient and hopeful despite the losses she has endured, and the years she spent in that alien country."

"What 'alien country,' Your Majesty?"

"Palermo. The court of her late husband, William. A place that straddles two worlds—ours, and the East. A Christian court, but one whose highborn women are kept secluded, in harems." She looked up with that brisk impatient expression I had come to know so well. "But now you must help me compose a reply to Joanna."

MY EXCITEMENT AND CURIOSITY TO meet the young queen soon became entangled with other, more complicated, feelings. Would Joanna resent my closeness to her mother? Would I be relegated to the side after her arrival and miss my customary intimacy with the queen?

Would I feel diminished, as I often had with my own family, and especially with my mother?

Or would those traits Joanna and I shared—we were the same age, had no husband, had suffered the death of infants—create an affinity between us? But then a chiding voice would emerge, and I would chastise myself for being foolish and unrealistic.

WEEKS LATER, ON A DREARY, rain-sodden day in May, queen Joanna and her retinue arrived, all rather bedraggled from riding in the downpour. Yet her woebegone appearance seemed to amuse, rather than distress, Joanna. "I must be a dreadful sight!" she told me, laughing, as she brushed off her soaked cloak. In looks she was reminiscent of her mother—rather tall, slender—with a similarly lively, darting way of moving. But her complexion was fairer and her features daintier than the queen's; her charming voice had a lilting, foreign intonation.

I curtseyed before her, and as I rose, she gave me a bewitching smile. "You are the fabled Lady Isabelle, I assume? Mother has often mentioned you in letters. She has decreed we are to become great friends"— this, with mock seriousness—"so we dare not disobey her." At that she took my arm, and any vestige of my previous disquietude simply vanished; I sensed I should like her very much.

Her visit of ten days was a singularly happy time—for all of us, but especially for the queen, whose pride and joy in her daughter, and whose concern for her, were palpable. Each time I observed them together I was struck by the queen's warm, uncritical maternal gaze—partly because it was a vivid, piercing reminder of what I had never experienced with my own mother.

SEVERAL DAYS AFTER JOANNA'S ARRIVAL, I introduced her to Marie. Having suggested we meet in the garden, I arrived there early with Marie, who was both excited and not a little nervous. "Come, let us see what has begun to bloom," I said, partly trying to distract her as we waited. We had only just begun to stroll along the paths separating the plots of flowering plants when Joanna appeared, trailed by her servant, the rather overbearing, swarthy woman I had noticed the previous day. "This must be Marie."

Marie stepped forward and gave a deep, graceful curtsey. "Your Majesty," she murmured.

"Up, up!" Joanna ordered, with a small, whisking gesture of her hand. "You are just as Mother described—charming! Everyone here sings your praises. My mother especially." Unusually bashful, Marie blushed; Joanna turned to her servant and said, "You may leave now, Malekakxa."

"What a strange name," I remarked to Joanna after the woman departed. "Where is she from?"

"She is of Greek parentage, and decidedly proud of it. It was helpful for me and Berengaria to have a Greek servant, and one with such fearsome looks, in the Holy Land. She frightened any number of Infidels." She laughed softly. "But come, let us walk a bit," she said.

The two of us conversed as we strolled along the allées while Marie, her eyes fastened on our visitor, listened raptly. To my delight, Joanna, no doubt aware of Marie's fascination, presently turned to address her. "You may not realize it, Marie, but there is something that you and I share. Did you know that I was brought up here, at the abbey—just as you have been?"

"Yes, Your Majesty. Sister Clementia told me. I have wanted to ask you about it."

"Then *do*—"

"Very well, then. How old were you when you first came here?"

"About five years of age. My brother John, the youngest, joined me later. He was beloved by the sisters, but always unruly," she added. "Some things do not change—he was an instigator then, and has remained so."

"Was the queen able to visit you here?" asked Marie.

"As often as her responsibilities would permit. I remember my joy when she swooped in to fetch us—we would take ship at Barfleur and cross the channel with her, to see our father, in England. Those were happy times, when everything seemed an adventure. Eventually I was sent to join Mother, in England. That stay with her helped prepare me for my marriage, after I was betrothed. I was twelve when I left England forever to live in Sicily."

"Were you frightened?" asked Marie.

"Oh yes, very!" she replied matter-of-factly. "But my older sisters had done the same, and Mother had taught me what was expected. I never questioned it."

"Do you ever now?" asked Marie, who had lost any trace of shyness.

"Not any more than I question my name, or my parentage, or the fact that the sun rises and sets," replied Joanna. "Even now, there is talk of my brother the king planning a match for me. . . ." Her voice had trailed off, and she seemed to withdraw into herself, but then her expression brightened. "And you, Marie," she went on, "you are devoted to your work in the scriptorium, I hear."

Marie described her work in a vivid, ardent way that clearly touched Joanna. "How blessed you are to have this passion, Marie," the latter exclaimed. "I would like very much to see your work. May I?"

"I would be honored, Your Majesty. I am just finishing a complicated page now. The light has been so poor these last few days." She looked up at the bright, clear sky. "I should take advantage of this sun and return to my work now."

"Then go at once!" said Joanna. "But only if you promise we will talk again before I leave, and that you will ask me any question you like."

"I shall," replied Marie with a thrilled smile.

After Marie left, Joanna turned to me. "There is a deep inner loveliness about her. You and Sister Clementia have guided her well."

"It has not been difficult—she was born with remarkable sensitivity, and a generous heart."

She gave a wistful smile, her eyes scanning the garden. "What paradise! I feel as if I did my penance with those long rides in the rain these past days. Today God has rewarded me with sun." She took my arm. "I have so many memories of being in this garden when I was a little girl. When I was a child here, there was a nun—very pretty and young—who instilled a love of flowers in me, just as Mother instilled a love of poetry." She took a few steps, as she pointed to one plant, then another: "That is leopard's-bane. And look"—she bent down—"the first blossoms of lady's mantle—what a vivid green they are! And that is feverfew—it rather resembles parsley, does it not?" After a few steps, she plucked some sprigs of lavender and then, eyes closed, inhaled the scent. "I had a splendid garden in Sicily," she said as we resumed walking, "and groves of lemon trees, too—there, and in Apulia, as well."

"I, too, had a garden I loved, at Ravinour—but no lemon trees! You would send lemons to the abbey from Sicily," I remembered as we continued to stroll.

"Yes—lemons from another time, another era." A certain melancholy had crept into her voice. "There was a woman in Palermo, an alchemist, who knew much about plants," she reflected. "About lemons and herbs, and other ingredients with which she concocted magic potions. She gave me several that were meant to help me conceive. To little avail, alas."

Her sudden despairing tone, and her story about the alchemist, both startled me and resurrected painful memories of my desperate expeditions to Anthusis. "You will return in a few days to Beaufort, I gather," I said, still trying to dispel those thoughts.

"Yes. And from there to Rouen, with Queen Berengaria. I must await my instructions from the king." She gave a small, stoical smile. "As I mentioned, there is talk of another marriage. It is only a question of when and how I might be useful." There was an almost indiscernible undercurrent of despair in the way she had pronounced "useful."

We came to a hedge of great, pale pink roses. She plucked one and held it gently in her hand. "The Infidels say that roses were born of Mohammed's sweat. The theory did not seem so strange in the Holy Land, but here—" She laughed softly. She began to pick the roses one by one, until she had assembled a small bouquet. "I shall take these to Mother."

"They will delight her," I said.

"I hope so," she murmured. "Mother has always loved roses." She held up the bouquet, scrutinizing it. "Yes, they are lovely. Except for this one, which is crushed"—she extracted one rose and tossed it to the ground—"good. Now the bouquet is *perfect*."

WHEN, THE FOLLOWING WEEK, IT came time for Joanna to depart, the queen remained in her chamber—"Far too despondent," she told me, to attend her daughter's leave-taking. Joanna herself trailed by, looked rather downcast as the abbess and Clementia gave their blessings, but broke into a smile when Aiglette gave her a bunch of posies. Marie, whose affection for the young queen had grown considerably over the visit, gave her a drawing she had been working on for days, and that I had not seen. I watched as Joanna unfurled it. "Ah, I will treasure this forever!" she exclaimed. Gesturing me to come closer, Joanna said, "Is it not exquisite, Isabelle?"

"It is *more* than exquisite," I said, glancing proudly at Marie as I studied the image. "It is wonderfully imaginative and original." An immense illuminated letter *J* both dominated and bifurcated the page, its strong, curving form intertwined with swirling, almost animate, leaves and spiky purple thistle. On the left side, a princess leaned over the rampart, below which a moat churned with high, whitecapped waves. On the right side of the *J*, Marie had depicted a crisp hedge maze, in the center of which stood an almost phantasmal lemon tree, and perched atop it, a great falcon with piercing eyes.

"This is among your very best work," I told Marie as Joanna thanked her profusely again before handing the drawing to Malekakxa for safe-keeping.

Then Joanna approached me. "You have brought us springtime, in all ways," I said as we tenderly embraced each other.

"I hope that is true," she said as we slowly drew apart, "but most of all, I hope I shall see you again before long. In the meantime, it cheers me to know that you are here with Mother. She has such affection for you," she added. "I should be slightly jealous"—here, an almost saucy glance—"if I had not come to have great affection for you as well."

"And I for you," I replied with emotion, thinking almost guiltily how baseless my early fears had been. "Take good care, Your Majesty, and return to us soon!"

"God—and my brother—willing," she murmured. Turning, she summoned the groom. "Come!" she commanded, in an imperious tone remarkably reminiscent of her mother's. "It is time to depart. My brother the king awaits in Rouen."

WEEKS LATER WE LEARNED THAT the queen's granddaughter Alix, the young Countess of Blois, was to join the order of Fontevraud.

"She is the child of the queen's youngest daughter from her marriage to King Louis," explained Clementia as we discussed her imminent arrival. "The queen has not seen her for many years. It seems they scarcely know one another."

"Perhaps her presence will compensate for Joanna's absence," I observed.

But that was not to be. It soon became evident that there would never be more than a pleasant, correct relationship between the young countess and her grandmother. About the same age as Marie, Alix was a dutiful, mouse-like girl who rarely spoke. "In looks and temperament, she reminds me eerily of Louis," the queen confided to me. "The same meekness, the same reticence. It is almost as if she has pledged herself to the path for which her grandfather would have been far better suited—serving God, at a holy place. She will make a fine nun."

ALAS, WE NEVER SAW JOANNA that autumn or winter; the following year we learned that she had been betrothed to Count Raymond of Toulouse. "Since he is known for his hot temper and his rough nature, I would have been against Richard arranging this," admitted the queen, "were not the alliance with Raymond so crucial. But with our help, Joanna will manage. Hopefully she will bear him an heir, at last."

"And if she does not?" I asked with concern, thinking of my own past.

"She *will*," she replied, then changed the subject.

MY AFFECTION FOR THE QUEEN, and my admiration and respect for her wisdom and strength, continued to grow during the four years that followed. That was the comparatively peaceful period of Richard's reign, when the tranquil routine of the abbey was enlivened by the queen's energy and presence.

Marie, increasing in skill and confidence, had come to apply herself to her work with an even greater sense of discipline and purpose. "She has become an extraordinary young woman," the queen remarked to me one day after Marie had presented some fanciful material she had just completed. "She is headstrong, intuitive, imaginative," the queen noted. "All the qualities of an artist."

"Yes," I mused, "and so very different from Aiglette. Only yesterday, Clementia told me, with no little approval, 'Aiglette does not bridle against ritual and rules, as Marie does.' Yet the two girls are devoted to one another."

Indeed, it became clear, as the girls grew up during those final years of that momentous decade, that Clementia had found in Aiglette what she had not, in Marie: the incipient, unquestioning piousness of a future nun. It touched me to see how close the two had become; indeed, Clementia treated the little girl with a tenderness that many remarked upon.

## CHAPTER 95

On the first day of the last year of the century—the first of January, of 1199—I awoke long before the bells tolled at dawn. It was still dark when I dressed, and dreadfully cold— the water in my basin was thickly crusted with ice. I must take a walk outside, I thought to myself, for I felt a need to reflect, and to comprehend what had happened in years past—the way my life had unfolded.

Just as the cock crowed and the sun was rising, I took a lantern and ventured outside. It was a clear, ethereal morning: snow during the night had dusted the greenery and the stone fences with a crystalline, white film. I walked with slow, meditative steps behind the high, proud apse of the church until I came to the frost-covered quadrants of the slumbering garden. For a while I stood quite still, recalling the frigid January day, not unlike this one, when I had arrived at the castle of Gerard. I thought of my wedding, of being a young married woman, and how much I had admired my husband before I came to fear him, and suffer by him. Even so, I felt less bitterness toward him now—the influence of the queen perhaps. She had taught me to value what I had learned from and experienced with him, rather dwell than on his failings.

A sudden rush of noise startled me—I looked up, at a flock of rooks, speeding across the sky. They made me think of Gerard's hawks and of his tragic end; the idea that he had burned to death with his cherished birds, in the mews he had lovingly built for them, still shocked me, and filled me with sadness, with horror.

I turned and began to walk toward the entrance of the cloister. As I unlocked the gate, a mouse, almost indistinguishable from the color of the stone pavement, scurried before me. There was no other creature about as I walked along the gallery; the sisters were still in their cells. I thought of them now—this singular universe of women, many of noble name—capable, intelligent, even learned—women who were reconciled to a life without men, without a husband. I could not completely say the same of myself, for there were times when carnal feelings surfaced within me, feelings that I had, on several occasions, voiced to the priest whom Clementia had chosen to serve as my confessor.

One day only months before, as I was walking with her, I asked whether she had ever regretted not having known married life. "No," Clementia replied, with beatific certitude. "The life I chose was always the right path for me, the *only* path. As for *you*, Isabelle"—she took my hand, pressing it warmly—"it was far better that you had known a man, that you had known marriage, before you came to us here. It has made you what you are."

I left the cloister and returned outside, walking in the direction of the gatehouse. Lothar—older now, and with an even more pronounced limp—hastened toward me as I approached. "Come quickly, Lady Isabelle," he said, with alarming urgency.

"What is it?" I asked, my heartbeat quickening: Had another baby been left for us?

He pointed to a dark mass huddled on the ground, in the shadows. I drew my lantern close, only to start when I glimpsed the woman's face: there was something about her eyes which reminded me of Anthusis. But this was not Anthusis: this rugged, filthy face was far coarser in feature, and much older.

"She says she can augur the future," Lothar told me with contempt, and yet—I sensed—with some fear as well. "I told her I would take her inside, and fetch her some food. But she refused to move. She told me she would not accept charity without giving us something in return—a prophecy." He looked at the woman, who had drawn her tattered cloak about her face. "She's a madwoman, I wager."

"Whoever she is, she is cold and starving." I knelt down by her. "Where have you come from, woman?"

"Far away." Her voice, though young, was deep and mannish.

"Do you have a name?"

"Seer, they call me."

"That is a calling, not a name."

"I have no other." She pulled aside her cloak—a small lumpy pouch tied with a red cord was nestled in her lap. She picked up the pouch, shaking it before me: I heard a small, hard rattling noise. "With these lots, I can divine the future," she told me. "Then, and only then, will I let you and the sisters repay me with food."

"Go ahead," I said. "Tell me your prophecy. But then you must keep your promise and come inside. The sisters and I will not allow you to linger here to die in the cold."

She opened the bag and tossed the contents onto the ground. The lots were made of sheep knuckles; some were boldly marked with an X, some with weird, incised oval symbols. She studied the pattern they had formed as a scholar would a manuscript; then grimly, yet triumphantly, she looked up. "I see two deaths. Both men. One dies without a murmur; the other, violently, by the hand of a stranger. And then there is something else"—her eyes narrowed as she scrutinized the lots— "Something white, cold, and opaque," she said, shaking her head. "But no, it is too cloudy to make out."

I felt relieved: there was no talk of women dying, of my girls' dying, of the queen or Clementia dying. Yet there was an authority to her voice and demeanor that still unnerved me.

"Come," I said, gesturing to her. The sun had risen high; the radiant light of morning seemed to dispel the momentary gloom, and the seeming authority, of the woman's words. "I have let you give your prophecy," I told her. "Now, *you* must keep your word. Follow me inside."

MONTHS LATER, DURING LENT, A letter from Fastrada arrived while I was working with the queen. (Alas, it was not delivered by LaFoi, who had long retired to a manor house granted him by the Hauteclares; his replacement, trustworthy if brisk, had none of his élan.) Any message from Fastrada sparked excitement, though only an iota of that elicited by her visits each spring. Her first encounter with the queen had been the most memorable: even Fastrada had been intimidated by the monarch, though not for long. As for the queen: Fastrada's verve and fearless style so captivated her that the two women soon came to forge a warm friendship. ("What joy to meet a woman who is not afraid to banter with me," the queen told me, adding, with a twinkle in her eye, "and whose keen sense of politics is only matched by her boundless reservoir of gossip!")

"Open the letter at once," said the queen, sitting up expectantly as the letter was placed in hand.

I did so, a smile coming to my lips when I glimpsed the great flourish of the *F* at the bottom of the page. But my smile vanished as I began to read:

My heart is heavy, dear Isabelle, as I pen these words, for I know only too well how much they will sadden you. Corbus has died. Gallien and Douceline are bereft; so are we all, for he had become a treasured member of our household, and one on whom Hugh depended for so much. It all happened very suddenly. Corbus had broken his leg on a foray in the forest. We had high hopes that the surgeon had set it properly, and that the leg would heal. For Corbus not to be able to walk would, of course, have been a terrible thing. Alas, an infection soon set in, and it became necessary to amputate both his legs. It was then he lost the will to live. One could see it in his eyes long before Gallien, who had become so adept at communicating with him, told me that Corbus had signaled "My time has come."

We have held his funeral and given him all proper rites. Hugh had a gravestone erected with the words: "Here lies Corbus, beloved of all God's creatures." No dates, of course, for no one knows how old he really was; he had retained that strangely elfin quality almost until the very end.

More I shall tell you when I next visit. If all goes well, that will be long before Easter, which falls so late this year. I yearn to see all of you.

I send deepest love, and my sympathy to you, who did so

much for Corbus. Embrace Clementia and the girls, and commend me to the queen.

*Fastrada*

My eyes brimming with tears, the letter still tight in my hand, I looked up at the queen. No words would come. I lowered my head and wept.

"It is always hardest when death claims those who are truly good," said the queen, who had heard so many tales about Corbus over the years. "I long to console you, dear Isabelle, but I know not how, alas."

"Simply by your being here with me, Your Majesty," I finally said, wiping my eyes as I looked up. "That is great solace in itself." But then a frightening chill came over me—

"What is it, Isabelle? You have gone quite pale."

"The prophecy," I whispered.

"What prophecy?"

"A woman who purported to be a seer came to the gatehouse months ago," I said. "She augured that two men would die. The first, she said, 'without a murmur.' And now Corbus has died. And without a murmur, of course, for he was mute."

"I urge you not to give this too much credence," said the queen—out of true conviction, or simply as a way to comfort me, I was not certain, for there seemed to be a hesitation before she asked, "And her second prediction?"

"That a man would die, violently, from a stranger's hand."

"Alas, an all-too-commonplace enough event, it must be said. Do not let yourself dwell on it." She reached forward and took my hand. "Come, let us walk to the chapel. Together we will pray for Corbus's soul."

# CHAPTER 96

One morning a week later, toward the end of March, two of the king's agents—tall, burly figures in helmets and hauberks—arrived at the abbey. After hastily greeting me and Clementia, they asked to be shown to the queen at once. "A vital matter," one added gruffly.

"Of course," said Clementia. As we proceeded to escort them to the queen, I stole occasional glances at the men—the urgency in their eyes, and in their demeanor, alarmed me. "Wait here," Clementia directed them when we arrived at the tall arched door that marked the entrance to the queen's quarters.

She slipped inside while I waited outside with the men. They had a rough, intimidating manner, and everything about them seemed at variance with the serene otherworldliness of the cloister. I wondered what terrible things, what violence, they had witnessed; most of all I wondered about the nature of the tidings they had brought.

I was on the verge of asking them a question when Clementia emerged. "You may go in," she instructed them.

I told Clementia that I needed to depart. "Aiglette awaits me. I promised to read with her this morning."

"Go ahead then, I shall escort the men to the stables when they are finished."

"And you will let me know what you learn?"

"Of course."

Aiglette had just begun reading her lesson aloud when I heard a knocking at the door: it was the queen's servant. "The king's men have just departed," she announced. "Her Majesty asks that you come to her at once."

I rose to my feet. "Continue your reading," I said to Aiglette. "We will discuss the parable when I return. Promise me to read it carefully!" Sensing something was wrong, the little girl nodded solemnly.

Moments later, as I approached the queen's chamber, I came upon Clementia, who was leaving it.

"What has happened?" I asked.

"The king has been wounded."

"How?"

"The queen dismissed me before I could learn the details. I only know that he has been in Châlus with his men. Looking for buried treasure, some say. But time presses! I must provide supplies for the king's men, for their journey back to Châlus. Tell me what you learn after you speak with her," she said, hurrying away.

I entered to find the queen in her customary seat; she was still, almost preternaturally still; her hands were clenched. "Ah, Isabelle—how relieved I am to see you!"

I embraced her, then drew up a stool and sat down opposite. "I heard the king has been wounded," I said, leaning forward and reaching for her hand.

"Yes—" She looked away, her eyes grave and full of pain.

"In battle?"

"No—that is what makes it all the more terrible! Not in battle, but in a freakish accident." She shook her head in despair. "It should never have happened."

"Tell me—"

"It was twilight. Richard was walking along the battlements, not far from the siege machines. He often does this at night—a way to relax a little, to speak to his men in his camp, to buoy their spirits. He was not armed, and carried no shield—a terrible, reckless mistake. Little did he, or anyone, know that an archer was poised at the ramparts—the son of a man whom Richard had once punished. His arrow pierced Richard in the shoulder. A petty act of revenge, they say." She had uttered those words with disgust. "The surgeon is attending to him now."

"But the arrow did not reach his heart—" I replied with relief.

"No—the shoulder, the left shoulder," she repeated listlessly.

"Then surely he will mend!" I exhorted, even as I struggled to contain my own fears. "He is strong and has suffered such wounds before." I took her hand.

Her eyes brightened. "Yes, you are right," she murmured. "A wound in the shoulder—many have recovered from such an injury. My uncle Raymond long ago, in the Holy War. My son Henry, in the lists—"

"Then we must have faith, Your Majesty. The king will recover—I know he will!" I offered her my hand. "Come, let us entreat God to help him." Together we walked to the prie-dieu, knelt, bowed our heads, and clasped our hands in prayer. "Please, Lord, save your good and valiant servant, the king," I murmured. It was then—in that moment of entreaty—when I felt a sudden awakening of a memory, and, with it, a jolt of terror: Had not the seer prophesied that a second man would "die violently, and by the hand of a stranger"?

Banish those thoughts, I told myself incessantly; but the dreadful words of the augury continued to echo, tainting my prayers.


SIX TENSE DAYS FOLLOWED. ON the morning of the seventh, Clementia and I, having just left the queen's chamber, saw Grecia running toward us. "The king's men have arrived!" she cried.

"When?" asked Clementia.

"Moments ago. Mother Mathilda—" She stopped, interrupted by the sounds of harsh footfalls at the other end of the cloister. "Look!" She pointed to the end of the passage. "They come now."

Two men in hauberks and with daggers at their waists strode toward us.

"It is highly irregular for you to enter without my being notified," Clementia told them icily as they approached.

"There is no time for such niceties right now, Sister," came the man's brusque reply. "The king has ordered us to escort the queen to Châlus as soon as she can make herself ready. It is urgent."

Clementia and I remained silent, too fearful to ask why such urgency.

"The king's condition has greatly worsened," the man continued. "She must reach him before—"

"Follow me," said Clementia as she led them into the queen's chamber.

THE QUEEN, HER CHAPLAIN, AND several servants prepared to depart for Châlus the following day. Mother Mathilda and Luke, the abbot of nearby Turpenay, would also accompany her. At dawn, Clementia and I gathered at the stables to bid the somber entourage farewell.

Only the queen's pallor, and the weariness in her eyes, hinted that she was distraught. Her control was admirable—indeed awe-inspiring—for a mother embarking on a journey to her son's deathbed.

"You and the king will be in my prayers—in *all* our prayers—every moment, day and night," I said, reaching for her hand as she sat astride her mount. "I only wish I could help you bear the anguish of this journey, Your Majesty!"

"I must be strong for my son," she said.

"Yes, you *must*," I said, tears coming to my eyes. "Pray to Radegonde. And to God—they will guide you,"

"She and God have deserted me," she replied bitterly; the stalwart mask had dropped, and for the first time I glimpsed anger, rather than acceptance, in her eyes.

"No, do not say that, Your Majesty—He will *never* forsake you!" That the king might die still seemed utterly implausible to me; surely God would intervene, He would save him, as He had many times before. There would be a miracle; one heard of such things happening. "You yourself have taught me to be strong, and never to cede to despair," I continued, gently taking her hand. "Now I beg the same of you."

She closed her eyes, as if she were willing herself to resoluteness. "Yes, dear Isabelle, you are right," she allowed, giving me a glance of tender gratitude. "I do not want to disappoint you, and I must not disappoint my son. 'You are always so brave, Mother,' he once told me. I remember the admiration in his eyes when he uttered those words. Yes, I remember that—" She bit her lip. "May God in all His mercy guide me now!"

I turned my face away so that she would not see me cry.

"You are ready, Your Majesty?" the leader of the king's men called.

"Yes," she replied in a strong, clear voice, having collected herself. She took the reins, and I wiped my eyes of tears.

I walked to Clementia's side, and together we watched as the queen cantered away. We stood silently for a long time, our eyes fixed on the stretch of road even after the entourage had vanished.

"Now we must wait. And wait," I said mournfully as we watched the gate close ever so slowly. "And if the king dies—"

"Then we will do our best to help the queen. To give her solace, and to help her through the ordeal," said Clementia in a steely voice. "It is God, finally, whom we must trust. There is always a reason for such things, Isabelle—even for the loss of a child. It is the way God metes out his lessons—it matters little if the one He teaches is a queen, or a servant girl. In His eyes, they are equal."

I refrained from replying, for I could not bear to tell her what I was thinking: only a woman who has never lost a child could possibly have uttered those words; and that if God chose to teach in that way, He must be a cruel taskmaster, indeed.

DAYS LATER, ON THE SEVENTH of April, as Clementia and I were walking along a passage within the cloister, we saw Lothar's helper running toward us.

"A messenger from the king has just arrived!" he cried.

Clementia and I hurried to the gatehouse. The moment we glimpsed the messenger's face and demeanor, there was no need to ask why he had come.

Trembling, I turned to Clementia; all color had drained from her face. "No, it cannot be," I uttered in a quavering voice. "It cannot be— the king is dead."

"Come, we must speak with the king's man and ask what we must do," said Clementia, with her remarkable calm. "This is the time to be strong." She placed her hands on my shoulders. "Remember, Isabelle, this is a moment when God is testing us, and testing our faith."

The messenger approached—his face was sun-scorched, and the double lions on his tunic soiled and weather-beaten. No doubt he had ridden fast, recklessly fast, to reach us.

"You come from Châlus, I assume?" asked Clementia.

"I do, Sister. With dreadful tidings." He bowed his head. "The king is dead."

Clementia dropped to her knees, her hands clasped; I followed suit. "May the king rest in peace," she said as we knelt on the stone pavement. "May God protect him in life after death, and grant him salvation," I rejoined. We made the sign of the cross, and slowly struggled to our feet. The abbey bells tolled; the three of us stood in silence.

Finally, turning to the messenger, Clementia asked, "What is your name?"

"Rufus," he replied. "I have been with the king throughout the siege. And well before." He was well spoken—a young knight, clearly on his way to greater things.

"Tell us what happened," I said. "We were told the king had suffered a wound in the shoulder—"

He nodded. "He dismissed it at first and rashly tried to extract the arrow himself. Then the infection set in and the doctor was called. But it was too late. The king had seen enough gangrene to know what it was, and what it meant for him. 'Summon the queen,' he told us, and then—"

"Did she arrive in time to see him?" I asked, fearing the answer.

"Yes, yes, she did. She was there when he was given last rites. She was there at the very end."

"And his body? The funeral?" asked Clementia. "Do you know what plans have been made?"

"Yes. That is partly why I have come—to inform you of these things. The queen will set off within days for Fontevraud. She will accompany the bier. His body will be laid to rest here, beside his father the king. He directed that his heart be brought to Rouen, to be placed near his brother Henry's tomb. Those were the king's instructions."

"And what are *our* instructions?" asked Clementia; I knew it comforted her to think of planning, of logistics.

"Prepare the abbey for the arrival of the cortege, and for the funeral," he said. "The queen will arrive with the king's body in a matter of days."

"And the funeral Mass?" I asked.

"It will be held on Palm Sunday," he said. "Here, at the abbey church."

# CHAPTER 97

The glorious spring weather seemed a mocking reminder of what we had lost: our fabled king in all his splendor. "And this senseless tragedy," I lamented to Clementia as we awaited the arrival of the queen and the funeral cortege, "because the king, on an evening stroll, was careless."

"God had protected him so many times before," she said. "Perhaps it seemed impossible that He would not continue to do so."

"Perhaps, in the end, his confidence in his position and prowess condemned him. Perhaps," I added, recalling a tale my grandfather had once told me, "he was afflicted with what the ancients called hubris."

"I would not attribute his death only to hubris," she returned rather sharply.

"To what would you attribute it?"

"He disregarded the ways of our Lord and acted against the laws of nature. He turned against his father. He indulged in cupidity—was not the search for treasure partly the issue at Châlus, after all? He engaged in licentious behavior—even in his last days, they say, he sought pleasure. And the siege of Châlus—its very timing—was sinful in itself: God forbids fighting during Lent."

"But you have never mentioned any of this before. Certainly not to me, and—"

"Certainly not to the queen, you would say. Of course not! The queen, however realistic, is a mother all the same. Richard was her favorite son, and it was all too easy to be blinded by his gifts and valor. As for the queen—she has never been greatly afflicted by matters of conscience." Her lovely blue eyes seemed to bore through me: "Surely, even *you* must recognize that, Isabelle."

"I do," I confessed. "She is a woman of light and shadows. Both parts of her fascinate me—her ambition for her children, even her ruthlessness. I do not condemn her for those traits."

"I pray for her, and for her salvation," was the extent of her reply.

"With every passing year," I reflected, "the queen seems more ardent in her faith. She has greatly increased the number of charters and donations she has granted."

"True, but I assure you, after she returns, it will be the family's legacy and the securing of John's power against young Arthur's factions that will preoccupy her more than anything else."

"What do you mean—Arthur's 'factions'?"

"Many believe he has as much claim to the throne as his uncle John. And his mother Constance is reputed to be as fierce and ambitious a mother as the queen herself."

"Is it not strange," I mused, "that there should be these two Constances, both immensely ambitious for their sons, and whose actions have, at various times, aggrieved the queen? One rearing a boy in Palermo; the other, a prince in Brittany."

"Yes," concurred Clementia. "But the boy in Sicily—Frederick, the Hohenstaufen—seems a somewhat more remote nuisance. Arthur, in Brittany, is quite different, and his mother a far greater threat. She will not give up easily. And she knows it will benefit Philippe to create more chaos by supporting Arthur against John."

"But Philippe and John have been allies in the past—"

"The past no longer matters, Isabelle. With the death of Richard, the position of the players on the chessboard has changed," she went on. "Mark my words—I predict a bitter struggle ahead."

CLEMENTIA'S WAS NOT THE ONLY prediction that preoccupied me. During those sad, anxious days in the aftermath of Châlus, I dwelt anew on the words of the seer. Her first two prophecies had already come to pass; now I tried, in vain, to recall the third. One afternoon when fog rolled in and blanketed the abbey in misty white, I suddenly recalled, with a chill, what it was: "There is something else, but it is too cloudy to make out," she had said. Being optimistic by nature, I tried, with only a modicum of success, to convince myself that the very nebulousness of the augury meant that nothing else terrible—no death of someone dear to me, certainly—would occur.

Uneasiness, intertwined with grief over the king's death, propelled me to seek relief in action, in planning. In this way, I suppose, Clementia and I were quite similar. I redoubled the frequency of Aiglette's lessons and asked to assist Clementia in the preparations for the funeral of King Richard. We learned his brother, the newly crowned King John, would come from Brittany, and the elusive Queen Berengaria, Richard's widow, would remain at Beaufort. Though we heard, at first, that Joanna was too distraught to attend, one morning Clementia told me, "It seems that is not the reason for her absence. I received word this morning that she is pregnant and has had some difficulties. It would not be prudent for her to travel."

"That Joanna is with child should bring great joy! Not only to her, but to the queen."

"One would hope," said Clementia with a sigh. "But I imagine the joy has been overshadowed by Richard's death."

"When do you expect the queen and the entourage to arrive?"

She looked up, scanning the cloudless sky. "If the weather holds—on the morrow."

THE WEATHER HELD; A CHEERLESS calm settled upon the abbey as we awaited the funeral cortege. I remember the gentle wind, and how I shielded my eyes against the sun, that callous spring sun, as Clementia, Marie and I gathered, with all the others, near the gate house. I looked about in wonder at the hushed, solemn throng.

Meantime we waited, and waited, until, at last, we heard the sound of horns—the royal entourage had been sighted. Slowly, mournfully, the gate creaked open. "Come," said Clementia. "Let us move closer to the entrance. It is important the queen see us first."

As we proceeded forward, we heard the distant, funereal sound of a drumbeat. "It is not long now," murmured Clementia.

The portentous sound of the drum came closer and closer. At last we heard Lothar shout, "They arrive!" The following moment, the king's lead guards, in red tunics emblazoned with double lions, came into view, their lances and flowing pennants held high: the sight of those fearsome men, on their magnificent mounts, drew a gasp from the assemblage. All the while, craning our necks, we strained for the first glimpse of the queen. Finally, flanked by the abbess and the abbot of Turpenay, she appeared—her face lightly veiled, her bearing, as she rode, poignantly erect.

And then—as the drum continued its relentless beat—the bier itself passed through the gate: a red and gold canopy upheld by lances shielded the king's body from the sun. We dropped to our knees and made the sign of the cross. All was silent save for the thud of horses' hooves, the monotonous drumbeat, and the dull sound of wagon wheels rolling across the hard, packed ground into the inner courtyard.

When the procession came to a halt, the queen, still astride, slowly drew away her veil—how haggard she looked, how grief-stricken her expression! Then, after looking slowly and searchingly at the crowd, she made a slight gesture of her hand—part thanks, part royal benison.

Mother Mathilda dismounted, then stepped forward to speak. "Your Majesty," she said in her clear, noble voice, "we have returned to our home, to the abbey, after a long and painful journey. Before all those gathered here, I entreat God to bless you, and your family, as we attend to the king's final journey. Let us never forget that he was God's son, as well as your own. May God grant him salvation. And may you, and your family, continue to trust in the wisdom of the Lord as we prepare him for eternal life."

I watched the queen's pale, drawn face; it had remained impassive, with the remoteness of a sleepwalker's. For many moments, she made no response. Then, as if awakening from a trance, she said, simply, in a voice that seemed to have aged a decade, "It does my wounded heart good to return here, to Fontevraud."

Of her faith in the Lord, she made no mention.

THE FOLLOWING FEW DAYS—THE DAYS when we kept vigil for the king—return to me as a vivid, somewhat jolting, succession of images: the first sight of the king's face, and his body, as he lay in state in the church—how shocking to finally glimpse the face of one so fabled, to glimpse his profile, and his brow, and his golden beard; how strange, for a king so allied with war, with strife, to see his face settled into an expression of such serenity. And yet, even cloaked by death, it was not hard to imagine how formidable that tall figure, with his crown and scepter, must have seemed to his enemies, and how thrilling and inspiring to those he led in battle.

Had I not seen the king first, perhaps the initial glimpse of his younger brother would not have been so jarring—that moment when, hand in hand with the queen, John entered the church for the funeral mass on Palm Sunday. "One would scarcely think they have the same parentage," I reflected as she and John proceeded to their places several pews in front of mine. He was small in stature, his looks wiry and saturnine; even then, at a time of great solemnity, there was a restlessness, a rageful energy, a carelessness, about him. I noticed his hands, laden with lavish rings, and how they took up the missal with visible impatience; I noticed his dark, flickering eyes, his long sharp nose, and his thin, dissatisfied mouth. That he felt any real grief for the death of his elder brother seemed unlikely; that he knew he needed his mother, and her support, was all too evident. His behavior toward her was almost cloyingly attentive; she seemed, in her grieving state, merely to submit to it.

Throughout the Mass—as voices were raised in song, as the heavenly host was presented, as we prayed for the eternal salvation of the king—I found my gaze again and again fixed on John. He brought to mind an image of Lucifer that Marie and I had once seen on the lavish page of a Bible. John fascinated in the same way the image had; and everything about him and the brutish, steely-eyed men who had accompanied him, seemed at odds with the blessed serenity and benevolence of the abbey.

DURING THE SEVERAL WEEKS THAT followed, the queen was called upon to shoulder one responsibility after another, leaving her little time to indulge in grief. She met with foreign envoys and local lords crucial to John's ascendance; she granted charters and bequeathed gifts to those who had loyally attended her late son. Included among these was a donation of property to the nearby abbey of Saint-Marie de Turpenay—a generous acknowledgment of thanks to its abbot, Luke, who had provided her solace while the king lay dying and also presided over the funeral rites.

On the Tuesday after Easter, John, who had departed for Normandy immediately after the obsequies, returned to the abbey with the king's widow, Queen Berengaria. Clementia and I met her shortly after she arrived: she was a gaunt, solitary figure with heavy-lidded dark eyes and an almost painfully self-effacing manner. "There is something tragic and lonely about her," I remarked as Berengaria left with the abbess to join the queen. "How sad to think of her sequestered all this time at Beaufort."

"I suspect life became even lonelier for her after Joanna married," said Clementia afterward. "And now, with the king's death, she has no further purpose."

"That seems rather severe," I remarked. "She could marry again, she could find another purpose."

"That is not what I meant. She has no further purpose to the queen. Nor to John and his court."

I made no reply, unable to deny the harsh reality of her remark. "Have you learned when John will be crowned?" I asked.

"If all goes well, and John's men subdue those in league with Arthur—next month, they say. At Westminster."

A FEW DAYS AFTERWARD, AS I arrived at the royal chambers, I came upon Clementia, who was departing, and heard a soft, lulling melody emanating from behind the door. "What is that music?"

"The queen's minstrel," she replied, one brow arched in disapproval. "Hardly in keeping with abbey decorum, particularly in a time of mourning. He arrived yesterday from Poitiers. She finds this sort of music 'comforting.'"

"That does not surprise me," I said, restraining myself from smiling at her censorious expression.

"Interesting," she said, her tone rather disgruntled, "that was precisely Mother Mathilda's reaction."

I entered the chamber and found the queen gazing out the window, her eyes half-closed as she listened to a young, fair musician strumming a lute in one corner. "You may stop now, Alardus," she told him after greeting me. "Wait in the antechamber while I speak with Lady Isabelle."

"What do you think of his music?" she asked after he had excused himself.

"It is lovely," I replied enthusiastically, drawing up a stool opposite her.

"Clementia does not approve, of course." The queen's expression, as she uttered those words, was one of amusement rather than pique. "But even *she* would not forbid a grieving old woman's caprice."

"You are not merely an old woman," I protested. "You are the dowager queen of England and the Duchess of Aquitaine."

"Yes," she said dejectedly, "but I am also a mother. A mother who has lost her cherished son. How I shall miss him!" She gave a deep sigh. "Even you, Isabelle, cannot imagine the horror of those days at Châlus. To see my Richard killed in that senseless way. I weep to think of it— a lion slain by a gnat."

"What happened to the young man—the archer?"

"In his final hours, Richard forgave him and ordered him released."

"A gesture of great charity," I replied. "A gesture worthy of the king, Your Majesty."

"Yes," she murmured, her eyes replete with both pain and pride. "The gesture of the mighty man he was. But his men were not so magnanimous. After Richard passed from this world, they had the archer flayed alive," she added in a bitter tone. She lapsed once more into pained silence.

"I can only imagine the sorrow of those final days, those final hours, Your Majesty," I said.

"I thank God most of all that I reached him in time, that I was there at the end. They say, at first, Richard had been cavalier. He had been wounded before. He did not want his men to know—for them to worry, to lose heart.

"We arrived by early nightfall. Inside the tent, his men, his loyal men, kept vigil, some weeping. They had lit candles and torches and placed them around his bed. My son hated darkness, you know—he always did, even as a little boy. Loving light was in his blood, as it is in mine—the blood of the Aquitaine. He had asked for music, and the men had fetched a minstrel from the village. 'Only joyous tunes,' he ordered him. I told him to eat; he did, lustily. Not out of appetite, I am sure, but simply because food meant life. And he loved life!

"Even then, as his condition worsened, he did not ignore affairs of state. We talked about the future, he and I. He made it clear he wanted John to succeed him. 'Constance has one goal—to rid Brittany of our influence,' he told me. 'If Arthur gains the throne, she will achieve it. Then, little by little, she will poison the others against us. Promise me, Mother,' he said. 'Swear to me you will do everything to assure that John is crowned.' I vowed I would do everything in my power.

"A few hours later, the infection turned deadly. The Abbot Milo heard his confession, and Luke administered the last rites." As she began to weep, I embraced her.

For a long time we sat together, the only sound that of her sobbing. Finally, she lamented, "If only I found comfort in weeping—if only my tears would resurrect him, I would spill an ocean's worth!"

But then she drew herself up. "Banish tears," she murmured, almost as if she were chastising herself. Then, to me: "Go fetch Alardus. I must have music."

# CHAPTER 98

S hortly thereafter, the queen learned that her promise to her late son would soon be fulfilled: John would be crowned at Westminster in late May. I was with her when she received the news. "Good. All is in order," she said, her eyes scanning the letter with the royal seal, which had just arrived from England. I saw little happiness in her face—or, if there was happiness, it was a very measured sort.

"This should please you greatly, Your Majesty."

"It satisfies me," she conceded, the roll of parchment tight in her hand, "but the fight is far from over. I assure you that Constance and Arthur lie in wait. There is much restiveness in the realm, both here and across the Channel. John has made enemies—many enemies—over the years. There is a limit to loyalty that can be bought."

"But surely, most of those who followed Richard now support John."

"That is a disappointingly naive assumption, Isabelle," she retorted. "Richard inspired loyalty. John must *purchase* it. And his cohorts are an entirely different sort. They are a rough, conniving lot with eyes fixed on gaining property here, and in England. I trust them as much as I would Roman money changers. Already many powerful lords here have chosen to go abroad," she went on. "Henri de Champagne among them. He and many others would rather risk their lives in the Holy War than ally themselves with my son." Her expression was caustic.

"You have already done so much to help John."

"Too much, perhaps," she murmured, as much to herself as to me. "Too much."

"Best to dwell on heartening news," I gently urged. "Your son has been crowned. And Joanna is with child. Soon she will have a brother or sister for her little son, and you will have another grandchild—surely that must gratify you."

"Yes. Even if—"

She did not pursue the thought, nor she did need to: I knew what she was thinking—that Joanna had paid a heavy price by marrying Raymond de Toulouse. Rumors had long circulated about his temper, his brutality. From what the queen had confided, I had the impression that Joanna felt as much alone as a widow or a spinster. "I am sure Joanna longs to see you," I said, "especially in light of her brother's passing."

"And I long to see her, and to console her, above all. How distraught she will be to learn about Richard!"

"She does not yet know?" I asked, astonished.

She shook her head. "It has been difficult to get word to her—her husband's lands are in turmoil, and she has been moving from place to place, struggling to quell the rebels."

"Where is her husband?"

"Elsewhere," she replied, with visible disgust. "Raymond has been trying to garner support among the Aragonese."

"I had no idea of this," I murmured with deepening alarm.

"She has had much to contend with," she said, her expression pained. "I have asked that she come to Niort next month, when I am there to meet with those who are wavering in their support of John. Our alliances must be shored up. After that," she continued briskly, "I shall turn my attention to Lenora."

"Lenora? Have there been new developments in Castile?"

"Philippe's son, the dauphin, needs a bride. Lenora has four daughters. Comely and intelligent daughters, I am told by our envoys to Burgos. The eldest has already been promised to the court of Leon. The wife of the dauphin must be chosen among the other three."

"The next eldest, then?"

"That would seem logical, to most." She gave a cryptic smile. "But not to me. It is too important a decision to be made according to convention." She had pronounced the last word with almost imperceptible disdain. "My granddaughter's birth order matters far less than her character. She must have the right mettle for a future queen of France. Much will depend on her—not only for France, but also for us. For our realm."

"And who will you entrust to make that decision?"

"Whom would you suppose, Isabelle?"

I was on the verge of saying "Lenora"—for the queen's daughter was reputed to be immensely capable and intelligent—but then, catching the queen's expression, I replied, "Yourself, Your Majesty."

"Precisely. I will go to Spain, and I will choose the bride."

"But that is an exceedingly difficult journey," I replied, astonished, for the queen had already passed her seventy-seventh year. "A long and arduous journey across the mountains to Spain, to Castile."

"I have made others just as long and just as difficult," she replied, in a tone that made clear the matter had been decided. "Come," she said, rising. "The sun is shining. It is a lovely day in May—and how many more months of May remain for me, after all?" She offered me her hand. "I long to stroll in the garden."

CASTING ASIDE GRIEF, AND WITH great force of will, the queen made plans for her circuit through the Aquitaine. "I must turn all my energy to the shoring up of alliances," she told me as she prepared her itinerary; a map of the Aquitaine was spread before her.

"But how, Your Majesty?" I asked. "Philippe has immense resources." I did not give voice to what I was thinking: Philippe had dealt with John in years past and knew his weaknesses, and how his venal mind worked.

"It is quite simple." She gave me a disarming, if steely, smile. "I shall woo those who vacillate in their support for John, and punish those who turn against him. And I shall be generous to all who help our cause."

"How long do you imagine you will be away?"

"A great part of the summer. I shall leave soon and begin here, at Loudun"—she placed her finger on the map—"and then go farther south, to Poitiers. I shall be there by early May, God willing. From there to Niort, where I hope to meet Joanna. Then I shall set off for La Rochelle and Bordeaux. If all goes well, I shall confer with Philippe in

July. I have asked Rupert to draft a message to him—a most congenial message"—here, a crafty glance—"requesting that he and I meet at Tours."

I did not envy Rupert, the queen's clerk, such a sensitive, and crucial, task. "Do you think Philippe would ever agree to this?" I asked.

"Of course he will! If only out of curiosity, to assess his father's wicked first wife."

"How I wish I could be there to witness that encounter!"

"You are needed here," she said firmly. "There is much work for you and Clementia to attend to. And you have your responsibilities to Marie and Aiglette."

"But surely, Your Majesty, I could be of help to you—I could pen your letters."

"Not the sort I shall need on this journey. Those will require scribes who are conversant with the language of treaties, with legal matters. That is Rupert's expertise."

"Of course," I reluctantly conceded.

"But I do promise," she added in a gentler tone, "to send word to you while I am away."

THE QUEEN AND HER MEN left for the Aquitaine on a Tuesday, the morning of April twenty-seventh. "How brave she is," Clementia marveled as we watched the brilliantly attired entourage depart, "and what energy and discipline she has! Only a few weeks have passed since she buried Richard."

"Ambition is what keeps her alive," I said. "As well as the fear that her beloved Aquitaine will be torn apart by strife."

We began to walk toward the abbey church. As we came close, we heard music—the lulling strains of chants. "Aiglette is waiting for me here," Clementia said as we came to the portal. "I told her she could listen to the choir as they practice. She must be encouraged to listen, to practice, and to sing."

Clementia's bond with Aiglette, and the affection between them, had become even stronger in recent years. Much of this bond had developed through music: Aiglette, who was now nine years old, had perfect pitch and great musicality. Indeed, the queen claimed that she had the "purest voice" she had ever heard—"The voice of a seraph." That Aiglette should be gifted in this way, that she could be trained to use that voice in the service of God, gratified Clementia immensely.

There were moments, I admit, when I felt a twinge of jealousy; it was hard to acknowledge that Aiglette had become closer to Clementia than to me. Sometimes, while watching them together, I thought how strange it was that they even had come to resemble one another: with their porcelain skin, delicate features, and remarkable blue eyes, one might even have thought them mother and daughter.

# CHAPTER 99

Weeks passed; meanwhile I waited, and waited, for word from the queen. At last, on an afternoon in late May, a messenger arrived with a letter for me bearing her seal. After the salutation, it continued:

Much has transpired since my departure. As queen, during this time, I have accomplished much even if, as a mother, I have suffered much.

Joanna arrived here, at Niort, days ago, after fleeing Raymond's lands. She had courageously attempted, these past weeks, to quell the rebellions against her husband's rule. Finally, accompanied by a few loyal servants, her young son, and several knights in arms, she managed to escape. Of her husband there is no word.

My joy in being reunited with her is clouded by my grave concern for her health. She is in need of rest and nourishment if she and her unborn child are to survive; that she learned of Richard's death while making her way north has only worsened her condition. The news filled her with wrenching grief; her only solace, she told me, would be to pray at her brother's tomb. "Let me go to Fontevraud," she implored. "It will comfort me to have the companionship of Lady Isabelle and to reside among the nuns."

I have made arrangements for Joanna's journey to Fontevraud once she is fit to travel. I pray that will be soon—next week, God willing. I shall send word to you and the abbess once she is expected to depart. The knowledge that she will be in your care shall sustain me as I continue my journey and the fulfillment of my duties.

Profoundly affected by the account of Joanna and her harrowing plight, I set the letter down. How courageous Joanna had been, not only to have defended her husband's demesne, but also to have escaped and endured the long journey alone, and with child. She was very much her mother's daughter. I ran my finger across the image upon the seal—the queen with a lily in one hand, a hawk in the other.

Quickly I rose, and left to inform the abbess and Clementia of the letter.

ONE AFTERNOON IN THE MIDDLE of June, the entourage of the young queen passed through the abbey gates. At first, not having glimpsed her among the riders, I was filled with terror—perhaps the very worst had happened. Only when the lead knight dismounted did Clementia and I learn that Joanna lay within one of the two curtained wagons. "This way," he told us.

We approached the wagon. Malekakxa pulled aside the curtain: lying upon thick cushions within, and gazing at us with eyes that seemed all the more immense and blue amid the ashen, emaciated face, was Joanna. "Isabelle," she whispered, struggling to sit up. "I must—"

"Stay still, Your Majesty," I entreated as Clementia and I exchanged fearful glances. "Where is my son?" she whispered frantically, struggling to raise her head from the cushion.

"He comes now," replied Malekakxa. A young servant approached, a little blond boy clutching her hand. "Look," the nurse said to him, "here is your mother."

"My darling," Joanna said, trying once again to lift herself up. "You must be tired—" The nurse held him up for his mother's kiss, then gently set him down. "Make certain he has everything he needs," Joanna implored.

"Do not try to speak, Your Majesty," said Clementia. Then, to me, "We must get her to a bed at once. Tell the men to bear Queen Joanna to the infirmary," she ordered the lead knight. "Sister Philippa will su-pervise her care."

OVER THE NEXT FEW WEEKS in late June, Joanna's condition slowly and steadily improved. To our relief, she gained some weight, and her face gradually recovered its glowing beauty. It was clear, from her ex-panding girth, that her baby, due at the end of summer, was growing apace.

Our conversations, as we walked in the garden or sat together in her chamber, deepened our friendship. We laughingly admitted we shared some of the same idiosyncrasies—a predilection for household gossip, among them. We spoke of the struggles in her marriage, and I alluded to my own. We spoke of the future; she asked, touchingly, if I might one day consider joining her court. "When Mother is gone, and Aiglette is grown," she gently added, "and you are no longer needed here quite so much."

One morning, as we strolled, she told me, "Each day I feel a little stronger. And I feel the baby moving more and more." Then, buoyantly: "I shall name him Richard."

"And if it is a girl?"

"I have not yet decided." She placed her hand on her belly. "Ah! A little kick. But it will *not* be a girl. It will be a boy."

"How can you be so certain?" I asked with an affectionate smile.

"The prophecy of a seer. A seer in Toulouse—an old, very wise woman whom I consulted many times."

"Did she then . . ." I murmured wistfully, and we continued to walk.

"I received a letter from my mother yesterday. From Tours. She told me the negotiations with Philippe have proceeded as she hoped. She has pledged homage to him for her lands, for the Aquitaine."

"Not an easy decision, but a prudent one. Do you not agree?"

She nodded. "We need a modicum of peace and order for John to assemble his counselors and consolidate his forces against Arthur. Constance will do everything to help her son wrest the crown from my brother. That is Mother's greatest concern," she added, "but there is something else that concerns me just as much."

"What is that?"

"The nature of the men around my brother. They are the worst sort of *arrivistes*—hungry for riches and land, here, and in England. A venal lot without a shred of loyalty." She lapsed into silence, her eyes with that drifting remoteness I recalled from our very first encounter. Then, suddenly, her mien brightened. "Mother says she will travel from Tours to Rouen, where John holds court. I intend to join them there," she announced with a defiant smile that reminded me uncannily of the queen's when she had told me of her decision to go to Burgos.

"Are you certain that would be wise, in your condition?" I asked, alarmed. "A long, exhausting journey, to Normandy? Along roads swarming with Philippe's agents and spies? I do not think this a wise idea at all! And what of your husband? I doubt he would sanction such a decision."

She gave a mordant laugh. "What my husband thinks matters little to me. I want my child to be born in Rouen—in *my* family's region." She gave me a charming, determined smile. "Yes, it is crucial I join Mother and my brother the king in Rouen." She took my arm. "And I want *you*, Isabelle, to come with me."

AN HOUR LATER, JOANNA SUMMONED me, Clementia, Mother Mathilda, and Sister Philippa to her quarters. "I have come to a decision," she announced. "I shall depart for Tours, where I shall join my mother, and then accompany her to Rouen. That is where my baby must be born—in *our* capital, in Normandy. And I have asked Lady Isabelle to accompany me."

There fell an uneasy silence during which all of us exchanged nervous glances. "Your Majesty, I can well understand your desire to go to Rouen," interposed the abbess in a slow, purposefully measured way. "But I do think—"

"I strongly counsel you *not* to make this journey," interrupted Sister

Philippa. "It would entail much too great a risk—to yourself and your unborn child."

"I must respectfully disagree with you, Sister," countered Joanna. "Each day I feel stronger. And I have made far more difficult voyages in the past."

"But, Your Majesty," Clementia intervened, "until very recently, you have been dreadfully ill and weak. And the baby is due in less than two months, is it not?" She turned to me with an almost desperate look. "Surely, Isabelle, you must agree!"

"I do. And I have already voiced my objections."

"That is quite true," said Joanna. "She has voiced her objections, and I have quashed them. Remember," she added, "I come from hearty stock. My mother traveled ceaselessly when she was pregnant, and so, I am told, did my grandmother Mathilda, even while leading her forces in England."

The abbess, her hands clenched, protested, "But surely—"

"I *will* go to Rouen," reiterated Joanna. "I have already sent word to the king, asking that the birthing chamber be prepared."

"Very well," conceded Sister Philippa, barely able to conceal her consternation. "But I entreat Your Majesty, at the very least, to travel by wagon. We will provide one that will be as comfortable and safe as possible. You *must not ride*," she admonished.

"Of course," Joanna replied amiably, if somewhat unconvincingly.

"I promise to do everything in my power to ensure that Her Majesty arrives safely in Rouen," I reassured them, even as I struggled with apprehensions.

"Lady Isabelle will be at my side throughout the journey, and in Rouen," said Joanna, with an affectionate glance in my direction. "As for my son—I think it best that Raymond remain here with you. It is a long journey for a little boy. And he has been so content here, among the sisters."

"You know we will take very good care of him," said the abbess.

"How long do you expect to be away?" asked Clementia.

"A few months," Joanna replied. "I shall return by late September."

The church bell had begun to sound. "It is time for vespers," said the abbess, making a motion to leave. We had just begun to file out when Joanna called: "Stay a moment longer, Isabelle."

I returned to her as the others departed.

"There is something else I must ask of you," she said, in a low, imploring voice. "Promise to stay with me while I am birthing the baby."

SOON AFTERWARD, ON A CRYSTALLINE morning, we departed for Tours.

Accompanied by the ever-watchful Malekakxa, the young queen had kept her promise and took her place in the covered wagon. Days later, we arrived at Tours.

There, in the upper reaches of the castle, we found the queen presiding from an improvised throne in the center of a richly decorated chamber. "How well my daughter looks!" she said, rising to embrace us. "You and the sisters have performed a miracle." My delight in reuniting with the queen was tempered by concern, however: she looked exceedingly haggard and careworn. "Come, daughter, you must rest after your travels," she said, beckoning to a servant to fetch us seats.

"You and Isabelle are fussing over me too much," Joanna teasingly complained. "I feel so well—as if I were strong enough to fight the Infidels myself!" She raised her arm in dramatic, almost comical fashion, as if she were brandishing a sword. "Indeed, I see no reason why I should be compelled to travel by wagon into Rouen. The sister of the king ought to enter the capital astride—not as an invalid borne by wagon."

"But Your Majesty," I pleaded. "Remember Sister Philippa's warning!" I looked with desperation at the queen, hoping she would countermand Joanna's wish; but her implicitly approving expression gave me little comfort. The dowager queen riding triumphantly into Rouen with her regal daughter at her side was, I knew, a powerful image of majesty and lineage she would find important for her own purposes.

Thus I was not entirely surprised when she went on to say, "Surely a compromise might be made. I suggest Joanna go by wagon for the next few days—until we reach Le Mans. Then, if she continues to feel well, she might ride—slowly, of course—for the rest of the journey.

From Caen to Rouen, perhaps. That is only, what"—she shrugged—
"twenty-five leagues or so. Then we can enter the city together." She
took Joanna's hands in hers. "How blessed I am," she said, beaming, "to
have such a brave, spirited daughter!"

"Not nearly as brave as you, Mother," said Joanna, her eyes shining
as she basked in her praise.

THE MERGING OF OUR TWO entourages made a grand procession
when, the following day, we set off; all the while I hoped that the queen
and Joanna would abandon the idea of riding into Rouen together.
After we reached Caen, however, my hope was crushed—Joanna announced she would forgo the wagon for her mount, and we set off for
the final stretch of the journey.

From there, alas, the conditions grew more difficult. We came to
swaths of roads destroyed by warfare and marauding bands; then, one
afternoon, a torrential rain came upon us. Joanna's mount slipped while
crossing a river, and, to my horror, she tumbled to the ground while
approaching the bank. However hard she tried to appear cavalier, she
was unnerved; even so she insisted on continuing on horseback.

To the queen's delight, we achieved the triumphal entry into Rouen.
Cheering crowds gathered to glimpse the dowager queen accompanied
by her pregnant daughter as we made our way through the gates and
along the winding streets. The moment Joanna dismounted and entered the palace, however, she gripped my arm several times, as if about
to faint. Terrified, I urged her to do nothing but rest. I knew she, too,
was frightened, for this time she agreed with alacrity. It was by then
late July.

At first, I remained mostly with Joanna in her private quarters as she
rested. It was not until a few weeks later, on the Feast of the Assumption, that the royal physician, after examining her, ordered that she
move into the birthing chamber. "I shall inform your mother that the
time draws near," I told her.

"I do not want her here while I am giving birth," Joanna said, gripping my arm. "She must not see me this way."

"But your mother is very strong—"

"Tell her we will summon her when the time comes," she whispered fiercely.

A HOST OF FRIGHTFUL MEMORIES assailed me when, at last, we were led to the birthing chamber; I girded myself as the great door hinged open. At the first glimpse of the massive bed, the array of talismans on the table, the objects of agate and coral, and the leather strap affixed to the ceiling, a wave of terror surged through me.

The midwives set to work at once—administering soothing potions and nourishing elixirs, rubbing her belly and hips with oil of violets and roses. When, days later, it seemed the baby had not sufficiently descended, the physician ordered Joanna be given frankincense to sniff. "This will provoke her to sneeze. And that, in turn, should provoke contractions," he explained.

Soon the contractions began; the leather strap was lowered from the ceiling. "Hold it," the midwives ordered as they urged Joanna to push, and push again. All the while I sat by her bedside, wiping her brow and murmuring words of encouragement, even as I inwardly roiled with terror, pity, and revulsion. Part of me wanted to flee from this chamber, from this writhing stranger, for Joanna had been transmuted into a savage creature, a creature of screams, and violent heaves, and rancid sweat. Still I held her hand tight, exhorting her to be brave as she endured the waves of pain.

On the second day, the sheets were soaked with blood; the midwives exchanged terrified glances. The physician was called. "She cannot afford to lose any more blood," he confided to us. "I am concerned about her heart. I fear for her, and the baby."

Hours passed; Joanna's condition worsened; yet she remained awake, all too conscious of the precariousness of her life and that of her child. The midwives had become strangely silent as they ministered to her, as if possessed of dreadful knowledge they dared not share; the physician's countenance had taken on a frightening gravity. The queen had been summoned and entered the inner sanctum.

The physician took us aside. "There is no hope for her," he told us. "We must cut her open if we are to save the baby."

The queen looked about wildly as I began to cry. "No, no, it cannot be—" she moaned, raising both fists in fury. "Why, oh why, has God forsaken her?"

"Your Majesty," said the physician gently, but firmly, "if you are to speak with Queen Joanna, you must do it now. There is not an instant to waste, lest we lose the baby as well."

I wiped my face of tears, and the queen managed to collect herself. Together we walked to Joanna's bedside. And then the queen—her eyes brimming with tears, her expression one of infinite sadness and horror—gently took her daughter's hands; I looked away, weeping.

"You have come to say goodbye," whispered Joanna, her frantic eyes full of anguish. "Name the baby Richard. And if a girl, Mary. Promise me! Bury me at Fontevraud, next to my brother. Near Father."

"All your wishes will be granted, beloved child," vowed the queen, her voice choked. "I swear to you, my darling!"

The physician approached. We embraced Joanna a final time before he and the midwives gently, but firmly, pulled us away. "Leave us now," he said tensely, "to finish our work."

The baby, a boy, was born soon afterward. Joanna lived only long enough to hold him in her arms. She died on the fourth of September, the small, frail baby a few days later, not long after he had been baptized.

The archbishop of Canterbury administered the last rites and granted Joanna's dying wish: that she take the veil and die as a nun of Fontevraud. A royal messenger bearing the queen's orders for the burial and funeral was immediately dispatched to Clementia; it was she who was also given the sad task of telling little Raymond of his mother's death.

THE GLORIOUS PROCESSION THAT HAD entered Rouen triumphantly little over a month before was now transformed, by the king's command, into a funeral cortege. We departed for Fontevraud in the second week of September, King John and the queen mother riding side by side. Of that journey all I can recall is a blur of tears.

Two days later, on a crisp, ethereal autumn morning, Joanna was laid to rest. Never had the nuns sung the funeral chants with such tender fervency; never had the abbey church—shafts of gold-flecked light intersecting its apse—looked as starkly beautiful and otherworldly. *In paradisum* we did indeed seem.

The king—his grim mien suggesting calculation rather than sadness—remained at his grieving mother's side throughout; once or twice I noticed his fingers, weighted with rings, tapping the front of his pew impatiently. The queen herself was the very image of woe: her weathered face frozen in a mask of grief, her normally fluid movements now strangely slow and leaden, as if ossified by Joanna's death. Her tiny grandson stood close beside her; several times during the Mass she would murmur to him or stroke the top of his head.

At the end of the ceremony, when the singing had ceased and the last blessing had been uttered, silence fell upon the assemblage as she and little Raymond knelt to pray before Joanna's tomb. As the queen rose, the king offered his hand; then, tears streaming down her face, her hand holding fast to Raymond's, she proceeded past us at an achingly slow pace as the bells began to toll.

# CHAPTER 100

I did not so much make my way through the days that followed as drift through them. I lost all appetite and had no energy to walk; songs and poems I had once loved now filled me with grief; I studiously avoided the garden. And one day, when Aiglette brought me the bronze falcon—"To keep you company," she tenderly explained—I asked that she take it away; for now it reminded me of Joanna and her plight.

It was not only the loss of Joanna that had so affected me, but the dreadful memories it had awakened: memories of the terror of giving birth and losing my babies; memories of Aiglantine and her death. With Joanna, too, there had been the same harrowing, and ultimately hopeless, bedside vigil; the moment when we knew she would die and were powerless to intervene. It was strange, I came to reflect, how both women—one a lowly servant, one a queen—had accepted death with such stoicism, such dignity. But while Aiglantine could find comfort and reassurance knowing that her daughter would be safe and well taken care of, Joanna had died knowing her baby would probably not survive, and that her son would be raised by a man she had come not only to fear, but also to despise. "Watch over Raymond," she had implored her mother at the very end, "lest his father—" Then her eyes had closed, her breath had stopped, and she had ceased to be.

FOR THOSE FIRST FEW WEEKS that autumn, the queen sought solace in prayer, in meditation, in sacred music. Many times I came upon her kneeling on the prie-dieu in her chamber, or pacing in the abbey church, rosary in hand, before the graves of King Henry and Richard. "Joanna's tomb, and that of her baby, will be here, next to theirs," she told me one such day. To this she added, with a painfully sad smile, "After all the quarrels, the fighting, the estrangement—how strange that both children asked to be buried here, with him. The closeness they did not enjoy with their father in life, they will now have, in eternity."

She lowered her head as she uttered these words; the harsh rays of noon light from the tall, slanted windows caught the sharp angles of her cheekbones and mercilessly threw into relief the phalanx of deep wrinkles above the long, thin lines of her lips. "And I shall be buried here, too, of course," she went on. "There have been many days recently when I have prayed to God that He take me soon. I used to fear death. I no longer do."

The talk of her death filled me with overwhelming sadness and terror; for her to leave me, too—no, I could not bear the thought. "You may not fear your death, Your Majesty," I said, taking her hands in mine, "but *I* do, very much. It is too soon for you to leave me!"

Tears had come to her eyes. "Bless you, dear Isabelle," she murmured, drawing her arms around me.

WHETHER MY IMPLORING WORDS THAT day succeeded in buoying the queen's spirits, I am not certain; but, to my relief, her will to live seemed to revive in the following days. She summoned her most trusted counselors in an effort to shore up support for John in the fight against Philippe and Arthur. And she began to set her thoughts on her journey to Burgos, to the court of her daughter Lenora.

To my thrill, she asked me to accompany her. "It will be an adventure for you," she said. "Not an easy adventure, of course, but, hopefully, a memorable and productive one. We will cross the Pyrenees. You will see Roncevaux, and the place where Roland fought so valiantly. And most of all you will see Burgos. All say it is a splendid city, and my daughter's a splendid court."

Despite my delight at the idea of traveling with the queen, I did worry whether or not she was fit for such a long, demanding journey. One frosty autumn day, as we studied the map showing our projected route, I said, "Do you not think, Your Majesty, that you should perhaps

postpone this trip? To cross the Pyrenees in winter will not be easy.
Those mountain passes will be treacherous. Treacherous enough for
someone young, let alone—" Realizing my gaffe, I stopped, awkwardly.

"Let alone an old woman like myself?" she asked, one brow imperiously raised; I could not tell whether she was miffed or slightly amused.
"Is *that* what you were about to say?"

"I meant a woman your age, yes," I admitted.

"I have no time to waste. No season that will be any better. Besides, one can never be held hostage to elements over which one has no
control—weather being among them. And who knows," she mused, "if
I shall have the strength for this journey, come springtime? No," she said
decisively, "I must go now. These responsibilities fall to me, and to me
alone—they are the burdens of queenship."

ALAS, CIRCUMSTANCES DID NOT DICTATE that I accompany her:
about three weeks before our departure in December, both Clementia
and Marie fell ill—a terrible inflammation of the lungs, which wracked
their bodies with fever and made us fear for their lives. Even Sister
Philippa seemed shaken by the extent of their bodily weakness, and by
the dreadful coughing fits that came upon them all too frequently and
rendered their nights sleepless.

One morning a week before we were to depart for Spain, the queen
accompanied me to the infirmary to visit the two women. "You cannot
possibly leave them now," she decreed as we left. "Sister Philippa feels
the same way, I am quite certain. I could see it in her eyes."

"Then I shall stay here," I replied at once, both crushed and relieved.
"Should anything happen to either one of them if I were away—"

"You would never forgive yourself," said the queen.

"Yes," I replied, adding, "you know me all too well."

# CHAPTER 101

To my immense relief, Marie and Clementia began to improve shortly after the queen departed. Once they had fully recovered, life at the abbey returned to a vestige of normalcy—vestige, I say, because the region was suffering from privations of every kind. The encroachments of Philippe in Normandy and farther south meant that supplies of all kinds were growing alarmingly scarce. Our meals grew more meager; the supply of grain dwindled, and the livestock began to suffer from lack of proper fodder.

"Each day becomes more of a struggle," Clementia told me one morning. "There is so much we need, and when I think of the long winter ahead—" The abject despair in her voice, and the doleful look on her careworn face, shocked me. "Many to the north are suffering from hunger. Folk seeking refuge here have told us of Philippe's depredations, and of the sickness and pestilence that have ensued."

"Surely there is *something* we can do—"

Slowly shaking her head, she touched the silver cross that hung from her belt and softly recited a prayer.

"The silver," I murmured. Then, eagerly: "We have many silver objects in the treasury. And on the altar. They could be melted down, and we could sell the silver to pay for what we need. Any precious stones could be taken out and sold."

"Impossible! Those are holy objects, and most of them bequeathed to us by the king's family and the queen herself. What you propose is *unthinkable*."

"It is more unthinkable to let the sisters and our livestock starve," I retorted. "Do you think that would *really* be God's will—to let those in His holy house suffer, perhaps even die, in order to preserve objects made of precious metal?"

"They are not merely 'objects.' They are *holy* objects entrusted to us by our patrons, by the queen and her family."

"The queen would *never* choose them over the welfare of our community."

I watched, holding my breath, as she pondered this. "That may indeed be true, Isabelle," she finally conceded. "But only the abbess has the authority to allow such a drastic action, and even I would hesitate to ask her—"

"Then *I* will."

"Even if you convince the abbess—and I doubt you will succeed—the responsibility would rest with you. It will be *you*, Isabelle, who would have to confront the queen upon her return and explain your decision."

"I understand, Clementia." Turning to leave, I said, "I will speak with her today."

I sought out the abbess at once and explained what I had proposed to Clementia. She listened quietly, inscrutably, and when she spoke, it was in calm, measured tones. "Only the queen could possibly sanction the melting down of those objects," she said.

"The queen will understand, I assure you! She will not only approve but also *applaud* the decision. She would never choose objects over life."

The abbess looked at me with such unnerving intentness that, for a moment, I almost doubted my judgment. Finally, she spoke: "Perhaps you are right—we must do whatever we can. Let us meet later, with Clementia, to decide *which* objects, and how many we will need." Her eyes bore into me. "But you must agree, Isabelle, to take full responsibility for this decision, and to tell the queen yourself upon her return from Spain."

"I do, and will."

ALTHOUGH CLEMENTIA AND THE ABBESS were deeply concerned about the queen's impending reaction, the melting down of the silver and the funds this provided lessened the privations we might have otherwise endured that Christmas.

My spirits lifted when I learned that a messenger from the Hauteclare household had arrived with a letter. Heartened, as always, to glimpse the large, florid *F* of the signature, I read it at once, delighted to learn that Fastrada intended to visit us in the spring. It was another part of the letter, however, that most absorbed me:

> Only recently Hugh and Gallien had an encounter that made me think of you, and your past life. In the early autumn, the men ventured to Valkenswaard to meet the breeders of the finest falcons. There they chanced upon the master falconer employed long ago by Gerard—that cruel fellow, Ragnar, who had treated Gallien so badly. Hugh, ever curious, was determined to speak with him, and chose a moment to strike up a conversation when Gallien was occupied elsewhere.
>
> Ragnar seemed decidedly uncomfortable at seeing Hugh, and even more so when the latter brought up Gerard's tragic death—the very mention of which seemed to upset Ragnar greatly, and which he clearly did not want to discuss. Hugh then asked him if he had a particular mission in Valkenswaard. Yes, said Ragnar, he was intent on a gyrfalcon. Hugh assumed that his new employer had commissioned the purchase, but to his surprise Ragnar told him proudly that he was purchasing it for himself. "You have done very well then!" Hugh said. Ragnar boasted that he had had a run of luck at the dicing tables. Hugh had long heard rumors in hunting circles that Ragnar was addicted to gambling, and made it clear that he had done so well that he no longer had to serve as anyone's falconer. Only out of duress, he asserted, would he ever choose to be employed again. "That is partly why I understand the ways of falcons," he said, with that strange brutal laugh. "Like them, I love my freedom."

I set the letter down and began, slowly and contemplatively, to pace the hall. The very sight of Ragnar's name upon the page gave me a chill; I thought of his withering gaze, his simmering resentment. . . . But I finally cast aside those dispiriting thoughts, and tried to focus, rather, on Fastrada's possible visit. I would tell the happy news to Marie and Aiglette, and hastened to them.

They were sitting before the hearth, Marie reading aloud. Beside them on the bench, as if a member of the audience, stood the bronze falcon. "What are you reading?" I asked.

"A story about a princess whose father will not allow her to marry her true love because he is of a lowly station," said Marie. "And so her beloved, a valiant young man, goes off to seek his fortune in Cyprus. And then, one day—"

"Go on," I prodded, seeing that they were quite entranced. I did not yet mention the letter from Fastrada, knowing it would only prove a distraction.

Marie continued to read while Aiglette listened raptly—indeed, the latter was quite as still as the bronze falcon who sat beside her. How docile the falcon now appeared! How different from how it had appeared in years past, when I had thought it so fierce, almost menacing. But in Marie's and Aiglette's eyes, I realized now, the falcon had been transformed into quite a different creature—a companion, a charming plaything. But then they had no idea of its history, nor of the nature of the man who had given it to me. I wondered whether there would ever come a time when I would tell them.

# CHAPTER 102

O n New Year's Eve day—the first day of the new century—
the world was utterly blanketed in white, as if God had
elected to make of the landscape itself a tabula rasa.

As was my wont, I had awakened at dawn. I lit the fire at once, for
it was bitter cold; for a long time I stood before the frosted pane of
my window, gazing at the blanched, denuded branches of the orchard
beyond. Then I walked to the prie-dieu, knelt, and began to say my
prayers: I thanked God that Clementia had recovered, that "my girls"
were thriving, that Fastrada would visit us come spring. I prayed to the
Virgin, asking that she continue to protect us as we made our way into
the thirteenth century.

Then—warmer now, for the fire had taken hold—I walked to the
window and gazed out again. This time I thought of the queen, and her
long journey, and wondered about her progress; I thought of the perilous, icy roads, and of her, at her advanced age, crossing the daunting,
snowy mountains into Spain. Most of all I marveled, as I often did, at
her courage and determination.

Still preoccupied by such thoughts, I returned to the prie-dieu,
knelt, clasped my hands together, and prayed with special fervency for
the queen—praying, most of all, that we would receive word of her
very soon.

OUR PRAYERS WERE ANSWERED A few weeks later, when Clementia
and I were summoned to the chapter house: a messenger had arrived, bearing a letter affixed with the queen's seal. We hastened there to greet him.

Awaiting us in the vestibule was a short, barrel-chested fellow of
middle age with a piquant nose and incongruously large, pointed ears,

which rather resembled a donkey's. There was a certain vivacity to the man's persona, and a canniness about his eyes, that immediately intrigued me.

"Here is the letter," he announced, adding somewhat proudly, "I have come all the way from Spain. From the court of King Alphonso."

After thanking him, I asked that he wait to the side; then I began to read the letter aloud to Clementia. It informed us the queen fared well, and that she and her party had arrived in Burgos on the second week of January after a tiring but mercifully uneventful journey; she expected to return to France, by way of Bordeaux, come spring—perhaps, God willing, by Easter. From there, the queen would accompany her granddaughter—*which* granddaughter was not indicated—to Paris, where she would meet her future husband, the dauphin.

The official tone and foreign hand made it clear that the letter had been penned by a Spanish scribe. Its dry, detached nature left me rather unsatisfied and still longing for more details: a few impressions of the journey, and of Spain, perhaps.

I gestured to the messenger and called him forward. "What is your name, fellow?" I asked as he approached.

"Savaric, my lady. I come from the region of Toulouse."

The mention of Toulouse made me think, with a pang of sadness, of Joanna. "And you made the entire journey from Burgos yourself?"

"I did, my lady. And not an easy one, at that. I have made it before, but this time was the most difficult."

"The mountain passes must be treacherous in winter."

"They are hard enough in springtime and summer—but now"—he shook his head—"had it not been for the guide, and the sleds, and the packhorses—no, even I cannot imagine how I would have managed it. The cold and wind and the ice were fearsome."

"And Burgos itself? Did you spend much time there?"

"A few days. A most fair and well-defended city. And a most generous court."

"Generous?" asked Clementia.

"The court treated us well," he replied. "Ample provisions, fine quality ale, and a good clean pallet at night. What you would expect from the court of Queen Lenora," he added approvingly.

"Why is that?" I asked, intrigued.

"Because she is our queen Eleanor's daughter. And very like her mother, too."

"In appearance?" I asked.

"A little. She is tall, like her mother—handsome, I would call her." To this he added: "And like her mother, she has her wits about her."

Clementia and I exchanged amused glances. "How could you tell that, pray?" I asked.

He shrugged. "In my work, you quickly get a measure of people. After I arrived, Queen Lenora asked to see me herself. She had many questions about my journey from France. The condition of the roads, whether I had encountered thieves or gypsies—only once, I told her, but Saint Christopher had protected me." He made the sign of the cross, then fingered the medal that dangled from his belt. "And she seemed to know the supplies I would need for the return," he went on, "and the route I would take. Not only to reach here, the abbey, but also for the final part."

"The final part?" I asked.

"From here I go north, to Rouen." He gave a dry laugh. "Not a long journey, but these days it may almost be as hard as crossing the mountains into Spain."

"What do you mean?" Clementia asked.

"The roads are not easy to pass. The King of France has his men, his agents, everywhere. But that is not all: to the west, by the border with Brittany, there are Prince Arthur's men—though some would say they are one and the same as King Philippe's, and just as well armed. No"—he gave a woeful sigh —"this is not the world we knew with King Richard. Much has changed—" Then, looking slightly abashed, he stopped.

"Go on," Clementia prodded. "You do us a great favor by imparting this information. It is important that we know. We are rather isolated here."

"There is no sense of order, Sister, only growing fear," he went on. "When I made my way here, I passed through Gascony, and then through Poitevin country. The folk in those lands are wild, as we know, and had no real liking for King Richard. But they respected and feared him. And *now*"—he shook his head in mild disgust—"now it is not the same. Even the men who fight for the king are not the same. They are mostly mercenaries and such vermin. Men from the Brabant, and others recruited from Wales and Ireland."

"We are in a new century, and we have a new king," I said, all too aware that this hardly sufficed as an explanation.

"Let us hope God protects us," he said vehemently.

"And may He protect you, on your journey to Rouen," said Clementia, blessing him with the sign of the cross. "Come—I shall escort you to the kitchen." She gave a small smile. "We, too, can offer you some ale—though I cannot promise it compares to that of Queen Lenora's household."

SEVERAL MONTHS LATER, IN MARCH, another messenger—alas, not Savaric— brought us a letter from the queen with details of her return journey. She planned to accompany her granddaughter only as far as Bordeaux; from there, escorted by King John, the girl would proceed to Paris, where she would meet her betrothed. The queen would return directly to Fontevraud, hoping to arrive at the abbey by Easter.

"What do you make of this news?" I asked, turning to Clementia. "I know the queen was determined to accompany her granddaughter to the court in Paris. She has never shirked from an encounter with Philippe."

"I suspect she feels the journey all the way to Paris would be too long, and too exhausting," she replied. "It is easy for us to forget that she has almost reached her eightieth year. It only seems odd that there is no mention of the granddaughter *by name*. I assume it will be the eldest of the remaining three, Urraca."

"I am not so certain," I replied. "The queen gave me the impression that the birth order mattered far less to her than other qualities. Whomever she has chosen will, in her judgment, have the mettle of the future Queen of France."

# CHAPTER 103

It was a visibly aged and exhausted queen Eleanor who returned to the abbey shortly before Easter. Upon her arrival, Sister Philippa urged her to rest; unusually, the queen did not resist, and even seemed to welcome Philippa's ministrations.

For once, I did not hasten to see the queen in private, so keenly did I dread disclosing my role in the melting down of the silver. Finally, on the day before Good Friday, I sat with the queen alone in her quarters. "There is something I must discuss with you, Your Majesty," I began. "Something that has been greatly weighing upon me."

"So *that* explains your reticence," she said, her gaze so penetrating that I became even more apprehensive.

I took a deep breath; then slowly, and deliberately, I explained what I had urged the abbess and Clementia to do, and why. "I take full responsibility for the decision. I realize these were not only pieces of great value, but part of your legacy, and treasured symbols of your patronage."

An expression of patience and understanding had come to her eyes. "I would have made the same decision myself, Isabelle, and am heartened, indeed proud, that you chose to. A sign of strength—strength and wisdom. I admire what you did, and will tell the abbess and Clementia so."

"Thank you, Your Majesty," I said with a rush of immense relief, taking her hands in mine.

"*Now* I understand why you have been so preoccupied. Why you have not yet pressed me with a hundred questions about my journey to Spain," she observed spryly.

"The very fact you say that cheers me, Your Majesty! It means you, too, are feeling better."

"I *am*, happily." She tilted her head back in that habitual way—both sly and magisterial. "Come now, Isabelle," she teased. "*Surely* you have some questions."

"You know me all too well, Your Majesty," I replied with a slight smile. "Tell me, why did you not choose queen Lenora's *eldest* daughter as bride for the dauphin?"

"Yes, the envoys from France also seemed quite puzzled that it was not Urraca who had been selected. But"—her mischievous expression lent her a momentarily youthful air—"there is no reason to rigidly adhere to custom with decisions of such magnitude. Therefore, I chose the third daughter, Blanca."

"How did you explain your decision to the French?"

"That I feared the name Urraca might seem too foreign to the French; that I knew their 'acute sensitivity to language' and that 'Blanca' was easier on the tongue. They seemed to accept this explanation—the *fools*." Her visible delight in the ruse made me laugh aloud. "It was clear to me, from our first meeting, that Blanca, rather than her elder sister, had the requisite character to be the future Queen of France.

"Over the weeks that followed," she continued, "I observed her closely, and I *tested* her. We went riding together. Once or twice, in bad conditions, she fell, but then she quickly remounted without a complaint, without even a murmur. I asked those who went hawking with her how she performed: whether she was brave and persistent. They confirmed she was. I asked her tutors about her facility with languages, and whether she had a steady, inquiring mind. All affirmed she did. And lastly, I arranged to play chess with her."

"As you did with me, when we first met—"

"Yes," she replied. "And I was right in discerning your keen intelligence, was I not? I did the same with Blanca. I have no doubt about my appraisal of her—that she has the mettle to be queen. And that is why *she*, not Urraca, is on her way to Paris now."

"And the journey itself?"

"The ride to Burgos was not so difficult. The return was far more challenging. The wind, the cold, the snow, as we made our way over the mountains. I knew it would not be easy. But nothing important ever is." She looked at me with piercing directness. "Remember that, Isabelle, when I am gone."

Of late, the queen had begun to intersperse the phrase "when I am gone" in her conversation—four words that filled me with inexpressible sadness. "I am not at all surprised that you achieved what you set out to accomplish," I said quietly. "I am only upset that I was not able to accompany you."

"One day, after I die, you must go to Spain, to Burgos." She seemed to have noticed the sadness in my eyes, for she quickly added, in a tone so comically imperious that I knew it was intended to cheer me, "Indeed, as my subject, I *command* you to do so." The next instant, however, her voice resumed its former gravity. "After I am gone, Isabelle, you must take my letters and documents—those I have not instructed you to destroy—to Burgos. Marie and Aiglette must go with you on the journey. I know Lenora will warmly welcome you."

"I promise I will do *everything* you ask of me, Your Majesty," I said, struggling with sadness at the idea of her death as I embraced her. After we drew apart, I asked, "How would you describe Lenora, Your Majesty—is she at all like Joanna?"

"She has *far* more of her father in her," she said. "Indeed, I would say, that of my daughters, she is the most felicitous combination of Henry and myself. And she is certainly the daughter most ideally suited to queenship. I discern the blood of her grandmother Mathilda in her. She is Plantagenet through and through." This was said admiringly: as the queen had aged, she had come to view her late, formidable mother-in-law with far more admiration and understanding than she had earlier in her life.

"And while Lenora is well suited to court life," she continued, "she also greatly values contemplation. Her faith is strong and unwavering. She has had a most marvelous abbey erected. It reminds me of Fontevraud—but an *English* Fontevraud. The overall plan, and its church—all quite Plantagenet in spirit. Her father would be very proud of her."

"How joyful it must have been for you to see her after so many years!"

"I wept tears of joy when I first saw her. She was only seven when I accompanied her to Bordeaux to meet the envoys from Spain. I shall never forget the feeling of her little arms around me, and how she clung to me, sobbing, when it came time to bid her adieu. I have done many difficult things in my life but giving up my daughters when they were little girls was among the most wrenching. To know that she is well, that she flourishes as queen and mother, gives me great contentment. God has blessed me indeed, with Lenora." With a deep sigh she added, bitterly, "If only He had let me keep my Joanna!" She rose and walked slowly to the window. "The garden will be in bloom before long," she observed, but with a surprising, and uncharacteristic, lack of exhilaration. "For the first time in my life," she announced, turning to me, "I have begun to feel weary of the world."

The admission stunned, even frightened, me. "Remember you have only just returned from a long, exhausting journey, Your Majesty. You will feel more buoyant with each passing day," I told her reassuringly.

"Let us hope you are right, and that my weariness will soon abate. Too many depend on me." She looked down, twisting her great amethyst ring. "And too much remains to be done."

# CHAPTER 104

The queen's thoughts turned with marked intensity to her own resting place and the design for her tomb. I found this an exceedingly painful subject; but, as was typical of her, she confronted the planning with fortitude, precision, and even, on occasion, a certain elegiac dreaminess unusual for her.

One day, as we walked to the abbey church, she reflected, "I shall never forget seeing the tombs I saw in Outremer when I was a young woman. Some in the environs of Constantinople, others outside smaller cities. They were built by the ancients and had figures of the dead carved upon them—many still had bright touches of paint."

Her description eerily sparked memories of what Bertuccio had recounted to me long ago. "One day, shortly after I married," I said, "a strange fellow, a peddler of relics and other artifacts, came to Ravinour. He told me about his journeys in Italy, and about a region with tombs that had been placed in deep, cave-like rooms; one had to descend below ground to see them. The tombs were sculpted with figures upon them depicting the deceased. They were so true to life, he said, that one almost expected the dead to rise and speak."

"I, too, saw such tombs years ago when I traveled from Sicily to Rome. They were indeed haunting—" Her voice trailed off. But then, the next instant, as we approached the entrance to the church, she resumed in her customarily definitive tone. "When I pass from this world, I want my resting place to be similar in spirit to those ancient tombs—I want to be portrayed as if I were alive." To this she added, "My tomb must reflect not only me, but also make *others* wonder about the woman I was. About the *woman* I was. It must at once capture me and have an aura of enigma. A paradox, you will say. But what is life without paradox, after all?"

"True," I mused, adding, "yet it surprises me that you said *woman*, not queen."

"That I was *queen* will be quite obvious," she returned as we descended into the crypt; the air here was cold, with a biting dampness, though outside the sun was shining. "Do not think for a moment that I intend to be depicted without a crown!" We came to King Henry's tomb. "I will be buried next to my husband, the king. And near my son Richard, the king, and near my Joanna. Moreover," she continued in her authoritative way, "I want to be shown with something that defines me."

"A scepter?"

"A most disappointingly unimaginative answer, Isabelle," she retorted. "No—I shall not be shown with a scepter, but with a *book*. When I think of my years in captivity, and of other crucial moments of my life, I realize it is literature, poetry, and books of song that have made me what I am, and which have sustained me in times of tribulation."

"No doubt it will be assumed that it is a book of prayers, a Psalter."

"Let them think what they will." She smiled slyly, arching her brow. "You and I will know the truth."

I WAS IN THE MIDST of transcribing dictation from the queen when a letter for me arrived several days later. It came from the household of Guy and was accompanied by a tiny packet tied with string. I opened the letter with some trepidation and began to read:

*To the Lady Isabelle, the Lady Ermengarde sends tidings*

> Your brother Guy has died. He had been in declining health
> for the past several months—an illness which robbed him of
> all appetite and overwhelmed him with abject melancholy. Our
> physician, a most eminent specialist, attributed these conditions
> to the imbalance of humors which had long plagued him. The

illness contributed, no doubt, to his dreadful moodiness and shortness of temper, all of which I forbore with my customary patience. (Indeed, I confess with some pride that he often likened my temperament to that of an angel's.) He was bled and given various potions and emetics—at great cost to me, I should add—but to no effect. He died several days ago and will be buried on the morrow. He requested the most austere funeral possible. "Bury me as you would an ascetic or a Cistercian monk, like the good Saint Bernard," he urged me. Thus, for his final resting place, I ordered a plain coffin of pine.

During his final weeks, Guy begged me to refrain from sending word to you and Amélie about his deteriorating condition. "I do not want to trouble my sisters," he told me with great adamance. "It would fill me with shame to be seen this way—so weak and sickly. Let me die in peace, with the good Lord watching over me. There is only one person on earth, one person only, who gives me true solace, and that is you, dear wife."

At the very end, however, he asked that I send you the enclosed—a keepsake of sorts.

*Fare you well.*
*Lady Ermengarde de Lapalisse*

I stared at the small, cramped signature; its constricted, miserly quality seeming to epitomize the character of the cold, uncaring woman to whom it belonged. I took up the little packet and untied the string warily: enclosed was a medal of Saint Christopher similar to the one from my father, which Guy had given me the last time we were together. So he had remembered that day—perhaps even our bittersweet conversation, with its sense of finality, and of the journeys both of us knew he would never take. And then I recalled the moment when, with overweening pride, he had told me about his betrothal to the Lady Ermengarde; and, later, his feigned, almost painful heartiness as he described their "satisfying and productive" marriage; the concern I had felt for him, and the rare moment of empathy between us as we sat together reminiscing after our father's funeral.

I held the medal in my palm and began to reflect sadly upon Guy, upon the past. . . . Melancholy overcame me, and I set the medal down. Then I threw the letter into the fire, watching with perverse pleasure as the leaping flames encroached upon, and then devoured, the pinched signature of Lady Ermengarde.

# CHAPTER 105

L ater that spring, and throughout the early summer, Normandy and the regions around us erupted in violence and disorder. A series of shifting alliances—many sparked by King John's various appetites and impetuosity—caused further chaos. In early August, the king enraged the powerful Hugh of Lusignan by spiriting away Isabella of Angoulême, a fabled blond beauty to whom Lusignan had been betrothed, and thus ensuring lasting enmity between the two men and their families. "I do not approve of the match, though I can understand why John is besotted by her," the queen told me when word of John's nuptials reached us. "Isabella is lovely, intelligent, and alluring."

"She sounds rather like *you*, Your Majesty," I said.

"Compared to her, I was already rather advanced in age when I married," the queen replied with a dry smile.

"How old is she?"

"Fourteen. But I am told she is still physically a girl. Let us hope, for once, John manages to be patient. Who knows how long it will take her to produce an heir?"

At first, the controversy surrounding John's marriage distracted the queen from other matters—notably, her hatred of her widowed daughter-in-law Constance of Brittany and her son, the queen's grandson, Prince Arthur. But then, one afternoon a few weeks later, as I sat in the royal quarters with her, an envoy arrived with news: Constance had died after giving birth to twin girls. The queen, her expression impassive, merely remarked dismissively, "What a pity," while I looked away, avoiding the envoy's eyes. A few days later, having been summoned to the queen's chambers, I learned that another envoy—from the French court, this time—had just departed. "He brought word from Paris," the queen informed me; I knew from the lilt in her voice that the news must have been heartening. "Blanca seems to have endeared herself to Philippe and the dauphin," she said. "For that, at least, we can be grateful. That development will help us—John, most of all."

"How grateful the king must be for all you have done for him, Your Majesty! It was *you* who had the perspicacity to choose Blanca. And *you* who took that long, hard journey to Spain to fetch her."

"Alas, if only he *were* grateful!" she cried. "But one has only to remember how thanklessly he treated his brother Richard, even after he had forgiven John for his treachery." She fell silent, her finger tracing the sword-wielding figures on the Becket casket beside her. "One never knows with John. He can be fulsome one moment, utterly condemning the next. But let us talk of other things."

ALL THAT WINTER NEWS CAME to us in the usual ways—through letters received by the queen, and sometimes by messengers themselves, though, to my disappointment, few were as observant and memorable as Savaric. It was often through itinerant peddlers and traders, as well, that we heard about events—not only in surrounding regions, but in those across the Channel, where the situation continued to darken.

During Advent, a royal envoy arrived bearing a letter, which I read to the queen. The king, it informed her, would soon depart for England. He would spend Christmas in Oxford; from there he intended to make an extensive journey to the north—Yorkshire, Northumberland, and Cumbria—in the new year.

It was only several months later, in February, however, and quite by chance, that we learned more about the king's progression through northern England; this, from Clementia and Marie, who had recently traveled to Le Mans to purchase supplies. There they had encountered traders who had recently crossed the Channel from England.

"The Englishmen were very well informed," said Marie. "And quite wealthy, to judge by the look of them. They told us they had heard much talk of the king's journey from folk they encountered near Newcastle. People said the young queen is ravishing, and that everyone tried to catch a glimpse of her. The king travels with an *enormous* retinue, they said, as well as crates of treasures." Almost breathlessly, her eyes shining, she added, "And he travels with an entire *library* of his own, as well. Imagine!"

"The king is known to have a lust for books," I told her. "The queen says he will go to any length to purchase them, or to commission splendid copies. But do continue, Marie—"

"It seems that the king had heard rumors of buried Roman treasure near a town called Corbridge," she went on. "Not far from the great wall crossing the north of England. Perhaps now you understand why I thought this story might interest you, Lady Isabelle. I remember you mentioned your grandfather telling you about that region, and about the wall built by the Roman emperor—"

"Yes," I replied. "He *did* tell me those stories, and he even mentioned rumors of buried treasure."

"The traders had had dealings with the monks at Hexham Abbey, nearby," Marie went on. "The king had lodged there while his men dug for treasure. The monks told them that the men conducting the search were a brutal lot—one of them, Vautière, especially, whose *nom de guerre* is 'The Vulture.' But you look as if your thoughts are wandering—"

"I was thinking of Richard and Châlus, and of John and Corbridge," I said. "Two brothers, both kings, both perpetually in need of money, both compelled to find buried treasure. Did they find anything?"

"Nothing of value," said Clementia. "Only some bits of lead, and bronze, apparently. But there is another aspect to the story, which Marie and I thought would interest you. Did you not tell me long ago about a Norman, Tancred de Bernay, who was among those you met at the court in England, when you resided there with the queen?"

"I did. He was very ambitious."

"It seems with John's ascent his fortunes have risen even higher. He is now among those in the innermost circle," said Clementia. "It was he, together with this notorious Vautière, who led the foray to Corbridge, and other such forays, too." She had pronounced "forays" with sarcasm. "The traders told us that Tancred and Vautière were known to be pitiless. They alluded to terrible incidents and the razing of villages that refused to cooperate with their demands."

"Have you told the queen about all of this?" I asked.

"Not yet," replied Clementia.

"I suggest you wait," I said. "John's search for treasure will only bring back bitter memories of Richard and Châlus. And the mention of Tancred will remind her of being in captivity, in England. Her health has been precarious, and many other serious matters preoccupy her. No doubt she will learn about this soon enough."

# CHAPTER 106

The death of Constance, the ill-fated expedition to Corbridge, the encroachment of King Philippe's forces, the plotting against "the usurper," her grandson Prince Arthur—those were among the events that contributed to the darkening landscape around us. How often, during those subsequent years, did I thank God for the relative peace of the abbey, and for the loving company of those I held so dear—Clementia, Marie, and Aiglette.

My relationship with the queen occupied another stratum: I loved, admired, and respected her but knew I would never quite know her to the extent I did Clementia and the girls. As always, the queen's ambitions continued to influence virtually all her actions—the alliances she sought, the commands she issued, and the family necropolis she continued to plan with imagination and precision. But increasingly, during the years I dwell on now, the earliest years of the new century, another element began to preoccupy, even consume, her: the preservation and safekeeping of her letters—both private and official—as well as the myriad documents and writs that had accrued during her long reign.

I often ruminated whether she would have been quite so intent on their safekeeping had the character of her only remaining son been different. With each passing day I knew, with more and more certainty, the answer to that question: while she had always been realistic about her son's flaws, it became clear that she had hoped—in a rare leap of naivete—that the assumption of power might bring forth his best self; that the crown, the scepter, and the oaths he had sworn as the sacred oil anointed his forehead might help diminish his worst inclinations. But as his reign continued, it became evident this was not to be: the flashes of statesmanship, of military brilliance, of judicious thinking, were all too few. If anything, power had unleashed some of his worst character-istics: greed, vengefulness, capriciousness, paranoia, and cruelty.

Those flaws would have been painful enough for any mother of a son to acknowledge, let alone the mother of a king. But then something else happened, something else that was even worse: she had come to distrust him.

ONE MORNING DURING ADVENT OF the year 1202, she summoned me to her chamber. Upon entering, I noticed a trunk of medium size, which had been placed near her chair.

"Take a seat, Isabelle," she told me. "There is another private proj-ect I would like to discuss. I want you to help me sort, organize, and preserve my letters and personal documents—in addition to compiling the transcription of our ongoing work. When I am gone, I must know that all my papers are in good hands."

I did not reply at once, for that phrase "when I am gone" still made me inwardly start. "I had always assumed that your papers and letters would be taken care of by the king and his chancellery as well," I fi-nally said.

There was a certain severity in her expression, and in her tone, when she responded. "Have I not taught you, Isabelle, to be wary of *assump-tions!* I should think it would be evident," she continued slowly and de-liberately, "that my son is not someone one would necessarily trust with such things. It is his *own* legacy that consumes him—I doubt he gives nearly as much thought to that of his family. Of course, he will make a modest effort to honor me when I am dead: something pro forma, no doubt. But in the end I am not convinced he thinks of anyone but himself."

"But *you,* Your Majesty," I interjected, "you have done so much to help him! Without your efforts, many powerful lords would not have chosen to support him. The Vicomte of Thouars, and so many others. You did not even condemn John when he stole Isabella of Angoulême from Hugh of Lusignan. And think of the troubles that have ensued from that single action! You have been unwaveringly loyal and generous to the king."

"And therefore, you think—you *assume*—that he would return my efforts in kind."

"Yes."

"Then you are *wrong*," she countered, with a small, sad shrug. For the first time, her mask seemed to fall: what I glimpsed was not so much a queen, but a mother who had come to acknowledge that she not only disliked her son, but also questioned his every motive. "After I die," she continued, reassuming her queenly, imperious stance, "I want you to make certain all my property—my letters, my most precious belongings—do not fall into his hands. Or into those of these new men around him. As soon as I am dead, you must take these things to Spain, to Lenora. *She* is the child I trust. She will make certain that my bequests are properly executed. That letters that I will bequeath to Blanca, for instance, will find their way to her in Paris. That certain documents I designate will be sent across the Channel to the royal archives. That the jewels I leave for Lenora and for those closest to me"—here she took my hand—"will not be filched by the others."

I knew what she had meant by "the others"—she, too, must have been told about Tancred and his methods, and about the new men who had come from Wales and Ireland, like the one they called "The Vulture."

"You entrust me with an immense responsibility, Your Majesty," I said, at once honored and proud. But then I felt some disquietude: there was now another royal clerk, William, who was even more possessive of his duties than the punctilious Rupert. "Are you quite certain that Rupert and William will not be resentful that you have chosen me for this task?"

"I have no intention of telling them. Nor do I care what they think, and nor should you. I have not an iota of doubt, dear Isabelle, that you will fulfill my every expectation. In the time to come, the time I have left," she resumed briskly, "we will review these things together." She paused, as if weighing a particularly important matter. "I suspect there will also be some documents—letters especially—which I will not want history to own, or indeed for anyone to see. These you will help me destroy."

"Are you quite certain this is necessary?"

"Yes. In the future, I will designate some letters and documents to be burned. And I will entrust you, as well, with that task."

"I shall not find that easy to do—"

"As I have told you before, what is important is seldom easy to accomplish." Again, she took my hand, pressing it hard, her eyes fixed upon me. "Swear to me on the Virgin that you will do what I ask of you, once I am gone."

"I will, I will," I promised; she smiled serenely. "When shall we begin?" I asked.

"Tomorrow."

# CHAPTER 107

One afternoon during the turbulent autumn of the year 1203, the queen asked to see me on an urgent matter; I suspected it concerned the designs for the tombs. No doubt the queen, whose powers of sight had sorely diminished, wanted me to describe the final drawings to make certain that the changes she had requested had been implemented.

I entered the queen's chamber, where she sat before the hearth in sober splendor. Her servant announced my name. "That is hardly necessary," reprimanded the queen with a sharpness I had come to notice in her later years. "I know Lady Isabelle's footsteps. Now let us be."

Her hand—frail and weighted with her favorite amethyst and ruby rings—groped for me. "Come, sit near here, close by." After I did so, the queen continued, "We have a matter of importance to discuss."

"If it concerns the drawings, Your Majesty, they have indeed been completed. I have not had the opportunity to study them yet, but I shall on the morrow. And then we can look at them together." I had tactfully said "together," for the queen's waning eyesight was painful for both of us to acknowledge.

"It is not the tombs I want to discuss," she replied at once. "It is something else—a command from the king. He has ordered us to assemble some books from the scriptorium for him. He is greatly fond of books and takes great pride in his library. As he does in many other"—a certain tightness about the lips registered her displeasure—"less elevated forms of luxury. He is no stranger to luxury, my son."

"Has the king specified which kind of books?"

"Bestiaries—not surprising, given his passion for animals, for hunting, for hawks. Several for him, and others—and this is most important—as a gift for the pope. Innocent's support is crucial to his cause." To this she added, in a slightly jaundiced tone, "His Holiness appears to be among my son's few remaining allies—but even he needs to be placated, it seems. Review the volumes in our collection," she continued. "See if there are any of suitable quality. Commission new ones, if necessary, and have them begun at once. I shall instruct the king to assign one of his trusted men, if such a person exists"—her expression was caustic—"to fetch them. Someone of rank and experience. This is not a mission for a mere messenger. Not these days," she lamented, "with Philippe's forces encroaching. His agents are everywhere, I am told. The roads are treacherous."

"I do not think we have any bestiaries that would meet the king's standards," I replied, for I knew him to be exacting. "The finest copies were sent to Poitiers not long ago. I would have to ask Marie, and the other scribes, to create new ones. And that will take time. If some are meant for the royal collection, and others for the pope, I know that Marie and her fellow scribes would only want to send their best work." What I did not say was that it would terrify me, for Marie's sake, to disappoint the rageful, punitive king.

"How much time will this require?" she asked.

"At least four months."

"The king will not wait any longer than that. He is by nature impatient." To this she added, with a sigh of resignation, "As we know all too well."

"If Marie begins at once, the books might be ready by Epiphany."

"No earlier?"

I shook my head. "Even that will be a challenge."

"I shall convey that to the king. If I tell him Epiphany, then Epiphany it will be. He may be king," she added, drawing herself up, "but I am still the dowager queen, and his mother, after all."

"He owes you much, Your Majesty."

"He owes me everything," she replied with bitter vehemence. "Even *he* knows that, I believe! And if he does not—" But here she stopped, abruptly, only to ruminate, woefully, "How very different he is from my Richard! How lacking in those qualities I treasured in my beloved son. . . ." Her voice trailed off in a way that happened all too often those days, as if she were grappling with memories and truths too painful to allow.

I stood up. "I shall leave you now, Your Majesty. If the books are to be ready in time, I must speak with Marie at once."

"Give me your hand before you leave," she beseeched in a softer voice, adding, "my sight may have dimmed, but I can still feel. Ah, you are wearing the ring I gave you," she murmured, my hand in hers.

"It will never, ever leave my finger, Your Majesty."

Her eyes closed, she continued almost mournfully, "The warm hands of youth! How strange to think that I was once young—young and daring." Then, with fierce poignancy, she added, "And what I dared, I *did!*"

"You did indeed, Your Majesty," I replied, overcome with sadness as I recalled the vital woman she had been when I had met her, twenty years before.

SEVERAL MONTHS LATER, CLEMENTIA URGENTLY sought me out. "I have just learned that the king's emissary will arrive within weeks," she told me. Her demeanor was somber, and she seemed unusually tense. "The messenger gave me his name: Roger de Vautière."

"You utter the name as if it had a special significance."

"It does. Do you not recall? Marie and I first heard about him from those traders at Le Mans. And then, more recently, his name was mentioned in a letter from our sisters at Amesbury. Vautière served the king in Ireland, and subsequently in England, for years. It seemed that he passed through the abbey at Amesbury last winter. He and his men liberally partook of provisions, then seized treasure, relics, and whatever else they could"—her tone was cryptic—"all in the name of the king. Vautière is known to be among the king's most ruthless commanders. 'The Vulture' they call him."

"Ah, yes, of course, now I remember your mentioning him," I murmured. Then I offered, "It does not surprise that such an emissary should have been chosen," I offered. "The queen told me she would instruct the king to send someone of rank and experience."

"Then the king has clearly heeded his mother's advice," she replied drily. "Vautière will stop first at the treasury at Chinon—then only a short ride to us here." She began to pace to and fro. "The foray to the treasury is vital. Word has come that the king's forces need money for arms and supplies for the siege of Gaillard. It will require someone of Vautière's authority and forcefulness to secure what is necessary." She seemed to hesitate before adding, "Particularly now, since the king has fled to England."

"The king—fled to England?" I repeated, astounded.

"He crossed the Channel a few weeks ago."

"But what of Château Gaillard, and its defense?"

She shook her head in despair. "He has left the siege to those he trusts most—to loyalists like Vautière and Robert de Vieuxpont. A dwindling number, alas—so many of his nobles have defected to Philippe. That is why the pope's support is critical. The gifts—the books Marie and the scribes have created—are a way to woo His Holiness and further strengthen his support. They are as valuable as any treasure." She continued to pace. "Do you remember a few years ago," she said, turning to me, "when we heard about King John's expedition in the north of England in the winter—the search for Roman treasure at Corbridge, near Hexham Abbey?"

"Yes—of course."

"Vautière was among the king's men then," Clementia continued. "We learned from those at Hexham Abbey that he razed villages and was merciless to the folk in the region. Although the king's men found no gold or silver, that did not seem to impair Vautière's position vis-à-vis the king—remarkably enough, since he was among those who had organized the expedition." Her face, with its vestige of its former beauty, looked especially pale, worn, and grave. "The idea that Vautière has been chosen only emphasizes the importance that the king—and the queen, as well—ascribes to these books." Then, even more urgently, "Are they ready?"

"Almost. It remains for Marie to add the final touches."

"Tell her she must finish as soon as possible," she ordered. "Tell her I permit her *every* liberty, *every* privilege, in order for her to complete the work." She leaned closer, her hand clutching my shoulder. "I know it is terribly cold, Isabelle, and the hours of daylight few. If she requires an extra supply of candles or firewood, we will provide it. There is not an instant to lose. Go and tell her that now."

# CHAPTER 108

After ten more days of intense work, Marie and the scribes completed the books; a few days later, on a bitter cold after-noon during Epiphany, Clementia's servant, Grecia, informed me that the emissary from the king had arrived. "A soldier," she said. She looked frightened.

"Did you hear his name?"

"It sounded like 'Vautour'—"

Vautière, I thought with disquiet. "Where are he and Sister Clementia now?"

"In the chapter house. She told me to tell you that she will give him provisions, and then a letter from the queen for the king, once it is ready. You must go to the scriptorium at once, she said. They will meet you there."

I arrived at the scriptorium to find Marie at her desk, quill in hand. It was damp and icy cold that day. No one else was there; only a scribe of Marie's obsessiveness would have chosen to work under such harsh conditions. She wore woolen gloves without fingers, pausing occasion-ally to warm her hands with her breath. As I approached, she looked up, her eyes both radiant and inwardly absorbed.

"The emissary from the king has arrived," I told her. "He is with Sister Clementia now. He will be here soon to collect the books."

"All is ready. We have set them over there." She pointed to a casket on a cabinet beyond. "I thought it best not to secure the casket, in the event he wants to inspect them first. I have left some cord to the side."

I rubbed my hands together. "How cold it is, Marie! You have let the fire die down. I cannot fathom how you are still able to work. It cannot be good for you."

She shrugged, "When I am concentrating, I do not notice things like the cold."

I glanced at the door, expecting Clementia to enter at any moment. "What are you working on?" I asked, partly to deflect my own nervousness.

"The Psalter I promised for the queen. The page with the Archangel—my very favorite!"

I leaned closer to examine the design in progress—a nearly completed depiction of Saint Michael transfixing Satan, an image from the Book of Revelations. A wide red border with delicately drawn flowers, hawks, and doves surrounded the startling central image of the glittering-eyed Archangel himself, sword in hand, as he slayed the green-tinged dragon and the writhing, grimacing devils at his feet. "This is among your very best," I began, only to be cut short by the sound of footsteps coming from the stairwell below.

The door opened. Clementia entered—a slender, stately figure in white followed by a tall, heavily bearded man in a chain mail hauberk.

"Sister Clementia," I said, greeting her in the formal manner customary for the occasion.

She acknowledged me in kind, with a solemn nod. "May I present Roger de Vautière," she said. "He has been sent by the king to fetch the books and to deliver a message to the queen. He has just come from Chinon."

I curtseyed and then exchanged glances with him, only to find myself drawing back, partly out of revulsion. One side of his face was disfigured by a thick web of scars; the look in his eyes was glacial, contemptuous. There was a brutality, a feral scent, about him; I thought of the mercenaries at Barfleur.

"I assume the roads were difficult," I said, struggling not to avert my gaze.

"We are accustomed to such roads and conditions," he replied in a strikingly low, guttural voice, all the while observing me with an intentness that made me uncomfortable. Then his eyes took in the chamber before finally settling on Marie, who stood at her desk, watching us. "And that young woman over there?" he asked. "Who is she?"

"She is one of our most accomplished scribes." I gestured to Marie, who made a deep curtsey.

"She may continue her work," he said, his eyes still fixed upon her as she resumed her seat. Clementia and I exchanged uneasy glances, for his lingering gaze had a disturbing, even sinister, undercurrent, as if he were thinking, What a pity such a comely young woman should be wasted here, at a nunnery.

"I assume the books are ready," he said.

"Yes," I replied. "They are ready for you to inspect, if you wish, before they are secured for travel."

"I shall leave you to that, while I see if the queen's letter for the king is ready," said Clementia. "The queen is somewhat slower in her dictation these days."

I had been trying, meanwhile, to invent a reason for Marie to leave. "I suggest Marie go with you to help the queen finish the letter, Sister Clementia," I said. "She is adept at taking the queen's dictation."

"Excellent idea. I shall take her with me," she replied, before turning to Vautière. "When you have inspected the books, Lady Isabelle will show you to the chapter house. I shall await you there. I am sure you must be eager to be on your way."

"You forget there is one *other* matter," he announced. "I must deliver the message to the queen from the king."

"It is customary for *us* to deliver all letters to the queen," she countered.

"It is *not* a letter," he retorted. "It is a message I am to communicate to her myself, privately."

"Very well." She beckoned to Marie.

After they left, a forbidding silence descended upon the chamber. A thick, obscuring snow had begun to fall; the windows, frosted over, were now opaque. "This way," I said. "I shall show you where we have set aside the books." I walked toward the cabinet. "Here." I placed my hand upon the casket and forced myself to look at him.

But he was not looking at the casket; he was looking at me closely, ferociously. I felt my cheeks redden. I wanted to flee.

He took off his gloves, slowly and deliberately, and tucked them into his belt. "Either you have no idea who I really am," he ventured in an oddly bemused voice, "or you are an even more accomplished dissembler than I thought."

Confusion overtook me; I had no idea what he meant, what he could possibly be talking about; but then, suddenly, when I glimpsed the supercilious look of his flickering dark blue eyes, and caught a certain angle of his profile, I realized, stupefied, that it was Gerard. "*No*, it cannot be!" I stammered.

"It can. And it *is*," he replied with a grim, triumphant smile, his eyes with a peculiar gleam. "I have long dreamed of this moment. There have been times when the plotting of it, the imagining it, have kept me alive—the thought of seeing the expression on your face when you realized I had survived."

"You never died—" I murmured.

"You look disappointed, Isabelle." His tone was weirdly, and almost imperceptibly, wounded.

"I am stunned. Stunned—" Slowly, ever so slowly, I was beginning to grasp that yes, it was, truly, Gerard who stood before me. "You escaped the fire, then," I murmured, my hands clenched tight.

"A brilliant deduction." He raised his brow. "So it would seem."

"But there was a body found—"

"Someone else was with me. He did not escape; *I* did." He seemed to meditate, triumphantly, on this. "I not only escaped," he continued, "I survived, I fled, I prospered. But one thing I knew and knew for certain: it was only a question of time before I would find you. Once I returned to France last year, to join the king's men in Rouen, I began to connive a reason to come to Fontevraud. To your holy fortress, as it were. I was prepared to volunteer for any mission that took me south, to this region. But in the end, the fates smoothed the way. The king ordered me to go to Chinon and then to come here, for the books."

"But your voice! I did not recognize it—"

"The result of a wound to the neck," he replied, adding mordantly, "happily, the base Irishman who inflicted it is dead."

Still struggling to comprehend, I murmured, "No one thought you could possibly have survived the fire—"

"Then they do not know how resourceful I am. Long ago I told you that even misfortune can provide opportunity to the brave and enterprising. In my situation, it offered a convenient way to escape the retribution of Richard and my other enemies."

"But where did you go?" I asked, still in shock and gripped by a dreadful wonder. "How did you manage to conceal yourself—"

"I disguised myself and took ship in Marseilles. From there to Sicily, and finally, to Malta," he replied with an unnerving crispness. "I did well in Valletta and Medina, setting myself up in trade and some soldiery"— his voice brimmed with pride and self-satisfaction—"and eventually made my way to Ireland, when John was subduing the rebels. I had heard he needed help in bringing them to heel. I knew how to provide that help. Men, weapons, strategy. I had already done the same for his brother the Young King, after all, years before." He was speaking more quickly, more fluidly now, as if the recitation of his feats had energized him. "You see, like you, I chose a new life," he continued, "and a new name. It seemed more"—he gave a sardonic smile—"*convenient*. And safer, especially in the days when Richard"—his voice brimmed with venom as he pronounced *Richard*—"was king. Even easier, of course, during those providential years when he was in captivity. And then fate intervened again, a few years later, when he was killed at Châlus. It was Richard's death that freed me. His death, and John's ascendance." A grim smile had crept to his lips.

I thought of King John—his unsavory personality, his cruelty, his ignoble band of accomplices and companions. "You were able to make yourself useful to John," I said, all the while trying to summon up the queen's steely spirit, and her advice—stave off fear, think clearly, take the measure of your opponent.

"What I was prevented from achieving with Richard, I have succeeded in achieving with John," he boasted. "Richard thought he could destroy me. After my supposed 'death' he made attempts to seize my land, my fortune. But even there, I outwitted him: months before, I had hidden enough gold and riches to protect Ravinour from his depredations. You see, my sense of honor was such"—his tone was mocking, his smile sinister—"that I had thought to provide handsomely for my widow. After my 'death,' I wanted her to continue to live in luxury, and for her to be able, through charitable acts, to perpetuate my name and legacy—to the church, to the poor. Alas, even that prospect afforded her little comfort: I hear she was beside herself with grief." He paused before adding with conceit, not sadness: "She died of heartbreak, they say.

"Thus, in the end," he went on, "it is not Richard, but *I* who have triumphed! It is *I* who have survived. And it is *Richard* whose heart lies in a marble vault at Rouen." He took a glove from his belt, twisting it in his hands. "Surely you, who prize survival, must appreciate my remarkable feat! And you, with your penchant for adages, will appreciate my own favorite—*Vincit qui patitur*. Yes," he mused. "'He conquers who survives.' It is *I* who have survived. It is *I* who have prevailed." He looked at me almost beseechingly, as if he were seeking my praise, my approbation.

"Yes, you have survived," I said. "But your falcons and your doves did not! You lost them all to the fire. When I learned of your death, and how you had died, I thought it was *better* you had died! I could not imagine how you could have managed to continue living, knowing all your birds had burned to death."

"'Managed to continue living'?" he repeated in a mocking tone, before adding triumphantly, "How naive you still are, Isabelle! It was *I* who set the fire! It was *my* plan, from first to last."

"*You?*" I gasped in horror. The white room seemed to spin around me; my hand groped for the table as I tried, trembling, to steady myself. "*You* who set the fire? It is not *possible*," I stammered, "that you could have—something so diabolical—"

"It was I," he replied calmly. "My plan from beginning to end."

"But all your falcons, your doves—you cared for them so, they were like your *children*—"

"And then I set the fire that killed them," he announced with frightening matter-of-factness. "I would have preferred, of course, to have done everything on my own," he went on briskly, "not to let anyone else know of my plan. But it was too complicated to execute without an accomplice. I settled on Ragnar."

"Ragnar," I murmured. "Of course—"

"It was not easy to orchestrate, I confess. Even I had to steel myself to the task at hand." Then, rapidly, and with a weird, almost voluptuous eagerness and thrill, he went on, in a cadence by turns feverish and contemplative. "No, it was not easy. Not easy at all, even for me. But after a few flacons of wine, it was not hard to get the deed done. When all was set in place, I poured oil on the rush matting, ignited it, and escaped. Ragnar had prepared a mount at a designated place in the forest, as well as money for my transport and a change of clothes. Both being crucial, of course, to the plan." Luxuriating in these details, his voice mounted in excitement as he added, "I disguised myself as a pilgrim—*me*, a pilgrim." He gave a harsh laugh, "*Imagine!*"

But that was not what I was imagining; I was imagining the falcons' uncomprehending eyes, the gentle doves engulfed by flames, the stench of burning feathers intermingling with that of roasting human flesh. . . . "You said someone else was with you. Who was it?" I demanded. "Whose body was found?"

"One that Ragnar had disinterred that very morning. A thief, according to Ragnar, who knew him before he was hanged for stealing some food. We dressed him in my clothes and placed my ring around his finger—*my* ring, on a *peasant's* finger." He chuckled at the irony. "I was able to escape almost unscathed." He ran his finger across the scarred side of his face. "The flames were high, very high, by that time, you see, and it was not easy to make my way through the burning door." Again, that eerie, almost needy look, as if he were seeking my praise for his ingenuity, his daring.

"I am *horrified* to think of what your survival cost," I told him, my body shaking with disgust, with rage. "Your cruelty, your murderous plotting. To have killed all those creatures, to have left them tethered to their posts to burn to death, while *you* escaped!" I held my head in my hands, trying to dispel the image of the shrieking birds struggling to free themselves from the engulfing flames.

"So you do not *approve?*" he jeered. "The idea of my survival, and what it entailed, offends your delicate sensibility, your scruples. *You*, of all people—*you* who deceived me, and cursed my life, by consorting with that witch. It is because of *you*—your spells, your machinations— that I have never been able to have a child. A son and heir." He slapped the glove down by the casket. "And what have *you* made of your life, what of your dreams of adventure, of seeing the larger world?" He cast a long, scathing glance around the scriptorium. "You have condemned yourself to *this* place. A place of walls and rules and silence. A place for unwanted women who have no other use. You might as well be living in a *coffin.*"

"I knew you were capable of cruelty," I replied, keeping my voice level, "but to kill the creatures you nurtured and professed to have loved"—I shook my head in woe—"no, I never imagined you capable of such a heinous crime! It *sickens* me." I felt a sudden desperate need to make some sense of this, to weave together all the disparate pieces from the past—everything I should have perceived, everything that had led to this hideous moment. "I saw glimpses of your cruel side, of course," I began rapidly, passionately, "and I had heard stories from others. But I tried to discount them. From Agnes, early on. She told me you would not give Aiglantine a length of fabric to swaddle her baby. Then there was the way you treated Gallien when you blamed him for losing Vainqueur. And then, years afterward, I learned from Raoul how vengeful you were to Aiglantine after I left—how you cast her out like a wounded dog. It was a miracle that she was able to make her way here, to the abbey, after you threw her out. She was near death, wasted and ill. She came looking for her child. We did our best to care for her in her final days."

"Her child?" He raised his brow.

"That young woman, Marie, who was with me here." I spoke even more quickly now, and with even less restraint. "That was *her* daughter! Aiglantine had left her here, at the abbey, when she was an infant. The baby for whom she wanted the swaddling. But even there, you denied her the fabric, the ennobling fabric, which might have helped the child survive. You made Aiglantine grovel, even for *that!*" Then, even more bitterly: "But she never left the baby in the forest, as you probably wanted, and as many thought she had. She would never have done such a thing! She left the baby *here*, at the gate of the abbey. The nuns found her and named her Marie. Sister Clementia and I have brought up the child."

"I watched you with the girl. She is very pretty. And very dear to you, I surmise," he added in a chilling tone.

"She is like a daughter to me," I said. "The most precious thing in life to me."

"As I am the most *abject* thing to you." He glowered.

"You have *made* yourself into the most abject thing. By your cruelty. By your evil. You are hardly even *human!*"

"How wrong, how utterly wrong, you are, Isabelle." The timbre of his voice suddenly became softer, smoother—a lulling voice I recognized from the past and which, in its silky seductiveness, frightened me all the more. "I assure you I am all too human," he said, "and as *vital* as ever." He came close and ran his finger ever so gently across my cheek; I shuddered.

"There was a time when my touch did not disgust you," he replied bitterly.

"That was another time," I retorted. "Had I realized—"

There fell a long, harrowing pause as he continued to look at me, angrily, mockingly. Then he walked to the desk where Marie had been working. I followed at a slight distance, watching, terrified, as he let his hand linger on the leaf she had been illustrating. I came closer, frightened that he would defile it, but to my relief he merely seemed to study the images. "What would you say," he asked, turning toward me, "if you were to learn that the blood of the vile creature who stands before you now—*my* blood—also flows in Marie's veins?"

"*Your* blood?" I scoffed.

"It was *my* child Aiglantine bore."

"You *joke*—that cannot be!" But the moment I uttered those words, myriad disparate pieces seemed to coalesce with harrowing logic in my mind. I thought of the fabric he had denied Aiglantine for her infant: had that been his way of punishing her for begetting a child he never wanted? Then there was the fear Aiglantine always evinced toward him—her resolute silence about the identity of Marie's father, which I had always assumed was born out of shame. I thought of her painful reticence around Gerard during the years of my marriage, and her terrible, indeed almost inordinate, fear of displeasing him. Finally, I thought of Marie—her eyes, how like in color, and in expression, I realized now, they were to Gerard's; her exacting nature; then of her love of falcons, of adventure. . . .

"Marie, your daughter," I whispered, almost unable to give voice to the repugnant thought.

"Yes," he exclaimed triumphantly, reveling in my shock. "My very own! And like me, against all odds, she, too, survived." He turned several leaves of the manuscript before settling on a page embellished with vivid images of falcons and doves. "These are her drawings?"

"Yes."

"Do hawks interest her?"

I nodded, too numb to utter a word.

"She is not without something of me, then," he mused. "I find that strangely heartening." Then, savagely, he muttered, "If only she had been a *son*, not a daughter! *You* could not even give me a healthy daughter." He reflected on this, bitterly, before adding, "Now that you know about my child with Aiglantine, you also realize why I knew the problems we had in conceiving were not due to *me*. They were *yours*, and yours alone." He leaned forward, closer to me, the veins at his temple throbbing; I flinched, which sparked another burst of his fury. "You were not able to bring a healthy child to life—you were cursed from the beginning, as much a witch as that creature, Anthusis, you consorted with. No, the problem was never with me—it was with *you*, and your womb, which were defective."

His expression was bitterly triumphant as he had uttered those last, piercing words; he knew they had wounded me. All the while, I struggled to shield myself against his insults, but it was hard, very hard. And he had not yet finished—"But Aiglantine's womb was not defective," he continued. "She was ripe, and fertile. How pretty she was then, how fresh! She did not have to be coaxed and tutored in bed, as you did. She knew from the first, as you did not, how to please me." I crumpled to the seat before the desk, my entire being reeling with hurt, fear, and incredulity—was it possible that this *monster* had once been my husband? That I had lived with him, that I had lain with him?

He continued even more rapidly now, and with the same bizarre self-entrancement he had shown earlier when describing his escape from the burning mews. "Yes, she was wonderfully trusting, and, at moments, appealingly afraid." He paused, and then, with a certain repellent mock ruefulness, added, "But she did not understand the game of life. She never would, as *you* never will. And, of course, it became inconvenient when she got herself with child. Foolish of her to have been so careless. And even more foolish to have *told* me about it. She should have crept away and had it in peace, in anonymity." He shook his head from side to side, marveling, "I came here for the king's books, and for the queen's letter. I never imagined I would also find my *daughter*."

"She is *not* your daughter!" I cried, springing to my feet; my heart pounded and my hands began to shake uncontrollably. "*I* have brought her up. *I* have taught her. She has my *spirit*!"

"She has my *blood*," he replied, striking the table with his fist. "No court of law would ever prevent me from taking her from you. Certainly no court that is under the jurisdiction of *this* king—for make no mistake, Isabelle, he is *my* king."

"Hurt *me* if you like, but not *her*!" I pleaded. "She still has her whole life before her." I stopped, realizing this tack would never move him;

I would have to find another. I took deep breaths, forcing myself to strategize. "The queen is greatly fond of Marie," I began, managing to steady my voice. "Take Marie from here, from us, and you risk making an enemy of the queen. I know the queen well, and for many years. She trusts me. Ask anyone here. She will never let Marie be taken from me. Or from the abbey!"

"The queen is old and has not many days left. Or so I hear."

"She is indomitable. And she is close to her son, the king. He owes her a great deal. Without her help, he would never have become king. Without her support, even more nobles will desert him. Would you really risk that, especially now, with all that is at stake, with the defense of Gaillard?" To my relief, he seemed to consider this. "If you cross her," I continued, "you will also cross the king. And however close you purport to be to John, you must also know his reputation for retribution."

"I have only to bide my time then, until the queen is no more." He shrugged. "That day will come, sooner rather than later. The old dragon is in her eighth decade. Even *she* cannot live forever. Once she is dead, she will be irrelevant."

I knew all too well the terrible, undeniable truth of that last statement. "And if the king should learn who you *really* are?" I asked, taking another tack. "And what vile deeds you have done? That your new persona is nothing but a lie?"

"*Who* would tell him?" he asked. "*You?* Do you really think the king would believe *your* story—the ravings of a deluded woman, spurned by her husband and shut up in a convent? He would give it as much credence as he would the vision of some holy lunatic."

"The queen will vouch for me," I replied. "Then the king will have no choice but to believe I speak the truth."

"I shall tell him how you lied to me, how you deceived me. And then I shall *destroy* you," he swore. "Yes, I will destroy you, and I will make sure that your precious Marie knows that you consorted with that witch, Anthusis, during our marriage."

"I told you long ago why I went to Anthusis—I wanted desperately to have a child. *Your* child. That was the reason I took her potions," I returned, struggling to keep my voice from wavering. "And that is what I would tell Marie."

"Once again you *lie*—as you lied to me again and again. You know in your heart you are far from spotless, that you committed a sin against God by *preventing* yourself from getting with child—a sin that forever cursed my marriage bed. What will the abbess Mathilda, and the virtuous Sister Clementia say, then? How will they, and Marie, feel about you *then*?"

"They would never, *ever* believe you!" I cried.

"I am not so sure." His lips settled into a menacing smile. "When I tell them the real story, detail by detail—about the amulet you left, about all your lies—do you think you would *still* be welcome at this holy place?"

I could not bring forth a single word; all life seemed to have drained from me.

"Now, for the king's books," he concluded triumphantly. "Time presses. And before I leave, I must deliver the message to the queen—fortuitous, is it not? That will give me occasion to assess the queen's health myself."

I handed him the cord and watched as he strapped it around the casket.

"Tell me, Isabelle," he said, turning to me as he thrust his hands into his gloves. "Have any of these been illustrated by Marie herself?"

"Many," I murmured.

"Good. There is some justice in that, then." He took up the casket. "Now, to the queen. I can find my own way, I assure you." As he came to the door, he turned to face me: "Remember, when the queen is dead, I shall return. *Then* we shall see whom Marie really belongs to."

CHAPTER 109

I could not move; I scarcely breathed. I shivered with cold—it was nearly dusk and the air was icy—yet my body felt afire; afire with shock, and shame, and fury, and terror.

I crumpled to the bench before Marie's desk and covered my face, trying to blot out the memory of his strange, gleaming eyes and of his strange new voice. I wanted to die; I wanted to flee. I wanted to erase the memory of each revelation he had bitterly, yet triumphantly, recounted. I ached to awaken as one would from a nightmare—ecstatic and relieved that the nocturnal terrors had merely been chimeras. But what I had just seen was no chimera. This was a monster come to life, and *he*— this monster—had once been my husband. What had just appeared before me was not Gerard but another being entirely: the soldier Vautière, "The Vulture," the infamous henchman of King John who had ravaged the abbeys and villages of Ireland and northern England.

Of the man I had once desired, admired, and lain with, there seemed no vestige: in his stead, a being so corroded by bitterness, thwarted ambition, and lust for vengeance that he seemed more fiend than mortal. Yet "I am as *vital* as ever" he had told me with that searing gaze; but now his vitality would be turned toward revenge upon me, toward tracking me down as he had once tracked down wild creatures in the forest or soaring birds in the sky. I would only be safe as long as the queen lived; at the moment of her death, all would change. "Then I shall *destroy* you," he had told me in that terrifying voice. "Yes, I shall destroy you." All of a sudden I recalled how, years ago, he had announced to me, "I am not a vengeful man." How *little* he knew himself!

And what of Marie, my darling Marie? Should I ever have guessed that she was *his* child, the daughter of this monster? Should I ever have discerned that her spirited curiosity, and her obsession with falcons, might have sprung from *him*? I had come to think of her as so much my own child that I almost imagined those traits as having been inherited from *me*—or, latently, from some unrevealed side of Aiglantine.

My reeling mind then turned to her—to pitiful, suffering Aiglantine, and the secrets she had carried to her grave; then to all the facets of her submerged self that I had either never perceived or had misconstrued. Never could she let me know the painful truth of her past; never could she let her daughter know the circumstances of her conception, and the dreadful character of her father. How crypt-like she had been in her ability to conceal! I thought of the day when Sigibert had been apprehended in the forest, for instance, and how, confronted by Gerard, she had given away *nothing*. A "cool dissembler" I had called her almost proudly, imagining she had acquired this skill from me. Little did I know how experienced she was—even more experienced than I—in keeping secrets.

And yet, in my heart, I knew she loved me dearly, and that any secret she had kept from me was simply out of shame—a deep, unfathomable shame for which I could only pity her; a sin for which I could now only forgive her. How fearful she must have been that I would one day discover the truth of Marie's parentage; that I would think less of her, that I might condemn her, that I might no longer trust her. But I knew now, as I had never known so completely, that it was never *she*, but Gerard, who had transgressed. He had done what Hugh had hoped to do during the hunt—hence, I realized now, Gerard's almost inordinate rage that evening.

What twisted pleasure it must have given Gerard to see her serve me, his new wife, and how discomfited he must have been to see us grow close, to see us become friends, when not so long before our marriage, he had used her for his pleasure. Yet that deed, too, he had wielded in his arsenal against me, though it had not been enough for him to describe *how* he had seduced her. No—he had saved even crueler anecdotes as weapons of humiliation: even in bed, he had told me, I had not compared to her. Here, as well, he not only delighted in seeing me suffer, but wanted me also to infer something quite specific: despite my noble name, my education, and my intellect, I had failed in that other, primal, domain—just as I had failed to bear his child.

I thought of those years of pregnancy and childbirth, and of my hurt when Gerard would insinuate that the problem was with *me* and my inability to bear a healthy child. All the while Aiglantine must have realized that his words, however painful, may have evinced some truth; for she had borne him a hearty baby girl.

Little by little, as if deciphering a coded message, I continued to unravel those years at Ravinour. I thought of his pleasure in swathing me in silk—a mere scrap of which he had denied her baby—and how, watching us, Aiglantine would become so quiet, so grave; how poignantly grateful, and wistful, she had been when, before my leaving Ravinour, I had given her those lengths of silk. . . . And what of his fury, the day when he discovered her wearing my bracelets? That, too, I now understood. No wonder he had resisted having her attend me in the birthing room.

Finally, with rageful horror, I dwelt on Gerard's "death" and the heinous crime he had committed. Was the killing of all those lovely, soaring creatures any less, or more, because they had been his own? And what of Ragnar in all of this—Ragnar, whom Hugh had seen that day at Valkenswaard. How else could Ragnar have afforded such costly peregrines, I now realized, had not Gerard amply rewarded him for his silence? Suborned by a bribe, he would never reveal the true identity of Roger de Vautière.

*Roger!* I thought, with a start, of the very name he had chosen—the name of his late, admired, older brother. "What is past is dead," he had once pronounced. But even there he had deluded himself: for his new life he had chosen a name from the past, a name that haunted him, the name of the dead brother to whom he had, I had always intuited, felt inferior. Yet Roger was not the only brother toward whom he had felt ambivalence or even bitterness: years later there would be another powerful figure—a prince, then a king—whom he would strive, unsuccessfully, to please; and his name would be Richard.

Finally, wearily, I looked up. The windows were frosted over; the room entombed me in whiteness. I suddenly recalled the seer's final prophecy—"something white, cold, and opaque, too cloudy to make out"—as I sat, all the while, at Marie's desk, thinking and thinking. . . .

The book she was in the midst of illustrating—the book he had seen, the book he had mocked—lay open before me. Just enough light remained for me to peruse its pages. I turned one leaf, then another, though I was hardly capable of really seeing anything. By and by I came to Marie's favorite—a splendid image of the Archangel Michael which, even in my upset, I could not ignore. I stared at the fiery, vivid image; at his splendid spear, and his face, exquisite in its intentness. How lovingly and with what exactitude Marie had labored over this image, over this book. She had always revered the Archangel because she loved heroes; had she not fantasized that her own father might have been a holy warrior, or a prince? She must never, *ever* learn the truth, I vowed.

I would *not* let him destroy me, nor would I *ever* let him destroy Marie. Her *spirit* would win over his blood. What had he said? That I did not understand the "game of life." Here, too, he was wrong. Had he not realized that I had been schooled by the queen these past decades, and that I had imbibed much of her strength, her wisdom—even her ruthlessness?

*Vincit qui patitur* he had mockingly told me, without realizing that the motto could equally apply to *me*. I, too, would conquer by surviving. I would not let him win—I would escape. I would make my way to Spain with Marie and Aiglette and embark on a new life; we, too, would survive. I would protect them, just as I would protect the queen's letters and possessions. But *how*, and with what means? Even at the best of times, it would be a long, dangerous journey across the mountains. I would need support. I would need someone to help me prepare, someone who would understand my urgency, someone to whom I could, without fear, confide.

There was only such person: Clementia. I rose and left, quickly, to find her.

# CHAPTER 110

*Friday, the second of April*
*Anno Domini 1204*

Upon awakening, I suddenly remember with stabbing sadness—the queen is dead. I was with her yesterday, my hand in hers, when she drew her last breath.

My body aches: only with great effort do I manage to sit up and reenter the world of daylight. It is just past dawn, and there is little light. I look about the chamber: the bronze falcon peers at me from the table by my bed. Aiglette had placed it here last night. I recall her tender words—"It will keep you company"—as I gaze into the falcon's eyes.

I place one foot on the ground; it is already April, but even so the stone feels frozen. Setting down the other foot, I remember—tomorrow they will bury the queen. But I shall not be there to see the monks lift the terrible stone lid and secure it upon her tomb; I shall not be there to bid the queen adieu. But I cannot think of that now, there is no time to indulge in sadness. This morning the girls and I will depart for Spain. I must make haste.

I stand up unsteadily, my thoughts interrupted by a knocking at the door: it is Clementia, her beautiful face haggard with worry and sadness. That Aiglette will leave with us is especially painful to her, though she is too controlled and self-abnegating to admit this.

As she enters I smooth my rumpled clothes and say almost apologetically, "I fell asleep fully dressed."

"It is not surprising," she says gently.

"I must go to the girls at once. To make sure they are awake. That they are preparing."

"No need. Grecia is helping them. Marie and Aiglette have been awake for hours. Out of excitement, no doubt."

Or out of fear, I think to myself. "Have you received any new word yet, from your emissary?" In March, Clementia had engaged a trusted agent, Robert, to track Vautière and report his whereabouts.

"Nothing to add to what Robert told me weeks ago," she replied. "That Vautière left for England in February—that he remains there, somewhere near Oxford, they say, with King John. William Marshal and his men are holding the environs of Gaillard." I wonder whether Tancred is among these henchmen. "The abbess and I shall send word of the queen's death to him only after you and the girls have departed," she reassures me.

"And you do not think that Vautière and his men have heard that the queen was dying?"

She shook her head.

"And the other preparations—the mounts, the carts?" I ask.

"Everything is underway," she says, in the calm, lovely voice I have come to cherish, and will miss very much. "The men who will accompany you are very experienced. They know the mountains and will guide you ably. All has been arranged, all will be well," she assures me, placing her hand on my shoulder. "Even if Vautière should come here looking for you, we will *never*, ever let him know where you and girls have gone. We will never let them harm you."

"And I shall *never* let him!" I cry. "I shall smite him with my own hands first. And Marie must *never* learn he is her father."

"How strange," Clementia says, looking at me with an expression of wonderment. "Your voice! For a moment I thought it was the queen speaking."

"May God grant me her fortitude and courage," I reply softly, ardently.

"Now you must dress and close your trunks," she tells me. "Heraldis will help you. She waits outside. But be prepared—she is distraught."

"The queen was very good to her," I say with a sad smile.

She opens the door and beckons Heraldis, her face swollen and red from weeping, to enter. "Make haste, Heraldis," Clementia urges. "The sooner Lady Isabelle and the girls depart, the better."

After the door closes behind her, I tell Heraldis, "I shall wear the things we set aside the other day. My traveling costume." As she fetches them, I think of the day when Aiglantine helped me prepare the same clothes for my departure from Ravinour.

Having laid the clothes on the bench, Heraldis glances at the bed-side table. "What about the falcon, my lady—shall I pack it?"

"Yes, with the little box from my brother. Put them in the small trunk that always stays with me."

BEFORE ENTERING THE GIRLS' CHAMBER, I gird myself: they must never, *ever* know how frightened I am. I touch the queen's ring upon my finger, and then the place beneath my robe, below my collarbone, where the memento from Arnaut with the serpent and the crocodile presses against my flesh.

I come upon them standing over a table: Marie is showing Aiglette the map she has drawn; it is not a real map, but an imaginary one based upon descriptions I have gleaned from others over the years—pilgrims, travelers—but especially from the queen's journey to Spain four years ago. "This is the way we will go," I hear Marie tell her.

They look up at me in unison. "We have made this map together," says Aiglette proudly.

"Marie told me about it," I say. "Think of all the things Marie has taught you, Aiglette. To read, and to draw—"

"And to ride!" interjects Aiglette, who has been practicing these past months.

"Yes," I say, "and now you shall have a chance to show us how well. We have a long journey ahead." Then, urgently: "And your trunks—have you closed them?"

"Grecia did," replies Marie. "The men have already brought them to the stables."

"Good. I shall see you there shortly."

At this, I notice their expressions change: in a matter of seconds, their former sprightliness has vanished. They look frightened, as if the idea of meeting me at the stables, of mounting, of setting off, has made the idea of leaving their home, of leaving Fontevraud, seem suddenly all too real and painful. "What is troubling you?" I ask.

"The servants and others have told me the roads are full of brigands and robbers," Aiglette spurts out. "And they say that the road over the mountains is very dangerous—even in springtime."

"I have tried to reassure her," Marie says almost pleadingly. "I have told her that all will be well! That you already know much about the journey, and the safest route to take. The queen instructed you about it, did she not?" she asks me, with poignant vehemence.

"Yes, the queen told me all about it," I say brightly, trying not to hurry, trying to seem serene. I take Marie's hand, and then Aiglette's, in mine. "You will meet Queen Lenora, and the princesses. And then, one day, I promise"—here, I cross my heart—"we will make a pilgrimage to Santiago de Compostela. *Imagine!* And then perhaps"—here, I glance at Marie, knowing the next detail will intrigue her—"we will go to a place called Finisterre on the sea, on the far western coast. 'The end of the earth' my grandfather once told me the ancients called it."

Their expressions reassure me; the stories have rekindled their excitement. Finally, I add, "And Sister Clementia has provided us with the best men, the best guide. She would *never* put you in harm's way, would she? And would *I? Ever?*"

"*No!*" they exclaim.

"Do I look afraid?"

"*No!*"

"There now, no more gloomy thoughts." I give each a kiss. Then I go to the table, my finger tracing the route that Marie has drawn so exquisitely; she has included the principal landmarks—Conques, Roncevaux among them—from Fontevraud to Burgos.

"It will go in my saddlebag," says Marie, "along with—"

"Radegonde," prods Aiglette.

I walk toward the door. "I shall go to the stables now." Then, in a low, commanding tone: "Meet me *soon*, my darlings."

EVERYONE HAS ASSEMBLED BY THE stables. The sun's rays are suddenly much stronger, radiant. I look about the courtyard, trying to commit the scene to memory. Lothar has just opened the gate. Mother Mathilda and Clementia stand in front with me, Marie, and Aiglette.

Clementia embraces Marie long and hard, tears glistening on their cheeks as they draw apart. Then Aiglette—dainty, blond, and still unaccustomed to her stiff traveling clothes—approaches Clementia. I can hardly bear to watch this leave-taking, knowing it will likely be the most painful of all.

"These are my parting gift for you, Sister Clementia," Aiglette says with somber eagerness, offering her a small bunch of flowers.

"Forget-me-nots!" exclaims Clementia, holding them close. Then she and Aiglette do not so much embrace as cling together.

I hear the abbess's voice: "Come, girls, it is time that I grant you my blessing." Marie kneels on the ground before her; Aiglette follows. "May God look over you, protecting you from darkness, fear, and all earthly dangers," says Mother Mathilda. She makes the sign of the cross; Marie and Aiglette rise to their feet.

I take Marie's hand, and Clementia, Aiglette's. "Come," Clementia says, having collected herself. "Lothar will help you mount." The girls nod solemnly and walk toward their horses.

Clementia turns to me. "You have the queen's letters, her documents and jewels, and all the other—"

"Yes."

"Repeat the password for me."

I repeat the same word I had been given when I had first seen the queen, in England: "Amethyst."

"Good, then—" She is about to utter something else when, suddenly, we hear a great commotion: a man, entering on horseback, rushes toward us and dismounts. Alarmed, I look at Clementia: "Who is—"

"Robert. My emissary. But I never expected him this soon!"

The man, caked with dust, moves toward me and Clementia.

"Tell me what you have heard," she orders him.

"The last information I received was not accurate, Sister. For that,

I beg your forgiveness. Rumors abound to the north, you see, all made worse by famine and pestilence. Vautière is *not* in England with the king—he is with William Marshal and his men en route here from Rouen."

"Vautière *here*, in France?" I ask, petrified.

"Yes," he says. "I am told they have learned the queen is on her deathbed."

"The queen passed from this earth yesterday, at eventide," Clementia tells him in a sorrowful voice.

At this, he lowers his head and makes the sign of the cross. "Who has been told of her passing?" he asks gravely.

"No one," replies Clementia. "The abbess and I will send word to the king as soon as we are able. How long will it be before they arrive here?"

"Within four to five hours. Perhaps less if they ride at great speed."

"And you are *certain* Vautière is among them?" I ask, terrified.

"Yes. Possibly at the lead. But that is not all I have heard. There is other news, of the Holy War—Frankish forces have almost reached the gates of Constantinople. It is only a question of time before the siege begins. Within days, they say."

"The world in chaos," murmurs Clementia. "May God protect them, and all of us." Then, turning to me, and in a voice of great urgency: "You must depart at once!"

She leads me to the abbess; I kneel before her, her hand upon my head as utters her blessing. Afterward Clementia takes my hands. "I shall pray for you and the girls every moment of every day," she says as we embrace. "I know that God in His wisdom will protect you."

I wipe my face of tears and eke out, "Thank you, dearest Clementia, with all my heart." We draw apart. "I shall write you as soon as I am able. We will meet again, I know we will."

"We will," she says simply. "Come, it is time."

The men who will guide us have mounted and moved toward the gate.

Lothar stands ready to help me. I mount swiftly, savoring the feeling of the reins in my hands and grateful, as well, for the gloves, which the sisters have lovingly made for me. I smooth the leather over my fingers, then the high gauntlets over my wrists.

Aiglette, alone, trots up beside me.

"What is the matter?" I ask, noticing the trepidation in her eyes.

"I am afraid," she confesses, in a tremulous voice.

"I am not," I lie.

Marie joins us.

"Ready?" I ask them, as cheerfully as I am able.

"Yes!" they exclaim, to my relief.

"It will be an adventure," I tell them jauntily, though my nerves are afire.

"A way to test our mettle," adds Marie brightly, repeating the very words I had once told her.

"Precisely," I reply. Turning, I wave to Clementia and the abbess, before calling out: "Onward!"

We pass through the gate swiftly, the guide in advance, Marie and Aiglette slightly behind me. Shortly afterward, slowing our gait, we come to the crossroad, with its statue of the Virgin. "Lady Isabelle," Aiglette cries, coming to a halt. "We must dismount here, to pray. It is the custom."

Just as I move toward the girls, terror seizes me: is that the sound of distant, thundering hoofbeats I hear, or is it merely a figment of my imagination? "We cannot stop now," I tell them almost harshly. "We have not a moment to lose."

I give the signal to our guide to quicken our pace and we set off, the road widening as we move south. We ride long and hard for a long while until, at the approach of another crossroad, my deepest fears suddenly resurface and assail me. Not fears for *myself*; these are far more agonizing fears—that I have placed the girls in danger, that Vautière will find us.

I turn around, intending to ride back to them, to reassure them yet again that I shall always protect them, that all will be well.

But there is no need, for they are smiling.

# ACKNOWLEDGMENTS

The seed of this novel was planted decades ago when, at sixteen, I first went to Fontevraud with my family. The trip was one of many such Michelin Green Guide–propelled journeys while I was growing up, for I am blessed to have parents who were as passionate about "broadening" travel as they were about nurturing a love of history, art, and literature in their children. "A stop at Fontevraud to see the abbey," I wrote in my diligently maintained travel journal. "Saw the tombs of the Plantagenets in the lovely church. Breathtaking cloister, and kitchen with Romanesque tower. The whole region is beautiful and full of Plantagenet history. One can almost imagine Eleanor and her sons plotting together!" I had little idea that this first glimpse of the abbey, which had just begun to be restored by the French government, would ignite a lifelong fascination with the world of Eleanor of Aquitaine.

I returned to Fontevraud Abbey many times in subsequent years, watching with delight as it grew into an important cultural center. In the early stages of research, members of the staff—Nathalie Dunème, Marion Demonteil, Anne Foucault, and Hervé Regignano—were unfailingly helpful. I have many happy memories of perusing the abbey's excellent bookshop, and of the back-breaking weight of my book-crammed suitcase when, after a night or two (either at the Hôtellerie de L'Abbaye Royale or the Hôtellerie de la Croix Blanche), I would return by train to Paris.

It was through Nathalie Dunème that I was introduced to Les Amis du Vieux Chinon, the staff of which put me in touch with the late Dorothée Kleinman, the learned custodian of the mysterious, cavelike

Chapel of Saint Radegonde. It is there, high on a wall, where a fresco of Eleanor and (at least it is conjectured) her children, was discovered in 1964. I spent an unforgettable morning there, in April 2007, enthralled by Dorothée's lore. Later, as I drove back to Fontevraud, I remember ruminating about the possible affinity between the rebel Radegonde and the equally rebellious French queen who lived centuries later.

I am indebted to my friend Paul Freedman, professor of history at Yale University, for his help and encouragement, and for steering me to many vital sources, including his groundbreaking work on the spice trade. I am grateful, as well, to other professors at Yale, whose seminars profoundly influenced me as an undergraduate: the late Deno Geanakoplos, who introduced me to the history of Byzantium, and the late Robert S. Lopez, whose studies of medieval commerce made an indelible impression. I was fortunate to have been able to attend John Boswell's alumni seminar on the Middle Ages which he led in 1991. Lastly, I must acknowledge my debt to the late George S. Hersey, professor of History of Art, who encouraged me to infuse my senior theses with imagination, as did his teaching fellow at the time, David Alan Brown. David went on to an illustrious career as head of Italian painting at the National Gallery, Washington, DC; he has remained a mentor and a treasured friend.

Other scholars and curators have also been generous with their expertise: Annalena Müller, medievalist at the University of Fribourg; Nicholas Vincent, formerly professor of Medieval History at the University of East Anglia; Dr. Stephen Bennett; and Robert S. Wiecke of the Morgan Library. I owe thanks to many at the Metropolitan Museum of Art: Sean Hemingway and Debbie Kuo of the Greek and Roman department; Deniz Beyazit in Islamic Art; C. Griffith Mann and Barbara Boehm of the Medieval Art department. Thanks, as well, to Stephen J. Davis, professor of Religious Studies at Yale, for his insights on Syria and Antioch; and to Harold Attridge, of the Yale Divinity School, for his vivid lectures along the Camino.

Rebecca Weigand and David Smith helped me, early on, with invaluable research from the New York Public Library. For later research,

I was fortunate to have the help of the brilliant Richard Prud'homme. I must also thank Carolyn Waters and the staff of the New York Society Library for their assistance in retrieving scholarly papers and books.

I have always been interested in falconry but knew little about it until writing this book. Meeting Lars Ingildsen in Utah was one of the great, serendipitous moments of my research; there, on a winter afternoon, my husband and I visited his mews and "met" his awe-inspiring falcons and his doves. I must also thank Jon D'Arpino, of the Connecticut Falconers Club, for his patience in answering my questions.

My curiosity about the influence of Arab world on falconry, and on medieval poetry, led me to the work of James E. Montgomery, professor of Arabic at the University of Cambridge. On YouTube, I chanced upon his talk on "Falcons and Abbasid Hunting Poetry," which he delivered at a conference at NYU Abu Dhabi in 2013. I subsequently emailed him a few questions. Not only did he respond, but he also sent me a selection of his as yet unpublished translations of Arabic falcon poems, one of which I have used as an epigraph to this novel.

I owe thanks to many in England: the late Lord Northbourne, and his wife, Marie Sygne, Lady Northbourne, Amanda Cottrell, and my dear friend, the late Gwendoline, Countess of Dartmouth. Jake Simpkin gave me an illuminating tour of Salisbury, Winchester, and Southampton, as did Graeme Stobbs along Hadrian's Wall. Philip Chin was invaluable in organizing many English forays.

I am also deeply grateful to Dennis Stanfill, my preternaturally capable brother, for his guidance on visual and graphic design elements. Special thanks to Phil Poole for designing the book cover; to Griffith Everson for computer help; to photographer Michael Waring for his patience; and to Wendy Samuel for organizing research materials. My debt to the steadfast Angelo Del Vecchio is profound. For their encouragement when this novel was in its infancy, I would like to acknowledge Betty Kelly Sargent, Kenneth Atchity, and Michael Carlisle. To my children, stepchildren, and all my friends who have been understanding of my incessant "cave dwelling"—thank you.

I would have been hard pressed to imagine someone as wise, fervently enthusiastic, and responsive as Sara Nelson, my editor and ballast at HarperCollins. She has been nothing short of extraordinary. I owe her and publisher Jonathan Burnham enormous thanks for embracing my novel, and for deftly shepherding it to publication: *merci mille fois* from a deeply grateful author.

The HarperCollins team has been exceptional: Mary Gaule, Lydia Weaver, and Milan Bozic, among them. Mina Hamedi and Michael Steger of Janklow & Nesbit have wonderfully caring and a joy to work with.

To Lynn Nesbit, who has represented me for years, I owe enormous gratitude. Her support sustained me, and her belief in this book was such that I have concluded her intuition borders on the clairvoyant. Even a novelist would find it hard to create a literary agent of her vivacious intensity and passionate intellectual acumen. That she manages this with style, with spirit, with sprezzatura, is even more remarkable.

I was fortunate to have Priscilla Gilman as my reader and critic while writing. She is both uncannily sensitive and, when warranted, exceedingly tough; at times hearteningly reassuring, at others appropriately critical. To this formidable mix add a stringent sense of language, style, and logic. Her spirit and sensibility have enhanced my creative life.

Finally, and most profoundly, I must thank my husband, Richard Nye, to whom this book is dedicated. It cannot always have been easy to have a spouse who is, let us say, no stranger to the *idée fixe*; who would cloister herself to work on weekends and holidays, and who, at various times, set off alone for research expeditions to Syria, Turkey, and Sicily, not to mention walking trips along Hadrian's Wall, and along the Camino to Santiago de Compostela. His confidence in me and this novel never flagged. No wife could have a more understanding husband, no writer a more ardent supporter. He is my Lionheart.

# Author's Note

I owe an immense debt to the brilliant historians and scholars who have written about Eleanor of Aquitaine, the Plantagenets, and the remarkable twelfth century. While I researched this novel, it was a joy to delve into their works, all the while armed with the novelist's magical prerogative to interpret, enlarge upon, and imagine what might have been. Any factual errors are mine.

I have chosen to mention only a few of the many works I read and consulted. Among the excellent biographies of Eleanor of Aquitaine, I primarily relied upon that of Ralph V. Turner (*Eleanor of Aquitaine*, Yale University Press, 2009). Another profoundly helpful work was the superb collection of essays from a symposium on Eleanor of Aquitaine held at Fontevraud in 2004, and published by *Revue 303, Arts et Recherches*. Its meticulously detailed chronology of Eleanor's life was indispensable, as were its essays, especially those by Martin Aurell, Ursula Vones-Liebenstein, and Alain Erlande-Brandenburg.

The details of King John's foray to Corbridge can be found in *The Annals of Roger de Hoveden: Comprising the History of England and of Other Countries of Europe*, Volume 2, translated from the Latin by Henry T. Riley. The letter from Hildegard to Eleanor is included in *The Personal Correspondence of Hildegard of Bingen* by Joseph L. Baird. The two verses from ballads come from these volumes: the first from *Lark in the Morning: The Verses of the Troubadours*, Ezra Pound, Robert Kehew, W. D. Snodgrass, eds.; the second from *The Poems of the Troubadour Bertran de Born*, Patricia H. Stablein, Tilde Sankovitch, William Doremus Paden, eds. *The Art of Falconry*, the thirteenth century study by the astounding Frederick II of Hohenstaufen, remains a crucial source on the subject.

The following works, listed in alphabetical order, were also invaluable:

Blaine, Gilbert, *Falconry*

Boswell, John, *The Kindness of Strangers: The Abandonment of Children in Western Europe from Late Antiquity to the Renaissance*

Caldwell, Carl Howard, "King John's Mercenary Captains in Thirteenth Century England"; PhD thesis, Indiana University, 1975

Sheila R. Canby, Deniz Beyazit, Martina Rugiadi, and A.C.S. Peacock, *Court and Cosmos, The Great Age of the Seljuks*, (Metropolitan Museum of Art)

Bull, Marcus, and Léglu, Catherine, eds., *The World of Eleanor of Aquitaine*

Church, S. D., *The Household Knights of King John*

Davis, Williams Stearns, *Life on a Medieval Barony*

De Hamel, Christopher, *Scribes and Illuminators*

Dronke, Peter, *The Medieval Lyric* (2nd ed.)

Duby, Georges, Jean Birrell, trans., *Women of the Twelfth Century*

Freedman, Paul, *Out of the East: Spices and the Medieval Imagination*

Geary, Patrick J., *Furta Sacra: Thefts of Relics in the Central Middle Ages*

Gillet, Philippe, *La cuisine et la table au siècle d'Aliénor d'Aquitaine*

Gillingham, John, *Richard I*

Green, Monica, ed., *The Trotula*

Guy, John, *Thomas Becket*

Heckscher, W. S., "Relics of Pagan Antiquity in Medieval Settings," *Journal of the Warburg Institute*, 1938

Johnson, Penelope D., *Equal in Monastic Profession, Religious Women in Medieval France*

Kibler, William W., ed., *Eleanor of Aquitaine: Patron and Politician*, (Essays from a symposium on the Court of Eleanor of Aquitaine, Univ. of Austin, Texas, 1973)

Le Goff, Jacques, Arthur Goldhammer, trans., *The Medieval Imagination*

Lemay, Helden Rodnite, *Women's Secrets: A Translation of Pseudo-Albertus Magnus' De Secretis Mulierum*

Marshal, William, *History of William Marshal*, ed. A.J. Holden, trans. S. Gregory, and notes by D. Crouch, Anglo-Norman Text Society, 2002

Panofsky, Erwin, *Tomb Sculpture*

Pastoureau, Michel, *Blue: The History of a Color*

Parsons, John Carmi, ed., *Medieval Queenship*

Powicke, F. M., *The Loss of Normandy: 1189–1204*

Riddle, John M., *Contraception and Abortion from the Ancient World to the Renaissance*

Stetkevych, Jaroslav, *The Hunt in Arabic Poetry*

Tunc, Suzanne, *Les Femmes au Pouvoir: Deux abbesses de Fontevraud aux XII et XVII siècles*

Warren, W.L., *King John*

Wheeler, Bonnie, and Parsons, John Carmi Parsons, eds., *Eleanor of Aquitaine: Lord and Lady* (Collection of essays by various scholars)

# ABOUT THE AUTHOR

FRANCESCA STANFILL was born in Oxford, England, and grew up in New York City and Los Angeles. She is a graduate of Yale University, where her studies included the history of art and medieval civilization. Her articles have appeared in many publications, including the *New York Times Magazine*, *New York*, and *Vanity Fair*. Her lifelong fascination with the pivotal twelfth century and its legendary queen, Eleanor of Aquitaine, propelled her to write *The Falcon's Eyes*. This is her third novel.

SET IN FRANCE AND ENGLAND AT THE END OF THE TWELFTH CENTURY, THE MOVING STORY OF A SPIRITED, QUESTING YOUNG WOMAN, ISABELLE, WHO DEFIES CONVENTION TO FORGE A REMARKABLE LIFE, ONE PROFOUNDLY INFLUENCED BY THE FABLED QUEEN SHE IDOLIZES AND COMES TO KNOW—ELEANOR OF AQUITAINE

Willful and outspoken, sixteen-year-old Isabelle yearns to escape her stifling life in provincial twelfth-century France. The bane of her mother's existence, she admires the notorious queen whom most in her circle abhor: Eleanor of Aquitaine. Isabelle's arranged marriage to Gerard—a rich, charismatic lord obsessed with falcons—seems, at first, to fulfill her longing for adventure. But as Gerard's controlling nature and his consuming desire for a male heir become more apparent, Isabelle, in the spirit of her royal heroine, makes bold, often perilous decisions that will forever affect her fate.

A suspenseful, sweeping tale about marriage, freedom, identity, and motherhood, *The Falcon's Eyes* brings alive not only a brilliant century and the legendary queen who dominated it, but also the vivid band of complex characters whom the heroine encounters on her journey to selfhood: noblewomen, nuns, servants, falconers, and courtiers. The various settings—Château Ravinour, Fontevraud Abbey, and Queen Eleanor's exiled court in England—are depicted as memorably as those who inhabit them. The story pulses forward as Isabelle confronts one challenge, one danger, after another, until it hurtles to its final, enthralling, page.

With the historical understanding of Hilary Mantel and the storytelling gifts of Ken Follett, Francesca Stanfill has created an unforgettable character who, while firmly rooted in her era, is also a woman for all times.

FRANCESCA STANFILL was born in Oxford, England, and grew up in New York City and Los Angeles. She is a graduate of Yale University, where her studies included the history of art and medieval history. Her articles have appeared in many publications, including the *New York Times Magazine*, *New York*, and *Vanity Fair*. Her lifelong fascination with the twelfth century and its legendary queen, Eleanor of Aquitaine, propelled her to write *The Falcon's Eyes*. This is her third novel.

HARPER
*An Imprint of HarperCollinsPublishers*

Fiction

ISBN 978-0-06-322789-7

51999

9 780063 227897

EAN

USA $19.99 / $24.99 CAN

0722

Cover design by Phil Poole
Cover photographs © Getty Images
Author photograph by Michael Waring